ZANE PRESENTS

From My
SOUL
to YOURS

ALSO BY DYWANE D. BIRCH
Shattered Souls

ZANE PRESENTS

From My SOUL to YOURS

DYWANE D. BIRCH

SBI

STREBOR BOOKS

NEW YORK LONDON TORONTO SYDNEY

Strebor Books
P.O. Box 6505
Largo, MD 20792
http://www.streborbooks.com

This book is a work of fiction. Names, characters, places and incidents are products of the author's imagination or are used fictitiously. Any resemblance to actual events or locales or persons, living or dead, is entirely coincidental.

ISBN-13 978-1-59309-124-8
ISBN-10   1-59309-124-9
LCCN 2007924152

First Strebor Books trade paperback edition November 2007

Cover design: www.mariondesigns.com

10 9 8 7 6 5 4 3 2 1

Manufactured in the United States of America

For information regarding special discounts for bulk purchases, please contact Simon & Schuster Special Sales at 1-800-456-6798 or business@simonandschuster.com

DEDICATION

To my mother, Alice; and to all of the wonderful women
I have known and loved...
Thank you for inviting me into your hearts,
sharing special pieces of you with me,
and for always loving me unconditionally.

ACKNOWLEDGMENTS

First and foremost I thank the Almighty Father for continuing to love me in spite of all of my flaws. I am—because of Him. I will continue to be—because of Him. It is through His grace and mercy that all things flow in abundance. I am truly blessed!

To all of my family: my mother & stepfather, siblings, nieces and nephews, aunts, and hosts of cousins, thanks for all the support and love.

To all of my dear friends (you already know who you are) for the love, the laughter, the friendship, and for making this journey much more exciting than it already is.

To my Maryland family & friends (you know who you are), I look forward to many, many New Year's and Labor Days with you. Oh, how these gatherings could be the makings of a good book. I know, I know…what's done in the mountains, stays in the mountains!

A special thanks to my agent, Sara Camilli, for always lending me an ear to bend, and allowing me to bounce ideas her way. I truly appreciate you.

Special thanks to Zane, Charmaine Parker, and the rest of the Strebor Books International and Simon & Schuster staff. Thank you for becoming the wind beneath my literary wings.

My author and literary friends: Danita Carter, Péron Long, Nakea Murray, Anna J., Allison Hobbs, Cashana Seals, and Collen Dixon (who I value and love more with each passing day), thank you for the support, encouragement, and camaraderie.

To my YDC peeps (you already know who you are), thanks for always spreading the word about my literary endeavors, and enthusiastically waiting for the next "treat."

To all of the book clubs for continuing to support my literary endeavors; and to all of the bookstores that welcome my books onto their shelves, thank you!

And last, but not least, all of the readers and "special" fans who continue to support and spread the word about my literary endeavors. Thank you, thank you, thank you! You continue to be my inspiration.

Indy, Tee, Britton, and Chyna are back one last time to invite you into their lives again. As you read their stories, I truly hope you will find this sequel to be just as engaging and entertaining as *Shattered Souls*. If nothing else, it will definitely be a very interesting voyage. With all that said, sit back, relax and enjoy the experience!

Until the next time…happy reading!

Soulfully,

Dywane D. Birch
Email: bshatteredsouls@cs.com
www.myspace.com/dywaneb

I

INDERA: *My Whole Life Has Changed*

Hello there. I'm baaaaaaack! Live. Direct. And in your damn face! Well, don't just stand there with my door open. Come on in and take a load off your feet. Oh my God! It's good to see so many familiar faces. Did you miss me? Of course you did. Well, Chile. Fasten your seatbelts 'cause Miss Indy is in the house and I definitely have some dirt to dish. But before we get started, I would like to thank those of you who kept me in your thoughts and prayers during that whole shooting ordeal. And to all the brothas who showed me mad love. Thank you. Maybe I was a little too hard on some of you the last time we were together. Please accept my apology. Even if you wanted to slide that dick up in my... What? Don't try 'n front. It was inevitable for you to want some of this sweet sticky molasses. I ain't mad at ya, though. Now, don't get too happy 'cause I still can't stand lying, cheating-ass men. But as long as you stay in your lane: everything's peace.

But make no mistake. If there were more women out here—like me—who let you know from the gate that cheating on wifey isn't cute, perhaps you'd think twice before creeping. And the same thing goes for you cheating women. 'Cause your grimy asses are no different. Some of you trick-ass hoes have fucked over some really nice men. But that's neither here nor there for me 'cause I have more important things to be concerned about. What you do behind your closed doors and on your mattress is your business. I am only concerned about what I'm doing. And the one thing I am *not* doing is sleeping with somebody else's man. Been there, done that.

Yes, ladies, you are finally safe from the likes of me disrupting your homes and dogging your cheating-ass men.

Now, with all that said, sit back and kick off your shoes 'cause Miss Indy is about to get this party started, 'cause you know a party ain't a party until I run all through it. So, let's just do the damn thing!

Well, let me see. Where do I want to begin? Hmmm. Now, I know some of you are just dying to see what I've been up to. Inquiring minds just wanna know, huh? Well, first things first. Britton is back in the States. I'm not sure for how long though. Right now he's in California, running behind that psycho Latin love of his. I can't understand for the life of me why he is still with her. He says because she's the mother of his sons. Please. The only thing that Burrito did was spread open her legs to deliver them. Miss Goya—oh, excuse me, Lina—is too damn busy with chasing stardom and licking pussies that she just can't be bothered being a mother to her sons. Now back in my day, I would just slap her ass for playing him out. I never liked her from day one but he has told me on several occasions to mind my business. So that's what I'm doing. I just keep my mouth shut. Surprising, huh? Trust me. A few times I really wanted to sling her across the floor. But I keep things peace out of respect for Britton.

Sometimes I don't understand him. I mean, it's not like he doesn't know that that heifer is sleeping around on him. After all, he walked in on her. Ooops! Don't let him know I told you that. He'd kill me.

Well, if his sons didn't look so remarkably like him, I'd wonder if they were his. But I guess, since she likes rubbing clits instead of riding dicks, there's no room for denying he's their father. Not that I have a problem with her being with other women 'cause, as some of you know, I had my share of the other side back in college. And let me tell you, it was good while it lasted. But to rub it in Brit's face is a bit too much. And I don't like it one bit. Well, like he said, it's none of my damn business. So, moving on.

Anyway, despite that piece of news, he's happy being a father to his beautiful twins. My godsons are so darn adorable I can't stand it. And spoiled rotten. I just love watching Britton's eyes light up every time they call out, "Daddy."

Now, Miss Chyna? She is still the picture of elegance. And she is finally doing *her*. Ever since her first speaking engagement at Howard University, homegirl has been traveling around the country addressing the plight of adolescents. Ole glamour girl's calendar of events for her own children has been replaced with speaking engagements and tours.

Between traveling and running Soul Quests, she is making major power moves. I just love seeing this take-charge side of her. All of her kids are grown and on their own for the most part, with the exception of wild-ass Sarina. That's another story. And I'm not going to waste my time with the details. All I'll say is, that girl constantly keeps shit stirred up. I hate to talk about anyone's child, but she is crazier than a bed bug in heat. But that's their baby.

Outside of that drama, Chyna is enjoying life with her husband, Ryan. While their sons Jayson and Ryan Jr. are managing their four funeral homes, they're vacationing along the Slovenian Coast. I never thought I'd admit having an ounce of admiration for Ryan Sr. but times have changed. He truly loves my soror and keeping the flame in their marriage burning seems to be his only focus. All in the name of love. That's a beautiful thing. Now, their youngest son, Kayin, is finishing up his last year at Morehouse and planning to attend law school next fall. And word has it he and Britton's niece, the one who goes to Spelman. Oh, I can't think of that child's name right now. But, supposedly they are head over heels for each other. Hmm. Young love. How sweet. If you ask me, they both sound whipped. But, you didn't hear that from me.

Okay. Moving on to my Damascus. Oh, excuse me—I mean Tee. Well, he's a bona-fide celebrity. You'll have to excuse me if I flip back and forth, calling him Damascus to Tee. It changes depending on my mood. Anyway, as you know he gave up that stripping scene and replaced it with putting pen to paper. His book *The Young Brotha Behind The Mask* has hit the bestsellers list. He's sold over four hundred-thousand copies of his book, and the sales are still flowing. *ChaChing!* He's just blowing up all over the place. And in between radio-and-talk-show interviews, he's mentoring a group of teenage boys in a youth detention center and working on his next book. Oh, and get this. He even transferred his Norfolk State credits to John Jay College and completed his degree in criminal justice. Seeing him go across that stage to get his degree brought tears to my eyes. And you know I laced him lovely, don't you? I sure did. With a 2000 Range Rover and a Cartier. I'm just so proud of him.

Of course he still has a flock of salivating women tryna bed him down. You should see how some of these trick-ass women bat their eyes and flirt with him. It is sickening. Humph. Most of them know him wearing his thong from his stripping days. And then there are those who know him with nothing on from his fucking days—and let me tell you. I never realized how many females he had banged his dick in until *after* we got together. I knew he was a pussy fiend, but damn! Wherever we go in the tri-state, there's usually one chick who's either lusted him, sucked him, or he's slayed. Talk 'bout a male whore. Geesh! He swears most of his conquests were strictly tea-bagging him (sucking his nuts) or piping him out, aka sucking his dick dry. Humph. Whatever.

Fortunately, I don't go to many of his book signings for the sake of keeping peace. I mean. It is so unnecessary the way some of these trollops throw themselves at him. He kindly dismisses them with an autograph. I stare them down. Although, there was one time when I had to pull this sista to the side and forewarn her that she was pressing up on my man. I tried to be ladylike about it when I approached her in the bathroom.

"Excuse me," I had said. "I don't appreciate you trying to brush your titties up against my man."

Well, homegirl tried to get ghetto on me talking 'bout "so." *So?* Now it's one thing to step to someone's man when you don't know his woman's there, and it's another to do it right in her face. Particularly in mine, okay? That is grounds for an ass beating. Don't you think? So when she went to click her heels toward the door, I snatched the back of what I thought was her hair. Miss Thing yanked her big head around to face me, then snapped, "You don't know who you're fucking with, bitch."

"Really?" I responded, slapping her face with her ponytail. "Then I suggest we get better acquainted." Before she could open her mouth to say another word, I had slung her into the bathroom stall and jacked her up against the wall. I dug my nails in her throat. "Listen up, bitch. I don't fight over a man. So if you want him you can have him. But don't ever think you're gonna disrespect me and do it in my face." I let her go. She tried to catch her breath, holding her neck. "Do I make myself clear?"

"Very," she said, glowering at me, heaving in and out. I slapped her again with her nasty-ass wig piece, then tossed it in the toilet. Baldheaded ho. She had the game fucked up, okay. Like I said. I will not fight over any man. But I'll be damned if some dick-thirsty bitch will quench her thirst at my expense.

So as you can see, I'm still the same old Indy. Still wreckin' and checkin' shit. Other than that, what's up with me? Well, you know how I do. I'm just flowin' and makin' things happen. The last time we were together, there was some discussion around me selling Weaves and Wonders. Well, I decided against it. As a matter of fact, I opened up another salon in Jersey and I'm looking at a potential spot in Connecticut. Shit. I'm a businesswoman. Okay? And trust me. This time, there is no room for anyone to steal from me. Not that I want to rehash old memories, but the last bitch who kept swiping a few dollars from the register ended up with her fingers cut off. So if anyone else is crazy enough to try it on my time, then they'll catch it too.

Speaking of catching it, that whole court ordeal with Alexi was a trip. Of course I was ordered to pay all of her medical bills for slashing her face up and I'm financially responsible for any therapy sessions she might need. That was the handiwork of my high-powered attorney. And let me tell you, she needs every bit of it. 'Cause Miss Finger-snapping, fly-guy Alexi looks a mess. Humph. She'd been better off if she'd kept the tribal gashes and slashes I gave her instead of that raggedy graph job her no-frills plastic surgeon gave her. The child looks like a circus ho, okay.

In any case, the charges of attempted murder and aggravated assault against me were dropped since it was deemed in self-defense. However, I was ordered to attend anger-management counseling—like *I* really needed it. Humph. Fine with me. But I betcha she'll think twice before pulling another cutter out. Oh, my bad. The only cutting she'll ever do *now* is with her teeth.

Chile, you should have seen that fifty-foot bitch coming into court waving her nubs in the air—being all dramatic 'n' shit—tryna accuse me of being responsible for her fingers being chopped off. Do you know that she-man tried to sue me for permanent damages? Oh please. The bitch had no evidence and no witnesses, so she looked like a damn crazy-ass, fingerless fool. And then he—oops, I mean she—had the nerve to try to attack me in the waiting area when I finger-snapped her and whispered— as she walked by, "You betta work, Miss Knuckles."

Anyway, as I was saying before I got sidetracked—there's always gonna be a need for the bald and knotty-headed, hairy-faced, crusty-footed sistas to have a place to go. So why not keep 'em coming to Weaves and Wonders, right? After all, we do offer the best service around. And now with my new lineup of Dominican and African sistas on board, "Weaves and Wonders" is wrapping, weaving and braiding the hell outta heads.

I'm also still very involved in Nandi's Refuge. The crisis shelter I created— in honor of my beloved mother—almost five years ago to meet the needs of victims of sexual and physical abuse. Quiet as it's kept, my heart goes out to all of the kids who enter those doors. And I make it my business to ensure they feel safe and nurtured for the time they are with us. Yes, as hard as it may be for you to believe, I do have a heart. I'm just not wearing it on my sleeve for all to see.

Anyway, whether it's in one of my salons or at the shelter, I expect nothing but professionalism from my staff. And when it's not, all hell breaks loose. Girl, I had to go off on my shelter director when I heard Miss Thing hollering and screaming at some of the girls for not following instructions. I almost said, "Bitch, you betta check yourself, hollering at my girls like that." Instead, I waited for her to finish her tangent, then invited her into *her* office for a little supervision.

"Girlfriend, are you sucking on paint chips?" I politely asked. I figured if she were neurologically impaired from lead poisoning then I might be willing to get her the proper help she needed. When she denied it, I fired her ass. I don't know where the hell she *thought* she was, but Nandi's wasn't where she needed to be.

Many of my kids come to Nandi's to get away from the verbal abuse that goes along with whatever physical and/or sexual abuse they've been exposed to. So why the hell would I allow them to be yelled and screamed at. That chick had the mission statement fucked up, okay. So now I have the task of tryna fill the position. And let me tell you. You should see some of the whack jobs that come stumbling in for an interview. Humph. I wouldn't trust 'em with a dead hamster. So, as you can see, I am a very busy woman these days.

I know, I know. You wanna know if Tee and I got married. We did. *After* he signed a prenuptial agreement and an affidavit forfeiting any claim to any of my business ventures I made before or during our marriage. Of course he hemmed and hawed about not wanting my money—which I'm sure is and was true. But I am no damn fool, okay. Love doesn't have shit to do with protecting my financial interest. And no man—husband or not—is going to enjoy what he didn't bring into this relationship. Make no mistake.

See. Tee will never know just how much I am worth. The only money he'll know about is the money *we* accumulate together. That's where so many people go wrong. They get so involved with someone and all of a sudden everything they've worked for becomes their partner's. Wrong answer. What you bring into a relationship is what you leave with. Especially when you're rocking a portfolio like mine.

And then there was the issue of where we'd live. He didn't want to live in Brooklyn—although he has agreed to until our home is built—and I refused to live in his brothel of a townhouse in Jersey. Because we both know, he had more tricks in and out of that den for whores than I care to know about. And, before I'd even go up in that spot, I demanded he get rid of every piece of furniture he might have been able to screw on. Of course, that just about emptied out the house. Which was fine by me. Oh, let's not forget the boxes and boxes of women's phone numbers I personally burned in the fireplace, along with his little black, booty-call book. "You won't be needing this," I snapped as I tossed it in the flames. He just smiled.

Well, of course, smart-ass Tee wanted me to toss out all of the expensive trinkets I've collected over the years from no-good, lying-ass men. Now you know Miss Indy was not having that. We must have argued for three weeks before I decided to give in. So I tossed everything. I sure did. Right into storage and into a safety deposit box. Okay? Give away diamonds and minks? I think not. He must have lost his damn mind. But, as long as he *thinks* everything has been disposed of, he's happy. And I'm all about keeping my man happy. That's right. My man. Not yours. Mine.

Excuse me? Did I hear someone say something slick? Didn't I have to read a few of you the last time we were together? Must I go there again? Oh. I thought so. Just because I'm a married woman now, don't think I still won't black on your ass. Please. Don't take me there. I'm tryna be a gracious hostess. But, if you force my hand, I'm gonna have to bring it to you. So please. Let's get along.

Anyway, after six months of house hunting and arguing over locations, we've settled on having our house built in the Fort Lee area of Jersey. Of course he didn't think it was necessary to live in a gated community. But we've compromised. I get the gated community and he gets to have his game room. Who would have thought deciding on where to live would turn into such a big ordeal?

I still don't understand why we can't stay here. Humph. But since he wants to move, our home is gonna cost him every dime he makes on his book deals and then some.

Wait a minute. Stop the press. Before I go any further, I think we better clear the air about a few things. Now what was this mess I heard about some of you not liking me? Well, let me fill you in on a little something: Whether you like me or not doesn't make me or break me. Okay? I was fly then, and I'm fly as hell now. So don't hate the playa; hate the damn game. And this mess about me being no different than any other ho because I slept around with your man? Bitch, please.

The difference was and still is that I slept with your man to break him down. Not because I needed *or* wanted his sorry ass. Somebody needed to let him know that cheating on your dumb ass was going to have consequences. And like I told you back then, it was all about money, sex, and control. I'd run his pockets—not that I needed *his* change—then send his tired ass home to you. And make no mistake, as most of you know, a broke man was a no-can-stroke man. Believe that.

Now, don't roll your eyes at me. It's not my fault your men loved trying to suck the guts out of this hot pussy. And since you wanted to go there, just remember every time you're kissing him you taste me on his lips. So, if I was a ho, I damn sure wasn't a broke one. Now flip open *your* checkbook and let's see what type of currency you working with. Another thing. If you don't like me so damn much, why the hell are you here all up in my business tryna see what I've been up to? Humph. Just what I thought: Nosey ass.

What? That's why someone shot my ass up, is that what you said? Now, let me tell you one damn thing. Yeah, I got shot. And? As you can see a bullet didn't keep a sista like me down. I'm still keepin' it movin'. So what's your point? I wasn't pressed when he pulled the trigger—well, actually, I was but I didn't let him know it. Shit. Even though I was *not* ready to die, I didn't beg his ass to spare my life, either. Please. I beg no one for nothing. So I took it like a soldier. Could you? Humph. I didn't think so.

Anyway, I guess pulling that trigger made him feel powerful. The poor thing couldn't handle having his card pulled, exposing him for the weakling he is. It's my understanding that his wife left him shortly after I put him on blast for all to see. Shit! If you ask me, he should have been relieved that I blew his cover. I mean. I just can't imagine him being happy living a double life the way he was. It was time for him to face the music and get it all out in the open so he could dance the dance—if you know what I mean. Oh well, the truth hurts. And so does a damn bullet to the chest, okay. But I'm still standing. And that's all that really matters, wouldn't you say so?

Anyway, he's out and about for the moment. But, you mark my words. It's only a matter of time before he's clipped and bagged. It's been almost three years and the police still haven't been able to track his ass but my "connections" have. Well, they *did* have him under watch up until the last four months. Homeboy is missing in action as we speak. And of course, I'm not the least bit happy about it. How the hell he dipped out is beyond me. But, like they always say: you can run, but you can't hide. So in the meantime, I'm having him hunted down like the rabid dog he is.

Excuse me? Oh, you want to know what I have in mind for him? Well, you tell me. What do you think should happen to a man who came up in my shop, shooting me, then beating me in my head with a blunt object? Hmm. Let's see. How about something really creative, something to let him know he fucked with the wrong one. Well, whatever I decide, you best believe he'll wish he never tried to come for me. Trust.

Again, as many of you know, Miss Indy is…well, let's say I know someone, who knows someone, who knows someone who can take care of *whatever* needs to get handled. Don't get it twisted. It's just too bad he did. But for now, he can live a little. But the minute he's found, it's a wrap! I'm gonna give him his just reward for trying to leave me for dead. Believe that! So as you see, he's sloppy with his.

If he were really on point he would have sealed his mission with a bullet to my head. Now don't you worry yourself about whom I'm referring to, just know it ain't over by a long shot. And if some of you keep trying to come for me, I'm gonna have something for your ass too. Okay?

So as I was saying before I was rudely sidetracked, I am now Mrs. Indera Fleet-Miles and my wedding was the most talked about social event for weeks. It was a true star-studded event. Dignitaries and celebrities of all sorts were there. So security was tighter than a buffalo's ass. If you didn't show your color-coded invitation, you didn't get in. Simple as that.

Anyway, my twelve bridesmaids wore slinky, ivory strapless gowns with matching slingbacks and elbow-length gloves. And Chyna—my Maid of Honor—was laid out in a sleeveless, silk crepe fan-tailed, hand-beaded gown with a form-fitted bodice. My four flower girls were precious in ivory Cinderella gowns. The ringbearers and groomsmen were hand-somely dressed in black Ralph Lauren tuxes while Tee wore black tails. He was just too damn fine.

And you know I was fierce from head to toe. My gown? Oh, I thought you'd never ask 'cause you know I'm not one for bragging. It was an elegant Vera Wang piece. Custom designed of course. Ivory silk, spaghetti-strapped with plunging neckline and cutout back, beaded with 10,000 Austrian crys-tals. Four strands of crystals and beads in the front and back are what held this masterpiece together. Glitter, glitter and more glitter. That's all I can say. Girl, it wrapped this body like a moth in a cocoon. Hell, with a body like this, there was no need to leave anything for the imagination. I figured I might as well let the Brothers drool and the Sisters gag. After all, it *was* my day to shine. And that is just what I did.

I even pulled out my twenty-carat, princess-cut diamond necklace and accessorized with a pair of Australian teardrop pearl-and-diamond earrings. And of course I wore my mother's tiara. Chile, it was glitz and glamour. Oh, how I wish my sweet mother could have been there to see her baby come down that aisle.

Girl, it was fierce when the trumpeters blew their horns, announcing my arrival. Everyone gasped when the double doors opened. Even the judge who officiated the ceremony couldn't keep his eyes off me as I swayed and sashayed down the thirty-foot aisle to Pure Soul's instrumental ver-sion of "We Must Be In Love." I was so happy my homegirls could reunite to sing for me. Humph. It's a shame they ended up one-hit wonders. They had so much potential. Anyway...

Oh, who walked me down the aisle? Chile, no one. I decided at the last minute to work the crowd solo. And just as I was preparing to take my place beside my sexy groom, my sistafriends sung their a cappella version of "We Must Be In Love" to declare to my guests what I was feeling. *Oh, yes! We must be in love*, I silently hummed.

Britton—being Tee's best man, and my dearest friend—stepped around to kiss me on both cheeks before resuming his place as I turned toward my handsome groom. Girl, that nasty man stared and licked his lips at me during the whole ceremony. I just kept smiling my most innocent smile, then winked my eye at him. *That's right. Eat your heart out, boy*, I thought to myself. *All this sweetness is for you.*

So we shared our personal vows and pledged our love and commitment to each other before three-hundred-and-seventy-five guests. I was a nervous wreck. But I refused to break a sweat and stain up my gown. And I damn sure wasn't going to let tears of joy ruin what little makeup I had on my smooth, flawless skin. And just as Tee prepared to greet my neatly painted lips with wet, warm chocolate-drop kisses, one hundred white doves were released from heart-shaped cages while thousands of pink rose petals dropped from the ceiling. Sorry you couldn't be there. But if you'd like, I'll send you a few photos. Better yet, you can peep us in *Ebony* and *Jet*, spring 1998 issues.

Our candlelit reception was a lavish paradise filled with hundreds of roses, orchids and birds of paradise where our guests feasted on marinated shrimp; deep-fried lobster tails; miniature crab cakes, and sipped on Cristal champagne until the main course was ready to be served. Chile, everything was scrumptious, and elegant. But, the most meaningful part of the evening was when Jesse Powell and Brian McKnight sang. Yes, they did. Girl, it was all over. Tee and I danced our first dance as husband and wife to Jesse's "You." And when Brian sang "Never Felt This Way," he poured so much of his heart and soul into that piece that when he finished the place shook with applause.

But honey chile, when my girl Mary J. got up from her seat and decided to sing "I Never Wanna Live Without You," I was shocked. And by the time she did her rendition of "Our Love," I was in tears. Girlfriend threw down! Do you hear me?

Tee grinded so deep into me I thought he'd rip a hole in my dress with that pipe of his. He smiled, then whispered in my ear, "I love you so much, baby." My pussy sucked in my thong as he slowly tongued me down. "You got my dick so hard, baby. Let's sneak away for a quickie." *You will not funk up my dress*, I thought to myself. *"But I'll give you a little sumthin-sumthin to tie you over.* I slowly licked and sucked on his bottom lip. "You want this sweet pussy," I teased. Everyone clapped and stomped as I led him off the floor toward our bridal suite.

And after dinner and before the party really got started, Tee's frat brothers and my sorors gathered on the floor, encircling us in a double circle with my sorors creating the inner ring and his frat the outer ring. Each took turns singing our hymns while Tee and I held hands, facing each other. When they were done, the place lit up with frat and soror calls. And then a few of his brothers, you know—the ones filled with one glass too many—gave everyone an impromptu step show of rhythmic hand clapping, stomping and chanting. And then a few of my younger sorors worked it out, kicking, sliding, clapping and hip jiggling. It was definitely a memorable night. Tee and I kissed. The DJ segued into "My Love is Free" by Double Exposure. Then that elegant ballroom turned into a sweatbox of house and club mixes for my old school club heads before giving way to some hip-hop and a little bump 'n grind, make-your-pussy-wet music, okay. Girl, we gave 'em a taste of Bentley's, Bond's International and the Red Parrot, partying until about 6 a.m.

The honeymoon? Well, we spent four weeks in Europe: Hungary and Austria. I'd really love to tell you all about Budapest with its Chain Bridge and beautiful scenery but that place left a bad taste in my mouth. I didn't care for that Transylvanian goulash, or chicken paprikash. And I don't do pork chops, so nothing they served appealed to me. Besides, the shopping was lousy. Still in all, we were enjoying the nightlife until a drunk Hungarian made a lewd comment to me, then called Tee a *nigger* when he stepped to him for disrespecting me.

Chile, listen. It almost got ugly. Tee had to yoke him up and was about to slide his wig back. But I stopped him. Racist bastard! If it weren't for a few witnesses, we would have been hauled off to jail. Imagine that. Miss Indy and Tee locked up and tortured in a foreign country. That would not have been cute, okay.

Now, Austria was absolutely breathtaking. Sailing the Danube River, climbing the Alps—yes, Miss Indy climbing mountains—strolling and shopping along the Graben and Ringstrasse, wining and dining, riding horse-drawn carriages, opera shows and did I mention shopping? Yes, shopping, shopping and more shopping. I loved it. Tee was full of surprises. Who would have thought he had such a romantic side.

Chile, listen. If you ever get a chance to go, you must do Vienna. And you must try their world-famous Sachertorte. Oh, and there's nothing like Austrian chocolate. Humph. It's almost as creamy and smooth as Tee's lovemaking. Now the coffee, I wouldn't recommend it to anyone unless you are a seasoned coffee drinker. That strong-ass mess had me shittin' for days.

Excuse me? Oh. You wanna know if I could handle him. Girl, listen. When I told you I was gonna need a big-ass bag of Epson salt to soak my pussy, I was not kidding. That fool tried to beat this love tunnel up something fierce. 'Cause you know I teased the hell out of him up until our wedding night. For eight months, I tortured the hell out of his ass. Hot-oil dick massages, phone sex, nude video clips of me with a few of my sex toys, you name it. Of course, he didn't get up in this sweet juice *until* he ate me inside out, okay. But once he got it right, I let him slide up in this sweetness and homeboy tore me down. Okay. And I *loved* every inch of it!

Now, now! Let's take it down for a minute. Close your mouths and wipe the slob from around the corners of your lips. There's no need for you to try to be all up in our bedroom 'n shit. 'Cause I know how some of you dick hungry hoes can be. But, I'm not pressed. However, in case you wanna try to get a little taste of his chocolate-coated love stick, make no mistake if he gives it to you, he's yours till death do you part. Which would be sooner than you'd like. Anyway, back to my story. Where was I?

Oh yes. My honeymoon. Well, let me say we might have been in Europe for four glorious weeks but we spent the first eight days locked up in our suite like two wild animals, feasting on each other's lust. And believe you me; I threw this love gravy on him. Hell, mama had to go into her trick bag and show him a few things. Okay? There was no way I was letting him think he put a spanking on me without showing him how I like to really get down. But afterward, chile, listen. All I can say is, thank goodness for yoga and meditation exercises; otherwise, I'd be checking in for a pussy implant.

Humph. Let's fast-forward. Close to three years now, and we should still be living happily ever after, right? Well, most of the time. But one thing's for sure: The honeymoon is definitely over. Trust me. And the one thing that has kept us from killing each other is the fact that I'm busy with my businesses and he's usually on tour with his book. Otherwise, it would be World War III up in this piece. Believe that.

I know I'm not always the easiest person to live with but Tee can be a real pain in my ass, literally and figuratively. I love him with all my heart and he's good to me. But living with him is a whole other story. I think we should have just shacked for a minute before jumping into a marriage. 'Cause let me tell you: being married is a lot of hard damn work. Hold up. I'm not saying we're having major problems. I've just never had any patience with a man or for any of his idiosyncrasies.

For starters: smacking his food when he eats or grinding his teeth at night. Then there's the issue of leaving the toilet seat up. This is not cute, okay? I've gotten one wet ass too many in the middle of the night. And squeezing the toothpaste out from the middle instead of from the bottom drives me crazy. Then him leaving his dirty underwear in the middle of the bathroom floor wrecks my nerves. And I can't stand when he doesn't rinse the tub out after he uses it. Please. I am not Suzie Homemaker, okay?

Well, Chyna made it clear that I would have to pick and choose what my battles would be if I wanted to keep my sanity. So I try not to make a big deal out of everything but sometimes I find myself ready to go off. Like when he comes home asking me if I've cooked dinner. Dinner? You better try take-out. Better yet, how about taking me out. Or when he's been home all day and the house looks a fucking mess. How can one person have a whole house upside-down in a matter of hours? Then there's the fact that I am still not used to waking up every day and going to sleep every night with a man in my bed. Now don't get me wrong, it's a wonderful thing when I'm horny as hell—like right about now. This kitty cat is throbbing for a strokin'.

Girl, sometimes I wake up early in the morning horny as hell, rolling up on top of that pipe and riding the hell out of it. Humph. It's times like this when I don't mind an all-day and all-night fuckathon, okay. But let me tell you—even when I'm *not* feeling it—Tee's nasty ass is tryna dig his dick in me. Yes, he gives it to me dickliciously. Make no mistake. But damn. His long-winded ass plunging that dick in and out of me three, sometimes four, times a night is a bit much.

I thought if I wore underwear and a pair of shorts on those nights when I'm not particularly in the mood would deter him from tryna get some. But, I'll go to bed clothed and wake up with one leg in and one leg out of everything. Now what kind of shit is that? It's like I have to stay awake just to keep my pussy safe.

Another thing that has thrown me over the edge is this dog he's brought home. Had he prepared me, I probably wouldn't have overreacted. But when I walked in the house and heard what sounded like big-ass hoofs coming at me, I snatched open my satchel and yanked out my road companion. "Freeze! Or I'll blow your fucking brains out," I yelled at this monstrous thing. I was wrecked, okay? Tee had the nerve to come down the stairs laughing 'n shit like the joke was on me. Humph. The joke woulda been two bullets to his friend's big head.

"What the fuck is that?" I snapped. A Rottweiler he tells me. Now you know I was too through.

"Well," I said, staring it down. "That thing is not staying in this house." He wagged his little stump of a tail.

"Damn, girl. It's only a puppy," he said, rubbing and petting him. "Look, he likes you." I looked down at his big-ass paws. My right eyebrow went up. My left eye narrowed to a slit. Tee grabbed him before he could run up to lick me.

I clenched my teeth. "Tee, get that thing out of this house. Puppy or not, it is too damn big to be up in here." Puppy? Humph. He looked more like a bull to me.

"No, he stays inside. This is his home, too," he said, wrestling with him in the middle of the foyer. "So you might as well get used to him." He grabbed his chain and headed for the door. "By the way, his name is Bullet." The door slammed. End of discussion.

"So you think?" I said, looking dumbfounded. Well, the minute he and *Bullet* went outside for a walk, I double-locked all the doors. And outside is where he and man's best friend slept.

Don't get me wrong; dogs have their purpose. And many of them are cute. But they can have their purpose and be cute outside. I am not feeling any dog in the house.

Lastly, Tee wants a baby. Well, actually he wants three. Now that is definitely something I'm not interested in. Not now anyway. And, whenever I am ready, I might be willing to pop out one, but three? Now that's asking a bit much. Humph. It'd be just my luck to give birth to three sex-crazed boys, running around tryna hump every little girl in sight. Having some girl's parent calling me up talking about my son was caught in their daughter's bed. Please. Or worse: boy-crazed daughters. Lord no. The last thing I want to deal with is some sex-hungry child.

Anyway, I have my reasons for not wanting children at this moment. First of all, I'm about making money, not making bottles. Second of all, changing designers is more appealing to me than changing shitty diapers. The only ass I want to wipe right now is my own. I told him we should wait at least four years before starting a family. But that's not good enough. He wants to start one now. What the hell is the rush? He had the nerve to say, "Isn't your biological clock ticking? It's not like you're a spring chicken." I wanted to slap the piss out of him. I'll have him know, I'll be one of those women who go down in history giving birth to a healthy baby at eighty years old. Until then, I would rather use this time learning to adjust to living together and getting to know each other better.

If things don't work out between us, I do not want to be stuck raising a child on my own. Not that I don't want our marriage to last but I have to be realistic. Shit happens. And I am not the one to be tied down to a house full of kids, chasing after a child support check. Besides, I am not too keen on fucking up my shape. There's no way I want my titties dropping and my ass spreading.

Of course, Britton thinks I'm being selfish and feels I shouldn't have married him if I wasn't willing to give him the one thing he wants: a family. I never said I wasn't willing. I just said I'm not ready. Britton is always tryna read into shit. He makes me sick when he does that.

He recently said to me, "Indy, you are gonna find yourself by yourself if you don't stop playing with Tee's emotions."

"Boy, what in the world are you talking about? I'm not playing with his emotions. I love him and you know I wouldn't do anything to hurt him."

"Then tell him what you've been doing for the last six months."

"I can't," I said, feeling cornered. "He wouldn't understand."

"Well, what do you think is gonna happen when he finds out? Don't you think he's gonna be hurt?"

I sucked my teeth. "I'm not doing anything other than protecting myself and keeping him satisfied at the same time. Besides, he's not gonna find out anything."

"Whatever," he retorted. "You seem to have it all under control. Just don't come to me when it backfires on your ass."

"Humph. I like your damn nerve," I snapped, rolling my eyes up in my head. "Tee knows I'm not ready to have a baby."

"Yeah, okay," he responded sarcastically.

"See. Unlike, Miss Hollywood, I'm not trying to have a baby unless I'm prepared to be its mother."

"Indy, don't start—"

"No. Don't you start," I interrupted. I felt myself about to go off for no apparent reason other than not wanting to hear his lecturing.

"You got some serious issues, girl... Amar put that down...stop banging on the window... Listen, I gotta go. Amar is trying to bust the damn window out. I'll call you when the kids are in bed." He hung up before I could respond.

The balls of him! I'm not the one with the issues. I'm very clear on what the hell I'm doing. He, on the other hand.... Never mind. I'm not gonna go there. Oh, I suppose you want to know what Britton and I were talking about. Well, that's for me to know and for you *not* to find out. The last thing I need is your busybody asses all up in the mix tryna shake shit up for me. It's bad enough I gotta hear it from Britton. All you need to know is that I love Tee and I am only doing what I feel is in my best interest. What's wrong with me wanting him all to myself without having a crying baby to tend to?

What? I know you're not still tryin' to come at me? Well, let me tell you one damn thing: This is my body and I'll do what I want to do with it. Other than my monthly flow, I control what the hell comes out of this pussy. Okay?

Unlike so many of your dumb asses, I'm not gonna have a damn baby just to keep some man. Do you really think he's gonna stay with your simple ass just because you were stupid enough to have his seed. Please. And some of you bitches are regular breeding machines. Out here fucking like bunny rabbits and got babies by three and four different men. Whatcha tryna do, build your own nation? And what about those of you who still sleep with him—even when you know he's with someone else—because "that's my baby's daddy." Silly ass. The only thing you are is an easy lay, a used-up piece of pussy. So why don't you wake the hell up and move on. He has.

Ugh! And let's not forget those of you who don't even know who your babies' daddies are. What, you had to pick another name out the hat because the last man who you *thought* was the father failed the paternity test? Nasty bitch! And let me not get on you crotch-rot hoes who have had five and six abortions like it's a fashion trend. Wake up, you dirty tricks, that's not birth control. And you Baby Mama Drama Queens are ridiculous using your kids as a weapon against their fathers or fighting his *new* girl because you can't accept the fact that your trifling ass was dismissed. Get over yourself.

Oh, and don't even get me started on you bitches who put a piece of dick before your children. How the hell you gonna choose a man over your flesh and blood? Neglect your kids for a stiff dick, and sweaty fuck. Bitch, you need to be beat down, then tossed in an incinerator. That's right. Up in flames your hot ass needs to go. Crazy ho.

And I know you don't want me to get on you welfare whores who think it's cute lying around collecting a check once a month, thinking the more babies you have the more money you'll get. Stupid ass. You'll pop out babies so you can get free milk and cheese. Bitch, please.

Humph. Do we really have to do this? I had hoped to share my story with no drama and no damn stress. But I see a few of you have a lot to say about what I'm doing. So before you come for me again, I really suggest you be careful. 'Cause if you don't, you will get a tongue-lashing you'll never forget. Now let's move along, before I have you pack your purse, and put your ass out.

Oh my phone's ringing. Excuse me for one minute. "Hello."

"Hey, baby."

"Hey to you, too. Where are you?"

"On the turnpike. I should be home in like forty-five minutes."

"Hmmm. I can't wait."

"Yo, baby, whatchu got on?"

"Nothing."

"Word? Yo, my dick is hard as hell. I can't wait to get up in that pussy. I want you so fuckin' bad."

"Ooooh, baby. And this pussy wants you. I'll be nice and wet for you."

"Damn, girl. You gonna make me bust a nut on the side of the road. It's been two weeks so you know I'm backed up."

"Boy, please. I know your nasty ass better than that."

"Yea aight. You know the score. It ain't the same as being up in you. And tonight, it's on all night."

"Why wait? Pull that juicy dick out now and let's get it poppin'."

"Baby, you ain't said nuthin' but a word."

Oh, excuse me. I would love to sit around and chat with you but Tee is on the line. As you see, he's horny and I'm getting ready to work him into a sexual frenzy. With a little phone sex, I'm gonna bring him on home with a stiff dick and wet hand. So I'll have to get up with you a little later. See ya.

2

BRITTON: *All That I Can Say*

I don't know how in the world I allowed myself to get caught up in all this mess with Lina. I never expected a one-night stand, on the beach in the Dominican Republic, would have me stressed the hell out. If it weren't for that night three and a half years ago, I'd probably still be living in my tropical paradise—stress-free, carefree and debt-free. But no, I had to go and let my raging hormones take control of my rational side and force me to release a stream of horniness into her eager canal. Now, I'm her baby's daddy.

If only I would have known what type of mother she'd be, I would have probably kept my lonely penis in my pants and continued entertaining it with my hand and blow-up dolls. Better yet, I should have dressed for the occasion and worn a damn condom. No. Like I said, I should have just stuck with solo stimulation and called it a day. I'm telling you, the hand never lets you down. Just nut and go. It's one sure way to avoid all this craziness. Oh, well. I'm now a nut short and three years too late to be crying over spilled milk.

What I should have done was left her ass when I walked in on her sexing it up with one of her girlfriends two years ago. But what do I do? I join in. And what's really foul is that I liked it enough to *ménage à trois*, not once, not twice but thrice. How was it? The bomb! I'm telling you. The pleasure of having two tongues, two lips and two wet love boxes wrapped around my manhood was enough to drive me insane. They sucked and licked and rode me until I was drained of sweat, sperm and plasma. In a word, they greedily tried to kill me with pleasure, taking all of my bodily fluids with them. I had to really catch myself before I got strung out. 'Cause I was truly one orgasm away from getting turned out. I see now why Tee used to love having more than one woman in his bed. It's definitely an experience, like no other.

But ever since I fell into Pandora's box, Lina has been trying to get freaky with it without exercising any type of discretion. Now the sight of her disgusts me. She thinks it's cool to bring her female companions into this house to roll around in the sheets at her leisure. Well, it was when I let my kinkiness get the best of me and was a horny participant. But now I'm done with her and her sexual excursions. I had to finally check her and let her know she would have to bump pussy somewhere else. It's not like I didn't know she was bisexual. It's something we openly discussed. And I'm cool with it. But the agreement was she could do her thing as long as she respected me, our sons *and*, this house. Unfortunately, she's done none of the above. So she can moan and meow on the side of the road as far as I'm concerned. But I'm not having it here.

I guess a part of me thought she'd eventually decide to let go of that part of her life since she was so willing to seduce me—okay, maybe I seduced her. But I didn't ask her to bear my children. Hell, I didn't even know she was pregnant or had given birth until she showed up at my doorstep three months after they were born. I can still remember—as if it were yesterday—the day she walked into my house acting as if not hearing from her for months was cool.

Granted, we both understood our two-month fling was just that, nothing more, nothing less. She would return to the U.S. and I would remain in the D.R. But she was insistent we keep in touch, which is what we did for several months until she stopped returning my phone calls. A courtesy call to say, "Hey, I'm not feelin' you anymore," would have been the decent thing to do. Instead I got nothing. No explanation. No regard. So I erased her name out of my phone book and went on doing my thing. Then out of the blue she shows up at my door, waltzes in giving me the lame excuse that she had been meaning to call but *things* were really hectic for her.

Then, when she waved for her friend Carmen—who was carrying a huge woven basket—to come inside the house, I actually thought she had packed a picnic basket full of treats to surprise me. What a laugh that was. Oh, I was surprised all right! Instead, she pulls back a white blanket covering two curly-haired, red-faced baby boys. And says, "Britton, I'd like to introduce to you, Amir and Amar. Your sons." My sons! I should have known then something was wrong with her.

Indy had warned me about her when she came to D.R. to visit me. For some reason, she didn't like Lina from the start. True, they got off on the wrong foot when Indy called the house to speak with me. But—instead of getting me—Lina had picked up and all hell broke loose. Not to mention, Lina called her a bitch which you know didn't sit well with Indy at all. I had to really patch that one up before the two of them actually met. Thank goodness their paths didn't cross when Indy showed up at my door. It woulda been ugly, I'm sure. I'll admit, Indy's much calmer than she was three years ago, but had she gotten ahold of Lina back then…there's no telling what she'd have done. I had to practically beg her to let it go. And surprisingly, she did.

Nevertheless, she didn't mix her words. She made it very clear, "Keep that *puta* outta my sight and I won't have to handle her." Truthfully, I don't think she really gave Lina a fair shot. But, as always, the problem is: Indy's worse than my sister Amira when it comes to my relationships with women. No one is ever good enough. She had said, "Brit, that Chicken Fajita is nothing but trouble. I know you like her and all, she may even seem nice and sweet, but I'm telling you her spots will change. Mark my words." Well obviously, I didn't listen. You see where I'm at: stuck between a rock and a hard place with two children and a woman I'm not in love with.

Don't misunderstand me. There was a time when I really thought I was falling in love with her. But what I soon realized was that I was in love with the idea of being in love. Truthfully, it had been a while since I'd opened up my heart to anyone. And she was the first woman—in a long time—I even considered worthy of entering my emotional space. I don't regret having met her. After all, she is the mother of my sons and was one of the most beautiful women I'd laid eyes on. And, as everyone who knows me knows, I've always been a sucker for a gorgeous girl with long, wavy hair. Well, I *used* to be. Lina has definitely helped confirm that beauty is only skin-deep. Because let me tell you, she has shown me another side of her that is uglier than sin. I just regret being so damn impulsive and not more responsible. Had it not been for that first night down on that secluded beach, I would have never tasted the fruits of her love garden or slid through the valley of her womanhood. Humph. And I damn sure wouldn't be here.

I will say this much, I miss the tranquility of the Dominican Republic. Don't get me wrong. It's good to be home—home being the United States. But home isn't where my heart is. My heart is back on sandy white beaches, bronzing under golden Caribbean rays and splashing in sparkling turquoise water. Instead, I'm restless under palm trees and sick to death of being surrounded by plastic, star chasers. Everyone here seems to have been under the knife for some type of body reconstruction: nose jobs, liposuction, breast implants, ass lifts; you name it, they've got it. I'm telling you, this place is just full of confused, chiseled-up fools. Half of the time, I can't tell if it's real or Memorex. I've never seen so many phony, pretentious people in my life. It makes my stomach turn. So if you ask me, the City of Angels is more like the Land of Make-Believe.

You don't know how bad I want to be back on my terrace in Sosua, sitting in the nude, sipping on iced-tea spiked with a tad of Barceló—an island rum, and enjoying life with my sons. Back in my impulsive days, I'd be on the next flight out of here. I guess fatherhood has calmed me. So here I am—heartless—in California, hoping that Lina will get her shit together and try being more of a mother to our sons. I understand her desire to be an actress, but at what cost? We have two beautiful sons who hunger for her attention. Yet, the only thing she can muster up is half-assed kisses and hugs when they're already in bed sound asleep.

Granted. When I came out here with the kids, I agreed to be the primary caretaker while she pursued her acting career. And I've had no problem being Mr. Mom. I wouldn't trade watching them meet their developmental milestones for all the mint in the world. But what disturbs me is Lina's nonchalant attitude. No matter how hard I try to involve her in our children's lives, it's painfully clear that being a mother isn't her number one priority. I can't believe I came out here with hopes of us raising Amir and Amar together—as a family. How silly of me!

I even convinced myself, against my better judgment, that she and I might be able to build a life together. But obviously, it was foolish of me to think that she and I wouldn't outgrow this love affair. I know one thing. It's a good thing when I opened the door to my heart I left the chain lock on. Otherwise, I'd be all fucked up. Believe it or not, I'm really cool with there being nothing between her and me other than sex. Yes, even though she disgusts me, I still sleep with her. Well… I did up until two months ago. I don't know what or whom she's doing these days. Condom or no condom, I decided it was better to be celibate than sorry. Oh she still creeps into my bed, trying to get an occasional dose of my love but—as horny as I get—I don't give in. Well, okay. A few times I let her wrap her lips around it. Come on. I have needs too. And when I'm tired of having her mouth milk my penis, I'll shut that down too. In the meantime, I do what I got to do. Slowly but surely, I'm even getting sick of that.

Every time I think about this, I want to scream. I could have kept my ass in the D.R. with my sons and she could have sent us postcards, updating us on her climb to fame on the silver screen. But no, I travel across the country to be the devoted fool. Now, I'm not one to bust anyone's bubble but, between you and me, she'll be getting no Grammies or Oscars anytime soon. With her non-acting, can't-remember-her-lines self. So she just ought to practice her role as a mother. Please don't think I'm bitter. I'm just keeping it real. And the reality is she won't make the A-list—or B-list, for that matter—in this lifetime.

I think back on my own life and I truly can't fathom not having had my mother in my life as a child. She was—and still is—the most important person in my life. Doesn't Lina understand that mothers are truly special, especially the ones who love you no matter what—unconditionally. Weathering all of your personal storms with warmth and understanding.

Praising you. Cheering you on. Pushing you to achieve. Well, that's my mother and she's the reason I am who I am today. My unexpected visit from her last month reminded me of how much she means to me.

"Mom," I had said, surprised and happy to see her when I opened my door. "What are you doing here?" I was wearing a big smile on my face.

"Is that any way to greet your mother," she had said. "I came to see my baby. Now are you gonna let me in or do I have to spend the night on the stoop?" I grabbed her overnight bag, stepping aside to let her in. We embraced.

"Why didn't you tell me you were coming out here? I would have picked you up at the airport."

"It was last minute," she said, scanning the room with her eyes before taking a seat on the sofa. "I was worried about you so Jay put me on a plane to come out here to see you."

"Aww, Mom. Why didn't you just call and ask me how I was?"

"Because, I wanted to see for myself how you were doing. I've been so worried about you."

"Mom, I'm fine," I said, sitting next to her. "You have nothing to be worried about."

She gave me a half-eyed stare, studying me before she spoke. "Boy, I carried you for nine months and I gave birth to you. When you hurt, I hurt. And I don't care how old you get, you will always be *my* baby. My heart told me to come out to see about you. So here I am."

"Mom, don't worry," I repeated, trying to reassure her. "Everything's fine." She scooted closer to me, wrapping her arms around me.

"If you say so, sweetheart." She kissed me on my forehead. "I would lay my life down for you and your sister because the two of you are all I have. I would die to keep either of you from hurting." I just hugged her. It took everything within me to keep from breaking down. Even at thirty-eight, there was still nothing more powerful than being wrapped in my mother's arms.

So the only reason I'm still on this corny, plastic-ass Pacific coast is because I hold on to the notion that Lina will eventually wake the hell up and realize our sons need her just as much as they need me.

For the sake of my sons, I stay because I know what life has been like for Indy and Tee growing up without their mothers in their lives. I don't want Amir and Amar to experience that. No matter how inconsistent Lina's involvement might be, she is still their mother and I don't want to be responsible for them feeling isolated from her. Although, she's doing a damn good job of that on her own.

Just the other night, I had said to her, "Lina, you need to make some decisions as to your role in our sons' lives because this part-time mothering…" I corrected myself. "I mean this lack of mothering isn't getting it." She just stared at me like I had spoken in a foreign language or something. "Hello. I'm speaking to you."

"Brit, I don't have time for this right now," she said, sounding agitated by my remark. She turned around and walked toward the kitchen. "I have to—"

I cut her off before she could go into one of her weak-ass excuses. "When do you ever have time?" I snapped sarcastically, following behind her. "Why don't you take this," I said, slinging her black leather daily planner over at her, "and find a day when you can pencil your sons into your busy schedule since everything has to be such a damn production for you." It landed at her feet.

"How many times do I have to tell you, you can't make me choose? We both agreed that you would take care of the kids while I pursued acting. And now you're trying to act like I'm abandoning them."

"Those are your words, not mine," I said, rolling my eyes up in my head.

"Well," she snapped. "I'm not giving up my acting career to sit home, if that's what you're asking."

"What career?" I asked in mock surprise, laughing. "It's been three years and you've done one TV commercial, one small part in a low-budget flop of a film, and you've been an extra on one overrated TV show. I wouldn't call that much of a career. So no. I'm not suggesting you give up anything. What I'm suggesting you do is spend more time with our sons. Better yet, why don't you try *acting* like a mother, or is that concept too abstract for you to comprehend?"

"Fuck you, Britton!" she snapped, storming out of the house, and slamming the door behind her. Okay, maybe I was wrong for laughing at her. I really wasn't trying to be condescending or anything. I'm just so damn sick of her neglecting her responsibilities as a mother. Hell. There are plenty of actresses who juggle their careers and parenting. And they seem to be doing a good job. So why can't she?

I mean, damn. I would be more understanding of her pursuing her career if she made an honest attempt at being a part of our sons' lives. But she doesn't. She'd rather run the streets, hobnobbing at premiere parties. Which would be fine if she realized her other duties as well. And it wouldn't hurt if she were pulling in some decent money on a regular basis.

Hell. What about my career? I haven't worked a full-time job in almost three years. Well, if you want to count the time I lived in the D.R. then I'd say I've been unemployed—by choice—for four and a half years. When it was just myself I could up and leave at the drop of a hat and not worry about anyone but me. Which is what I did when I left Jersey for the Dominican Republic. This young heart threw caution to the winds and ran free. But, now I can't. I have two kids who have to have a roof over their heads, clothes on their backs and food in their mouths. And everything out here is expensive.

I have bills up the ass and my savings has dwindled down to almost nothing. It's a good thing I have my consultant work, otherwise I'd be standing in line at someone's soup kitchen and checking into a shelter. What I really need is a full-time job to maintain a comfortable lifestyle 'cause this check-to-check living isn't cutting it. But every time I get a halfway decent job, I wind up having to quit because no one can handle Amar. He's been thrown out of three daycare centers in the last six months. All three being white owned and operated. Not that I'm prejudiced or anything. But let's face it, many of them are not in tune to our children's developmental needs and they damn sure aren't always culturally sensitive.

Three months ago, I had to have a school meeting with the director of one of his preschools. She insisted that Amar was ADHD and needed medication. When I asked her how she'd come up with her diagnosis for my son, she stated, "Well, Mr. Landers, Amar tends to have difficulty playing quietly and he often butts into other children's games." I just sat there, staring at her in a daze.

"And?" I responded. She continued, shifting in her seat while darting her eyes around the room.

"And he often engages in physically dangerous activities without considering he might get hurt." I folded my hands in my lap, then ripped into her.

"Let me explain something to you, Ms. Duncan. My son is far from ADHD. If you knew anything about children—particularly boys—you'd know that fidgeting and rambunctiousness are typical behaviors for *many* of them. You'd also know that half of normal children are more active, more inattentive or more distractible than average."

"Mr. Landers, I'm only suggesting—"

"No," I interrupted, placing my elbows up on her desk, then clasping my hands together. "You're assuming. I don't know where you got your credentials but the last time I checked you weren't a psychiatrist. Now, I would think Amar would need to have at least eight symptoms that fit the criteria for an ADHD diagnosis, wouldn't you say so? Based on my calculations, you are five short."

"Well..." She paused. There went those darting eyes again. It was like she were playing a tennis match with her eyeballs. "There are other behaviors as well, but the ones I've mentioned are of much concern. Mr. Landers, I believe your son could benefit from a trial of Ritalin or some other medication to—" I cut her off before she could finish.

Ritalin? I couldn't believe this woman was sitting in front of me with her bouncing eyeballs, suggesting my child needed medication. He's only three! Aside from the side effects, there is very little research on its safety and effectiveness in kids under four. So no one really knows what the long-term dangers might be. It just really disgusts me how more children are haphazardly diagnosed with Attention Deficit Disorder (ADD) and Attention Deficit Hyperactivity Disorder (ADHD)—and placed on medications as young as three, all because some professionals would rather base their diagnosis on subjective observations rather than considering the possibility of other factors that may be responsible for ADHD-like behaviors.

I know many parents and teachers want a quick fix when it comes to dealing with children who present behavioral challenges. But what many parents don't know is that for every child diagnosed with ADHD, only two to three percent are truly affected by it. Believe me when I tell you, Amar is *not* one of them. So, I'll be damned if I'm having him drugged the hell up based on the observation of a wandering-eyed director.

"You don't know jack about what my son needs. And he damn sure can't benefit from being in a setting where he is constantly harassed. Did you consider he might just be an overactive child who needs redirection and positive reinforcements; something he clearly doesn't get from here. The only thing you are concerned with is getting your monthly fees while ripping off hard-working parents." I wanted to tell her I thought she needed medication for all that rapid eye movement she did; instead, I excused myself from her office, grabbed my son's things and stormed out of there.

I don't know whom the hell she thought she was dealing with. But, I'm not the one. Call it what you want, but the bottom line is—and was, there are too many African-American children in special education settings and/or on medications due to misdiagnoses. Which in the end—as far as I'm concerned—does more harm than good.

I apologize for going into another one of my tangents about the educational system, but stuff like this burns me up. Anyway, before I went off course, I was saying how I'm unable to keep a job because no school has been able to handle Amar. And since Lina's behind is always too busy or no where around, that leaves me to "pick him up immediately." Which is what I do without any hands-on disciplining—something I like to refer to spanking as. But last week, I lost my cool when Amar's teacher called, demanding I come get him.

"Mr. Landers. This is Mrs. Thimball from the Children's Day Center."

"Hello, Mrs. Thimball," I politely said, bracing myself for her news. "How can I help you?"

"You can help me by coming to pick up you son, *now!*" she yelled. "I am a patient woman but I will not tolerate an unruly child, especially one who bites. Now come get him or I will sit him out on the curb!" She slammed the phone down in my ear before I could say another word. I snatched up my car keys and ran out of my office. The only thing I kept thinking during my twenty-minute ride there was that this deranged woman had my son sitting on some curb, waiting to be picked up like a trash can. I was heated. Now, I don't believe in hitting a woman but I *was* prepared to run her ass over in my car.

Luckily for her, she didn't follow through on her threat. When I pulled up to the entrance, she greeted me with a limp, dragging Amar behind her. "Take your son and keep him home. I will reimburse you for the rest of this month's tuition."

"Well, can you at least tell me what happened?" I asked, scratching my left temple.

"Your son bit me on my ass! That's what happened," she snapped. I blinked my eyes in shock. I'm not sure if it was because I had never heard this prudent woman curse or if I couldn't believe what I heard he had done.

Apparently, Amar was mad at her for placing him in timeout for the fifth time for talking loud and disrupting the rest of the class. So while she was writing on the chalkboard, he ran up behind her, then sunk his teeth into her flat rear end. She screamed bloody murder while he clamped down on her butt cheek, leaving his teeth marks. I can't tell you how embarrassed I was and how bad I wanted to say something to ease this woman's mind or give her something to soothe her behind. But, I didn't and I couldn't because there was nothing I could say or do to make her feel any better. So I did the only thing I thought was right. I asked Amar to apologize. He refused. "She twisted on my ears, Daddy," he said, glaring up at her. Tears welled up in his eyes. I quickly glanced at his left ear. It was still red.

"Amar, apologize to Mrs. Thimball," I directed. "She's mean to me," he said, trying to hold back his tears. I ignored Mrs. Thimball's mumbling under her breath. Something about young people having babies and not being able to control them.

"Amar, this is not a debate. Now apologize." Again, he refused. So I asked him two more times, each time much sterner and with more bass. And still he refused. So I grabbed him by his arm, pulling him into me. I then pulled down his pants and spanked his bottom until it was red. I opened the car door, directing him to get in and sit still. He climbed up onto the seat, screaming and wailing. And before Mrs. Thimball could storm back into the building, I caught up with her, asking her to *please* clarify Amar's claim that she had pulled on his ears. I purposefully walked up a few steps further to make sure we were out of Amar's view.

"I most certainly did," she replied with indignation in her tone. "He was pulling on another student's ear, laughing. I asked him if he'd like it if someone pulled on his. So I yanked both of his little ears to let him see how it felt. Then I put him in timeout."

"Did you twist them?" I asked, trying to maintain my composure. My heart was beginning to pick up its pace. I could feel it beating in my throat. She stood there with a blank look on her face.

"Your child bit me. That should be your concern, not whether or not I pulled *or* twisted on his little ears."

My head was starting to pound. "Mrs. Thimball," I said, taking in a deep breath. "Did…you…pull and twist my son's ears?"

"Yes, I did. To teach him that pulling on other children's ears is not nice. Nor is it acceptable behavior in my class." I stepped in closer to her, then spoke in almost a whisper.

"Mrs. Thimball," I said, clenching my teeth. "That was inappropriate on your part." And before she could open her mouth to say anything else to defend her actions, I grabbed the top of her right ear and tried my best to twist it off. She yelped in pain. "Don't you ever put your hand on my child." I let go, turned around, then walked back to my car with her holding her ear and rubbing her behind as she made her way back to her classroom.

On our way home, I tried to explain to Amar why he was spanked and how I was really upset that he would behave in such a manner. I wanted him to understand that he can't go around biting people when he gets angry. See. When I discipline—whether it's timeout, loss of privileges or spanking—I try to use it as a form of teaching and I hope they learn from their mistakes. Amar, however, just looked at me like I had three heads or something. Obviously, paying me no mind.

Being a parent, I now understand what my mother meant when she'd say, "This hurts me more than it hurts you," because, although I tried not to show it, I was all broken up inside. So I did the only thing I could. I pulled over on the side of the road, got out the car and opened up the passenger side door for Amar to get out. Kneeling down, I took his shoulders in my hands, and locking my eyes, I said, "I'm sorry for spanking you but you have to listen when Daddy tells you to do something. Do you understand?" He nodded with his bottom lip poked out. "I don't like it when I have to spank you. I gave him a hug. "I love you." He just stood there, glaring at me with his lips poked out.

I rack my brain, trying to figure out where in the world he gets his temperament. My mom says he's just how Amira was. Mean. Amira agrees, laughing. But what I know she really means is, he's just like my father, 'cause that man—God rest his soul—was evil. I just have to shake my head sometimes. 'Cause wherever this side of him comes from, it's the nastiest streak I've ever seen in a three-year-old. Oh, he'll get mad at you and before you know it, he's either thrown something at you or clopped you upside the head with it. He has no problem using his little heavy hands to get his point across. Something I don't put up with. That kind of aggression is a clear indication of him potentially becoming a bully. And I'm not tolerating that. Period.

He's also very stubborn. Now *that* he probably does get from me. I'll tell him to do something and he'll just stare me down. Well, two can play that one. So we stare each other down until I start counting to five. By three, he knows he had better start moving, or else. I try very hard to be patient with him. But he really tries to push the envelope to the edge with his falling out and making scenes when he can't have his way. I usually don't feed into it. I just leave him in the middle of the floor, road or wherever he falls out and keep it moving. Then he finally decides to get his behind up, stomping and screaming at the top of his lungs. But when he gets the best of me, I snatch him up and give him a one-two swing. That generally snaps him out of his fit. Like I said, I don't make it a habit of spanking but every now and then I gotta warm his bottom as a last resort. I'll be the first to admit, he's a handful. But he can also be very loving.

Now Amir has a much calmer disposition. He's every bit of me. Moody. So when he gets into one of his little funky states, I just give him his little space. Eventually, he comes around. He's also quiet and tends to keep to himself. Like me, he doesn't bother anyone. He just sits and observes everything and everyone. But if you press him the wrong way one time too many, he will fight you. But fighting is clearly not his nature.

Most of the time you don't even know he's in the house unless you get up to check on him. And nine times out of ten, he's into something he has no business being in. But all you have to do is give him one of those looks and he stops whatever he's doing. I have to admit, the boy's a little manipulator. He has a habit of looking up at you with his big round eyes, giving you the saddest puppy-dog face I've ever seen. And then for added effect, huge crocodile tears cling to his long lashes. You wanna know something? It works!

With both of these boys, I have to have eyes and ears in the back of my head at all times. Amir likes scissors and markers; he'll write on anything in sight. Amar likes hammers; he'll bang the whole damn house down if you let him. The boy is so daggone destructive it's nerve-racking. If he's not flooding the toilet, he's breaking up his toys, or climbing up on tables, trying to swing or jump off of something.

So as you can see, I don't get a moment's peace until they are sound asleep. By the time I get back from the park or zoo with them, feed them, bathe them and get them settled down it's already eight o'clock. Then it's good night, sleep tight; don't let the bedbugs bite. And by the time I shower, attempt to manually relieve my sexual tensions, then finally fall asleep, it's time to start my day again.

I tell you, it never ends. Sometimes I just wanna scream, "Where's my goddamn help around here!" But I don't. I simply take it in stride and handle my responsibilities as a man, and a father. Bottom line: my sons didn't ask to come into this world, so they shouldn't have to suffer because they have a mother who chooses to be irresponsible and irresponsive.

I tell you, sometimes I feel like I'm about to lose my mind when I'm dog-tired and they're running around, making more noise than I can stand. I just feel like beating them quiet. But then, out of nowhere, my voice of reason takes over, reminding me that they are just innocent children. So I pop two Advil instead, and let them be.

But I will say, when everything is all said and done—regardless of how trying my day might have been—tucking them into bed at night and kissing them on their foreheads makes everything worthwhile. Being able to tell them how much I love them is something I wouldn't change in this world. And hearing the word *daddy* is the most wonderful feeling.

And although having children has slightly altered my life, I've grown. I'm focused. And I'm very happy. I just wish Lina could feel all that I do. I can't imagine not waking up to their morning ritual of jumping on my bed, yelling for me to get up. Not hearing the pitter-patter of their little feet across the wood floor would drive me insane. As much as a handful they can be, I can't imagine my life without them in it. That's one of the reasons I have a difficult time understanding how any man can walk away from his responsibilities as a father. I don't think I could ever look myself in the mirror every day and honestly feel good about myself, knowing I abandoned my children.

Making a baby damn sure doesn't make you a man. And walking out on them—be it financially, emotionally, physically, or mentally—makes you even less of one. All I can say, nothing but death will keep me out of their lives. I'm prepared to take the good with the bad, the bitter with the sweet. And this is coming from a man who was adamantly against ever having children. But things change. And as Lina has shown, people change. Well, I'm prepared to move forward with my life for the sake of them. Sadly, Lina will soon realize that all good things must eventually come to an end.

3

SARINA: *Crazy Maze*

If only we lived in a world absent of prejudices, a place where we could love each other, regardless of preferences. Free to love a sista or a brotha. Free to show displays of affection if you dare. With a man or woman, who should care? See. I am as easy and free as I wanna be. Blowing in the breeze, fucking and sucking and choosing my own destiny. Oh, can't you see. It's only by chance that I'm a victim of circumstance. Oh, that's me! Standing up to fight adversity. Don't you see? I deserve a chance to grow, to roam. To be free to love, free to be me. As freaky as I wanna be. 'Cause my back is aching, my belt's too tight. My coochie's aching from the fuck I had last night. HeeHeeHee.

You know. I could have been a famous fashion designer by now, if it weren't for all those playa-hating bitches in my class, plotting to steal my ideas. Oh, I heard the whispers, "Will you look at what she has on... What in the world?" I saw the wide-eyed stares and the sidelong glances. But I fixed them. I kept all of my sketches in a locked portfolio, then slipped my portfolio into a locked briefcase. And I kept the keys hidden in the sole of my shoe. There was no way I was going to let those fashion frauds get a hold of my masterpieces. Didn't they know I'd been breaking fashion barriers since high school? Well, of course they didn't. That's why I dropped out of art school and decided to take my show on the road without any interference from anyone. And now I'm the proud owner and designer of Sarina Creations, specializing in one-of-a-kind patterns and designs. Yes, the outfit I have on now is one of my very own. A deer fur halter-top with matching hip-huggers. See. I even have fur-covered slingbacks. The handcuff belt and dog-collar choker are for added effect. You like?

You should see how I turn heads when I prance up and down the runway. Okay, the sidewalk. Big deal. Runway, sidewalk, same difference; it's still my show. Okay, here we go. I lick my red-painted lips, bat my curled lashes and, at times, I might even blow a kiss at a friendly yet unfamiliar face. And then I bring it…serve it…work it. Sashaying down the catwalk during rush hour. Strut, spin, and pose. Strut, spin, and pose. And all eyes are on me. It's always the jealous ones who laugh at me but I always get my share of whistles and, every now and then, someone might throw a few dollars in my tin bucket.

Last week I made ninety-eight dollars. Humph. Not bad for a day's worth of work. But I never get a standing ovation. Who cares, though? I'm still going to be famous with or without their support. By the way, I'll be up and down Kennedy Street signing autographs tomorrow around noon, just in case you want to come out and show me some love. What? Kennedy Street where? Duh, Washington, D.C., where else?

Oh, excuse me. For those of you who might not have heard about me, let me formally introduce myself. I am Sarina, the twenty-year-old daughter of Ryan and Chyna Littles. The black sheep of the Littles' clan. I guess you can say, I was born into this world with two strikes against me: being the ugliest, and the blackest, of their four children. Before me, my light-skinned mother—with her silky hair and emerald-green eyes—gave birth to three beautiful boys; light, bright babies with green eyes and straight hair. Then me. Soot-black with dark eyes, knotty hair—okay, so it was thick and long before I cut it off. But it still wasn't silky. Then there's this wide nose and my big lips. Yet, she claims I was her precious bundle of joy; her beautiful baby girl. Please. How could anything looking like this be precious? If you ask me, it seems more like a curse.

To this day, I still have a difficult time believing that she's my mother. I'm certain she stole me from my real mother. I know she did. I don't care what anyone says. I mean. How could the law of genetics allow a woman who can pass for white give birth to someone with deep, dark skin. My father—whose skin is as dark as mine—insists that she did in fact deliver me from her womb. I still have my doubts; however, I'll take his word for it. After all, he was there. And he would never lie to "Daddy's little angel." Well, he did. There were no little angels—dark as night—living in hell. But, I accept what he says, nonetheless. After all, I am the spitting image of him, from his wide nose and thick lips to his dark-brown eyes and dimpled chin. I am my father's child. Oh, sure that impostor has always tried her best to smother me with undeserving hugs and kisses. She always told me—even if they were lies—how beautiful I looked and how special I was and how much she loved me. I just didn't feel worthy of such adoration.

One thing I can say; as ugly as I was, my parents never treated me any different than my brothers and they never let them tease me. They were always so nice to me, probably because they felt sorry for me more than anything else. They most likely were thinking what I was already feeling: poor thing.

But no matter how hard they tried to make me feel wanted, no matter how many kind words she might have said, I still never felt like I belonged. I can still remember the first time I brought my third-grade friends home from school to play and one of them asked me, "Who's that lady?"

"That's my mommy," I had said. They all stood there with their mouths hung open in shock.

"That white lady's your mommy?" they asked in unison.

"She's not white," I snapped with an attitude. "She's black."

"But she's not black like you," Blue-eyes responded.

"So, she's still black," I argued.

"Well, how come you don't look like them?" Blondie asked, pointing at the picture of my three brothers and me. There I was: the dark spot sitting in the middle of the two youngest with my oldest brother standing behind us. "But you're so black. You don't look *anything* like them." I took that as an insult and put them little snot balls out. I never invited them over to play again. I think I cried the whole weekend. My mother tried her hardest to comfort me but nothing she said changed the way I felt.

"Sweetheart," she had said, rocking me and wiping away my tears. "Black is beautiful. Don't you ever be ashamed of your skin tone; you are Mommy's beautiful angel." I heard her every word but it didn't matter. Unless she was able to scrub the black off me, there was nothing she could do. Nothing she would say could ever change my ugliness. That was the first and last time I'd shed a tear over the color of my skin. From that moment on, I would accept my curse dry-eyed and unmoved.

Oh, of course, she *claims* she never favored my brothers over me. She has tried desperately to reassure me that I was her favorite, telling me her lies about how she saw black as beautiful and how she believed having babies with dark, rich skin would validate and solidify her blackness. Ha! She even had the nerve to take it a step further to say, *I*—Sarina Dalon Littles—represented everything beautiful for her.

Nonsense. I don't dislike my brothers. I don't fault them for their being everything I should have been—light-skinned and beautiful. The blame falls on that woman with the flowing, butt-length hair and beautiful creamy skin. Those sparkling green eyes should have been mine. Do you know, I have dreams of cutting out her eyes and wearing them around my neck like emeralds. Oh, I think they would go fabulous with this green-feathered pantsuit I designed out of goose feathers. No, silly! I didn't kill any geese. I took the feathers out of all the goose-down pillows in Chyna's house, then dyed them green. For Heaven's sake!

Anyway, she wants me to accept her excuse that she gave my brothers more attention because she didn't want them to go through life like she did, being confused about who they were. She claims she wanted them to develop into strong men who were proud of their blackness, knowing their lightness would make it hard for them to feel connected to any ethnic group. Hog balls!

Between you and me, I don't believe none of that shit about her feeling worthless until she gave birth to me. What kind of fool does she think I am? She doesn't know shit about feeling worthless. I spent my childhood wishing I could disappear. At ten, I read the *Bluest Eye* by Toni Morrison and cried. Then I saw white flashes. I think it was then that I had my first hallucination. I couldn't imagine there being someone else in this world as ugly as me. Pecola became my best friend. I was so happy to have Pecola in my life. My playmate and I had things in common. We were alike in our ugliness and our hunger for attention. But we were also very different. She wanted blue eyes and I wanted green. Her parents fought. Mine rarely spoke. She was raped. I wasn't. I'm glad my daddy didn't rape me. Oh, how my heart went out to Pecola. Still does. That's why I protect her from harm's way. I will never let anyone hurt my sweet Pecola again. She's been through enough in her life. It's such a shame. So, I guess looking back I wasn't so bad off, after all. I just didn't think anyone could be worse off than me. Hell. Come to think about it. Back then no one ever had to rape me. They still don't. I'm usually willing to just give it away.

Thinking back, I sure did give *it* away a lot. HeeHeeHee. I started pulling my panties down in sixth grade, showing the boys my hairy cooch. Thanks to my mother, that's all I could do since she had me chained to her hip. Those girls would call me names but they sure didn't have titties like mine or have hair between their legs. So I had all the boys as my friends. Ha! I'd sit on the back of the private school bus and play "peek-a-boo" with all of them. I showed those snotty, flat-assed girls.

But, baby. Once I turned fourteen and was able to convince my father to allow me to attend public school—which was no easy task, thanks to my busybody mother—I had the boys lining up to get some of this poon-tang. It didn't matter to me that they called me "tar baby" and "charcoal" behind my back. In my face, they always said how good I made them feel. I knew they didn't like me for me. It didn't matter. The only thing that mattered was that I got their attention. I learned to accept my ugly blackness because as long as I had a bangin' body it didn't matter what my face looked like. So my big basketball ass and cantaloupe-sized titties became my prized possessions. My mother would have the nerve to tell me to be proud of my skin color because "black is beautiful." Well, if black is so damn beautiful, why the hell did the kids at school tease me?

Well, my sophomore year was the last time anyone called me out of my name. That's right! Enough was enough. Once I fought these three bitches—at the same time—no one else dared to dis me. I guessed all those karate lessons paid off. This ugly, black whore, as they called me—over some stinking boy, no less—whipped their asses real good. All because I fucked one of their boyfriends and he gave her syphilis. Big deal. Like it was my fault he didn't wear a condom. Just take your dumb ass down to the clinic and keep it moving. Please. Those boys knew I liked it raw. Come to think about it. Those nasty dogs were probably the reason I'd had numerous STD's. Oh don't worry. I haven't had anything in a long time, and I've never gotten anything I couldn't get rid of. Syphilis, chlamydia and trick-o-molasses—hahahaha! I mean trichomoniasis—are the only things I've had. So who cares? Life goes on. One thing's for sure: all the boys loved this pussy. HeeHeeHee. A few even told me how big it was.

Shoot! I keep me a diary of all the boys I've been with. Last time I checked I was at seventy-eight. Oh, no! Wait a minute. Let me recount. Umm. You know what. I forgot to add the two men I did in the bathroom of that Shell gas station last week. And then the other day I was in the backseat…no, scratch that one. Sucking dick doesn't count. Anyway, once I reach two hundred, I'm gonna get someone to make a mold out of my pussy so I can sell it. HeeHeeHee.

Oh, I know what you're thinking. You think I'm just downright nasty. Well, at least I've never been pregnant. Half the girls my age were either having babies or having abortions. Stupid. My parents didn't even know I was fucking until my nosey-ass mother walked into my room—without knocking—and caught me in the act. I was seventeen then.

See. I was slick with mine. Little did she know, I had been sneaking boys—and girls—in and out of my bedroom window since I was fourteen years old. Before that, we just did it on the side of the house or in the woods. And do you know she had the nerve to beat me? Sure did. She took an extension cord and tried to strip the skin off me. See here. I still have the scars to prove it. That was the first time she had ever laid a hand on me. And I almost think she would have killed me if my father hadn't kicked the door in to save me. Can you believe it? My own so-called mother wanted to kill me.

Okay. So maybe I called her a white bitch and attacked her first. I didn't appreciate her barging into my bedroom and throwing my company out. I was right in the middle of a climax. She could have at least waited until we were finished. What would have been so wrong with that? I'm sure she wouldn't have liked me to storm into her room without knocking. Not that she was getting any. HeeHeeHee. She thinks I don't know, but I know. I know all about her and my father sleeping in separate bedrooms while she tried to act like all was well. Ha! She probably was too frigid for him. Pathetic sow! She spent her lonely nights, running around meddling in my business instead of tryna get her groove on. I bet you the only thing being squirted in her was an old dirty douche. Heeheehee. Anyway, Miss Perfect wouldn't know how to back that thang up if her life depended on it. I bet you.

Oh well. That's now water under the bridge. They are back together, playing the happy couple. And I guess she's finally getting some. Either way, I'm just glad that woman finally has a life of her own and is staying the hell out of mine. She's the cause of me being in all this mess anyway. As a matter of fact, it's her fault I was placed on a nut ward when I was seventeen. The only reason I was hiding under that desk in my room, naked and with a knife in my hand, was because someone had come into my room trying to rape and kill me. Why else would I be screaming? They said I was a danger to myself, and others. Go figure.

Since then, every time I turn around someone is trying to have me put away because they feel I engage in bizarre and self-injurious behaviors. Bizarre? Please. I don't know where the hell these people get this donkey crap. Just because I shaved my head bald and my eyebrows off, doesn't mean I'm exhibiting bizarre behaviors. I had a legitimate reason: there were bugs crawling in my hair and on my face. Is it my fault that no one believed me? Besides, I like wearing wigs. I have a different wig for every day of the week. As a matter of fact, I have a wig in every color and every style imaginable.

And this mess about me being self-injurious? Please. I've never heard such nonsense. These stupid-ass people are still talking about shit I did two and three years ago. Like the time I had been missing from home for three weeks and was found in Baltimore walking in the middle of oncoming traffic. Big deal. I was seventeen, carefree and liked living on the edge a little. So what if I was drunk.

Then there was the first time I slit my wrists. I was eighteen. It wasn't like I wanted to kill myself. I was trying to rid myself of this person inside of me. She kept whispering and taunting me to let her out. So I said, "Okay, bitch. You want out, you got out." So I took a serrated knife and sliced into my skin until blood freely flowed, releasing her from her misery. I woke up two days later on another psychiatric ward. Four weeks later, I was discharged.

Now, the second time I slit my wrists it was to release the poison that flowed through my veins. You see. The waitress at this little diner I used to go to—before they banned me from entering their establishment— tried to kill me. Oh yes she did. She sprinkled rat poison over the croutons in my salad. I'm certain of it. So I attacked her. I took off my wig and beat the everlasting shit out of her. Yes sirreeee buddy. That'll teach her to tamper with my food. They even had the nerve to have me arrested. I couldn't believe how the police humiliated me. Placing those damn cuffs on me like I was some dangerous criminal. I tried to tell them I wanted to file attempted murder complaints on that scraggly heifer but they wouldn't hear of it. Instead they charged me with assault.

My mother had to come down to bail me out. Hahahahahaha! I went upstairs to my room, pulled out my razor—the one I kept hidden under the rug—and, with quick, deep motions, I sliced my wrists. So off I went, back to the looney bin, where I vegetated for eight weeks. Both times, I tried to explain to those idiots that I wasn't suicidal but they wouldn't hear of it. Not even my parents believed me. Now do you think I would inflict that kind of pain on myself if I was really trying to kill myself? Let's be for real. Cutting your wrists hurts.

So, if you haven't figured it out. Everyone thinks I'm crazy but to hell with what they think. I'm probably the sanest person you'll ever meet. If you ask me, my parents are the crazy ones for spending thousands of dollars on shrinks and medications. Since I was thirteen, I've had every type of counseling invented. I've had four psychiatric hospitalizations in the past three years and, in the past two years, I've gone through five psychiatrists and not one has been able to change shit about me. Don't they get it? There is nothing wrong with me. They are just educated idiots. I can't stand them.

Well, I did like Dr. Rogers but he got scared when I got up from my chair and showed him my pierced clitoris. HeeHeeHee. He snapped his pencil in half and broke out in a sweat. He was scared of this young stuff. Hell. I thought a fine-looking black man in the business of probing minds might wanna try probing my insides instead of my thought processes. I dared him to stand up to let me see his hard-on. Scaredy-cat. Anyway, outside of him, the rest of those doctors are jack-offs.

For one, most of them are usually some tight-assed, abuse survivor who's in recovery of some sort. And most of them are either on medications for some underlying disorder themselves, in treatment, or both. Humph. All that tells me is that they are just crazy-ass, credentialed nuts, getting off on trying to get inside someone's head. Particularly mine. Well, I'm too smart for that. I always flip the script on them. And before you know it, I've assessed all of their insecurities and diagnosed any and all psychosis in their pathetic lives. Just the way I did yesterday with Dr. Shapenski, my therapist for the last six months.

"Hello, Sarina," he begins, smiling. His upper lip curls under, showing the top of his big gums. "How are you today?"

He waits for my response. I just stare at him. His nose begins to inflate and deflate like a balloon. I laugh.

"Okay," he continues, flipping through his notes. "Last week, I gave you an assignment. I wanted you to write down all the things that you like and dislike about your mother so we could discuss them today. Were you able to do that?"

For the life of me, I can't understand why this pasty-faced fool doesn't just read the damn back notes. Every report, every session says the same damn thing: I hate that bitch! She has done nothing but try to ruin my life. So there is nothing to write down. He should already know this. She knows it. The whole world knows it. So why in the name of Pippy Longstocking does he insist on wasting my damn time *and* his?

I take my hands and gently rub my nipples in slow circular motions over my white blouse. They begin to swell like ripened fruit. I continue to rub until the gnats in my mind stir with excitement. He doesn't flinch, seemingly unnerved by my protruding nipples. Doesn't even shift his eyes from mine. He waits for me to finish. Then the fruit flies decide they don't want to play anymore. I stop.

"So, Doctor, tell me something. Do you love yourself?"

"How is that question relevant to this session, Sarina?" he asks, shuffling papers in my thick manila file. He makes me sick, answering my questions with a question. I glance down at his fat stubby fingers as they grip his Reflections pen. They remind me of swollen Vienna sausages. He writes something illegible in my progress notes. I silently laugh to myself, imagining him jerking off, then licking his fingers.

"Sarina, tell me how are you feeling these days?"

"Horny," I respond, crossing, then uncrossing my legs. I spread them wide, then fan them shut. Open. Shut. Open. Shut. His eyes never leave mine. I make a mental note: *Next time I'll wear a short skirt and no drawers.* I glance down at his fat feet stuffed into his Cole Haan loafers. *Limp dick,* I think. I burst into laughter.

"How are you sleeping at night?"

"Alone. Do you love yourself, Doc?" Again, he ignores my question. I feel his brown eyes trying to pierce through me. I stare him down, fanning my legs. Open. Shut. Open. Shut. *Tell him to lick your bloody pussy.* I ignore the voice. Open. Shut. Open. Shut.

"Sarina, you seem somewhat distant today. A little preoccupied. Are you taking your medication?" *Would serve him right if you got up and slapped him.* I will myself still.

"Are you taking yours?" I ask, smirking, shifting my weight in the leather chair. He raises his eyebrow. Ah-hah! I slip my hands under my thighs, then kick off my heels, plopping my bare feet on his oak coffee table, then stretching open my toes. He continues to not answer me. But I'm patient. Patient, get it? HeeHeeHeeheeheehee.

"So, how are things with your family?" he asks, waiting to see what I'd say or do next. I smile. But inside I'm laughing.

"How are things with yours?"

"Everyone's doing well, thanks for asking. Now, I'd like to know how things are going with you."

"When did your wife leave you?"

"Excuse me?" he asks, shifting his eyes from mine.

"Your wife, when did she leave you?" He sighs, clearly getting frustrated.

"Sarina, what makes you think my wife left me?"

"Your socks aren't matching. You have on one black and one blue sock." His face turns red as he glances down at his feet. "Let me guess. She left you for a younger man." I wait for his response. He shifts in his seat instead. I remove my feet from his table, slipping my feet back into my shoes.

"I don't blame her. I woulda left you too. I guess she got tired of your impotence and premature ejaculations. You know there are surgical procedures and medications for such sexual inadequacies. I bet you ejaculated as soon as your wee-wee touched her warm, moist coochie?" HeeHeeHee. "Two pumps and a hump, and you were done." He closes my file.

"Sarina, how do you expect to get better if you don't take your medications as prescribed? You can't stop taking them when you want."

"The same way you expect to. Like you, I can do whatever I want. Whatcha gonna do, tell my mommy and daddy? Call my big bad probation officer?" I ask, sarcastically. "I'm a big girl now, Doc. And before you start asking me your goddamn stupid-ass questions again. No, I'm not suicidal. No, I'm not homicidal. No, I'm not hearing voices." He brushes over his hair with his left hand. That irks me. It reminds me of an old dirty rug. *Go 'head, snatch it off his head.* "Why don't you take off that stupid-looking toupee?" I shout.

"Sarina, I think that's it for today," he says, glancing down at his watch.

"I'll see you again next week. I'm going to write you another prescription before you leave." I get up to walk toward him, then lean into him. My nose almost touches his. His breath smells of old coffee and stale cigarettes.

"The hell if you will," I snap, raising my voice in his face. But I know better than to give him an invitation to have me put away. I refrain from threatening him or becoming physically aggressive. I lower my voice, then smile. "I am no more crazier than you are, Doctor." I grab his face, then kiss him on his forehead. "God loves you even when you don't. Now have a good day." I grab my purse, then head for the door, leaving him flustered.

Quack-ass doctors, to hell with 'em all! Who needs medications? I stopped taking mine three months ago and as you can see, I'm doing just fine. Trust me when I tell you, I might be black and ugly, but I damn sure ain't crazy. As a matter of fact, I've decided to take my one-woman show on the road and take a bite out of the Big Apple. So eat your heart out, 'cause Sarina is in a New York state of mind!

4

DAMASCUS: *Give Me The Lovin'*

After two weeks of touring and promoting my book, *The Young Brotha Behind the Mask*—which has gotten mad reviews from *The New York Times*, *The Washington Post*, *Kirkus Book Reviews*, *Newsweek* and the list goes on—I'm glad to be home. Waking up in a hotel room with a stiff dick and nothing but my hand to pop off these nuts was starting to throw me over the fuckin' edge. Not that I have a problem with busting a nut in my hand, I just enjoy having a snug, hot hole to bury this log in, feel me?

See. Back in my stripper days, I'd have more wet holes to slide this pole in and out of than I knew what to do with. I had pussy up and down the East and West coasts begging for this big, black...well, you should already know the rest. Women would drop their drawers and pay to take a ride on all this. Word is bond. I banged a lot of backs out in my day. Hell, I even tried to crush a few windpipes, na' mean.

But now, instead of dropping dough to feel this pipe or suck down these nuts, they're spending it to read my book. Yep. I'm happy to announce, the days of Tee, aka T-Bone—my stage name—waking up to dick-thirsty beasts and trying to fill an empty heart with empty sex is long gone. Word up. The only woman I'm stripping for these days is my wife. And my heart is filled with more love than I ever thought possible. Do I miss all the pussy? Nope. Hell, most of the time, my dick was in it but my mind was somewhere else, feel me?

I mean. Bustin' the nut was good but the shit that went along with it was beat. Like chicks wanting to cuddle and kiss after I've just busted a load down their throats. I'd be like, "Yo, what the fuck! Your tramp ass just let me nut in your mouth. And you want some extras? Yo, get real." My motto was: Stick 'n move. And that's just what I did. Stuck it and kept it movin'.

Hell, being an author is really no different from when I was a dancer. I still got chicks tryna check for me. Yo, peep this shit out: A couple of weeks ago I was in Jersey City doing a signing at Sacred Thoughts Bookstore when this thick-hipped sista with a small waist and wide ass asked if she could take a picture with me. I was like, "No problem, baby. Do you." So she gets one of her girls to snap the flick for her. Man, listen, this chick stood up on her tippy-toes and licked my damn neck while pressing her pussy up into my thigh. Her girl snapped the damn flick before I could jerk away. Yo, I wanted to really check her ass but I just bit my lip. I figured it was only a picture and I wanna keep my readers happy as long as they don't get too out of hand, know what I'm sayin'? However, I know if Indy had been there it woulda been on up in that piece. 'Cause the one thing she's not havin', and that's a sista tryna play her close. Word up.

But, between you and me, I'm glad she stays home. 'Cause I don't need the stress, feel me? Hell, when I'm doing a signing somewhere, I'm out there tryna sell books, not knock boots. Now, if I were single, it would be a different story. I'd have that back crackin' and the pussy smackin' but I'm on some different shit now, na' mean?

Yo, but you wanna hear some crazy shit. A few months back I did a book signing at Ourstory Books and Gifts in Jersey and there were like six chicks up in that piece who had let me beat the pussy up at one time or another. I was buggin'. And of course, that just happened to be one of the signings Indy decided to attend. But after the signing, I had to let her know that I had broken my dick off in a few of 'em. Yo, I know I didn't have to tell her, but what the fuck. That's the one thing we both agreed to do, let the other know when someone we've hit off is in our space.

Hell, it ain't no secret that I was the meat man, packing beef and butchering the hell outta some pussy. So depending on where we're at, we sometimes run into a few old customers, feel me? So to keep down on the confusion, I always let Indy know what time it is, and vice-versa. That's just how we do it. But keeping it real with you, I don't like it when she points out some cat she was gaming. Even though I know Indy has a past—like I do—the idea of knowing some other nigga was up in my wife just doesn't sit well with me.

Anyway, after I told her, she shook her head, then leaned in, whispering in my ear, "I know you didn't fuck big girl standing over there in the blue dress too, looking like a damn grizzly bear." I shrugged my shoulders, throwing my hands up in mock surrender. "Ugh. I forgot. You'd fuck anything with a hole *back* then." She planted a kiss on my lips, then walked off, making it perfectly clear—without saying a word—that I was no longer available for their sexual pleasures. Every woman in that piece cut their eyes at her as she made her way around the room, smiling and shining. Two of them were even bold enough to flirt with me when they thought Indy wasn't looking. And another tried to be on some slick shit, slipping me the digits on the sly.

Yo, I'm telling you. If you a single cat making moves, there's no reason for you not to be getting pussy on a regular. If you aren't...nah, I ain't even going there. Bottom line: if you ain't hittin' skins, then something must be wrong with your ass. Shit, with all the women available to brothas, even a little-dick nigga can get his nut off if his game is tight.

But for the life of me, I can't understand how some of these sistas just play themselves out the way they do. Do you know, just the other night I had a sista who had read my book walk up to me and ask me if we could have a fling. All because, as she put it, "I heard you packin.'" I was like, "Be easy, Ma. Slow it down." I had to shake my head 'cause it was shit like that that kept me knockin' backs out and scraping knees up back in my pimp-daddy days.

Man, listen. I could write a book on some of the things women have said to me after I've banged up their insides, like "I want respect." Yo, now that's some funny shit. I'd laugh at that one, then hit 'em with, "Baby, you just sucked me and my boy off, you nasty. So, no man's gonna respect you when you can't even respect you." Some of 'em just couldn't grasp that. I guess it was a little too far outta their reach.

A few have even hit me with, "I love you so much, Tee." Now, that's a laugh! I mean, how you gonna catch feelings for a cat who just slayed you *and* your girl at the same time? C'mon. The only thing any of them were lovin' is this big, long dick. Issues. That's what they have. A whole lot of unresolved shit going on. Word up! So, hell nah! I don't miss the pussy one bit. Besides, Indy knows how to give it to me just how I like it.

Don't get me wrong. It's been a few times when I almost caved in and let some chick suck down these milk duds. Not because I was feelin' them, I just wanted to nut. Like, last week while I was down in New Orleans at the Essence Festival. Man, let me tell you. There were some freaks out there willing to put in some work. I ain't gonna front, a few times my dick tried to entice me to give in. But then, out of nowhere—before I could even make a conscious decision on my own to bounce—I'd hear Indy saying, "Let that bitch suck your dick if you want." It's like she has eyes and ears every fuckin' where. So, I'd just take my ass on up to my hotel room, jump in the shower, beat my dick, then get on the phone and talk to her until I fell asleep. Besides, I'd rather not let some chick who doesn't mind getting her knees dirty fuck up my thing. Keeping it real, it's really not worth it. I don't care how much brain (head) she gives. Call it pussy-whipped, call it strung out, call it whatever you want. The bottom line: this brotha's grounded *and* in love.

And even if I wasn't focused, I still don't think I'd be beat, especially now that I'm stacking my paper right. See, a cat with a little paper and celebrity status will get all caught up in the hype and be quick to trick off without thinking about the consequences. And then *bam*—before you know it, you're all fucked up in the game with hot drawers talkin' 'bout you tried to rape her. Yeah, she mighta been more than willing to get that back knocked out; but—the minute she feels slighted, she'll flip that shit on you. Word up. On some real-for-real, I'd rather beat my dick, then get all jammed up. The hell if I need that kinda stress on my back, feel me?

Anyway. Man, listen. I don't know what it is about being married, but this wedding band is a magnet for women. I don't care where I go or what I'm doing, chicks will see the ring, and still try to press up. Yo, what the fuck is up with that? I'll tell 'em, "Nah, baby. I'm cool. I gotta wife." But instead of them movin' on, they'll hit me with the digits or practically beg me to beat the pussy up anyway. I guess it's that whole idea of wanting something you know you can't have—then again, I know many cats who'll buckle at the thought of getting away with creepin'. Yo, if you ask me, that's because them niggas on some weak shit, na' mean? But, I ain't with it. Not when I got a good thing at home, feel me?

Besides, most of the women coming at me can't touch Indy. She has 'em beat hands down, even on a bad day. Word is bond! See. Indy takes me places I never thought I'd go sexually. From role-playing to rough 'n dirty, she really brings it out in a nigga, have me callin' out her name 'n shit. My baby got mad skills. No joke. Hell, a few times she made me feel like I was climbin' the fuckin' walls. Now that's when you know the sex's slammin.' Word up. So on the real-for-real, she got my shit wide open.

Now hold up. There are a few things I won't get down on: like her wanting to put on a strap-on dildo and do me. Fuck that! I told her little ass, "You musta bumped your damn head if you think you stickin' a dick in me." Yo, I don't care if it is fake. It's still a damn dick! And I'm not big on her wanting to handcuff me, either. Hell, knowing her freaky behind, that's when she'd try to take the ass, feel me? So no handcuffs! But everything else is a go. I mean everything. Any way she wants it, my baby gets it. So getting home to climb up in that pussy was the only thing on my mind the whole time I was flying down the turnpike. I couldn't wait to wear that ass out.

Man, listen, when I flipped open my cell to call home, I knew her ass was in heat the minute she started talking low 'n sexy on the phone. But, when she hit me with "baby, my pussy is sucking the skin off my fingers right now… It's so tight and hot… Hurry home and get some of this wet pussy," I knew it was on and crackin'. All the way home she had my dick so fuckin' hard I could have cracked the steering wheel with it. I'm telling you. She had me so 'roused, I actually pulled out my dick and jerked off while driving. Yo, I almost ran off the side of the road when I splattered my nut up on the sunroof and dashboard. Word up.

Damn. My baby knows how to keep Big Daddy happy, is the first thing I thought the minute I walked through the door. My baby was butt-ass naked, standing in glass-heeled slippers with whip cream in her hand. The minute I stepped in the house, she pounced on me like a tigress in heat, pushing me up against the door, then dropping to her knees. Before I could say a word she had my dick out of my pants and had sprayed it with the whip cream, then let her lips and tongue slide across it, around it, and all over it. "Damn baby. It's good to be home," is all I could say.

Yo, between you and me, I've had my dick sucked by many women and no one has ever made my knees buckle the way Indy has. The girl can suck the hell outta some dick. Word up. Damn. I know I shouldn't be telling you all this, but my baby has a wicked-ass tongue. Word is bond! And before I knew it, she had sucked and jerked me to another fuckin' planet.

Yo, by the time Indy finished bouncing up and down on my dick, it was three in the morning. The girl literally tried to fuck my brains out. Now I've always been able to fuck all night but she drained this hose dry. By five o'clock I had to sneak down to the kitchen to get an ice pack to soothe my dick and balls. And at seven, she had her pussy hovering over my face, talking 'bout, "Wake up, sleepyhead, it's time for breakfast." Indy never ceases to amaze me. I opened one eye and noticed she had the tip of a peach slice hanging out of her. I smiled when she lowered her sweet hole on my lips. I closed my eyes, then let my mouth and tongue feast on its meal. That was the best breakfast I'd had in a while. Word up.

Aiight. Aiight. Before Indy tries to blow my spot up, I'm gonna keep it real. When we first got married, I didn't know shit about eating pussy. And she wasn't havin' it. Indy was adamant if I didn't eat her pussy right, I couldn't slide my dick up in her. Of course, I was like, yeah, whatever! But yo, she wasn't bullshittin'. You don't know how bad I wanted to get up in her. And rubbing her pussy with my fingers to get it wet was not working for her. And there was no damn way I was gonna be on my honeymoon and have to settle for her grinding her pussy on my dick or sitting back, watching her hit herself off with a dildo. Nah, fuck that, I was putting this dick up in her.

So I enrolled in the Indy school of pussy eating. Word up. She'd lie back, spread open her legs and dictate how she wanted me to lick and suck her pussy. "Either eat my pussy, *and* eat it right or get the fuck off it," were her exact words to me. And every time I didn't do it right, she boxed my ears by slapping her thighs shut. Damn, she had a nigga's ears ringing. And check this shit out. I couldn't even get her to suck my joint. She was like, "Not until you learn how to eat my pussy right." So I spent the first three days of our honeymoon learning how to eat my wife's pussy. Now ain't that some shit?

Hell. Back in the day, I never had to concern myself with eating no pussy 'cause chicks knew I was strictly into layin' the pipe and having it sucked dry. All I had to do was give 'em this dick real good, and a chick would lose her damn mind. Yeah, I'd rip a chick's back out and have her screaming my name, begging me for more—but not Indy. She was no joke. Aiight.

Yeah, I knew how she got down before we got married. But I thought if I read a few books and watched a few fuck flicks that I'd have it down packed. Damn, was I wrong! This cat didn't know shit. And Indy had no problem putting me on blast. Yo, fuck that. That was then. And this is now. And *now* I eat the hell outta that pussy. Word up!

"Damn, girl, you missed Big Daddy, huh?"

"Boy, don't flatter yourself," she said, jumping out of bed before I could slap her on her fat ass. "I just wanted some dick. Now I'm well-fucked, refreshed and ready to keep it movin'."

"Yeah, a'ight. Keep talking slick," I shot back, sliding my hand up and down the length of my dick, then swinging it from side to side. "And I'm gonna whip you with this wood."

"Well, before you whip it," she snapped, standing in the middle of the bedroom to do a handstand. "You betta lick it," she finished saying upside-down while spreading her legs into a Russian split. Her agility and flexibility are things I love about her. Plus, she's double-jointed. So with her legs in the air, I jumped out of bed quicker than Flash Gordon and licked the hell outta that fat pussy. Because I was gonna whip this dick on her and make her call out "Big Daddy" if it was the last thing I did. But I already knew with her stubborn ass it was going to be a long morning. And it was.

Yo, on the real. Indy knows she can get freaky. Not that I'm complaining. Like I said, she never ceases to amaze me. She really bugged me the fuck out the other night when she climbed into bed, then on top of me, straddling my waist and nibbling on my earlobe. She stuck her tongue in my ear, then sweetly whispered, "Tee, baby. I want you to fuck me in my ass." My dick snapped to attention. Not too many woman have been able to take all this back there.

"You sure about that?" I asked, grinning from ear to ear like a kid at Christmas.

"Hmmm, hmmm," she purred, grinding her wet pussy onto my stomach. She kissed me, then started sucking on my bottom lip, reaching around and grabbing my bozack. Slowly jerking it. Up and down, gently rubbing her thumb along its slit. "I want it deep in me. But first, I want you to eat my asshole."

She got up from me and shifted her body around, lowering her soft ass in my face, then putting my joint in her mouth. I stared at it, then lightly licked around its opening. For a quick minute, I thought it winked at me.

"Stick your tongue in it, baby," she ordered, licking the head of my dick. I obliged. I spread open those soft, fluffy cheeks and stuck my long, thick tongue deep inside of her ass. Word up! That hole was tasty. "Open Sesame," I said in between licks and kisses, sticking my fingers in and out of her. "Big Daddy's about to tear it up." She moaned and sucked me until I was ready to pop off.

Yo, it was like she unlatched the hinges of her jaws to swallow every inch of me while massaging my hairy nut sac. *Damn, baby. Damn…Yeah baby, just like that,* my mind whined. Man, listen, she had me so fucking hot, my balls were rumbling. She had taken me to another level.

I really started to get into it when she abruptly stopped, reaching under the bed and pulling out a vibrator and a tube of KY jelly. She climbed off of me, got on her knees beside me, then spread her ass up and out. "Put your dick in." You damn sure didn't have to tell me twice. I grabbed the KY, lubed up, rubbed a glob into that forbidden entrance and prepared to mount. The minute the head of my dick touched that little hole and was able to enter she clicked on her vibrator, sticking it in and out of her pussy until her chocolate tunnel loosened up, sucking in all of me. "Damn, baby. This ass is hot."

"Hmmm. Give it to me, Tee."

"Yeah, baby," I said, pulling her ass cheeks open, watching my dick go in and out. I slid it in, then slowly pulled it out to the head, then slowly back in again. I repeated several more times until I picked up my speed. Yo, she was handling this pipe. "You want this dick, baby?"

"Yes. Oh Tee. Fuck this ass," she moaned, swinging her hips and flipping her vibrator on high. "Hmmmm. Hmmmmmm. My pussy's so wet, baby."

Yo, between Indy's moaning, her tight asshole gripping my dick, the hum of her vibrator and the swish-swishing of her pussy, I was about to lose my damn mind. Word up. I placed both of my hands on either side of her soft hips and dug my dick deep in that hot booty hole.

"Uh. Oh. Hmmm. Give it to me, daaady. Give me that sweet dick, baby. Uh." I pumped harder. Deep-dicked her until my knees wobbled. "Oh. Hmmm. You like this ass, baby?"

"Yeah, baby. Whose ass is this?" I asked with my left arm around her waist and my right arm up under her while rubbing her clit with my fingers.

"Yours. Uh. Oooh. Yessss. Yessss. Fuck me, Tee. Hmmm. It feels so good in my ass. Hmmm. Make my pussy nut, baby."

Yo, the dirtier she talked, the harder my dick got. The harder my dick got, the deeper I dug. Indy had my head spinning. We moaned, groaned and sweated until we both erupted sticky nuts of pleasure. Word up! We did it up real lovely.

Oh, don't get it twisted. She tries to be stingy with it most of the time. But I usually find a way to get around that. All I have to do is start licking and sucking on her hot spots and it's a wrap. There's no way I'm lying next to all that ass and not be hittin' it every night. She's out of her damn mind.

Like I told her last week, "You mine, baby. From the top of your head to the bottom of your feet, to the crack of your ass—you mine. So don't think you gonna hold out on keeping my dick wet."

She laughed, then headed to the bathroom. When she came out, she tossed a cup of water between my legs and snapped, "How's that for keeping your dick wet?" I got up and chased her ass through the house, finally tackling her down on the floor in the living room where I slid all this eleven inches up in her until she gasped and wet my dick with ecstasy. She knew the score.

Nah, hold up. I'm not sayin' shit is always sweet between us. 'Cause word up, Indy can really vex the hell outta me with her moody, funny-style ass. But, I usually nix her off 'cause I ain't with a whole lotta beefin', feel me? I tune that ass right on out and keep it movin'. That shit just pisses her off even more. I don't know what it is about women, wanting to bitch about shit that doesn't even make sense to me. Yo, so the fuck what I leave my boxers in the middle of the floor. Damn! Either pick them shits up or step over 'em. Why do I have to hear about it? And how the hell you gonna wake a nigga up, talkin' 'bout "cut down on that snoring."

Man, listen, she'll wait until I'm rollin' in a deep sleep to shake me like she just lost her fuckin' mind, talking that crazy shit. I told her ass to buy some earplugs. Hell, I don't complain when she's scratching the back of her throat like she has mites in her mouth or when she's soaking up my side of the bed with her drooling. And I damn sure don't say shit when she wakes up looking like she was smacked with an ugly stick. She wakes up with her lips swollen, eyes all bulged out, and her breath bangin'. But as scared as I am, I still give her ass a good morning kiss and just take it all in stride. I'm telling you. She really kills me. Half the time, I laugh at her ass. Word up. My baby is funny as hell.

Speaking of babies, I'm tryna make a few of my own. Seeing Brit with his boys makes me want children even more. I told Indy from gate how bad I wanted kids. And now that we're married, I want our family to grow beyond her and me. It's taken a lot of emotional convincing, because of her reluctance, but she's finally agreed.

"Well, she said. "If this is what you want, then I guess we'll have to start planning."

"Damn, baby. Why you have to say it like it's some ungodly task or something? Damn, I thought you wanted a baby."

"Tee, that's not what I'm saying at all. And of course, I would like to have a baby."

"Then what's the problem?" I asked, rubbing the back of my neck. Every muscle in my body was beginning to tense. My head was starting to hurt. I tried to keep my frustration in check.

"Tee," she said, pausing again, then sighing. "I'm just not ready."

I sucked my teeth, studying her. "You're not ready? What kinda shit is that? What is there to get ready for? It's not like you have a lot of time on your side." That came out of my mouth before I could catch it from slipping off my tongue. She raised an eyebrow, tilting her head. It was about to be on. "I didn't mean it like that," I said, tryna clean it up.

"Oh, really?"

"Look baby," I said, tryin' my best to not let this turn into a you're-sleeping-your-ass-on-the-sofa night. "You act like there's something wrong with wanting a child with the woman I love."

"I didn't say that—"

"Sounds that way to me." She shifted her eyes, drifting off to another place. I brought her back to our conversation with the touch of my hand. Her hazel eyes met mine.

"Tee, I just think we should wait until the time is right."

"When the time is right? We're married, we've survived the first two years together and I love you. What else is there to wait for? I'd say this *is* the right time." I rubbed her hand while she fidgeted in her chair "Baby, you're my life." Her facial expression softened. She traced my lips with her index finger. I kissed its tip. "And I want the love we share for each other to bring us a child."

"I know, Tee," she said, smiling. "And I love you, too." There was a long pause before she spoke. It was almost as if she were tryna choose her words carefully. "And, you're right. There'll never be a right time. So there's no time like the present. I'll give you a baby." Instead of questioning her on the "I'll *give* you," as if she were doing me some kind of favor—as if it were an act of kindness toward the downtrodden, I kissed her gently on those pretty-ass lips of hers. I didn't care about anything other than having a baby with the only woman holding the key to my heart. I carried her upstairs to our bedroom where I filled her up with all the love that's in me.

That was six months ago. And she's still not pregnant! I've even bought a few books to show which positions you should make love in to have either a boy or girl. Of course Indy thinks the books are a bunch of bullshit. "I don't know why the hell you waste money on a book that has no damn control over which sperm gets the egg first."

Whatever. Bottom line: we sex it out every day and night until she is. I can't seem to figure out what the problem is. I know this sharpshooter is aiming right and shooting more than blanks. I've asked her if we should be concerned but she says no. Yo, I ain't gonna front, I'm disappointed every time her period comes. But, fuck it. We'll keep going strong until it happens. It's all gravy, 'cause you know how much I love to fuck.

In the meantime, if she'd only take her ass in the kitchen to cook me a hot meal. I'm not asking for her to slave over a stove seven days a week, just hook a brotha up from time to time. Damn. A couple of weeks ago I called her on it and things got a little heated. I fucked up when I mentioned how I never had any problems getting those chickenheads I used to smash to keep the pots hot. Well, that set her off like Fourth of July fireworks.

"Motherfucker, you want a hot meal, then take your happy ass on back to those dumb-ass bitches. 'Cause this sista ain't cooking shit." I knew that shit was gonna cost me. 'Cause any time I fuck up, Indy's gotta hit me in the pockets. I ended up spending over three hundred dollars on roses and buying her a new Gucci watch and still had to sleep in the spare bedroom.

By the third night, I had had enough of her cold-shoulder treatment. I brought my ass back to our bed. I slipped my boxers off and slid up beside her warm body. My dick snapped to attention. I pressed up against the crack of her soft ass. She yanked around and blacked.

"Motherfucker, I know you don't think you gonna get any of this good pussy after tryna talk slick about some chickenhead bitches cooking for you."

"Aye, yo," I whispered.

"What I tell you 'bout talkin' slick?" She glared at me.

"Damn, girl. How long we gonna go through this." My dick throbbed. My balls ached. "I'm sorry, baby. I don't wanna beef." *I just want some damn pussy.*

She squinted her eyes at me, then softened. "Me neither," she said, leaning in to give me a kiss. She licked my lips, then stuck her tongue in my mouth. I smiled, squeezing my dick. She got up outta bed and shook her bare ass into the bathroom, closing the door behind her. I smiled. *Yeah, my baby's about to ride this stiff dick into tomorrow.*

I rolled over on my back, massaging my swollen nuts—anxiously waiting for her to climb up on this trunk. About five minutes later, she came back out wearing a black wetsuit. "Let's see you get up in this," she snapped, snatching the covers up over her, turning her back to me.

"What?!" I snapped mad as hell.

"Good night," she said, dismissing me with the flick of her hand.

I looked down at my stiff joint, *Well, buddy, it's just you and me*, I thought to myself. I sucked my teeth. "Fuck it!" I snapped, rolling on my side to face her. I jerked off until I splattered a thick, gooey nut on the back of her wetsuit, then took my ass to sleep.

You know. Sometimes, I really just wanna black on her ass but can't 'cause some of the shit she does cracks me the hell up. Like three days ago when she broke down and said, "You know, baby. I've been thinking about what you said. And you're right. I should cook for you. We've been married for almost three years and I haven't cooked not once for you. There's absolutely nothing wrong with me hooking up a meal from time to time. So tonight I'm gonna serve you real proper."

"Now that's what I'm talkin' 'bout," I said, smiling from ear to ear. Finally. My wife was gonna take it to the kitchen. So after spending the day down in Jersey, I get home to a candlelit house, Maxwell's "A Woman's Worth" blaring through the speakers, and Indy wearing nothing but a black lace apron and black spiked heels. I don't even need to tell you how thick the beef got. It was about to be on up in here. Word up!

"Dinner is ready to be served, your Royal Highness," she said, pulling my chair out for me to sit. My stomach growled. I watched her bare ass bounce and sway as she headed back to the kitchen to bring her man his meal. I rubbed my dick, 'cause we both knew what dessert was gonna be. So she comes back out and sits a silver tray in front of me, pulls up the silver plate cover and *voilà!* Dinner was served.

"Yo, what the fuck is this?" I snapped.

"It's your dinner. You wanted a hot meal so you got it. Now stick that on your list of things I don't do." She had the nerve to hit me with a no-frills TV dinner. I wanted to scream on her but I sat and ate my damn food 'cause I was hungry as hell. She pranced her ass up the stairs, cursing. "That'll teach your black ass. Telling me what the fuck some dick-whipped bitch used to do for you." She slammed the door. A few minutes later, she came back down fully dressed. I looked up at the clock. It was ten minutes to eight.

"Where the fuck you going?" I asked, getting up from my seat.

"Out."

"The hell if you are," I said before she could get out the door. "You make me sick with this, girl. You always harboring shit, I thought we were done with that. I said I was wrong for saying what I said. So can we move on? Damn." I walked up on her and tried to kiss her. She turned her head. "Come on, baby. How long you gonna put me through this? You know I was only fuckin' with you."

She stared me down with her hand on her hip. "Tee, don't fuckin' stand here and try to patronize me. We both know your ass was serious." Okay. I saw where this was going so I decided I had better take another approach.

"Damn, baby. I said I was sorry. What else I gotta do?" I pleaded while grabbing her around the waist.

"Get the fuck off me."

"Come on, girl. You ain't going out tonight so you might as well go on back upstairs and put back on that little apron and finish serving me the rest of my meal." I licked my lips.

She turned around and flipped up her skirt, showing me her bare ass.

"Lick my ass." I didn't bother asking her hot behind why she didn't have on any drawers. But one thing was for sure; we weren't on the same page. She was ready to beef and I was ready to fuck. And this particular night she wasn't gonna get her shit off.

See. Sometimes I gotta manhandle her ass to get her to take it down a notch. Otherwise, she lets her mouth get the best of her and starts talking out the side of her neck. So, I snatched her up over my shoulder and proceeded to carry her up the stairs, while she kicked and cursed me out. I pinned her down on the bed, pulled up her skirt and commenced to lick her bare ass until she stopped running her damn mouth. She stopped squirming, stuck her butt up and out, and spread open her legs. "If you're gonna lick it, then lick it right," she snapped. "And while you're at it, you might as well eat my pussy, 'cause I know that little TV dinner didn't fill you up." I burst out laughing, then helped myself to dinner, hungrily licking her into ecstasy.

5

CELESTE: *I've Been in The Storm Too Long*

Lord knows my life has been a well-traveled road with one detour too many. At forty-one, I've had my share of bad days and lonely nights. I've had to climb more hills and cross more valleys than I would have liked. And I know what it's like to be dragged and kicked through the mud. Make no mistake, I've seen the dark side of life and I have skeletons I wish could stay where they lay. I guess you can say I've been to Hell and back. Yet, I still stand.

When I reflect back on my journey, I can't help thinking about the song "We Fall Down." Every time I hear it, it brings tears to my eyes. Partially out of guilt for not always getting up when I fell. But now I understand why. You see sometimes I just didn't know how. Sometimes I didn't have the strength to. And other times I was too ashamed to. There were many times when it felt safer lying in a muddy lake rather than standing up to face ridicule. Sometimes it was too hard to face what I would see in the mirror of my life. What I had become.

Sometimes I'm haunted by the misdeeds of my past. And it hurts. But I can't change the past nor can I predict my future. I can only stay focused on today and pray I continue to have the strength to overcome whatever obstacles are placed before me. I've come to accept the fact that all that I've gone through in my life has been more of a means of me finding myself. It's unfortunate my path of self-discovery has been trekked at a painful pace. Clouds of despair have hovered over me, dumping a cascade of loneliness on me.

Sad to say, most of my life has been a monsoon of loss and emptiness; an emotional swamp of misery. You see my first loss was at sixteen when I lost my virginity and innocence to a nineteen-year-old boy I would never love or ever be loved by. Ignorance is what brought us together. Fate is what forced us apart. He ended up being sentenced to twenty-five years behind bars for shooting a man in the face and I ended up giving birth to a child I never wanted. Never loved.

And now it's too late. I'll never have an opportunity to know what it would have been like to love her. Just when we were beginning to develop a mutual respect for one another, she—along with my mother and father—was taken away from me. Four years ago, a man fell asleep behind the wheel of his truck and hit them head-on, killing my daughter instantly. My parents died one week later: my mother from cerebral hemorrhaging and my father from internal bleeding.

At twenty, Anqelique's life was ended, haphazardly at the expense of someone else's ignorance and self-indulgence. Not only was the driver's alcohol level almost three times more than what state law permits for drivers—he was uninsured. And although he's serving a twenty-year sentence for aggravated manslaughter, my whole family is gone. Just like that! As soon as I was getting my life together and beginning to develop a relationship with them—particularly my daughter—some selfish bastard caused the end of my beginning. His reckless decision to drink and drive killed three innocent people. He took away a mother, a father, and a daughter. Despite my strained relationship with them, they were the only family I had. And now, I can only wonder what might have been between us.

Not that I deserved to have my daughter in my life. It's not like I was in hers. Sad to say, Angelique didn't even know I was her mother until her thirteenth birthday. That was the day I barged into my mother's two-story home (with wide-eyes and ashy lips) and told her—without considering the consequences or repercussions—that Octavia was *not* her mother. I was. As heartless and as cold as this might sound: I didn't care. I wanted her to know. As long as the secret was out in the open, I didn't care how it sounded or who got hurt. I needed her to know how I hated when she called me *Celeste*.

I wanted her to give me the respect I hadn't earned. I'll never forget the look in my own mother's eyes when she raised her hand all the way back and slapped me to the floor—in front of all her guests.

"Get out!" my mother yelled. "How dare you come into my home with your drunken nonsense."

"I'm not drunk!" I screamed back at her, holding my bruised face. "Tell her the truth."

"I'll do no such thing," she snapped, shaking with anger. "I've never raised a hand to your selfish, unruly behind, but if you don't get out of this house I'll beat you with everything in here."

"It's the truth and you know it, Mother," I challenged, standing to my feet. "Tell her," I screamed, pointing over in Angelique's direction. "Tell her how you tricked me to give her up."

My mother lunged at me, knocking me back to the floor. "Why you ungrateful, little scatterbrain… "

"Please, Mother," Angelique pleaded with tears in her eyes.

"Sweetie, I'm your mother," I interjected. "It's time you knew the truth." My mother slapped me again.

"You shut your ever-lying mouth." My mother scowled. In all of my years, I had never seen her irate. Everything about her was always controlled. She would never dare to embarrass herself in front of others. But this time it didn't matter. She had a look on her face I had never seen before. And it frightened me.

"Avia," my father warned in his booming, baritone voice, "let her be." He gently grabbed her by the arm, trying to lead her out of the room. My father was a man who usually spoke very little. But when he did, he got your attention. Unfortunately, this time, my mother paid him no mind.

She scowled, snatching her arm from him. "I'll do no such thing. I will not allow her to continue with her slanderous comments." As I pulled myself up from the floor, she turned her attention back to me. "If you open your mouth to say another cotton-picking thing, I will kill you dead with my own bare hands. How dare you come into my home with your half-baked scuttlebutt, disgracing my good name?" Her eyes bore through me as she squinted balls of fire. She clenched her teeth. "Don't you ever, as long as you live, step foot back in this house." She glared at me with disdain carved on her face as I whimpered. "You are lower than the debris floating in the gutters. From this moment on, you are dead to me."

My own child stood in shock, looking down at me as if I were something vile. It was almost as if she had stepped in animal waste and was disgusted with having gotten it on the bottom of her shoe. That's how she made me feel. I think that hurt me more than any slap my mother could have ever given. I think her look, the same look Octavia always gave me, is what pained me the most. In her eyes, I was nothing but trash.

I want you to understand that in the beginning, I tried my best to love my daughter but something in me wouldn't let me. I wasn't in the right frame of mind. And after years of playing *big sister* to her, I've come to realize I lacked that maternal connection a child needs to thrive. I was too young and too emotionally unprepared for motherhood. Nor did I really want it.

Besides, my aristocratic mother was insistent that no decent man was going to want spoiled goods. So I abandoned her. I willingly gave my parents all of my parental rights. After all, in the fall I was going to be one of the fly girls at Howard University. With all the campus parties and fine, eligible men around, there would be no time for diaper bags and feeding schedules. It was going to be all about me. So I went through life without a care in the world, pretending.

You see, at seventeen, life was sweet. Or so I thought. With thick hips, wavy brown hair and an attitude to match my designer outfits, I had my pick of any campus brother I wanted. So my life became a big party. But then in my junior year, a young freshman waltzed into my creative writing class and swept me off my feet without ever looking at me or saying a word. I was so used to guys chasing behind me that I expected him to as well. But I was invisible to him. I refused to entertain the possibility that maybe he wasn't attracted to me. That could never be. So, he became my challenge. I secretly vowed I would have him if I did nothing else and then drop him like a hot potato for not acknowledging my existence. But any time I saw him, I became more consumed with thoughts of him. My desire for him only magnified with each passing day.

He was one of the finest brothers I'd ever seen and had the words *good catch* written all over him. He had smooth, reddish-tinted skin with a sexy mole on the side of his face, thick curly hair and long lashes wrapped around big, brown bedroom eyes that lured me to him. His lack of interest in me didn't matter to me. I pursued him until he gave in to me. And the first time we made love it was magical. He was the man who warmed my heart and filled my loins with pleasure. And I wanted to ensure his seeds of promise would take root inside of me; perhaps produce a plentiful harvest. So I poked holes in his condoms. Yes. I trapped him. I loved him and knew he would grow to love me too. How could he not, if I were the mother of his child?

From the moment of conception, I loved my baby with every breath I took. Then with the blink of an eye, my love child was snatched away from me. You see: God doesn't like ugly. Little did I know that I would be struck down and eventually have to bear the heaviest cross of my life: Giving birth to a stillborn son. That was my second loss. And the loss of my will to live was my third. The agony of having to bury my baby was the most excruciating pain I could ever imagine. I remember lying in that hospital bed, yelling and cursing God for taking my son from me. Isn't it ironic, I didn't want my daughter, but lost the son I loved?

Looking back, I suppose my deceitfulness had sucked the life out of him, along with forsaking my firstborn. Still in all, no matter how much time has gone by, I still mourn. I will always mourn. I don't think any parent can ever get over losing a child, particularly a mother. Having to sit there and watch them lower his casket into damp soil was the most agonizing, heart-wrenching experience I've had to live with. The pain and emptiness has been etched in my heart forever. And sometimes, in the still of the night, it comes to remind me of how cruel life can be.

I suppose my fourth loss: losing the only man I'd ever love—the father of my son and *my* husband—was inevitable considering the circumstances that brought us together and the events that separated us. A few months after we buried our son, we both agreed to leave D.C. and Howard University for Norfolk, Virginia—where in the fall we'd both transfer to Norfolk State University.

I truly thought the change would bring us closer. Well, the only thing it did was strip me of what little dignity and self-worth I had left. Norfolk was where I'd sold my soul. It was there that I'd fall on my knees scratching and itching. It was in my corner of misery that tiny white specks of paranoia would have me crouched down, feeling the floors for God knows what. It controlled me. I became its whore. It became my pimp.

There was nothing anyone could do for me. I'd let it straddle my back and ride me to hell. I forced it to push my family away from me. Abandon me. Nothing hurt more than my mother telling me I was no longer welcomed in her home. "You are a disgrace to this family," were her last words to me before slamming the door in my face; leaving me to weather a cold winter storm, wet and alone. But that didn't stop me.

I allowed it to chase my husband away, leaving me with nothing but stained memories. To this day, I can still feel the warm droplets of despair that escaped from his eyes as he embraced me for the last time. "Celeste, I can't take seeing you like this. I love you, but I just can't do this with you anymore… It's killing me," he had said to me the minute I walked in the house after a three-day rendezvous. I slapped and kicked him. I threw things at him and screamed obscenities. The only thing he did: grab his suitcase and slowly walk out of the door and out of my life, never looking back. They always say, "How you get him, is how you keep him." Well, I got him with lies, and I lost him with lies. So you tell me, does that saying really hold true?

I couldn't believe he'd turn his back on me—the mother of his child. I was hurt and scorned, and I swore I'd make him feel the pain I felt. Three weeks later, with my eyes as big as flying saucers and my hair tossed every which way, I marched right over to Norfolk State in my wrinkled clothes and waited until I saw him coming across the campus. There he was. Fine as wine, standing in front of Godwin Student Center talking to two girls. I quickened my steps, my heart pounding. The thought of aggressing caused froth to form around the corners of my mouth. He tried to ignore me. He did his best to avoid me. But I cut him off, blocking his escape from me. I refused to let him dump me without getting another piece of my mind.

"You ain't shit. You weak-ass motherfucker," I yelled at him. "I hate you. You pretty-faced bastard...I'm gonna have your face cut," I threatened. He said nothing. He just stared at me with pity. I saw the hurt in his eyes but didn't care. Why should I? After almost two years of marriage, he had left me to fall into the bottom of a pit. Before I knew it, I had summoned up a paste of thick, brown phlegm that stuck on his face. That was my dare for him to strike me. Instead, he walked away, leaving me in the center of campus looking like a crazed-fool.

Truthfully, I had no reason to blame him. He had begged and pleaded with me to get help. Yet, I continued to walk my tightrope of lies. Lies I sometimes had trouble remembering and keeping track of because I had told so many. Despite his threats to leave me time and time again, I continued to dance with deception. What else was I supposed to do? It whispered sweet nothings in my ear in the middle of the night. Teased me. Enticed me. Forced me to sneak a few dollars from him, then slip out into the darkness in search of its companionship.

Before the night was through I'd have snuck in and out of the house three, maybe four, times with money I'd *borrowed* out of his wallet. And, when there was nothing else left to borrow, I'd remove items from our home. How dare he try to force me to give up my feelings of euphoria? It was the only thing that kept me sane. He was just too self-righteous to understand. Still, I wanted him. I still do. After all, he had promised to love me in sickness and in health.

Nevertheless, I hated him for leaving me hostage to little white rocks of death. But each time I saw him I'd break down and beg him back. And in between clouds of white smoke, I cried rivers of sweet sorrow and self-pity. Hoping. Desperately wanting the strength to keep my life from unraveling. From becoming unglued. But the burning desire to keep chasing that first hit kept me chained to a pipe, and a crystalline powder called crack.

Yes. Call me Crackhead. The reigning Queen of Crack, if you will. Call me anything you'd like for that matter. Just know that for the last ten years I've been clean. And I owe it all to my savior Jesus Christ. Now don't get me wrong, I'm not some born-again religious fanatic. I am just at a point in my life where I've learned to give thanks for my blessings. I mean. After three failed rehab attempts and countless NA meetings, it was nothing but the grace of God that the taste for drugs was removed from my mouth. How else could I have the strength to throw down my pipe and never look back? It was HIS mercy that lifted me out of my hole of destruction. And I am thankful. Nothing more. Nothing less.

I am living proof that all things are possible. I spent seven years of my life enveloped in self-hatred and bitterness. And I sealed it with countless lines of cocaine and vials of crack. Thousands of dollars wasted on clouds of smoke. With the strike of a match, my life was sucked away through a glass tube. To only wake up and find myself looking up from a dark, lonely pit. The reality is, no matter how loud I screamed or how long I cried, I was my own worse enemy and no one could save me. I had to be ready to save *me* from myself. And I did.

So I am here today to tell you that this sister has moved upward and onward with her life, leaving old people, places and things behind. Never again will I allow drugs to control my existence or rob me of my life. There is no way in hell I'm ever going back to the way I used to be. I have a successful career, a new lease on life and now I'm ready to love again.

In the past, I had nothing to give of myself because I didn't know whom I was or what I was supposed to give. I had to learn how to love myself—first—before I could ever truly love anyone else. And I have. Now I'm ready to give all that is within me to the only man who has consumed my thoughts for the last seventeen years. I often wonder if he still thinks of me, or if I've become a dusty memory in the back of his mind. The thought of someone else having his heart saddens me. As strange as it may seem, I can't imagine anyone else ever loving him as much as I do or being worthy enough of his love.

I don't want you to get the wrong impression of me. I'm not some psycho fatal attraction or anything like that. I'm just a woman still in love with a man I lost to stupidity. I want him back and I am ready to do whatever I must to have him. And I do mean *whatever*. Sometimes I am overwhelmed by the intense emptiness his absence in my life brings. And even though I've had my share of relationships—and a few one-night stands—none of them have ever been able to fill the void in my heart. Even in the company of other men, I still felt lonely. Loneliness is a terrible thing. It's like a thief in the night, smothering you. Stealing your heart and soul. I refuse to embrace it, ever again!

All I need is one chance to prove to him that I am no longer that confused and lost girl he once loved. I am a woman. A woman willing to give him all he'll ever desire. As crazy as this may sound, I can't let go. As hard as I've tried, something within won't let me. A deep aching in my heart tells me he still loves me. So I hold on. And somewhere, somehow, I am going to make him love me all over again. He has to give my love another try. No matter what it takes, I won't let him give up on loving me.

I've had many sleepless nights searching my mind's eye for traces of his love. And only after I've conjured him up from the depths of my soul, am I able to peacefully rest. In my dreams, his smile invites me to taste his lips. It is his lips and tongue that whisper sweet lullabies over my body. Painting me with warm wet kisses. It is his hands that glide across my body, causing every nerve to tingle with excitement.

My insides, wet with desire, lovingly greet him. It is his entry that causes me to see streaks of red and fire-orange. A thunderous moan escapes me. My hips rapidly meet his thrusts like the crashing of waves against a jetty. A fire of overwhelming desire ignites. Flames of passion engulf me. But then…I awaken.

"Good afternoon, Celestial Consultants. Celeste speaking. How may I help you?"

"Just thought you'd want to know, everything's in place. You'll be leaving out on Thursday at ten thirty a.m. on flight 683. First class, of course."

I smiled. "Perfect."

"Now don't forget," my confidante and friend said, reminding me of the shopping spree I had planned. "You'll need to pick a up few exquisite pieces for added effects. Otherwise, you'll just be another face in the crowd."

"And we don't want that," I added. "But, don't you worry. I have everything under control. I plan on doing some serious shopping."

"Then return everything when you get back," she said, laughing.

"Ooh, how tacky." I paused, joining in her laughter. "I'll just return what I don't use."

"Well, whatever you do, don't scratch up the watch I picked up. Otherwise, you'll be selling everything you own to pay for it."

"That much, huh?"

"A mint and then some."

"I'll be sure to take very good care of it," I said, thinking of my mother. *I don't know where you get your poor-trash, two-dollar tramp ways. But, you had better start acting like a Munley or you'll be disowned.* I shook her voice from my head. "I better get going. I'll give you a call in a few days."

"Enjoy!"

"Thank you."

"Oh, and Celeste."

"Yes?"

"Good luck."

"Thanks," I said, taking in a deep breath, then slowly exhaling, hoping to blow out the huge butterflies that beat in my stomach. Finally, after months of planning, the time had come for me to make my debut. Yet, I was nervous. I felt like a swimmer, treading my way to an unknown land in an unpredictable sea.

I smiled, glancing over at his picture on my desk. Soon it would all be over. In a matter of time, I'd be able to lay in the comforts of my man's arms. I miss him so much. I can't let all I've done over the last two years to have him back end in vain.

I need you to understand. Through all of the rain and mud, I have never stopped loving him. And now the sun is shining down on me, warming my desires for him intensely. If everything goes according to plan, I will be wrapped in his warm embrace. And this time, *nothing* will keep us apart. Not even my past.

Trust me. There's a new sheriff in town— and she's back with a new look and a new attitude to match. And I'm here to reclaim my husband. Oh yes. I have come from out of the storm and I am ready to face a brighter day. *Wherever you are, my love, I will find you.*

6

INDERA: *A Ride In the Sky*

I was truly pleased with what I saw when I stood in front of my floor-length mirror this morning; girlfriend was *fierce*. I looked good enough to eat if I do say so myself, laid out in my mint-green jump-suit with matching handbag and pumps. Of course, I accessorized with my diamond-and-emerald choker and matching bracelet. With the exception of my Gucci luggage, from my outfit to accessories, I was a walking bill-board for Chanel. I tossed my shades over my head, then blew myself a kiss as I prepared to finish packing my last piece of luggage. Sistagirl was heading to Las Vegas with about fifty sorors for seven days of glitter, glamour and gambling. And let me tell you, it's a good thing I'm married because I was ready to drain me a few ballers and shot callers. Trust me.

Anyway, despite feeling a little queasy, I was in good spirits and floating on cloud nine until my phone started ringing off the hook. Something told me to let the answer machine greet my caller but for some reason I decided against it. Wrong move. It was Chyna calling me from Slovenia, rambling about Sarina being somewhere in New York. I thought I would fall out. I was so tempted to tell her to back off and let Miss Thing do her. But hearing her level of concern forced me to bite my tongue. Which was the worst thing I could have done, 'cause now my dear sistafriend has entrusted her deranged daughter in my care.

"Hello."

"Hi, Indy. It's Chyna."

"Hey girl."

"Did I catch you at a bad time?"

"Not really," I said, plopping myself on my king-size bed. "I'm just trying to finish packing."

"And where are you off to so early in the morning?"

"Vegas."

"Oh that's right. The Spelman chapter reunion."

"And you know it. I haven't seen most of my line sisters in years. And some of our sorors from NSU and Hampton are going to be there as well. So you know we are gonna cut up something fierce."

"I know that's right. Just don't blow too much money gambling."

"Girrl, please. Scared money, don't make money. You should know better than that."

She laughed. "I know that's right."

"So where are you?"

"We're in Ljubljana, Slovenia."

"You betta work it out," I said, finger-snapping. "So are you loving it or what?"

"Indy, it's absolutely breathtaking. And relaxing. I'm really going to hate to leave."

"What's your rush? It's not like… Wait a minute. I know you are not calling just to chitchat, so what's going on?"

"Well," she said, sighing. "We've been trying to reach Sarina for the last four days. I was wondering if you might have heard from her."

I rolled my eyes while shaking my head. That damn girl again. The last time I saw that child I wanted to knock her in her head. She was cursing Chyna out so bad it gave me a headache. Chyna took it in stride, letting her call her every name in the book. Well, I didn't like it one bit. "Sarina, you need to show your mother some respect," I had said, calmly.

"Well, you need to mind your damn business," she responded without blinking an eye.

"Excuse me?" I asked, tilting my head to one side.

"What, you deaf? You heard me the first time. I said, 'mind your damn business.'"

"Sarina!" Chyna snapped, slamming her hand on the table. "You can say what you want to me, but don't you dare disrespect my company. Now get out!" Sarina continued arguing while knocking things off the counter. I kindly got up and walked outside to collect myself before I tore Chyna's house up. I strolled over to the gazebo in the backyard, sat down, crossed my legs, then waited for Miss Mouthy to make her way back to the little cottage her parents allowed her to move into so she could have her own space and a sense of independence. Whatever! They still pay the bills, okay.

Anyway, a few minutes later, Sarina stormed out of the sliding glass doors, heading toward her bungalow situated in the far corner of Chyna's four-acre property. Apparently, she didn't see me sitting out there—or if she did, she ignored me—'cause she walked by mumbling to herself, gesturing with her hands. When she got to her destination, slamming the door behind her, I kindly got up and leisurely made my way down the stone walkway to her front door. I knocked.

"What?!" she screamed, swinging the door wide open. "Oh, it's you." She slammed the door in my face. I knocked again.

"Sarina, dear," I said in my most gentle voice. "Open the door. I want to speak with you." In the background all I heard was "bitch" this, "bitch" that—referring to me, I'm sure. I knocked again. And the minute she opened it, I pushed it so hard it almost knocked her into the wall. I stepped into her filthy place, then slammed the door behind me, locking it. The smell was atrocious.

"Let me tell you one fucking thing," I said, clenching my teeth. "See. You might have Chyna and everyone else around here walking on eggshells but I'm not the one." She just stared at me. I continued. "Now what was that mess you were talking about, telling me to mind my damn business?"

"Just what I said, you high-priced cooch." Yes, she called me a *cooch*. A high-priced one at that! Her face started twitching and she began mumbling. Before she could move another muscle, I made sure I had enough distance between us in case she tried to come at me.

"You listen here. Chyna may be your mother but she's *my* sister so how you treat her *is* my business. I don't care how crazy you act, if you ever let me hear you talk to her like that again I will have your—"

"Indy?" Chyna called out, banging on the door. "Are you in there. Sarina, open this door. Sarina! Indy!" I sidestepped over to open the door, never turning my back on her, okay.

"Calm down, girl," I said, swinging the door open, smiling. "Miss Sarina and I were just about to have a little heart-to-heart." You should have seen the frantic look on Chyna's face. She was wrecked. Poor thing had been looking all around the house and outside for me. And came rushing over to Sarina's when she saw that my car was still in the driveway. I guess she figured I'd be paying Miss Cuckoo Puffs a little visit. "We're finished for now," I said, looking over at Sarina who was now walking around in circles, saying things like, "You told that bitch." She'd start laughing, then say, "who the fuck she think she is."

"Come on, Indy," Chyna said, pulling my arm. "Let's give Sarina her space."

I smiled. "You're right. Let's." We walked out, leaving Sarina in her own little world gently closing the door behind us. She swung it back open.

"I ain't scared of you, bitch!" she yelled, slamming the door so hard her windows rattled. I closed my eyes, taking in a deep breath. Of course, Chyna wanted to explain to me the seriousness of Sarina's illness. And how I should be careful to not say hurtful things to her because it would only *exasperate*—as she put it—her situation.

Chile, please. I was not tryna hear it. My mind was already made up: The next time she made my friend shed a tear or spoke to her in a hurtful way, I would have her voice box cut out. Period! You can gasp all you want. I mean what I say. Yes, I know that's her daughter. And yes, I know she'd be devastated if something happened to her baby. But, having her larynx cut out wouldn't be the end of the world. She'd still be alive. She just wouldn't be able to run her damn mouth. She's put my sistafriend through enough. And I'm tired of it.

Well, a few days after that incident, she was put away for almost two months. And during that time, Chyna had to hire a professional cleaning service to go in and clean the child's nasty place. They had to pull up the carpet, power wash, then repaint the walls and throw out all the furniture because that kook had used colored markers on anything she could to sketch her designs. Truth be told, she's quite talented. Anyway, that was over a year ago. I haven't seen her since. And don't want to if I can help it.

"Now you know me and Miss Sarina don't see eye-to-eye," I said, returning to my present conversation. "So what makes you think she'd call me?"

"Well, the boys said she was somewhere in New York."

"New York? Lord no." *Just what we need, another crazy fool wandering the streets*, I thought to myself. "When did she get here?"

"Girl, your guess is as good as mine. Neither Ryan Jr. nor Jayson have seen her in about three weeks. It was by chance that her therapist called the house looking for her because he couldn't reach her at her place."

"Well, what makes everyone think she's here?"

"Because she told her therapist she was coming out there for a few weeks."

"Oh, I see." I looked down at my watch. I needed to cut this short before I missed my flight. "Well, if she's here, I haven't seen or heard from her. But if I do, I'll be sure to send her home."

"Indy, you know Sarina will not come home unless she wants to. So if she does try to reach you, please try to find out where she's staying and keep an eye on her for me. I'm worried sick about that girl. If she's missing her therapy appointments, then I'm sure she's not taking her meds. Ryan and I are gonna come home to look for her."

"Chyna, please. When are you gonna stop letting that child run you ragged. Sarina is a grown woman. Let her be. You rushing back to hunt her down is gonna do you or Ryan no good. New York is too big. She could be anywhere. Don't worry yourself. I'm sure she's fine."

"Indy, she's impulsive. So, I can't help but worry. Anything can happen to her."

"Girl, listen. You need to give Sarina a little more credit. If she can handle the streets of D.C., then she can surely handle the boroughs of New York. Besides, I don't doubt Miss Sarina can rumble with the best of them."

"That's what I'm afraid of." She sighed, sounding more distressed. "There's no telling what kind of trouble she'll get herself into. Indy, if she contacts you *please* find out where she is."

"If she calls I promise I will do my best to get her to call you. Other than that I can't make any promises."

"Thanks, girl. That's all I ask. Just make sure she's safe. Please."

"You know I will," I said before I could catch it from rolling off my tongue. I guess she could sense my reluctance.

"Indy, if it's too much trouble, Ryan and I will be on the next available flight."

"Girl, please. Enjoy the rest of your trip. If I hear from her, I'll make sure she's alright." I sure will. I'll make sure she gets greeted with a B.D. O.A—Beat Down On Arrival—if she tries to get funky with me. Miss Sassafras will be swung all around this piece, okay? But of course I didn't think it was necessary to share that with Chyna. It would only make her more of a basket case.

"I love you," she said, sounding slightly relieved.

"I love you, too, and make sure you bring me something nice back," I said before hanging up. I could have kicked myself for committing to keeping an eye on that busybody if she shows up here. I should have told Chyna, hell fucking no. But I knew that would only make matters worse. There was no need for her to disrupt her trip trying to track that child down. Besides, we've been friends for a very long time—since 1981 to be exact—and Chyna has been there for me on more than one occasion. Not to mention the fact that I *am* Miss Thing's godmother, like it or not. So it was the least I could do.

Humph. After all the shit Sarina has put her mother through I don't understand why Chyna hasn't cut her ass off and let her fend for herself. That girl has been nothing but nasty and disrespectful to her; yet, she continues to run behind her. I spent many a night on the phone with my homegirl, listening to her cry her eyes out over that child. I know she loves her daughter but enough is enough. It's time to let go. Crazy or not, she's a grown-ass woman. Humph. Maybe I'm missing something. But I know one thing: no damn child of mine would put me through half the shit Chyna's gone through and live to tell about it. Then again, I guess I don't really know what I'd do unless I was in that situation… Hmm. Oh hell no! They'd have to lock me up and throw away the key, 'cause I'd have fucked her up a long time ago.

"Oh shit," I screamed when I glanced at my watch and saw that it was ten minutes to eight. I started running around the bedroom like a wild woman, trying to make sure I had packed everything. My flight was at ten-thirty. I threw the rest of my things in my carry-on, wrote Tee a little note then headed for the door.

By the time I stepped out of my limo, it was already nine forty-five. Thanks to tunnel traffic, I barely had enough time to catch my breath. And to top it off, I felt sick as a dog. *Probably because I hadn't eaten*, I surmised as the chauffeur opened my door. When I stepped out, you should've seen how the men were breaking their necks to get a peek at who was stepping out of a stretch, rocking the fly gear, with two large pieces of designer luggage.

Girl, I know. I pack like I'm going away for months. Well, you never know what you may need. And when I travel, I like to have the comforts of home, okay. Anyway, I handed my skycap a handsome tip for all his troubles, then strutted to the counter for first-class travelers, returning the wave of several sorors.

Anyway, let me tell you. I can't stand a phony-ass bitch. If you got something to say, say it and keep it movin'. You know what I'm sayin'? Don't be cheesin' up in my damn grill like we all coochie crunch, then try to talk shit behind my back. And whatever you do, don't spread lies. 'Cause when it gets back to me—which it does—I'm gonna call your ass on the carpet. I don't care where we are. I don't care what time of the day it is, how long ago it was or what the hell I have on. I'm gonna bring it to your ass, simple as that. And that is just what I did in the middle of Newark International Airport when I spotted one of my so-called associates walking toward the Delta Airlines ticket counter.

Mind you, I hadn't seen Belinda in over three months. We both had attended Spelman so on the strength of that, I used to give her free coupons to Weaves & Wonders to keep her knotty-ass hair pressed and dressed.

That's until one of our mutual associates and I were having a conversation which led to her telling me how she wanted to have sex with two men. She then politely slipped and said she had heard I had been with three men and wanted to know how I enjoyed it. Well, I thought I'd snatch her tongue out of her mouth. "Bitch, where in the fuck did you get that from? I have never fucked three men," I snapped. She apologized, trying to backpedal her way out of me slapping her damn face. "I'm about to really get ugly on your ass for tryna disrespect me," I warned.

Well, she wasted no time telling me which dog passed that bone along. Miss Belinda felt it her duty to share that I used to be one of the biggest freaks on campus. A freak? I might be a little freaky—alright, a whole lot of freaky—but I'm damn sure no fucking freak. And I sure wasn't one then. There's a big difference, okay? Hell. I didn't *willingly* start giving up this love funk until I was about twenty-one. So, get a grip.

Anyway, it's my understanding that Miss Belinda's conversation went something like this, "Please, between me and you, Indy is one of the biggest hoes around. She tries to play like she's all Miss High Post. But she'll fuck your man quicker than a cat will piss on cotton. It's funny how she let her success go to her head. Someone needs to remind her where she came from 'cause I remember when she was the talk of the whole campus for letting three men run a train on her nasty, freak ass." Well—when I heard that—I was too through. This bitch has a face like a chow and she wants to get fierce. Oh no! You know girlfriend was gonna catch it.

First of all, I've *always* had bank and I've been rocking stilettos, designer bags and diamonds long before that bitch stopped wetting the bed, okay. So *who* the hell was that homeless strumpet gonna have remind *me* of where I came from? That ho doesn't even have a mailing address. She might have a roof over her head but she's staying in someone else's home, living out of boxes and storage bins because she can't afford her own place. Please. She might as well be living in a henhouse as much cock she has coming in and out of her, okay. Now, I didn't wanna have to go there, but that bitch tried it on my time.

Second of all, just because you like dead-end jobs and sit around waiting for a man to take care of you, don't hate on my success because you don't know how to get in where you fit in. Is it my fault your ass isn't motivated enough to make power moves? I'm so sick of these *Mahogany* wannabe bitches who don't know where the fuck they're going. They wouldn't know success if it bit 'em on the ass. Dumb, lazy bitch! Hell, like they always say, how you gonna soar with the eagles if you're pecking with the chickens, okay?

Furthermore, why would anyone feel the need to bring up shit that supposedly happened almost twenty years ago? I mean really. That makes no sense to me. And if you're gonna tell my business, tell it correctly or keep your damn mouth shut. To think of all the times people would talk about her big-ass head sitting on her shoulders because she doesn't have a neck, looking like Mrs. Potato Head, okay. Not once did I ever go there with her. Instead, I defended her ass. So the minute I saw her wide Mack-truck ass strutting past me, I walked right over to her, tapped her on her shoulder, then lit into her, like a match to lighter fluid.

"Indy, girl. Oh my God! How you doing, girlfriend?" She attempted to give me a hug and a kiss. I put my open hand up to her chest.

"Save the phony shit, bitch. I know you've been talking shit about me."

"Indy, g-girl," she stuttered. "What in the world are you talking about? You know we cool."

"Cool, my ass," I snapped. "I should punch you in your big dick-sucking lips for spreading lies about me. Where the fuck you get off saying I let three men fuck me? And if I did, what business is it of yours? I don't go around telling people how many muthafuckers you've sucked and fucked in bathroom stalls, now do I?"

This bitch had the audacity to look at me dumbfounded. Like I had lost my mind or something. Chile, listen. The last thing you want to do is play stupid with me when you know *I* know *you* know what the hell I'm talking about. Let me tell you. I was a split second from knocking her block off. That trick walks around with her clitoris in her throat, doing more dick washing than a Laundromat does clothes and she wants to dish dirt. I was not having it.

"Not once have I broadcasted you having venereal warts. You nasty bitch! But since you wanna get fierce, I'll show you fierce, you neck-less slut." That's when I blew her spot up and let everyone in earshot know how Miss Head and Shoulders likes to stroll boardwalks and peruse adult bookstores, looking for old, nasty married men to give her rotten pussy to. I let 'em know how she rides the PATH train, picking up men, then bringing them back to Jersey to fuck 'em. Please. I aired that ho's dirty laundry out for all to see. Come for me? I think *not!* By the time I was done with her, she was wrecked.

"And another damn thing, you crusty-ass scavenger," I continued. "For the record—since you think you know so damn much—I didn't let anyone run shit on me, you dumb-ass ho. So, the next time you open your mouth to say something about me, make sure you got your information correct."

She stood there looking at me in shock. I blinked my eyes real hard and saw myself beating her face in for running her damn mouth about something she knew nothing about. I really wanted to scream on her ass. This fat bitch tried to put me on blast and didn't even have her motherfuckin' facts straight. I wanted to grab her by her throat and slam her head against the counter. I tightened my fists until my nails dug into my palms. Little did she and many others know, I was drugged and sodomized by a weak-ass man and his two punk-ass partners who spread those lies about me letting them run a train on me.

Yes, I was the talk of the campus. However, the truth did come to light. And when it did, I made sure that that sorry son-of-a-bitch would never rape another young girl. Trust me. I made sure every time he dropped his pants he'd have scars to always remind him of what he did to me. Thanks to his stinkin' ass I ended up transferring to Hampton University to get far away from any memories of what he had done to me.

"That's not what I meant, Indy. I thought—"

"You *thought?*" I interrupted. "Well, you thought fuckin' wrong. So now I'll give you something to think about on your flight, you greasy bitch." *Slap!* Before I could catch myself—not that I tried—I had slapped the shit out of that fat, blemished face of hers. "Don't ever open your mouth and spread lies on me. 'Cause the next time you'll get more than a slap." Three strapping security officers walked over and kindly escorted me away. She declined signing complaints against me, stating it was a sisterly disagreement. Yeah whatever.

Lord knows I've come a long way. 'Cause a few years ago, I would have really dug in that ho's ass. The only reason I didn't hurt her up in there was because I was basically over it. But, had I got to her when it was brought to my attention, I would have mopped her ass across that floor. I really can't stand bitches whose sole purpose in life is to spread lies. Just straight-up hatin'. Oooh, that shit burns me up. My thing is, if you're gonna say something about someone know what the hell you're talking about and be woman enough to admit you said it when your ass is confronted. That's one of the reasons I've never had many female friends. Most of them can be catty, petty and downright sneaky. They just can't be trusted. I have many associates but very few friends. I can count on one hand the number of women I can actually call true friends. One, two—Chyna and my homegirl, Val.

Over the years, I've come to realize that I'm hated by many, loved by few and envied by most. And you know what? I don't give a damn. Bottom line: What you see is what you get. I'm not biting my tongue for anyone. Period. And I'm sure as hell not going to talk about you behind your back. And if I do—trust and believe—it's gonna be about something I've already said to your damn face. But, I'll be damned if I'm going to lie on you. You can talk all the shit you want about me. Just don't lie. I'd rather you step to me and say whatever's on your mind, instead of smiling in my face, then tryna dog me out behind my back. And if you're gonna come for me, come correct.

Anyway, after that face-slapping incident, I strutted back over to the America West baggage check area where Val and five other sorors were waiting. Three of them were Spelman graduates, the other two I was unfamiliar with.

"Indy, you haven't changed a bit," Val said, hugging me in a sisterly embrace. "Still turning people and places out." She looked wonderful in her black stretch gabardine jumpsuit and matching blazer. Although we've spoken over the phone regularly the past year and a half, it dawned on me that I hadn't seen Val since my wedding. She looked six inches taller in her Charles Jourdan black stretch-leather knee boots. Her cinnamon-coated skin was flawless. She pulled her curled bangs behind her ears. I smiled, admiring my friend's natural beauty.

"Girrl, you are workin' those boots," I said, shaking my finger from side to side.

"Thank you, darling," she said, giving me a fashion two-step and pose. We giggled.

"Girl, you're too much," I said, reaching over to hug her again. We embraced a few seconds more before beginning the introductions.

"You remember Lea and Janie, don't you?"

"Of course I do," I said, smiling. "It's good seeing you both." We exchanged hugs.

"Same here," they said in unison. They also wore black. Lea wore a black pantsuit with a pink wide-collared blouse. Janie sported a black floor-length, sleeveless knit pullover dress with a matching sweater.

"Hi, I'm Tradawna," a tall, brown-skinned sister said, extending her neatly manicured hand. I accepted and smiled. She wore a hunter-green mini-skirt and matching two-button blazer, serving cleavage for days and showing off her pierced bellybutton. I glanced down at her four-inch sandals. Her toes were painted in soft pink polish. She was ova.

"Girl, I'm feeling those heels."

"And I'm lovin' the jumpsuit," she said. "All this black was about to have me mourning up in here." We laughed, then hugged.

"Girl, black is where it's at," Val snapped while high-fiving Lea and Janie.

"And black don't crack," Tradawna interposed with a neck roll and finger snap.

"And once you go black," Lea added, shaking and waving her hands in the air, "you don't go back." Everyone laughed.

"I know that's right," I said, still smiling, then turning my attention to an attractively tall, cocoa-skinned sister. She was a statuesque Amazon of a woman, wearing a low-cut, black knit dress. Her huge breasts were practically busting the seams open as if they were fighting for breathing space. Humph. I don't know why these big girls insist on wearing skimpy pieces. It was like seeing a whale stuffed into a sardine can. I started to say something but decided against it. "Oh I don't think we've met. I'm Indy."

"Yes, I've heard so much about you. I'm Dietra."

"Oooh girl, whatever you do," I said, looking around as if I were expecting someone to blow my cover. I leaned inward as if I wanted to talk privately with her. "Don't believe everything you've heard." Everyone laughed.

"Alright, ladies. Let's get this show on the road," Val directed in her take-charge tone. "We have a plane to catch."

"And you know it," Tradawna said. "Show me the ballers, shot callers."

"Girl, please. Show me the money," Lea sang.

"'Cause scared money, don't make money," I snapped.

"Amen," an unfamiliar voice chimed in. I smiled, turning my head to see the owner of the voice. There stood a walnut-brown sister with wavy hair pulled neatly back in a curly ponytail, wearing a slinky green Gucci dress and green Gucci leather stilettos. The sista had shape for days and her make-up was done to perfection. *You betta work*, my mind snapped. Her face was hidden behind her green-tinted Gucci frames. But, whoever she was, it was clear girlfriend was high-fashion down.

"Oh it figures, you would say something like that," Val cracked, turning her attention to me. "And of course, you'd agree."

I rolled my eyes. "Don't hate, girl. Hi, I'm Indy," I said, smiling and extending my hand.

She removed her shades, returning the smile and sticking her tongue out at Val. "Hello, I'm Celeste." For a split second, I thought I knew her from somewhere.

"Did you graduate from Spelman?" I asked, staring into her slanted eyes.

"No, Howard."

"Oh, an Alpha Chapter soror," I joked.

"Actually, I pledged Omicron Alpha Alpha grad chapter in Connecticut."

"Well, it's nice meeting you, either way." We embraced. "Humph. It looks like you and I are gonna have to show these girls how to win the money."

"Girl, the jackpot is definitely calling."

"And so is our plane," Val yelled over to us. "Now bring your prima-donna behinds on." Celeste and I looked each other up and down, then over at Val. "Don't hate," we said in unison as we broke out in laughter, heading for our terminal.

Well, lo and behold. Celeste and I hit it off like old-time acquaintances. Notice I didn't say like friends. Anyway, sistagirl had a little class about herself and I liked that. Not only did she know how to rock the fashions, girlfriend had no time for economy travel. We ended up sharing a seat in first class, while the rest of the girls sat coach. I peeped her 18K Baume & Mercier with mother-of-pearl dial, glanced over at the rest of her jewels, examining the quality of her ring, earrings and bracelet. *Real diamonds*, I said to myself. I smiled my stamp of approval, then fastened my seatbelt, preparing for take-off. I closed my eyes, said a prayer and crossed my heart. I don't care how many times I fly, I'm still spooked every time the plane ascends and descends. I don't do plane crashes, okay.

Anyway, everything was going well. We had successfully taken off. I got comfortable in my seat and decided it was time to strike up a conversation with my new travel partner when she beat me to it. "Your ring is gorgeous," she said, admiring my six-carat solitaire diamond with matching, six-carat diamond-encrusted band.

"Why thank you." I smiled, letting its sparkle dance around the cabin.

"How long have you been married?"

"Two and a half years and counting."

"Oh, you're still newlyweds."

"Well, on paper," I said, searching through my satchel for a stick of Doublemint. "But it seems like we've been together forever." *Now where in the hell is my gum*, I thought to myself. *Oh here it is.* "Have a piece?" I asked, holding the unopened pack in front of her. Sista felt like doing a little click-clacking, okay?

"No thanks," she replied. "So tell me. How's it being married to a famous author?"

"Truthfully, I don't see him as famous. He's just my husband." I reached down, pulling my carry-on from under the seat in front of me. I zipped open one of its compartments and pulled out a copy of his book. "Here's his book. Have you read it?"

I watched her with a sidelong stare as she flipped through the pages, reading the acknowledgments, then turning it over to the back cover. She stared at Tee's picture.

"Umm. No, I haven't," she said, fumbling and almost dropping the book. "It looks very interesting though. I'll have to remember to pick up a copy." She handed it back to me. "Your husband's very handsome. I guess you stay very busy trying to keep the women off of him?"

"Not hardly," I said, twisting my face up. "I am not the one. If you leap and he catches, you can keep him. Trust and believe." Her eyes widened in shock.

"I heard that. So, do you have any children?" she pried.

"Girl no," I said, shaking my head and rolling my stick of gum in my mouth. "We have plenty of time for that. Right now we're just tryna live and love."

"Well, judging by the size of that rock, it looks like somebody's loving a very lucky woman."

"Absolutely," I said, beaming. But in reality, luck had nothing to do with me having someone to love me in my life. What man in his right mind wouldn't want to have a woman like me with brains, beauty and good pussy? And on top of that be able to make his toes curl when she's sucking his dick and licking his balls. That's right, honey. I love licking the back of those hairy barbells, then taking them in my mouth, twirling my tongue around 'em while I'm massaging his perineum. Oh, I'm sorry—I mean the area between his balls and asshole—I forgot I'm talking to some of you who are illiterate hoes. Ooops! My bad.

Anyway, that drives him bananas. Girl, that shit makes his nut pop like a champagne cork spilling forth the thickest, creamiest cum you can imagine. Humph. I can't wait to get home. Now, don't get it twisted. As long as he's sucking my fat pussy and licking my clitty-clitty, I'll reciprocate all night long. Know what I'm sayin'?

Bottom line: I know how to keep him satisfied in and out of the sheets, okay. You see. The key is making him feel like he's losing his mind, while giving him a taste of this sweet pussy. When I ride his dick, I ride his mind. When I suck his dick, I suck his mind. So ladies, when you're fucking your man, don't just bounce up and down on his dick, fuck his brains out. Don't just lie there like a dead fish. Throw that pussy at him. And if he wants a little backdoor loving, give it up. It's a nice treat—especially on special occasions, like Valentine's Day, your anniversary or his birthday.

Yes, it'll hurt the first few times, but once you get used to it, you'll be taking that dick like a pro. Not to mention, keeping your man happy. Now don't scrunch your face up. I know some of you old closet freaks love being fucked in the ass, okay, so don't even give me that "I'll-never-let-my-man-fuck-me-in-the-ass" look. Lies.

Chile, listen. It's a good thing Tee and I don't live in one of those nine states that ban consensual sodomy 'cause the way we get down in the bed-room, we'd be put away for life. Can you believe that shit? You can't even fuck or suck the way you want in your own damn house. If I want to suck my man's damn dick or give him some of this ass gravy, what damn business is it of anyone's? Go figure.

Anyway, back to keeping your man on his toes. Sometimes I leave Tee little notes, inviting him to meet me in the dining room or kitchen in five. And when he comes in, I'm already spread out on the table or counter—lying on top of rose petals, with knees bent and legs fanned wide open—waiting to serve him his treats for the day: Pussy pie and ass pudding. Other times, depending on my mood, I may crawl under the table—with crushed ice in my mouth—while he's eating breakfast, lunch or dinner and start sucking his dick. Hmmm. Girl, it drives him crazy.

Oh shoot! Here you go, getting me sidetracked again. All this sex talk has gotten my thong moist. Now as I was saying—honestly speaking—regardless of how much Tee gets on my nerves he's the man for me. He's fine, sexy, has the body of a Zulu warrior and keeps my pussy smiling. And he knows how to get down for his, financially speaking. But most importantly, I know that he loves me. So in retrospect, I guess you can say, I'm blessed. Of course I wasn't gonna tell her all that. "What about you, is there anyone special in your life?"

"No," she replied somberly, then quickly changed her tone. It almost seemed as if she had drifted into deep thought. "I mean yes."

"Well, which is it?" I asked with a raised eyebrow.

"Well," she continued, shifting in her seat. "Let's just say I've kept my heart open to him."

"Girl, give it time. Your dream man will come."

"He already has," she said, smiling. "I'm just patiently waiting." I gave her a quizzical look, probing further.

"Hmmm. Sounds like a lost love."

"For now," she said, rubbing a gold wedding band hanging from a diamond-cut rope chain she wore around her neck. "Do you mind if we change the subject?" She untied her silk scarf from around her neck, neatly folding it in her lap.

"Oh, I'm sorry. I didn't mean to open up old wounds."

"Trust me. No wounds, just love sickness."

It's a good thing I didn't give her honorary diva status. No diva sits around waiting for some man to come back to her. She keeps it moving. *Humph*, I thought. *There's a lot more to this chick than I thought.* I studied her for a few seconds, imagining some man ripping her heart from off her sleeve, then throwing it in her face. Probably some married man she fell head over heels for. I privately rolled my eyes up in my head. *Lord. Don't tell me I'm sitting next to another dumb-ass woman.*

The more I stared at her, the more I was certain I knew her from somewhere, but where? That was the million-dollar question I was sure to get an answer to. Or my name isn't Indera Fleet-Miles. I glanced over at her again. This time taking in her hair's wavy pattern, her skin's smooth tone. My eyes zoomed in on the dent over her eye, the scar along her neck. I continued my interview until the airplane hit its third air pocket. Suddenly, I felt a wave of nausea come over me. I had never felt so sick to my stomach in all my life. I broke out in a sweat and everything started spinning.

"Soror, are you alright?" Celeste asked, waving her hand to get the flight attendant's attention. Before I could respond, I threw my guts up all over the place, then everything else became a blur.

7

BRITTON: *It's Too Late*

"Amar, if you don't get your behind down from that counter, you're not going to watch Barney today."

"I don't care, Daddy. He's ugly," he responded, jumping down from the counter onto the kitchen chair, then to the floor. "I'm gonna watch SpongeBob SquarePants today." I have to admit, I had to chuckle. He said that as if a sea sponge living with his pet snail in a pineapple can was any better looking. Where in the world do they come up with these outlandish cartoons? Whatever happened to the days of Speed Racer, Krazy Kats and Winkie Dink?

"Well, I tell you what, Mr. Smarty Pants. You won't be watching him, either. And since you don't care, then you don't care about going to bed while Amir and I have ice cream at snack time," I said, standing in the doorway while he dragged the chair back to the kitchen table. I shook my head.

"That's not fair," he whined.

"Well, it's not fair when you don't listen to me, either. How many times have I told you to not climb on things in the house?"

"A whole bunch," he said, slapping his little forehead, clearly trying to be a wise guy. "That's a lot of times, Daddy."

"Exactly. And you still ignore me. So there'll be no ice cream for you. Now get yourself upstairs."

"Why?" He pouted.

"Because you don't listen. Now move," I said, pointing toward the stairs. He didn't budge. "Amar, did you hear me?" He still stood there, looking at me like I had two heads or something. "One…two…three…"

"I'm not your friend anymore," he whined, stomping up the stairs.

"Good. I don't want any friends who won't listen. Now get your little fresh behind upstairs." He started yelling and screaming at the top of his lungs, then slammed his bedroom door. Just as I was about to go up and have a little talk with him, the phone rang. I looked up at the clock, shaking my head. *She cracks me up, calling here so early.* I picked up on the fourth ring.

"Hello."

"Boy, why haven't I heard from you?"

I smiled. It was my sister, Amira. "Well, hello to you too. I see you're up with the chickens this fine morning," I said sarcastically. It was ten a.m. on the East Coast.

"Boy, please. I've been up since six, and not by choice. Alona was up at the crack of dawn, making a mess. This girl is such a damn busybody. Into everything." I laughed. Alona is my three-and-a-half-year-old niece, the youngest of my sister's nine daughters.

"Welcome to the club. As you can see, this house is up with the roosters. So how's the Brantley army doing?"

"Everyone's fine. We're just trying to plan for Ashley's wedding." Ashley is my twenty-six-year-old niece. "I still think she's too young to get married."

"Well, the wedding isn't until next year, Amira. She still has time to change her mind. Besides, look who's talking? I recall you getting married younger than her."

"That's besides the point," she snapped. "I don't want her rushing into anything like I did. Now don't get me wrong. I love me some Wil and I have no regrets about getting married or having so many kids. But if I could do it all over again, I would have waited until I traveled the world a little. Maybe I would have gone away to college or a technical school."

"Amira, you're a good mother and wife. And there's nothing wrong with that. Besides, it's never too late to go to school."

"Boy, please. I am too old to be sitting up in somebody's classroom. I live my college life vicariously through my children." She laughed, then quickly returned to her point. "The other girls are so independent and ambitious but that Ashley. I don't know what I'm going to do with her.

I've always been so hard on these girls because I don't want them to end up like me, especially Ashley. She doesn't know what she wants out of life. And you know like I do, you have to love yourself first, before you can expect anyone else to love you. But for some reason she thinks getting married is going to be a quick fix. I'm telling you, Britton. I think she's making a big mistake but I know she has to live her own life and make her own decisions.

"I just don't want her to wake up twenty years from now and have nothing to show for her life but a house full of kids and a pocket full of worries. I know I got married young, but times were different back then. And I was fortunate enough to marry a man who has loved me for all that I am. He loved me before *I* even knew how to love me. And he put up with all of my shit." She paused, then started laughing. "And you know back in my day, I was a handful."

"What you mean *was?* You still are," I said, joining in her laughter. "Lord knows I sure wouldn't put up with you. I really have to give it to Wil for staying with you this long. He's definitely a remarkable man."

"Oh, boy be quiet," she said. "Well, these young couples today don't know anything about that. They jump into marriages without fully understanding the meaning of loving and standing by your mate through thick and thin. The slightest disagreement and they run to the nearest judge, crying 'irreconcilable differences.' When I married Wil, I knew the minute I said 'I do' that I would grow old with him and die with him. And believe me, it hasn't always been easy."

Amira was sixteen when she had Ashley and—like our mother—nineteen when she married her husband, Wil. She'll kill me if I told you what his real name was. Oh well. Anyway, Wilfucious Lee Smothers Brantley—ten years her senior—took one look at that "wild thang" from Jersey City and declared his undying love for her. Of course, me being only fifteen, I thought he was a stone-cold, country fool for wanting to get anywhere near her. Then again, I was glad someone wanted to marry her mean, bossy behind. The sooner she got out of the house, the better.

Amira was so mean-spirited I began to almost feel sorry for the poor man. But the brother was persistent. He must have chased her down for almost a year before she finally gave in. Like I said, no one thought she was ready for marriage because she was too young and so wild. Even our father flew in from San Diego to try to talk some sense into her. But she made it very clear, "I'm tired of these broke-ass little boys. I want me a man with a job and some life experience. And Wil said if I marry him, I won't have to work unless I want to."

Well, that's all she needed to hear 'cause girlfriend liked sitting on her behind all day. Still to this day, I have to laugh because, although he kept his word, he failed to tell her he wanted to keep her barefoot and pregnant. Every time you turned around, she was popping out another baby.

You know. It's amazing she never ended up in jail as much as she carried on in the streets fighting. In high school, she was notorious for boxing and biting anyone she thought was talking slick. She'd box you like a man, then once she got you on the ground she'd bite your face up. By the time someone was able to get her off of you, you'd have teeth marks across your forehead and cheeks. No one at Snyder High School dared to cross her. She couldn't even keep a boyfriend without beating on them.

Once she graduated, she took to carrying a fork in her pocket. Instead of biting you, she'd stab you in your forehead, leaving four bloody prong marks. She'd call it her "beat-down stamp." I guess it took a country boy from Greenville, South Carolina to tame her. I have to say, she really lucked up and got herself a really good man. However, I'm still trying to figure out how he puts up with her. 'Cause here they are twenty-three years and nine daughters later, and they're still together.

"Amira, have a little faith."

"Please. I have all the faith I need. What I don't have is enough money for this damn wedding. Poor Wil is so stressed."

"If I were in his shoes," I said, laughing, "I'd be stressed out too if I still had eight more daughters to marry off. That man is going to have to file bankruptcy messing with all you women in that house."

"Well, he should have given me all boys."

"Yeah, yeah, yeah. Blame it all on the man." I snickered. If it were up to Amira's behind she'd keep getting pregnant until she had her son. Fortunately, my brother-in-law said, "Enough is enough." So now Mother Hubbard has to wait until she has grandsons. In the meantime, she likes spoiling my sons rotten. "So how's the weather in Jersey?"

"Oh, it's gorgeous today. But it's supposed to drop in the fifties by Friday."

"That's Jersey for you. Unpredictable. Just like women."

"Boy, I know you're not talking," she snapped, laughing, "as many times as your ass has packed up on whim."

"Hey, I like change. Didn't you know variety is the spice of life?"

"I wouldn't know about all that. But I do know I miss you." Awwwww. I was touched. I was expecting her to say something smart like she normally does. Fact of the matter, I've missed her too. Even though she tends to get on my last nerve sometimes with her meddling and opinions, we've always been close.

"How's Noelle doing down at Spelman?" I asked, staring at the mess the boys made in the kitchen. There was Kix cereal all over the floor. Milk was splattered on the table. I pulled a chair out from the table and sat down.

She sucked her teeth. "Humph. She *was* doing fine until she got herself knocked up."

"She did what?" I asked, not sure I had heard her correctly. "No."

"You heard me."

"When?"

"Last month. I forgot to mention it the last time we spoke. Of course she begged me to not tell you." She indicated my niece was more concerned about what I was going to say or think than she was with Amira beating her ass—or worse, her father finding out. Out of all my nieces, Noelle and I have always been the closest. "That damn girl has two more semesters left and she turns around and gets herself pregnant. I told her ass we didn't send her down to that school to get knocked the hell up. She cried, saying they always used protection but the condom broke. I told her ass if she can't keep her legs shut, then she better make sure he either buys bigger condoms or she better check the expiration date on them. I'm telling you, these damn girls are going to drive me crazy."

I wanted to laugh but knew she was being serious. From the beginning, Amira has preached to my nieces about not getting pregnant until after they got their college educations and had decent jobs. She wants them to be self-sufficient in the event they have to raise a child on their own.

"So you're gonna be a grandmother—"

"The hell if I am!" She scowled, cutting me off. "She's taking care of that little situation next week. And you know I cursed that little green-eyed Negro out to no end." *That poor boy*, I thought. If he had to be on the receiving end of my sister's wrath, then I pitied him. If I know Amira, she chewed him up, spit him out, then stepped all over him with that mouth of hers.

"I wonder what his parents are saying," I blurted as an afterthought, "particularly Chyna."

"I doubt if he even told them." She scowled. "Damn knucklehead."

"Now, Amira don't you think you're being a bit hard on him? After all, he didn't get her pregnant by himself."

"Oh, don't think I haven't had some choice words for her hot tail."

"Well, they're both legal age, and able to make their own decisions," I reasoned. "Including whether or not they practice safe sex."

"Humph. Whatever! All I know is, I told them both they'd have to pay for this with their own money 'cause she wasn't using our medical insurance to pay for their carelessness."

"What did Wil say when he found out?" I asked, standing up to look out of the kitchen window. A mangy dog with a broken tail was outside digging in my neighbor's trashcan. He whimpered off when someone threw an old boot at him, hitting him in the back of the head.

"Boy, are you crazy?" she snapped. "I haven't told him. And I'm not going to. I told Noelle she should be the one to tell him. Hell, I probably wouldn't have known either if she hadn't called here all hysterical."

I *tsked*. "Keeping secrets like that from your husband is a no-no. He's gonna be irate with you when he finds out."

"A 'no-no,' my ass," she mocked. "Like you said, she's of legal age. So let her be the one to tell him. I'm not interested in hearing his mouth."

"Hmm… I'm surprised she's gonna have an abortion."

"Well," she sighed, "to be honest with you, I'm a bit surprised too. But it was their decision. And it's fine by me. This is probably one of the more responsible choices they've made. Of course, they both claim they're always responsible in their relationship. Please. If these damn girls don't kill me, I don't know what will."

I chuckled. "Oh, please. You'll survive just fine."

"I know that's right 'cause I'm not taking care of no one's babies. I had my kids and I raised them. I never looked for anyone else to take care of mine. When I came home pregnant with Ashley, Mom didn't lift one finger to help me, and I didn't expect her to. I made my bed and I laid in it. And that is what I expect from these fast-ass girls of mine."

"Well," I said, trying to block out Amir and Amar's arguing over who was playing with whose truck. "I'm sure they've both learned from this and will be more careful... Will you boys *please* knock it off up there with all that hollering...I'm sorry for yelling in your ear."

"Humph."

I continued. "Well, I won't be surprised if they end up getting married." I smiled, thinking about the young lovers. Noelle and Kayin have been together since her freshman year at Spelman and have been inseparable since. They both say it was love at first sight, but what do I know.

Funny thing, neither of them knew I was connected to either's side of the family until Noelle mentioned—six months into their dating—that she wanted to introduce him to her uncle in the Dominican Republic. She was shocked when she found out I was close friends with his mother and he was even more surprised to find out I was her uncle.

"Oh, please," Amira said. "She better keep her ass in those books and try to find herself a damn job instead of worrying about that boy. I'm telling you, I think the damn girl is dick-whipped."

I laughed. "Amira, they're just 'in love.' You remember how it was, being their age."

"Yeah," she said, drifting off into thought. For a brief moment, I followed behind her until she broke my reverie of my campus flings. "I sure do: Young, dumb and full of cum—"

"Daddy," Amir interrupted, stomping down the stairs, tattling. "Amar's jumping on my bed and he won't let me watch *Blue's Clues*."

I rolled my eyes up in my head, inhaling, then quickly exhaling a deep breath. "Go tell him I said to stop jumping on your bed and to let you watch your show or he's gonna be on punishment."

"Amar!" he yelled at the bottom of the stairs. "Daddy said to cut it out for he beat your butt real hard." He hopped up the stairs, one by one, finally making his way to the top. "Did you hear, boy? Daddy's gonna beat your butt if you don't let me watch TV."

"Is that my sweet nephew in the background making all that noise?" Amira asked gleefully, getting off track from our conversation. "My sweet babies are getting so big."

"You got that right," I chimed. "They're three going on thirty. I wish they'd take their behinds back to bed. …If ya'll don't stop slamming that bedroom door and stop that yelling I'm going to Magic Kingdom without you," I snapped, hollering for the second time in Amira's ear. "Sorry about that. They are really tryna pluck my nerves this morning."

"Sounds like they are running you ragged."

I shook my head, smiling. "From sun up to sun down. But I love it."

"Well, let me welcome *you* to the club." She snickered. "Don't worry, this is just the beginning. Wait until you're faced with teenagers."

"Damn," I said, opening up the half-empty refrigerator, sticking my head all the way in as if I were looking for some hidden meal. "Thanks for reminding me." I grabbed the carton of chocolate soymilk, then shuffled over to the pantry where I grabbed a box of Wheaties Energy Crunch. I was starving. While holding the phone in the crook of my neck, I grabbed a bowl and spoon from the drain board, then sat at the kitchen table where I prepared my morning feast. My stomach growled when the milk splashed against the honey-toasted, whole-grain flakes. I said grace, then dived in, smacking in my sister's ear.

"Damn!" she exclaimed, giggling. "Slow it down, cowboy."

I laughed.

"So when am I going to see you and the boys? Your nieces want to see their adorable little cousins."

"Well," I exhaled in between scoops of cereal, blocking out Amar and Amir's bickering. "The boys and I are taking the train to Disney World—"

"Disney World," she snapped, cutting me off. "Why in the world would you travel across country just to see Mickey Mouse when Disneyland's right there?"

"Been there, done that," I offered, waiting to hear her dismay. I scraped the bottom of my bowl with my spoon to get the last bit of cereal, then put it up to my lips. I was tempted to lick but drank instead.

"Don't you think that's a bit extravagant for someone who's not working?"

"Absolutely not," I snapped, sucking my teeth, then chuckling. "I've applied for welfare. I'm just waiting for my checks to come in. So mind your business." Although I was joking, the thought of going down to the local welfare office to apply for benefits didn't sound too bad. Hey, if some of these young girls can use their welfare checks to get their hair and nails did, why couldn't I use mine to take my sons to Disney? Hmmm. I wonder if I can apply for Section 8 housing. I know in some states, you can get some really nice homes, and you can even transfer it from state to state. Shoot! Every two years I'd be moving into a new home, acting like I just bought it.

"Humph. You so damn silly," she said, giggling. "And I'll report your ass for welfare fraud."

"You make me sick," I teased. "Always player hating."

"Yep," she continued, laughing. "Will turn your ass into the authorities quick, fast and in a hurry."

"You so stupid, girl. Anyway, like I was saying before you rudely butted in, I'm going to Disney World in a couple of weeks so I'll probably visit everyone on my way back."

"Well, that would be nice of you to grace us with your presence."

"Amira," I blurted. "Shut the hell up with your smart ass." We both started laughing. "Anyway, I need to pay my tenants in my condo a little visit. They seem to have a problem paying their rent on time."

"That's a damn shame. Don't they know being put out on the streets ain't cute?"

"Apparently not. But they will real soon."

"Why you scoundrel!" she replied in mock exasperation. "You wouldn't dare."

I laughed. But the truth of the matter is I had been wrestling with the thought of putting them out for the past six months. Besides the fact that every other month something needs to be repaired or replaced, they consistently have an excuse as to why their rent payments are late. Last month I was told they couldn't pay me because there was a death in their family. The month before that someone was in a car accident and this month I was told that another relative's home had caught fire.

Now I try to be very patient, but this is pushing it. What the hell does that have to do with them paying me my damn money on time? When she called me this month, crying hysterically, I told her she and her family had too much damn drama for me, and that I wanted this month's rent along with the three months' arrears or they'd be looking for a shoebox to live in. I might play dumb, but I'm damn sure not slow behind the eight ball. So if they knew like I did, they'd pay up and stay up or be out on the streets.

"Yeah, okay," I said. "Let 'em try me and see what happens."

"Well, if you want, I'll go over there and collect your money for you." She giggled. "And I'll bring a nice shiny fork with me, just in case I have to stamp my business card in her forehead to remind her of her debt."

"Amira, you crack me up. No. That won't be necessary. Let's leave the forks at home for now. But, I'll keep it in mind."

"Oh, before I forget. When I was over Mom's last week, some woman called the house looking for you."

"Did she say who she was?" I asked, grabbing the dishcloth, wiping milk from the kitchen table, then putting the cereal bowls in the sink.

"No. She claimed she went to school with you."

"Humph. That could be anyone," I said, pulling the broom from out of the closet, then sweeping the floor. I swept hard, shaking my head, annoyed about the mess Amar and Amir had made.

"Well, whoever she was, she was definitely anxious to track you down."

"And what did you tell this mystery woman? I know you didn't give her my number?"

"Boy, please. And have to hear you damn mouth for the rest of the year? Not! You know me. I drilled her ass to no end but she stuck to her little story of trying to track down classmates for a class reunion."

"Well," I sighed, dumping the contents of the dustpan in the garbage. "She'll be one classmate short because I'm not reachable." I returned the broom to the closet, then sat at the base of the steps.

"Anywhoooo," she chimed in my ear. I scrunched my face up. I hate when she does that. It sounds so damn ignorant. But I kept my comment to myself. "How's Miss Lina doing?" she asked, knowing she could really care less.

"Who knows and who cares," I snapped, glancing up at the wooden wall clock. Lina hadn't been home since our last argument, which was over four days ago. She had come home agitated about something, taking it out on the boys. She slapped Amir, leaving her handprint on his face when he excitedly jumped up on her. Damn! All he wanted was a hug. Amar, taking up for his brother, waited until she was resting on the sofa, then bit her on her ankle. She screamed bloody murder, then whipped him. Although I didn't agree with his actions, I politely pulled her to the side—out of earshot of the boys, of course—and told her she had no business spanking or yelling at either boy since she is never around to do anything with them. I had to make it very clear to her that I was sick of her emotional neglect and that if she couldn't be here to teach them how to tie their shoes or write their names or help with the potty-training or give them hugs and kisses or be a part of anything else pertinent to their development, then I'd rather she not try to discipline them. And beating on them out of frustration was definitely out.

I told her if she couldn't be around to give them love and praises, then she needed to keep her damn hands off of them. I didn't want to come off nasty—although I was mad as hell. I just wanted her to understand the importance of them knowing her as a mother who takes pride in loving them, not beating on them. Well, she didn't like that one bit. She stormed up out of here and I haven't seen or heard from her since. Not that it matters. That was just another one of her excuses to get out and stay out. Whatever! I like it better when her erratic ass isn't here anyway.

"Oh, don't tell me there's trouble in paradise," she said, jokingly. "Sounds like you and the rising Star are heading for a separation."

I took in a deep breath, slowly releasing memories of happier times back in the D.R., where caressing tropical rays and cool breezes was my fondest pastime. I shook my head, trying to figure out when things had become so damn complicated. "Trust me," I relented. "Sooner than you think."

"Well, good. I never liked her anyway."

I chuckled. "That's nothing new. Who have you ever liked?"

"I liked that Keisha girl, didn't I?"

I burst into laughter. "Amira, you are hilarious. I was in the eighth grade. And Keisha was buck-toothed and cross-eyed." I don't know how I could forget about Keisha Jenkins. She wore these huge round glasses that were so thick that, when the sun glared on them, it looked like she could burn a house down if she stared at it hard enough. I used to feel really bad the way other kids used to tease and make fun of her, calling her things like "glassy-glassy" and "Oooga Booga." I never laughed at their jokes in front of her. I think that's the reason she liked me.

But between you and me, I was scared of her. I was always afraid she'd bite me with those long, wide teeth with the jagged edges. Sometimes I'd wake up to nightmares of her swinging my chewed-off limbs in her mouth. So I was always nice to her. And as a result of my kindness, she'd leave me notes on my locker, asking me to be her boyfriend. And every day I'd return it saying, "No." She just followed me around like a lost puppy, wagging her flat behind and licking her ashy lips. Everywhere I turned, she was there haunting me.

"Exactly," Amira concurred. "She was hard on the eyes, but she was a nice wholesome girl. Unlike those nasty, stuck-up heifers who were always chasing after you, she was a sweet girl."

"Amira, please!" I exclaimed, trying not to laugh. "That child made my eyes hurt every time I looked at her. Ugh! You suuuuuuure is ugly," I said, doing my best impersonation of Shug Avery in *The Color Purple*. We were both cracking up. I tried to get serious, feeling guilty for talking bad about her—truth or not. "That's not nice. We shouldn't be making fun of her like that. It wasn't her fault."

Amira became quiet for a moment, matching the silence upstairs. *Hmm*, I thought. *Those boys are being a bit too quiet.* I decided they must have fallen back to sleep. I snapped back to attention when Amira blurted, "You're absolutely right. It really wasn't her fault." She paused. "I blame her parents! They shoulda been beat with a stick, then hauled off to jail for bringing that ugly child into this world. That child had some big-ass teeth, didn't she?" I opened my mouth to comment but she continued, clearly on a roll. "She looked like a cross-eyed camel with matted braids." I burst out laughing.

"There's no reason," she continued, "they couldn't have gotten her teeth fixed and bought her some corrective lenses. And you know it. Isn't there some kind of law against ugliness?"

"Amira, you're a mess," I said, trying to compose myself. "I'm sure she looks nothing like that now."

"Well, for her sake, I hope not. The thought of waking up to that face is unthinkable. Any man who lays down with her will have to wrap her face three times with the American flag and say he's doing it for our country." I was in tears from laughing so hard. My sides began to ache.

"Amira, please. You're making my stomach hurt," I pleaded, still laughing and wiping my eyes. "I'm sure her inner beauty has prevailed." I almost slipped and told her how I ran into Keisha about eight years ago in New York, coming out of Citibank on Park Avenue. She had swung the door open almost knocking me over. And before I could say something, she recognized who I was. I'm telling you, I was floored. She had her teeth shaved down and capped, and had undergone some major reconstruction. I must say I was truly impressed. The days of a knock-kneed "Ooga Booga" were long gone. That ugly duckling had been transformed into a beautiful swan. We ended up walking down to Houston's on Twenty-Seventh Street where we ate, drank and laughed for hours until nightfall. Somehow I ended up back at her place, being ridden like Amtrak. Nice wholesome Keisha was now a freaky sex-machine.

"I hear she's living somewhere in New York," I offered, "working as a fashion designer."

"Hmm. Lucky her." Silence. "So when can I expect to see my favorite brother and two handsome nephews?"

"I'll give you a call to let you know exactly when," I said. Then I heard,

Bam! Screaming followed. Someone had fallen. "Amira, I got to go check on these kids. I'll talk to you later." *Damn. Can I get one day when they're not doing something*, I thought to myself.

"Give 'em kisses for me."

"After I give 'em ass whippings," I snapped. "Oh, and Amira."

"Yeah?"

"I miss you too."

"I know you do," she said. I could feel her smile through the phone. She blew me a kiss, then hung up. I returned the phone to its cradle, then leaped up the stairs to see about my little men.

When the door slammed shut, I was sitting on the sofa watching the six o'clock news. I braced myself and concentrated on keeping my mouth shut. Not because I had much to say about her running in and out whenever she wanted—as far as I was concerned, she was just a boarder anyway. But she had assured me when she called the other day that she would be home Tuesday evening so I could conduct the weekly teen-parenting workshop I run over at the KinderCare. But because she was a no-show, I ended up taking the boys with me, which was a true test of my patience, 'cause Amar showed out something terrible. In all honesty, it was probably my most productive session because the group got to see firsthand what it's like having a precocious, headstrong toddler. It really opened up a lot of discussion about the trials of parenting, disciplining, and setting firm limits. I'm telling you, I really wanted to wear his little behind out with my strap.

Anyway—productive group session or not—that still doesn't negate the fact that Lina is too damn unreliable. She knows how I don't feel comfortable leaving them with a sitter. I mean, nowadays you don't know whom you can trust. There's so much stuff going on with kids being abused by their babysitters. I can't—and I won't—risk that. I don't care how many background checks I ran on them, if I did have to resort to having a sitter, I'd have every room in the house rigged with tape recorders and video cameras, and would be ducking down between the bushes, peeking in the windows to see what the hell was going on. Call it paranoid or overprotective if you want. Better safe than sorry.

Between you and me, I'm even hesitant about leaving them with certain family members. 'Cause you just don't know. Hell, look what I went through. My mother was working and going to school, trying to better herself and make sure my sister and I had a better life—and I was home, being sexually abused by a cousin. So, you just don't know. But, the one thing I do know and that is, Lina won't ever have to worry about me asking her to watch *our* kids again. I asked her to watch them one day out of the damn week, and she couldn't even do that. That shit burns me up. Then again, she really did me a favor 'cause—given her flighty ways—I have to wonder how safe they'd be left alone with her.

So here it is Friday night and now she decides to flit her behind in the house like she doesn't have a care in the world, announcing her wonderful news of finally getting the lead role in a movie. Interestingly, my attitude instantly changed when I heard the news. I was truly happy for her, despite everything else going on between us. I had hoped it would be the big break she'd been waiting for. A part of me was beginning to feel that maybe I was being a little too hard on her, maybe even a little selfish and insensitive. After all, I did understand that for every one door that opens, another three have already been slammed in your face. When we first moved out here, I saw firsthand what that did to her. She cried many a night. And I prayed many more for her.

Regardless of what I thought of her acting ability, I knew she wanted this more than anything else. So despite the tension between us, hearing her news was grounds for a celebration, or so I thought. To my dismay, Lina had already celebrated without us. Nevertheless, I tried to be happy for her until she informed me what she'd be doing.

"Brit," she exclaimed, grinning from ear to ear as she pranced around the house, "I'm so excited about this lead role." She was bubbling over with joy *and* alcohol. I forced a smile, hoping my words would sound sincere.

"Again, congratulations," I said, getting up from my seat to give her a hug. "Boys, Mommy's going to be in a movie."

"Yea Mommy!" Amir and Amar screamed in unison, running around the living room, then jumping on her. "Can we be in the movie, too, Mommy?"

"No, sweethearts, not this one," she explained, pushing both boys off of her. "This movie is for grown ups only."

I raised my eyebrow at her brushing our sons off, but I kept my smile painted on my face. "Come on, Amar and Amir, it's bath time." I looked over at Lina who was glowing and clearly pleased with her accomplishment. "Lina, would you like to do the honors?"

"No," she quickly replied, "I'll pass. I have a thousand phone calls to make and then I have to head over to Brielle's." Brielle was her latest conquest. "You do understand, don't you?"

I glared at her. "It's crystal clear," I said, heading to the bathroom with both boys in tow. Thirty minutes later, I had finished bathing, dressing and getting them ready for bed. I returned to the living room where I found Lina on the phone whispering, then she burst into laughter. Her giddiness subsided when she looked up and saw me staring at her. She said her good-byes to her caller and hung up.

"So Lina, what's the name of this new movie you'll be starring in?"

"*Lust Between the Sheets,*" she said in almost a song. It rolled off her lips as if it were a lullaby.

"*Lust Between the Sheets?* That sounds a little seedy, don't you think?"

"Brit, this movie is going to give me a lot of exposure and the opportunity to really show off my acting skills."

"That's great," I said, trying to sound happy for her. Yeah, this was an opportunity, all right. The opportunity to expose her bare ass and show the world how big of a freak she is. Like I said, I might play dumb, but I'm damn sure not stuck on stupid. "So, what type of movie is it?"

"I told you," she responded, sounding slightly annoyed that I would ask her for any details. "An adult movie." Okay, so now she wanted to continue being elusive with me. She picked up the remote control and began channel surfing, stopping her search when she got to the Lifetime channel.

"An adult movie like in rated 'R' or as in rated 'X'?" I asked, studying her. I reached for the remote control, pushing the off button. All eyes on me!

She sucked her teeth and let out a deep sigh. "Britton, why are you asking me so many questions?"

"Because," I began, turning around to see where the boys where before I continued. I had a feeling things were about to get heated. "I would like to know what kind of movie the mother of my children is going to star in with a title like *Lust Between the Sheets.*"

She rolled her eyes up in her head. "I told you it's a once-in-a-lifetime opportunity, and could open doors for me. So why can't you just be happy for me instead of badgering me?"

I got up from the sofa, peeking up the stairs to make sure the boys were in bed. When I didn't hear any noise, I returned my attention to Lina, sitting in the easy chair. "Don't think I don't want to be happy for you. I do. But how can I be when you won't even share what your starring role is." I paused to allow my words to hover around in the air. "Now if you ask me, from what I'm hearing, the only thing this movie is going to do is have you rolling over on your back, opening up your legs for every Tom, Dick and Harry. So, again, I ask is this an R-rated or X-rated film?"

She glowered at me, narrowing her eyes to thin slits of agitation. "It's rated 'X,'" she snapped. "Now. You happy?"

I shook my head. "I see. So you'd rather sell your dignity and self-respect for a role in a movie, all because you want to make the silver screen?"

"Don't even go there," she hissed. "You've known how bad I want to be an actress from day one. You know how important this is for me."

I opened my mouth to speak but nothing seemed to come out except for a heavy and disgusted, "Humph."

"You can 'humph' me all you want. But this is my big break and I'm going to do whatever it takes to get to where I need to be in this industry."

"So it seems," I said, trying to maintain calm. But inside I was screaming, *"You nasty-ass ho!"* I eyed her for a moment longer before continuing. "So, you're saying you'd sleep your way to the top?"

"I'm saying I'm gonna do *whatever* I have to."

"By any means necessary, huh?" I asked, staring at her. I couldn't believe this was the same woman I'd met over three years ago. There was definitely something remarkably different about her. Maybe it was always there, but perhaps I had been too infatuated with the idea of her being something she wasn't. Or maybe I was too preoccupied with my sons to really care. In either case, this particular night I noticed it as clear as day.

Although, I've never seen any telltale signs, I remember that same glazed look from so long ago. I'm familiar with the hot flashes and profuse sweating. There was no sense in denying it any longer. That would explain some of her erratic behavior and extended excursions. It would explain the wild eyes, the constant sniffling and why her nose is always red. Allergies my ass! She's on drugs.

It's common knowledge that many of Tinseltown's elite battle with drug and alcohol addiction. Many of whom are hooked on coke and booze, in and out of rehabs. Where upscale places—like Betty Ford and Promises—become temporary shelter from the havoc drugs have created in their lives. I remember going to the elaborate home of one of Hollywood's top executives where champagne and cocaine went hand in hand. I'm almost certain the champagne was also spiked with some type of narcotic. I stood there in utter shock, watching these polished fools climb walls, strip down to their skivvies and Victoria Secret's and dance on top of tables and speakers. I didn't eat or drink anything. And I clearly didn't fit in, so I politely excused myself, leaving Lina in her glory with her industry friends.

"Absolutely," she snapped, narrowing her eyes. "Nothing or no one is going to stop me."

"And what about our sons?" I asked, feeling like that was one of the dumbest questions to fall out of my mouth as I already knew they didn't matter. I just hoped she'd prove me wrong. But like my mother always said: when you ask a question, be prepared for the answer. I just didn't think it would affect me the way it did.

"What about them? Those are your sons. Not mine. Why else do you think I brought them to the Dominican Republic, surely not for a visit? I don't have any interest or intentions of being a mother. Not now, anyway."

Her words stung me. Her callousness practically sucked in the air around me. I slowed my breathing, trying to calm my beating heart. Hearing the truth hurts, and it's sometimes even harder to swallow. But it's always better to face the truth than try to obfuscate.

"Then I guess there's nothing else we have to say," I said, shifting back in my seat. "You got your movie deal and I got my sons." I shook my head in disgust, then stared at her with a slight tilt of my head, trying to figure out how the hell she'd become this cold, uncaring woman. "You know, you're really pathetic." It was in that moment that something in her snapped. Her eyes bulged, the veins in her neck and forehead popped out.

"No!" she snapped, slamming her hands down on her hips, "you're the one who's pathetic."

I held my breath for a few seconds, then blew it out through my nose, slowly. "Lina," I said, trying to not let anger control me. "I think it's best you leave before one of us says or does something we'll regret later. I don't—"

"Fuck you!" she hissed, walking up in my face. "I'll leave when I'm good and goddamned ready. I'm so sick of your self-righteous, uptight, corny ass. This is just as much my place as it is yours so— " She had her finger in my face, waving it like a nightstick. I shifted back in my seat.

"Lina, I'm asking you nicely to get out of my face."

"Or what," she snapped, wriggling her finger and rolling her neck in sync with her words. "You don't tell me what the fuck to do." I looked up at her as she hovered over me. "Humph, just what I thought. Punk ass." I counted to ten, forward—then backward. I pressed rewind in my mind, trying to understand what went wrong. When I came up with blanks, I pressed fast-forward. Her words began to twirl through my ears as she rattled on, sounding like one of the Chipmunks. "You and them damn boys—"

"Get out of my face," I snapped, cutting her off while pushing her finger out of my face, "before I throw up. The sight of you is making me sick." I paused, glaring at her. "You're worse than pathetic. You're fucking disgusting." *Slap!* It felt like something sharp had grazed my skin, breaking flesh.

I rubbed my hand along the side of my hot face. It burned. I looked at my hand. Blood was on my fingertips. Her fingernails had scratched their way into memory. I closed my eyes, then took a deep breath. It was then that the room started to spin. The sound of her hand hitting my face echoed in my ears. Bloody walls, bruises and black eyes clawed at my conscience. I clamped my eyes shut and held my head in the palms of my hands. Soft flesh being beaten by heavy hands pounded my mind. She was still hovering over me, screaming and cursing, but her words collided. I clutched my fists together. My jaws tightened. The trunk of my fears snapped open. Flashes of smashed windows, shattered glass and flipped-over tables spilled open, cluttering my thoughts. Doors hanging off their hinges swung from the corners of my mind.

"Lina," I said slowly and deliberately, almost methodically. "You have three seconds to get out of my face before I hurt you up in here. I'll be anything you want me to be, but the one thing I won't be is your punching bag, now or never. So, I'm telling you to get. The. Fuck. Out. My face. Before—"

"Before what?!" she screamed. She stared me down through bloodshot eyes and flared nostrils, then pulled away from me. And in one swift motion she dug deep within the pit of her gut and hacked up thick phlegm that stuck on the side of my face. I cringed. She had spit on me. I wiped the side of my face with the back of my sleeve, heaving in and out. I tried to restrain myself. I tried to muster up the will to get up and walk away, but something within me wouldn't let me.

Instead, I jumped up and swung her into the wall. It was in that split second that I had almost snapped and beaten her head in. She had awakened the ugly beast in me. I stood there breathing heavy, glaring at her with fire in my eyes, knowing if she came at me with another raised hand I'd kill her.

The last thing I ever wanted to do was leave on bad terms. If nothing else, I had hoped Lina and I would part without any animosity. Maybe even be able to maintain a level of civility. But she's ruined any chance for that.

I've spent most of my life avoiding relationships and situations out of fear that one day I'd wake up and become the man I spent my life despising. I am adamantly opposed to domestic violence. I swore I'd never hit a woman. No matter what, I'd never raise my hand to a woman. Yet, with the snap of a finger, I almost became my father and went upside her head. Had I not seen Amir peeking around the doorway, I would have beaten the mother of my children. I can't live like that. And I damn sure don't ever want my sons to see me raising my hand to any woman.

I watched my father beat the shit out of my mother and there was nothing I could do to help her. Nothing. I would lie in my bed at night trying to block out her screams and his yelling—calling her every degrading name in the book—as he beat her with his fists and anything else he could get his hands on. I refuse to be the batterer or the battered in any relationship. And I refuse to be involved with any woman who drinks, smokes, snorts, dips or chews. And you better believe I damn sure refuse to have my kids subjected to that kind of life. Period. So, to hell with Lina. Good fortune and good riddance, I'm outta here.

8

SARINA: *Wind In My Mind*

Tell me. What do you see when you look at me? Is it the sway of my hips or my thick full lips? Is it the contours of my behind that invite you to stare? Or is it my dark skin and knotty hair? Tell me. Perhaps the gap between my thighs keeps you mesmerized. Does your disdain for me keep you from looking into my eyes? Tell me, you fool. What do you see? Is it a faceless body with legs spread apart? Big breasts? Or is it my soft, hairy spot for your tongue to rest? Is it my oooohs and aaaahs, my moans and groans that keep you around?

Tell me when you'll be ready to pull back the layers of my flesh to see that I am an oxymoron. I am a cascade of melted glaciers, rippling waters of uncertainty. I am a tear-stained image of yesteryears, tattered memories of what used to be. I am a bouncing ball of confusion and fear. Patiently waiting for that day when you can see the beauty in me. In the meantime, tell me, you fool. What do you see?

Ooooh Wee! My mind is racing a thousand miles a minute. Whew! New York is full of so much excitement. I strutted through Penn Station, smiling and greeting my new fans. All the way up the escalator to Seventh Avenue, I turned heads in my latest creation, a one-piece leopard print leotard with matching spiked heels and headscarf. Of course, I know they're not looking at me the woman; it's the body and my wears that keep their eyes fixated on me. So what! I don't give a damn. I got their attention and that's all that matters.

Instead of waltzing up and down the street, I decided if I was going to get my fame, I had better take my show onto Fashion Avenue. But before I did, I decided to sit on the steps of Madison Square Garden and people-watch. And let me tell you. New York has some sights for the sore-eyed, along with a few sights for the cockeyed. Well, just when I was about to regulate me a Black and Mild, my cell phone starts ringing. I had forgotten to turn it back off. "Hello, Sarina Creations," I answered. "How may I direct your call?"

"Sarina? Thank goodness."

"Who is this?" I asked annoyed, lightly rubbing my cigar between the palms of my hand, then removing the tobacco and cancer paper.

"Sarina, it's your mother."

"Humph."

"Your father and I have been worried sick. We've been trying to reach you for the last several days." I repacked the tobacco, then lit my cigar.

"And?"

"Where are you?"

"Why?"

"Your brothers said you were in New York. And I just want to make sure you're okay. Where are you staying, sweetheart?" I rolled my eyes.

"Where are *you* staying?" I asked, sucking in my cigar, letting the smoke twirl around my tongue. I slowly blew it out.

"We're still in Slovenia but we're flying home tomorrow morning—"

"Oh, you're still in Slooooooveeeeenia," I sneered, leaning back on the concrete step. "Whoopty do. Like I give a hoot." I paused, savoring the burning in my chest. I held it in, then forced it out in one blow. "Well, don't rush home on my account. I'm doing just fine without you all up in my face."

"Sarina, you sound really hostile. Is everything alright?"

"Sareeeena, you sound really hostile," I mocked. "Oh please. You make me wanna bite steel wool. Like always, you just wanna be all up in my damn business. If you were so concerned, you woulda left me a damn credit card and some money before you went off gallivanting around the world."

"Sarina, are you taking your medications? Your therapist said you've cancelled two appointments." Now that did it. She was getting a bit too damn nosey for my liking. "What business is that of yours? I'm a grown woman. So why don't you go scratch a monkey's ass."

"Sarina—"

"Oh, shut up!" I snapped. "You're nothing but dirty dishwater."

"Sarina, do you have Indy's phone—"

"Hello. Hello. I can't hear you. There seems to be a bad connection," I said, pressing the end button and shutting the power off. That woman has been nothing but a thorn in my side. Who the hell does she think she is, trying to steal my joy? It's bad enough she's taken everything else away from me.

First my car, so what if I had an accident. All I did was sideswipe a man on a bicycle, knocking him off his bike. It wasn't my fault that old fart didn't look both ways. Then my credit cards, so I ran them all up. Big deal. Why should she have cared, they were in my father's name, not hers. And now she wants to take away my freedom. That woman has even tried to turn my own father against me. She makes me stone-cold sick. She's tried to control my life far too long. One of these days, I'm gonna have to put a stop to her meddling once and for all.

I finished my cigar, flicked it onto the sidewalk and stood up to execute my plan. It was a beautiful day. "What da fuck you looking at?" I yelled at this four-eyed geezer with a big wart on his nose, watching me, trying to hide behind a pole. "I see your ugly ass!" Everyone within earshot looked at me, then around to see who I was talking to. But I saw him. And I knew what he was up to. He was following me. He wanted to know where I kept my friend. Ha! I'll suck horse milk before I let anyone hurt her again or find out where I keep her hidden. I promised her, I'd keep her safe from harm's way, and that's what I intend to do. At whatever costs! So I fixed him. I sat back down on that step, smoked me another cigar, then waited for nightfall. It would be easier to sneak around to the other side to make my escape.

I sat. And sat, glancing down at my watch. Time was slowly ticking away. That motherfucker! He was gonna make me late for my photo shoot. I jumped up, ran over to that pole and gave him a piece of my mind. Then I slapped him. Of course he denied my accusations, but I know better. I slapped him again, grabbed my things, then left him standing there in a daze. I hurt my damn hand too! I think I broke his jaw. Serves him right. Owww! My hand really hurts.

HeeHeeHee. Guess what? I met me a fine man in Port Authority who I strolled along Forty-Second Street with. We laughed, talked and shared four fried chicken wings, a side order of vegetable fried rice and two egg rolls. And then I invited him to my rat trap of a motel room. Mmm-hmm. I sure did. How could I resist five feet eleven inches, one hundred and ninety pounds of hairy, long-tongued man, he's just too sexy. It didn't matter to me he was homeless. Shit. Homeless men need love too. So what if he's a little dusty? With a haircut and shave he'd be good as new.

Once in my room, I pulled out my clippers and scissors and cut down that nasty bush of hair on his head, then shaped up his mustache and beard. He was a work of art in progress and I was his sculptor. Yes indeed. And tonight my masterpiece was going to be all mine. We drank a bottle of Wild Irish Rose and a forty-ounce of Steel Reserve, then we sparked up a blunt. Betcha By Golly Wow, if I didn't get horny. HeeHeeHee.

You wanna know what I did next? I made him brush his teeth and take a hot shower. And when my homeless love stepped out, "Oh my!" I exclaimed, then backed this chocolate caboose up, taking in all of him. That's right, doggie-style, baby!

Well, just when my poontang started poppin' and the party was getting started, lame nuts ejaculated deep inside of me, then had the audacity to ask me for fifty bucks. I thought I was hearing things so I asked him to repeat himself. And sure enough, he said, "Let me get fifty bucks, sweetness." *How dare he*, my mind screamed. *I've been good to him, feeding and fucking him and this is how I'm repaid!*

I jumped off the double bed and lunged at him like a bat out of hell, screaming, "Who the fuck do you think I am, you goddamn street urchin!" I scratched his face and neck up. I sure did. Damn fool-assed man. Here I was giving up free pussy and he wanted to disrespect me, asking me for some damn money. "Cut him, cut him, cut him," rang in my mind as I snatched the empty beer bottle and smashed its base against the edge of the night table, chasing him out the door and down the hall, with my titties and ass bouncing in the air.

You should have seen him running. HeeHeeHee. You woulda thought someone was tryin' to kill his Johnny-Come-Quick ass. I don't know if I was mad because he wanted money or mad because he gypped me out of a good fuck. Here look. See how wet my pussy is? HeeHeeHee. If I stick my fingers in it, white stuff comes out. Here look. It looks like cottage cheese. HeeHee.

Come drag your tongue across my womanhood. My punany. Twat. My oochie-coochie yah-yah. HeeHeeHee. The essence of soiled flesh.

"Who wants to fuck, who wants to fuck," I chanted, knocking and banging on every door until I found me somebody in this rat hole to finish the job. Door number six opened. Bingo!

"Yeah," a short, stocky guy with short dreads asked, swinging open the door. He reminded me of someone from *The Little Rascals*.

"Hey, Buckwheat," I said, holding my titties together in my hands, then licking each nipple. "I wanna fuck. Can you handle that?" I widened my stance. He glanced down at my furry nest.

"Aye yo, get da fuck away from here with dat shit," he snapped, trying to slam the door in my face. I stuck my foot in before he could get it closed, then pushed it in, knocking him backward.

"I said I wanna fuck."

"Yo, Cee, who dat at the door, money?" someone with a deep voice asked.

"Some trick ass, I'm about to knock da fuck out."

"Well, what she want?"

"Talking 'bout she wanna fuck."

"Then let that ho in," another voice said. "I'll knock her back in." I smiled. Buckwheat stared me down. HeeHeeHee. I turned around and bent over, giving him a quick view of my twat. He stepped aside to let me in, then closed the door.

"Who's smoking trees up in this bitch?" I asked, bee-bopping toward a cloud of smoke. "Let me get a hit of that," I said to the guy lying across the bed in a white Calvin Klein T-shirt and boxers. His eyes almost popped out of his head when he looked up and saw me standing there in the nude. The other guy was sitting at the desk, rolling more blunts. He was bare-chested and looked fresh out of prison with his bulging muscles and homemade tattoos.

"Got damn!" "Boxer Boy" said, looking at my big titties, handing me the spliff. I took a heavy pull and smiled.

"Yo, she wanna fuck," Buckwheat repeated, grabbing at his dick.

"Word?" "Bare Chest" asked, grinning.

"Then let's bust that ass," "Boxer Boy" said, getting up, then pulling out his dick. I took another hit of his spliff, then dropped to my knees— HeeHeeHee, taking his pecker in my mouth. "Bare Chest" got up and walked over with his dick hanging out and over his gray sweat pants. And with one dick in each hand, I sucked them both until I heard a wrapper tearing. I craned my neck around, then smiled when I saw Buckwheat rolling a condom on his dick. Hmmm.

"I want you to lie down so I can ride you," I said to Buckwheat. "And you can stick this in my ass," I said to "Boxer Boy," yanking his dick. He looked at me in shock. I licked the head of his dick. "That's right," I repeated. "Grease it, ease it, put it in my ass and let me squeeze it!" HeeHeeHee.

"Nah, let me get the ass," "Bare Chest" said.

"Nope. You can bust your nut in my mouth," I said to him, pulling back the extra skin on his uncircumcised dick. It smelled like Taco Bell. Hee-HeeHee. Oooh Wee!

I had me a good ol' time. I smoked up all their shit, fucked all three of them, then went back to my room to get ready to hit Times Square, singing "Where Were You When The Lights Went Out In New York City." HeeHeeHee.

9

CELESTE: *Woman to Woman*

I must say, when I saw Indy slap that woman in the airport I was a little taken aback. Particularly coming from a woman who is noted to be a successful entrepreneur and philanthropist. Every graduate and undergraduate chapter in our sorority has heard the name Indera Fleet or read an article on her at least once in their lifetime. I have to admit, her bio is quite impressive. According to the sorority gossip mill, it is rumored that she's worth hundreds of millions of dollars. Unbelievable!

That's why when I saw her going off on that poor woman who looked half frightened out of her mind, my first thought was "They failed to mention this social icon was also a little on the crazy side." But once we finished our formal greetings and got settled on the plane, I decided that Indera was a rich woman who thought she could say and do whatever she wanted and get away with it. I guess her money and social standing afforded her that right. Hmm. She almost reminds me of my mother, the one and only Dr. Octavia Munley-Randolph—a silver-spooned society matron bred from old money who thought she owed no one anything because of her birthright. She believed the right name, the right address, the right friends, the right education were synonymous to one's level of success. And, as far as she was concerned, the Munley name held marvelous things.

When Octavia stood, it was as if she were posing for the cover of *Glamour.* Appearance was everything. Head up, back straight, shoulders back, hips forward, one leg behind the other. She commanded attention, and her presence alone demanded drum rolls and the red carpet. "Celeste, you are a

Munley. And Munley women use their brains and beauty, not their booty to get the things they want out of life."

I unfortunately was never able to live up to her high standards for in my eyes I was a Randolph, after my father whom she—if you let her tell the story—married because of his family's social status and that they grew to love each other. But later on in life, I learned she had gotten pregnant during her three-month courtship and was forced to marry him to keep from shaming her good family name. Then to add salt to injury, my grandfather stipulated in his will that if she divorced, she would lose her inheritance. Yet, she walked around with her head in the air like she was above reproach.

The eldest daughter of Drs. Harvest and Lenora Munley, one of D.C.'s most affluent families, Octavia was a summa cum laude graduate of Spelman College, as were her mother and grandmother. Her father, grandfather and great-grandfather were Morehouse scholars. The Munley tree was rooted with a long line of judges, doctors, lawyers and educators. After all, her father was one of D.C.'s finest Supreme Court judges, her grand-father was a former chancellor of Howard University and her great-grandfather was a prominent lawyer and close friends of Mary McCloud Bethune and Madam C.J. Walker. My mother was proud to announce her great-grandfather's association with W.E.B. Du Bois. And she prided herself on her family's social standing and grace.

After all, the Munley home was a place were Kwame Nkrumah—past president of Nigeria—and Alain LeRoy Locke—the first black Rhodes scholar—ate from her family's china and sipped from their crystal. So, as far as she was concerned, anyone born of simple origins was not worthy to be in her company. And she had no problem looking down her thin, pointy nose at anyone she viewed beneath her. Including me. Nothing I did was ever good enough.

When I graduated tenth in a class of two-hundred-and-thirty, she said I didn't try hard enough. When I came home pregnant, she said I was noth-ing but a loose floozie. It didn't matter that it was my first and only sexual encounter. I can still hear her saying, "Celeste, I am appalled at how you have embarrassed me. You have brought nothing but shame to this family and our good name."

I'm sure if he had been the son of a successful businessman or judge, it wouldn't have mattered as much 'cause she would have married me off. But because he was "roguish" and a "good for-nothing" who ended up in prison, I was a disgrace. But Octavia would take care of everything. She'd ship me off to Memphis where I would have the baby, then return like nothing ever happened. "We will say this is a distant cousin's baby whom we have adopted, and you will go on with your life and try to make something of yourself. Do you understand?" Although it was more of a demand than a question, I nodded, signing over my maternal rights.

When I opted to attend Howard University instead of her alma mater, she said I was being spiteful. Then she declared me a lost cause when I became pregnant the second time—marrying a young boy of simple means, as she put it. And she really lost her mind when we transferred to Norfolk State. She blamed my drug use on "that filthy environment." Little did she know, I had been sniffing coke with all of my "well-to-do" friends all during my freshman and sophomore years at Howard. It was a well-kept secret that just escalated after I buried my son.

If she were still alive, I can only wonder what she'd have to say about my association with Indy. Sitting in first class—next to this modern-day princess—was clearly a far cry from my days nestled in the corner of some crackhouse, cavorting with drug dealers. Octavia would most likely be ecstatic and say something like, "Celeste, dear. Indera is the proper company to keep. She is of fine stock." Of course she'd be referring to her money and the fact that she too was a soror. Yes, my mother lived and breathed *her* sorority. After all, its symbols represented the epitome of beauty, class, and culture. And any *fine* young woman could only have been raised by a *soror*, with the exception of me, of course.

My lovely departed mother would say the nastiest things to a person and still maintain a smile on her face while cutting you with her words. Oblivious to the damage she'd done. I suspect the only difference between the two of them is that Indera is a part of the nouveau riche. Old money, new money…what difference does it make? It all spends the same. And no matter how you spend it, a snob is still a snob. At that point, I knew befriending Indy would be a definite challenge, especially when she started probing me about my past, present and future.

"So, Celeste, where are you from?"

"D.C.," I said, proudly.

"Hmmm. The city of scandal and corruption," she remarked, pursing her lips as if she were pondering her comment. "Every time I think of D.C. I can't help but think about that ex-mayor. He just really played himself."

"He made a mistake and hit rock bottom," I said with annoyance, trying not to let her hit a nerve. I just get so sick of people equating D.C. with the past mistakes of one mayor.

"Well, I guess you're right about that. Now I just wonder when that singing diva is gonna hit the bottom. She's always sweating like a pig on stage. Chile, I just wanna snatch that hot-ass wig off her head and beat her with it." She paused, shaking her head. "Humph. Lord knows she looks like a scarecrow on crack right about now. Someone needs to chain her ass to a rehab bed and toss out the key. And that washed-up, one-hit wonder husband of hers, I bet his ugly ass was the beginning of her downfall." I really wanted to laugh at her comment but given what my battles have been, I knew it was no laughing matter. I gave her a sidelong glare instead.

"Indera, dear. Don't ever think you are too big to fall from grace."

"Oh. Trust and believe, *dear*. I know what goes up must come down. But while I'm up on top, I'll be damned if I'm falling off for a hit or a line. I don't care how rough things get."

"Girl, never say never. Anything can happen."

"Well, I beg to differ. 'Cause I know for a fact. That's one thing I will *never* do willingly. I'll be the first to say, that I've been through a lot of shit in my life, and it has affected me in one way or another; but not to the point where I'd turn to drugs for validation. It's all about self-love. When you truly love you, you don't allow nothing or no one to disrupt your flow. And you don't allow anything to contaminate your mental, spiritual or emotional space. And I love me. So don't get it twisted." Although her eyebrow raised and her forehead furrowed, she kept a smile pasted on her face.

I frowned, then took in a deep breath. "Well, sometimes it's not that simple. Sometimes people fall because they're pushed."

"Then you get your ass up, brush yourself off, and keep it moving."

"It's not always so cut-and-dry."

"Hmm. I guess." She placed her hand over mine, gently patting it. "You know, soror, it almost sounds like you speak from experience hitting rock bottom and falling from grace," she spoke matter-of-factly. I kept my composure. But my insides were beginning to churn. How dare she!

Yes, I had fallen from grace. I already told you how my addiction pushed me into a yawning gulf of squalor, living in filthy rundown woebegone shacks, smoking crack all night. I blinked, shifting in my seat. Every time I put that stem to my lips, I allowed it to control me. It owned me. And I surrendered my life to its will.

"Maybe, maybe not." I paused, mostly to smother my growing frustration than for effect. "The fact of the matter is: people can *and* do change. When we fall, we can all get back up. Some of us just need a little help standing until we're strong enough to stand on our own." I waited long enough for my words to linger in the air. People like her make me sick with their holier-than-thou attitudes. Always talking about what they'd never do.

Do you think I wanted to be an addict? Do you think I wanted to be on my knees, begging some dealer for my next hit, or being slapped around? I thought I had it going on. I thought I had everything under control. But I didn't. And before I realized it, I was already pulled under its spell. I had gone from fly girl to fly-by-night junkie with the snap of a finger. You know, it's sad. But women like Indy see people like me as weak because we fall victim to circumstances. Well, no one wakes up saying, "Today, I think I'm going to be a drug addict, or an alcoholic."

I hate people like her who talk about "picking yourself up, and keeping it moving." Sometimes people can't just pick themselves up and keep it moving, because they don't know how. But my thing is, when I fell—or when someone else falls—where the hell were you? Sometimes, we need someone to reach down to help us up. Not kick us down, to keep us down. So please.

"You know," I continued. "I can't understand for the life of me why people are always so quick to judge others without having ever walked in their shoes."

"I agree. People do change but as far as I'm concerned—no matter how much changing you do—you will *always* be remembered for what you were."

I smacked my lips. "Well, we all have a past."

She broke out in a wide smile. "That we do. But no matter how hard you try to run from it, don't ever forget—your past will always find you." Her hazel eyes bore into me. I shifted my eyes, twisting the ring dangling on my chain. Silence consumed the air between us. She rummaged through her designer saddlebag. I snapped my eyelids shut, ruminating until her voice disrupted my thoughts. "So, is D.C. where you live now?"

"No. I live in Hartford," I responded curtly.

"Hartford, *really?* I'm planning to open up a new salon in the Hartford area."

"Well, congratulations," I said. "I'm sure you'll do very well there."

"I don't doubt I will. You know I had to go up there to check out the competition first, just to see whom I'd have to blow out of the water. But to my surprise—"

"Turning Heads in Bloomfield," I interrupted, "is the only salon that'll give you a run for your money."

"You think?"

"Girl, I know. That's the only place I go to get my hair done. And them girls can do some hair. Besides, I'm friends with the owner."

"Well, lucky her. Just make sure you let your girl know while she's busy *turning heads*, I'll be weaving wonders all around her."

I chuckled. "I'm sure Regina is armed and ready."

"Oooh, soror, what happened to your neck?" she asked, staring at the four-inch scar neatly tucked under my jawbone, barely missing my jugular. Many people have noticed it. I mean it's not like I try to hide it. But no one has ever dared to ask me about it in such a bold manner. I rubbed its indentation, remembering the sticky blood flowing through my fingers as I held on to my neck desperately searching with pleading eyes for someone, anyone, to save me.

"Bitch! What the fuck you think you doing?" he yelled, walking into the bedroom catching me scooping out six vials filled with shiny white rocks from one of the Ziploc bags he kept locked in a briefcase. I had picked the lock.

"Uh, I...I," I stammered, visibly shocked. "Rocky, I was—"

"What the fuck I look like?" he asked, cutting me off. "You think I don't know your trick ass been swiping my shit?" I tried to scurry around the bed, stumbling backward, knocking the lamp off the nightstand. He cornered me, slapping me with a backhand that sent me flying over the bed, then crumbling to my knees. He hit me again and again. Each time, the impact of his gold lion's-head ring breaking skin, causing blood to seep through, then slowly roll down my face.

I had promised myself time and time again that I wouldn't let my use put me in harm's way ever again. But with the strike of a match or the flick of a lighter and six hits later, I'd suck in every promise I'd made and blow it out into a whirl of white smoke. Nothing else mattered but where I'd get my next rock. It had already been my third time sneaking into my drug-dealer boyfriend's stash without getting caught so I figured one more time wouldn't matter. But it mattered more than I'd ever imagine. And there was a price to pay.

"No, Rocky! Please!" I begged. "I'll make it up—"

"You damn right you will," he snapped, punching me in the mouth before I could finish my sentence. Blood spurted from my bottom lip, spilling onto my chin. I fell backward, my head slamming hard against the wall. My eyes must have closed for a spilt second, because before I could see it coming, before I could duck or scream, his fists hit my face, causing stars to float before me. He had punched me in my left eye, then again just above my right one. Each punch caused more skin to burst open. I dropped to my knees. He cursed and screamed obscenities at me, yanking me up, then dragging me out of the motel room and shoving me into the back-seat of his two-door Chevy Blazer, screeching out of the parking lot and onto the empty highway.

"Rocky, please!" I begged, crying and holding the sides of my bruised face. Blood from the gash over my eye continued to drip into my eye. He turned around, his eyes ablaze and swung his closed fist into my mouth again, causing me to slam backward into the seat. Blood gushed out, fill-ing my mouth, wrapping around my tongue, then rolling to the back of my throat. I coughed and gagged, bringing it back up.

"Shut up, bitch!" he bellowed. "You wanna fuck with my shit. I'm gonna teach your trick ass a lesson you'll never forget." My mind and heart raced in fear. I had known Rocky to be dangerous when crossed, but I had never experienced his wrath firsthand. He slammed on his brakes, made a wild U-turn in the middle of the street, heading toward Rock Creek Park. When he found a secluded dark area, he parked, then jumped out of the truck, swinging the door open. He reached in the backseat to pull me out, but I backed away, kicking and screaming. He got ahold of both of my legs, then pulled but I was holding onto the back of the passenger seat.

"Noooooo! Please, Rocky!" I screamed. "Please. Help me! Somebody help!"

"Bitch, didn't I tell you to shut the fuck up!" He let go of my legs, climbing into the backseat, slapping and punching me. When he punched me in my jaw, I shrieked in pain. He then snatched me out from his truck and dragged me into a wooded area where he continued to beat me. He then forced me to take off my jeans and remove my underwear.

"Please, Rocky," I begged in almost a whisper. "Please."

"You want some rock, bitch-ass whore!" He threw me down on the ground, pinning me on my back, pressing his forearm deep in my neck, shutting off my airway. "I'll give you some rock, trick bitch!" Forcing my legs open with his own, he then rammed his penis into me, pounding inside of me, punching me about the head and face until he ejaculated. When he was done, he grabbed me by the back of my head, yanked me up, snapping my neck back as far as it would go, then flipped open his switchblade. With ringlets of my hair coiled around his hand and fingers, I pleaded one last time as I saw my life flash before me through bloody swollen eyes. And when I looked into the sky I saw nothing but streaks of darkness. In one swift motion he brought his blade across my neck, then left me there— naked from the waist down—to bleed to death. Had that switchblade sliced through my skin a few inches deeper, it would have cost me my life.

"Wrong place at the wrong time," I responded, glancing over at Indy who was staring as if she could see through my scar. Why I even allowed myself to get into this with her was beyond me.

"Well, chile. I've had a few battle scars of my own. But I know this fabulous plastic surgeon whose work is remarkable. I'll refer you to her if you'd like."

"Oh, that won't be necessary," I replied, smiling. "This scar is a reminder of where I've been in my life, and where I never want to return. So removing it is out of the question. Besides, I think it gives me character." I don't actually believe that but it's what I wanted her to think. Honestly, I see it as a hideous reminder of how cruel life can be. But I've learned to accept its presence as a part of my living and breathing. And I need to see it there in order to maintain my sobriety.

"If you say so," she said, smiling. I could feel her eyes piercing through me, searching for my tiny box of secrets.

Between you and me, I was beginning to wonder if I would be able to stomach her interrogation much longer without telling her to mind her damn business, which I'm sure would have caused tension between us. But one thing's for sure: God works in mysterious ways. She started throwing up all over the plane. I know this might sound horrible but I was relieved. Not that I'd wish anything bad on anyone, I just wanted her to keep our conversation simple. In some situations, less is always best. There was no need for her to know any more about me than I already knew about her. I flew in silence the rest of the flight, smiling.

Of course we all stopped in at one time or another to check on how she was doing. One thing's for sure, Indera might have been sick but she wasn't missing out on one ounce of luxury. I smiled when I entered her plushy twenty-ninth-floor, two-story penthouse suite with elevator, marbled bar and magnificent view of the Las Vegas skyline. The girl definitely lived the life of the rich and famous. *Hail to the Queen*, I thought.

"Soror, thanks for stopping by," she said, opening the door wearing sky-blue Versace loungewear. I had expected her to look a mess, considering being sick. But to my surprise, her hair and face were all in place. When they said she was a diva, they never lied. She was stunning.

"I hope I didn't catch you at a bad time," I said, stepping into her palace. "You look wonderful for someone who's been bedridden."

"Girl, let me tell you. Just because I'm under the weather, that does not mean I have to look weathered, okay? I make it my business to look my best even under distress or duress."

"I heard that," I responded, smiling. "Well, I just wanted to stop through to check in on you and see if you needed anything."

"That was so sweet of you," she said warmly. "But you didn't have to come all the way up here for that. A phone call would have sufficed, but thanks just the same. Since you're here, please come on in and have a seat." She walked me through the foyer into the living room. I could hear Cherokee's "Steppin' Stone" playing softly in the background. "So how are you enjoying your time in Vegas?"

"Oh, it's just wonderful. I'm really glad I was able to come."

She smiled, then asked, "Can I get you something to drink?"

"No thanks. I can't stay long. I'm meeting Tradawna and a few other sorors down in the lobby in a few minutes to head over to the Bellagio to see the Dancing Water show."

"Oh, that sounds like fun." She sat across from me on the edge of the long burgundy sofa, reminding me of my mother. Back straight, legs crossed at the ankles, manicured hands, one on top of the other, neatly placed over one knee: a true lady. At that moment, snatches of "Pomp and Circumstance" came to mind. I smiled, more to myself than at the staring eyes, frantically searching for things they didn't need to see. I diverted my attention to an elegant sterling silver picture frame positioned on the huge coffee table. In it was a picture of two beautiful boys. I smiled.

"Oh, they are so adorable," I said, breaking her concentration. "Are they your nephews?"

"Thank you. No, those are my godsons Amir and Amar," she replied, smiling. "Spitting images of their father." Silence immediately filled the room with awkwardness thick as fog until she sliced through it with her questioning. "Soror, what did you say your last name was?" she asked, with a slight tilt of her head.

I shifted in my seat. "I didn't. But since you've asked, it's Munley. Why?"

"Because I am certain we've met somewhere before, I just can't put my finger on it."

"No. I don't think so," I said. "We might have seen each other in passing at a boulée or one of the regional meetings but I'd definitely remember meeting you. Anyway, you know what they say about us all looking alike."

"Hmmm. Maybe."

"Oh, my goodness," I said, glancing down at my watch. "I better get going. The show starts in twenty minutes."

"Well, enjoy," she replied, getting up to escort me to the door. "Thanks for stopping by."

"No problem." I clasped my hands over hers. "Take care. I hope you feel better soon."

She smiled. "I already do."

After spending five days locked up in her MGM suite, hugging her toilet bowl while the rest of us got our gamble and drink on, Indy shocked us all when she made her grand appearance through the casino, looking as if she'd just returned from a photo shoot instead of a sick bed.

"Girl, you look fabulous," I commented, giving her a hug. I sincerely meant the compliment. She wore a gorgeous sleeveless brown mohair sweater dress with matching five-inch mules and purse.

"Why thank you. And so do you."

"Well, it's good seeing you up and about," Val chimed in. "We were beginning to worry you might end up spending your whole trip in bed."

"Please. You should know better than that. There's no damn way, I'm letting a little food poisoning or flu keep me down. Besides, those damn MGM lions kept roaring, 'Money over here, money over there.' And you know how I love money."

"You ain't never lied about that," Val responded, collecting her half-empty bucket, then getting up from her stool. "Well, I don't know about ya'll but I'm going over to the blackjack table. Maybe I'll have better luck over there. Let's all meet up at Olio's around, say, seven. I'll make reservations."

"Sounds good to me," Indera replied.

"Me too," I said, as we both watched Val switch her way toward her next chance at winning big, fading into the sea of gamblers. "So where are you now off to?"

"Chile, I'm going right over there and play me a few slot machines. One of those machines is about to buy me a new mink."

"Mind if I join you?" I asked, laughing at her comment.

"By all means. Just don't disrupt my flow 'cause mama's on a mission." I smiled, following her over to the twenty-five-dollar slot machines where she claimed three machines, flipping open her Chanel purse and sliding five crisp one-hundred-dollar bills into each machine. Of course my eyes almost popped out of my head as she prepared to blow fifteen-hundred dollars like it was nothing. Although I have a successful consulting business, there is no way I was willing to blow away my hard-earned money. So I found myself a machine four stools down and slowly slid in two one-hundred-dollar bills, rubbing my hands together, taking in a deep breath, then slowly pulling the lever. In a matter of seconds, I was minus two hundred and digging in my purse for another two. When I lost that, I dug in my purse for two hundred more. I was relieved when three lion heads popped up and the bell rang. I was happy to have won most of my money back.

"Girl, don't tell me you're packing it in already?" she asked, pulling all three levers of her machines with the speed and grace of a gazelle.

"Absolutely. I won my money back and I'm done."

She paused for a minute, staring at me with her face frowned up. "What kind of mess is that? Girlfriend, either play to win or play to lose but don't waste a seat, playing to break even."

"I'm not a gambler," I explained. "So as long as I'm not losing what I put in, I'm alright."

"Honey, if you're pinching pennies, then perhaps you should go over to the nickel machines." And with that said, she turned her back to me, slapping down her levers. I was speechless, to say the least. *This bitch*, I thought to myself. And just as I was about to gather my things, bells rang, red lights flashed and hundreds of silver coins clattered into their bins. Indy had hit the jackpots on two machines, simultaneously. And then five minutes later, her third machine hit. It's always the ones who don't need the money who seem to always win. In less than an hour, Indy had won over eighteen-thousand dollars. "Not bad for a sick bitch, huh?" she asked, grinning from ear to ear. "Like I said, you gotta be in it to win it."

"So I see."

After Indy cashed in her winnings, she sauntered through the casino to the Rainforest Café to the Lion Habitat shop, then along Studio Walk where she bought souvenirs and expensive trinkets. While I only purchased a key chain and magnet for my secretary, I was amazed at how this woman spent money. Never looking once at a price tag.

"Oooh girl. Let's go over to the Forum Shops at Caesars Palace. I want to hit the Louis Vuitton and Gucci stores before we hook up with the others," she blurted, glancing down at her watch. "I'm already five days behind in my shopping."

Well, she left out we'd also stop along the way to shop in Versace, Dolce & Gabbana and Chanel. Nine-hundred dollars later, I walked out of one shop with one pair of shoes, and a matching leather handbag. I was done for the day. As much as I love my designer wear, there was no way I was going to try to keep up with her spending. She was out of control.

"Celeste, so finish telling me about this mystery man of yours," she requested while trying on a pair of Gucci boots.

"I don't remember starting," I replied, giving her a raised-eyebrow stare. For the life of me, I couldn't understand why she was so interested in my life story. "Are you always so inquisitive and suspicious of people?"

"Well, since you asked," she said, smiling. "I'm always skeptical of anyone who is grinning in my face. And I'm even more suspicious when I think someone is tryna hide something. And I'm always inquisitive about any woman who is holding her breath waiting for a man to walk back into her life—"

I don't know where she got the impression I was holding my breath waiting for my man to waltz back into my life. Even I knew better than that. Like I said before, *I* intend on walking back into *his* life, claiming my rightful place in his heart.

"Excuse me, Indy, but if I choose to not discuss something with you, it doesn't mean that I'm hiding anything. It means it's none of your business and it's something I'd rather not share with you."

She pursed her lips. "Hmmm. I didn't mean to step on a nerve."

"Trust me." I smirked, staring her in her eyes. "When you step on a nerve, you'll know it."

"Really?" she asked in a tone so sweet it dripped with sarcasm.

Yeah bitch! my mind snapped. But my mouth settled for, "Really." I checked my watch. It was four-thirty. "Oooh, soror. I gotta get back to the hotel. I'll meet up with you at Olios."

"*Ciao!*" she said, dismissing me with the flick of her wrist while trying on her eighth pair of shoes. I walked out of the shop, angrily swinging my bags through Caesars Palace and out the sliding glass door where I hailed a cab back to MGM. I'd had enough of her.

"Has anyone seen Indy?" Val asked as we were seated at our tables. "I tried calling her suite before coming down but there was no answer."

"Well, I left her at Caesars around four-thirty," I said. "The way she was spending, she's probably somewhere still shopping."

"Well, I hope we're not waiting for her before we order. I don't know about ya'll but I'm hungry enough to eat a horse," Dietra remarked.

"Girl, you're always hungry," Tradawna said, laughing. "This afternoon you were hungry enough to eat three cows."

"Listen, dear," Dietra retorted, "ain't no shame in my game. I'm a big girl who loves to eat."

"Hello. Can I get you ladies something to drink?" the dark-haired, muscular waiter asked.

"Yes, I'll have the Bada Bing," Dietra said with a coquettish grin.

"What in the world is a *Bada Bing?*" Tradawna asked no one in particular, then turned to the waiter for clarification. After he explained it was a Cosmopolitan made with Absolut Mandrin, shaken with fresh lime juice and a hint of cranberry, she naively smiled and said, "That sounds delicious. I'll have one as well."

"I think I'll have the Olio cocktail," Janie said.

"And you?" he continued, looking at Val.

"Oh, I'll have water with lemon, please." The rest of us ordered our drinks, then smiled as he took off to fill our request.

"Now that was one fine white man," Dietra snapped, staring over at the bar in his direction. "He can dip his stick in my pudding any day."

Val clucked her tongue, thumbing through the menu. Tradawna rolled her eyes. Lea gave her a half-eyed glare. I smiled.

He returned with our drinks. "Is everyone ready to order?"

"Yes. I'll have *you* along with the seafood platter," Dietra said coyly. She stuck her index finger in her mouth, then slowly removed it. The waiter turned beet-red.

"And what about you?" he continued, turning his attention to Tradawna, then to the rest of us.

"I'll have the chicken marsala with mushroom ravioli," she said. I ordered the Alaskan crab cakes and baby spinach with Sambuca sauce. Val opted for the braised sterling salmon with spinach and grilled artichokes. Lea and Janie ordered the chicken Alfredo. Dietra licked her lips as he walked away.

"Damn, girl. Do you think you can go one night without throwing yourself at a man instead of acting like some hard-up maiden?" Val asked, clearly annoyed with Dietra's flirtatious behavior. She didn't care about race, religion, or marital status. If she wanted you, she went after you.

"Nope. I love men almost as much as I love to eat. Besides, I don't see anything wrong with two consenting adults having casual sex. Please, you know my motto: If you wit it and wanna hit it, come git it."

"Well, let's see how casual you are when you get it and have to take your ass down to the clinic because you can't get rid of it." Tradawna snickered. "With all that's going on in this world why would you want to play Russian roulette with your life?"

"You ain't never lied," Val agreed.

"Tradawna, girl," Dietra snapped. "I know you're not talking with all those little hood rats you got running behind you."

"Now wait a minute. Just because I like my men in Timbs and Uptowns— Airforce Ones, that is, for you fashion illiterate." She grinned. "That does not make 'em hood rats. Please. I'd rather have a brotha who rocks a hoody and Timbs than some fake-ass rockin' knock-off designer wear. And for the record, I'm not boppin' every brotha I see."

"Girl, please," Val snapped, rolling her eyes in her head, "Dietra isn't concerned with what any man has on, it's how fast he can take it off and get it up that matters."

"Well, like I said, there's no shame in my game. I like what I like and I want what I want. Maybe if you stuck-up biddies stopped fakin' and frontin' and kept it real, you'd be getting your backs knocked out on a regular 'cause there's definitely enough dick to go around for all. And—" Dietra stopped in mid sentence with her tongue wagging when she spotted a tall brown-skinned man the color of Nestlé chocolate. "And tonight I want that fine piece of man right there." She gestured with her eyes for us all to take a peek at her next victim. Turning our heads in his direction, we agreed. He was one handsome, broad-shouldered black man. "Excuse me while I go over to weave my web." She scooted around the table, almost knocking Tradawna out of her seat.

"Damn, girl. Break my shoulder, why don't you, with that buffalo ass of yours." We all laughed, watching her pull the suction out of all that rear end, then flip Tradawna the finger.

"Oh my!" I exclaimed. "Soror is a mess."

"That she is," Val concurred, looking down at her watch. It was nine-forty p.m. "I wonder where in the world Indy is." Most of us had already finished eating and were either having dessert and coffee or more drinks.

Somewhere minding someone else's business, I thought before saying, "Well, from what little I know about her I get the sense she's a woman full of surprises." Val smiled.

"Indy is fierce," Tradawna interjected, smiling. "I just love her energy."

"You know when I first met her," Lea stated. "I didn't think I was gonna like her." Val shot her a look, warning her to be careful what she said about her friend. Lea continued, oblivious to Val's stare. "But I have to say, she seems like a lot of fun." Then everyone around the table began singing her praises. Indy this. Indy that. I smiled. It was like she either had these women brainwashed into believing she was this Saint or they truly admired her. My mind wandered to sweet thoughts of my husband and how wonderful it would be seeing his smile. Feeling his touch. Then I thought about what I had to do. What I needed to do. If I wanted to have him back in my life, there was no way getting around it. I would do whatever it took. In the end, it would be worth every miserable moment. Val caught me rolling my eyes up in my head.

"What was that about?" she asked, causing everyone else to look over at me.

"Huh?"

She repeated the question.

"Oh, I have something in my eye," I said, gently pulling my eyelashes away from my eye. She gave me a quizzical look, then returned her attention to her half-eaten chocolate mousse. Dietra returned, slamming her pocketbook down on the table, then plopping down in her chair. She was clearly annoyed.

"What's the matter with you?" Janie asked. Dietra gave her a half-eyed glare.

"Nothing," she snapped, digging through her purse, pulling out her compact and lipstick. She evenly applied a fresh coat of burgundy-wine paint to her full lips. "Fuck him," she replied, smacking her lips together, then snapping her compact shut.

"Oh Lord!" Tradawna blurted. "Don't tell us the Chocolate Prince turned down the Love Goddess."

"No," she corrected. "*I* turned him down."

"And why was that, Miss I Want That Fine Piece of Man?" Val asked.

"Because that chocolate nicca likes his milk white," she said with disgust, rolling her eyes, then pursing her lips. "And I don't fuck no nicca who sticks his dick into white pussy."

"I don't know why not," Tradawna said. "You fuck everything else."

"Now, now," Val stated. "It's good to see she has *some* standards. So what if he likes white women? We all have our preferences. Different strokes for different folks. Besides, just a few minutes ago, you were ready to jump our waiter's bones. And he's white. So practice what you preach."

"Here, here," Tradawna chimed. "I second that emotion."

"Humph," Dietra grunted, dismissing the comment. "Whatever. Big Mama is gonna get it knocked down regardless so who cares." She paused for a moment as if pondering her remark and added, "He probably had a little dick anyway." We all looked at her, gathered our things, said our good-byes, then headed for the door, leaving her deep in thought—sulking.

DAMASCUS: *Young, Gifted & Black*

Man, listen, of all the book signings I've done, there's nothing like the love I get from African-American-owned bookstores. I don't care where I go I'm embraced real proper. And today was no exception. I spent three hours doing a book signing at Kujichagulia Bookstore out in Paterson owned by Stacy Foster—this young sista's makin' power moves for real for real. The girl is fly, focused and definitely has flavor. Word up! But what was most impressive was her passion for reaching out to youth, empowering and encouraging them to read and write daily. I'm really diggin' her style. And I was about to call her to thank her again for the warm hospitality when my phone rang. I picked up on the third ring.

"Hello," I said, removing my clothes and tossing them across the sofa. I walked through the kitchen and opened the back door to let Bullet in. He charged in the house, almost knocking me over.

"What's up, boy?"

"Brit, my man. What's poppin', nigga?" I asked, glad to hear his voice.

"I can't call it. Just thought I'd give my two favorite people a call to see how things were."

"Yo, I'm chillin'. Just got in from a book signing out in Jersey. Other than that, everything's everything."

"So, Mr. Big Time author, has celebrity status gone to your head yet?" I chuckled. "Nah, never that. I'm still just everyday peeps."

"I heard that. Oh yeah. I saw the article written on you in the *Black Issues Book Review*. Very impressive, boy! I'm really proud of you."

I smiled. "Thanks, man. Yo, I can't front. I was kinda shocked when the editor called me and said they wanted to write a piece on me."

"Tee, c'mon now. I don't know why. The book is deep as hell. I mean the fact that it addresses the plight of many of our youth gives readers something to really think about. And the fact that you experienced a lot of what is in that book and was still able to come out on top makes the message even more powerful. I know what your struggles were and I think it's great that you share your story with the world. Reading your book or hearing about your life may save someone else's. Each one must reach one."

I laughed to myself. I knew Brit was about to get wound up and go into one of his speech modes. He was right, though. If anyone needed to give back, I did. Especially to young brothas who let the streets control 'em. There was definitely a time when I lived and breathed the streets. Hell, that's all I knew so where else was I supposed to be?

When you grow up without peeps who give a damn about you, you look for love and acceptance in the streets. Nah, hold up. I'm not sayin' my moms didn't love me. She loved me the best way she knew how. And I'm sure she loved me more than she loved her drugs. At least that's what I've told myself all these years. Should it matter that she kept me locked in a room, watching a little black-and-white TV while she used drugs or turned tricks? Or that she was missing for two and three days at a time? Not all the time, some of the time. Fuck. Maybe she didn't care more about me. Nevertheless, she was still my moms. And, since she's dead, I'll never know so it doesn't really matter now.

But dig, like I was sayin', the fucked-up thing about the streets is, most of them cats in the street don't really care about you, either. On the bricks they might be like "Yo, you my nigga; yo, you my dawg for life," but, when push comes to shove, it's just do or die. You don't *do* right, you *die*. Word up! You gotta always be on point 'cause if you sleep on a cat, he just might take your face off, feel me?

I know a lotta the shit I did was fucked up. But back then my mentality was like, "Whatever!" See. When you homeless and hungry, you do *whatever* the fuck you gotta do to make it through another night. You handle your business, yo. Feel me? At fourteen, I shoulda had my young ass home in bed. But I didn't have a home and I damn sure didn't have a bed. And the few beds I did have were either temporary or they were shared with some chick who liked young dick. So lying up in a warm bed—fucking—was much better than sleeping on the streets or in some rat-infested abandoned building. Besides, it kept my stomach full and my dick wet.

What's really fucked up is that most people can't even begin to imagine the number of kids living on the streets because of either running away or being thrown out by their peeps. You wanna know what really cracks me the hell up? The mindset of many people who think kids choose to be on the streets. Yo, what the fuck! Every kid wants to have a safe, warm place to sleep at night. What they don't want is some bitch-ass nigga beatin' on them or someone constantly crawling in their bed at night, tryna get a nut. Feel me?

When I was on the streets I had to worry about where I was gonna get my next meal, where I was gonna rest my head and how the hell I was gonna wash my ass. Sometimes I slept on the subway. A few times I slept in the park. And I damn sure wasn't too proud to rummage through a Goodwill bin for clothes. Sometimes you do what you gotta do—not by choice but by force. I know I did. I hit the streets because I was tired of bouncing from one placement to another and I was sick of being beat on. I didn't need anyone else to remind me I was nothing when I woke up every day, having nothing; feeling like nothing. So I jetted.

I shot craps and stole cars for a few months or so. But then I learned the art of selling drugs and immediately became sucked into the drug-game. The money and power became my high. I was somebody. So it became all about slinging drugs and dick, all in the name of survival. I learned to use what I had to get what I needed—by any means necessary.

When I look back on my life, I know I am fortunate. Nah fuck that. I'm blessed. Word up. I'd probably still be on the streets if I hadn't gotten locked up at sixteen. Those eighteen months in detention mighta taught me how to be a better hustler but it also helped save me from myself. And I know in my gut if someone hadn't reached out to me while I was there,

there are only two places I'd be: dead or rotting away in jail. It just took me getting bagged the second time—at twenty-four—for me to realize that jailin' wasn't me, na' mean?

Those three years on lockdown—and the other three on parole—was enough for me to never allow them gangstas to get me by the balls again. Aiight, aiight, I still did my thing, pushing weight for a minute. But I stacked my dough and knew when it was time to dip outta the game, feel me?

See, some of these cats get so caught up in makin' the cheddar that they become too blindsided to know when it's time to flip that shit into something legit, dig what I'm sayin'? They'd rather bubble up and bling-bling instead of tryna stay low pro. It's just really fucked up they can't see any farther than the fast cash, fast cars and fast ass until it's too late. And what's really fucked up, is the fact that many of these cats don't have shit to show for the work they put in on the block. Yeah, they might stay dipped in the illest shit, might even have a fresh whip but—at the end of the day— they still living at home or with some chick in Section 8 housing. And when they get popped they don't have shit to come home to. No investments, no savings. Nothing but a chick who let his mans run up in her while he did his bid. Yo, I ain't hatin'. And I'm damn sure not knocking the hustle. Just stack the cash and get the hell outta the game before it's too late, feel me?

Yo, I've been there. And I understand the mentality that when you're on the streets, you gotta learn how to get down for yours, and not give a fuck about who you gotta step on to get it. And I've seen what that "baller-shotcaller" life can get you: death or incarceration. Eventually, that shit comes crumbling down on you. Believe that! A lot of the cats I was running with are now either hemmed up in the legal system, drugged out or dead, for what? Damn. B sure knows how to say shit that hits home. He definitely knows how to keep a cat grounded. That's one of the reasons I got mad love for him. Now that's my dawg for life.

"I feel you, son."

"You just keep writing, boy. Besides Indy, I'm your biggest fan. Oh, speaking of Miss Indy; is she home?"

"Nah, she's in Vegas with some of her sorors, spending money left and right I'm sure."

"I don't doubt that," he said, chuckling. "Especially, now that you're one of the top best-selling authors in the country. Knowing Indy's behind, she's lovin' those checks more than you."

"Yo, tell me about it." I said, shaking my head. "Between this damn house we're building and all of her shopping sprees, I'll be lucky if I have enough money left for a McDonald's Happy Meal."

"Poor thing," he *tsked*, trying to sound sympathetic. "So when's the house gonna be ready?"

"The hell if I know. Every time I turn around Indy's adding some new fixture or having the contractors tear something out because she doesn't like it. And of course it costs more money. She's a real pain in the ass when it comes to wasting money. If this keeps up, I'm gonna have to go back to stripping just to make ends meet."

"Yeah, okay," he said, laughing. "And Indy will have *both* of your heads chopped off." Yo, he found this shit real amusing. "Well, that's what happens when you marry a high-maintenance diva. If I were you, I'd put a pad-lock on that wallet of yours and start digging in hers."

"Yeah, aiight," I said, sitting at the kitchen table, flipping through a stack of bills. Indy's ass is sitting on more cream than she knows what to do with, yet she'd rather spend my shit up. All I wanted was a nice, simple house with a big yard and a finished basement for a game room and gym. But no, *she* wants to live in a gated community. *She* wants marble fireplaces and Italian-marble floors. Who the hell needs three fireplaces and four bathrooms in one damn house? *She* wants vaulted ceilings with skylights. *She* wants a gourmet kitchen with granite countertops and stainless steel appliances. What the fuck does she need all that shit for? Her ass doesn't even cook. Man, listen. This whole damn house thing is one big fuckin' headache. I'm telling you, I've about had it. I changed the subject before I got vexed. "So how are the boys doing?"

"Fine. Big and busy."

"I heard that." I let silence fall between us for what seemed like an eter-

nity while I imagined what my sons would be like. I wondered what kind
of father I'd be since I didn't have one to emulate. Hell. I wondered if I'd
ever know fatherhood the way things have been going. Indy's still not
pregnant. That shit just fucks me up. I've never wanted anything more
than being a father.

My thoughts drifted further trying to recover any traces of a man in my
life known as *Dad*. My search was the same as any other time: nothing.
With the exception of scattered images of a twenty-two-year-old drug
dealer—the same one I'd catch my moms on her knees with in the stairwell or occasionally sneaking out of her bedroom in the middle of the
night—nothing remotely resembled that of a dad. Damn. What was that
cat's name. Jake? Snake? Black? Yeah, that's it: Black.

He'd peel me off a few dollars for ice cream and candy. And anytime I
was out after midnight, he'd snatch me up and send me home, then threaten
to put his foot in my ass if he caught me out again, bitching that no four-
year-old should be out that time of night. Yo, how the fuck was I supposed
to know. It's not like I had anyone paying attention to me.

You know, there was some fucked-up rumor that he was my pops. So
when I was like five, I asked him. And instead of denying it, he simply said,
pulling out his dick, "Check this out, young blood, if you gotta big, black
dick like this here, then yes. If it's little, hell fucking no!" My eyes popped
open in disbelief and shock as he swung and shook his dick in my face.
"Now take this dollar and go buy yourself some ice cream." I took off
running not certain if it were out of fear of what I had just seen or in
anticipation of all the treats his money would buy. In any case, I gotta
long, thick dick and it's black as night so does that mean his young ass
knocked my moms up?

"Earth to Tee, are you still there?"

"Yeah," I said, snapping back to the present. "I'm here. I was thinking
how lucky your boys are to have a father like you."

"Damn, Tee. You sure know how to lift a brotha's spirits. Thanks. But,
honestly, I'm the lucky one. I have two beautiful sons who fill my life with
purpose and meaning. There's nothing I wouldn't do for them. They are
my life."

"Yo, I feel you, son. So what's up with you and Lina?"

"Not a damn thing. I'm leaving her," he said, sounding defeated. "I gave it my best shot and it's time to pack it in."

"So just like that, you bouncin'?" I asked. "What about the twins?"

"What about 'em? When I go, they go. I have no more time for bullshit and I've had enough of hers. So I'm stepping *with* my sons."

I couldn't believe he was really gonna jet with his sons. Damn. I don't think I'd have it in me to raise kids on my own. But one thing about Brit, he's always been in a class by himself. So there was no doubting his ability to make it happen for him and his children with or without that fine shorty. I have to give it to him, though. He knows how to bag some of the finest honeys around. The fucked-up thing is, they start buggin' out and bringing him grief. It's like he has a hex on him or something. But when it comes to him doing his thing, he just goes with the flow. That's Brit for you. He lets shit roll off his back.

"Yo, you know if you need anything, I got your back?"

"Thanks, man," he said. "You and Indy have already done enough."

"Nigga, you my boy," I snapped, saying it with enough emotion to let him know it was coming from the heart. "So if I got, you got. Feel me?"

"I feel you," he replied, chuckling. "But, reliable daycare is all I'll need, for now."

"So, what's up with the job thing?" I asked, looking in the 'fridge for something to eat. *As usual*, I thought, *there's nothing in this bitch*. I slammed it shut. On the counter was a glass bowl with two red apples, one pear and three bananas. I grabbed a banana, peeled its skin back, then took one huge bite.

"I'm credentialed and marketable so I'm not stressing the job scene too much. I'll probably just work from home for a while until the boys are in school all day. Then I'll beat the pavement. In the meantime, I already got a spot to rest at. So everything should work out."

"Brit, knowing you, you'll make a way out of no way. Word up," I said, walking into the living room, chomping on the last bite of my banana. "Oh shit!" I snapped. "Bullet, what the fuck you doing?" He had the nerve to have his big ass stretched out across the sofa, chewing the heel of one of Indy's designer shoes. "Yo, B, I gotta bounce, Bullet done got a hold of Indy's shoe."

"Oooh, Indy's gonna fuck ya'll up." He laughed, hanging up. I chased Bullet's ass down the basement, put him in his cage, then gated the doorway off, cursing when I saw the note she had left me: *Tee, baby. Make sure you keep the gate up. I don't want that dog eating up my shit. See you when I get home. Love you.*

"Damn you, Bullet!" I yelled, tossing her mangled shoe in the trash. Hell, I figured she wouldn't miss it since she never wears the same pair twice in the same year anyway.

Man, don't even ask. I don't care how many times I tell her she needs to chill out on the shopping she still brings bags up in this piece. I've never known anyone who shops as much as her. No joke, she has enough shit hanging in her closets with tags still on them to open up her own boutique. And I'm still tryna figure out why the hell she has so many damn shoes. No exaggeration, she has a closet with over six-hundred pairs of shoes stacked in boxes from the floor to the ceiling; and not one pair under three-hundred dollars. Yo, that shit is ridiculous. But like she said, "As long as I'm not spending *your* money, don't worry about my shopping habits. Besides, I don't hear you complaining when I hit *you* off." Her point was well taken, so I keep my mouth shut and let her do her.

"Bullet, shut that damn noise up," I yelled at the top of the steps leading to the basement. He was down there barking for me to let him out. "You fucked up. I'm the one who has to hear Indy's shit, not you. So your ass is hit." I went upstairs, showered, then tried reaching Indy on her cell. I left a message.

Just as I was getting ready to head out to the Pathmark to get some groceries, the doorbell rang. I looked out the peephole and opened the door, grinning. It was Pedro, the young cat Indy and I had met in the Dominican Republic three years ago when we were visiting Brit. Indy was so distressed when she had heard he wasn't able to finish school because his family couldn't afford to pay for his uniforms and supplies that she gave them a few thousand dollars—besides the seven-hundred dollars she swiped outta my wallet to give 'em. Yo, sometimes I still laugh at that shit. But, at the time, I was heated—but four months later she sent for him and his family to live in the States where he could get his education and become the doctor he aspired to be. That shit really touched me.

Between you and me, I think what really hit her was his story of losing his parents in a hurricane when he was four, leaving him and his younger brother in the care of his sixteen-year-old sister. On the strength, Indy has a real soft spot for orphans. Anyway, over the last three years, Pedro's gone from a shy, little boy from the D.R.—who spoke broken English and had minimal grade schooling—to a well-spoken straight-A student. Yo, I'm proud of him. Word up.

"Pedro, my man," I said, opening the door. *"Que pasa, amigo?"*

"Nada," he replied, smiling. We shook hands. I still can't get over how he's shot up over the last year. At fourteen, he was almost as tall as me.

"Don't tell me you've come back for another spanking on the pool table," I said, closing the door behind him. "'Cause I got a stick with your name written all over it."

He laughed.

"You only win 'cause I let you," he said, teasing.

"Oh, word?" I asked, going into one of my shadow-boxing moves, gesturing to give him body shots. Over the past three years, he and I have developed a very close relationship. Since he doesn't have a father figure, I've kind of taken him under my wing so sometimes he comes by and we shoot the breeze, lifting weights, shooting pool or hitting the hoops.

"Well, let's rack 'em up and see what you got," he challenged, heading down to the basement. "I'll even let you break." I laughed at that. 'Cause the truth of the matter, the cat's got game. If I don't break hard and run the balls fast, it's over. I followed behind him.

"Yea, aiight, money," I said, grabbing my stick from off the rack. "You 'bout to get whooped on real good." I chalked my stick, then broke the balls, sending four balls in: three striped, one solid. I looked up at Pedro who was mapping out his strategy in his mind. I grinned, chalking my cue. "Stripes. Now, get ready for your beating."

"Not a bad break for an old-timer," he said, keeping his focus on the table. "But, it's not over till it's over." He had his right arm across his chest, with his left elbow on his right hand while resting his chin on his thumb and his index finger over the bridge of his nose.

"Oh, aiight," I shot back, sinking in another ball, then another. "You just sealed your fate, lad."

"We'll see."

"Confidence," I said, chalking my stick. "I like that. Eight ball corner pocket." He started whistling. I scratched. "Damn!" Pedro burst out laughing. I was heated but I tried not to show it. *How the hell did I scratch?*

"Told you," he replied, still laughing while tossing me the triangle.

"Aye, yo. You jinxed me."

"Rack 'em up, old-timer." I laughed at that and then housed him the next two games, showing him no mercy. After he finished getting his beatdown on the table, I ordered two large pizzas, we kicked back and ate, then watched a few DVD flicks.

Saturday, at 7:30 a.m., the phone rang. I picked up on the first ring, thinking it was Indy since I hadn't heard from her last night. We had agreed that anytime one of us was away from home we'd check in, to at least say good night. Instead, it was Yolanda Allen, owner of Eden Books and radio host of WDAS in Hartford, Connecticut, confirming my nine o'clock phone interview. After I told her that I'd remembered to call the station, I hung up, then grabbed the bottle of coconut oil, pouring some into my left hand and over my dick. It was time for my morning nut. I rubbed my balls and slowly jerked off imagining Indy straddled over me, riding this wood. I gripped tighter and stroked harder as if it were her wet pussy clamping around my dick.

Yo, Indy has a pussy like a Venus Flytrap. That shit grips and pulls my dick. I love when she twirls her hips down the length of my pipe, then slowly rocks and rolls down onto the base. Damn, my shit is harder than a muhfucka just thinking about that pussy. I can't wait to bust that ass when she gets home. Word up! My shit is throbbing.

Anyway, thinking 'bout Indy had me so damn roused my balls throbbed. I needed to bust off so I gripped my shit tighter. My strokes became deeper. Longer. Harder. Faster. Until I moaned, "Damn, baaaaby!" splattering a nut thicker than oatmeal across my chest and over my shoulder. I turned over on my side, glanced over at the clock, then picked up the phone. It was time.

"Good morning, everyone. Welcome to 'Something for the Mind.' Hartford's best-kept literary talk show. Joining us today is Damascus Miles, author of *The Young Brotha Behind the Mask*," Yolanda said. "So, Damascus, without giving away too much of the story, tell us a little bit about the book."

I cleared my throat, rubbing sleep from my eyes, before I flipped into professional mode. With the help of Indy and a public relations and speaking agency, I pretty much have this interviewing shit down packed. Although I sometimes feel like I'm reading a script or some shit, I put on my mask and talk the talk. Feel me?

"Good morning. Well, *The Young Brotha Behind the Mask* is an autobiographical novel about a young man's journey through a life of abuse, neglect and abandonment and how he allowed drugs, criminal activity and promiscuity to define his masculinity." Now in layman's terms, it's about a young homeless cat who hustled and fucked for survival. I want to hit her with it raw but I don't. I stick to my script.

"Well," she said, "there is definitely a message to be learned by reading your book, that's for sure. There was just so much emotion in each chapter. When you talk about your emotional loss due to your mother's addiction, then the physical loss you experienced as a result of her death, I cried. When you talked about some of the abuse you experienced in the foster care system, I cried some more. It's definitely a great read."

"Thanks. I appreciate that. I want people who read my book to know that many times, when you see a young brotha who appears fearless and emotionless, that underneath that aloofness could be someone who is hurting, lonely or confused. Many times young brothas feel pressured to prove their masculinity so they adopt a very aggressive or detached stance. They have trouble communicating their feelings; thus are oftentimes overlooked or misunderstood.

"You know many of them have misplaced ideas of what being a man is supposed to be. I know growing up I did. And I sometimes wonder what my life would have been like if I would have had a positive adult role model in my life. But I understand if the only people you look up to are the cats selling drugs, in gangs or standing on the corners, then that's whom you have to emulate. That's how you define yourself. If you've never seen anybody successful in your life, living a positive lifestyle, you can't feel that you can do anything other than what you're doing.

"I don't blame anyone in my family for what I went through in my life. But, maybe if I had gotten the love, support and self-worth that can only come from family—be it immediate, extended or communal—I wouldn't have turned to the streets for validation. Who knows, maybe I wouldn't have made some of the choices I made in my life, feel me?"

"Oh, I feel you," she said, "and I think anyone who reads your book will feel the same thing. You know. The underlying theme of your book seems to be the need for love."

"Absolutely," I said. "Even the roughest, toughest kid needs love."

"I know for me. Being a parent, I just can't imagine my child or anyone else's for that matter, being subjected to any of those experiences."

I pause before I respond 'cause I feel my mask peeling off. I shuffle through my mental cue cards to keep from flipping the script. "Well, believe it or not, it's happening every day. Somewhere, there's a child going through some form of abuse or neglect. Somewhere there's a child who is home-less or who is exchanging sex for food or shelter. Somewhere there is a child who is in a foster care or other placement that is worse than being left at home. I don't want people who read my book to lose sight of that."

Yo, on the strength, I want peeps to realize that the young cat they see standing on the corner ice-grillin' may be the same cat who's homeless or hungry. He might feel lost and unloved or be lonely. I want peeps to under-stand that everything they see on the outside of a young brotha isn't always what it seems, feel me? Sometimes you gotta go beyond the surface. Dig deeper.

"Oh, believe me," she said. "After reading your book, there's no way anyone with a conscience can ignore what's going on. It's definitely an eye-opener."

"Then I've done what I set out to do. Hopefully, it'll make a difference in someone's life."

"I'm confident it will." There was a slight pause, then she continued. "So Damascus, are there any writers who you feel have influenced your writing?"

"Umm. Not really," I said, sitting up on the edge of the bed. "My writing is influenced by my experiences. But there are books I've read that I could really relate to."

"Such as?"

"Well, Claude Brown's *Manchild in the Promised Land*, umm, Ralph Ellison's *Invisible Man* and Nathan McCall's *Makes Me Wanna Holler*. Just like in those books, Trigger Jones—the main character in my book—struggles with issues around his identity and his quest for manhood."

"I have to say, the minute I opened your book, I was hooked. I mean, although there were a lot of painful situations being told, there was also a lot of humor and erotic stuff going on as well. Ladies, let me tell you. When I read the chapter on Trigger Jones' life as a stripper, I lusted." She chuckled.

I smiled, flicking dried remnants of my morning nut off my chest. "Oh word?"

"Hmmm-hmmm," she purred. "That Trigger sure had his way with the women."

I laughed. "Nah, Trigger just let the women have their way with him."

"And that they did," she said, giggling. "Well, judging by how well your book is doing, I guess it's safe to say your days of stripping are long gone, huh?"

"Most definitely," I said, laughing. "Besides, my wife would kill me."

"I know that's right." She laughed. "Well, sounds like the days of Trigger Jones are over, and there's a happy ending after all."

"No doubt," I replied, lying back on the bed, glancing over at the picture of Indy on the nightstand. I smiled. "Yea, life could never be better."

"Oh well ladies," she cooed, feigning defeat. "I tried." We both laughed. "So, Damascus, tell us. When can readers expect your next book?"

"My next book, *Caged*, is due out in the spring."

"Hmm. Catchy title. Will it be a spin-off of *The Young Brotha?*"

"Not exactly. It's more of a diary-letter-based story."

"Do you mind telling us a little bit about it?"

I coughed. "Excuse me," I said, clearing my throat. "Not at all. It's a story about a young cat's life in prison. I think we all know someone who has been (or is) incarcerated. Loneliness is a terrible thing, and when you're behind the wall, it can really eat away at your spirit. And when you lose a loved one, be it a family member or significant other due to death or abandonment, there's a huge sense of helplessness and hopelessness that begins to consume you. Well, this book will speak of the love, loss and loneliness he has experienced during his imprisonment."

"Sounds very interesting. And what can we expect from book three?"

"To be honest with you, Yolanda. I can't say at this time; one thing's for sure, it will give Zane's *Sex Chronicles* a run for its money, feel me?"

"Oh my!" she exclaimed. "I feel you alright. I can't wait. Well, folks you've heard it here on WDAS. Thank you for tuning in to this morning's segment of 'Something For The Mind.' If you're in the Hartford area, don't forget to stop by Eden Books at 680 Blue Hills Avenue to pick up your copy of *The Young Brotha Behind the Mask* by Damascus Miles."

After Yolanda and I exchanged our *thank yous*, I rested the phone back in its cradle and lay back across the bed, wondering whatever happened to Mr. Tillman and Ms. Rivers, the two social workers at the Youth Detention Center who not only made sure I obtained my GED while detained but helped me get accepted into Norfolk State University as well. They even went to court on my behalf, convincing the judge to not sentence me to a state facility for juvenile offenders. They were the first adults who actually put their necks on the line for me, showing me that there were adults who genuinely cared about my well-being. I can never forget that. And that's why I make it my business to give back.

That's why I devote time going to youth detention centers, reaching out to hopefully instill in them a sense of hope. I strive to restore their sense of worth and value in a world that would rather build more fuckin' prisons than help these young brothas work through their anger, fear and pain. Dig, these young brothas—like I did growing up—need responsible, productive men to teach them what being a responsible black man means.

These young brothas need to know, they need to understand, that they too are worthy of love and validation. And they sure the fuck can't learn that behind bars. Damn! This shit is real. We need to learn to be better brothers, fathers, husbands, and friends so that we—as men—can step up to the plate and assume responsibility for our young brothas. Maybe then, each one will be able to reach one, and save one.

You know. It's kinda funny how life turns out. I would have never guessed in a million years that I'd be one of those brothas jumping in the trenches, as Brit would say, tryna reach out to others. Not that I wasn't down for doing the community service thing before. Sure, I'd hit someone less fortunate than me with a few dollars here, a few dollars there. But that's it.

Keeping it on the real for real, I never really saw myself as a role model until now. I was so emotionally fucked up from all the ripping and running and sexing I did, I never imagined I could use those experiences as a basis to help other cats in similar situations—or brothas heading down that same path of self-destruction. 'Cause here I am now—ex-con, ex-hustler, ex-stripper—a progressive and evolving being who is a husband and a best-selling author, making it my business to kick some knowledge about the effects street life and self-defeating behaviors can have on you. Damn. I almost sound like Brit. Now ain't that some shit! I guess all those brotherly heart-to-hearts over the years about giving back finally paid off.

Yo. Every time I walk through those steel doors, an eerie feeling settles in the pit of my stomach. But I keep my head up, smiling as I flash my visitor's ID badge. And the first thing I see when I step through the double doors is a sea of young, black brothas lost in a social wasteland.

For many, it becomes a barren landscape of forbidden freedom and forgotten dreams. For others: a way of life. I think it's really fucked up how some of these young cats think it's all gravy to have spent time in jail. I just wanna snap when I hear that shit. Did you know that as of June 2000, there were 791,600 African-American male inmates in state, federal, and local jails? Yo. That shit ain't sweet. WE need to wake the fuck up!

Every time I look in the faces of many of those young brothas, I see the reflection of a fourteen-year-old boy in their eyes: Lost. Hardened by social ills. Sadly, they will become products of a corroded system that doesn't give a fuck about the socially hazardous consequences of locking them up and throwing away the damn key if professionals give up on them.

You know. That's why I make it my business—no matter how bleak some of their situations may be, no matter how racist the system may be—to come out to rap to 'em. See. It was behind those same walls that someone finally took the time to look beyond my facade, seeing the soul of a lonely boy. It was there that a young social worker brought me into his office, sat me down and challenged me to want more out of life. He dared me to be better than what I was. He challenged me to remove my mask and see what I really was: Young, Gifted and Black.

11

INDERA: *Don't Explain*

Girl, let me tell you, my feet are killing me. I shopped 'til I almost dropped. Oh my God! I worked the hell outta those salespeople. Had them scrambling around like chickens. Chile, I get a kick outta them fools, shucking and jiving for a commission. And let one of them not put my change or receipt in my hand. Strike! You will return everything back to its place on the rack or shelf and refund me my damn money. Okay? I don't care how bad I might want something.

And let 'em follow me around the store like I'm beat for their shit. I will turn that mother out. Think I won't. Or let me ask to see something and they give me the price before showing it to me—as if to say, "Sorry, dear. But you can't afford this." Giiirl, listen. I flip open my designer wallet, slap my American Express Black card down on the table and demand to see a manager. And just to fuck with 'em, I'll buy the most expensive piece in that bitch, making sure someone else gets the commission. And then I go back two weeks later to return it.

What? Why you giving me the eye? Oh. You wanna talk about my interaction with Miss Celeste. Please. What's there to talk about? Oh, I see. You think I was a little short with her. Well, get over it. I don't know what it is about her, but something doesn't sit right with me. She's sneaky and I don't trust her. Now hold up. I'm far from jealous. I'll give it to her. Girlfriend can put it on. But that still doesn't dismiss the fact that she has some kind of hidden agenda. And don't think I didn't peep how she started fumbling with Tee's book, getting all nervous and shit, after flipping through the acknowledgments. Now what was up with that, huh? Exaaaactly!

And no. I'm not being paranoid. I know women like I know the folds of my damn pussy. And any woman who is smiling and cheesing all up in my face as much as she was wants something. Trust me. But like I told you on the plane, I will get to the bottom of it. So until I do, I will keep my ear to the ground and my eye on that ass 'cause I know homegirl is up to something and it ain't pretty. I don't care what *you* say.

Now before some of you start rolling your eyes up in your heads—not that I give a damn, saying I'm up to my shit again—you should know I will only pull your card when I suspect you tryna be slick. Other than that, I'm mad cool. *Most* of you should know that by now. Hmmm. Now isn't it something when the hunter, gets caught by the game? That's right, fall right into your own damn trap. Well, just thought I'd throw that out there to give you a little something to think about.

Anyway, I'm friendly with any and everyone as long as you come correct. But make no mistake, while I'm laughing and cheesing with you, I'm peeping everything about you. I sleep on no one. Please, a diva must always know whose on her team and *who* her opponents are, okay? And that's why I pulled out my little black book, flipped open my cell, dialed the digits, then waited for the voice on the other end.

"Yeah," the voice on the other end responded.

"I need some information on a Celeste Munley. I want you to kick over every rock and every stone until you come up with something. I don't care what you gotta do. I want to know everything from the number of times she shits to whose pussy she came out of." I gave him what little information I had gathered from my chitchat with her and a few other sorors: age, hometown, college she attended and current residence. Of course it wasn't much, but it was enough to get this research project started.

"Got it. How soon you need it?"

"Yesterday," I replied, then snapped my phone shut. I raced toward the bathroom, slapped up the toilet seat, then hurled my guts out. I don't know what the hell is going on with me, but it's not cute. This throwing up is wearing me out. But I'll be damned if I'm gonna waste the last few days of my trip hugging a damn toilet bowl. Oh my God! I know what you're thinking. Don't even say it. Wrong! Sister Mary checks in monthly and, on top of that, I'm armed and ready just for safekeeping, okay.

Now don't give me that under-eyed glare. Well, how else am I supposed to protect my interest? I sure can't ask Tee to wear a condom, now can I? Humph. Let's not start. We've been having a good time so far, so let's get off this subject before one of us says something we can't take back. So let's move along, and get along.

Anyway, I'm going down to meet the girls so if you wanna hang, by all means you're welcome to tag along but remember, what we discuss stays between me and you. Got that? Cool. Damn it. Hold one minute, it's the phone. "Hello."

"Aye yo, where you been?"

"What?"

"You heard me. Don't start showing your ass, girl."

"Tee, lick my ass, okay?"

"Yeah. Talk slick if you want," he snapped with an attitude.

"Can't you say hello, first, before you start your shit?"

"Hello. Now where the fuck you been?" Okay. Now he's trying to get on my nerves.

"In Vegas. Where the hell else you think I've been?"

"Who knows; I haven't heard from your ass in two days. And every time I call your damn cell, it's not on. I've left your ass three fuckin' messages and you still didn't have the decency to pick up the phone to call. You cheatin' on me or what?" Humph. As you can see, he's tryna get some shit started so y'all go on without me. I'll catch up with you later. So if you'll excuse me, I need to get back to my phone call. Oh, and lock the door on your way out.

"Boy, shut your paranoid ass up. You're so damn silly. First of all, I haven't had the phone on since I've been here. I just turned it on a few minutes ago. Second of all, you know the number here so you should have called the hotel. Now like I said, LICK MY ASS!"

"Yeah, aiight," he said, trying to hold in his snicker. "Talk greasy if you want." He paused for a moment. Then he spoke again as if he had come to some realization only he was aware of. "Don't make me fuck you up."

"Humph. What*eva*."

He lowered his voice. "When you coming home so I can plant this nut in that ass?"

I grinned. "Why?"

"Why you think?"

"You miss me?"

"What you think?" he asked, then deepened his voice. "What you got on?"

"Why?"

"Yo, won't you quit it."

"You so fucking nasty," I said, laughing. "Get your hands out your damn boxers."

"You got clothes on?"

"Yes. Why?" I asked, coyly. Of course I already knew why: His ass was horny and he missed this sweet pussy. I just wanted to hear him say it.

"Yo. Take them shits off and lie across the bed."

"Why?"

"Aye yo. Don't play with me."

"Look, boy. Ain't nobody playing with your ass. I gotta meet the girls downstairs."

"What? Fuck them hoes."

"Don't be calling my sorors hoes," I snapped, rolling my eyes up in my head. "I told you about that. Now if I call 'em that, that's one thing, but don't you."

"Aiight, my bad. Damn. I know you coolin' with them stuck-up...your girls and all but you mean to tell me you can't spare a few minutes for your man."

"Now here you go. You know damn well I always have time for you."

"Aiight. Act like it then." He paused for a moment. His breathing was slow and heavy. I closed my eyes and imagined him with his shiny dick in his hand, long-stroking it. Up. Down. Up. Down. Thick veins pulsing, head engorged. Hmmmm. My pussy twitched. Before I knew it, I had unzipped my pants and slipped my hand down in my Victoria's.

"You gonna let me bust this nut or what?"

"That depends," I responded, while rubbing my pussy. I widened my stance, dipping and rocking at the knees. My kitty kat drooled. I slid one finger in. Then two.

"Yeah, aiight. You know the score?" His breathing quickened which said he was jerking off with fast, hard strokes. "You gonna let me stick this big dick in that fat pussy or what?"

"After you lick it."

"Yeah, baby," he whispered. "I'm gonna lick that pussy for you...Damn, baby. You got pussy like honey."

Okay. Now we were getting somewhere. Fuck dinner with the girls. My pussy is soaked and I want some deep dick action in me. Hmmm.

Oooh. I wanna feel his heavy balls slap against my asshole. I cupped my hands between my legs and let my fingers massage the back of my pussy, pressing my palm against my clit. I pressed in harder when Tee said he was gonna lick my pussy from the back to the front, then from the top to the bottom. My pussy juice dripped from its lips, trickling down my inner thighs. I removed my hand, then started licking my fingers. Hmmmm. My pussy tasted so good. When I finished sucking my fingers I slid them back down between my legs, and worked my spot with circular motions of my index and middle fingers.

"Hmm. Suck my pussy patch," I moaned, pulling my fingers from off my clit, then slipping out of my clothes and removing my pink, laced thong. "You miss this sweet pussy?"

"Yeah, baby. Yo, you got your toy with you?" I smiled 'cause he knew damn well I didn't go anywhere without my road companion. "Go get that toy and stick it deep in that pussy for me. Aiight, baby?"

"Hmmm-hmmm." Needless to say, I grabbed my ten-inch dildo, rubbed it along my pussy lips and clit until my hole dripped a puddle of excitement, then slowly slid the head in. Out. In. Out. In. I teased myself until my lips flapped around it. I stuck and pulled until my pussy begged for it. "Oh yes, Tee." I squealed, pushing it in deeper. "Oh yes. Whose pussy you fucking?"

"Mine, baby," he said in a slow deep voice. "All mine. That's my pussy, baby." He lowered his voice to almost a whisper. "Yo, let me hear that pussy smack." I smiled, removing the phone from my ear. Then taking it with my left hand, I placed the receiver down toward my pussy while I held my road companion by the base of its balls and pumped it up in me. My pussy slurped and gulped it all in. "Damn, that sounds good. That's right, baby, give me that wet pussy."

Chile, that's all I needed to hear to finish myself off. I pumped and moaned. Moaned and pumped until I squirted a fountain of pleasure that ran down the crack of my ass, drenching the towel beneath me. I was spent, okay.

By the time I showered—wait a minute. Don't start! Yes, I did just finish having phone sex, working myself over. *And?* I done told y'all before about doing whatever floats your man's boat. See. That's the problem with some of you: you're too damn close-minded. And then you wonder why your man creeps. Humph. Just because you get him, don't mean you gonna keep him, if you know what I mean. So, you had better recognize before someone else does.

Well, there is no shame in my game. Believe that. Tee knows all the right things to say to get this pussy poppin' and I give it to him just the way he likes it. So if my man wants to phone bone, then that's what he gets. I'd rather run up a phone bill, letting him get his nut than me having to go to jail for fucking him up because he crept on me. Please.

Girl, sometimes he'll call me up on his cell when he's just around the corner to get me all hot so that by the time he walks through that door, he's as hard as a brick and my pussy is flowing like a river. We'll get each other so worked up with all that dirty talk that when he finally slides up in me, my kitty kat is sucking the skin off his dick until he pops that thick, sticky treat. Humph. Chile, please. You better ask somebody.

Let me tell you. If Tee wants me to walk around wearing chains and swinging a whip, then that's what I'll do. Now don't get it twisted. There are a few things I won't do: fuck animals or let him shit or piss on me—not that he's asked. But that's where I draw the line. Oh, and I refuse to swallow. Chile, one time I was just a licking and sucking and slurping him off when he had the nerve to ask me to swallow his cum. I almost choked. I lifted my lips up off that dick and told his ass, "Motherfucka, when you bust your nut up in me, then eat my pussy out afterward, *that's* when I swallow your shit. Until then I suck and spit."

See now. Once again, you got me bouncing all over the place. Anyway— as I was sayin'—by the time I got dressed and made my way down to Olios, it was ten-thirty. Of course everyone was gone except for Dietra. She was sitting at the bar with some thick-armed, wide-nosed man. They were eating Buffalo wings and sipping on drinks. And clearly wrapped up into each other's every word.

Mack Daddy was truly in need of a Weaves and Wonders makeover. Boyfriend was rocking a knotty-assed Gumby and had thick, bushy sideburns. Girl, he even had the audacity to have about ten gold chains draped around his long neck. And big gold nugget rings on every finger except his two thumbs. I cringed.

Dietra had on a pair of denim low-riders. You know the ones I'm talking about: the ones that show your ass crack. Excuse me. I mean butt cleavage. Ugh! All you could see were two big ass cheeks. A small strip of her black thong—which looked more like a piece of dental floss in the crack of that wide crater—was showing. Humph. I don't know why, but seeing all that back fat shaking and jiggling made me think of that McDonald's commercial: "Two whole beef patties, special sauce, lettuce, cheese, pickles, onions on a sesame seed bun." Disgusting! And as soon as I get home, I'm selling all my Golden Arches stock.

I know that's not nice. And I'm not talking about her. I'm just stating the facts. It was downright nasty! I would have thrown up right there on the spot if I hadn't already done so before I left my suite. Anyway, I guess she thought she was being chic. She swiveled around on her stool to greet me.

"Hey, soror. How are you?" she asked, standing up to give me a hug. "We were wondering where you were." She towered over me, swooping her big arms around me. She stumbled a little. A clear indication she had had one drink too many.

I smiled. "I'm doing wonderful, thanks. Too bad I missed everyone. I got caught up on the phone." I gave her a once-over, from head to toe. Nice hair. Attractive. Beautiful skin. Pretty smile. Tight shirt. Gut bulging. Ugh! Ass hanging out of jeans. *Oh my God! No she doesn't have her toes hanging over her sandals, touching the ground.* I made a mental note to discuss her fashion violations the next time I saw her, privately of course.

"Yeah, I think most of them were going over to the Monte Carlo. I know a few of the Hampton sorors were going dancing at some club they heard about." All this information was fine and dandy but what I wanted to know was where Miss Celeste was. "Oh, I'm sorry. Leonard, this is another one of my sorors. Indy, this is Leonard."

"Nice to meet you," he said, scanning every inch of my body with his hazel eyes, courtesy of LensCrafters. I laughed to myself, watching his Adam's apple bounce up and down in his throat as he talked. He licked his lips, then smiled. Dietra's eyes darted back and forth between him and me. She moved in closer, placing one hand on his shoulder and the other on her hip. I suppose to mark her territory. *Oh please*, I thought to myself, cutting my eyes at her. Of course I kept my composure. I just smiled and gave him a half nod, then returned my attention back to Miss Hungry For A Stiff Dick.

"Do you know where Celeste and Val are?" I asked, trying to not seem interested.

"I think Val and Lea went over to New York, New York to ride the roller coaster. I'm not sure where Celeste is. I think she said something about having some phone calls to make." She shifted her weight from one foot to the other, giving me the eye signal that she was trying to get her fuck on. I felt like saying, "Bitch, I'm not interested in standing around looking at you or your busted-up date, so sit your nasty ass down and get over yourself before I slap you with one of those Buffalo wings." But I continued smiling instead.

"Well, I'll let the two of you get back to your tête-à-tête." Gumby looked at me like he was stuck on dumb. I just kept grinning. "Enjoy your evening," I continued. "Dietra, I'll see you in the morning."

She gave me a sly grin. "Make that the afternoon."

"Humph. Do you," I said, laughing. I pirouetted on the balls of my feet and headed toward the exit, shaking my head. That poor man looked like he'd just stepped out of a time capsule. I hoped he knew what he was getting himself into. I had heard that ole girl was known to break headboards *and* damage backs. I could just see it now. A big-assed bison on her knees, taking in the dick of a giraffe.

Just as I was making my way over to the Baccarat table, I spotted Tradawna sitting at a twenty-five-cent slot machine, playing Wheel of Fortune while laughing and talking with a tall, slender man.

Unfortunately, I couldn't see who he was since his back was toward me. From behind, it looked like he had it going on. Strong back. Small waist. Nice ass. Well dressed. She was just a smiling and giggling. It was obvious he was trying to charm his way into her drawers. *Be careful, girl!* I warned her to myself, heading to get my gamble on.

I graciously took my seat—in front of number four on the table lay-out—between an attractive white woman, smoking a stinking-ass cigar on my left, and a delicious piece of cocoa-dipped man on my right. I turned my face up at the smell of her cigar. It clung in the air like old funk. There were three men on either side of them. My stomach started to churn. *Okay, Indy be nice*, I said to myself. *You can just get up and move to another table.* But it was too late. I had already laid two thousand dollars on the table and had been given my chips. I shifted in my seat, cutting my eye over at tar breath, then smiling at the croupier, or caller I should say, when I caught him glancing at me. He gave me a reassuring eye as if to say, *Honey, I know.*

When the shoe, oh, I'm sorry I forgot some of you aren't gamblers. Not that I'm in need of Gamblers Anonymous or anything. I just like to gamble hard and win big when I *do* gamble. Anyway, after the dealer shuffles, then reshuffles the deck of cards—there's usually six or eight decks of cards being used. Damn. Do I have to explain the whole damn game? Anyway, the cards are placed in a covered box called the *shoe*. Are you with me? Okay. So as I was saying, when the shoe finally got to me, I was wrecked. Not only was that ho on her way to smoking her second cigar, a man—wearing a big, black cowboy hat and black tuxedo with a white fringed shirt—had the nerve to light up as well. Ugh! His gear was tired and late with those funky-ass cowboy boots. Now I had smoke coming from both ends, slowly cutting off my oxygen. Chile, I could hardly think straight. Before I knew it, I had snatched her cigar out of her mouth and…

"Bitch, I'm about done with you and this stinking-ass cigar," I snapped, banging its tip into the ashtray. "Now light up another one and I'm gonna slide your ass off that stool."

"I beg your pardon," she said in her uppity Southern drawl. She almost reminded me of that dumb-ass Scarlet O'Hara in *Gone With the Wind*. Humph. She looked at me as if she wanted to say, *"Frankly, my darling, I don't give a damn."* I turned my chair toward her. Back straight, head in a combative tilt. Giving her my "your-next-move-better-be-your-best-move" look, ready to knock the wind out of her.

"I *said* I will beat *your* ass if you light up one more fucking cigar." Interestingly, my voice was calm. She tried to stare me down with those blue eyes of hers. But I think my smile is what spooked her 'cause girlfriend damn sure didn't strike another match. "Now let's play." I swiveled back in position, placing eight hundred dollars' worth of chips in the bank box. The three dealers looked at me, then her, then back over to me, smiling with their eyes.

Needless to say, after another hour on the table, I walked away with forty-eight-hundred dollars. While the dealer on my right came over to handle my payoff, I flipped open my Gucci bag, pulling out my compact. *You betta work, girl*, I said to myself as I checked to make sure my face was still in place. Of course it was. Please. You can say whatever you want and call me whatever you want, but the one thing you will *never* be able to come at me on is my wears, hair or face. I keeps it laced and in place, and you know this.

Well, the cocoa delight sitting next to me decided it was time for him to leave as well. *Humph*. His ass shoulda left the table fifteen-hundred-dollars ago. But that's neither here nor there. Instead of him just staying in his lane and keeping it movin' he decides he wants to stop me for a little chitchat. Lawd knows. These men never learn.

"Hey, pretty. I'm Marcellus and you are?" He asked, extending his wide hand. My head snapped to my left, crimped hair swinging to stay in its place to get a good look at this fine specimen of a man with the deep creamy voice. He flashed me his million-dollar, Crest-stripped smile. Hmmm, dimples. I looked down at his outstretched hand.

"Married," I replied with a smile, taking in the crisp scent of his Bvlgari pour Homme while allowing his firm grip to cover my whole hand. He placed his other hand over mine. Soft, strong hands as warm as sunshine. Chile, I quickly pulled my hand back.

I slowly let my eyes travel along the length of his six-foot-something frame, starting from his close-cropped head to his hefty shoulders. His gray silk-ribbed muscle T-shirt wrapped his chest and biceps like a glove. I continued my journey to his thick waist with the black leather belt then allowed my eyes to linger where the fabric of his black silk pants clung against a meaty bulge that seemed to have a life of its own. I ventured down to his black Ferragamo loafers. Size twelve I guesstimated. Yes, I made it very obvious that I was checking out his *goods*. So what! Men do it all the time, okay.

"Can I invite you to a drink?" he asked, looking me straight in the eyes.

"Drinks and then what?" I asked coyly.

"Well, the night's still young. Let's start with drinks, then see whatever else your heart *or* body desires." He flashed me that winning smile again. He was too damn fine, too damn sexy and up to no damn good.

"It's Marcellus, right?" He nodded. "Now Marcellus, what would your wife think if she knew you were having drinks or *whatever* else with another woman?"

"She'd think I was just being friendly."

"Is that so?" I snapped, shaking my head. "Well, she's a damn fool. 'Cause let me tell you, if my husband ever *thought* about having a friendly drink or whatever with another woman I'd fuck him up so bad he'd never be able to swallow or do *whatever* with anyone else." He stood there looking at me in wide-eyed amazement.

"*Daaaaaaaam!*" he exclaimed, mouth agape.

I had one-foot forward, leather straps—bearing the weight of my six-hundred-dollar bag—resting in the crook of my left arm and my right hand on my round hip. I touched my lip with the tip of my tongue, then allowed my eyes to wander his manly body again before I spoke.

"Now close your mouth and let me give you some advice: Take your horny ass home to your wife or go back to your hotel room to call her up to let her know how much you miss her and appreciate her. 'Cause if you don't, you may end up laying up with some chick who will have no problem blowing your cover *after* she drains your damn pockets, if you know what I mean." He stared at me with inquisitive eyes.

He placed both of his huge hands on his narrow hips, shaking his head and smiling. "Damn, I hope your man knows what kind of woman he has."

I smiled. "I think he does. But if he doesn't, his dick *and* balls will be conversation pieces sitting on my mantelpiece. Trust and believe." I gave him a quick wink, then flounced my way through the crowd, looking over my shoulder to catch him still smiling—this time at the sway of my hips and the bounce of my ass. He winked. I returned the smile and kept on steppin.'

Now you know—back in my other life—I would have run his pockets, leaving him with nothing but lint. And if he wanted to get up in my sweet juices, I'd make him suck my pussy until my uterus collapsed, then send him home to his wife with a limp dick and bruised lips along with a lovely care package en route—especially picked by yours truly, okay? Humph, if that fool only knew. The only thing I can say is, times have sure changed.

"Goooood Morrrrrning, sorors," I sang as I strutted through the café in my brown monogrammed stilettos—draped head-to-toe in Louis Vuitton. I served it up lovely in a brown long-sleeved, flare-armed, scoop-neck dress that hung just below the ankles and clung only enough to show off my perfect curves. Then I accessorized with a monogrammed silk scarf wrapped around my head with a matching Ellipse-style handbag.

"Good morning, soror," several sisters from Hampton responded in unison.

"You go, girl!" Rebecca—another Spelman soror—chimed, giving me the thumbs up in approval of my fashion. So you know I had to go into one of my mannequin poses, then strut off toward the buffet.

You know, I always liked Rebecca. She's a bit snobbish but it's nothing that a good read every now and then can't cure. Trust me. She and I had a few run-ins—when we were on line together—because she was number one on line and I was number two. And every time line sister number one wasn't around or didn't know her greetings or her history, guess who got it? That's right, line sister number two, okay?

See, Rebecca actually believed she was exempt from learning the Greek alphabet, the sorority pledge and facts about the founders. Or marching, greeting or doing anything else related to pledging. This knock-kneed child thought she could just make line and bat her eyes and it'd be a done deal because her mother—like many of our mothers—was a soror. Well, let me tell you, that didn't fly with none of the big sisters and it damn sure didn't fly with me. Humph. After a few days of her messing up, I decided it was time I took care of her lackadaisical ass.

So one night, right after one of our grueling pledge sessions with Big Sister Thunder and about forty other big sisters from surrounding schools, we limped back to our hiding place and I transformed into Big Sister Beat Down. And before she could justify her shortcomings, I whipped her ass. Girl, it was a mess. It took all eight of my line sisters to get me off of her. And from that point on, we all made a pact that whomever wasn't on point for our pledge sessions they'd get a beat down. A few weeks later, Rebecca dropped line. Poor thing couldn't handle the pressures that went along with pledging.

Chile, back in the day, we pledged hard, do you hear me? And I mean *pledged*. None of this orientation mess they got going on now. Anyway, it took sistagirl three times before she finally crossed the burning sands. Each time she made line the sisters put her through the wringer. But I have to give it to her: she was a bad bitch to pledge after my line sisters and me 'cause we took her through it. And because she stuck it out, she got mad respect from all of us.

"Indy, over here," Val called out, waving her hand in the air to get my attention. Seated at the table with her were Lea, Dietra, Tradawna and two other sorors I wasn't familiar with. Val stood up to give me a hug when I reached the table. Girlfriend was sharp in her green leather jumpsuit. I smiled. "What happened to you last night? We missed you."

"Girl, I got held up," I said, looking over her shoulder as we gave each other a one-arm hug to avoid toppling my plate of grapes, strawberries and cantaloupe. "Good morning, ladies."

"Hey, soror," they responded in unison.

"You betta work," Tradawna snapped, shaking a finger at me. I smiled. "You don't look so bad yourself. I'm lovin' that blouse." I had to give it to her, she was decked out in a purple Donna Karan blouse that criss-crossed in the front and tied in the back and a pair of black hip-huggers. She returned the smile, standing up to give me a hug, then head back toward the buffet. I couldn't help but notice that killer shape of hers. "No, *you* betta work," I finger-snapped as I sat my plate down, then took my seat between her and Dietra.

Lea introduced the two unknowns as Monique and Renee. They too were fly as hell: flawless skin, neatly arched-eyebrows, hair and nails done to the T. And jewels for days. We exchanged pleasantries. I had to smile to myself as I scanned the room, noticing all my sorors. Most of them were fierce. And I mean *fierce!* Of course there were a few who were in violation of fashion codes: like mismatching high-end designer wears with low-end pieces—you know, rockin' Gucci with Old Navy—or frontin' a fake handbag. Ooh, there's nothing worse than a fraudulent sista tryna be fierce. "Girl, just leave it alone," I said to myself. And that's what I did. They were all lovely women, regardless. It was just nice to see beautiful black women of all shades, shapes, sizes and economic backgrounds coming together to celebrate sisterhood.

"Girl, is that all you're eating?" Val asked, finishing up her plate of French toast and a vegetable omelet.

"Chile, I'm afraid I might start throwing up if I eat anything else." Of course she suggested I get checked out when I got home. But sistagirl was already way ahead of her. I have an appointment with my doctor the minute I get home. Renee gave me a warm smile when she realized I had peeped her staring at my diamond-encrusted bangles. Her eyes were filled with compliments so I smiled back a "thank you."

"Where's Celeste?" I asked to no one in particular.

"Oh, she said she was going to sleep in today," Lea volunteered. "She said she didn't get much sleep last night. Said she tossed and turned all night."

"Oh that's a shame. Poor thing," I said. *Hmm. What's that all about?*

"She said she'd see us at the sorority luncheon," she added.

"Good," I said, then leaned over toward Dietra. "Girl, I'm surprised to see you so early."

She sucked her teeth.

"Girl, please. Coming down here for breakfast is more exciting than the night I had with that farting-ass man I was with." I shot her a look of amazement while the others looked at her, waiting for her to elaborate on the details of her evening. "Well, after you left, we had another drink and finished off our food—"

"Chile, you mean to say you ate *again*," Lea interrupted.

Dietra glared at her, then rolled her eyes. "Annnnnyway," she continued, ignoring Lea's remark. "After we finished eating, I positioned myself in front of him while he was seated and started rubbing his meat to let him know what I wanted for a nightcap." She grinned, then rolled her eyes up in her head. "But do you know that nicca had the nerve to shift his weight on the bar stool, lift his ass cheek to one side, then let out a fart loud enough to blow a hole in his drawers."

"Whaat?!" we all asked in disgust and disbelief.

"No he didn't, girl," I said, trying not to laugh.

"Yes, the hell he did. I almost passed out. He stunk so bad he could have wiped out a whole city. Girl, I was so damn embarrassed. And I don't embarrass easy."

"Chile, I know you left his stank ass, sitting right there," Renee stated, fanning a hand in front of her nose.

Dietra looked away, trying to hide her face with her hand.

"You did leave, didn't you?" Tradawna asked, catching the tail end of the story as she sat down. The rest of us waited for her answer.

"Well, not exactly," she said, sighing. "I sorta, kinda ended up back in his room. I mean passing a little gas—alright, a lot of gas—isn't the end of the world, right? I figured he thought it would be a quiet fart. So I gave him the benefit of the doubt. Besides, I liked what I was feeling."

"Humph," Val grunted, rolling her eyes.

"No you didn't?" Lea snapped knowing Dietra had lain down with funk butt.

"Yes, I did," she cringed, then gave us the abridged version of how she had straddled him and was riding him into the sunset—with his head banging up against the headboard—when he announced he was about to cum. So she went buck-wild on him, bouncing up and down, squeezing her pussy muscles around his dick when all of a sudden he yelled, "I'm cumming!" And as he came, he started farting. She said he was farting so loud and so long it sounded like a foghorn blowing. We were all laughing.

But the worst part was when he went to get up to go to the bathroom. She had rolled over on her back; feeling something wet on her ass, she moved over thinking it was from her juices but when she inspected—it was a wet puddle of shit. Her fuck of the night had shitted in the bed. The table erupted in laughter.

"It was an absolute mess," Dietra explained, trying to be serious. "I was too through."

"Girl, what did you do?" Monique asked, wiping tears from her eyes.

"I jumped up, threw on my clothes and was out the door before he returned. I was in such a rush I left my good pair of underwear."

"Serves your behind right," Val said, holding her sides while laughing. "You're always so quick to jump some man's bones."

"Girl, it could not have been me," I said, placing my fork across my plate, then wiping my mouth with my napkin. "There's no telling what I would have done to that fool. Then again, I wouldn't have given his ass the time of day anyway."

"I know that's right," Renee responded.

"I still can't believe he was letting out wet farts while you were getting your groove on," Tradawna stated, still laughing at the thought.

"Well, believe it," Dietra said in disgust. "The next time I lay up with a man, I'm gonna make sure I bring some wipes and a bag of Depends with me." We laughed. She sat with her face scrunched up.

"Well, I wanna know this, was the sex good?" Lea asked.

"I guess it could have been if I didn't have to spend most of the time holding my damn nose. I mean, the brotha had it going on in the meat department but I was too busy trying to concentrate on holding my breath without keeling over to really enjoy it."

I tried to imagine this big, six-foot, two-hundred-and-something-pound woman, holding her breath while tryna get her fuck on from a man busting his nut *and* his ass at the same time. Chile, I was hysterical. Do you hear me? I was laughing so hard tears were falling from my eyes. "Girl, I've heard it all," I said, trying to pull myself together.

"Oh, no!" Dietra snapped, trying to hide her face.

"What?" we asked in unison.

"That's him," she said, truly embarrassed for giving his toxic ass the time of day. He spotted her and started strutting like a peacock toward our table. He had on a burnt-orange double-breasted suit and a brown shirt with an orange-and-brown-pin-striped tie.

"Girl, the nicca is heading toward the table," Tradawna said, talking out the side of her mouth. "And he's tore up from the floor up." Oh my God! We all watched as he glided like he was the Don. He looked like something out of an old *Dolemite* flick.

"How you ladies doing this morning?" he asked us while grinning and licking his lips at me. Everyone gave him a polite nod. I twisted my face up. "Dietra, baby, can I speak to you for a moment?"

"Not now," she said barely looking at him. "Don't you see I'm having breakfast with my girls?"

"Well, when you get done, come check me. I'll be sitting right over there with my partners." He pointed to the far left of the room toward a table where two men were sitting. They weren't bad looking. They just looked like they had stepped off the set of *Starsky and Hutch*, looking like Huggie Bear's twin cousins in those wide-brim hats and polyester suits. Girl, they looked like they had been frozen in the seventies with that outdated fashion.

"Cindy, why don't you come over too? I wanna introduce you to one of my boys." *Cindy?* Now you know he was about to get read real quick if he didn't step off. Val put her head down 'cause she knew he was about to catch it. The other girls tried their best to hold in their snickers.

"Negro, please," I said. "I don't think so. First of all my name is Indy. That's I-n-d-y. Not Cindy. Get it right. Second of all, there's nothing your friend can do for me."

"My bad, baby," he said, trying to sound like Billy Dee Williams. "Indy, Cindy. Same difference." I raised my left eyebrow.

"Let me tell you something," I said, snatching my purse open. "There's a big difference. But judging by the way you look, I can see you wouldn't know any better."

"Damn, baby. Don't be so hard on a brotha for making a—"

I cut him off before he could finish, "I think you have me mixed up with Dietra, okay? I'm not your baby. So I'd advise you to go glide your farting ass over to the other side of the room before you get your feelings hurt. And while you're at it, take this with you." I threw him one of my panty liners. "Just in case you shit on yourself." The whole table rolled with laughter. He glared over at Dietra while backing away from the table, visibly embarrassed. She shrugged her shoulders, then started making farting sounds.

"So beat it, shitty drawers," Tradawna blurted, still laughing. Let me tell you. We were hysterical. I'm telling you, I hadn't laughed so hard in a long time. We all got up, leaving in tears.

Chile, all of a sudden, I broke out in a sweat and felt a wave of nausea come over me. "I have to use the bathroom real quick," I said, racing in its direction. "I'll meet up with ya'll later." I busted into the bathroom, swung open the nearest stall door, then leaned over the toilet, gagging.

Ugh! *I'm really getting sick of this shit*, I thought to myself, flushing the toilet, then slamming the lid down. I walked to the sink, dampened a napkin, then lightly dabbed my forehead. "I don't know what the hell is wrong with me. But I know I'm not pregnant," I said reassuringly to myself.

Now, had my period not come on I wouldn't have been so sure. Thank

God! I glanced in the mirror, pulling the edges of my scarf down around my forehead. For a hot second, I didn't like what I saw, looking back at me. Guilt was staring me right smack in my damn face. And then I had the nerve to speak as if what I said was going to make it better. "Tee," I said to myself in the mirror, "I know how bad you want a baby. And I'd like nothing more to be able to give you one, but I can't. Not right now. I have to be sure."

Believe it or not, I was really torn up about what I was doing. Oh, please. Don't give me that look, "like yeah right." I was. And Miss Indy's not the one to feel guilty about jack, okay. But this had me going through it. However, as bad as I felt about it, I had to keep on keeping on. So I shook the guilt off, and stepped.

Well, just as I was about to make my way back over to the slot machines, I ran into Tradawna talking to the same man I saw her starry-eyed over the other night. I started to just go on about my business until I got a good look at him. His eyes caught mine. Oh. My. God! I knew that fine nigga. Chile, I did the only thing any respectable woman could. I walked over to bust up their little party. Hmm. Hmm. I sure did.

"Tradawna, dear," I said, cutting my eye at her admirer. "If I were you, I'd be careful who I let in my space." He shifted his eyes from me to Tradawna, then back to me, becoming visibly startled.

"Hello, Indy," he said in his smooth, baritone voice. If you closed your eyes, you'd swear you were talking to a thin, chiseled version of Barry White. Humph. "It's been a long time."

"Not long enough. But then again, I forgot Vegas is where you like to do tricks."

"The two of you know each other?" Tradawna asked with surprise all over her face.

I smiled. He fidgeted with his drink.

"We sure do," I said. "Chester and I go way back. Isn't that right?" Way back is right. Chester Barnes was just another one of those no-good, lying-ass men I had to dog inside out about five years ago. We had meet at one of the Magic Marketplace fashion shows they have twice a year here in Vegas. If you've never been to one, you must make it your business to come out to one. Girl, there are ballers everywhere. And you get a chance to see some of the latest and hottest fashions for African-Americans, okay.

Anyway, sexy, smooth-talking Chester the Pussy Molester thought he was gonna play both sides of the stick, if you know what I mean. Boyfriend would press me hard, lying about his family. And that's one thing I can't stand: a stinking-ass man, stepping out on his family. So when I found out he was married, it was a done deal.

Actually, if you wanna keep shit real, it was a wrap the minute he stepped out of his damn boxers. Girl, I looked down at his turkey-link dick and acorn-sized nuts, and rolled my eyes long and hard. *What a damn waste,* I thought, *a fine-ass man with a nice body, and no damn meat.* Ugh!

But being the gracious hostess that I am, I was willing to let him eat my pussy until the walls caved in; but—after four licks, and a few damn slurps, I felt something wet, and warm spurt on my leg. Homeboy came all over himself, and *me.* Then had the nerve to roll over on his back like he had just sleighed me. I was too through, okay. Chile, I screamed on him.

"Motherfucker," I snapped, jumping up from the bed. "I know you don't think you just did something spectacular. You got the nerve to think you a fucking don, and you can't even hold your damn nut. What the fuck!"

"Damn, baby," he said, flabbergasted. "It's been awhile since I had some so I got a little excited. Give a brotha a minute to get it right."

No he didn't just go there, I thought. I glared at him. "*Little* is right," I snarled, glancing down at his dick. "But that has nothing to do with you eating my damn pussy, nigga. So get back on the damn clock and act like you know. Or I'ma turn this bitch out tonight." Needless to say, he punched back in, and ate me out like there was no tomorrow, trying to make it all good. Girl, he even had the damn nerve to say he wanted to keep seeing me when it was all said and done. Please. He'd be seeing me all right. But not in the way he wanted. I had a little trick for his ass.

A few weeks later, I showed up at his mansion, ringing his doorbell, then handing his wife all of the diamond trinkets he had bought for me.

The Mrs. initially thought I was playing a sick prank of sorts until I rattled off dates and times he'd spent wining and dining me. She ended up inviting me in and we talked for hours. By the time I was finish blowing up his spot, I wound up having to console the poor soul. I really felt bad for telling her. But, as far as I was concerned, she had a right to know what kind of man she was dealing with. But the crazy thing is, she knew her man cheated on her and she was okay with it. Humph! I wanted to slap her silly ass.

Now don't give me that look. I mean. As women, we really need to unite instead of fighting each other, and stop letting these men get away with shit. Like I always say, a man is only gonna do as much as you allow him to do. So, as long as women allow—or accept—men walking over them, they will continue to do it. And I am *not* the one, okay.

Anyway, he was wrecked when he walked in and saw me perched up on one of his kitchen stools sipping tea with his six-month pregnant wife. "*Surprise!*" I wanted to shout but I tilted my head and pursed my lips. Girlfriend went ballistic, okay. And I quietly gathered my things and walked out of their home, leaving him in the middle of tryna explain his way out of cheating on his lovely wife with yet another woman.

"How's your wife doing?" I asked, giving him a one-eyed glare.

"Thanks to you," he replied with a tinge of resentment. "She left me." Apparently, his wife had finally come to her senses and had had enough of his trifling ways. She walked out on him a few months after their child was born, then divorced him a year later. Boyfriend now has to pay out the ass.

"Well, good for her," I said, glancing over at Tradawna who looked lost. "Soror, remember what I said. Be careful."

She smiled her innocent smile. "Oh, we were just talking," she explained. He licked his lips, then grinned.

"Don't you worry, this pretty lady is in good hands."

"Hmm. For your sake, let's hope so." And with that said, I excused myself and headed for the elevators. I know what you're thinking. You want to know why I didn't tell Tradawna about his ways. Chile. That wasn't my place. I did what I needed to do when I forewarned her. Now, what she did with that piece of advice was up to her. She's a grown woman.

Damn it! It's my cell. Hold on. "Hello."

"That information you requested yesterday is gonna take a little longer than I thought to get."

"And why's that?" I asked, opening up my handbag to retrieve my lipstick. I applied a fresh coat while looking into the huge ceiling-to-floor mirror by the elevators.

"Well, it appears my contacts are unable to locate any info on a Celeste Munley in the D.C. or Maryland area. However, we were able to locate a Benjamin Munley in Northeast. And about nine other persons with that same last name."

"Is that so. Well, with a name like Munley, I'm sure it won't be too hard to determine if there's any connection."

"I agree."

"Well, did you— speak with your contacts in the Connecticut area?"

"Yep. And still came up with nothing."

"Hmm. Interesting."

"Very. But, I'm on it. I'll get back to you when I have something more to add."

"I'll be waiting," I replied before disconnecting my call. Alrighty then. And the plot thickens. Now, you tell me why my research assistant can't find anything on Miss Celeste, huh? Exactly. That's not her last name after all. So, why do you think someone would give you a wrong last name? Hmm. Because as I said the other day—she has something to hide! I don't know about ya'll but I think I should pay my soror a little visit to see how she's doing, don't you think?

12

BRITTON: *You Can't Do It Alone*

"PBBBTH! PBBBTH! PBBBTH! PBBBTH!"

"PBBBTH! PBBBTH! PBBBTH!"

"If y'all don't stop that spitting," I snapped, opening my eyes. "I'm gonna pop both of you." I glanced down at my watch. It was three fifteen p.m. "I can't even close my eyes for ten minutes without the two of you doing something." They had spittle all over the window. I reached in my backpack, handing them both two napkins. "Now take this and wipe that window off." I shook my head.

"Daddy, are we almost at Disney World?" Amar asked, handing me his damp napkin.

"Almost," I said. "Now sit down and be quiet."

"Daddy, is Mommy gonna be at Disney?" Amir asked.

"No!" I snapped. I didn't mean to. It just came out. I guess I was hurt and frustrated that he'd asked about her for the umpteenth time. Not that I expected them not to. It's just that…well, this was my time with them and I didn't want to spend it talking—or thinking—about their no-count mother. Believe it or not, I invited her to come with us. And you want to know what she said? "Thanks. But I have a film release party to go to. Maybe some other time." You don't know how close I was to calling her the *B* word. I'm telling you, I had to really bite my tongue to keep from calling her every dirty name in the book. I couldn't believe that witch. I still can't. Well, actually I can. I thought. Hoped. Ah, never mind…forget it!

"Why come?"

"It's not why come. It's how come," I corrected.

"How come, Daddy?" He pushed.

"Because Mommy has something else to do," I replied, trying to keep the edge off my voice. But inside I was screaming, *"Because she's too busy tryna be the next Heather Hunter, somewhere fucking her brains out!"*

"Daddy, I'm gonna buy Mommy a toy." Amar announced.

"Noooooooo! I'm gonna buy Mommy a toy first," Amir whined.

"Am not!"

"Am so!"

"Am not!"

"Daddy. Amar said I'm not gonna buy Mommy a toy first."

"Hey, guys," I said, tapping my chin. I wanted to immediately defuse the situation before it escalated, more so for me because I was afraid I might accidentally say something unkind about their mother. As much as I'm disgusted with Lina, I don't ever want them to hear me saying anything negative about her. Regardless of my feelings, she is still their mother. "I have an idea, why don't both of you buy Mommy a toy."

"Yeah!" they squealed. "We gonna buy Mommy a toy. We gonna buy Mommy a toy!"

I leaned forward in my seat, pinching the inside corners of my eyes with my index and thumb to keep the wells of my eyes from spilling over. You tell me, how am I supposed to explain to them that their own mother doesn't want them, huh? I don't want to be bitter toward Lina. I really don't. It's bad enough already that I don't like her. But right now, I am really starting to hate her. For making her sons miss her. And for having me hate her.

Whether Lina understands this or not, this is not about her or me anymore. It's about our sons. And believe me when I tell you, I wrestled many nights wondering if I was doing the right thing by packing up and leaving with them. I really tried to give her a chance to redeem her self. But when she agreed to give me full custody, I knew I had no other recourse. *Snap!* Just like that. She signed her name on the dotted line without blinking an eye or dropping a tear.

"Are you sure about this?" I had asked, trying to give her an opportunity to reconsider.

"It's for the best," she replied, nodding, then throwing her head back as if she didn't have a care in the world. "I can't give them want they need. I wish I could but I can't." She paused for a moment, then looked me in my eyes. "Promise me you won't let them forget who I am." For a split second, I thought I saw a glimmer of emotion—perhaps regret—behind her vacant brown eyes.

"Lina, if our sons grow up never having any recollection of you, I promise you, it won't be my doing. You can look in the mirror for that."

"Take care, Britton," she said, reaching for my hand, then squeezing it.

"Whatever you're searching for I hope you find it. Be safe," I said. She hugged me tightly, then headed down the long corridor, turning left and walking out the double glass doors stepping out into the thunder and rain.

I closed my book, *Simon Says* by Collen Dixon, and stared out the spit-and finger-smeared window. I glanced down at Amar and Amir, sitting on the carpeted floor playing with "Yano the Storyteller." They giggled when he spoke, blinking his big eyes and moving his arms. I'm still trying to figure out why I bought that talking fur ball for them. But Yano—as ugly as he is and as expensive its cartridges are—he entertains and enlightens them so that's all that matters. I smiled as he began telling the story of Yana and The Magic Fish.

You know. It's amazing how life can sometimes seem so surreal. Just when you think you're floating off into a land of fantasy, reality kicks in to remind you that it's not a dream world you're living in. And just when you think life can't show you any more surprises, something happens to prove you wrong. These two boys sitting before me, my sons, are my affirmation that life goes on. You live, love and learn to let go. You never forget; you go on living, loving and learning.

For a split second, my father came to mind. Since his death almost four years ago, I've thought of him quite often. Although I never liked him, I was finally able to come to terms with my feelings toward him and absolve him of his past deeds. If I hadn't gone to Germany to see him, I wouldn't have had the chance to see who he had become, nor would I have been able to give him the opportunity to embrace me one last time. The frail man I saw lying in that bed definitely wasn't the same man I remembered in my nightmares; and he surely wasn't the same man I swore I'd never have anything to do with. The cancer had eaten away his frightening presence embedded in the corners of my mind. He was just a dying man. A man I truly had no love or sympathy for.

As cold as that may sound, it is what it is. Nevertheless, I'm really glad I saw him before he died. If nothing else, he was able to leave this earth knowing I had forgiven him for scarring my life. And in forgiveness came healing. And for that I am thankful. At least, for the both of us, there was closure. And I was finally able to move on with my life without carrying someone else's baggage.

I can honestly say I'm not the same man I used to be three, even four, years ago. I'm at peace with myself because I was able to choose understanding over hate, facing the men—my father, and my cousin Bryce—who had brought suffering into my life.

My father for the impact his beatings on my mother had on me, and Bryce for raping my soul as a child. I've come to accept that in the end, I wasn't the one who would hurt the most. They'd both have to carry the weight of their mistakes. And I wouldn't have to bear the burden of bitterness and silence any longer. I'm free. And that, my friend, is a beautiful thing.

Hmm. I sat in my seat looking at my sons, and smiled. I never thought my life could ever be filled with so much love. There was a time when I felt so empty. Like something was truly missing. The feeling wasn't one of loneliness; it was a dull aching deep within me. I don't know if that makes any sense to you. It's kind of hard to explain. But having my sons has changed all of that. I never imagined my life would turn out this way. Complete. I guess because I never thought I'd ever have children or experience the joys of fatherhood again.

To this day, I still can't believe how much they resemble me when I was their age. From their big brown eyes and long, thick eyelashes to their high cheekbones and reddish complexion, from their thick curly hair to the mole on the side of their faces. It's almost like looking into a mirror. The only difference: I'm seeing double. And the older they get the more distinct their features become.

Somewhere between the boys' chatter about all the cartoon characters they wanted to see at Disney World and Yano's dialogue about the little girl who catches a fish, lets it go, then is granted wishes because it's a magic fish, my mind drifted back to my conversation with my sister. Bless her heart! I can always count on that busybody to know when to say the wrong things at the wrong time.

"Brit, don't you think you're being a little unreasonable?" she had asked me when I told her of my decision.

"No, I don't."

"I mean it's one thing to leave her, moving around the corner and it's another thing to move across the country."

"Oh well," I responded, hoping she'd get the hint that I didn't want to get into a long, drawn-out discussion about my plans. She didn't.

"You do know it's not going to be easy," she reasoned.

"I never said it would be."

"Well, as much as I admire you for wanting to parent the boys on your own, I can't see you raising two children by yourself."

"Why, because I'm a man?"

"No. Because I know how you are." I don't know what she meant by that. But whatever she meant, I didn't like how it sounded.

"Hello, newsflash: You don't know half of what you think you know about me. If women can do it, so can men. And this man can and will."

"I didn't mean it like that," she said, almost apologetically. But she had already pinched a nerve with me so I wasn't ready to drop it.

"Whatever, Amira. You know, you'd be so much more helpful if you learned to keep your mouth shut sometimes." There was silence between us. I'm sure she was thinking back when we were children living in California and our mother decided to pack us up and leave our father to return to her Jersey roots. Amira unconditionally loved the man who beat our mother, regardless of the impact his abuse had on us. And it took her many years to accept that it was over between them. But she visited him every summer and on holidays, developing an even stronger father-daughter bond despite the distance. Back then I had no interest in forgiving him or understanding his emotional struggles. But this is—and was—a totally different situation. I know in my heart of hearts, she was only trying to play devil's advocate, but what I needed from her at that time was her blessings, not her bullshit.

"Brit, as much as I don't like that child, I don't think it's right for you to move so far away. She *is* their mother."

"And *I'm* their father," I snapped. "You ought to be glad I'm heading back to Jersey instead of the Dominican Republic where *I* want to be." The nerve of her! I couldn't believe she was taking Lina's side over mine, acting like I was ripping her sons away from *her*.

Not to sound petty or anything, but I'm the one who has been raising them for the last three years while she's been running around La La Land, doing God knows what. I'm the one who sits in the doctor's office for hours when they're sick—after being up all night with them. I'm the one who feeds them and bathes them. I'm the one who reads them their bedtime stories and tucks them in at night. I'm the one who teaches them the alphabet and how to say grace and how to pray. I'm the one who hugs them and praises them. Not her. So why the hell is my sister having so much sympathy for her. My pressure was beginning to boil. I took three deep breaths, trying to check myself before I said something I really didn't mean. But she kept on going.

"And how is she supposed to be a part of their lives if you're three thousand miles away?"

"The same fucking way she could have been in their lives, when we were living under the same fucking roof." I didn't mean to curse at her. But she was really getting on my nerves and I had had enough of her interrogation. "She didn't give a duck's fuck about being a part of their lives *then* so what makes you think she'll be any more interested now?"

"Humph. Now was all that cursing really necessary?" I almost laughed at that question as much cursing she does. But I was too damn mad to go there. She sucked her teeth. I could see her rolling her eyes up in her head while pressing both fists into either side of her hips.

"So how do you expect to take care of them? It's not like you have a steady job."

"I'll get one. And your point?"

"My point is," she said, sighing. "Those boys need their mother just as much as they need you."

"Well, what they need and what they don't need are two separate issues; which is why I'm leaving her. What they need is a mother who is going to be there to love and nurture them, not some woman who wants to run in and out of their lives. Being a parent is about commitment. Not convenience. So when Lina is ready and willing to be a mother to our sons, the door is open. She knows how to find us. But until then, it's a done deal. So get over it."

"Well, excuse the hell outta me," she chimed. "Sounds like you have this all figured out."

"Yep. So either be supportive of my decision or shut the fuck up."

She paused. "Keep being flippant if you want. But don't think I won't get with that ass when I see you."

Flippant? She's never used that one before. I laughed out loud. It never fails. I don't care how mad Amira gets me, she always says something that will crack me the hell up.

After all the times she's beat up on me growing up, she still thinks she can whip my ass. That shit is hilarious. Fortunately for her, she hasn't tried to in a long while. And if she did, my nine nieces would gang up on their mother if she even dared to beat up their favorite uncle.

"Oh what's that, one of your new words for the week?" I clapped. "Wow, what an expansive vocabulary. I'm impressed."

"Brit, kiss my ass. You know what the fuck I mean."

"Well, unlike you, hoochie, Mom has my back." Now I knew that would get her going. She hates when I make it seem like our mother is the only one who is there for me. When in actuality they are both always in my corner. It's just that my mother will speak her peace and let me be.

Whereas, Amira will challenge everything I say, turning it into a big ordeal.

"Boy, you know goddamn well I got your back. I just want to make sure your impulsive ass knows what the hell you're doing."

"Well, I can't tell," I said, feigning a pout.

She sucked her teeth. "I just don't want to see you making a big mistake."

"And if it is, then it's one I'll have to live with. Not you."

"Well, sounds like there's nothing else to say."

"Nope. You've said enough for one day."

"Only because I care about you and I want what's best for my nephews."

"I know you do. But it's my life, Amira. And these are my kids. So let me do what I feel is best. Now give me a kiss and let's make up." There was a pause. Then she kissed me through the phone. "Ewww! That was a wet, nasty one."

"Kiss my behind, boy."

"I love you too, smoochie coochie momma." We laughed, said our good-byes, then hung up.

I snapped out of my trance when Amar got up from the floor. "I'm sleepy," he said, rubbing his eyes with the back of his hand while climbing up on the seat. I lifted my left arm so he could lean his body into mine. I let my arm cover him. Amir had already climbed up in my lap twenty minutes earlier and was sleeping with his head resting on my right shoulder. I shifted him around so that he wouldn't get a crick in his neck, then leaned my head back, lowered my eyelids and allowed my mind to take me back to a place I visit often. The past. I used to dwell in it; but, now I use it for self-reflecting and for counting my blessings and giving thanks. I use it as a means to measure where I've been, where I am, and where I want to be in my life.

Oftentimes I find myself thinking about my...I mean sometimes I wonder what my life would have been like if my firstborn were alive. I try to imagine what type of father I would have been at that age. I know I would have done the best I could with what little I had, to be the best I could be. But, I don't think it would have been good enough. Not at nineteen. I was still too young to take on that kind of responsibility.

Financially and emotionally, I wasn't prepared to care for anyone else. I could barely take care of myself. Let alone a child *and* a wife. But for the sake of my child and the love of my life, I would have done whatever I had to do. I truly believe everything in life happens for a reason.

In hindsight, I know I jumped into a marriage for all the wrong reasons. But when you're young and when you think you're in love, nothing else seems to matter. And anything anyone says to try to reason with you simply falls on deaf ears. So you end up living with and learning from the mistakes you made. At least I did. And I have no regrets. Sometimes, I think about my estranged wife and I wonder how life turned out for her. I would hope she's in a much better place, mentally and emotionally. And I would hope she's still not bitter toward me for walking out on her the way I did. I had no choice. I did what I had to do in order to keep from hurting. I needed to hang on to what vestige of sanity I had left.

Bottom line: Life is just too damn short. I know plenty of people who stay in unhealthy relationships for the sake of something other than peace of mind: for the kids, for security, and the list goes on. And it's sad. But who am I to judge. I know we can't control another person's behavior, but we can definitely control whom we allow in our personal space, and how we allow them to treat us. And I refuse to allow anyone to disrupt my flow, mentally, spiritually or emotionally. Period. I'm not built for the drama. And now I have children I have to consider. Because whatever decisions I make will ultimately affect them as well.

I know part of moving forward in one's life is letting go. So I'm letting go. Just like I've let go of all the ghosts from my past that haunted and tormented me for so many years, I'm letting go of Lina. And I'm *finally* letting go of my long, lost wife. As soon as I get back to Jersey, I'm filing for my divorce once and for all.

I opened my eyes, stared at my sleeping sons, then silently thanked God for blessing me with the gift of life. I kissed them both on their foreheads, then returned to my place in my book. There was no longer any doubt as to whether or not I could do this alone. For I knew in my heart I could and I would. I leaned back and smiled, anticipating the adventures of Disney World with my sons.

Whew! Seven days in Orlando, Florida has worn me out. I am exhausted, to say the least. You don't know how happy I was to see Jersey when I got off that plane—yes, plane! After three days of being on a train to get there, I had had enough of Amtrak. There was no way I was taking another train going anywhere. Luckily, we had a sleeper. Otherwise, I'd probably have lost my damn mind, trying to sleep in a reclined position. So the minute I got to our hotel, I called Continental and booked a return flight. It made no difference to me how much money I wasted.

After getting our luggage, I picked up my Hertz rental, loaded the car, strapped Amir and Amar in the backseat and headed for Maplewood. I was so glad they nodded off the minute I pulled out of the terminal and merged onto routes 1 & 9 'cause I didn't feel like hearing any noise. I needed a minute to mentally collect myself from all the running around I'd done trying to keep up with them. I never thought I'd need a vacation from a vacation just to recuperate from all of the excitement. My back is aching. My feet are sore and I'm beat down. Let me tell you. If you ever decide to travel across country with two toddlers, going to Disney World. Word of caution: Don't ever, *ever* do it! I'm serious. Take it from me. Don't do it to yourself.

Don't misunderstand me. The boys had a blast. Okay, alright already. So did I. I probably had more fun on some of the rides than they did. You should have heard me singing and clapping to "It's a Small World" as we rode through the tunnel. I even got mad when we didn't get picked to be contestants on Nickelodeon. I guess it was for the best 'cause I wasn't too keen on having them dump a bucket of green slime on me, and neither were the boys. So we sat in the audience.

Still, Amar and Amir ran me ragged. From the Magic Kingdom to Universal Studios to Sea World, the lines were long and the sun was blaring down, scorching the hell out of us. They'd ask to go somewhere—like Woody Woodpecker's "Kid Zone" or Snow White's Scary Adventures, then once we got there, it was nonstop whining, "I'm tired, Daddy…Pick me up, Daddy…I'm hot, Daddy." Or they'd bug me to no end about seeing the Disney characters. So I'd stroll them from Adventureland all the way over to Toontown's Hall of Fame—in the hot sun, mind you—then after standing in that long line, one of them wouldn't want to cooperate with getting his autograph book signed or taking a picture. So I ended up getting the books signed and taking pictures with the characters.

A few times Amar decided to go into one of his screaming-and-falling-out fits because he didn't get something he wanted. So I'd gather our things and march right back over to our hotel and I'd put his behind to bed. So actually, him having a few tantrums did me a favor. Little did he know he had given me a chance to nap!

I would have loved to have someone pushing me around in a stroller, picking me up when I was too tired to stand, buying me ice cream and winning me stuffed animals. Hell. I'd love to have someone rubbing my feet and massaging my back right about now, come to think of it. And we won't even talk about the deprived muscle between my legs. I could sure use some attention there too.

I was so aggravated with all the traffic on Interstate 78 I wanted to scream. It was bumper to bumper, thanks to some idiot who decided to be reckless, causing a three-car accident and traffic being backed up four miles long.

By the time I reached my destination, turning onto Hilton Avenue it was 4:45 p.m. A fifteen, twenty-minute ride had taken an hour and a half. However, my road rage immediately disappeared the moment I spotted the three-bedroom, brick-front bi-level called home. I pulled up behind my mother's burgundy Lexus. A gift she treated herself to after she earned her master's degree in social work last year. I smiled.

A single mother, who escaped a life of domestic violence, attended night school, earned her GED, enrolled in college—receiving both an under-graduate and graduate degree—and is now the coordinator and therapist for a battered woman's shelter. In my eyes, she's the epitome of success.

I woke Amir and Amar, gathered some of their things from the car, then headed for the door. I let Amir ring the doorbell. Then Amar. I shook my head, smiling at their copycat behavior.

"Here come my precious babies," my mother sang, swinging the door open to greet us. "Come here and give your grandma some sugar." The smell of home-cooked treats greeted us, tickling my nose. My mouth watered. Mom was dressed in a pair of jeans and her white "Grandmas are Special" sweatshirt embroidered in gold. I smiled when the boys ran into her arms as she kneeled down, hugging and kissing them both. "Tell Grandma all about Disney World." They giggled while squirming in her arms.

"We saw Mickey Mouse and Donald Duck—" Amir offered.

"And Winnie the Pooh," Amar interjected.

"And we saw the parade at the Magic Kingdom," Amir added.

"Is that so," my mom said, amazed at how well they talked.

"I didn't like Minnie Mouse, Grandma," Amir stated.

"And how come?"

"'Cause she had ugly shoes." My mom tried her best to hold back a laugh.

"Grandma, Amir was crying when he went to take a picture."

"Did not!"

"Uh-hunh. I saw you crying."

"Okay, boys. That's enough," I said, walking in with the last of our things, then closing the door.

My mother stood up and placed her hands on her hips, smiling at me with loving eyes. She opened her arms wide and I walked into her embrace. "Hi, baby. It's so good to see you."

"It's good to see you too, Mom," I said, kissing her on her cheek. "I love you." She hugged me tighter.

"I love you too. Now, let me get a good look at you," she said, taking a step back to give me a once-over. "You look good. A little tired but still as handsome as ever."

"You don't look too shabby yourself," I said, smiling. Her reddish-brown skin was still smooth and practically wrinkle-free save from the ones around the outer edges of her eyes. Her hair was silver-white and neatly cropped in a Halle Berry cut. For sixty-three, she didn't look a day over fifty. She was beautiful.

"Daddy, I wanna tell Grandma about the Magic Kingdom," Amar stated, pulling my pants leg to get my attention.

"Me too, Daddy," Amir said.

"You can finish telling her after we put our things in our room, okay?"

"Okay, Daddy," they said in unison.

"I can't get over how big they've gotten since I last saw them."

"I know. One minute they're babies and the next minute, they're grown midgets."

"Daddy, I'm not a midget," Amar declared. "I'm a big boy, right, Grandma."

"Yes, you are," she said proudly, reaching over to hold his face in her palms. "You're Grandma's big boy." She kissed him on his forehead and then let him go. I grabbed him before he runs off.

"Oh, no he's not!" I stated, picking him up and tickling him. "You're Daddy's midget man." He laughed and squirmed, trying to break free.

"Do me, Daddy," Amir requested, raising his arms to be picked up. I put Amar down, then picked up Amir, giving him the same treatment. He too erupted in laughter.

"Ah! Ah! You're Daddy's little midget man." I put him down, then began tickling both boys simultaneously. I stopped and let them jump on me while they tried their best to tickle me. I laughed and begged for them to stop. My mom laughed along.

"Go get Grandma," I said, laughing. Of course they declined the offer and continued jumping on me. We played for another ten minutes or so before I got up, then directed them to get their Disney knapsacks.

I walked them through the foyer, then upstairs to their room. When I opened the door, I couldn't help but smile. The room was painted blue and white with royal-blue carpet. Two twin beds were neatly made up with Mickey Mouse comforters and matching pillow shams. In the corner, there was a blue easy chair with boxes of gifts wrapped in Spiderman paper. The boys squealed with delight. "Daddy, look what Santa Claus brought."

"Those aren't from Santa Claus," I tried to explain. "They're from Grandma Santa Claus."

"Grandma's not Santa Claus, Daddy," Amir said, giggling while pulling off his Mickey Mouse ears and throwing them on the floor. I walked over to inspect the boxes. Each boy had six gifts apiece. I gave them the boxes with their names on 'em and watched as they tore open their packages, jumping around the room in delight with each new toy.

When I saw my mother standing in the doorway, smiling at them with adoring eyes, I walked over to her, and whispered, "Mom, you didn't have to spend so much money on them."

"Nonsense," she said, swatting at the air with her hand. "It's not every day I get to see my grandbabies. Besides, Jay said to buy them whatever I wanted." She beamed as if she were a schoolgirl when she said my stepfather's name.

"Where is Mr. Jay?" I asked, admiring the love I saw in her eyes for him. They've been married for almost sixteen years and—after all that time—I still haven't been able to call him anything other than "Mr. Jay."

"Oh, he's working late tonight," she responded, chuckling. "He says he has to keep working just to keep his baby living comfortable." I smiled.

"Look, Daddy! Look what I got," Amir exclaimed, holding up a Speak and Spell.

"Me too!" Amar said, showing the same learning game, only in a different color.

I gave my mom a raised-eyebrow stare. "What?" she asked, feigning innocence. "I couldn't buy one without buying the other. Just wait until you see what your sister has for them." I gave her a look of astonishment, then shook my head.

I wanted to lecture her about overindulging them with gifts but I knew it would do no good. She had made it very clear that those were *her* only grandsons and she'd buy them whatever she wanted, whenever she wanted. And saying anything to my sister about spoiling them was like talking to a mute. So I shook my head and said, "I don't know what I'm gonna do with you women." I wrapped my arm around her shoulders, kissing her on the side of her forehead. "Did you buy me anything?" I asked, putting on a sad face.

"Nope," she said, "but I made you all of your favorite dishes." My lips parted into a wide, toothy grin.

"Well, that'll just have to do," I said, rubbing my stomach. "'Cause I'm starving. If you weren't my mother, I'd bite you."

"Boy, you're too much," she said, smiling and wrapping her arm around my waist, then gently squeezing. She looked down at her watch. "Oh my! I better get back downstairs to check on dinner. Your sister and her crew should be here soon."

"Okay," I said, giving her another kiss. "I'll be down in a minute."

"Take your time." She closed the bedroom door, making her way back downstairs.

When I returned downstairs, Mom was in the kitchen putting her finishing touches on her famous coconut cake. I peeked into the four pots simmering on the stove, then pulled open the oven. I smiled. She had made candied yams, baked macaroni, barbecue chicken, fried chicken, collard greens, cabbage, and her melt-in-your-mouth biscuits were waiting to be browned and served. And in the refrigerator she had a big bowl of potato salad and banana pudding ready to be devoured. My stomach growled.

"Gee whiz, Mom! Looks like you've cooked enough food to feed the U.S. troops."

"Well, I just want to make sure I have enough food. Besides, the way your sister and her family eats, it's almost like feeding troops." I laughed. She smiled, scooping white fluff with coconut flakes mixed in out of a glass bowl with her spatula, then spreading it across the cake. She repeated the process until the bowl was empty. Then she dug into a plastic bag, sprinkling additional coconut flakes on top.

"I can imagine. I sure can't wait to see everyone."

"It's been a long time since I've had my children home at the same time," she said, looking up from her masterpiece. She wiped her left brow with the back of her hand, then sat her spatula across the top of the glass bowl. "I don't get a chance to see much of you and now with the babies..." She paused, trying to hold back a choking sound, then continued before she broke down. "I want to spend more time with my grandbabies."

"I know, Mom. I promise I'll try to visit more often." I walked over to where she was sitting and started massaging her shoulders. I kissed the top of her head, then leaned in and wrapped my arms around her neck, letting them hang down in front of her. She dabbed her eyes with a napkin; I suppose to stop any tears from escaping.

"So tell me, sweetheart. How are you *really* doing?" I knew by the way she asked that that she already knew about my leaving Lina, thanks to Amira running her mouth. I lifted my body up, then looked down at the brightly waxed floor. I thought I saw my reflection looking back at me.

"I'm fine, Mom," I said, "I mean given the circumstances, things couldn't be better." The way she looked at me told me she wanted to know how it all had come to this. So I told her.

I walked over toward the counter, leaned back against its edge, folded my arms across my chest, then opened my mouth, spilling out everything that had been going on in my life: from my failed relationship with Lina to her lack of interest in being a mother; from my financial stressors to my problems with Amar in daycare. I held nothing back and she listened intently, clinging to my every word.

"I see," she said when I finished. "Well, try no to be too hard on Lina. Whatever her struggles are, she has to be the one to go through them. She has to be the one to deal with it. You can't make her be something she's not prepared to be."

"I know, Mom," I said, sighing. "I stopped trying a long time ago. But it still hurts to see what it's doing to those boys in there. Maybe it doesn't really bother them now, but what happens when they get older and start asking questions."

"Then you answer the best way you know how. Without judgment or ridicule."

"Hopefully, that's what I'll be able to do. But until then, I'm raising them on my own. So, if she wants to be a part of their lives, she'll have to come here to do it."

She got up and walked over to me, placing her hands on either side of my shoulder, looking me directly in the eyes, then asked, "Are you sure about this?"

"Yes," I said, looking up at the ceiling, then back into her eyes. "I've never been more sure of anything than I am of this."

She stared at me, almost as if she were studying me, then rubbed the left side of my face with the back of her hand. She began to speak. Slow and deliberate. "Anytime you start to feel like you can't do this alone, you pick up that phone and you call me. I don't care what time of the day or night it is. You call me. Understand?" I nodded. She embraced me and continued, "I'm here for you."

I wrapped my arms around her, resting my chin on the top of her head. I breathed in her Crème of Nature shampoo and smiled. "It's good to be home," I said, wishing—at that moment—I could stay wrapped in her arms forever. "I've missed you, Mom."

"I've missed you too, sweetheart." We relished in the moment for a few more minutes before she pulled away and said, "Now come on and help me get this table set before the troops get here." I broke into a hearty laugh, then grabbed a stack of china to set the table.

"Dinner was absolutely tasty," Amira said, rubbing her over-stuffed stomach. "Mom, you really outdid yourself this time."

"Well, of course I did," Mom replied jokingly. "I'm glad you enjoyed yourself. Now come on in here and help me with these dishes."

"Aww, Mom," she whined, playfully, "can't Brit do them this time. He always gets out of doing the dishes."

"Absolutely not. You have nine daughters and six of them are still home, so I know you haven't lifted a dish in years. Now get in here." I silently giggled, then stuck my tongue out at her.

"Well, the way you licked your plate clean, it's the least you could do." I laughed. "You sure were hungry." She had gobbled down two large helpings of food, then found room for a slice of Mom's signature coconut cake.

"Oh, shut up!" she barked, rolling her eyes at me. "You make me sick, boy. Paris, Kayla and Taylor, come up here and help your grandmother." Mom stopped what she was doing, then looked over at Amira with amazement.

"You let them girls be," she snapped.

"Yes, Mommy?" Paris called. Kayla and Taylor were standing behind her, each carrying one of the boys on their hip. I smiled at how beautiful they were. Paris was now fourteen and preparing for her freshman year in high school; Kayla was sixteen, entering her junior year as a track star; and Taylor was a seventeen-year-old college-bound senior. Milira, eighteen, and Nicole, nineteen, were already gone. They had hurriedly eaten their food, given everyone kisses, then bolted for the door in pursuit of teenage adventures with two young men they referred to as *flavors of the week*.

"Never mind. Your grandmother has decided to put me to work instead." They looked at each other and giggled. "Oh, it's funny, huh?"

"Quick, go get, Daddy," Kayla said to Alona who had just come upstairs from the basement carrying her dolls in her arm.

"Uncle Britton, can my little cousins come to my house to play with me?" she asked, ignoring her sister's request. I laughed, considering she's only a year older and nowhere near as tall as them.

"We'll see," I said, picking her up. "Give your uncle some love." She kissed me on the cheek, wrapping her arms around my neck. "You being a good girl?"

"Yes." She giggled. "Uncle Britton, are you staying over Grandmom's house or at our house?"

"Grandmom's," I answered, putting her down, then removing the rest of the dishes off the table to bring into the kitchen. I sat them on the counter. "Is that okay with you?"

She nodded as she sat her three chocolate Barbie dolls in one of the dining room chairs. "Mommy, I'm gonna stay with Uncle Britton, and my cousins, okay?"

"Did you ask Grandma?" Amira asked, rolling her sleeves up to begin her chore of dishwashing.

"Grandma, I'm gonna stay at your house today, okay, Grandma?"

"Sure, baby," Mom said, smiling. "Amira, you need to put a little more elbow grease on those dishes. I don't want my plates greasy." Mom winked at me. I held back my laughter. Growing up, Amira was notorious for half-washing the dishes; there'd be more soap and water on the floor than on the dishes.

"Humph," Amira grunted, then mumbled, "I don't know why in the world you just don't use the damn dishwasher." Lucky for her, Mom had already gone downstairs to check on my brother-in-law and my stepfather, who were both probably sleeping.

"Oooh, I'm telling," I said teasingly. I walked up behind her, then wrapped my arms around her waist.

"Don't come over here now, trying to be all lovey-dovey. Traitor."

"Oh, booger bear, be quiet. Here, I'll wash and you dry and put away."

"Oh, now you wanna help when everything's almost done." I burst out laughing, 'cause the only thing she did was rinse the plates and utensils, then stack the dishwasher. She turned it on while I washed and scrubbed the pots. Mom was standing in the kitchen doorway with her hands on her hips.

"Girlfriend," she said. "I *know* you don't have my dishwasher going."

"I sure don't," Amira shot back. "Brit does." I gave her a sidelong glance, then shook my head. "He's still hardheaded. I told him not to mess with it, but you know how he is."

"Hmm-hmm." Mom chuckled, snapping a picture of Amira and me cleaning up. "And your behind would lie your way out of a paper bag."

"That's if she didn't eat it first," I added, flicking water on her.

"You think," she responded, popping me across the butt with the towel. It stung.

"Ooooow!" I yelped, scooping a handful of wasted cake off a plate, then smearing it in her face.

"Oh, it's on now," she challenged, sticking both her hands in the remaining half of Mom's coconut cake.

"Amira!" Mom shouted, "Don't you dare." It was too late. Homegirl had already thrown a big chunk of cake at me. I ran over to the table, grabbed the rest of the cake in my hands, then chased her through the house. "Britton, Amira. Ya'll knock it off. You two are worse than kids." Amira and I ignored her and kept running through the house, laughing and teasing each other the way we used to when we were growing up. She ran out the front door. The kids came running upstairs and then outside to see what was going on. I was on top of Amira smearing cake all over her face and in her hair. Everyone was laughing, except Amir.

"Nooooo, Daddy. Don't do that to Auntie Mira."

"That's right, baby," Amira said, laughing and trying to catch her breath at the same time. "You help your auntie. I'ma fuck you up for breaking my damn nail."

"Auntie, that's a bad word," Amar informed her, still laughing.

"I know, baby, Auntie sorry but I'm still gonna beat your daddy up." Amira and I were so busy tussling on the ground and laughing we didn't see our mother come from around the back of the house with the water hose. She gave us both a good hosing down. The water was ice-cold.

"Ahhh!"

"Oooh! That water's cold."

"You kids wanna play," Mom said, chasing us with the hose. "Then I'll show you a thing or two, messing over my good cake like that." You should have seen Amira and me scrambling, slipping and falling, trying to get away from Mom and her twenty-foot hose. We didn't know she had enough pep in her step to keep up with us but she did. By the time she finished with us, we were soaked.

"Okay, Mom," we shouted in unison. "We give up."

"Yeah! Grandma," Amir and Amar shouted in unison, clapping.

"Look at Mommy's hair and face," Alona said, giggling. Kayla took pictures of her mother and me looking like two wet rats. Amira whispered one of her schemes in my ear. I laughed.

"No way, girl. Mom will kill us for sure."

"Oh come on. It'll be in fun."

"Well, you hold her," I said, trying to take the lesser of the evil.

"Ready?" she asked.

"Ready." We ran up behind Mom with Amira grabbing her around the arms while I yanked the hose out of her hand, turning it toward her.

"Mom," I said. "This is gonna hurt me more than it hurts you."

"Don't you dare," she said, laughing. "I mean it, Britton. Amira, let me go."

"Sorry," I replied, shrugging my shoulders, then drenching her.

"Amira! Britton! You rats," Mom squealed with laughter. "I'm gonna get the both of you." Amir, Amar and Alona came running over to us, wanting to join the fun. I wet them too, then handed the hose to them so they could take turns wetting one another. With Amira and me on either side of our mother, we planted sweet kisses on her cheek.

"I love you, Mom!"

"Me, too!" Amira said.

"I love you brats, too. I'm so glad to have both of my wet babies home."

"Awww!" Amira and I said in unison. We burst into laughter when Kayla came back out from hiding, snapping our picture. That was the most fun I'd had in a long time. We ended up staying outside laughing, joking and talking until the wee hours of the morning. It was sure good to be home. I had to smile. With the love and energy of family, how could anyone ever be alone?

13

CELESTE: *Drown In My Own Tears*

I was yanked from my sleep as the shrill sound of a baby's cry chased me through barren land. I jerked up from the bed, looking around the room, trying to absorb my surroundings. My face and pillow were wet with tears. Sweat rolled along my spine as I suddenly realized I was still in the hotel. My breathing was heavy and quick, matching the racing beat of my heart.

The illumination of a full moon peeked through the slit of the room's half-drawn drapes, causing an eeriness to stir around me. *Pull yourself together*, I thought to myself. *It was only a bad dream.* I shuddered, glancing at the digital clock on the nightstand. It was two fifteen a.m. I had fallen asleep after returning from dinner. Thank goodness Tradawna was still out and about, doing God knows what. The last thing I needed was someone to bear witness to my turbulent sleeping. Or worse—overhear the wailing of my womb. I shivered. Goose bumps clung to my skin like a cold rag, causing me to shake with chills.

Judging by the way my covers and pillows were on the floor, I had thrashed about the hotel's queen-size bed, fighting demons as I was held prisoner to visions of a woman being buried in a pine box. As the box was slowly lowered into the ground, the woman kicked and screamed, beating her fists and dragging her nails frantically against the top of her wooden trap. Blood dripped from her fingers as splinters ripped the skin from under her nail beds. She was being buried alive.

I have had that same horrible dream for the last ten years of my life. Usually I awaken just before the last nail is being hammered along the edges of her coffin, sealing her fate. But this time…this time the earth had opened up to receive her. This time, dirt was being thrown down on her. There was no escape.

I peeled myself out of bed, removing my damp nightgown, then headed for the comforts of a hot shower to wash away the scent of fear. While the steamy water jetted out of the nozzle, I pulled my hair back into a ponytail, then eased my way behind the white curtain. I stepped under the spigot, releasing tears.

"We find the defendant guilty," the brown-skinned woman said, facing the judge. Her words reverberated in my head like the clanging of bells.

"Nooooooo!" I remonstrated, collapsing onto the huge wooden table. "Noooo!"

"Order!" the judge snapped, slamming down his gavel. He peered over his black-framed glasses, cutting his eye over at me, then my attorney. "Mr. Piney, I advise you to get your client under control. *Now!*"

I must have stood under that water, crying for what seemed like hours, trying to rinse away my trail of deception. "Stop this craziness," I scolded myself aloud, letting the water beat against my face. I tightly pressed my eyes shut, scrubbing my face. "You've paid for your mistakes twofold. You can't keep beating yourself up." Although I try to convince myself of this time and time again, I'm still haunted by the woman holding a glass stem to her lips. No matter how many times I bathe, my dirty past still covers me. I turned the water dial to the hottest temperature my skin could stand, hoping to scald these memories away.

By the time I finished showering, I was as wrinkled as a prune. *You and your slatternly ways will come to light.* I shook the voice out of my head, wincing at the thought of someone finding the key to my safe box—the place where I've kept my twisted skein of lies. *Impossible*, I thought to myself as I applied almond oil over my skin. *No one will ever find out.* I repeated that in my head over and over; however, I refused to acknowledge my reflection in the mirror. Something within me told me if I stared back at the image, I wouldn't like what I saw. If I weren't careful, everything I've worked for would come crashing down on me.

"Ooh!" I shrieked, jumping when I stepped out of the bathroom. "Girl, you almost scared me half-to-death. I didn't hear you come in." It was Tradawna. I glanced over at the clock. It was four in the morning. She tossed her purse on the bed.

"My, aren't we up early," she said, removing, then throwing her clothes in the corner. She covered her mouth, trying to stifle a yawn. "Excuse me. Girl, I'm so beat." She went into the bathroom, leaving the door open. I could hear the release of fluids escaping her body. I wrinkled up my nose, wondering why she didn't close the door. A few seconds later, the faucet water turned on, then she stepped back out into the room, applying Noxema over her face. "Are you just getting in or just getting up?" she asked, putting one arm behind her back, then with a snap, removing her bra. Her breasts seemed to sway. I turned my head.

"Up," I replied, sitting at the foot of my bed.

"Well, giiirl. You shoulda been with us. We were over at the Monte Carlo, chilling with L.L. and this new rap group Blind Ambitions. Girl, it was off the hook. There was Cristal and Moët all over the place." She was clearly in her glory as she shared her adventures with the G.O.A.T. and his entourage. I half-smiled. "Oh my God! I couldn't get over how fine L.L. was. He has the bomb body. And that group Blind Ambitions can definitely rock the mic..."

"Hmm," I said, trying to sound interested; yet not be too encouraging for her to continue talking me to death. I kept myself from rolling my eyes up in my head. She's a really nice girl, just loquacious, if you know what I mean. "Sounds like you had a lot of fun." I forced out a yawn, stretching my arms over my head.

"No doubt," she said, going back into the bathroom. I sighed, wishing I had been asleep when she came in. But I was relieved when I heard the shower turn on. At least there'd be a moment of silence. When she returned, I had safely slipped back into bed, hoping the break of dawn would keep the nightmares at bay, and cradle Tradawna to sleep. I leaned back against the headboard, prayerfully closing my eyes before drifting off to sweet thoughts of the only man I'll ever love.

When the phone chimed in my ear, I thought I was dreaming. I pried my eyes from my slumber, scanning the room. Tradawna's bed was empty.

I let out a relieved sigh, then looked over at the clock, reaching for the phone. The red numbers read: 10:00 a.m.

"Hello," I said, rubbing my eyes.

"Hey, soror, are you coming down for breakfast?" It was Lea.

"No. I'm gonna pass," I responded, trying to shut off the aching in my head.

"Oh, okay." She paused for a moment, sensing something uncertain. "Umm, is everything alright?"

"Yeah. I'm just tired. I didn't get much sleep," I offered without thinking. "I'm going to stay in bed and hopefully get some rest. But I'll be down for the luncheon."

"Okay. We'll see ya then." We said our good-byes and hung up. I pulled the covers up over my body, then slowly floated back to sleep.

I had only fallen back asleep for two hours when I heard the knock on the door. For a moment, I thought it might have been housekeeping; but dismissed the thought when I recalled placing the *do not disturb* card on the door handle. The tapping continued. I got up, pulled on my robe, then fluttered toward the door. *Tradawna must have left her key*, I thought as I opened the door. Shock registered on my face as my visitor stood there, wearing a smile that hid an agenda.

"Hey, sleepyhead," she said, waltzing her way through the door. I stepped aside, letting her in before she knocked me over. "I was worried when you didn't come down for breakfast. So I thought I'd come up to check on you." She tilted her head, standing model-like: poised, assured. She was remarkably beautiful.

"Hello, Indy," I said, pulling my robe tight around my waist, feeling tattered. I forced a smile. "Please come in. You'll have to excuse me. I'm just getting up."

"Oh, you look just fine," she replied, maintaining a smile laced with cynicism. "You must have had a rough night?"

"Why'd you ask that?" I asked, shifting my uneasiness from one foot to the other. *Whatever you do, stay calm.* A thousand thoughts trampled through my mind like a herd of elephants.

"Girl, it's almost noon and you're still lounging in your pajamas. The day is ticking away. Do you mind if I have a seat?" she asked, surveying the room, then—without waiting for my response—sat in one of the wing-back chairs neatly positioned on either side of a round Birchwood table. She placed her purse on top of the table. "Chile, you missed an enjoyable breakfast."

"I'm sure it was," I said, keeping my tone light. "Good to see you're finally able to keep something down. I guess whatever you were coming down with has passed."

"Thank goodness." She hesitated, taking in the room. Her wandering eyes soaked in the unmade beds, Tradawna's crumpled clothes in the corner. Then like a hawk, she zoomed over to the nightstand. I casually glanced over to where her eyes became locked. The book. I had read and reread the acknowledgments, flipping back and forth to the color photo of the author on the back cover. *How could I know*, I thought, feeling trapped in. A feeling of awkwardness began to boil, but slowly dissipated when she continued without mentioning she had spotted it. "Not much can keep a sista like me down," she said, pursing her lips. "I know one thing. I can't wait to get back home. Vegas is cute, but seven days is a bit too long for me." She rubbed her stomach, staring at me. "Whew! I'm stuffed." I smiled knowingly.

"I know what you mean," I said, sitting on the edge of Tradawna's bed, "about being ready to get home. I've had a wonderful time, but I'm sure I'll have a million things to catch up on when I get back. I'm sure my desk is flooded with messages."

"Oh, don't even mention it. I'm trying hard not to think about it." She paused a beat, then continued, "Exactly what do you do, if you don't mind me asking?" She crossed her legs, cupping her hands over her knee.

"I'm a consultant," I said, matching her gaze. "I have my own agency."

"Is that so?"

I nodded.

"And what type of consulting do you do?" I gave her the *Readers Digest* version of my agency's responsibility to provide sports, events, and enter-tainment marketing along with offering advertising and public relations services throughout the Greater Hartford area. "You go, girl. I should have known you'd have it going on."

I smiled. "It definitely keeps me busy. But I love every minute of it."

"You graduated from Howard, right?"

"Yes."

"So your degree is in communications?"

I nodded. "And journalism," I added, shifting in my seat. The air around me was beginning to thicken. I was choking. She was trying to flip through my dossier. *What in the world is she after*, I wondered as she clung to my every word.

"Do you have any business cards with you?" she asked. "I'm all about networking and drumming up business for my people."

"As a matter of fact I do," I said, getting up to walk toward the closet. I grabbed my purse, then pulled out my cardholder, handing her one of my cards. "Here you go." She looked it over, then smiled, placing it in her purse. I sat in the chair next to her.

"Thanks. I'm going to check out your website when I get home, and—if I like what I see—I'll be giving you a call to coordinate the grand opening of Weaves and Wonders III." I coughed. She paused, curling the tip of her tongue up, touching her upper lip. "For a handsome fee of course."

"Well," I offered, trying to conceal my skepticism, "if my schedule is free, we can definitely discuss it further."

She grinned, staring into my eyes. "Hopefully, it will be. I'd love to work with you." I shifted my weight in my seat. Although my smile widened, every muscle in my body tightened.

I took in a quick breath. "That could prove to be quite interesting I'm sure."

She pursed her lips, removing her silk designer scarf from around her head, then tossing her head to the side. Her hair fell freely to her shoulders. "Trust and believe. It will be one of the most talked about grand openings Hartford has ever seen."

"Indy, I don't doubt that one bit."

There was a pause. Indy tilted her head, running her fingers through her ultra-silky hair. "So tell me, soror. Is D.C. where your parents live?"

I swallowed hard, trying to dissolve the lump forming in my throat. "They're deceased," I said in a husky whisper.

"Oh, I'm sorry to hear that," she said thoughtfully. "Are you the only child?"

"No," I stammered. "I mean, yes." She raised her eyebrow. "I mean I had an older brother, but he was killed in a carjacking a few years back."

"That's terrible," she offered, placing her hand over her heart. "Girl, it sounds like you've been through a lot."

"And then some," I said, sighing, getting up from my seat to pull the curtains back. The sun's rays brightened up the room, but did nothing for my restless spirit. "But, I try not to think about it. I'm a survivor," I added, shuffling toward the dresser, pulling open the top drawer. I removed a pair of black stockings and underwear.

"Well, through all of the good and the bad, life is what you make it. That's for sure. So here's to survival," she said, lifting her hand in a mock toast.

"Here, here," I responded, pulling out a black pantsuit from my leather garment bag. I pulled the spread back on my bed, laying the suit across it. I then pulled out my suitcase, removing a pair of black leather pumps. Indy watched my every move, smiling.

"Do you have any children?"

Her question seemed to wrap its words around my neck in a chokehold. I silently gasped for air. The veins in my head pulsed. "No," I said, trying to keep my voice steady. "No children, and no family that I'm close to."

"So, then it's just you against the world."

"Basically."

"I know that's right. Well, I will say this: I know what it's like having to fend on your own. I'm just thankful…" Her thoughts drifted before she continued. "I know it would have been one lonely journey for me if I didn't have the love and support of my friends. And of course, my husband has been extremely supportive."

"You're extremely fortunate," I replied.

"True indeed," she said, staring over at the nightstand. "So, tell me. How are you enjoying the book?"

"Huh?" I asked, startled.

"The book," she repeated. "How are you enjoying it?"

"Oh, I haven't had a chance to start it yet. I've just flipped through a few chapters. But, from what I can tell so far, it looks like it's going to be a really good read."

"Well, I'm sure Tee..." She clarified whom she meant when I gave her a confused look. "...Damascus. Everyone calls him Tee."

"Oh," I said.

"Anyway, I'm sure he'd love to hear your feedback once you've finished it."

"Then I'll be sure to give it." I smiled, keeping myself busy around the room while she talked. I began removing clothes from the dresser drawers, then packing them into my suitcase. Her voice clattered around the room, ricocheting off the walls, causing my head to ring like two cymbals being slammed into each other.

"Did you ever meet him?"

"Who?" I asked confused.

"Tee."

"Not that I can recall," I said, catching her gaze, then shifting my eyes. "Why?"

"Well, if you didn't know. Before he was a writer, he stripped for a living. I just thought you might have seen him at one of his performances. He was quite popular in the Connecticut area, especially Hartford."

I shifted my weight from one foot to the other. "No. I can't say that I have. I really don't do the club scene much." I silently held my breath, then blew it out slowly through my nose.

She smiled. "I don't blame you. You definitely weren't missing much. I was never into seeing a bunch of hard-pressed women, clawing and pawing over some half-naked man anyway. Besides, most of 'em are a bunch of sex-deprived hoes hopscotching around the country to see which dancer they can take home. Nasty tricks. I could never figure out what a woman gets out of spending up *her* money on some man whose only focus is to humiliate her ass on the dance floor, or stage."

My mind drifted back to five years ago. I was still new to the Hartford area, didn't have any friends and didn't really know my way around yet.

And the only person I knew was a girl in my apartment complex. She had taken me out a few times to show me the happenings in the area, and to get me out of the house. Although she was a bit loud and could be vulgar, she was friendly, and really had a kind heart. She had knocked on my door repeatedly until I finally opened it.

"Girl," she said, placing her hands on her thin hips. "You just need to get on out of that funk and come on out to Club Voodoo tonight. There's a male revue from New York there tonight and they are gonna turn that mother out."

"No thanks," I said, closing the door behind her. "I'd rather stay in."

"And do what," she asked, scrunching her face up. "Pick your toenails? I'm telling you tonight's the night to have a real good time. It'll be well worth it."

"I'm not into strippers."

"That's because your country ass hasn't seen niggahs like these. Buffed, thugged out, and every brotha packing at least a nine." I looked at her, unsure of what she meant. She rolled her eyes. "Nine as in nine, thick inches of dick."

"Oh."

"You probably haven't had good dick in a long while, anyway. So you might as well come on out to at least get a look at what you're not getting at home. You don't have to tip unless you want, and I'll even pay your way."

I smiled.

"Girlfriend," she snapped. "You won't regret it. Especially after you see the niggah with the pierced dick. He's all that." She quickly licked her lips and fingers. "Tonight we 'bout to get things poppin' for real." And on that note, I got dressed and rode over to Club Voodoo with reservations, and curiosity all wrapped in one.

When we got there, the parking lot was packed. The line extended down to the other side of the plaza where the club was located. I couldn't believe all the women standing in line waiting to get inside. After twenty-five minutes of waiting, we finally got inside. The club was nice. There were two large rooms. In one area there was a stage and rows of chairs practically filled with eager patrons. The other area was a huge dance floor with two bars and a flight of stairs, leading to the VIP lounge. I looked up and saw about fifty men—I assumed to be the dancers, since there were no other men besides the bouncers and bartenders in sight—and a few women, standing around, eating and drinking. The bass from the music booming from the speakers vibrated through me.

"Here, girl," Trena said, handing me a drink. "Something to calm your nerves before the show starts."

"What is it?" I asked over the music, sniffing it.

"Long Island Iced Tea." I took a sip. It was nice. I could barely taste the liquor. Trena smiled at me.

"I'd go easy on that if I were you. The night's still young."

"I can handle it," I said. Well, by the time the show started, I was on my third Iced Tea and was feeling no pain. I was feeling good. Trena was also a little full from her drinks. I was really beginning to have a nice time. Then the lights dimmed, the strobe lights turned. And then stepped out the dancers. These beautiful men came in every shade of black. And looked like they could have been centerfolds for one of the male calendar editions. One by one, they showed us what they were made of, wearing anything from bath towels to cut-up jeans and sweats. Women were stomping, clapping, screaming. You name it, they were doing it. Even I got caught up in the moment, pulling out a few ones to tip a brotha who caught my attention. But when the emcee, a beautiful Hispanic woman, announced the men of the hour, Hammer and T-Bone, the screams were deafening.

When I asked Trena where they got their names, she simply said, "'Cause Hammer bangs down the pussy. And T-Bone is juicy and thick, like that. And has enough meat to feed the hungry."

"Oh," I said even more curious. I ordered another drink. Hammer came out, wearing a hooded sweatshirt pulled over his head, a pair of sweat pants and shades over his eyes. The crowd went wild. And when a bald, dark-skinned brotha with a tribal band tattooed around both biceps came out, wearing a pair of unlaced Timbs and blue-and-white boxers, I think every woman almost fainted. He looked as if he had been sculptured from the finest clay in the world. When he licked his lips, then wagged his pierced tongue while grabbing his crotch, I thought the building would collapse from the thunderous applause and screams.

"Girl, this is what I was talking 'bout. Wait until you see that niggah T-Bone up close and personal." I couldn't believe how much of a rush I was getting watching them perform lap dances, and hip-grinding movements. I pressed my legs tight to hold in the excitement that had already begun stirring inside of me, waiting for release. It had been a *long* time since I had been intimate with anyone. Trena was right. It was long overdue.

When Tee and Hammer finally made their way over to Trena and me, I had drunk enough Long Islands to wash down whatever inhibitions I'd had before I got there. Before I knew what was happening, T-Bone was dancing up against me, and breathing on my neck. I was losing myself to the music, the smell of his scent and the feel of his muscles against me. He was too much. And just before he could go on to his next victim, Trena and I had grabbed the strings of his mesh thong, snatching it off. He didn't even blink an eye. He just kept on dancing, bumping and grinding—naked for all to see.

"Girl," Trena purred over the ruckus. "We doing his fine ass tonight. Him and his boy." My eyes got big.

"You can't be serious?"

"Oh, don't bitch up now." She smirked. "Have another drink," she said, handing me a twenty. "'Cause we 'bout to get our groove on." By the end of the night, we had become the same girls Indy was sitting in my hotel room talking about. I had spent every dime I had in my wallet. And we were following behind two chocolate Adonis, heading to their hotel room.

In the morning, I had awakened nude in a strange bed, alongside Trena with a hoarse throat, sore jaws and...I'm just too embarrassed.

Bits of that evening were coming back to haunt me. I quickly shook the only thing I remember hearing him say before he grabbed the back of my head, ramming his penis down my throat, then ejaculating in my mouth. *Yeah, suck that dick like a twenty piece.* I remember Trena being on her knees with Hammer in back of her while she sucked on T-Bone's testicles. Oh my God! I never considered one indiscretion could catch up to me, and possibly ruin everything. I'm begging you to not mention any of this to her or anyone else. Please. Then again, we never told them our names and I'm sure he's been with plenty of women, probably too many to keep count. If I ever run into him, I'm sure he won't remember me. There's no way.

I took in a quick breath, crossing my fingers. "I guess it's safe to say you never went to any of his shows."

"Please," she snapped. "Absolutely not."

"Well, how do you handle knowing he's had his body exposed to—and I'm sure touched by—hundreds of women?"

She chuckled. "Truthfully, I could care less."

"That's noble of you," I said cautiously. "You must really trust him."

"I have no reason not to. His dancing days were way before my time. I knew what he did before I married him. And I know *a lot* of women have let him knock their insides around. So I can't hold any of that against him. I only concern myself with what or who he's doing now. Like you said on the plane, we all have a past. And whatever is done in the dark will come to the light. Believe that. And when it does, I'm usually right there; front and center."

I cringed. Her eyes were smiling. "Oh my!" she snapped, glancing down at her timepiece. "Look at the time." She stood up, catching her reflection in the oval wall mirror. "I gotta get upstairs to freshen up before lunch." I stood up as well, gingerly walking behind her, trying to conceal my eagerness to see her leave. "I guess I'll see you in an hour or so."

I nodded. "You sure will," I said with a wide smile, opening the door, desperately wanting her out of my space.

"Good," she replied, leaning in to give me a hug. She lowered her voice to a whisper, "Soror, if there's anything I can ever do for you, don't hesitate to call me."

I smiled. "Thanks. I appreciate that." She tightened her hug before gliding out the door toward the elevators, leaving behind a whirl of contradictions. I closed the door behind me, pressed my back against it, then slowly slid down to the floor, covering my face, feeling like the walls were closing in on me. I cried, trying to reassure myself that my past wouldn't catch up to me. I wiped my face and went into the bathroom to shower. I needed to get ready for my sorority luncheon.

An hour later, I was dressed and ready to sit through another grueling event with a group of cliquish women who were honoring the biggest snoot of them all—Indera Fleet. She was being honored for the sorority's 2000 Humanitarian Award for all of her contributions to the African-American community in education and business. How thoughtful. Every time I turned around, Indera was being recognized for something. Not too long ago she received the Allstate Insurance Company's "From Whence We Came: African-American Women of Triumph" award for her accomplishments, and now this.

In all honesty, I'm a little envious of her. She has it all. And she's the daughter my mother would have wanted me to be. Poised. Beautiful. Graceful. Which is probably why a part of me finds the High Priestess quite enchanting, to say the least. I guess after sharing with you what I had done with her now husband, I don't have any room to talk about her or anyone else. I'm not perfect. And I've made mistakes. But it's not like I'm saying anything bad about her. She's definitely an enigma. And I'm sure in another lifetime, I could really like her—not that I dislike her now. I...let's just say, she's the means to an end for me.

"Celeste," my confidante had said a few weeks prior to my official induction into an organization that exemplifies the high ideals of finer womanhood, scholarship, and service. "I understand your reasoning for going through all this, but don't you think there's another way to do it without joining a sorority you care nothing about?"

I sighed. "Unfortunately not. Desperation calls for desperate measures," I reasoned, staring at the wedding photo in the *Jet* "Society" section. I almost fainted when I came across the article of this illustrious wedding—over two years ago—in the magazine. I couldn't believe my dead-end search was finally over. I now had a lead I intended to follow. I didn't care how far-fetched the idea was. As far as I was concerned, it was the only viable plan. I read and reread the names of the bridal party over and over, gazing bleary-eyed at the man with the bright smile. I kissed the tip of my finger, then slowly traced his lips and face.

"I hate women like her," she commented, referring to the bride, "they think they have the world in the palm of their hands."

I sighed. "Most of them do. Particularly her. Just look at her. No matter what happens, she seems to bounce back on her feet quicker than a cat with nine lives."

"It's sickening," she barked, sucking her teeth, and glaring at the photo. "Bitch."

I rolled my eyes. "Rochelle, I really wish you'd let it go." Besides being my only friend, Rochelle has been my lifeline since relocating to Connecticut almost four years ago. I really don't know what I'd do without her. She's been with me every step of the way with trying to find my husband. And I've been with her every step of the way with trying to help her get over hers. She blames everyone else for his shortcomings, except him. He was the one who betrayed her trust, not the woman who knew nothing about her being his wife. Sometimes, I have to remind her of that. "The only person you have to blame for your misery is your husband. Now stop sulking, and help me get ready for my orientation session."

"Humph. I still think this is all a waste of time."

"Well, do you have any other suggestions?"

"Yeah," she sighed. "How 'bout you just ring his doorbell and say, 'Hi, honey. I'm home.'" She laughed. I frowned.

"Wrong answer, silly. If it were that simple I would have done that already." I shook my head in aggravation. For years, I've tried tracking him down. I called the Alumni Office at Norfolk State hoping they'd have current contact information on him. And I even tried his fraternity's member directory. To no avail, both searches had nil to offer.

I even contemplated calling directory assistance in every state, hoping there'd be a listing under his last name. But that would entail going through every city on the map. It felt as though he never really existed. Like he was a figment of my imagination. It was like he had vanished off the face of the earth. I had even considered hiring a private detective, but didn't know if I would be able to afford the fees for a lengthy search. So, stumbling on his picture in *Jet* was a godsend. I knew then what I had to do.

"Okay," she continued. "So you become a member. Then what?"

"Then I become familiar with sorority protocol. Attend regional conferences, boulées, participate in community service projects until I can strategically plan a way to meet the phenomenal Indera Fleet."

"And then?"

"I don't know," I said, sighing. I was getting frustrated with my friend's inquisition. "I do know she's the key player in me getting to him." I pointed to the groomsman's picture. "All I know is, I've been trying to find him for years. And here he is, right smack in my face. Now if that's not fate, I don't know what is. It's the break I've needed. I just need time on my side until I'm able to figure out my next move."

"What if he's involved with someone else? Or better yet, won't take you back."

I looked at her dumbfounded. "I don't care if he's involved with someone else, he won't be for long. And he will take me back. I won't give him a chance not to."

"For your sake," she said, shaking her head. "I hope it's that simple."

"I don't think it'll be easy. But it won't be impossible. After the initial shock wears off, he'll be all mine."

"Hmm. Well, since you seem to have it all figured out, the only thing I'll say is: If you're trying to get to him through her, be careful. From what I hear she can be a vindictive bitch when she feels crossed."

I flicked her comment off with my hand. "Vindictive or not. I'm a woman who'll stop at nothing to get what I want. Even if it means joining an organization I despise."

She grunted. "Whatever."

"Rochelle, sometimes you have to go through the bad in order to get to the good." I shut the magazine, stuffing it in my purse. "Besides," I continued half-jokingly, "my mother—the socialite that she was—would be pleased knowing I joined *her* precious sorority."

Anyway, it was a slow start, but after a whole year of planning—and preparing—I am finally in the company of Indera. *Hmm*, I thought, pulling on my jacket. *There is definitely something you can do for me.* I broke into a wide smile. Working on her grand opening wouldn't be such a bad thing after all. In the end, we'd both get what we wanted.

You disgust me with your low-down trampish ways. I shook the voice from my head. "Not today, Mother," I whispered, looking up. "You will not get the best of me today." I adjusted my sorority pen on my blazer, checked my hair one last time in the mirror, then fastened my beaded choker around my neck, covering my scar. I took a deep sigh. I was looking forward to getting home. *One more day*, I reminded myself as I walked out of the door.

When I stepped onto the elevator, I wondered if I had bitten off more than I could chew with this charade. But immediately erased the notion from my thoughts, for I had my eye on the prize. I smiled, savoring the warmness that flowed through my body anticipating the end of this madness. I straightened my back, threw my head up and waited to face the day with a newfound confidence. Nothing was going to stand in my way. *Soon, baby*, I said to myself, stepping out of the elevator into the lobby.

14

SARINA: *Mind Trips*

I loved New York—the big city of raggedy dreams— until today. The day everyone turned their backs on my friend. How could you stupid people see someone lying on the ground in distress, and you act like it's nothing?

"Help me," the voice cried. At first I thought I was hearing things but then I heard the voice again; this time, calling out my name. "Sarina, please help me."

I couldn't believe it. Without hesitation I ran toward the familiar voice, falling to my knees, cradling my lost friend in my arms. I hadn't seen her in years. And here she was in Washington Square Park. She was beaten and in a lot of pain. Yet, despite these unfortunate circumstances, we were finally reunited.

"Pecola. Who did this to you?" I screamed with tears running down my face. "Who hurt you?" People walked, skated and rode by, looking down at me without offering to help my injured friend. "What the fuck you people looking at. Get me some help!"

"Sa—"

"Sssh," I said, lifting her up. "It doesn't matter. I'm here now. I'll keep you safe." I was sure whoever had done this to her was somewhere nearby, waiting to finish the job. My gut told me it was the same man who'd been following me. Now he had others watching as well. If they did this to her, then I'd be next. Things were getting too dangerous here. I had to get somewhere safe until I was able to get back to Maryland. And I knew just where I'd go. "Come on," I said to my sweet friend, opening up my suit-case to get something to wrap around her. "Let's get you out of here. I promise I won't let anyone hurt you."

15

INDERA: *You Got Me Going In Circles*

You know. That damn Tee works my last nerve. I am so sick of him. Do you know that muscle-head fool had the audacity to tell me I needed to start taking care of home more? The balls of him! He knew damn well I was a career woman before he married me, so if he thinks he's gonna domesticate me after two years of marriage, then he's lost his damn mind 'cause this sista is not the one for cooking and cleaning, or laying up underneath no damn man. I have no time being a house trophy, okay. I didn't build a multimillion-dollar empire, having emerged from the shadow of *any* man, famous or not. I'm a sista making shit happen. It's not all about the diamonds and pearls; it's about profits and progress for me. And—make no mistake—when it's all said and done, I will be a household name. I *thought* I had made that very clear to him. Well, obviously I didn't.

"Look," he had said to me at breakfast. "I understand you're a woman on the move but all of your outside activities are starting to interfere with you taking care of home."

"What?" I snapped, giving him a look of disbelief.

"You heard me."

"And what is that supposed to mean?" I asked, getting up from the kitchen table to place my bowl in the dishwasher.

"It means I want you home more."

"Home to do what, may I ask?"

"To spend time with *your* man," he snapped, folding his arms around his bare chest. "That's what."

"Tee, don't start your shit, okay? I do spend time with you."

"Oh, is that so? When is the last time we had dinner together, can you answer that?"

I took a deep breath, blowing out my growing attitude. "Sometime last week."

"Yeah. Aiight. Try two weeks ago. You leave this house early in the morning and don't walk back up in here until late at night. Since you got back from Vegas, I barely see you."

"I can't help it if things come up that require my attention."

"Hmm. And I don't?"

I sucked my teeth.

"We sleep in the same bed," he continued, "and I still feel distant from you. I can't even get you to make love without having to beg you for it."

"Well, when I get home I'm tired and I just wanna sleep."

"Then maybe you should think about freeing up some of your time."

I looked up at the crystal wall clock. It was 7:15 a.m. "You know what," I said, yanking my satchel off the counter and grabbing my keys. "I can't get into this right now. I have a nine o'clock board meeting to get to."

"See, this is the shit I'm talking about. You're always off and running some damn where. Call out." He got up from the table and walked over to me, grabbing me around the waist and planting his thick kisses under my earlobe, then dragging his long tongue across my neck. He pressed his hard body into me. "Play hooky with me."

"Tee, I can't," I said, sidestepping him. "Not today."

"Then when goddamn it! I need my wife." His tone didn't sit well with me. *Oh, he has some fucking nerve, raising his damn voice at me.*

"For what! Some pussy?"

He stood there in the middle of the kitchen in his boxers with his hand on both hips. The muscles in his chest twitched. His nose flared. "How about for some conversation, or maybe for some companionship. And yeah, some pussy would be nice from time to time." Oh my God! Some pussy from time to time would be nice. Now isn't that some shit? This fool would keep his dick packed in me around the clock if I'd let him, okay. Chile, if I had had enough time, I would have pulled up my skirt, hopped up on the kitchen table, spread open my legs and yanked my lace panties to the side, then screamed, "Come get some pussy, nigga!" But I didn't. So I quickly shook the thought out of my head. I felt my pressure rising.

"All you ever think about is keeping your dick wet. Do I ever complain when you're gone for weeks at a time, touring around with your book, do I?"

"Come off of it! And every time I go on the road, I ask you to come along. But you always have some fucking excuse."

"You know I have to work."

"Bullshit! Mighty funny you didn't have to work when you wanted to fly your ass to Vegas to cackle with a bunch of stuck-up..." He paused when I glanced down at my watch. He glared at me. "Take your ass on to your fucking board meeting. I'll see ya when I see ya."

I stood there, fuming. Blood had rushed to my head so damn fast the room started to spin. I was glaring at him so hard everything around me began to blur. I was getting ready to go off. Felt like a pressure cooker about to explode. But the lid was on so tight the only thing able to spill out of my mouth as I headed for the door was, "Kiss my ass, Tee."

"Yeah, aiight," he shot back. "And when shit starts falling apart in this marriage, you'll have no one to blame but *you*." Now that did it! I stopped dead in my tracks.

"What the fuck is that supposed to mean?" I yelled, slamming my purse down on the table.

"Just what the fuck I said. Take it however you want." That blew my lid straight to the roof. Steam was coming from everywhere. I blacked on his ass.

"Let me tell you one fucking thing. If you feel you have to step outside this marriage to get satisfaction, then you do it. But don't you dare put it on me. 'Cause whether I'm home or not, if that's what you're gonna do, then that's what the fuck you'll do. So do it and be done with it. Forgive me for not being able to lie around the motherfucking house all day with a wet pussy ready to be fucked at your convenience, *but* I do have a life outside of the fucking bedroom. There's money to be made and I'm there to make it. So you can say what the fuck you want, and do what the fuck you feel you gotta do, but *don't* make excuses for wanting to do it."

He *tsked* me, shaking his head. "You just missed the whole fucking point."

"No, motherfucker!" I snapped. "*You* missed the fucking point." His jaws tightened.

Chile, if you could have seen the expression on his face. It looked like he was ready to whip my ass. The pupils in his eyes became tiny dots of anger. But he contained it. And I stood my ground. "Now like I said before, lick my ass!"

"Fuck it! Do you, baby."

"You know—"

"Yo, shut the fuck up! I ain't beat for your shit. So get the fuck out!" He walked out and went back upstairs, leaving me standing there, seething. That motherfucker told me to get the *fuck* out of my own damn house. I was shocked, to say the least. Chile, the only thing I could do to keep myself from running up those stairs and jumping on his back was to grab my things and slam the front door. You know, now that I'm repeating the story, he really told me a thing or two, didn't he?

Well, that was two weeks ago, and he's still acting funny. Okay, so maybe I overreacted. I don't know what has gotten into me lately. But you know what? Oh well! He'll get over it. Unh-huh. Don't you start too! It's bad enough Britton is siding with him. I called that man up for some emotional support and do you know what he had the nerve to say. "I read somewhere that two-thirds of all black marriages end in divorce. So what I encourage you to do if you don't want to end up another statistic, you need to learn how to balance being an independent woman and a woman devoted to making her marriage work. It's about compromise, communication and sacrifice, things you are too selfish to consider. Anyway, you should be discussing this with your husband. You do remember who that is, don't you?" I slammed the phone down on his ass.

I know marriage is about compromise and communication and all that other stuff. But, I'm telling you this marriage mess is more work than I bargained for. I'm starting to wonder if I made a mistake. I mean, I don't know if I'm cut out for this 'cause you know a sista like me likes to answer to no one.

Between you and me, I don't know if I can give him what he wants. Tee really has a good heart. Lord knows he does. But I don't know if I have the patience needed. Slowly, I feel like I'm... Humph. I don't know where all this ambivalence is coming from all of a sudden but it's starting to eat at me. I guess you want to know why the hell I married him. Well... because I know he really does love me. Believe it or not, I do love that man but I'm so...let's change the subject. I flipped open my cell phone, and called home.

"Tee?"

"Yeah?"

"What are you doing?" I asked, pulling out of Woodbury Common, heading home. I don't usually do outlets but I've been so stressed lately that I decided an afternoon of shopping would ease my tension. Well, two thousand dollars later in Prada and Gucci, I'm still agitated.

"I'm on the computer, working."

"On your book?"

"Yeah, why?"

"No reason," I said, slightly annoyed he was still acting shady toward me. But I guess I deserved it, considering my last outburst. Unh-huh! Don't give me that "yes you do" look. "Sweetheart. I know I don't always act like it and I forget to say it sometimes, but I do love you."

"Then stop neglecting me. Stop putting walls up between us." See what I mean? He still has this stinking attitude. "Look, I gotta go."

"Wait a minute!"

"What?"

"I thought maybe we could go to the movies or something."

His tone softened. "What, you asking me out on a date?"

"Something like that."

"Then call back and ask me the right way." *Click*. My mouth hit the floor when I heard the dial tone. Well, instead of calling back, I tossed the phone over in the passenger seat and kept it movin'. *Next stop, Saks Fifth Avenue. Louis Vuitton, here I come.*

Needless to say, when I got home—with over ten shopping bags, mind you—the only thing I was greeted to was Bullet's big ass sprawled out on my motherfuckin' white sofa, chewing on my fucking seven-hundred-and-twenty-five-dollar Gucci heels. I must have thrown every damn bag I had at him. You should have seen his behind scurrying back downstairs where he belongs. That fool-ass dog ate up my damn shoe and had the nerve to bark and growl at me when I went down to put him in his cage. Yes, he did. Showed me his teeth and everything. Can you believe that?

That did it! I tried to knock his block off. I'll be damned if some animal is gonna get nasty with me. He has the nerve to chew my shit up and then get funky. I think not! "Don't make me send your ass to the pound," I snapped, smacking him with the fly swatter. "I will fuck you up in here! If you ever growl at me again, I'll bash you. Now get your ass in that cage." He reluctantly got in. I slammed its door shut.

"You got one more time to eat up something of mine and I'm gonna have your fucking teeth knocked out." He laid his big ass down real quick on his blanket and turned his head away from me. He sure did. That block-head dog lays around here eating up everything, doesn't pay a lick of bills and has the nerve to ignore me. Oh, I got a trick for his ass, okay. I kicked his damn cage. "You got one more time," I reminded him, going back up the stairs, "and I'm gonna fuck you up."

I don't know how many times I've told Tee's ass to keep the gate up so he can't get up the stairs. But no, he lets him have full reign of this house. Of course, Tee was nowhere to be found. Actually, he didn't bring his ass home until way after midnight. Hmm-hmm.

Well, let me tell you. That went on for the last three nights with him boppin' in this house late and wrong. Now, the first two times I let it go. But honey chile, last night it was on and poppin' up in here. The minute he walked into the bedroom, flicking on that bright-ass light, I was sitting up in bed just a waiting. And you wanna know what he had the nerve to say when I asked him where he'd been?

"Don't question me," he said, slipping out of his clothes, then heading for the bathroom. Well, I thought I was about to lose my damn mind. Chile, I jumped up out of bed and stormed into the bathroom behind him. He was sitting on the toilet.

"What do you mean, 'don't question' you?"

"Yo, do you mind. I'm tryin' to take a shit."

"Well, I asked you a question," I said, walking up on him, then looking down at his blue Ralph Lauren boxers draped around his ankles. I turned my face up when he grunted, letting out a string of plop-plops.

"What the fuck. I'm taking a shit. You don't like the smell, then get out." He grunted again, then farted a few times. I held my breath, glaring at him. He wiped his ass, then flushed the toilet. I stepped out of his way while he went to the sink to wash his hands. I stared at his back while he brushed his teeth. *Funky ass.* I had to count to ten. I really felt like banging him in back of his head.

"What the hell you staring at?" he asked, looking at me in the mirror, smirking.

"I'm waiting for an answer," I said with one hand on my hip.

"If I wasn't home, then that means I was out," he responded, stepping into the shower. The water turned on. The steam from the shower started to fog up the mirror as I stood there, contemplating my next move. I picked up his boxers and peeked inside. And *NO* I didn't sniff them. I just looked in the crotch area for cum deposit. Humph. Nothing. *Lucky him*, I thought to myself while I moseyed over to the shower. *I should scald his smart ass.* I reached in and turned the dial all the way to the left. *Now, that'll cool his hot ass off.*

"Yo, what the fuck!" he snapped, swinging back the shower curtain. Soapy water dripped from his face and rolled down his body. I looked down at his long dick. "Why the fuck you always gotta play?"

"I'm *not* playing, Damascus."

"Whatever man!" he snarled, swinging the curtain shut, turning the water dial back toward warm. *Whatever man?* I think not! I snatched the curtain back, stepped into the shower with my nightgown still on. "What?" he asked, soaping up his rag, then washing under his arms and across his chest. He turned his back toward me to let the water rinse the front of him, then he turned back around, acting as if I weren't there. He started singing some shit. Right now, I can't think of the man who recorded it. But, Tee was definitely trying to irk me with his "You'll Never Find Another Love Like Mine" bullshit.

I stood there staring him down while he continued washing his body and humming his tune. I concentrated on the heavy stream beating against his back. Before I knew it, I had wrapped one hand around his dick and clamped the other onto his balls, yanking and squeezing. "Don't make me hurt you up in here," I said, pulling harder.

"Aye yo, go 'head with that," he snapped, dropping his washcloth and bar of Dial, grabbing my wrist. I twisted. He winced. "Damn, get off my shit before I hurt you."

"I asked you a fucking question and I want an answer. Now where the *FUCK* you been? You got three seconds before I rip these motherfuckers off." I squeezed his balls harder. He scrunched his face up in pain.

"Aiight! Aiight! I was in Jersey to see Brit. Damn. Now will you get off my balls?"

"Three nights in a damn row?" I let go of his big, hairy balls.

"Yeah. Now get off my fuckin' dick!" *Hmm.* I thought. *He better not be lying. Then again, why would he when he knows I'll ask Brit myself the next time I talk to him?* There's one thing I can be sure of: Britton isn't covering up for anyone. But make no mistake. I was gonna be on the phone first thing in the morning just to be sure. I let go.

"You gotta lot of shit with you," he said staring at my nightgown clinging around my hard nipples. He stepped closer toward me. His breathing was low and controlled. He moved in more, extending and bracing his arms against the checkered blue-and-white tile. I turned my head before his lips touched mine, then attempted to step out of the tub. He grabbed me by the arm, pinning me up against the wall.

"Get off me," I snapped, trying to free my arm.

"Oh hell no. You wanna play, then let's play."

"You're hurting me," I said, trying to wriggle my way out of his grasp. He tightened his grip. "Oww, get off me, Tee."

"You shoulda thought 'bout that before you grabbed my dick." Well, before I could say or do anything else, that fool had shoved his tongue down my throat and had his hand up my wet nightgown, rubbing my pussy. I tried to be strong. I tried to shut my legs tight so he couldn't play in my treasure chest. But I'm so sensitive down below. All you have to do is blow on my pussy and I start dripping, okay. So, I stopped fighting. He stuck his middle finger in my pussy, playing with my clit with his thumb. Then his index finger joined in, searching for a wet treat. I snapped my head back and let him have his way with my love nest. Girl, it was all over the minute he placed those soft lips on my nipple, sucking it over my nightgown. I wrapped my left leg around his waist so he could slide his fingers deep in me. And then without saying a word, he removed his fingers, replacing them with his thick, heavy dick, thrusting deep in me. Awakening pleasure zones. Chile, I was slipping into a sexual coma when he grabbed my other leg around his waist, then lifted me up on his dick.

"You like grabbing on my dick, huh?"

"Hmm-hmm" is the only thing I could say.

"Then let me see you grab it with your pussy." And with the hum of the showerhead beating its water against our bodies, he rammed his eleven inches in and out while my creamy pussy sucked and pulled him deeper in me, gobbling up every inch of him. "That's right, baby. Give me that wet pussy." Girl, need I say more. He banged this pussy up until I screamed in ecstasy and the water turned cold.

Let me tell you. This month has flown by! And I'm glad. If it's not one damn thing it's another. I have been going crazy. Between providing coverage at the shelter, maintaining my two salons and preparing for the grand opening of my third shop in Hartford, I haven't had a moment to think straight.

On top of that, I have my dance studio and Camp Safe Haven—the summer camp I operate for underprivileged youths up in the Poconos. And to add to that, I have the annual winter Cotillion and Scholarship Ball right around the corner. This year's gala will be held in February at the Waldorf. It's in its fifth year and so far—with tickets selling at five-hundred dollars a pop—I have raised over four million dollars to provide full four-year scholarships to outstanding students around the tri-state area.

Of course, these aren't things you would know about unless you ask. Hell, most of you think I'm just some materialistic, cold-hearted bitch. Well… I am. But I'm also very giving *unless* you cross me. Oh, I know it's a little pricey but it's for a good cause. Besides, you know I only rock with the shakers and movers. Hold up. Now who in the world is this calling my cell? It's nonstop. Excuse me for one minute.

"Hello."

"Mrs. Fleet, sorry for disturbing you. This is Charlie over at Minus Contracting. I think we may have a problem."

"And what might that be?"

"We accidentally used the wrong stones for the fireplace in the study, and we put the gas fireplace in the master bedroom on the wrong side of the room."

"Doesn't sound like a problem to me."

"Well, I was wondering…"

"Listen, Charlie. There's no time for wondering. I want everything in my house as specified in my contract. So, the only thing you should be wondering is how long it'll take you to correct your errors, otherwise you'll be *minus* a j-o-b. Now have a good day." *Click*.

Oh my God! I never knew having a house built could be so damn stressful. Every other day the contractors are calling about something or they have to rip something out because they didn't follow instructions. Every time I turn around I'm back on the highway, heading to Fort Lee to see what the heck is going on. Although they assure me the house will be completed on schedule, which is supposed to be in November. Humph, at the rate they're going, I'll be surprised if we're moved in by spring. And of course, Tee blames me for all the delays and confusion. Please. It's not my fault those fools don't pay attention. If I have to move out of my brownstone, then I'm moving into a house that has everything the way I want it. Period. That's right. Fifteen-thousand square feet of living fit for a queen, okay.

But, I tell you one thing. If Tee weren't so insistent that we move, I'd break that damn contract. Oh, please. I already know. That would really throw his ass into a damn conniption. Humph. That's the last thing I need right now, with everything else going on. Trust me.

Damn it! I got off track again. Oh, like I was saying. I don't know if I'm coming or going. All this running around is beginning to take its toll on me. Even getting out of bed has become a task within itself lately. And as you already know, Tee thinks I should either give up or cut back on some of my activities. Unfortunately, that's not an option at this time. But don't tell him I told you that. Hell, I told him if he stopped tryna dig his dick in me all hours of the night I wouldn't be so damn tired. He laughed it off. But I was serious as hell. I had to let him know that my pussy was going on sabbatical.

But on a more serious note—not that my hole being stretched open beyond repair isn't serious, it's just not the immediate priority at this moment—I had been pulling my hair out the last few weeks trying to hire another shelter director because the one I hired two months ago, quit! Yes, she did. After putting in four days of work, Miss Betty Wilkshire left the building for lunch and never returned. She had the nerve to call three days later stating she couldn't handle being cursed at by the kids. Can you believe that? Now, I know some of the girls can get a little mouthy at times, and will let loose a string of curses from time to time. But you have to know how to check 'em.

Sadly, the girls didn't like her. So they would call her names like Big Foot Betty, or Patty Pancake. Well, the woman did have big feet—size twelve to be exact, and a flat ass—not that it made it right for them to be disrespectful. But one thing about teens, they are very perceptive and— if they don't like you, they will zero in on your flaws and deficiencies and use them against you. I had encouraged her to nip their name calling in the bud before it got out of hand but she couldn't seem to rein them in. Humph. Well, between you and me, I'm glad they chased her up out of here. That woman kept a bad case of suction. And let me tell you, there's nothing more disgusting than a flat-assed woman walking around think- ing she's cute with a crack full of fabric sucked in her ass. Ugh!

Anyway…See, these kids don't play with me. I mean, don't get me wrong, a few have tried it on my time—like the young lady who strutted up in here, last week with her mother, thinking she was running things. Chile, listen. My admissions coordinator had buzzed my office when the little darling decided to curse out one of my social workers, then proceeded to use the wall as a punching bag—putting not one hole but two holes in my wall. Now you know I was too through.

So here I come, stepping up toward the office—sharp as a tack in my green beaded Christian Dior blouse and green knee-grazing skirt with the back slit—when I peek through the door and see a sixteen-year-old girl, looking about twenty-five. She was *Goach* down—hat, purse, belt, and shoes—yes, I said Goach. G-o-a-c-h, not Coach, okay. Chile, it was a designer nightmare.

Anyway, a pair of 14-carat doorknockers the size of hula-hoops hung from her ears and she had the nerve to be click-clacking her gum and talking shit to the social worker.

"I ain't signing shit 'cause I ain't staying here," she had said. "What the fuck I look like staying in some stupid-ass shelter with a bunch of fucked-up bitches."

"Well, I'm sorry but you have no other place to go. Going home doesn't seem like an option at this time," Susan responded with frustration registering all over her face.

"Bitch, I got someplace to go!" she snapped at the burgundy-haired social worker then, glared at her mother. "But she won't let me. I don't know why the fuck I can't just live my life." Susan spotted me at the door then politely excused herself while she came out to speak with me in private. The young lady argued with her mother, screaming. She took it down a notch when her mother threatened to knock the taste buds out of her mouth. But she still ran her mouth. A little more than I would have stood for.

I focused on Susan, temporarily blocking out the ruckus that child was making. Although she maintained her professionalism, Susan was clearly agitated. "Indy, I will not go back in there and have to deal with that child talk to me any kind of way. She's called me every name except a child of God. Do you know, that little snot had the nerve to spit her chewing gum at me? I'm sorry, but I don't get paid enough to put up with that kind of abuse."

"Why don't you go 'head and take the rest of the day off," I offered. "I'll finish up in there."

"Humph" she grunted. "Good luck. I'll see you in the a.m." I smiled as she briskly walked in the opposite direction. If I didn't know any better, I'd think she was practically running out the door.

"Hi, I'm Indy," I said, walking back into the room. "I'm going to be finishing up this intake." I extended my hand. Her mother shook it. The young lady stared at it, rolling her eyes while sticking a fresh piece of Wrigley's in her mouth. I stood there for a moment, placing my hand on my hip.

"What the fuck you want?" she asked, with an attitude as wide and as nasty as the Hudson River.

"Colette! Watch your mouth," her mother snapped, then looked up at me. "Do you see what I have to go through?"

"I don't care. That bitch ain't nobody." *Click-clack. Click-clack.* Sistergirl was working that gum.

I parted my lips into a wide phony smile, then asked, "Mrs. Searing, do you mind stepping outside for a moment? I'd like to have a little talk with Colette alone, please." She gave me a nervous smile, slowly getting up from her chair.

"Colette, you mind your manners," she said, glancing over at her before leaving the room.

"Whateva!"

"Oh, she'll be just fine," I reassured, smiling so wide my face would have cracked if it were cold. "Isn't that right, Colette?"

She sucked her teeth. Her mother closed the door behind her.

"Okay," I said, looking directly at her, taking my place behind the desk, then flipping through her intake packet. "Let's get started. I see here your mother reports that you have been staying out late, have become sexually involved with older men and have been cutting school. Is this correct?"

Click-clack, Click-clack.

"Is there any particular reason why you choose to be disrespectful?" *Click-clack*. I let her swim in her thoughts while I continued reading her paperwork. Her mother reported she was unable to manage her daughter and was afraid to discipline her because social services had threatened to press charges on her if she used any form of corporal punishment—whipping her ass, in layman's terms. *Humph*, I thought. *I wish the hell some agency would tell me how to raise my child after I carried them for nine months, wiped their ass and cleaned their snotty nose. I'd go upside that worker's head, then she'd have a reason to press charges.* I almost laughed, imagining me attacking some caseworker for stepping up in my house, talking slick. I pressed on. Hmmm. Her mother also indicated that Miss Click-Clack pushed her down. See. That's why I'm not having kids. 'Cause the first time he or she tried it on my time, I'd end up in jail for sure.

Let me tell you. I lost my mother when I was eight years old and there's nothing I wouldn't do to be able to pick up the phone to hear her sweet voice or to see her beautiful face. Nothing. So, I usually rip into these girls when I hear about them fighting or disrespecting their mothers. I continued skimming the rest of the presenting information, then abruptly stopped when I came to her sex history. She had already had two miscarriages and had been treated for syphilis and gonorrhea. My eyes became glued on the section that asks if she ever had been the victim of a sexual assault. The mother answered *yes*; raped by three teenage boys at knifepoint.

Click-clack. Click-clack.

I got up to walk around the wooden desk, then knelt down in front of her. Perhaps a softer approach would work. "Colette, sweetheart. I know you're angry about being here. And that's okay. But I want you to know that I understand your pain. I know what you're going through."

Click-clack. Click-clack.

"I want to help you get through this," I continued. "I know you're hurting but if you don't let it out, it will only get worse." Now mind you, I never put my hand on her and I am as sweet as can be. She flicked something from under her fingernail toward me. Now she was starting to work my last nerve but I remained calm. "I know firsthand what holding on to your pain can do to you. It will destroy everything you touch."

"Fuck you!" she snapped, screaming. "You don't know shit! So get the fuck out my face! I don't have to fucking talk to you if I don't want." She gave me eye contact. Brought her face inches away from mine. Stared me down. "I said get the fuuuuck out my face, bitch!" The word *bitch*—coming from a child—grated along my flesh worse than the sound of someone dragging fingernails across a chalkboard. I pursed my lips tight. Alrighty then. I got up and walked over to the door, locking it. Then I took off my earrings, my two tennis bracelets and rings. I laid them on the desk in front of her, then kicked off my six-inch Dior stilettos. Pain or no pain, hurt or no hurt, it was about to be on up in here. She watched my every move.

"Let me tell you one damn thing, Little Miss Thing," I snapped, slamming my hands on the desk. "As long as you breathe the same air I do, if you *ever* call me out my name again, I will snatch your tongue out your mouth and whip you with it." I placed my palms flat on the desk, then leaned in toward her, clenching my teeth. "I'm not your mother and I'm not your friend. I don't care how old you are and I don't give a fuck where you're from. You think you're hot shit 'cause you talk to your mother any kind of way, and lay on your back with old-ass men. Well, let me tell you something, Miss Grown Ass, your mother might be afraid to get with that ass up in this piece but I'm not. After I beat some manners into you, I'll call protective services myself and think nothing about it. So stand up and let's get it on." I came from around the desk, then took my fighting stance, waiting for her to make her move. She sat stone-still.

Now say what you want. I don't care if it wasn't professional of me. I might have some postgraduate professional training in mental health, okay. But my degrees are not in psychology. And being pragmatic, forget it! I don't go in for anyone's child talking slick, okay. And I don't discriminate. I don't care if you're six or twenty-six. You come out your face wrong and it's on. I have no problem getting down on my knees to fight a toddler if I have to, okay. You can laugh if you want. But I'm serious. I will sling your ass.

Anyway, I didn't really want to go there with her but I had to let her know she wasn't movin' no mountains here. And she damn sure wasn't pumpin' no Kool-Aid, okay. We were here to help her and that *is* what we were going to do, even if it meant I had to beat her down first.

I snatched her purse as she was getting ready to dig in it, and threw it across the room. Chile, listen, I didn't know what the hell she was gonna pull out and I wasn't gonna stand around to find out. And you know like I do, these kids nowadays like using weapons, okay.

"Oh no, dear," I said. "We don't do weapons here. You wanna rock, then we rock with the hands. Now let's go." Girlfriend was shook now. 'Cause she wasn't expecting a fly-ass *bitch* like me to step to her like that. So to make a long story short, she changed her tone real quick and we finished our admission without further incident. That was almost a week ago. She's still giving staff and some of the other girls a run for their money. But she has settled into being here, has patched those holes up and painted the wall, and is now—although still a little resistant—working on her issues, okay. Nandi's here to teach these girls how to continue loving themselves when no one else will.

Wait a minute now! I'm not advocating that approach. I'm just letting you know how I had to check her. For the record, there's nothing in the world I wouldn't do for my girls, but if you come off wrong, I'm checkin' you with the quickness, okay. 'Cause sometimes you have to throw out that crap about 'sugar and spice, and everything nice' and get down and dirty, if you know what I mean. Oh, don't give me that look. You know as well as I do that some of these girls are mean and nasty. They tease, insult, threaten and can be downright malicious. But make no mistake that situation with Colette was the last straw for me. I don't have the patience I used to with some of the more challenging teens. And I know if I didn't do something quick, fast, and in a hurry, I'd end up on Riker's Island. So, I got on the phone and called the one person whom I knew could run this shelter with a firm yet compassionate hand.

"Britton, I need your help," I said the minute he picked up.

"Indy, what's wrong? Is everything okay?"

"No, it's not. How would you like to be the new director of Nandi's?"

"You're kidding, right?" he asked, laughing.

"No. I'm dead ass. I've gone through two directors in the last six months and four social workers. I'm in a state of crisis. I need someone who can get in here and hit the ground running. That person is you. I know you've only been home for a few weeks so I'm sure you haven't had time to look for a job, yet. Well, I have an opening." Whew! I was talking so fast, I had to stop for a deep breath. "And I need someone here with the proper credentials. Britton, you have the skills needed at Nandi's."

"Indy, I'm flattered…but I mean. I love you and all, but I don't know if I could work with you or for you." Chile, listen. I was starting to hyperventilate. I was desperate, okay. And he was my only hope.

"Don't worry, you can run it however you see fit. I trust your professional abilities."

"Well…" He paused. "I don't know. I like the idea of working my own hours—"

"Well, you can."

"I tell you what. Why don't I help you find someone?"

"No!" I snapped. "I want you. Now name your price, damn it! Whatever you want. It's yours."

"Girl, you know I'd do anything for you 'cause you've always been there for me, but I'm here in Jersey and Nandi's is way up in Chester. That's like an hour-and-a-half commute one-way—depending on traffic—and with a twenty-four-hour facility like that, it would require some late nights."

"You can set your own hours. I already told you that. I'll even put you up in one of the new condo or townhouse developments here and throw in a new car as an extra perk."

"Hmmm. And then I'll have to worry about daycare."

"No, you won't. I already have a daycare facility on grounds for staff. Anything else?"

"Damn," he said, laughing. "You've thought of everything."

"Absolutely. So will you at least think about it?"

"Indy, if it were anyplace else I'd probably jump on it but *Chester, NY?* That's not an appealing location for me." Hmm. He's playing hardball.

"Would seventy thousand to start be appealing enough for you?"

He started coughing. "What did you say?" *Got 'em!*

"I *said*, how's seventy thousand?"

"And, I still get the house?"

"Yes. I'll even buy you a new wardrobe if you'd like. 'Cause I know how poppa likes to shop." Of course I'd have to run the salary offer by the board of directors, not that it mattered because they were all on my team, if you know what I mean. So I get what I want.

"Well," he said, laughing. "With an offer like that how can I resist?"

"You can't," I said, smiling.

"Hmm, hmm," he said, "And if you start your shit, I'm out."

"Oh, boy, please. Not me. I promise, you won't even know I'm around." He started laughing. "What? You don't believe me? I'm serious. I'll be as silent as a lamb. Well, at least for the first few months. Then I can't make any promises I might not be able to keep."

"I mean it, Indy. The minute you start up, I'm bouncing."

"I heard you. Now when can you start?" He paused. I'm sure to make me sweat it out a little longer.

"Umm. Well…Let me see. Hmmm. How about in two weeks? I have some things I need to take care of first."

"Perfect!" I clapped. "Boy, I'm so glad you're home. I don't know what I'd do without you. I love you, baby."

"I know you do. I love you too. You just make sure you have enough money in your budget to pay me, 'cause this is gonna cost you. And I still want that car, 'cause you know a brotha gotta have a ride to get around up in those woods."

"Oh, don't you worry," I said, laughing. "I got you covered." I blew him a big kiss, then hung up. Chile, I was ecstatic. I would be killing two birds with one stone: we'd both be helping the other and this would ensure he hung around for a while. That man has done more moving around than a nomad so there's no telling where his impulsive behind would end up next if I hadn't come up with this plan. Call it selfish if you want. The bottom line, I just want my friend around, okay.

Anyway, I don't know why I hadn't thought of this sooner. Come to think about it, why didn't any of you think of it. Damn! What's the point of having you around if you can't even offer me some sound suggestions? Humph.

Nevertheless, in another eight days, Britton will come in here and whip this place back into shape in no time. Knowing that, that'll be one less thing I'll have to stress over, I'll be able to concentrate on other things. And although I really hate to do it, I'm seriously considering the possibility of having more free time before I end up having a breakdown or something. 'Cause, between you and me, I'm so fucking tired right now. I could pass out. For once, I have to agree with Tee—I need to be home more.

Speaking of which, I was getting ready to call him to let him know I was coming home early so he could take *me*—oops! Did I say me? I meant so *we* could go out for dinner when my cell phone rang. I looked at the caller ID. It was the shop.

"Hello."

"Hello, Indy?"

"Speaking."

"Hey, girl. We have a situation down at the shop that needs your immediate attention."

It was Coffee, my shop manager. Actually, her name is Coffeena but everyone calls her Coffee because of her deep-brown complexion. She's a full-breasted, thick-hipped sista with a slim waist, standing about five nine. Girlfriend rocks waist-length locks and has the most beautiful brown eyes I've ever seen. The girl is gorgeous and doesn't even know it. I know you're waiting for *but*, but there's none. Humph. I don't know why you think I always have something bad to say about people. I give compliments when and where compliments are due. Damn.

"Well, what's the problem?" I asked, getting concerned. Out of all the managers I've had, Coffee is the most competent. She's a no-nonsense sista who knows the hair business like the back of her hand. We met a few years ago at one of the Bronner Brothers hair shows in Atlanta and clicked right from the gate. So when she approached me last year about the possibility of working for me, I snatched her up without blinking an eye. She's been working for me ever since. What I like most about her is she can handle any situation without breaking a sweat. Homegirl rarely calls me about anything, so if she's blowing my phone line, it must be major.

"There's a woman here, ranting and raving about someone chasing her.

And you saying something about giving her a job until the coast is clear."

"Until the coast is clear? Chile, I don't know anything about anyone starting a job. Unless you fired someone or someone quit, there are no chair vacancies."

"I know. That's what I told her but she's insistent. Says she's not leaving here until she speaks with you."

"What's her name?"

"She wouldn't give her name. She mumbled something about it being confidential information. Said you'd know who she was."

"Well, what does she look like?"

"Tall, attractive, dark-skinned, wearing a long black-and-white wig, and dragging a suitcase. If you ask me, she seems a little touched."

Touched? Oh no! That could be no one other than, "Sarina!" I shouted. Of all the days to show up at the salon, she picks Friday, one of the busiest days of the week. In the background I could hear someone yelling, "What the fuck you looking at?"

Someone responded, "You."

Then I heard, "Bite me, bitch!"

"Damn it!" I snapped. "I'll be right there. And whatever you do, don't let her leave."

"Well, hurry up," she urged. "It might get ugly up in here real quick." I slammed down the phone, grabbed my keys and jumped in my 745i. I pushed play on my CD remote and waited for Syleena Johnson's *Chapter 1: Love, Pain & Forgiveness* to entertain me while I made my way to Manhattan, pushing ninety miles per hour on Route 17 to I-87 for the New York State Thruway.

And let me tell you how I was cruising along—had just merged onto Palisades Parkway South—minding my own business, jamming to my beats when a white couple—who had to be doing every bit of a hundred, if I was doing ninety, ninety-five—cut over into my lane without using their blinker. Then he cut back over. Chile, it almost scared the shit out of me. Then the fool had the nerve to give me the finger when I pressed down on my horn, speeding up alongside them, like "what the fuck!" You should have seen us with our windows down, arguing. I had my passenger side down while he had his driver's side down. Then he pulled off, crossing over into my lane—again—where he decided to brake in front of me. The fool was trying to cause an accident. And he was plucking my nerves, okay. So I pressed the menu button on my car phone, scrolled through my phone-book, then pressed talk.

"Hello," the woman on the other end said.

"Girl, I need you to run this fool's plates and get back to me." I gave her his N.Y. tag numbers.

"I'm on it," she replied, hanging up. That's right. I called my girl down at the Brooklyn DMV and she will pull up all the info I need. 'Cause in the morning when that bitch ass man tries to drive off in his shiny new Porsche, he'll need a flatbed to do it, okay!

Anyway, by the time I screeched in front of Weaves and Wonders it was four o'clock. I had made it there in a record-breaking forty-nine minutes and-twenty-six seconds. And before I could even walk through the door, I was greeted by Coffee. Through the window I could see it was packed with women tryna get their hair and nails *did* for a night of cocktailing and hip shaking. As you know, Weaves and Wonders caters to a mixture of clientele, from the bourgeois to the ghetto-fabulous and everything in between from male, female and confused.

"Girl, I'm sure glad to see you. I don't know who that child is, but the bitch is crazy. I had to stop two customers from smashing her chin."

"Where is she now?" I asked, walking through the glass doors, sweating like a horse.

"She's in your office."

"*Whaaat?!*" I snapped.

"It was the only thing I could think to do to keep her quiet and out of sight." I ran toward my office with her saying, "Don't worry, everything's locked up."

"Hey, Indy," a few customers called out to me. I threw them a quick wave and smile. I heard someone say, "If I didn't just get my nails done, I woulda slid that bitch."

"I know that's right," another customer responded. The only thing on my mind was what the hell Miss Sarina was doing. You should have seen me racing to my office. The last thing I needed or wanted was her ass ransacking my shit. I swung the door open in anticipation of catching her red-handed. Instead, I walked into a room full of smoke. I stopped dead in my tracks, fanning the air around me. I coughed. Homegirl was lighting one cigarette after the other, wearing a hole in my plush carpet, pacing the damn room.

"Well, it's about damn time," she snapped, taking a long pull of her Newport, then tossing it in my green leather trashcan.

"Girl, what the hell do you think you're doing?" I asked, rushing over to put out her smoldering cigarette before she burned my place down. "Have you lost your damn mind?" I shut my office door, then opened the ceiling vents.

"Oh, chill out, whinch biscuit. There's nothing in there but a bunch of papers."

Whinch biscuit? Now what in the world is that? But instead of responding, I caught myself before I said something unkind. "So what brings you to New York?" I asked, trying to figure out what the hell she had on. Girlfriend was in a yellow lace mini-skirt with a matching lace bikini top under a long-flowing satin three-quarter blazer. She wore a pair of yellow thigh-high converse sneakers to set her suit off. She looked like she was ready to do a video shoot for "Send in the Clowns."

Chile, you could see right through that mess. She plopped her ass up on my desk, sitting with her legs wide open. I gagged when I caught a glimpse of her pussy hairs sticking out from around the edges of her yellow thong. Oh my God! It looked like a wild jungle of nastiness. And then Miss Thing-a-ling had the nerve to do a scratch 'n sniff. Yes, she did! She scratched her pussy right in my face, then sniffed her fingers. I was too through. *Nasty cuss*, I thought, twisting my nose up. "Sarina, do me a favor. Get your ass up off my desk."

"I'm on tour," she replied, pulling off her waist-length wig, then leaning back on her forearms. *No, this crazy bitch didn't ignore me*, I thought to myself.

"Sarina," I said, with a forced smile. "Don't make me hurt you up in here. Now get your ass off my desk." She tossed her wig over onto the green leather sofa and slowly dragged her ass along the edge of my desk. *I'm about to snatch this bitch real quick.* I slowly counted to ten. She got up and sat her ass down on the sofa. "Now what is this about being on tour?"

"Ugh! I'm showcasing my Fall Collection of Sarina Creations, duh."

Let it go, girl. For Chyna's sake, just be happy she's safe and alive. I pressed on. "So where are you staying?"

"Under cobwebs," she replied, picking her nose. She flicked something to the floor. I took a deep breath, trying to keep a straight face. *She's special needs,* I reminded myself. *Be patient.* I continued, trying my hardest to keep everything Chyna had said to me about her illness in the forefront of my mind. Chile, it wasn't easy.

"Oh. I see," I said, taking a seat in the chair across from her. I crossed my legs, placing my hands in my lap. "So how long will you be in town?"

"Well," she sighed, crossing, then uncrossing her long, shapely legs. "I'm not sure." I had to admit, girlfriend—nutty or not—had some gorgeous legs. And honestly speaking, she's a very pretty girl. The poor thing has her father's rich, dark complexion and facial features and her mother's beautiful, smooth skin and gorgeous shape. I'd say she's very lucky, considering what her father looks like. Girl, I love Chyna to death, but I still can't figure out how the hell she's able to wake up every morning to that man's face. Chile, it's enough to scare E.T. home. That's all I'll say. Humph. Well, he's good to her so that's really all that matters.

"I see. Well, have you spoken to your mother?"

"I don't have a mother," she snapped, smoothing down the sides of her wig. She burst into laughter. "My mother died when she gave birth to me."

Chile, I was at a lost for words. "I'm so sorry you feel that way."

"Oh, please. She was nothing but a garden of rotted skunk cabbage anyway." Alrighty then. Moving on.

"Well, I'm sure your father and brothers are worried about you."

She cocked her head to the side, raising her right brow. "Now, I don't think that's any of your business." She was definitely asking for it, don't you think?

"Girlfriend," I said, trying my best to keep a smile on my face. "You're in my shop, sitting in my office, so it is my business. So don't go there."

She laughed in my face. "You so silly. If I tell you something, you have to promise me you won't repeat a word of it." She paused, placing her wig back on her head. For the life of me, I can't understand why she'd rather wear wigs when she has a head of beautiful thick hair—well, she does when she's not chopping it off. "I don't want this leaking out to my fans."

Oh Lord! "Of course," I said, getting up from my seat to sit with her at the far end of the sofa. I turned to face her. Now you know, the whole time I was thinking, *I need to get in touch with Chyna* ASAP!

"I'm being watched," she whispered. "So right now, I don't know how long I'll be here."

"Oh my!" I said, feigning worry. "Who's watching you?"

"There's these pilgrims with fangs trying to kill my best friend. They've been following me every since I got to New York." I had to catch my mouth from dropping open. I studied her face for a moment, trying to see if she'd crack a smile. She didn't. I hoped it was only a sick joke. It wasn't. She was as serious as a heart attack.

"Well," I said, looking around the room, "where's your friend, now?"

"I've hid her. But—"

"We need to call the police then," I offered, cutting her off.

"No!" she snapped. "They'll kill us for sure."

"Sarina, we have to get you some help."

"Sssh," she said, putting her finger to her lips. "The walls have ears." I stared at her with wide-eyed amazement.

"Nonsense, girl. No one is listening to us."

"Hush!" she snarled, getting up to look under the sofa, between the cushions, then under my desk. "I think your office is bugged." Now you know it was time to get up and make that phone call.

"Sarina, dear," I said, trying my best to keep my tone even. "Why don't you come back and have a seat?" She started pacing the room. "Sarina, did you hear me. Come sit down." She continued, back and forth. I sat and watched her looking around the room, staring at the walls. She started counting. I glanced over at her luggage, then back over at her, picturing her wandering the streets of New York, dragging her suitcase behind her the way a vagabond meanders through life. And do you wanna know something? For the first time in a very long time, my heart ached for her. I saw my best friend's child beginning to fly over her cuckoo's nest, right before my eyes.

"You have spiders all over your walls." She burst out in laughter. "You better go hide before they eat you." She started making biting gestures and clacking sounds with her teeth, sitting back down, smiling. Then out of nowhere, she started crying as she sang "The Itsy, Bitsy Spider."

"This song makes me so emotional," she said, rocking from side to side, humming. She removed her wig again, wiping her face with it.

"Sarina, I'll be right back," I said, grabbing my purse and keys. Please. There was no way I was leaving my keys for her to bounce in my shit. I'd have to beat her down for sure. "I need to check on a few things out front. You sit tight, okay?" She nodded, pulling out another cigarette. "Unh-huh, don't you dare," I snapped, glaring at the matches in her hand. I kindly walked over and confiscated them and the three lighters in her satin drawstring purse. Then I made her stand up so I could pat her down to make sure she didn't have anything else that could burn the roof down.

Chile. Let me tell you. When I bent down to feel around her ankles, I almost passed out. The smell from her ass almost killed me. It smelled like she had soaked in chitlin juice—Oh, I know it's chitterling juice. Chitlins. Chitterlings. Who the hell cares? The bitch smelled like shit, okay. Ugh! I got lightheaded from quickly snatching up my head. Girl-friend was a walking funk box.

"You wanna look in my nest too?" she asked, giggling. "That's where I keep my spider eggs." Girl, listen. I popped my hips down the hallway, went into the staff lounge and flipped open my cell, leaving a fierce message for Chyna to call me *immediately*.

16

CHYNA: *Lost Ones*

If this were a perfect world we lived in, I'd still be in Slovenia, strolling along the streets of Ljubljana, enjoying the picturesque streets latticed with stone bridges over the Ljublanica River and hemmed by weeping willows. I'd be sitting outside an open-air café, sipping on cappuccino or eating their beloved gelato while playing footsies with my husband. Or I'd be in Piran—a city with Venetian Gothic architecture and labyrinth-like alleys—with Ryan, holding hands as we walked, taking in the crisp blueness of the Adriatic Sea, along the narrow curve where Italy becomes Slovenia and Slovenia becomes Croatia. But instead, I'm on 95 North, heading to New York to pick up my daughter.

Sometimes I don't know if I'm coming or going. The last three years have been wonderful on one hand, and stressful on the other, to say the least. Ryan and I have never been more in love. I've spent twenty-six of my thirty-nine-and-a-half years with him. And for that, I'm grateful; he's not only my husband and lover, he's my friend and soul mate. Although there was a time when the flame in our marriage had blown out, and I became consumed with the possibility of Ryan and me drifting into separate corners of the world, Ryan loved me enough to want to strike another match. He's the man I gave myself to at fourteen, bore his four children, and have loved with everything that is in me. Truth be told, I couldn't imagine life without him in it.

And to think I almost allowed my own insecurities and uncertainties to drive him away. I had allowed my imagination to get the best of me, creating images of him having an affair with the woman I saw him dancing with at the Georgetown Country Club. Not to mention, having Indy to add fuel to the fire with her "I hate cheating men" slogan. So for two years I said nothing.

Instead of confronting him about what I thought I had seen, I threw him out of our bedroom and went on shutdown. I let the thought of his infidelity fester, isolating myself physically, mentally and emotionally. And for whatever reason, his guilt enabled him to distance himself from me as well. So we lived under the same roof, going through the motions of being the picture-perfect family for the sake of appearance. I was unhappy.

But what I soon learned was that my unhappiness was more internal than external. Yes, my marriage was in a state of disarray, but so was I. And until I figured out what I needed for me, first—instead of putting the needs, desires and wants of my children and husband before my own—I would always be miserable. I'm not saying there was anything wrong with meeting the needs of my family. Sometimes we have to put their needs before our own. But when you create your whole existence solely around them, you begin to lose yourself in the process. Which is what I did. Bit by bit, I had allowed myself to become so consumed with the needs of everyone else that I lost sight of what was important for me—and to me. You see. My children were my life. I had given so much of myself to them, and to Ryan, that there wasn't anything left for me to give to myself. Does that make any sense to you? I felt drained. I was confused. And I felt lost.

So I found temporary solace in pursuing two master's degrees, which I completed simultaneously in three years. Yet, no matter how many degrees I obtained, there was still something missing. I knew it. Felt it. But just couldn't put my finger on it. It almost felt as if I had been sucked into a vacuum. Sadly—when you got right down to it, at the end of the day, I was an overeducated housewife. And as much as I didn't want to admit it, Indy *and* Sarina had been right. I needed to "get a damn life," as they both so eloquently put it.

Once the boys were out of the house, and Sarina was quickly approaching eighteen, the reality of their words became painfully clear. On the surface, I lived a beautiful lifestyle, but knew nothing about living a life of my own. With all of my education, I had nothing. And it was scary. Indy had warned me time and time again, "Girl, you had better start doing you. If Ryan ever decides to walk out on you, or God forbid something happens to him, what are you gonna do?" Sad to say, I honestly couldn't answer her. A part of me wished I could have been more like her: strong-willed, independent, and focused. But then I probably wouldn't be with the man who soothes my soul. And I wouldn't have had my four beautiful children. Ryan Jr., Kayin, Jayson and Sarina were what kept me going when I felt like giving up.

Oh, yes. There was a time in my life when I contemplated suicide. I didn't actually have a plan or any intent. It was only a fleeting thought. But the idea was there just the same. And if you asked me, "why?" I really couldn't tell you. All I know is I'm thankful I didn't act on it.

Nothing is worth taking your life, at least not for me. But I can honestly understand how one might feel when their back is up against the wall and they feel like the walls are closing in on them, leaving no where to turn and no way out. Or when you feel as though your life has no real meaning. Or when you want to throw your hands up, and scream. I've been there. However, I also know that there's a light at the end of every tunnel. And no matter what obstacles are placed before me I can overcome them with faith and prayer.

Nevertheless, I knew as long as I continued carrying around my own emotional baggage—particularly scars from my childhood, I would never be able to move forward as a mother or a wife. As long as I remained detached from my own feelings and held on to the secrets of my past, I'd always be going through the motions with no sense of time, direction, or purpose. I'd be wandering through life, feeling like nothing; looking for nothing.

Consequently, I knew I would never be able to help my daughter unless I took a truthful look at my own issues, and addressed them head-on. I am so thankful I made that call to Dr. Mills, a wonderful psychologist who helped me identify and process my own self-defeating behaviors. She helped me see that I am a woman—first—then a wife and mother. And that it's okay to need and want time for me. And I was able to come to terms with my checkered past, and move forward. And for that, I am forever grateful.

With the help of Dr. Mills, I was able to evolve, progress, and grow—not only as a woman—as a mother, wife, lover and friend. And through my journey of self-discovery, I found me. And as a result of my own healing process, I've been able to help others, particularly children, who have felt unwanted, unconnected or undervalued in the world.

Soul Quests—a day treatment program I developed—has been going strong for the last three years, helping to instill self-love, self-pride, and self-respect in adolescents who struggle with identity issues and are faced with racist attitudes among peers and within their families. Through ongoing counseling, mentoring, and cultural activities, Soul Quests has been able to help our youth develop positive self-images and increase their feelings of self-worth. The goal is to help them love, respect, and be proud of who they are in an ever-changing world. Isn't it ironic how I'm able to make a difference in the life of someone else's child, except my own?

You don't know how distressing and frustrating it is trying to help someone who doesn't want to help themselves. Particularly when it's your own child. But as the saying goes, you can lead a horse to water, but you can't make them drink it. Unfortunately, no matter how many times I replay those words in my head, it's still hard, accepting the truth. And right at this moment—the reality is, trying to help Sarina want to help herself is the most stressful part of my life.

My beautiful and talented daughter fights me tooth and nail when it comes to addressing her psychological and emotional needs. For whatever reason, I'm her enemy. The one she sees as trying to bring her harm when in fact she's her own worse enemy. However, with love and patience, I am hoping that one day she will be ready to tear down her self-built prison walls to free herself from her turmoil. That's all I can do. Hope and pray.

So for the last three years, I have been trying to help Sarina find the strength to face her future optimistically. And she's been combating me every step of the way. She's always had aspirations of becoming a fashion designer. I mean the girl really has a gift if only she stayed focused. She can draw, sketch a design and make patterns with her eyes closed. She even attended school for a brief moment; but, of course, it was short-lived since she became bored with the process of learning. And then she felt her peers were trying to sabotage her. So she stopped going.

It's been like this for years. In high school, she'd start a project, then lose interest before she even completed it. Or she'd disrupt the class or not go. I was so disappointed when she dropped out of high school in the beginning of her senior year, I almost cried. But there comes a point when you have to let your child make his or her own decisions, no matter how wrong you feel it is. Besides, like Ryan said when I told him Sarina wanted to sign out of school, "What difference does it make, she's never in school anyway." As true as that was, I still had hoped he would have argued, even demanded, she finished her education. He didn't. And I had to come to grips with the fact a traditional school setting wasn't for her. Fortunately, she did complete her GED. And I couldn't help but be proud, because if nothing else, she stuck something out, and achieved a goal (then again, she was on her medications, and taking them regularly at that time). Unfortunately, she doesn't have the coping skills to achieve more. Particularly now since she refuses to take her medications.

And sadly, without the proper direction and life skills, Sarina will not be able to live a healthy productive life in society. And that saddens me. Because I know that Ryan and I aren't always going to be around to care for her. No parent wants to accept the possibility that there might be something wrong with their child. And the truth is sometimes hard to swallow. At least it was for me.

For years, I was in denial. I denied Sarina was in a state of psychiatric distress. And I denied my family's mental health history, and how that might potentially have an effect on my children. I thought if I acted like it didn't exist, then it wouldn't. And whatever behaviors Sarina exhibited that resembled anything remotely consistent with a psychiatric disorder would disappear. But it did exist, and became more apparent as time went on. And had it not been for Sarina having her first breakdown three years ago, I'd still be denying her mental health issues, the state of my marriage, and my own sense of worthlessness.

See, Sarina suffers from schizophrenia—a serious psychiatric illness that strikes young people in their prime, making it very difficult for them to distinguish between what is real and what isn't. Although the usual onset is between sixteen and twenty-five, thinking back, I suspect she developed the telltale signs of the disorder when she turned fifteen. On second thought, now that I'm sharing this with you, her personality actually began to change when she turned thirteen. 'Cause before then, she was the sweetest child you'd ever wanted to meet. It was almost as if that magical number—thirteen—triggered a hormonal imbalance, causing her to be defiant, oppositional and extremely aggressive without provocation. But I chalked it up as typical adolescent behaviors, dismissing any thoughts that her out-of-control behaviors were the result of something more serious. I allowed my love for my only daughter to blindside me from the horrible truth.

Even as a toddler, Sarina was always testing limits and was extremely moody, oftentimes having uncontrollable outbursts that would last for hours on end. And her imagination was always getting the best of her. She'd come running into the room, screaming, "Purple sheep are trying to bite me!" Or she'd be sitting by her window for hours, and when asked what she was doing, she'd simply say things like, "I'm waiting for my spaceship to come." I wanted so bad to believe she said—and did—odd things for attention instead of there being an underlying psychiatric disorder.

However, the older she got, the more bizarre her behaviors became. And she always seemed to be daydreaming endlessly. Gradually, she began to display inappropriate emotions. I can recall one particular incident—when she was about sixteen—when I received a phone call from my neighbor, informing me that another neighbor's daughter had been hit by a car and was in critical condition. Since Sarina had gone to school with her and they were friendly, I expected her to be somewhat distressed by the news.

Instead, she grinned, then burst into laughter, saying the girl was a cascade of falling water in a dirty cloud. I was taken aback to say the least.

As time went on, her style of dress became more eccentric. She began wearing outlandish outfits that I initially chalked up as self-expression. But when she started shaving her head bald, and her eyebrows off because she believed bugs were crawling on her, I knew something was remarkably wrong. Yet, in all the years we spent in individual and family counseling, I still said nothing about my family's history of psychiatric illness. There was nothing wrong with me. And my three sons were unaffected by any genetic predisposition. So I wanted Sarina to be exempt from it as well.

But like my twenty-one-year-old manic-depressive mother who committed suicide a few hours after secretly giving birth to me, and my grandmother who suffered from psychotic episodes—causing her to ultimately stab my step-grandfather to death, Sarina, too, was affected by this dreadful brain disease. A lifelong disease that can be controlled but not cured. Nevertheless, I still refused to acknowledge her illness.

And it wasn't until I found her hiding naked under a table in her bedroom, holding a butcher knife, that everything I tried hard to ignore, or forget, came flashing before my eyes. The first twelve years of my life in New Orleans under the guardianship of my paranoid and delusional grandmother. A life of horror and isolation I never discussed or mentioned to my husband, or anyone else for that matter, out of shame and embarrassment. Truth of the matter, mental illness is something most families would rather keep hidden in a closet than discuss or admit it exists.

I guess it's a wonder I turned out the way I did, considering everything I witnessed as a child. The ritualistic hand washing, the chanting, the drinking animal blood, the ranting and raving about "the darkie coons stealing babies," the locking and double-locking of doors, and a long list of other disturbing and strange behaviors was life behind closed doors with Lucretia Devereaux; a woman with mesmerizing beauty and a closet full of demons. She was a woman people feared.

Thinking back, I can't recall one time when she put her arms around me, or said she loved me. Displays of affection were unheard of. The only emotions shown were that of anger and rage. Instead of kind words and a loving embrace, outbursts and violent acts—or being completely ignored for days—were the only things I was exposed to. I suppose, despite it all, it's a blessing she never physically harmed me. Consequently, I haven't figured out which was the lesser of the two evils: being physically abused or emotionally neglected. Interestingly, I don't blame my grandmother for anything. She wasn't a well woman. And she wasn't in her right frame of mind. I've accepted that. But, it's still hurtful, and it's left scars as reminders.

However, I guess her hospitalization saved me. Who's to say her dangerous delusions wouldn't have commanded her to harm me? There were many nights she'd frantically run through the house wielding a butcher knife, screaming. When I was removed from her home and sent to live with my aunt in Norfolk, it was then that the secrets of my family's past began to unravel. Had my aunt not disclosed that the woman whom I had been living with for twelve years was really my grandmother, I would have continued through life thinking she was my mother. Not that it mattered anyway. She's the only mother I knew. God rest her soul. And I would still have thought my step-grandfather was just that, instead of being the man who carried on a four-year sexual relationship with my grandmother's daughter—my mother. The consequence: my birth. Guilt and shame caused my mother to take her life, and my grandmother to take the life of someone else. Regardless of everything, I like to believe that both women are now in a much better place.

I do thank God for my aunt Chanty being in my life, though. She tried her best to make sense out of all the madness. And she did her best to show me the love I never knew. For she understood what I had been subjected to. She had lived it, and escaped it, never looking back.

But I was already so deprived emotionally that nothing she said or did made me feel loved, or liked, for that matter. Despite my exotic beauty, I felt like a freak. A creature. The color of my skin and texture of my hair were my curse. And I hated everything I saw. Ambiguity. I felt black. But didn't look black. I struggled trying to blend into a culture that didn't embrace me, understand me or even want me. I was trapped. Lonely. Invisible.

It has taken me years to finally be comfortable in the skin I'm in. Sadly, the color of my skin and hair texture was not only a source of contention for me as a child. But, it's been one for Sarina as well. I never thought I'd live to see the day when my own daughter would despise me for being who she feels she should be: light-skinned with long flowing hair, and piercing green eyes. I grew up feeling like I had been cursed, wanting desperately to be smothered in the rich heritage of our blackness. Yet, Sarina hates the skin she's in. My beautiful daughter feels cursed for having rich, dark skin as smooth as chocolate. She'd rather be me.

For those of you who don't know, my family lineage is that of French, Irish and African. My great-great-great-grandmother was an African princess who was ripped from her family and homeland, and brought to America in shackles. But—through repeated rapes by her wealthy slave owner, multiple births and arranged marriages—her beautiful, rich features were weakened, bringing forth a legacy of fair-skinned, blue or green-eyed, blond-haired men and women who refused to acknowledge their African roots. It was a sin to be black. "White was right." The lighter the skin, the better. Passing became their way of life.

Yes, because of their sick, twisted way of thinking, my bloodline has been so diluted that I, too, can pass. I lived my first twelve years of my life, speaking French and living like I was white because that's what I was forced to believe. But, something deep within me told me differently. See. I was mesmerized by beautiful black skin. And like my aunt Chanty—who was shunned and disowned, I chose to live my life as a black woman. Which *is* what I am. Beautiful. Strong. And Black.

Anyway, on top of everything else I had to go through, I spent most of my adulthood fearing I'd turn out like my grandmother. I went through life holding my breath, waiting for the day when the voices would come steal my sanity away. I didn't know the minute or the hour, but I believed in my heart the day would come. And it has—through Sarina. And you don't know how consumed I was with guilt, for not speaking up sooner.

I blamed myself for Sarina being stricken with this illness rather than me. But keeping to tradition, the secrets were kept. And it has cost me, dearly.

Although I know I'm not to blame for Sarina's mental health issues, I could have gotten her the proper treatment instead of spending thousands of dollars on counseling interventions that weren't addressing the underlying cause of her behaviors. Fortunately, through my own counseling, I've been able to move past my guilt and focus on getting my child the help she needs.

And with the help of NAMI—the National Alliance for the Mentally Ill—which offers support groups, conferences, and education programs, I have found the network system I need to help my daughter get through this. I have learned that I am not alone in my fight to address issues related to Sarina's illness. And I'm empowered. So, no matter what, I refuse to give up on her. She's my daughter, and I could never turn my back on her.

There are so many people who are mentally ill, living on the streets because mental health institutions have either closed their doors on them or been shut down due to budget cuts or unsafe conditions. Or loved ones have turned their backs on them, forcing them to live without any support. So they take to the streets, being unheard and unwanted. Considered social outcasts. Oftentimes labeled "bag ladies," "bums," and "tramps." The tattered and torn. The same men and women we see pushing shopping carts—carrying all their worldly possessions, or walking back and forth or standing on corners, having what appears to be conversations with themselves. These are the ones we see suffering. What about the ones who have slipped through the cracks unseen? What happens to the ones who remain in hiding: invisible and miserable?

What about the men and women who become funneled into the criminal justice system under the watch of correctional institutions that are not trained or equipped to provide these offenders with the type of mental health interventions needed? Sadly, many become violent (or commit nonviolent offenses) due to refusing to continue on their medications so they end up being arrested instead of being hospitalized.

I refuse to let any of that happen to Sarina. People with schizophrenia or other psychiatric disorders, need understanding, patience, and reassurance that they will not be abandoned. And the one thing that will always be constant in Sarina's life—no matter what—is my love, and support. With hope, motivation and proper care, there can be recovery for the mentally ill.

Oh Lord. If only she'd get past her denial. The thought of Sarina wandering around New York without her medications frightens me. She's likely to do anything. And to be honest with you, I do fear for her safety as well as for the safety of others. The last thing I ever want is for a situation to occur where Sarina hurts someone else because of her paranoia and delusions. If she feels ridiculed or threatened, she's liable to act out violently. And that worries me.

Right now. I have to close my eyes and let out a heavy sigh. Relax. Relate. Release. That's all I can do at this moment. Otherwise, I will drive myself mad. I say all this to say, if you're a parent and you have a child who alleges seeing things and/or hearing voices which are not real; withdraws from family; has a hard time making and keeping friends; has ideas that people are out to get them or talking about them and/or begins behaving like a younger child—I urge you to seek help from your family physician or pediatrician. Get a referral to a child and adolescent psychiatrist who is specifically trained and skilled at evaluating, diagnosing, and treating children with schizophrenia. It's an illness that affects all of us.

There is no race barrier. Believe me. I know. I wish I had been honest with the therapist in the beginning instead of trying to conceal pertinent family history. Maybe Sarina wouldn't be in the state she's in now had I gotten her the proper treatment. I had to learn the hard way. No professional can help you get to the bottom of what's going on with your child behaviorally if you opt to withhold information about your family's background.

Each year, it is estimated that approximately 100,000 people are newly diagnosed with this disease. And although there are studies suggesting that changes in the brain, biochemical and environmental factors, and genetic predisposition play a major role in this illness, the exact cause is unknown. But in my case, it's clear that genetics were the cause of my daughter's problems. Schizophrenia affects the women in my family, dating as far back to my great-great-great-grandmother. A part of me wonders if this was the end result of my family's history of inbreeding—in order to preserve their Caucasian features.

Um. Forgive me if I'm rambling on. It's been so long since we've talked, and so much has happened. I'm so worried. I don't know what else to do. Like I said, I won't give up on Sarina. But she has consumed so much of my time and energy that I am drained. I am truly exhausted. But if I don't keep on pushing on, who else will she have? I mean, Ryan loves his daughter, but he's frustrated. And he's fed up.

"This nonsense with Sarina," he had said on our flight returning from Slovenia, "has got to stop. Something's going to have to be done."

"I don't know what to do," I said, sighing. "I wish I had the answer."

"I think we need to think about having her committed." I clutched my chest. I couldn't believe he'd say something like that. Yes, Sarina needs help. But I believe she can get it in a less restrictive environment. I refuse to see her put away indefinitely. My grandmother spent twenty years institutionalized until she withered away and died. That's not the life I want for Sarina. I believe she can still live a healthy, productive life in the community if she acknowledged her disability and committed herself to getting well, and staying well.

"My goodness, Ryan. You say that like you want to see our daughter placed under lock and key for the rest of her life."

"Well, if it's going to keep her safe then I'm all for it. I'm just as concerned for her psychological and physical safety as you are. But, I'm also concerned about the safety of others. We can't even turn our backs for one minute without having to worry about when she's going to disappear or act out. Every time she takes off we're on pins and needles, worrying if we're going to get a call in the middle of the night, informing us that something terrible has happened. I can't take seeing you pace the floors at night with worry."

"It's part of being a parent," I said, squeezing his hand. "I can't give up on her."

"Sweetheart, I don't want to give up on her, either. But we can't make her want to get well. She has to want it for herself. And until she does, we're beating a dead horse in the head. We should be enjoying our life. But look at us. We're rushing back to track down Sarina, *again*. I love her, and I'll always be there for her, but I don't know how much more of this I can take. We've been going through this for far too long. And enough is enough."

I let my thoughts drift to Sarina's last hospitalization over a year ago when she barricaded herself in her cottage for four days, refusing to let Ryan or myself inside. Anytime we knocked on her door, she screamed obscenities and threw things at the door. By the fifth day, we had to call the police and Crisis Response Team for assistance. And after seven hours of coaxing, the clinician was finally able to persuade her to open the door to let her in. Eventually, she was brought out—unkempt and dressed in a bloodstained nightshirt. She had to be taken to the emergency room for lacerations to her arms and legs for attempting to "drain the poison."

When Ryan and I entered her living quarters we almost passed out. She had literally destroyed every room in the small carriage house we allowed her to move into in order to give her a sense of independence. Oh, it was awful. It reeked of urine and feces from her going to the bathroom wherever she wanted. The walls were covered with drawings of bodies without heads, or with grotesque sexual organs. And there were cigarette holes and burns in the furniture and rugs.

But that was only the half of it. When I walked into the kitchen, I thought I would vomit when I saw maggots slithering over the meat that had been left out on the counter, rotting. I screamed when I saw the body of a dead kitten lying on the table. I found his head in the microwave. We ended up throwing out everything and spending thousands of dollars to repaint, repair fixtures and refurnish. Something had to definitely give, and soon.

"I agree," I replied, taking a deep breath. "But, it's hard."

"I know it is," he said, kissing my hand. "But, it's going to be even harder if she ends up hurting someone, or ends up dead." Everything he said was right. My heart dropped into my stomach. When Sarina isn't on her medication, she starts to feel persecuted, believing she's being watched or followed. Sometimes she hears voices that are threatening or condemning.

Or…Oh, I shudder to think…encouraging her to kill herself. I wanted to burst out in tears right there. Ryan put his arm around me, pulling me into him. He must have sensed my fears.

"We'll get through this," he said, consoling me.

I nodded. "I hope and pray we do."

So for two weeks, I prayed and waited while Ryan faxed flyers and photos of Sarina to every police department in the five boroughs of New York. It would take a miracle, but I knew it was possible for Sarina to be found. And I held on to my faith.

"Thank you, Lord," I whispered when I heard Indy's voice on the answering machine earlier today, saying Sarina was at her salon. I burst into tears. You just don't know how relieved and extremely anxious I was. Knowing Sarina was alive and safe was a load off my mind. However, Indy's tone told me what I dreaded most. Sarina was deteriorating. When I returned her phone call, I told her that Ryan and I were on our way to get her. I asked her to please not let her know we were coming. Sarina would take off without blinking an eye. I feared the *next* time we wouldn't be able to find her.

So, when the cell phone rang for the third time since leaving Maryland, my heart leaped in my throat. Indy had already called twice. The first time to let me know she was taking Sarina home with her, and the second time to say, " I don't know how much more of her stinking ass I can take." I flipped open my cell and answered.

"Hello."

"Chyna?"

"Hey," I said, bracing myself for what would come next. "Is everything okay?"

"No. Everything's not okay," Indy snapped. "How far are you from Brooklyn?"

"We not too long ago got on the New Jersey Turnpike…Honey, what exit did we just pass?" I asked, looking over at Ryan.

"Two," he replied, giving me a look of concern.

"We've just passed exit two. I guess we have another hour an a half or so to go."

"Wrong answer," she barked. "You have an hour to get here, or you'll be picking Miss Honey up in a body bag. Let me tell you what the fuck this bitch did—"

I cringed, hearing her refer to my child in that manner. Regardless of what she'd done, she's still my daughter. And hearing her being called names is hurtful. But I know enough to know that anytime Indy speaks in that tone about *anyone*, it only means one thing, she's about to go off. "Indy, please calm down and tell me what Sarina did."

"Calm down hell!" she screamed into the phone. "I'm a hot second from splitting her damn wig up in here for talking shit, and coming at me like she's ready for some work. No bitch is gonna be in my house, talking slick. Not even your crazy-ass daughter. Now you had better tell Ryan to press down on that pedal and get the hell here, before I put her ass—"

There was screaming in the background and then I heard, "Suck my bloody pussy, bitch!" My stomach tied in knots. Sarina was in rare form. "Fuck you! Fuck you! Fuck you! You tried to hurt my damn friend. Dirty bitch, I'll kill you." Then I heard something slam. A door I hoped.

"I'ma show you a bitch," Indy screeched, throwing the phone down.

"Indy? Indy?" The only response was the sounds of screaming and glass smashing. I dreaded what the end result would be. Either way, I knew in my gut it wouldn't be good. The only thing I could do was pray. "Oh Ryan, please hurry," I begged, rocking in my seat while holding my cell phone tightly pressed against my ear, listening to the commotion between my daughter and dear friend. Only God knew what I'd see when I finally arrived. And when the phone went dead, my heart told me nothing would ever be the same.

17

INDERA: *Chain of Fools*

Oh. Please. Don't even say it. I've heard enough from Britton's ass about the way I went off on Chyna. Sistafriend or not, girlfriend had no business stepping up in my home snapping about me having her grown-ass daughter tied up and gagged, okay. Yes, I had her crazy ass wrapped and tied down like a damn billy goat until they got here. *And?* Did you see what the hell she did to that bedroom? Girlfriend disrespected my home, and she disrespected me, okay.

And no bitch, crazy or not, is going to get that off. I don't care whose child you are. Now you tell me, what would you have done, huh? Humph. Well, they're lucky I didn't call the cops on her behind and have her hauled off to jail. Better yet, they should be glad they're not making funeral arrangements, okay.

Here I was being nice, bringing Sarina home with me until Chyna and Ryan were able to get here to pick her nutty ass up. And instead of being thankful, I get damn attitude. I should have let her behind wander the damn streets with the rest of the displaced, and disturbed. Humph. Then we wouldn't be having this conversation. And Chyna and I would still be speaking. Oh, well. Fuck it. My motto is, stand by you child, and get knocked down right along with her. No. I didn't go upside Chyna's head. Not that I didn't want to slap her ass into reality. But no matter how mad I get, I could never do it. Then again, with everything going on with me lately, I can't be sure what I'd do 'cause it definitely almost got messy up in here.

Anyway, getting to the story. From the moment I got Sarina's stinking tail in my car to bring her home with me, the nut started cracking. I mean. She was already buggin' in my office earlier; but if I would have known girlfriend was on the verge of snapping the way she did in my home, I would have hit Clarkson Avenue and dropped her ass off at the Kingsboro Psychiatric Center, then kept it goin,' okay.

Chile. It seems like the minute she walked in my house she zoned out, mumbling and laughing to herself. At first I thought Girlfriend was just trying to get a reaction out of me. So, doing my best, I ignored her. But then she started getting under my skin with all of her pacing 'n shit, dragging her damn suitcase across my floors so I took her upstairs to chill out. Hell, I figured, she'd be safe up on the third floor until Chyna got here. Ha! Little did I know that—in less than an hour—the bitch would throw shit in the mix and disrupt my whole flow, okay.

Chyna was so damn concerned Girlfriend would take off if she knew they were on their way that I agreed to keep it on the hush. But I damn sure didn't agree to let that nasty bitch use her tampon as a crayon, okay. Yes, that's what the hell she did. Miss Crayola wrote "Bitch" on my damn walls with her menstrual blood. And then had the nerve to have her tampon laying on top of the dresser. I'm telling you. I wouldn't have believed it if I hadn't seen it with my own damn eyes.

Nor did I agree to allow her to have some wounded, dirty-ass pigeon— that she had packed in her funky suitcase—lying on top of my damn white comforter with all his nasty-ass feathers, and drippings. And I damn sure didn't agree to let her think she could jump up in my face popping shit when I told her to get that thing out of my house.

Now the cursing, I could have tolerated. And I probably would have let her get it off with slamming doors. But when Girlfriend broke bad, threatening to kill me and throwing her hands up, I had to take her down. And it wasn't easy, okay. That's a strong bitch, okay. But she got served—*well*, I might add. Oh. She got hers in. Trust me. I'll give her that 'cause, as you can see, my eye's all blacked the fuck up. But I beat that bitch *down*. For every slick thing she's ever said to me, I slid her ass. For every tear she's made her mother shed, I rocked her.

Hmm. Hmm. We fought through the whole third floor of my house, tearing up every damn room. From boxing like two men to kicking and slapping like two crazed women, we thumped up in this piece, okay. Ugh! Chile, please. Girlfriend wore me out, though. I am so damn sore, okay.

Where was Tee's ass? Please. The hell if I know. The only thing I did know, there was no damn way I could let some twenty-something girl whip my ass in my own home. That was not an option. So I had to really get focused, and beat her with everything I could get my hands on. But it wasn't until I knocked her in her head with a lead-crystal vase that she took it down. And kept it down. And the minute she hit the floor, I was on her.

Surprisingly, I didn't beat her skull in. I banged her in her mouth two good times, knocking her teeth loose and splashing blood every which way. Then I ran to my utility closet, snatching up some rope and two rolls of duct tape, then commenced to tie her ass up, wrapping the tape around her body mummy style. I taped her damn bloody mouth up, dragged her down three flights of stairs, then through the kitchen, throwing her to the floor of the back porch.

Chile, listen. For a second, I really thought I might have killed her, because she was out cold. But I placed my fingers on her jugular to be sure. And breathed a damn sigh of relief when she had a pulse. Lord knows I really didn't want to have a dead body in my home, or on my hands. But if need be, it would be.

Anyway, after I was done with her, I went upstairs, showered, then came back down refreshed and dressed, sitting on the sofa patiently waiting for Chyna and Ryan to show up at my doorstep for their wrapped package. When I looked over at the clock on the end table, it was 8:30 p.m. *They should be pulling up any minute*, I thought as I made my way back into the kitchen to check on my houseguest. She was still out. And a part of me was beginning to feel bad for her pathetic ass. So, I went into the cabinet, pulled out a five-gallon pot, filled it with cold water and three trays of ice, stirred the cubes around for a while, then tossed it on her. She jerked up. "Rise 'n shine, bitch," I snapped. Her eyes blinked rapidly as she thrashed around, trying to break free from bondage.

"Don't look at me like that," I said, glaring down at her. "You thought

I was gonna let you whip my ass, didn't you?" She grunted, violently moving around. I bent down beside her on one knee. I slapped her face. "You really fucked up, putting your hands on me, sweetie." I slapped her again. "The only reason you're still breathing is because of your mother. You, know. The woman you hate so much. I understand you have issues, but you picked the wrong time to get crazy, and you *really* picked the wrong one to fuck with." I paused, preparing to slap her again when the doorbell rang. I banged her in the head with the stainless steel pot, then stood up. "Looks like you've been saved by the bell."

Just as I was getting ready to open the door, the phone rang. It was Tee. "Hey, baby."

"Hey," I said, opening the door. "Where are you?"

"Indy," Chyna said frantically, giving me a hug. "Is Sarina still here?" I nodded. Ryan said his hello, then gave me a hug. I smiled.

"I'm just leaving Brit's. I should be home in about an hour."

"Alright," I said, closing the door behind them. "I gotta go. Chyna and Ryan are here."

"Oh word. They've found Sarina?"

"You could say that," I said, gesturing for Chyna and Ryan to have a seat. "Look, let me go. I'll talk to you when you get home."

"Aiight. Well, tell 'em I said whaddup." We said our good-byes, then hung up. Chyna's mouth flew open when she saw my eye.

"Oh my God, Indy!" she snapped, placing her hand over her mouth. "What happened to your eye?"

"Your daughter attacked me."

"Are you alright?" Ryan asked, walking over to me. His face was etched with concern.

I nodded. "I'm fine. But—"

"Oh, Lord," Chyna interrupted. Her eyes were filled with worry. "Where is she?"

"She's in the pantry," I said, gesturing with my head. Chyna whisked through the living room, heading toward the kitchen. Ryan stared at me and sighed.

"I really don't know what we're gonna do with her. She won't take her medications."

I shrugged my shoulders. "Humph," I grunted. "Then perhaps she should be put away before she ends up—" I stopped in mid sentence when Chyna screamed hysterically. Ryan ran out to see what the problem was. I sat on the sofa, leaning back, then crossing my legs. When the tape was removed from Sarina's mouth she yelled, and screamed.

"Indy," Chyna screamed, walking back into the living room, looking distraught. "What in the world did you do to her?"

I furrowed my eyebrows together. "Excuse you? What did *I* do to her? I kept her from tearing up my shit."

She frowned at me. "Did you have to hurt her?"

"Be glad she's still breathing," I said, shifting my body around to face her. I was surprisingly calm. I tucked my leg underneath me.

"And what," she began, cocking her head to the side, "is that supposed to mean?" Girlfriend had the nerve to give me attitude, okay. "You know she's not well. You didn't have to beat her upside her head or hit her in her mouth. Her gums are swollen. I think she has teeth loose." I raised my eyebrow. *Oh well.* She paused, trying to contain her anger. She slammed her hand on her round hip. "And you didn't have to tie her up like she's some animal. That's my daughter in there."

I could feel my pressure rising. I took a deep breath. Counted to ten before I went off. "Chyna. Don't fucking stand there, and give me the third degree about what the fuck I did to *your* daughter. The bitch attacked me, and I beat her ass. Simple as that. And like I said, be glad she's still breathing." I got up from the sofa, walking over to her. She moved out of the way. "Now get her the fuck out of my house." Ryan walked in carrying Sarina in his arms.

"I hate you!" Sarina screamed, foaming at the mouth. Blood and spit flew from her mouth as she ranted. She tried to break free from Ryan, but he had her tightly secured. Apparently he didn't have a problem with his child being tied down because he damn sure kept her feet and hands roped up. "You hurt my friend, you stinking bitch! I hate you!"

"Sarina, stop it!" Chyna snapped.

"Fuck you!" she hissed at her mother. "This is all your fault. You had Pecola killed." Chile, listen. Even I had a look of bewilderment plastered on my face when she said that. *Who the fuck is Pecola?*

"She's a little banged up," Ryan said, looking at me, "but she'll survive until we can get her home."

Humph. Next time I'll be sure to throw acid in her face, I thought, acknowledging him with a nod.

"I hate you!"

"Knock it off," Ryan barked at her. "Or I'll tape your mouth up myself." She began mumbling under her breath.

"Sarina, sweetheart," Chyna said, "everything's going to be okay."

She burst into laughter. "Oh, please tighty-whitey. You make me sick."

Chyna remained calm. "We're going to get you some help."

I rolled my eyes up in my head.

"I'm not the one who needs help, Chyna."

I shook my head; more at Chyna's foolish ass than at Sarina's comment 'cause had that been my child I would have knocked the shit out of her. But then again, it's not. So let me keep my mouth shut, okay. Humph.

"All right, Sarina. That's enough. I think we better get going," Ryan said, lifting her up over his shoulder. "Indy, I'm sorry about all this. Whatever damages she's caused just send me the bill and I'll handle it."

I half-smiled. "Thanks," I replied, appreciative of the gesture.

"Ryan," Chyna said, glaring at me with tears in her eyes, then walking over to open the door for him, "I'll be out in a minute. I have a few things I want to say to Indy first." She waited until he was down the steps before she closed the door, then turned her attention back to me, folding her arms. I stood with one hand on my hip and the other balled into a fist.

"How dare you," she screeched. "I don't appreciate you referring to my daughter as crazy or calling her a *bitch*."

"Well, she is," I snapped. Her eyes bulged. Mine narrowed to two thin slits. "You might let her curse you out, and beat your ass. But, she can't get that on my time."

"Don't you understand, calling her names only exacerbates—"

"You know what, Chyna. Save your excuses, and save that medical bull-shit for someone who really gives a fuck. I did your ass a favor, okay. You know that *bitch*..." Her nose flared. "That's right I said, bitch, B-I-T-C-H. And what? You know damn well her ass is violent, and all you want to do is stand here acting like it's okay for her to fuck my house up and come at me wrong, and I'm just supposed to accept it because her ass is a certified nutcase."

Fire shot through her eyes. "How dare you!"

"No!" I snapped. "How dare you. Next time, I'll just put the bitch out of her misery."

Her eyes widened. "I feel really sorry for you," she said through clenched teeth. "You're a cold, nasty *bitch*." Chile, I was shocked, okay. In all the years I've known Chyna, she's never used that word. Come to think about it, she's never cursed. "You're insensitive. Hateful. And downright vicious."

"No dear," I shot back, walking up on her. She stepped back. "I feel sorry for *you*. Then again, I guess I shouldn't since the fruit doesn't fall too far from the tree." I brushed past her, walking to the door and swinging it open. She stood there slack-jawed. "Every time that child disrespected you or had you in tears, I was there for you. And I always bit my tongue. And you're right, she's your daughter. Not mine. So from this point on, the next time she assaults you or tries to kill you, don't call me.

"As a matter of fact, I hope she fucks you up really good. Maybe then you'll wake the hell up, and stop being so damn stupid. You really got the game fucked up. I got nothing but love for you, but I'll beat your ass in a New York heartbeat if you ever come in my home and talk shit to me. Now get the fuck out, you silly bitch." She stood there, glaring at me.

"As long as I live," she replied, walking toward the door, "you'll never have to worry about me or my problems again."

"Good," I snapped, slamming the door behind her.

And there you have it. That was over three weeks ago. And she and I haven't spoken since. Britton feels the things I said to Chyna were hurtful and he thinks I should apologize. Yeah, okay. Hold your breath. As far as

I'm concerned, she owes *me* the apology. Oh, don't get it twisted. That's still my girl and all. And I'll be damned if I ever want to see any harm come to her. But, for now, it's best that she and I space it out from each other; you know, love each other from afar.

Anyway, moving on to more interesting matters. Chile, do I have some scoop for ya'll. Guess who spent time in a state prison for reckless endangerment and abandonment? Celeste Munley. Mmm. Hmm. Only her last name isn't Munley. It's Randolph. Which is the reason my research assistant had a hard time digging up skeletons in her backyard. Humph. I knew that bitch was a fraud. I just couldn't put my finger on it.

Well, get this. Girlfriend was sentenced to five years in a D.C. prison for dumping her newborn child in a dumpster in thirty-degree weather. Supposedly, she only served two years due to good behavior. Humph. Chile, I wouldn't have believed it myself if I didn't read the news clipping with my own two eyes: Baby Survives 10 Hours in Trash Bin. Girl, I was shocked. The article went on to say that the baby's mother, Celeste Randolph, had given birth to the newborn in a motel room, then placed him in a garbage bag before dumping him into a dumpster. She had the nerve to say she had gotten pregnant by an ex-boyfriend who had raped and beaten her, and had dumped the baby hoping no one would find out she'd given birth. Ugh!

According to a police report, the infant was found wrapped in a filthy blanket with its placenta still attached by a homeless man, rummaging in the bin for food. The man heard a noise and fished the child out. Can you believe it? That nasty bitch! Thank God the poor thing was still alive. Chile, with all these programs out here, and places you can go to drop off an unwanted child, why the hell would you leave an innocent baby for dead?

Chile. You should have seen her face plastered on the front page with her knotty-ass hair and eyes as big as golf balls. Girlfriend was one sloppy sight, okay. And don't think I haven't made a copy to share with her for old time's sake.

Please. Scandalous is right. But that's not what really has my stomach in knots. My research assistant has also discovered that this trick is married.

Now, don't give me that "so what look." Girlfriend's full name is Celeste Randolph-Landers, okay. Chile, the bitch is Britton's wife. Now, you know I'm wrecked. And I can only imagine how he's going to be when he finds out this two-bit-pipe-sucking-trick is back in action. I knew she looked vaguely familiar to me. I just couldn't put two and two together. And now that I have, you know sistagirl is going to be paying Miss Celeste a little visit.

Oh my God! It's all coming back to me now. Britton never talked much about his marriage, but it is one thing he did share with me during one of our trips back to Virginia after spending the weekend in New York, clubbing, of course.

At first I thought he was playing but then I realized he was serious when he pulled out a picture from his wallet of the two of them together when they were first married. She was very pretty. Actually she was fly. Humph. Not that she looks busted now. But, upon close inspection you can tell she's been through it. It's a damn shame what drugs and the streets can do to you. Chile. It couldn't be me.

I recall thinking how happy they looked together. But he quickly corrected my assumptions when he told me all about feeling trapped after they had gotten married, but wanting to do right by her because he had gotten her pregnant. *Humph, the bitch probably did try to trap your fine ass*, I thought, listening to him. 'Cause you know how grimy some women can be. Anyway, he even shared with me how they lost a child, and how she started using drugs. I listened as he shared his story. "I couldn't take it anymore," he finished. "So I just walked out on her."

"Would you take her back?" I asked, paying the toll for the Delaware Memorial Bridge.

He shook his head. "Nah. Not after hearing she was tricking. She's done too much dirt. And I don't think I could ever trust her." Chile, that was over fifteen years ago when he shared that story with me, making it very clear he had erased her out of his life. And when he was done, he tore the picture up. "Oh, well," he said, tossing the torn pieces out of the window. "That was then. And this is now. So out with the old, and in with the new."

And now this chick thinks she's gonna pop back on the scene and it's going to be all sweet. Humph. Not if I have anything to do with it. Now, I know you're not giving me that look like I should mind my business and stay out of it. Yeah, okay. I know Britton has a right to know. And he will be told, but not until I have a little chat with that scuzzy ho. Oh, don't worry. I'm going to come at her very ladylike and give her the option to either bow out gracefully or end up…Let's just say, if I have to pull out my trick bag on her, it might get a little messy, okay.

Well, I guess I'll find out exactly what my soror is up to all in due time. Oh, excuse me. I can't seem to stop yawning. Chile. I don't know about ya'll but I'm beat. So, if you don't mind. I'm gonna take it down for the night. But, first thing tomorrow, let's be up and ready to roll, okay.

When the phone rang early this morning—two a.m. to be exact, I actually thought I was in a dream when the strained voice on the other end said, "Grace is dead."

"What?!" I asked, rustling out of my warm bed to go into the bathroom to speak. Tee stirred lightly in his sleep. I blew out a sigh when he didn't wake. "When?" I whispered into the receiver, closing the door behind me. I pulled down the lid to the toilet, then sat down, crossing my legs. Excitement raced through my body. This was too good to be true.

"I found her last night." There was a slight pause. My heartbeat raced with anticipation. "She died on her knees." Apparently she had gone to bed around seven p.m. because she wasn't feeling well. When he went up to check on her—about four hours later—he found her on her knees with her head facedown on the bed, as if she had been praying.

Humph, I thought, picking my cuticles. *Good for the bitch*. Given the situation I decided it was best I kept my remarks to myself. Particularly since nothing I felt was kind. I know him calling me was hard enough, considering how I feel about his wife. Cockeyed bitch.

"So when's the funeral?" I casually asked.

"The day after next."

Please. After the three years of hell and torment that woman put me through she's lucky she lived as long as she did. I squinted fury from my eyes, rubbing the small cigarette burn neatly hidden by hair at the nape of my neck. The smell of burning flesh has haunted me for many years. The best thing he could have ever done was move back to Grenada with that ugly, beady-eyed woman; otherwise, she would have been disposed of a long time ago. Fortunate for her, I do have a heart.

Well, don't give me that look. I didn't want to take her life, anyway. I wanted her to always remember what she had done to me. I smiled to myself, remembering back over thirteen years ago when I made the call to have *her* tortured for beating and abusing me.

Well, most of you already know all this. But for those of you who don't: Yes, I had the bitch's arms chopped off. See. Without arms, she'd never pose a threat to another child's safety. She'd never be able to pick up another object to strike or beat anyone else.

"I see," I said, yawning. "Oh excuse me. Well, as much as I would like to be sympathetic to your loss, I can't say that I am. There's no love lost on my part."

"I didn't expect there would be," he slowly replied. "I just thought you'd want to know." I closed my eyes, taking in his words. Even though he speaks English very well, I've always found his Caribbean accent delightful. But he still makes me sick.

"Well, thanks for sharing."

"Indera, I stayed because it was the right thing to do." His guilt must have been eating at him.

"For who?" I asked, rapidly tapping my fingers on my knee. In a matter of minutes, he was going to say the wrong thing, and I was going to black on him.

"I couldn't abandon her."

I shook my head. "So you abandon me instead? You knew what she put me through; yet, you chose to stay and take care of that crazy bitch."

"Indera, please. Respect the dead."

Blood rushed to my head. My jaws tightened. "Fuck her. And fuck her being dead. You chose her over me—your only child. You chose to be a better husband to her than the woman who loved you more than life itself—my mother. So fuck her. And fuck you."

Silence.

"I loved your mother."

"Don't you dare talk to me about loving my mother. I saw the pain in her eyes. I saw her loneliness. So spare me, 'cause you damn sure didn't love her enough to leave the streets and your whores alone. But you catered to that pink-lipped, wiggly-eyed ho's every whim."

"You don't know what you're talking about."

"Don't tell me what I don't know. I know my mother died in my arms, and you were no fucking where to be found. I know you shipped me off to a boarding school, and forgot about me. I know you married a woman who beat and degraded me, and allowed her perverted brother to crawl his big, nasty ass into my bed every night. And I know you were no fucking where around. So I know more than you think."

"You don't know the whole story. And now's not the time to get into it. I've made a lot of mistakes and you've never let me forget them. But I can't take back what happened in the past. If I could I would. But I can't. I just want to make things right between us now. Will you ever find it in your heart to let me back in your life, and forgive me?"

I sighed, standing up to stretch. I flipped on the light and stared into the mirror. I almost wanted to laugh at him. Isn't it funny how the chickens come home to roost every time? I think if I saw this man right now, I'd slap the shit out of him—father or not. Oh, don't you start with that forgiveness shit too. As far as I'm concerned, the bond of a father and daughter should be sealed with the purest love imaginable—something Robinson Fleet and I never had. Whatever we did have between us was tainted the day he left me in the care of his wife. So you'll have to excuse me if forgiving him hasn't been in the forefront of my mind.

Do I love him? Well, I haven't brought any harm his way, so I suppose I feel something for him. I just haven't figured out what that is. Please. I barely know his ass. Although we speak, I haven't physically seen him since I was twenty-five. And before that, he was too busy making moves—if you know what I mean—so he was never around, be it by choice or chance. Now don't sit there and act like you don't know what I'm talking about. Do I have to spell out everything, damn! Yes, I'm the daughter of a fucking... Ugh! You figure it out.

Anyway, it was the week after my birthday when he shared with me he was leaving the States to care for his psycho wife because he feared for her safety. Can you believe that shit? Not once did he concern himself with my well-being but he feared for the life of a woman who spoke ill of my dead mother and harsh to me, among the other cruel, sadistic things she enjoyed subjecting me to. Chile, the only thing I can do is, shake my damn head.

So off he went with his handicapped, crazy-ass wife. I swore then he'd never see me again as long as he stayed with that woman. And I meant it. However, that hasn't stopped him from sending me large sums of money throughout the years. And—*yes*—I graciously accept every damn Benjamin. Please. Just because I don't want to look in his face, that doesn't mean I won't spend his change. Oh, don't get it twisted. I know he's kept his eye on me from a distance. Please. He flew back to the States and was at my bedside when he found out I had been shot.

Although I'm not supposed to know, it's my understanding he was not only broken up behind the incident, but he swore whoever was responsible would pay. Girl, the only thing I can do is laugh at that. He must have forgotten who I am: a grown-ass woman who rocks and rolls on her own. So, I damn sure don't need him to handle my work. Nonetheless, I suspect my assailant hadn't expected me to survive. Not that it matters. Because whether I was dead—which I'm not—or alive, he'd still be served. See, 'cause if I can't get to him, Robinson will, okay.

What? Oh, you thought I said I haven't seen him since my twenty-fifth birthday? I haven't. I was still in a coma when he arrived—a day later—at the hospital. And, although I couldn't see him, I felt his presence. Anyway, my point is, his contacts have kept him well informed. Trust and believe. If we have nothing else in common, we both have eyes and ears everywhere.

"Now that that bitch is dead," I said, wiping a tear from my eye. "Maybe." I clicked the phone off, leaving him with the dial tone. I stood in front of the mirror, staring at the vision before me: A young girl, standing in the middle of a kitchen with a bloody butcher knife wrapped tightly in her hand. I rinsed the image from my head, splashing cold water on my face. "Make no mistake, bitch," I mumbled. "You may have died, but you're far from dead. And I'll be damned if your soul will rest." I flipped off the light, smiling. *Well, looks like my little visit with Celeste will have to be put on hold*, I thought, stepping out of the bathroom with the sway and swagger of a woman with a grand plan. *Something much more important has come up.*

I felt energized. The thermostat in my love snatch went up several notches seeing Tee lying on his back with his nude body half-exposed from under the covers. My pussy sucked in the string of my black teddy. *That's right, kitty girl*, I said to myself as I pinched my clit and left nipple, *momma's gonna feed you real good.* I slipped out of my lingerie, climbed into bed, then took his meaty dick in my mouth, sucking him to life. In a matter of moments, he was fully erect and ready to go. It never takes much to get him 'roused. Big Daddy always rises to the occasion, okay. Hmm. Just how I like it: long and strong. He let out a deep groan, then opened his eyes with a wide grin on his face.

"What time is it?" he asked groggily.

"Time for you to buckle up and enjoy the fuck of your life," I said, sticking my tongue in the crack of his ass, then gliding it up under his balls. I took them in my mouth one by one, gently sucking and rolling my tongue around them. He widened his legs, moaning. "Damn, girl."

"Whose dick is this," I demanded in between licks, kisses and slurps. I slobbered him down, watching him open and close his toes.

"Yours, baby," he moaned.

I smiled as I slowly crawled up over his body, lightly brushing my pulsating pussy over his stiff dick before reaching around and sticking it deep into my overheated hole. Hmmm. It was like sliding down on a long pole. I galloped on his dick, squeezing my pussy muscles around it until I let loose a fountain of pleasure. Chile, the thought of giving my father's wife a grand "going home" threw me into a horny frenzy. Before I knew what had come over me, I was talking in tongues, riding and sucking Tee until he begged *me* to stop. When we both came, I collapsed on top of him with his dick still inside of me, falling fast asleep.

"Aye," Tee said, tapping me on my shoulder. "It's almost ten o'clock. Aren't you going to work today?" *Now what the hell is he doing up*, I thought before opening my eyes. *After the fuck I put on him, he should be worn out.*

"No," I grunted, rolling over, stretching and moaning all in one swift motion. Kitty was full. I was exhausted, and truthfully—felt queasy. I'm not sure if it were my nerves from this morning's news finally settling in or from the thought of touching the soil of the "Spice Isle." Whatever the case, I needed to beat these butterflies the hell out of my stomach 'cause I had things to do.

"Ah, shit!" he snapped with a wide smile on his face. "It's about to be on up in here."

"Slow it down, tiger," I said, pushing him back before he started pawing me. Of course his dick was hard. Horny ass. I got out of bed, walked into the bathroom, grabbed my crystal tumbler, then filled it with water from the Aqua Cool Cooler. I turned the water on for the shower, then closed the door to let the bathroom steam up. "You've gotten all the pussy you're gonna get for one day," I said, walking back into the bedroom.

"What?!"

"You heard me."

"Yeah, aiight," he said, getting out of bed. I must admit. My chocolate warrior is sexy as hell. I scanned his chiseled body as he walked toward me. "Come here, girl," he said, pulling me into his arms. I obliged, leaning my head back, closing my eyes as he pressed his lips against mine. His big hands traveled along my back, then found their way to my bare ass. He squeezed. "I love you, girl."

"Still not getting no pussy," I replied, sidestepping him and his engorged sword.

"That's fucked up," he snapped, looking down and grabbing his dick. "How 'bout putting in some lip work?"

How 'bout you clock in and eat my pussy. The nerve of him to stand there and suggest I suck his dick after all the sucking I did last night—well, early this morning. All he had to do was lie back and enjoy the service. Not once did I squat over his face and lower my sweet pussy on his lips. So he had better get a grip. I started to curse him out, but rolled my eyes instead. "Wrong answer. We have to get packed."

"Packed? You never mentioned anything to me about going anywhere."

"I'm telling you now," I said, running into the bathroom. I almost forgot I had the shower on. Steam burst out of the door.

"And where are you jetting off to now?" His tone was tinted with attitude. Apparently he didn't hear me when I said *we* had to get packed.

"Grenada," I said, stepping into the shower. He stepped in behind me.

"Grenada? What the fuck for?"

"My father's wife died."

"Damn, sorry to hear that."

"I'm not."

"I figured that much. So explain to me why you're going to Grenada?"

"Correction. *We're* going to Grenada."

"Okay, so why are *we* going to Grenada? You don't even like the woman."

"Exactly," I said, smiling. "I can't stand her ass. But I still have to pay my respects. There's no way she's going to be buried without me seeing her one last time." Tee stared at me for a moment, studying me as I lathered my body. "What?" I asked, feigning innocence. "Why you looking at me like that?"

"Oh hell no! Your little ass is up to something."

"Boy," I said, taking the bar of soap, rubbing it across his chest, then slowly over his nipples, "what makes you think I'm up to anything?"

"I know you," he said, taking the soap from my hand. "And you aren't going way over there to pay your respects to someone you can't stand. Particularly your stepmother, so what's the deal?"

I sucked my teeth, handing him his washcloth, then stepping out of his way so he could wash and rinse his body off. "Stop letting your imagination get the best of you. Regardless of my feelings toward her, she's still my father's wife." He burst into laughter.

"I don't believe you."

"I'm being serious, Tee."

"Come on now, you barely talk to the man. And you haven't seen him in years."

"Well," I said, getting out of the shower, reaching for my towel, then wrapping it around my breasts, "for your information we've been talking at least once a month for the last three years. I just haven't said anything."

"Oh, word?" he asked, turning the water off and stepping out behind me. I grabbed his towel, wiping him off. He stood with his legs spread apart and his arms up over his head as I dried him down while explaining to him how my father and I have engaged in regular conversations since the shooting ordeal. Like clockwork, he calls the first of every month. Chile, the calls are brief—my doing, of course—but it's definitely a big change from the once-a-year call I used to get for my birthday. Between you and me, I look forward to hearing his voice, even if he does piss me off. Oh, alright. I guess I still fantasize about being a daddy's girl.

Anyway, my father was crushed when I didn't share with him I was getting married. He called me to let me know he had seen the article in *The New York Times* society section, announcing my engagement. I was like, "Okay, your point." I could hear the hurt in his voice when I told him he wasn't invited. How could I allow him to be a part of one of the most important moments in my life when he wasn't there when I needed him the most? As far as I was concerned, he hadn't earned the right to walk me down the aisle or bear witness to my happiness. Of course, Tee thought I was dead wrong. And tried to wreck my nerves about it. But I gave him a look that said, *Stay in your lane, and let me handle mine.* And when he continued to press the issue, I cursed him out so bad there almost wasn't going to be a wedding. I lit into that ass, okay. So, now when it comes to anything pertaining to my father, he keeps his mouth shut and minds his business.

Nonetheless, my father not being invited to the wedding didn't stop him from sending me a monetary gift of one-hundred and fifty-thousand dollars in the form of a wire transfer—which I kindly put in the trust fund account I have for my godsons. Nevertheless, he's been trying to win his way back into my life. Of course, I haven't made it easy for him. But slowly he's breaking me. And now with his bitch out of the way, there's a slim chance he can take his rightful place in my life.

Tee smiled. "That's good news, baby. Damn. I'm finally gonna get a chance to politick with the ol' playa."

"Humph. I don't know about all that. But I do know if you don't hurry your ass up, you'll be left in the wind 'cause we have a flight at five. So are you coming or not?"

"Is my dick hard?" he asked, staring at me with lust in his eyes. I smiled. "Then I'm cumming. So come on and break me off some more of that good lovin'. *Oh what the hell*, I thought, grinning. *We still have time before the limo gets here. Besides, Kitty can go for another feeding.*

"I'm not wet," I said with my hands on my hips—lying.

"Yo, I got something for that," he snapped, sticking his long tongue out, then rapidly flapping it up and down before turning me around. I spread open my legs, then bent over, grabbing my ankles and exposing two overly eager pussy lips. He got on one knee and stuck his tongue in me. Chile, I was wetter than a lake, long before his tongue even touched me. I just wanted him to eat my pussy from the back before I let him get up in this sweetness, okay. And just as I had hoped: he sucked, licked and kissed my pussy until I dropped down on my knees, begging him to bust his nut in me.

"Beat this pussy up, baby," I moaned, swinging my hips. He jabbed his dick deep in me. "Uh. Give me that hot nut."

"Damn, girl. Throw that pussy." Chile, the way he kept pulling his dick out real slow to the tip of its head, then slamming back in was driving me bananas. I was so heated I felt my insides boiling.

"Stop teasing me," I snapped, looking over my shoulder, tossing my hair out of my face. "Work it like you mean it." I leaned over on my forearms, pumping my hips forward and backward. "Show momma what you working with."

"Yeah, baby," he grunted, slapping me on my ass. "Keep talking slick."

"Give me the dick, boy," I urged, twirling my hips, and squeezing my pussy muscles.

Oh my God! When he pulled my ass cheeks open as wide as they could go, and dug his dick in my pussy, pounding in and out, I thought I would faint. It felt so damn good. "That's right, daddy…Hmm. Fuck me, baby." And that's just what his nasty ass did.

From the moment we boarded flight 1745, I was covered with a quilt of emotions. I don't think it was because I was going to finally be face-to-face with my father after all these years. And I don't believe it had anything to do with seeing Grace in her coffin. Actually, I was looking forward to that. Her death was closing another chapter of my life. And with that, I found comfort. No. This trip's ability to stir my emotions had everything to do with visiting an island I hadn't seen since I was seven years old. Granted I have business dealings there. Not that I really want to get into my money matters with you. But, thirteen years ago—actually, around the same time Grace had her *accident*—I turned my mother's summer home (the one I inherited) into a magnificent twelve-room bed and breakfast, overlooking the inner harbor. And it's doing fabulous, okay. Bottom line: I wanted Grace to know that wherever they were, my mother's spirit would be right there—and I'd be somewhere close by, waiting in the winds.

And, yes, my Fleet blood runs as thick as the lush tropical mountains on the island. Still in all, it isn't just the place where my father was born, and lives, it's also the place where my mother and her family spent their summers and holidays. It's also the place where my parents first met, and fell in love. Little did I know, this trip would become more than bidding my stepmother a farewell; it would become a walk into a past I knew very little about. It was there that I learned my mother would visit Grenada as a child with her Nigerian father and British mother—frolicking under the sun with a poor, little Caribbean boy, with eyes shaped like almonds and skin the color of copper.

I thought back to the first time I visited the island. It was for the funeral of my mother's family's loyal housekeeper: the widow who cooked, cleaned, and did laundry for a living while raising seven children in a two-room, tin-roofed flat. Fiona Fleet. My grandmother. I closed my eyes, trying to conjure up images of St. Georges, Grenada. Sadly, there were none.

The minute the airplane descended, Tee reached over, planting a passionate kiss on my lips. I smiled as he rubbed the side of my face. "You aiight, baby?"

I nodded. "I'm fine."

He winked. then quickly pecked my lips again. "That's my girl." He then leaned in and whispered, "I'ma bust that ass when we get to the house."

"Negro, get a grip," I said, rolling my eyes. I glanced down at my watch, then back over at him, shaking my head. It was the wee hours of the morning and the only thing on his mind was climbing up in my love nest. Please. After five hours en route to Puerto Rico, a four-hour layover in San Juan. then another two-hour-and-twenty-minute flight to Port Salines Airport, the only thing I was dropping were these eyelids, okay. Besides, I just finished jerking his horny ass off under the gray wool blanket—compliments of American Airlines—less than an hour ago. "The only thing you gonna do is *bust* some zees 'cause the pussy train is full."

He smirked. "Yeah, aiight." He stood up, stepping into the aisle, grabbing our bags, then stepped back so I could get in front of him. The white couple sitting across from us smiled when Tee smacked me on my ass.

"You so damn silly," I snapped, backing my butt up into him. "Now smack that." I glanced over at the woman, stylishly dressed in a tan-and-brown-checkered Chanel suit accentuated with a knotted silk scarf. I peeped her, checking out my wears: Roberto Cavalli jeans; a Christian Dior blue satin crepe blouse; a fly-ass, sapphire belt; and a pair of blue Cesare Paciotti mules, okay. Chile, I don't normally mix and match designers, but the ensemble was so fierce I had to rock it.

Anyway, I returned a half-smile before turning my back to her. Girlfriend was attractive—in her late forties, I surmised. Although with women it's sometimes hard to tell our exact age, especially when we're well kept. And the size of her diamonds told it all, okay. Well, after she gave me the once-over, she cut her eyes over at Tee who was standing there, looking all thugged out in a baggy blue velour Sean John sweat suit, a pair of blue Timbs and a Sean John fitted pulled down over his face, covering his eyes.

"You must be newlyweds," the blue-eyed gentleman said, smiling. His companion nodded in agreement. But by the way she was looking at us, I'm sure she was thinking something else. If I coulda read her thoughts, I'm sure I woulda had to slap the shit out of her.

"Not really," Tee responded. "We've been married almost three years."

"Oh, that's still new," the neatly coiffed brunette offered, leaning into her man. "We've been married almost twenty years and we still treat each year as if it were our first. Isn't that right, honey?"

"Sure is, sweetheart," Blue-eyes replied, smiling. "Every day is a honeymoon." His dimpled chin gave him a handsomely rugged look. I pictured him as a banker or investor of sorts, sitting there in his traditional blue, pin-striped suit. His crisp white collar was unbuttoned and his tie hung loosely around his neck. They kissed. I smiled, then cut my eyes up at Tee. He shrugged his shoulders. It was clear their cocktails had kicked in. Little did the drunken lovebirds know—or remember, Tee and I had overheard brunette threaten to leave Blue-eyes if he didn't fire his young, spunky secretary when they returned from their vacation. Her exact words: "It's the little bimbo or me."

When we exited the plane and stepped into the airport I smiled as we were greeted by the sounds of calypso. Tee and I walked hand in hand, heading for our car service. The minute we walked outside and stepped into the car, I felt relaxed as I inhaled the calmness of the night, while the driver made his way up and around the narrow hillside streets to Nandi's Guesthouse.

At eight a.m. I was standing on the balcony of our suite, enjoying the splendor of the most breathtaking view of the prettiest harbor town in the West Indies. Chile, the whole town is nestled along the slope of hills and puts any magic-book story to shame with all of its sheer beauty. I was enthralled. I looked up into the crisp blueness of a cloudless sky and whispered, "I love you, Momma." I smiled, taking in the heady, exotic aroma of the spices the island was known for: cinnamon, nutmeg, cloves and ginger. And then my thoughts drifted to what brought me to this tropical wonderland in the first place: Grace.

I pressed my eyes shut, blocking out the whimpering of a young girl who had just been beaten with a razor strap. I shook the cries loose from my head, then fast-forwarded to the day I snatched a butcher knife out of the dish drain and slashed her ass up for throwing her bedridden father's bedpan at me, tossing piss and shit on me. The penalty: one hundred and ninety-six stitches across her chest and arms—long before they were removed, of course. The sight of her blood, and the panic in her eyes, triggered a point of no return for me. At fourteen, I knew then, that *no one* would ever mistreat me, and get away with it. Never again!

You may have beat me, but I'm not beaten, bitch. I still came out on top. And I am here to serve notice on your ass. My lips parted into a wide grin as I finalized her farewell in my mind. I read somewhere once that revenge is best served cold. That may be true. But in this case, it's better served hot 'cause tonight Grace was about to get the fireworks of her life.

Tee snuck up behind me, slipping his arms around my waist and pulling me close. He kissed my neck, then nibbled on the back of my earlobe. "Damn, this view is hot. I just wanna take you right here." His hands found their way over my breasts, massaging and squeezing my nipples. A firecracker popped inside of me, causing me to moan.

I smiled, leaning my head back on his chest. "Take it then," I teased, grinding my ass into him, then hiking up my silk robe just enough to expose the bottom of my ass cheeks before spreading them open, releasing a steam of wetness. My insides were on fire. And without saying a word, he pulled open his robe, dipped at the knees, then slowly slipped his dick deep in my smoldering hole until he unleashed a nut as creamy and rich as coconut milk.

Chile, I was so full of energy that I felt as if I would explode if I didn't get out and do something. I wanted to take in every inch of the island. From our shopping—well, browsing, because they damn sure didn't have any major shop happenings—down at the Market Square, to our stroll along the waterfront of the Carenage on the inner harbor where we sat on the pedestrian plaza under hanging planters, eating banana bread and drinking sweet tea while enjoying the gentle breeze splashed with a hint of spice; to Grand Etang Lake and the Seven Sisters Falls, Tee and I were in awe.

But you know the funny thing is that everywhere we went, it felt like we were being watched. Someone was clearly keeping tabs on our—or should I say, *my*—every move. But it didn't matter. 'Cause I knew, Robinson knew I had landed. I looked down at my watch. It read: 5:21. It was time to get this show on the road.

"Damn, girl!" Tee exclaimed when I came stepping out of the room, wearing a fire-engine-red, scoop-necked mini-dress with matching three-quarter jacket. Odd color for a wake, I know. But I was *fierce* and on fire, standing there in my red Gucci stilettos—the ones with the mother-of-pearl heel. And I wanted them to know it when I stepped up in that disco inferno, okay. I smiled, humming as I put on my red coral, gold-and-diamond-cuff bracelet, and teardrop earrings before handing Tee the matching choker to fasten around my neck. The dress gave just enough cleavage and curves to stop traffic, okay. And with over two hundred-thousand dollars' worth of jewels on, I was a walking vault. It was just the look I wanted. "Don't make me have to go in somebody's mouth tonight," he said, pressing his lips up to my ear. "You gonna have these cats drooling and running off the road."

"Let 'em drool." I said, turning around and giving him a long, deep kiss. "I only have eyes for you." He handed me his diamond-and-platinum cuff links to put on, then kissed me on the lips again.

"Yo, you just too damn fine."

I smiled. "I know. And I'm all yours."

"Yeah, that's wassup," he said, grinning with a mixture of love and lust in his eyes. Hmm-hmm. I have to say, Tee was looking quite scrumptious himself in his black silk custom-tailored Ferragamo suit. It was nice to see him out of those damn Timbs and baggy-ass clothes for a change. But one thing's for sure, when he puts it on, he does his thing. I looked down at his size fourteens in his black Versace loafers and smiled. Humph. I've always had a thing for a big-footed man rocking an expensive pair of shoes, okay. Chile, there's nothing worse than a brotha tryna be fly with a pair of busted-ass kicks on. Ugh!

I remember when we first got married Tee used to always bug me about taking it down a notch. Talking 'bout, "Damn, girl. All you do is wear heels 'n shit. I don't know why you can't chill in some Timbs sometimes."

Humph. All the years he's known me, I've always pushed a heel and handbag, okay. So ain't nothing changed. But one day, he worked me so bad that I decided to give him what he wanted. It was the day he decided to tell me he was having a few of his "mans 'n them" over to shoot pool, and play a few games of spades. And he wanted me to play hostess to their girls. Yeah, okay.

So I went uptown and bought everything I needed: a pair of gold fronts for the grill piece; a pair of fourteen-carat doorknockers the size of mini rims for my ears; five gold rope chains, and a pair of powder-blue, six-inch Timbs. Then I found these cute little bootie cutters, and a matching midriff shirt that crisscrossed in the front. I threw my hair up into a ponytail, snapped on an Enyce baseball cap, and stepped out like, *What, nigga? What!* Chile, you shoulda seen his face when I came down the stairs in my wears. He was too through. But you should have seen how his boys' eyes popped out of their sockets. Even their girls gagged.

"Yo, let me talk to you for a minute," he said, grabbing me by the arm and leading me into another room. "Yo, what the fuck you doing?"

"Yo, dawg," I said mockingly. "I'm chillin', son!"

He cut his eyes. "Don't fuckin' play with me."

"Yo, son. Chill wit dat shit," I shot back, smirking.

"Yeah, aiight. You got jokes, right?"

"You wanted me to take it down so I took it down."

He clenched his teeth. "Yo, don't stand here and fuckin' play me. I said take it down. Not have your ass and titties out in front of all these muh-fuckas. Got these cats looking all up in your pussy." I glanced down between my legs. Humph. He did have a point. The shorts clung so tight you could see the imprint of my fatness. Boyfriend was stewed. "Yo, get your ass upstairs and get some fuckin' clothes on."

I stared him down. "I think not! This is what you wanted, so this is what you get." I snapped, snatching my arm back, then marching back to enter-tain his guests. I had everybody in tears when I shared the science behind my getup. They were hysterical. Eventually, I did go upstairs and put on something more presentable. Still in all, Tee didn't speak to me for almost two weeks behind that. But I bet you he won't ever come out his face about me taking nothing else down, except my thongs, okay. Please. Don't no man—husband or not—tell me how to fucking dress. *Especially* when I've been serving it up the same way from day one, okay.

Anyway, back to Tee looking good in his suit. After he stopped ogling, he gave me a serious look, walking up to me. "Yo, baby, you sure 'bout this?"

If you only knew, I thought, reaching up and adjusting his silk tie. "I've never been more sure than anything in my life."

"Let's roll then," he said, taking me by the arm and guiding me toward the door and down the stairs.

I smiled. "Let's."

By the time we stepped up into John Paul's Funeral Parlor, there was this sudden calmness over me. I took a deep breath, then slowly exhaled, walking into the double doors where the viewing was being held. The room was filled with about thirty to forty people, paying their final respects. The ugly bitch even had a bunch of beautiful floral arrangements around her casket. *What a waste*, I thought. Tee held my hand, squeezing lightly to keep me reminded that he was there with me. I smiled and shifted my eyes ahead. A young woman dressed in a black dress was on her knees crying in front of the bronze casket, while another woman, also dressed in black, tried to console her. My heart jumped when I spotted the back of a man sitting in the front row with two dark-skinned women on either side of him. He had one arm around each of them while they wept. I knew without seeing their faces exactly who they were: My father and Grace's two crispy-critters, Iliana and Portia—my stepsisters.

"You want me to go up there with you?" Tee whispered, putting his arm around me. I shook my head. "No. This is something I have to do, alone." He hugged me tightly, then squeezed my hand one last time, kissing me on the cheek before sitting down in the aisle chair in the back row.

"You worthless, bitch! You can't do anything right…You're just like your mother,

a dirty whore...You little spoiled bitch." Her raspy voice followed me as I made my way toward her casket. Slowly I moved, one foot in front of the other. Graceful. I felt like I was floating. "*You can do what you want with her black ass, just keep out of my girls' bedroom.*"

And then I saw her brother's face. "*I'll make Grace stop beating you, if you let me make you feel good.*" His hands went inside of my panties. "*Be a good little girl, for me.*" I threw my head back, fighting tears that I thought had long dried up. The beatings were one thing, but to have that much hate in her to allow her forty-five-year-old brother to rape an eleven-year-old girl—me—is beyond forgivable. And there *is* a price to pay even in death.

The only thing I heard when I reached the casket was the air being sucked in around me. They all sat stone-still, shocked. I cut my wet eyes over at my father and his stepchildren, then down at the two women crying in front of the casket.

"I'd like a moment alone with my stepmother," I said to them, staring at the dead woman's pasty face. At first they didn't budge so I clenched my teeth, and slowly repeated myself, "I said. I want. To. Have. A moment. Alone. With. My. Stepmother." They stared me up and down before moving. I stepped out of their way, then moved closer to the casket. She didn't have on her thick, Coke-bottled lenses, but everything else about her was the same: from her yellowish-blonde hair to her wide nose and big red lips—her grill was still wrecked. The bitch looked like a pit bull in the face, okay. *Who in the hell put pink lipstick and blush on your ugly ass*, I thought before glancing over my shoulder. Someone's hand had touched me. It was my father's.

"I knew you'd come," he said softly. I kept my back to him, breathing in his presence.

"Get your hands off me," I said, keeping my eyes locked on Grace. She was dressed in a white lace gown with the stubs of both arms neatly pressed at her sides. He removed his hand. "Go on back over there with your stepchildren and console them. I want to be alone with your wife, if you don't mind."

"Indera—"

I turned around, cutting my eyes at him. He put his hands up in surrender, slowly backing away. Although he didn't say anything else, I could see it in his eyes. Fear. The corners of my lips curved into a slight smile. He was afraid of what I might do. I eased his mind, "She's safe, *for now.*"

I turned my back to the staring eyes. I overheard someone ask, "Who is that?" Followed by another voice, "What's she doing here? I swear if she does anything, I'll—" She stopped in mid-sentence when I snapped my head in her direction, staring dead in her brown eyes. I cut my eyes over at Iliana, then my father before returning my attention to Grace.

I could hear the group of women in back of Iliana and Portia speaking in hushed tones as I leaned into the casket, speaking into Grace's ear as if she could hear me. "I've patiently waited for this day, you evil woman. You beat and abused me, and turned your head when your brother molested me. You did everything you could to break my spirit. You tried to strip me of my self-worth, and steal my sanity. But, make no mistake. You underestimated me. I knew enough to love me. And I survived your hell. I'm rich. I'm beautiful. And I'm here to let you know, you will burn a thousand deaths before your soul ever rests. So ashes to ashes, dust to dust, bitch." I turned, glanced back over at my father, then headed to the back of the room where Tee waited. He stood up and hugged me, walking me out the door.

Is that it? Yes. That's it. Well, don't sit there with your mouths open, acting all surprised 'n shit. I know you didn't expect me to go up in there, tossing her coffin up. Now you know damn well I don't carry on like that. Well, okay. I have been known to shake it up a bit. But not at someone's viewing. My goodness! I mean out of courtesy to her family and friends, letting them have their moment of mourning, was the most gracious thing to do, don't you think?

Chile, I told ya'll I only wanted to pay my respects. I had no intentions of going up in there, causing a scene. I said what I needed to say, and kept it moving, okay.

And at five minutes to twelve, I quietly eased out of bed from under Tee's embrace and walked out onto the balcony, softly singing, "*Burn, baby, burn…*

disco inferno…burn, baby, burn." And at the stroke of midnight, I took in a deep breath, spreading my arms open and closing my eyes, then exhaling as the sound of sirens, and fire trucks made their way to the flames on the other side of the island. That's right. Someone slipped into the parlor, opened Grace's casket, doused her stinking ass with kerosene, then struck a match on her misery.

By the time anyone reached John Paul's, it would be burned down to the ground and Grace would be nothing but ashes. I smiled when a cool breeze swirled around me. I stared at her obituary, crumbled it up, then placed it in the glass ashtray on the rattan table, setting it aflame.

"I told you, I'd be waiting in the winds." I stared into the fire, then picked up the hot glass. *"Arrivederci*, bitch," I snapped, tossing it and the ashes of her memory over the balcony.

Now, what's that look for? Oh, I know I'm going to hell. But make no mistake. I won't be going alone. And, anyone who fucks with me, I got something for them there too.

18

DAMASCUS: *I Don't Wanna Be The Last To Know*

Man, listen. I don't know what the hell is going on with Indy's ass. But ever since we got back from Grenada, she's been buggin'. Word up. One minute we're chillin' 'n shit, then the next minute she's snappin' my fuckin' head off. I don't know how much more of this hot-and-cold shit I can take. A nigga can't even get a decent nut around here anymore without grief. I mean damn. In the last three weeks I'm lucky if I got some pussy twice. And each time, I had to practically take it. What the fuck! I had to step to her about it the other night 'cause I had had enough of her shit.

"Yo, you fuckin' around on me or what?" I asked, standing in the doorway of the bathroom. She was lying in the tub with her head back, surrounded by bubbles. She snapped her eyes open, then slowly turned her head toward me.

"Tee, what the hell are you talking about?"

"You been acting feel funny and shit. I wanna know if somebody else is beatin' my time 'cause I ain't beat for that cheatin' shit. So if you fuckin' I need to know now."

She sucked her teeth. "You so fucking stupid. What the hell I look like, I can barely deal with your ass, besides having someone else to put up with. Get real."

I folded my arms across my chest. "Yeah, aiight."

"You're too damn paranoid," she said, rolling her eyes, then lifting her head up and body forward.

"Yeah, aiight. Don't make me fuck you up, Indy."

She rolled her eyes again. "Humph. If you say so."

"Oh, you think I'm playin'?"

"No. I *think* you're trying to start your shit. But I'm not gonna let you suck me into it. Not today." She lathered up her rag and began washing the front of her body. Then she leaned back against the back of the tub and slowly lifted one leg out of the water, extending it up in the air while her washrag glided across her smooth skin. Then she slowly lifted the other. Streaks of water ran down each leg. Yo, my dick jumped. I licked my lips, gazing at her pretty toes. She emerged both legs back under her soapy water when she caught the way I was looking at her. "Do me a favor and wash my back, *please.*"

I walked over and knelt down alongside the tub, taking the pink-and-white washcloth from her hand. I stuck my hand down in the hot water, soaped up the rag, then washed her smooth back. "I don't know what's gotten into you," I said, staring at her profile. She was so damn fine. I felt the urge to lick the water as it slid down her back. But I restrained myself. I swallowed my drool, washing down my lust. "You really be on some flip shit."

She sighed. "Tee, I've been really tired lately. And every little thing seems to set me off." I twisted my lips, half convinced.

"So you bite my head off every chance you get? That shit makes no sense to me."

"I don't mean to snap on you. It's just that you make me sick sometimes, and I don't know why. It's like, you'll say something and I want to scream. Or you'll walk into the room and I want to slap you."

I scrunched my face up and shook my head. "That's fucked up."

"I know. But it's how I feel."

"So what you sayin'? You need a break or something?"

She shrugged her shoulders. "I don't know, Tee."

"Well, I tell you what," I snapped, getting up. "Let me know when you figure it out 'cause I ain't beat." Yo, keeping it real. My feelings were hurt. Yeah, I know. It was how she felt. But it stung just the same. Who the hell wants to be told by someone they love that they're sick of you? That shit ain't cool. I tossed the rag in the water and walked out, slamming the door behind me. *Talking 'bout she feels like slapping me.* What kind of shit is that? If I would have known marriage was going to be this damn stressful, I would have stayed the fuck single. Word up. 'Cause I really ain't with all the extras, feel me?

Britton hit me with the fact that I had to take the good with the bad. That's fine and all. But damn! Do I have to take all the bullshit in between too?

"Just be patient," he said last week when I spoke to him about it. "I'm not sure what she's going through, but whatever it is, just try to be understanding."

"Yo, man. I'd have no problem understanding if I knew what the hell it was I needed to understand. Shit, she doesn't even know. I'm telling you, B. I'm really trying to be patient. But Indy isn't giving me anything to work with. She's cool for a day or so, then it's bitch city up in this piece. I'm telling you, man. I don't know how much more of her nitpicking I can take. She makes me want to strangle her ass, sometimes."

"Well, my friend," he said, sounding serious. "Look at it like this. If the two of you don't end up killing each other, you'll be able to sit back and laugh at this when you're sitting in your matching rocking chairs, brushing each other's dentures." He burst into laughter. Yo, shit wasn't funny. If I were a weak cat, fucking with Indy's ass would have me wanting to blaze a few trees—a spliff to the head. That's all it would take. Word up!

"Yeah, right," I responded, massaging my left temple. *Women.* "Yo, dawg. I'll get up with you, I need to hit the gym to relieve some stress before I do something crazy."

"Well, call me if you still need to vent. You know I'm here for you."

"Thanks, man."

"Be easy."

"One," I replied, hanging up. I went downstairs and worked out until I was too damn exhausted to think about anything else, but sleep.

So here we are a week later, and her ass is still beefing about shit. Yesterday, she blacked because I didn't put the toilet lid down. And? Pull the shit back down. Damn! Hell, she acts like it's my fault her ass got wet. If she looked before she sat down, she'd see the lid was up. Then this morning she went off because I didn't put the butter back where I found it in the refrigerator—in the little compartment with the lid. Can you believe that shit, bitching over butter? Who the hell died and left her ass icebox monitor? That was it for me.

"Yo," I snapped. "Why don't you just shut...the...fuck...up! You talk about being sick of me not doing this, sick of me doing that. Well, I'm sick of your ass, bitching all the damn time. So just get the fuck up off my back."

"Who the hell you talking to like that?" she barked.

"You. Who the fuck else? All you want to do is beef. And I'm sick of it. So, shut the fuck up!" In all the years I've known Indy, I've never raised my voice to her, at her or around her. But she had it coming.

She stood there, looking at me stunned. "Kiss my ass!"

"No," I shot back, *"you* kiss mine. And when you're done doing that, you can put your mouth to use, and suck my damn dick." The last part slipped out before I could catch it. *Oh shit*, I thought. *I done fucked up now.* Fuck it. She vexed the hell out of me. So if she can come out her face and tell me to kiss her ass, then there's nothing wrong with me telling her to suck this dick, right? She blinked real hard, trying to absorb what I had just said.

"What did you say?"

"You heard me," I said, adding extra bass to my voice while grabbing a handful of my crotch. "I said, suck my dick." Her facial expression hardened and before I could duck or move out the way, with the speed of a Hank Aaron pitch, she snatched an unopened can of Carnation milk off the counter and threw it at me, clocking me upside the head.

"Now suck on that, fucker!" she yelled.

"Oww!" I hollered. "You really gonna make me fuck you up in here." I stood there, rubbing my forehead. I could feel the beginning of a lump forming. She slammed her hand on her hip, pointing her finger and twirling her neck around like she was Linda Blair and shit.

"Motherfucker, don't you ever fucking talk to me like that 'cause the next time, you'll get more than a can upside your big-ass head." She stared me down, waiting for me to leap. I clenched my jaw.

"I'm out," I snapped, walking out of the kitchen. My head was beginning to throb. *Fuck! I can't believe she hit me in my damn head.* I was so heated, I felt like punching holes in every wall. That's how mad I had gotten. But, I grabbed my keys instead, and headed for the door, ignoring her. She followed behind me. The last thing I heard before slamming the door on her ass was: "You better save that shit for your fan club 'cause you got me mixed up with one of your hoes on the street, telling me to suck your goddamn dick like I'm one of them trick-ass bitches." Whatever!

Yo, I got me a room at the Brooklyn Marriott where I was able to watch TV, leave the lid up, and drop my boxers—wherever the fuck I wanted— in peace. Funny thing, I woke up in the middle of the night, reaching over to grab her; but the only thing I felt was an empty space. *Women!* Can't live with 'em, can't live without 'em.

But let me tell you. After two days of solitude, I walked back up in this spot well rested. And I needed it. Word up. 'Cause I was really feeling like I was 'bout to snap. Between you and me, the way things have been lately, I almost hated to come back. But I did. I love Indy's little ass to death, but she's gonna have to get a grip, and soon. Or I'm out. Feel me? 'Cause all this damn beefing we've been doing is real beat. All I wanna do is keep shit light, instead of getting hit with all this damn grief. It's not like I'm some difficult cat to get along with, 'na mean? Hell, it doesn't take much to keep me happy. All I wanna do is lay back, and just be on some cool-out shit. And poppin' a few good nuts would definitely ease the tension. But even that's a wrap. My damn balls are so fuckin' heavy I can't walk straight. And jerking off hasn't been cutting it. Bottom line: I want me some ass bad.

I've been so damn horny lately that I've been actually buggin'. Word up. The other week I was beatin' my shit and smellin' a pair of Indy's lace underwear. That day-old scent of her pussy had me so damn roused I ended up licking the crotch area, and popping a hot nut thicker than grits. No joke. She really has my head twisted, for real for real.

By the time I reached the top of the stairs, my dick was already at attention and I had all of my clothes off. Beefing or not, we were 'bout to get it on, feel me? I slowly opened the bedroom door, then stood in the doorway for a few minutes, playing in my mind how good it was gonna be layin' this pipe. Word up.

Yo, between you and me. I was glad to see Indy's ass was still sleeping 'cause I didn't feel like hearing her mouth. The only thing I wanted to feel was that hot pussy wrapped around my dick. She was lying on her back, which made things easier for me. I wouldn't have to fight tryin' to get up between them smooth legs. I smiled when she let out a soft snore. *Look who's snoring now*, I thought, pulling back the white comforter and straddling her nude body. *Damn, my baby gotta bangin' body*, I said to myself, sliding my tongue over her right nipple, then lightly blowing on it. She stirred. I continued licking, cupping her breasts. She snapped her eyes open.

"What the fuck you doing?" she asked in a husky whisper.

"What does it look like?" I shot back, kissing her on the lips.

"Oh, you think you can just walk up in here after being gone for two days and get some pussy."

"Yep." I planted more kisses on her lips. She turned her head.

"Get off me."

"Nope." I licked along her neck, then down the center of her chest. She lay stone still. I wasn't beat, 'cause I knew once I hit the right spot, it'd be on and poppin.' I dipped my tongue in her belly button. Slid my hand between her soft legs. She flinched.

I reached up, pinched her left nipple while my tongue found its way further south to where my fingers had already gone. I looked up. Her head was pressed deep into the pillow. Eyes closed. I smiled.

"If you take my pussy without permission," she whispered, placing her hand on the top of my head and pushing me further down to her spot, "it's rape."

"So," I said in between licks and kisses. She widened her legs. Began moving her hips.

"You want this dick, baby?"

"Hmmm."

"You gonna give me some of this pussy, baby?" I asked in between jabs of my tongue in and out of the folds of her fat lips.

"Nope," she said, moaning.

"Yeah, you want it," I urged, sucking and licking on her clit. "Beg for it."

"Hmmm."

"I'ma give it to you real good."

She sighed. "Lick my ass, Tee."

"Yeah, baby," I said, jerking my dick. My shit throbbed. "Want me to put this dick in you, baby?"

"Lick my ass," she said again, trying to push my face away from her pussy.

I squeezed my dick, jerked harder, kissing and licking the bottom of her plump ass. "Yeah, baby. I'ma lick it for you." My balls ached. I stuck my tongue in her tight hole, pulling her ass cheeks apart. "Hmm. Your ass tastes good, baby."

She thrust her hips forward. "No, Tee." She pushed my face away with her hands. "When I said lick my ass, I meant: Lick. My. Ass!" She slammed her legs shut, pushing me off her.

My eyes widened. My dick pounded in my hand. "Aye, yo. What the fuck!"

"You're not gonna talk slick to me, then think you can slid up in this good pussy like shit's all sweet."

I sighed heavily. I was about to explode, sexually and mentally. I really don't know how much of this I can take. "Yo, what the fuck does one thing have to do with the other? Can't you just put the beef aside so we can get it on, instead of harboring shit? You haven't hit me off in weeks."

"And until you know how to talk to me, it'll be months before you slide back up in this again. I don't appreciate you telling me to suck your damn dick the way you did."

She got out of bed, glaring at me. I rolled over on my back with one arm extended behind my head, facing her. My dick bounced across my stomach. She tried to keep her eyes off it. I stroked it, then held it upright at the base.

"See what you do to me?"

She sucked her teeth. "Get a grip."

"How 'bout you come grip it?" I requested, stroking it up and down.

"Wrong answer," she snapped. "How 'bout you go to hell?"

"Yo—"

"Don't 'yo' me."

She is really fuckin' tryin' me. I closed my eyes tight, took a deep breath and blew it out, slowly. "Yeah, aiight. You got that," I said, straining to keep my cool. *I'm tryna get some damn pussy and she wanna be on some bullshit.* "Come on, Indy. I ain't tryna argue with you so can you *please* chill. Please, baby."

"Humph." She walked over to the dresser, pulling out a sheer white, spaghetti-strap nightgown. She slipped it on. I could see the soft patch of hair between her legs. Her nipples were standing at attention. Man, listen, Indy's got a lotta shit with her, word up! She's not givin' up the pussy; but she'll put on a skimpy-ass nightgown just to fuck with me. I smiled to keep from screamin' on her, shaking my head.

"What the fuck's so funny?"

"You," I said, rolling out of bed, walking up to her. She put her hands on her hips, glancing quickly down at my brick-hard dick. "You always gotta have the last word. Always gotta be so damn tough." I grabbed her, pulling her into me. I stared into her eyes. "Why don't you chill, aiight? I don't wanna beef with you. All I wanna do is make love to my wife. That's it. So can you, please, not deny me?"

She licked her lips, placing her hand around my dick. She squeezed and jerked it. Damn, her hands felt good. "You want me to suck this long dick for you?" My mind raced as she stroked my dick up and down. Yo, as bad as I wanted her to get down on it, something wasn't right. She had flipped the script too damn quick. And knowing Indy's spiteful ass, she had something up her sleeve.

"Nah, that's aiight," I said, pulling her hand from around my shit.

"You sure?" she asked, grinning. "'Cause I'll clock in, if you want."

Oh, hell no! I wasn't falling for that shit. She'd fuck around and try to bite my dick off for coming at her wrong. I shook my head. "Nah, I'm cool." I backed up from her and headed for the bathroom. *She's a real fuckin' trip,* I thought as I walked into the bathroom, closing the door behind me. *A nigga can't even get his dick wet around here.* I jumped in the shower and beat my dick under the water, letting a nut of frustration slide down the drain.

An hour later, Indy showered, got dressed and stepped out, saying she was going shopping and didn't know what time she was coming back. *Like she doesn't have enough shit already*, I thought to myself. *Do you.* It was for the best any damn way 'cause if she stayed her ass home, she'd find something to bitch about, 'na mean?

Besides, I needed to finish my manuscript and have it on my editor's desk by Tuesday. The last thing I needed was her riding my damn back too. She's cool peeps and all, but she's no-nonsense when it comes to deadlines 'n shit. She sort of reminds me of Indy. So having the house to myself would give me time to finish up the last two chapters of *Caged*. Yo, between you and me, this book is gonna be a sizzler. I'm really diggin' the characters. And the ending is off the fuckin' meter. Word up! Nah, no sneak peeks. You'll have to wait until it hits the streets.

Anyway, by five p.m. I had eaten, popped another nut and finished my book. *Two books down, and one more to go*, I thought while clicking my PC off. And I was relieved. This whole writing thing is cool; but keeping it real, it's not something I see myself doing for a lifetime. I mean. I'm under contract for three books and that's peace. But once I blaze this last book, it's a wrap. I did the writing thing, now I just wanna step out and do something new, 'na mean? Don't get me wrong, being an author has been a rewarding experience but it's not where my heart is. Not long term anyway. Ever since I started visiting detention centers, I've been really thinking about going to law school or doing something in juvenile justice. I feel like that's where I can make the most difference, feel me?

I know I already hit you with all this a while back; but it's like every time I step through those doors, I can feel those young cats' pain. I can hear their cries. I know what they feel 'cause I've been there. And I feel like I need to be a part of their healing process. In some small way, I wanna feel like I made a difference in someone else's life. The way some-one did in mine, feel me? Not that I think I'm gonna save every young brotha. But, hopefully, I can get them to see that life doesn't have to be the way they know it, or have lived it.

Of course Indy feels I can do it all. Write books, go to law school, and still work with the young cats. And on the real for real, she's probably right.

She's been encouraging me to go back to school ever since I got my bachelors last year. Funny thing, if she had her way, she'd have me getting a doctorate in something. Damn, yo. Now that I'm sitting here telling you all this, I have to shake my head and smile. As mad as she makes me, and as much of a moody, pain in the ass she can be at times, Indy has always had my best interest at heart.

Yo, someone's at the door, hold up.

"Hold your horses," I snapped, walking toward the buzzing doorbell. "Who is it?"

"Police," a booming voice said as I opened the door. I had a puzzled look on my face.

"Can I help you with something?"

"Good evening," a tall, dark-skinned brotha, sporting a bald head and goatee said. "We were hoping we could speak with Ms. Fleet. I'm Detective Anderson and this is Detective Frenchskins," he added, pointing to the short, stocky white man with wire-framed glasses and a receding hairline. He looked vaguely familiar. I unlocked and opened the storm door, inviting them in. I sized them up before speaking. The brotha was built like an athlete, a little taller than me. Six-four or six-five; the other was much shorter with a Pillsbury Doughboy shape.

"I'm sorry. She's not in. Is there something I can help you with?" They looked over my shoulder—for what I don't know—then returned their attention to me. "I'm her husband."

"Ah, yes," Detective Frenchskins said, smiling. "I knew you looked familiar. You were the gentleman I spoke with down at the hospital—"

I nodded, acknowledging his recollection. "Right. Does this visit mean, you have her attacker in custody?"

They shifted their eyes, glancing at each other. The brotha spoke. "We'd really like to discuss this with Miss, I mean Mrs.—"

"Miles," I offered.

He smiled. "Mrs. Miles. Do you know when to expect her…" At that moment the door opened.

"Here she is now," I said as she strolled in carrying shopping bags from Saks. She scrunched her face up.

"What happened?" Although we're still beefing, I thought it best to put on my happy face, feel me?

"Baby, these gentlemen would like to talk to you about the shooting."

"Oh," she said calmly.

"Mrs. Miles," Frenchskins said, "We'd like to have a moment of your time, if you don't mind."

She smiled. "Not at all. Just give me a moment to put my bags up."

Both men smiled, nodding. "Not a problem." They both obliged when I offered to take their coats. Anderson was casually dressed in brown slacks and a thick brown sweater. His sidekick's navy-blue suit looked as if he'd slept in it. There was a grease stain on his tie.

Indy glanced over at me before making her way upstairs. "Come in and have a seat," I said, extending a hand toward the living room." I looked up toward the stairway, but Indy had already vanished into the bedroom. I hung up their coats. Both men were still standing.

"Please. Sit." Both sat on the sofa. I sat across from them in the loveseat. No words were spoken between us. Frenchskins flipped through his notepad.

"Nice place you have here," Anderson said, breaking the growing silence.

I smiled, wishing Indy would hurry the hell up so I could hear what they had to say that couldn't be discussed with me—her husband. "Thanks."

Indy strolled in, seemingly pensive. I studied her, but it was hard to read what was going on in her little head. Trying to figure her ass out sometimes makes my head hurt. I let it go. "So, officers. What brings you here?" she asked, walking over to me, then sitting down on the edge of her seat. She crossed her legs.

The short detective cleared his throat. "Well, Ms. Fleet. I mean…Mrs. Miles. We think we know who shot you."

"Is that so?" Indy asked, sounding unmoved.

"You mean you have him in custody?" I jumped in, feeling relieved that this lunatic was finally off the streets, and justice would be served. After three years there'd be some closure. If I could get my hands on him, I'd split his shit for what he put her through, feel me?

"Well, not exactly," he continued. I gave them both a quizzical look. Indy remained expressionless. "I mean. Yes. And no."

"Okay, which is it?" I asked, getting frustrated. "Either you have him or you don't."

"Mrs. Miles," the brotha interjected, shifting the questioning. "Do you know a Randall Brown?" He pulled out a black-and-white five-by-seven picture, handing it to her.

"Not that I can recall," she responded, taking the photo. I glanced at it. "Oh, you mean Randi. Not personally. But *Miss Thing* used to frequent my shop a few years back, why?" Instead of leaving it at that, Indy had to put all the man's business on front street, telling them how he was friends with one of her ex-hair stylists, Alexi—who happened to be a transvestite—and would come into her shop to get his nails done for nights of bar hopping and dick sucking dressed as a woman. I shook my head. Indy doesn't care what she says.

"His personal life is not of interest to us," Frenchskins stated abruptly.

Indy cocked her head, interlocking her hands over her knee. "Then state your purpose for being here so I can unwind from my day."

"Would he have had a reason to want to harm you?" Anderson interjected.

Indy pursed her lips. "Well, a few years ago I put him on blast in church. So he might have been a little salty with me for airing his secret life in front of his wife, and the rest of the congregation. Why you ask?"

"Well," Frenchskins said, leaning forward, "we have evidence, suggesting he's our assailant."

"Has he admitted to it?" Indy asked, uncrossing her legs then shifting back in her seat.

"Well, no."

"Then how do you know he did it?" she challenged.

"Because we received a note, along with a gun and billy club, stating he had attempted to kill you." Frenchskins glanced over at Anderson. "And his fingerprints match the ones we found on the weapons."

"Interesting," Indy said. I gave her a sidelong stare. She was too damn calm for me. "So where is he?"

"The morgue," Anderson stated coolly.

"What?" I asked, scooting up on the edge of my seat, leaning forward. Indy remained still. "What happened to him?"

"He was beheaded."

"Oh shit!" I snapped.

"Same thing we said," Anderson replied, shifting in his seat. Two months ago, they had received an anonymous call from someone indicating they knew who had attempted to kill Indy. The caller didn't remain on the line long enough for the call to be traced. However, the next day they received a package from a delivery service with a man's hand cut off and a typed note, stating: *This was the hand that pulled the trigger*. A few days later, they received another package from a different delivery service with the weapons. Sure enough, Forensics was able to confirm the allegations. Then last week, they received a third package, this time a much larger box, from yet another delivery service. When they opened it, they were greeted with a man's head packed in dry ice with a handwritten note nailed into his forehead: *This was my punishment for trying to kill Indera Fleet*. They indicated that his head was badly beaten and his scalp and face were so burned (from someone setting his hair on fire) that they had to use dental records to identify him. They had yet to uncover the whereabouts of his torso. I cringed. Indy didn't blink.

"Is that it?" she asked, getting up.

"Well, not exactly, ma'am," Anderson continued, clearing his throat. "We received another piece of information, attempting to link you to the crime."

"Say what?!" I snapped, shaking my head in disbelief. "Nah, that's some bull."

She remained standing. Hands on hips. "And what might that be?"

"Two days ago we received a letter written several months back from someone we believe to be the assailant/victim. The handwriting matched the other letter." He paused, wiping his brow. "We believe it was written before he was decapitated."

"Okay," Indy responded. "So what does that have to do with me?"

"Well," he continued, "it stated he was being watched and that he feared for his life. The letter went on to say that he had instructed a friend to mail his letter if something were to happen to him. He alleged that you knew he was the one who attacked you, and that you were out to get him as payback."

My mind slipped in and out of the conversation. *Did she really have something to do with this shit*, I wondered. I pressed rewind in my mind, recalling situations where it had been speculated Indy had something to do with "things happening" to people she felt crossed her, for one that Alexi chick who worked down at her salon. I thought about how Indy had slashed her up because she pulled a box-cutter on her. The fact that the chick had her face sliced up, needing over sixty stitches, wasn't enough for Indy. She had to take it a step further, stating she was going to be "handled" for stealing from her. Then, months later, Indy's accused of having the chick's fingers cut off. There was no proof, but Alexi was sure it was Indy's work.

I continued. I thought about some of the things she'd done to cats who had come at her wrong. Like sending that videotape of that brotha she fucked in the ass to his wife, *and* his job. Although she couldn't be linked to the tape because her face wasn't shown, she had cost him his family, and career, without a care. Then there was the brotha—about six years back—who called her a "stuck-up bitch" at a hair show in Atlanta. Instead of blacking on him, like she's known to do when a cat talks slick, she smiled, saying he had better enjoy himself now because he'd never be able to open his mouth to call another woman a "bitch." She stepped off, saying nothing else. Two days later, his tongue was cut out.

And the most recent ordeal: that Grenada trip. Indy has never minced her words about how much she hated her stepmother. Yet, she flies down to her funeral, talking 'bout she wanted to pay her respects. Yeah, aiight. Then all of a sudden, the damn funeral home is burned down to the ground. Indy didn't blink an eye when her father came to the guesthouse to confront her about it. And when her stepsisters came at her, she looked at them like they were crazy. She didn't admit it, but she damn sure didn't deny it, either. And there was definitely no evidence found to confirm their suspicions. The only thing Indy said was: "Well, she was going to burn in hell anyway. So what's the big deal?"

Damn! These were a few incidents that were too coincidental that I was aware she was suspected of having *something* to do with it. I don't want to even think about the shit I know nothing about. I shook my head. Am I married to a gangstress, or what?

I watched Indy's face and body language, studying her response for any signs of nervousness. Nothing. "Let me explain something to you. This man came into my shop, shot me in my chest, and severely beat me, causing life-threatening injuries. And you have the audacity to sit up in my home, telling me about some letter written by a disgruntled drag queen claiming I might have had something to do with his head being chopped off. Please. As much as I would love to take credit for his demise, I can't. So, unless you have some solid evidence linking me to his death, I suggest we conclude this meeting. Now get up and get out."

"We didn't mean to upset you," Anderson said, getting up. "We—"

"Mrs. Miles," Frenchskins interrupted. "I recall in the early stages of this investigation you saying you didn't know who shot you. Now I hear you saying he did it."

"No," she snapped. "Get it right, detective. What you heard was, me repeating what you just sat here and said. If I'm not mistaken, *you* said you had evidence suggesting he was my attacker. Not me. Perhaps you should lay off the donuts and pay more attention to what you say."

His face turned beet-red. His partner stepped in. "We appreciate your time, Mrs. Miles. Sorry for disrupting your evening, or causing you any inconvenience. We just thought you'd like to know that we're closing our investigation at this time." He extended his hand. She shook it civilly. "We'll be in touch if something should change."

She smiled. "Well, I thank you for putting some closure on this matter. I'll sleep much better now, knowing he's off the streets. I can finally get on with my life." Get on with her life? Hell, her ass hasn't missed a beat. Did she tell ya'll she's working on her own cosmetics and perfume line? She didn't, did she? Figures. Hell, I wouldn't have known either if I didn't overhear her talking on the phone to a chemist. And I'm sure she hasn't mentioned her new entertainment company. Yeah, she'll sleep better all right—straight to the damn bank. I kept my mouth shut. I shook both detectives' hands, walking them to the door.

When I walked back into the living room, Indy was sitting on the sofa with her right leg tucked under her, flipping through the mail. I stood behind her, staring at her. What the fuck is up with her ass? The cops walk up in here, hitting her with this news and she acts like it's no biggie. I needed to know something.

"Yo, you mean to tell me, all this time you knew who shot you?" I asked, standing in front of her.

"I never said that," she responded, tearing open her American Express bill, then shuffling through the ten or more pages.

"You didn't have to."

She looked up, catching my stare. "So what are trying to get at?"

I took a deep breath, blowing it out slowly. "I'm trying to figure out what's going on with you. It's like you on some secret squirrel shit, and I'm not diggin' it."

She *tsked*. "Tee, let's drop it, okay?"

I frowned. "Okay, nothing. The cops just left up out of here, talking 'bout they were sent the hand and head of a man they believe to be your attacker, and a letter alleging you were behind it. And you sitting here, talking 'bout 'let's drop it.' Negative. I don't think so."

She tossed the mail on the table, pulled her foot from under her and shifted in her seat. She squinted. "Okay, look. What do you want to know?"

"The truth," I said, sitting down next to her. "And don't try to give me the fluffed version. I want it straight, and to the point."

"Well, if you're asking me if I had something to do with his unfortunate fate, the answer is no. But I don't give a damn that someone took his head off. He tried to kill me, okay. So as far as I'm concerned, he got what he deserved."

"So you knew all along who shot you?"

"Basically."

"So why didn't you tell the police—or me, for that matter?"

"Because, it was my life he tried to take, and it was my choice to seek justice, not the police. Oh, I planned to turn him in, but *not* until I was done with him. The reason I didn't tell you I knew who had shot me was because I knew you would want me to go to the police with the info. And my mind was already made up. If I survived, he'd have hell to pay." A part of me understood what she was saying, but I still wanted to know who died and left her judge and jury.

"But I'm your husband. If no one else knew, I should have."

"I didn't want you brought into the middle of it," she offered, turning to face me.

"What the hell you mean, you didn't want me in the middle of it? I went through that shit with you. I was there from the rip. If I woulda caught the nigga, he woulda caught a hot one. Word up. I'da capped his ass myself—on the strength."

"And that's what I didn't want. Not that it matters now because he's dead."

"And you had nothing to do with it?"

"I just told you that."

I stared at her.

"Don't look at me like that."

"Like what?"

"Like you don't believe me."

"I don't know what to believe anymore," I said, getting up. I lowered my voice. "All I know is a lot of crazy shit's been going on lately, and you seem to be the common denominator."

She cut her eyes at me. "You can believe what you want. But know this, if I wanted him dead, I wouldn't have waited three years later to have him done, okay. He would have been killed from the jump. And *that*, you can believe."

Yo, I just looked at her ass, shaking my head. She returned to her stack of mail as if I wasn't there, and as if she didn't have a care in the world. I walked out of the room, believing my wife was off the damn chain.

Bright and early, Saturday morning, the tires of my Range screeched as I pulled out of the Amoco gas station on the corner of Flatbush and Lefferts avenues. I had gotten up early to wash and gas up the whip and decided at the last minute to head up to see my man Brit. It had been a minute since we'd really had a chance to hang, and shoot the shit. Keeping it real. I missed the raps. And right now, I really needed to bend his ear. Word up. That shit Indy had hit me with had me bugging. I mean damn.

I knew her ass had a mean streak, and had no problem getting down for hers, but damn. She's vicious.

I called home to let her know I wouldn't be back until late. The phone rang six times before the answering machine clicked on. I glanced down at my watch. It read: 10:08. *Damn. I know her ass isn't still in bed*, I thought, leaving my message.

While on my way up to Chester, I stopped at Woodbury Common to pick up a couple of Timbs for Amir and Amar at the Timberland store. Then hit the Burberry and Prada stores, picking up a few things for myself. Like a leather laptop case for my PC, two pair of gloves, a scarf, and some other shit. Nothing major 'cause it was too damn busy with heads tryna find the hot shit for bargains. It was like a hundred buses and a thousand people out there, running around like cattle. Word up. That's why I don't like fuckin' with them outlets. It's too damn hectic. I got my shit and bounced my way over to Brit's.

"Yo, B," I said, walking through the door. We gave each other a brotherly embrace. "What's poppin'?"

"Nothing much," he said, smiling. "Just tryna survive. What's in the bags?"

"Oh, I picked up some things for the boys," I responded, handing him the bags.

"Thanks," he said, shaking his head. "You and Indy have them spoiled rotten."

"Nah, just a little sumthin'," I said, taking off my coat, then hanging it up in the hall closet. "I hope everything fits." He looked through the bag, pulling out the boxes.

"Three pair of Timbs each?" he asked, opening the boxes. "These boys are growing like weeds. By next month they'll be too small."

"Then I'll hit 'em again," I shot back, plopping on the sofa. "Yo, where they at anyway?"

"My mom's," he replied with a puzzled look on his face. He shook the two empty bags out and scratched his head.

I stared at him. "What?"

"Damn, man. I could have used a new pair of Timbs too." He stuck his bottom lip out, pouting. "You know I'm up here in these woods broke down and busted."

I laughed, looking down at his Nike-clad feet. He had on a bangin' pair of gray-and-red Air Max that cost 'bout a buck forty. "Yeah aiight, nigga," I snapped, grabbing one of the boy's action figures off the sofa and throwing it at him. "And I'm Spiderman."

"And that you are," he replied, laughing. He excused himself to put the boots in the kids' room.

While he was upstairs, I leaned my head against the back of the sofa, wondering what the hell Indy was up to. I really needed to know when and why things got so crazy between us. You don't know how many times I've beat myself in the head thinking that maybe it was me. Maybe I was smothering her. Maybe I'm not giving her what she needs. Nah, fuck that. I threw the thought right out the window. Maybe she's just gotten on my last damn nerve with all of her bullshit. 'Cause I give her all the space she needs to do her thing, feel me? So I know this shit's not about me. It's about her. And she needs to check herself before she fucks up a real good thing.

"Something the matter?" Brit asked, walking back into the room, disrupting my thoughts. "You look like you lost your best friend."

I sighed. "It almost feels like it," I said, catching his stare.

"I'm listening," he said, sitting next to me. "What's Indy up to now?"

"Who the fuck knows," I snapped, resting my elbows on my knees and placing my face in the palms of my hands. I rubbed my hands over my face. "B, she's driving me fuckin' crazy. Word up. One minute, I'm ready to just say fuck it, and bounce on her ass. Then the next minute, she throws the lovin' on me, and I'm whipped all over again. It's like I can't get enough of her." I paused.

Brit leaned back and folded his arms across his chest and waited for me to continue.

I exhaled. "I love the hell out of her, B. But she's a real bitch sometimes." I turned to face him to check for his facial expression. There was none. As always, he was gonna let me say what I had to say, the way I had to say it, without judgment. "I think she's fuckin' around on me, B."

"And why do you think that?" he asked diplomatically. This time he paused. I twisted in my seat.

"Has she said or done something to give you reason to believe she's creeping on you?"

I shook my head. "Nah, not really."

"But you think she is?"

"I don't know. I mean. I don't think she would. But then again, I know how females get down. They'll have you thinking it's all about you; playing you like a fiddle while they're out fuckin' the next man. I don't think she'd play me like that. But let's keep it real. Chicks can get real grimy. And you know how Indy is."

"Exactly," he replied. "And I know that's not how *she* gets down. And you should too. I know the two of you are having problems but I seriously doubt it's because Indy is out here fucking around on you." He shook his head. "Nah. I don't think that's it at all. Hell, as much as she can't stand cheaters, it wouldn't make any sense."

"And neither does a fire marshall who goes around setting forest fires. But he does it anyway because he doesn't think he'll get caught."

"Your point?"

"My point is I don't know what the hell she's capable of."

"Okay, then let me ask you this. Are you cheating on her?"

"Hell no!" I snapped. "I love her little ass too much for that."

"Hmm. But you don't think she loves you enough?"

"I didn't say that."

"Okay, so what are you saying?"

"I'm saying my wife has me buggin.' Word up." I paused, looking over at him. "Yo, Indy's ass is crazy."

He burst out laughing. But I was serious. "I told you. But you said it didn't matter."

"Man, listen, it didn't. But now that we're married…it's like I'm living with the *Two Faces of Eve* or something. Seems like ever since she agreed to get pregnant, she's been trippin'."

A look of surprise flashed across his face. "When did ya'll decide to have a baby?" he asked excitedly.

"A few months ago. I thought you knew."

He shook his head. "First I'm hearing it. But it's about damn time. I'm glad Indy finally came to her damn senses. I was so sick of her taking those damn…" He stopped himself, slapping his hand over his mouth.

I leaned forward, raising my eyebrow. "Taking those what?" I asked, facing him.

He stood up. "Nothing," he snapped, moving quickly from one side of the room to the other.

"You know something I don't?" I asked forcefully.

He turned to face me. "Huh?"

"Don't stand there looking stupid and shit. What was she taking?"

He lowered his eyes, then looked up, staring at me for a long moment. "Let's forget it. It's not important."

I frowned. "The hell if it's not. You know something, and you're just gonna stand there and leave me hanging. That's real fucked up, B. Word up."

He opened his mouth to speak but the words seemed to stick to the roof of his mouth. "I…umm. Tee, listen…" Then like a ton of bricks it hit me. I plopped back against the sofa. Hurt. Stunned. And fuckin' betrayed.

I swallowed the lump in my throat. "She was taking birth control, right?" He lowered his eyes. "Ain't that some shit. And you knew all along. All the times I told you how bad I wanted to have a baby with her, you fuckin' knew she was playin' me." I slapped my knees as I stood. "Yo, that's some real foul shit. Word up, B."

"I didn't mean for it to slip out," he explained. "But it wasn't my place to say anything. I'm sorry."

"Yeah, right," I said, brushing past him to get my coat from the closet. I sighed, heading toward the door.

"Wait," he called out behind me, placing his hand on the door. "What are you going to do?"

"I don't know," I said, holding back my fury. My eyes burned. "But I gotta get the fuck up outta here."

"Listen Tee, don't do nothing crazy. Maybe you should stay the night and leave in the morning when you're calmer."

"Nah. I'm cool," I said, pulling open the door and walking out.

"Yo Tee, man?"

I kept walking. Nothing he had to say mattered. I held my breath, clenching and unclenching my jaw. I don't remember breathing until I pulled out of his parking lot, and was halfway down the hill out of his development. If I knew nothing else, I knew it was about to be on.

I had driven around the city for a while, up and down the West Side Highway before finally making my way over the Manhattan Bridge. I don't know how fast I was going or exactly how long I'd been driving but when I eventually screeched in front of the house, it was a little after eleven o'clock. All of the lights were off, except for the nightlight in the hallway.

I walked in the living room, picking up the framed picture of her and me off the end table. I stared at it, shaking my head. *What the fuck was she thinkin'?* I thought, tossing the photo on the floor, then walking toward the dining room. I flipped on the light switch to go into the kitchen but stopped in my tracks when I spotted her green leather Gucci bag. Now, before you go saying something, hear me out first. I have never gone in Indy's things looking for anything. But as far as I was concerned, I had a right to know what the hell my wife was up to. And I needed to see proof for myself, feel me?

I picked up her pocketbook and then sat it back down. *Nah, nigga, don't even go there*, I thought. *Just ask her.* "All she'll do is try to lie her way out of it," I reasoned to myself. *Fuck it!* I picked up her bag again, this time dumping the contents on the carpet. Out fell three cell phones, a can of mace, brass knuckles, and a .357. Man, listen, I stood there like, *what the fuck!*

"What the hell is she doing with this shit?" I asked, rummaging through the rest of her things, more concerned about finding her pills than trying to figure out why she was carrying around weapons.

I picked up the matching leather pouch, unzipped it, then pulled out its contents: a string of metal balls, a pen-sized vibrator, and—bingo, a pack of pills! I flopped down in one of the dining room chairs, staring at nothing for what seemed like hours before I actually counted the pack. Eight pills were missing. And then I snapped up as if I had a vision: an epiphany or some shit. I stormed up the stairs, taking two at a time until I reached the bedroom door. I swung it open, flipping on the light switch.

"Yo, wake the fuck up!" I ordered, shaking the bed.

She jumped, seemingly startled. "Whaat?!" she snapped, adjusting her puffy eyes to the light.

"Aye, yo. What the fuck is this?" I asked, holding the pack of pills for her to see.

"Where'd you get those?" she asked, stirring under the covers before sitting up.

"What you mean, 'where you get those'? What the fuck are you doing with 'em?" I shot back.

"Tee, I'm really not feeling well. Can we talk about this tomorrow, please."

"Yo, fuck a tomorrow!" I yelled. "I wanna know what the fuck you doing taking these pills without discussing it with me."

Her head snapped and jerked sideways. "Excuse you?"

"You heard me. Now what the fuck are you doing with them?"

"First of all, what the hell were you doing in my pocketbook?" Instead of her just answering the damn question, she wants to answer a question with a question. She was really trying my patience. "Second of all, I don't have to discuss shit with you. It's my body and I decide when and what I do with it."

Can you believe that shit. Man oh man! She was about to really catch it. "Yo, don't fuckin' come at me like it's no big deal that you've been fuckin' lying to me."

"I haven't lied to you about shit," she snapped. "So what are you talking about? Yes, I *was* on birth control. But, I've been off of them for over a month. So get a fucking grip." She got back under the covers. "Now do me a favor, and cut that damn light out. I told you I'm not feeling well. And you want to argue over a pack of old-ass pills."

Oh hell no! She's always fuckin' talkin' slick, and I'm always letting her slide. But I'll be damn if she was gonna get it off this time. I blacked.

"Fuck you not feeling well," I barked, yanking the covers off her. "I'm sick of your shit, Indy. You have me thinking we were trying to have a fuckin' baby when all along you were fuckin' playin' me. I don't appreciate that shit. Not one damn bit."

"Have you lost your damn mind?" she asked, shocked. "I'm fucking sick, okay? So I don't feel like talking about this right now."

"I don't give a fuck about you being sick! Everything always has to be about goddamn Indy. Indy this. Indy that. Well, when the fuck are you going to realize that there's more to life than fulfilling your own motherfuckin' needs. When the fuck are you going to start realizing that everything isn't always about you and what the fuck you want. What about me, huh? What the fuck about this marriage, huh, Indy?" I snatched her by the arm, yanking her up.

"Oww," she winced, trying to get out of my grip. "What the fuck is wrong with you? You're hurting me." I was enraged. All I ever did was try to love her ass and she wanted to be on some slick shit.

"Oh, now you're hurt," I snapped, shaking her feverishly. "Well, guess what? You're hurting me, and you're hurting this marriage with your bullshit. Don't you know I love your little ass, and all you're doing is hurting me?" The room began to spin. My head ached. The air around me thickened. "You're gonna make me hurt you up in here, Indy. You hear me?" I yelled. "I'm sick of you fuckin' playin' me like I'm some crab-ass nigga!"

"Get your motherfucking hands off me!" she snarled, swinging her fist and hitting me in the chest. I mushed her in the face, causing her to fall back against the headboard. She jumped up ferociously swinging her arms slapping and punching me like a wild woman. "You must have lost your goddamn mind, thinking you can put your motherfucking hands on me. No fucking man puts his hands on me, and think he's gonna live to tell about it."

I blocked her blows, ducking and dodging her fists until I was able to grab her by the wrists and throw her down on the bed. I never realized how strong she was 'cause it was almost as if I were tussling with a grown-ass man. Word up.

"Get the fuck off of me!" she screamed.

"Not until you calm down," I said, trying to catch my breath. "I don't wanna hurt you up in here, Indy. So calm the fuck down."

"I want you to hurt me, motherfucker. Bitch-ass nigga! Yeah, I took birth control pills. So the fuck what! It's my fucking body, and my fucking pussy so I don't have to answer to you about a motherfucking thing. So fuck you!" She frantically kicked her legs, trying to flip me off of her. But I held on steadfast. She continued to hurl hurtful words at me, saying, "I hate your ass! I wish I never met you. I want you out of my house. And out of my fucking life." And in that split second, I raised my arm up over my head, balling up my fist to knock her block in. But just as I was about to come down on her grill, something stopped me in midair. It was like someone else was in the room, grabbing my arm. Indy stopped screaming and moving. Her chest heaved in and out. Her eyes shot fire. "I dare you. Go 'head, take your best shot, motherfucker." I let her go, getting up off of her.

"You're a real fuckin' bitch," I said, walking toward the door, dabbing my busted lip with the back of my hand. I wiped blood on my shirt.

And with the speed of a cheetah, she reached up under the mattress while leaping up off the bed in one swift motion, pulling out a gun, then shooting up the bedroom, spraying bullets all over the room. "You lowdown stinkin' bitch-ass motherfucker!" I ducked bullets. "I'll show you a bitch, nigga," she screamed. "I'll blow your motherfucking face off." In all my years knowing her, I've never seen her like this. It was like she was possessed. And I was scared as hell. Word up! I ran—nah, fuck that! I jumped down the stairs and hauled ass, fleeing for my damn life.

19

BRITTON: *Is It Love You're After*

You already know, Tee is my boy and all. And I love him dearly. But I'm telling you. He has got to get the hell up out of here. I figured I'd give him a few days to get himself together, then he'd take his ass back home to his wife. But no! Two weeks later and he's still here. That's going a bit overboard, don't you think? Okay, I understand why he walked out on Indy. I'd probably have done the same thing. But, damn. Two weeks? And the messed-up part about all this is that I'm the one catching it from both ends of the stick.

On one end, I have Tee. Stressing. Complaining. Blaming. Hurting. And the list goes on. He just keeps himself locked up in that room upstairs, typing on his laptop and playing Donny Hathaway CD's over and over and over. I think if I heard "I Love You More Than You'll Ever Know," "Giving Up" or "I Know It's You" one more damn time, I'd thrown myself over the fucking George Washington Bridge. He was driving me crazy. So I asked him to stop playing that shit repeatedly. So what does he do? He puts on the Stylistics and starts running them in the ground with "It's Too Late," "You're As Right As Rain," and "My Funny Valentine." I had to go into the room and threaten to cut the wires to the stereo if he didn't put some earphones on. He did.

I don't think he's eaten or slept in days. And he damn sure hasn't bathed. I know 'cause the few times I walked in to check on him, the odor was enough to make anyone from a Third World country wanna run out and buy some deodorant. I know that's not nice, but it's true. He doesn't stink. He stanks!

"Tee, don't you think it's time for you to go home and work this out with Indy?"

"Nah, B," he had said to me a-week-and a-half-ago when I confronted him after his fourth day here. "After that stunt she pulled, I'm just not feeling her."

"So what you saying?" I asked, watching him pace the floor. "You ending it?"

"Yo, I don't know," he replied with a mixture of frustration and hurt registering on his face. "I'm really fucked up right now, know what I'm sayin'?"

"I hear you. But I think the two of you need to talk this out."

"B, I'm telling you. There's no talking to her. She's not a rational woman. Her ass is bugged the fuck out. I mean. I knew her ass was crazy, but her ass *is* crazy! Word up. You shoulda seen how she snapped. She just flipped the fuckin' script like I was the one tryna play her out. Then she got on some Shotgun Annie type shit, pulling out heat and shooting up the fucking room, like she was Mae West 'n shit. Yo, I ain't with that." He took a seat on the edge of the brown leather chair. He rubbed the week-old growth of hair on his face, then placed his face in his hands, massaging his forehead in wide, circular motions. "Yo, I seen another side of her, that I'm just not—"

"Do you remember when you and Indy came down to the Dominican Republic to tell me about your engagement?"

He nodded. "Yeah. Why?"

"I asked you then if you knew what you were doing. And what did you tell me?"

He turned his head in my direction, scrunching his face up. "Yo, what the fuck that got to do with anything? I married a crazy-ass woman and you asking me to remember what the fuck I said before I married her ass." He sucked his teeth.

I didn't back down. "What did you say to me?"

He blew out his frustration. "I said I finally bagged her and I wasn't letting her go."

"And?"

"That I knew all I needed to know. I said I didn't give a fuck about her past as long as I had her in my present and we were able to build a future. I told you, as crazy as her little ass was, I'd die loving her no matter what. There. You happy?" He got up and started pacing again. "But that doesn't have shit to do with the price of tea in China and it damn sure doesn't have shit to do with her ass tryna get slick."

"Did you mean it?" I asked.

"Yeah, I meant it," he replied as if I should have already known the answer. "But she has more shit with her than I can…Yo, I ain't feelin' her ass."

"Listen, Tee. I'm not saying what she did was right. She was dead wrong. But at least pick up the phone to call her. Or at least let me let her know you're here."

"Nah, nigga," he said, glaring at me. "You knew what her ass was up to and you didn't say shit. So you don't let her know shit!"

"I hear you," I said, rubbing my temples, "but she's worried about you."

"So the fuck what! She wasn't worried about me when she was playin' her fuckin' games." He paused, then turned to look at me. He stared at me for a few seconds. "Yo, we supposed to be fuckin' boys. And you went along with it."

"Unh-uh," I said, shaking my head, "you can't get that. I didn't go along with anything. Just like I'm cool with you. I'm cool with Indy. When you tell me shit, I don't go back and tell her so what makes you think it'd be any different for you? That's my girl and, although I don't agree with what she did, she's *still* my girl. And you're still my boy. But I'll be damned if you gonna put this on me. You act like I enjoy being in the middle of this mess. If my name were Bennett, I wouldn't be in it. But I am."

"Yo, you right," he said, sitting on the sofa a few inches from me, laying his head back. He let out a weak laugh. "Yo, she got my shit fucked up, B."

"Uh-huh."

"I can't mess with her, B," he continued, not sounding too sure of himself. He sat up, leaning his elbows into his thighs and holding his face in his hands. He shook his head. "I'll end up having to really hurt her ass."

"Daddy!" Amir screamed, stomping down the stairs. "Amar is jumping on the bed. And he won't leave me alone."

"Amar!" I yelled. No response. "Amar! You hear me calling you?"

"Huh?" he said at the top of the stairs. I could see him in my mind with his little hands on my white walls, peering around the corner.

"Not 'huh,'" I snapped. "Get your butt down here, now!" He crept down the stairs, dragging his feet into the carpet, finally making it over to me. "What I tell you about jumping on that bed? Do you need a meeting with the strap?" Tee looked over at me when I said that, I'm sure trying to figure out what a "meeting with the strap" was. It's my nice way of asking him if he wants a behind whipping.

"No," he said, pouting.

"Then you'd better knock it off. Now, both of you get upstairs and get in the bed. And don't let me hear another sound outta either of you. You got that?"

"Yes," they said in unison.

"Now come here and give me and your uncle Tee a hug." Amir jumped on me, giving me a big hug while Amar gave Tee one, then they switched sides. I kissed them both on their foreheads.

"Ya'll be easy," Tee said, giving them both five.

"Now good night," I said, pointing toward the stairs.

"I'm not your friend anymore," Amar said to Amir when they reached the stairs.

"So, I'm not gonna be your friend too," Amir replied. I shook my head. Tee gave a faint smile. He got lost somewhere in his own thoughts before breaking the silence between us.

"All I asked for was a baby," he said in almost a whisper. "She didn't have to play me like that."

"I know."

"Then why the fuck she do it?" His voice was filled with anger but his eyes were sad.

I looked away, taking in a deep breath, then letting it out slowly. "She's scared," I said, twisting and pulling the braids along the back of my neck.

"So why the fuck didn't she say something?"

"She said she tried."

"Bullshit! If she didn't want a baby she should have kept it real from the gate." He got up and went back upstairs, leaving a trail of anger and me sitting in the middle of it.

Then on the other end of this madness, I have Indy. Yelling. Screaming. Complaining. But underneath I can hear her worry 'cause she hasn't heard from him and she has no way to track him since he left his electronic leashes—cell and two-way—home when he left. And to ensure she wouldn't be able to find him, he even went as far as hiding his truck in a parking garage, then catching a cab here. Humph. I don't know how many times she has called here looking for him, asking me if I've heard from him. And as you already know I actually had to lie. That hurt me to my heart.

As wild as Indy gets and as much as she goes off, *I* know her better than anyone. And the one thing I know. She is worried, trying to figure out where he might be. I know she loves that man upstairs more than she's willing to admit. But sooner or later she's going to have to fall off that horse called Pride and come to terms with her feelings. If not, she's gonna end up losing the one man who truly loves her. And in the end, they'll both be unhappy.

"Britton," she had said a few days ago. "This is not like him. We've had our beefs but he's always come home or at least called. But it's been over a week and I *still* haven't heard from him. I called his agent, she hasn't heard from him. I've gone through his Palm Pilot and called every number listed. And I've called every hospital in New York. He's nowhere to be found."

"Indy, I'm sure he's somewhere trying to get his mind right. He's pretty bummed out. Give him some time. He'll be home."

"Well," she said, sighing heavy. "I'm not going to sit around waiting for him to figure out what he wants to do. This shit is too damn stressful for me right now."

"Indy, be patient," I said, carefully choosing my words. I couldn't believe she actually parted her lips to say this situation was too "stressful." I almost laughed. Had she forgotten that she was the one who started this mess? I shook my head, continuing our conversation. "I will say this, Indy. I know Tee loves you. But he's hurting. I'm telling you, he *will* be home."

"I know you've heard from him, Britton. If he's called no one else, I know he's called you." My head ached. My eyes stung. I caught my reflection in the mirror. I didn't like what I saw, lying to my best friend. I tightly closed my eyes, pressing my forehead into the palm of my hand. I was on the verge of cracking. But I promised him I wouldn't tell. I promised. I took a deep breath.

"Indy, do you love him?"

"Of course I do. What kind of question is that?"

"No," I said, shaking my head with my eyes still closed. "I'm not talking about the way you love Gucci or Louis Vuitton. I mean do you *love* him? I mean really love him." It was quiet on the other end. So quiet I couldn't hear her breathing. I continued. For the sake of my boy's sanity, I needed to know. "I ask this because I know that man loves you. And you hurt him, Indy. I'm not placing blame or pointing fingers. I love you and I love him. But you hurt him. And I need to know. Do. You. Love. Him? 'Cause if not, let him go. End this madness so the both of you can go on with your lives. If the shoe were on the other foot, I'd be asking him the same thing."

No response.

"Indy?"

"I heard you."

"Well?"

"Brit," she said, trying to stay cool. "I can't...Please. I can't talk about this right now." Silence again. Then she spoke, slowly in almost a painful whisper. "If you see or talk to him, ask him what he wants me to do with his things. He has one week to get back to me. If I don't hear from him, I'm putting everything out on the curb." She hung up. But I could hear the sadness in her tone. I heard what she said, but I knew it wasn't what she meant. So that's one message I wouldn't be passing on.

I'm telling you. I'm so damn mad at her right now, I could scream on her for putting my boy through this shit, and for having me all mixed up in it. But on the other hand, I wanna hug her and let her know I'm here for her too. Regardless of what happens because I know she's hurting too. Even if she does cover it up. But right now, Tee is of most concern to me.

I'm really worried about him. I've known him for years and I've never seen him like this. Never. I knew Indy had the potential to crush a man's spirit but I never thought in a million years it would be Tee's.

You know, he actually broke down and cried. Do you know what it's like to see a six-foot-something, two-hundred-and-ten solid-pound man cry? It tore me up. I had to leave him in his tears so I could find a private place to shed my own. That's how bad it was. That's when I knew it was time for me to take matters into my own hands. So, I did the only logical thing any friend would do, particularly since I felt partially responsible for all this confusion. I got up early Friday morning, got the boys dressed, then packed them enough clothes for the weekend. I was heading to Jersey to drop them off at my mother's, then hopping onto Route 22 toward the Holland Tunnel, taking my ass to Brooklyn. Destination: Indy's.

When I pulled out of my driveway, I spotted one of my neighbors walking with her son (well, I assume it's her son.) She smiled and waved. I did the same. I've been living up here for almost three months and to this day don't know—or speak to, for that matter—any of the people in this development. I like to keep it moving, if you know what I mean. But for some reason, this lovely sista piques my curiosity. I watched her in my rearview mirror as I made my way down the street. I smiled at the way her hips swayed and butt bounced in her Enyce sweats as she headed back to her house. I shook my lusty thoughts loose when Amar broke into song at the top of his lungs.

"A-B-C-D-E-F-G...H-I...J-K...L-M-N-O-P... Now I know my ABC's, next time won't you sing with me?"

I lifted my hands up off the steering wheel, quickly clapping. "Good job, Amar," I said, looking at him in the rearview mirror. "But you didn't finish the rest of the alphabet. You still have ten more letters to go."

"I'm saving the rest for later," he said, counting to ten. I smiled, shaking my head.

"I know my ABC'S too, Daddy," Amir shared. "Watch." He began singing over top of Amar which immediately turned into a screaming match between the two of them about whose friend the other wasn't anymore.

"Okay, let's turn this noise down," I said, raising my voice. They quieted down. "How 'bout we all sing together." They both nodded. So from Route 17 to the Garden State Parkway we sang the alphabet, "This Old Man," and every Barney song created.

I pulled into my mother's driveway, walked the boys inside, quickly gave her a hug and kiss, then headed for the door. There was no time for chitchat. I was on a mission. Misery loves company, and I was no longer in the mood to entertain it—or my pain-in–the-ass houseguest. They both had to go.

As soon as I got through the tunnel, bearing around for the Manhattan Bridge. I tried calling her, but there was no answer. I tried again when I got near the PC Richards on Flatbush Avenue. No answer. I tried her cell phone. No answer. I called both salons. Indy hadn't been to either place in over a week. They were told to only call her for emergencies. I thought about calling Nandi's but knew she wouldn't be there. Since I've been on board, she only comes through there once a week, if that. *Where in the world can this girl be*, I thought as I made my way around Grand Army Plaza.

When I reached her street, I made a left, then continued on until I reached her brownstone. I blew out a sigh of relief when I saw her 745i parked out front. I pulled into the space behind her.

I rang the doorbell. No response. I looked down at my watch. It was eleven in the morning. There's no way she was still sleeping. I rang it again. No response. Then I held down on it until it buzzed in her ear like a pesky fly.

"Go away," I heard from behind the wooden door. I shook the glass handle to the wrought-iron storm door. It was locked.

"Indy, girl…open this door or I will beat it down."

She knew the voice but decided to ask anyway. "Who is it?"

"It's Britton, fool. Now open up this damn door," I demanded, banging on the door. I shook my hand in pain when I hit it a bit too hard. "Ouch, damn it!"

I held down on the doorbell again. Finally, the double locks clicked. The wood door swung open, she unlocked the storm door and turned around to go back to wherever she had come from. I walked in, shutting the heavy door behind me.

In the background, Cynda Williams' voice filled the room with her Acapulco version of "Harlem Blues," warning you to not try to figure out what was in a man's mind 'cause even if you wanted to, there was no use of trying—especially if he was from Harlem. *How fitting*.

There were boxes all over the living room. Pictures were taken down from the walls. Holes were the only reminders of what used to be. There was a stack of photo albums over in the left corner of the doorway leading to the dining room. Over the fireplace hung a huge oil painting of Indy's mother. I stopped to admire it.

With the walls bare, it was the first time I really took a good look at it. She was absolutely stunning. Her thick hair was neatly pinned up in what looked like a French roll. Her smile was wide and bright. The detailing made everything about it seem so lifelike. She was standing in a grand foyer, wrapped in a white floor-length mink. Her bare cocoa-colored shoulders were exposed. Diamonds as thick as ice cubes hung around her neck and from her ears. I smiled. *The epitome of elegance*, I thought as I made my way to the kitchen. My mouth flew open when I entered. It was a mess. Dishes were overflowing in the sink. The garbage was stuffed beyond capacity. Three empty containers of ice cream were sitting on the countertop, along with a half-eaten box of Veniero's cheesecake. I couldn't believe my eyes. This was serious.

She was standing by the back door, staring out of the small glass window—wearing a white Dolce & Gabbana sports bra with a white-and-black sarong wrapped around her small waist. I tried not to focus on her curvaceous body. But it was a distraction. It looked as if she had put on some weight. Not in a bad way. But in a way that made her hips thicker and her already plump behind plumper.

"Girl, what in the world is going on?" I asked, peeling my eyes from her backside while taking off my jacket and draping it around the back of one of the beige double-padded rollback parsons chairs. "This kitchen is a mess." The ceramic-tiled floor had a gritty feeling when you walked on it, and it looked as if it hadn't been swept or mopped in days. The round marble-top table was covered with pots, pans, dishes and flatware.

"Well, hello to you too," she said, keeping her back to me. I stood. She said nothing else for what seemed like forever while I surveyed the mess in her kitchen. "Do you know I put his dog out? He kept chewing up my things. Wouldn't fuck with nothing else but my shit. I didn't want to bang his teeth out so I packed his shit and put him out." She shook her head. "That fool-ass dog whined and barked as I was leaving. I can't get his yelping out of my head."

I didn't let on that I already knew she had boxed up him and his things and sent him on his way. I was afraid to ask where she had taken him. I thought it was best I not know. I knew more than I wanted or needed to know as it was.

"What's up with all the boxes?"

"We closed on our house the other day," she answered in a strained tone. Not once did she look at me. She became silent. I had nothing but time on my hands, so I said nothing. She took in a deep breath. "I decided to move with or without him."

"Is that so?"

"Hmm-hmm." She was leaning up against the frame of the door with her right hand on her hip. Her left arm was wrapped around the front of her stomach. She stared out into a yard of nothingness, contemplating. "I love this house."

"I know."

"This is where my mother loved me until the day she died in my arms." I could tell by the sound of her voice that all the packing had brought on thoughts of her childhood when her mother was alive.

"You have a lot of wonderful memories here," I said, pulling out a chair, removing stacks of newspapers and sitting down. I crossed my legs at the ankles.

"And some horrible ones," she added. "There are too many ghosts in this house."

"So you're all ready to move?"

"Yep. I'm tired of 'alternate-side-of-the-street parking.'" She offered a weak laugh before softly continuing, "I need new memories." I nodded my head, understanding exactly what she meant. I used that remark as my chance to segue into my reason for coming there.

"And do any of these new memories you seek to make include your husband?" It was then that she turned to face me. A pair of black D & G shades covered her eyes.

"You tell me. Should they? I don't know where he is or what his plans are."

"Do you care?"

"What do you think?" she asked, removing her shades. I tried to hide my shock. Her eyes were swollen and looked sore from days of salty tears running down her face like Niagara Falls. A flash of all the tears and laughter she and I had shared. The parties. The brother-sister fights. All of the love we've always had for each other. The secrets. I stood up and opened up my arms to comfort my dearest friend. She fell into my embrace.

"What have I done, Britton? Tell me what in the world have I done." The walls of her heart were falling brick by brick, layer by layer. She broke down. "I hurt him. I didn't want to hurt him. He wouldn't let up. He kept going at me, yelling and cursing. My head started pounding and before I knew it, I went off. You have to believe me, Britton. I never wanted to hurt him." My beautiful friend cried her eyes out. "Why couldn't he take it down a notch? Why couldn't he ease up when I asked him to?"

"Sssh," I said, rubbing her back. We stood there without words, for what felt like hours with me holding her. With Indy sobbing and Cynda whining about her man surprising her, leaving her note saying he was gone for good, I felt an aching pain stab at my brain. My friend had her own troubles. The last thing she needed to be doing was listening to someone else's blues. "The two of you had your first big fight, that's all."

"Are you kidding me?" she asked, looking up at me. "It was more like a nuclear war up in here. You didn't see the look in his eyes. I think I went too far." Although I agreed with her, I decided to keep it to myself. Saying "I told you so" didn't feel right.

"Indy, you have got to get your anger in check, girl."

"I thought I did have it under control. But for the last two months or so everything seems to set me off. I've been having mood swings like crazy."

"Have you seen your doctor?" I asked, rocking her. She shook her head in my chest.

"I have an appointment to see her again today to go over all my lab work. Brit, I think I'm on my way to having a breakdown or something." Then she shared with me her concern that she might be having some residual symptoms indicative of post concussion syndrome—a neuropsychological disorder caused by traumatic brain injury. She'd had a concussion from being beat in the head the night of her shooting three years ago. I tried flipping through my memory bank for any familiarity with traumatic brain injury. I had none. And then it hit me as if a ton of bricks had been dumped on me: Indy was worried about dying. Her swollen eyes and sorrow were not just a result of her fight with Tee. Her tears ran much deeper. All of the women on her mother's side had died at an early age. Her mother died at forty from an aneurysm. Her maternal grandmother died at forty from brain cancer. And now she was approaching forty. It all made sense to me now.

I swallowed hard. I refused to embrace the possibility.

"You're just stressed out," I said, trying to sound optimistic. "Before you know it, everything will be back to normal."

"I don't want to think about it right now," she said, hugging me tightly before letting go. She shook her head, shaking her worries off the way a dog does fleas. Then she threw her head back, dabbing under her eyes with the back of her two index fingers. She unsnapped her hair clip, releasing her thick mane. Her hair fell to her shoulders. "Look at me. I'm a mess. Standing here crying over a man."

"He's not just any man, Indy. He's the man you exchanged vows with. He's the man you promised to love, honor and…Umm. On second thought, scratch that part 'cause we both know Miss Indy doesn't obey anything but the traffic signals." She cracked a smile. Even in her darkest moment, her smile lit up everything around her. "He's the man you said you would cherish and love in sickness and in health 'til…until the two of you are too old to do anything else." I couldn't bring myself to say "till death do you part."

"I know, Britton. I know. But—"

"Do you want him back?" I asked, cutting her off. Her tear-filled eyes said all I needed to hear.

"No more *secrets* then," I said, taking her by the hand to go into the living room where we sat on the sofa. I wrapped my arms around her. Lisa Stansfield's soulful voice erupted through the speakers with her "Just To Keep You Satisfied" from the *Inner City Blues* CD.

"Britton," she said, wiping her face. "There's so much Tee doesn't know about me."

"Give him a little more credit than that. Tee knows more than you think. And he damn sure knows you're no angel. He just doesn't say anything." She looked up at me with quizzical eyes. "Not because I told him anything." She glared at me. I smiled. "He knows you're not perfect. But you've always been perfect enough for him. Don't you know that man loves everything about you? *Everything.*"

"I know," she said, picking up the sterling silver hand mirror off her octagonal marble table. She stared at herself. "This is not cute. I look whipped." I snickered.

"Yep. But even *you* can have a bad day. And your breath stinks," I added, waving my hand in front of my nose. She playfully slapped me on the arm.

"Be quiet, boy." She sat up, shifting her body to face me. Her wrap gave way, exposing her firm upper thigh. She readjusted it, keeping her eyes on me, then shifting them, looking around the room. The brilliance of the diamond cross hanging around her neck caught my attention. In all the years I've known her, I can't recall a time I've ever seen her wearing one. She looked up at the ceiling before speaking again. She looked down at her wedding ring. "I love him, Britton. And that scares me. All my life I've never allowed myself to get attached to any man. I never needed them to affirm who I was as a woman. I've never needed them for anything. And I still don't."

"So I guess you don't need Tee in your life," I said, playing devil's advocate. "You can write him off. Just like that," I added, snapping my fingers.

"Brit, honestly. I want him in my life. But I don't *need* him in it. If he decided to bounce, I'd be okay. Trust me. I'd be hurt, but I'd get over it and I'd keep it movin'. I'm not like most women who need a man. I'm not a woman who can't live without a man. I learned a long time ago that I was responsible for loving me, no one else. So I have never needed to step outside of myself for love or acceptance from anyone, especially a man. I've held it down solo just fine." She paused, shaking her head. She smiled. "Then here comes Tee's ass, chasing me down, disrupting my flow. Wanting to love me. Wanting me to love him."

"And you damn sure gave him a hard way to go," I said, chuckling. She smiled again.

"I didn't want to love him. But he was always there—waiting."

"Yep. No matter what you said, or what you did, Tee let you know what he wanted from you."

"A chance to love me," she replied in almost a whisper. She picked up the Waterford crystal frame sitting on the marble end table. It was her wedding picture. Tee was standing in back of her, holding her tightly against him with his arms wrapped around her waist—kissing her on the cheek. She was smiling with her eyes closed. They looked so happy. She stared at it, wiping the tears that clung to her lashes before they fell. "And for me to love him back."

Dionne Farris' "Food For Thought" filled the room with her wisdom. She wondered if she were the only one using food for thought when faced with finding and knowing right from wrong, wondering how to pay for the things her mouth had bought.

I looked over at Indy. A part of me wanted to preach to her, counsel her. Tell her that she was dead wrong for tripping the way she did. I wanted to remind her that she wouldn't be in this predicament if she stopped her antics. But, she was dealing with something much bigger than using birth control behind her husband's back. Besides, she already knew where her faults lay so I settled for, "Then stop your foolishness and let him love you, Indy."

She raked her hands through her hair, pulling it up into a ponytail, then letting it drop to her shoulders again. "My mother drilled in my head to never trust a man with my heart. And I lived by that. I swore I'd never end up like her, giving all of herself to a man, then ending up with nothing but...my mother loved my father more than life and she ended up dying from a broken heart. I held her in my arms, Britton. I saw the look in her eyes. And I swore that would *never* be me."

"It won't be. You have to trust in the love you have for Tee. And believe in the love he has for you. Sure there's a chance either or both of you will end up hurt. But nothing worth having comes without some risk. Do you know there are so many women out here who would love to be in your shoes? You're beautiful, talented, rich, and you have a man who is not only faithful to you, he loves the ground you walk on. And did I mention you're filthy rich?" She laughed. But I was serious.

See. Unlike everyone else, I know the real deal behind Indy's dollars, and what she does with them. I mean, she might brag about her shopping sprees but when it comes to her community involvement, she's very tight-lipped. She'll never let you in on the fact that in addition to her two—excuse me, I mean three—hair salons, shelter and camp, she owns a real estate development firm that specializes in urban projects. With a portfolio valued at roughly three hundred and fifty-million dollars, it includes fifteen apartment buildings and nine office buildings in about eight states, including New York, Jersey and Connecticut. She'll never share with you that her firm is responsible for building and/or rehabilitating low-to-moderate-housing developments, which are based on income.

And she sure as hell is not going to let you know that she has declined twice to be featured in *Black Enterprise* magazine. When I asked her why, she simply said while writing a check to the United Negro College Fund for twenty-thousand dollars, "'Cause I don't want them nosey asses knowing my business." I got a kick out of that.

She giggled. "You so damn silly."

"I know," I said, smiling. "But I'm also being serious. There are some women who'd kill to have what you have, especially that man of yours. But, he's taken so they can only dream. My point is, be thankful for what you have: a man who loves you and only you. From your moody-ass ways to all the little things you do for others. He loves your smile. Your eyes. Oh Lord. And your sex." I burst into laughter.

"He didn't?" she said, blushing. "You mean to tell me, he's told you what we do?"

I smiled, raising my eyebrows up and down. "No. Not *everything*. But I heard it's da bomb!" She burst out laughing.

"Humph. Don't act like you don't know," she said, taking me back to the time when she and I'd had our sexual encounter—I mean encounters. Truthfully, I was shocked that she'd bring that up since it's something we've never talked about. We did it. Enjoyed it and just let it be what it was, an experience between two good friends. Come to think about it, I don't even know how we ended up on top of each other. It wasn't planned. It wasn't something we ever thought about or discussed. I mean, it simply happened. I know. I know. Nothing like that just happens. But I'm telling you, it did.

I guess you want to know, right? Well, alright. I guess I can share. We had just gotten back from North Carolina from the Aggie Fest and I was tired from all of the driving. So instead of heading back across the bridge to Norfolk, I decided to stay the night in Hampton at her condo. So, to make a long story really short, I asked her to wash my back while I was in her tub, soaking my weary bones. She commented how nice my body was.

"Boy, I did not know you had a body like that," she had said, staring at my chest and abs. "You better work."

I laughed it off, splashing water on her for making me blush. She continued washing my back, then my shoulders. And before I knew it, I had pulled her into the tub with me and…that's all she wrote. I tell you, the girl is dangerous in and out of the sheets. Trust me. She definitely taught me a few things. And yes. I had to lick her love box first. Does Tee know? Not from my lips but he's always suspected something. Not that it matters though. It was long before the two of them really became friends. Besides, the common denominator in their friendship ever developing was me. Anyway, when I look at Indy, it's in a brotherly way. And vice-versa. We share an unexplainable love for each other; a bond that no one will ever understand.

"Oh, please," I said, smiling. "You took advantage of me. You jumped my bones when I was most vulnerable."

She *tsked* her teeth. "Yeah, right. Well, if that's your version of the story, then you damn sure didn't try to stop me." The truth be told, there was definitely more than one version of the story. If you let Indy tell it, she'll tell you I practically begged her for a ride on her sex wagon. I laugh at that one, but neither of us will ever tell the real deal.

"That's because I was scared of your ass," I said, laughing. "I was afraid if I didn't give in, you'd fix it so I'd never be able to have an erection again. And you know a brotha gots to be able to get it up."

"Oh shut the hell up," she said jokingly, "before I hurt you up in here."

"Temper, temper," I shot back, shaking a finger at her. "Your temper is what got you in all this mess as it is." She reached over and touched my face. Her hands were soft.

"I don't know what I'd do without you."

"I used to wonder about that myself. But I guess we'll never know 'cause wherever I am, I'm always gonna be here for you."

"And you know I'm a ride-or-die kinda chick when it comes to you. I got your back always."

"Oooh wee!" I exclaimed, slapping my forehead. "You ain't never lied about that."

We laughed. 'Cause Lord knows she'd bring down the walls of Jericho when it comes to me. Talk about overprotective.

"I love you, Britton."

"And I love you." I reached for her hand, interlocking our fingers. I kissed it. "So what are you gonna do?"

"I don't know," she said, sighing. "I don't know how to be strong and soft at the same time."

"It's your strength Tee loves."

"He's the only man I've opened my heart to."

"I know. And you've made him very happy." Her lips parted into a slight smile. "He's the first man I've ever let my guard down with. Besides you, he's the first man I trust. And that scares me. Being vulnerable scares me."

"Indy, you are my girl. A true diva. But being a diva doesn't mean you have to be strong all the time. You're human. You have emotions and feelings. And there's nothing wrong with exposing your heart to the one you love. That isn't a sign of weakness. Don't you know when you open your heart to someone, loving them makes you vulnerable? And it makes you do some crazy things. Love makes no promises, and there damn sure are no guarantees. Love can hurt just as much as it can feel good. But you continue loving and fighting to keep that love growing."

"So I'm learning."

"And while you're loving, you have to learn how to eat humble pie and swallow your pride. And it doesn't always go down easy."

"So I see," she said, picking at her cuticles. She looked over at me, smiling. "How did you get to be such an expert in matters of the heart?"

"The hell if I know," I said, laughing. "It's not like I have a love life of my own." Not that I wouldn't want to have someone special in my life. I refuse to allow chaos in my personal space. I don't have the personality for a lot of bickering and foolishness. And the minute you start up, I'm out. And I'm not into this breaking up and making up madness. Once I say it's over, it's a done deal. I'm not down with none of that back-and-forth craziness. You go your way, and I'll go mine.

When relationships fail people are always complaining about what the other person did or didn't do. What's the point of pointing fingers? I believe there are always telltale signs of something not being right in a relationship. But for some reason we choose to see it, or ignore it; be it by choice or convenience. If I choose to stay in an unhealthy relationship I have no one to blame but myself. So, I'm not going to throw stones on someone else for being who they are when I allowed them in my space in the first place. That makes no sense. I used to believe in the old saying, "I can do bad all by myself." Well, since my own failed relationships, I've adopted a new motto: I can do *better* all by myself. And that's what I live by. I refuse to carry around anyone else's baggage or issues when I have my own I'm trying to keep in check. It's not an option. Period.

"That's because them stupid bitches don't know how to treat a man like you."

I smiled. "Perhaps. But, don't you become one of the stupid ones. You need to talk to your husband. You and I have been best friends for years and we always will be. We've shared many things together. Secrets. Laughter. Tears. Nothing will or can ever come between us. But Tee's your husband and he should be your bestest friend. Those are the things you should share with him now. You should be able to talk to Tee about any and everything."

"Britton, there's so much about me he'd never understand. Some things are better left untold."

"You say you love him and you trust him. Then trust him with the truth. The two of you need to have a heart-to-heart."

She nodded. "I guess you're right."

"And when you do," I said, standing up to walk toward the window. "Leave that damn gun at home." I looked over my shoulder, winking. Her eyes widened.

"How'd you know about that? I didn't say anything about a gun...You *have* spoken to him. I knew it. You make me sick," she said, throwing a white pillow from the sofa at me. She threw another one. I ducked before it hit me in the back of the head. "I don't believe you had me worrying all this time and you knew where the hell he was. I worried myself sick, boy. How could you do that to me?" Yes, Indy was worried, but we all know if she *really* wanted to find Tee, she would have. Besides, deep in her heart, she already knew I'd be the first person he'd reach out to, no matter what.

"I know you did. I didn't want to, but he made me promise. And you know how I am about promises. I feel really bad about it, Indy. But tough love is what you needed."

"Tough love, my ass," she snapped, giving me the finger. "I thought he was hurt somewhere. I've been stressed the hell out for two fucking weeks and he's been with your ass. That's really fucked up."

"Okay, it is what it is. But don't think it's been a picnic for me. I'm the one in the middle. But now it's time for *you* to do something about it."

"And what might that be?" she asked, running her fingers through her hair again.

"What the hell you think! Go get your husband and bring him the hell home."

"I haven't even heard from him. He knew I was sick and he didn't even pick up the phone to see how I was doing. I could have been in this house dead."

I sucked my teeth. "Girl, as many times you blew my phone up he knew your ass was alive, and he knew how the hell you were doing. I kept him updated."

"Hmm," she purred with a hint of sarcasm. "That was nice of you. But he still could have called."

"Yeah. Yeah. Yeah. Shoulda-coulda-woulda. Big deal. He didn't call. There are things you shoulda did, but you didn't. So let's get over it."

"Humph," she grunted, dismissing my statement. "And what makes you think he wants to come home or see me for that matter?"

I stood in the middle of her living room, placing both hands on my hips with a look of disbelief and amusement. "Because he's the only man crazy enough to want to spend the rest of his life with your ass." She stared at me, then sucked in her bottom lip.

She threw another pillow at me. I sidestepped it.

"You're probably right. The rest of 'em scared to death of me." We both laughed.

"You got that right. Scared you might blow their spots up or their heads off."

"Damn," she said, slipping deep in thought. "I sure did some crazy shit to some of 'em. Not that they didn't deserve to be shaken up a bit."

"Look," I said, walking back over to the sofa, plopping down, "I'd love to stroll down memory lane with you but you need to get your ass in gear. I want Tee outta my house. I'm tired of him moping around in my damn spot." I tossed her my house key. "Go to your doctor's appointment, do whatever you gotta do, then go get your man."

She didn't say a word. Just snatched up the keys and jumped up with relief written all over her face, running upstairs to shower and get ready to face her man. I sucked in the air around me, then blew it out like a candle. My job was done. I pulled off my Dr. Love-Dr. Ruth-Dr. Phil hats, kicking my feet up on her table.

"Get your damn feet off my table," she yelled out of her bedroom. *Damn, how the hell did she know that?* I thought, then started laughing. I had forgotten. Indy knows everything. I sat back with my arms over the back of the sofa and my legs spread apart, smiling. The music was off, but Dionne Farris continued playing in my mind. I sang, *Wanting to lose the negative but all I lose is time, there's a constant battle going on, a chained heart and mind who's winning...*

After I left Indy's I decided to head over to the Newport Centre in Jersey City. It's not that often I get out without having the kids with me so I decided to take advantage of it. I had planned on catching a movie, but quickly ditched the idea and went shopping instead. I bought each boy a pair of black Air Jordans and a pair of wheat-colored Timberland boots. Then I made my way over to Sacred Thoughts, the bookstore Tee raved about when he did a signing there a few months back. The minute I walked through the door I was greeted by an attractive brown-skinned sister with thick, shoulder-length locks—wearing a black leotard jumper.

"Good afternoon, brotha. Welcome to Sacred Thoughts." I smiled. "Can I help you find anything in particular today?"

"No, thank you. I'm just looking right now."

"Well, my name is Shondalon."

"Nice to meet you, Shondalon. Nice store you have here."

"Thank you. Just let me know if I can help you with anything," she said as she walked behind the counter, picking up the ringing phone. I half-listened as she began fussing someone out over the phone. I smiled when I came across Tee's book. After a few moments of perusing the bookshelves, and admiring the African masks and art collections, I decided to buy a jar of coconut-scented shea butter, and two books: *Shame On It All* by Zane and *Shattered Souls* by Dywane D. Birch. After reading a few pages of *Shame On It All*, I knew the freaky Whitfield sisters were just what I needed to compensate for my sexual drought. And when I finished reading the back of *Shattered Souls*, I knew I had to know more about the four friends who were bonded by unconditional love and repressed childhood memories that reminded them of the hurt and pain they were forced to endure at the hands of the people they trusted. Hell. I know a few shattered souls myself, so I was definitely looking forward to cracking it open.

Shondalon was hanging up the phone as I approached the register. She smiled. "You are going to really enjoy these two good books," she said, taking my items and ringing them up. "I can't keep either of them on my shelf."

"Yeah, they both seem quite interesting."

"Oh, trust me. They are all that and then some. Especially this one here," she said, holding up *Shattered Souls.* "It'll have you laughing and crying one minute, and horny the next."

"Well," I said, handing her my credit card, "I definitely can't wait to start them." She handed me the receipt slip and a pen to sign for my purchases, then gave me my copy as we said our good-byes. Her face lit up when I mentioned Tee was my brother.

"Now, that brotha," she said, smirking, "has all the women drooling with his fine self. You should have seen the line of women waiting to get his autograph. I need to get him back in here to do another signing real soon." I laughed. Some things never change.

"Yeah, that's Tee for ya. I'll be sure to let him know. "

"Please do," she responded with a wide, toothy grin. I nodded and threw her a half wave, making my way out the store, up the escalators and out the door to my car.

By the time I picked up the boys from my mother's and finally pulled up into my garage, it was well after six. "Daggone it!" I snapped when I realized I didn't have any food in the house.

"Ooh, Daddy," Amir said, "you said a bad word."

"I'm sorry," I said, smiling. If I closed my eyes, I'd swear I was talking to someone much older. Sometimes, I have to do a double-take when they speak. They're both so advanced for their ages. It amazes me. I guess the fact that I always preferred having regular conversations with them as opposed to cooing and baby-talking them has helped their comprehension and vocabulary. I backed out of the garage, heading back out of the development to the nearest Pathmark.

"Unh-uh," Amar interjected. "Daddy didn't say a bad word."

"Did so. Daddy, did you say a bad word?"

"No. Not really," I explained, looking through my rearview mirror. "That's a word grownups use when they don't want to use a bad word."

"Okay," he said, sounding like he understood. He paused. "I don't like that word, Daddy."

"Well, I'll try not to use it. How's that?"

He nodded. "Good."

"Daddy can say it if he wants," Amar scolded.

"Unh-uh."

I jumped in before they started bickering. "You're right, Amar, Daddy can say it if I want. But I won't because your brother doesn't like it. Just like I won't say words you don't like, okay?" He nodded, satisfied with my response. "Now let's go inside and buy some food," I said, pulling into a parking space and turning the car off.

After thirty minutes of trying to figure out what to buy, we finally made our way up to the register with one loaf of wheat bread, two half-gallons of Soymilk: chocolate and vanilla, carrot sticks, dried pineapple chunks, one box of oatmeal, two boxes of cereal, three jars of Delmonte tropical fruit salad, four cans of red salmon, a package of smoked turkey wings, and two pounds of string beans. I figured we'd have salmon patties and string beans. But, of course the boys begged me to buy them a box of pizza so I ended up giving in which is something I usually don't do. Amira is always saying I take the joy out of being a kid because I don't allow Amir and Amar to enjoy junk food. I do. I just monitor their intake. Which is something I think all parents should do.

"My. Aren't we eating healthy," the voice said in back of me. I looked over my shoulder. It was my neighbor, standing in back of me with a wide smile and twinkling eyes. Her caramel-coated skin was blemish-free and glowing as if it had been freshly buffed. I smiled.

"I try," I said, trying to keep my voice steady.

"You live in thirty-three-twelve, right?" I nodded, surprised she knew. "We haven't officially met," she said, extending her hand. "I'm Myesha."

"Britton," I offered, shaking her soft, warm hand. "Pleased to meet you…"

"Daddy, can we have candy?" Amir interrupted.

"No. Now put it back and get over here. And those are my boys, Amir and Amar," I said, pointing at them as they walked over with their lips poked out.

She smiled. "Aww. How old are they?"

"Three."

"They're adorable," she replied admiringly. The cashier gave me my total, then started bagging.

"Thanks," I said, swiping my MasterCard through the machine. "And a handful. But I love every minute with 'em. By the way, where's your little guy?"

"My little guy?" she asked surprised. "Oh. You must be talking about my nephew Tyler. He's with his grandparents."

"Oh," I replied, smiling, placing my bags in the shopping cart. I stood over to the side and continued talking while her groceries were being rung up. I was glad to be having a conversation with a beautiful woman so I was in no rush to get home. "He looks so much like you."

"That's what everyone says…" Her voice was coated with love, trailing off. "He's my twin sister's son." *Ah, a twin*, I thought, smiling. *Interesting*.

"So that explains the remarkable resemblance." She returned the smile. "I assumed he was yours."

"He is," she said, beaming. "I've helped raise him off and on since he was born." She shared that she had moved her six-year-old nephew and sister into her home when her sister had taken ill three years ago, and has been caring for him full time since her death from Hepatitis C. She had contracted the virus from a drug-involved boyfriend.

"Sorry to hear about your loss," I said, grabbing Amar's hand. "…Amir, take your brother's hand. I commend you for taking him in and raising him as your own."

"Thanks. It's what she wanted," she added, walking out the sliding glass doors behind me. "And I wouldn't have it any other way. That's what family does." I nodded knowingly. We continued talking until we reached my car. I put my groceries in the trunk and opened the back door to let the boys in. Then I walked her to her car, which was four parking spaces over from where I was parked. I stood and watched as she loaded her trunk, then slip into the driver's seat of her silver Volvo. In that short time, I learned she was a principal at an alternative school in Manhattan, lived in Chester for the last three years, and was happily single; but open to new possibilities. I smiled. "Well, neighbor, I guess I should let you go. Don't want to hold you any longer than I already have."

As fine as you are you can hold me all night if you want. "Oh, you're not holding me," I blurted. "I've actually enjoyed our conversation."

"So have I," she offered, holding out her hand. "I'm glad we finally had a chance to meet."

"Likewise," I said, squeezing her warm hand in mine. I gazed at her, catching the sparkle in her eyes; a warm feeling shot through me, causing me to blush. "Have a good night."

"You too." I stepped away from the car as she backed out, then walked back to my own car. Just as I was getting in, she backed up and blew the horn, rolling down her passenger side window. "How 'bout we get together one day soon to finish our talk?"

My mouth parted into a wide grin. "How 'bout tonight over salmon patties and string beans." I couldn't believe I had just invited a strange woman into my home. But she was beautiful, and it felt right. And interestingly, the boys were well behaved. Any other time one of them would start whining or yelling about something. But for whatever reasons they were quiet. It had to be a sign. I crossed my fingers.

"Say the time and I'm there," she said, giggling. *Yes!* I screamed inside.

I glanced down at my watch. It was already seven-thirty. "How's eight-thirty?"

"Perfect. See you then." She pulled off, leaving me floating on cloud nine as I backed out of my parking space, heading home to prepare dinner for the lovely Myesha.

20

DAMASCUS: *Where Do We Go From Here?*

Man, listen. This stunt Indy pulled has me wondering if I really know who the hell she is. I mean, damn! She's always talking 'bout trust 'n shit, yet she turns around and does some sucka shit instead of just laying the cards on the table. Maybe she did try to be straight up with me. Maybe I only heard what I wanted to hear. Maybe I'm just a damn fool. Who the fuck knows! All I know is, I'm mentally beat the fuck down right now. Yo, I almost feel like a damn junkie, trying to shake a bad hit. My body aches, my head hurts. I feel sick. I can't deal with this shit. I don't know if I'm coming or going.

Damn! I miss the hell out of her little ass. But, she really got the game fucked up, if she thinks I'm just gonna let her shit on me. I ain't built for that shit. I'm telling you. I really wanted to go in her mouth. Word is bond. I wanted to bust her grill in. But I couldn't. I think that's the shit that has me so fucked up. The fact that I wanted…I mean, I almost lost control. Fuck! Why the hell she have to try to play me like I'm some chump or sumthin'?

I've been lying around this piece, depressed as hell, feeling lower than I've ever felt in my life. And her ass is probably out somewhere shakin' and movin' while I'm here fuckin' miserable. Why? "What the fuck I do to deserve this shit?" I asked Brit this morning. "All I ever did was try to love that damn girl."

He looked at me, clearing his throat. "Well, Tee. Do you ever think about all the women you dogged out—or should I say, dicked over—in your life? Maybe this is your payback for all the hearts you've broken or the backs you've ripped open."

Yo, you see this shit? I asked him a simple question and, instead of helping me figure it out, he hits me with some extra shit. I wanted to black on his ass. I ran my tongue across the thick film on my teeth. *Damn, I need to brush my teeth.* "Yo, what the fuck you talking about, B?"

"Look," he said, "all I'm saying is, you've been with a lot of women in your time and I'm sure along the way you've done and said some things without caring about anyone's feelings."

I clucked my teeth, sucking in the air around me, then blowing it out. "Yo, them chicks were fucks. That's it. They knew it and I knew it. I wasn't kidding myself or them into thinking there was a chance for anything more than me beating the pussy up. I think I gave it to them straight, no chaser. I wanted a nut. And they wanted dick. As far as I see it, it was a mutual exchange. But that still has nothing to do with Indy, and what the fuck she did. I married her ass. Gave her my fucking heart and she tried to clown me." I stared at him for a moment, shaking my head.

He got up from the sofa. "You know what. I understand you're hurting. And I'm doing my damnedest to be understanding and supportive. If you want me to just listen then cool. I'll listen. But, don't ask me a question or my opinion, then get an attitude when my response isn't good enough. You sit here acting like you walked in on her fucking someone else. Okay, she exercised *her* right as a woman to do what she wanted with *her* body without discussing it with *you* first. I'm not saying it was right or wrong. But damn! Do you think maybe you could have handled the situation differently? I understand you were upset, but did you really have to go up in there cursing and screaming? Was that all really necessary?"

Damn. Here comes another lecture, I thought. No matter what I would have said at this point, he wasn't going to understand that this shit is much bigger than Indy being on some slick shit with the pills. It's about trust. And right now, she's fucked that up. All I ever asked from her is to keep it real with me. I mean, damn! Is too much to ask?

"Aye, yo B," I said, tryna check my anger. "You right. My bad." He disregarded my attempt to apologize.

"If you want to sit around, having a pity party instead of trying to resolve this mess then you're right. It is your bad. This is like the fifth time you've snapped on me. So do me a favor, take your ass home to your wife and work this shit out. Otherwise, I'm putting you out." Yo, the nigga didn't crack a smile when he said it, either. True, he was only tryna help and I was taking everything out on him. And he was right about it being Indy's right to do what she wanted with her body. But do you think I could have been let in on it too? I mean, knowing that he knew about this shit bothers me. But, I have to respect his loyalty, so I really had no reason to lash out at him.

I opened my mouth to say something.

He put his hand up to stop me. "I'm gonna give you some space. You have three more days to wallow around. So you had better figure out what you wanna do. In the meantime, I'm going to Jersey for the weekend. I'll be back on Sunday." He headed upstairs but then turned around to say something else, "And, do you think you can do me a favor while I'm gone?"

"Yeah," I said, looking over at him, "what's that?"

"Wash your ass!" And with that said, he bounced from the room, leaving me slack-jawed.

So after he left, I forced myself to sift through this shit and decide what it is I really wanted. I lay back, closed my eyes and willed myself to do some serious soul searching. The minute I shut my eyes I saw Indy's face, her smile. I saw her coming down the aisle at our wedding. I saw her lying in my arms, singing to me. Yea, the girl can blow when she wants. I saw her beautiful body and remembered the time she performed this ballet piece in the nude. Yo, that shit was hot. I ended up beating my dick, then making love to her. Aye, yo, I know ya'll think busting a nut is all I think about. But you just don't know what the hell that girl does to me. Anytime I think about her, my dick gets hard. My shit has a mind of its own. And it loves being up in that pussy. But, don't get it twisted. There's more to Indy and me than just sex. Aiight, aiight. Yea, that's all I wanted from her at first. Can you blame me?

I mean, damn. I was big on this girl, long before she even knew I existed. Believe that. From the first moment I opened up that *Jet* magazine, flipping through its pages, stumbling on the centerfold beauty. I was like, "Whoa! Now that's a keeper." I knew then, she was the one. I just didn't know what "the one" actually meant. Yo, I actually thought about jumping in my BMW, driving to Atlanta and riding around Spelman until I spotted her sexy ass. That sounds crazy, right? Yo, I'm telling you, I was buggin.' But, I checked myself real quick and settled for tearing her picture out and pinning it up on my wall.

Then check it. Two years later, I'm in Hampton, standing outside, chilling with a few of my boys. You know, talkin' shit, checkin' out all the ass coming and going into the Phi Beta Sigma-Zeta Phi Beta function and just before I'm about to dip out, here come three fine-ass sistas, laced to the nines, walking up to the line. Yo, cats were tryna holla at 'em, but they gave 'em no rhythm. Man, listen. It was definitely all about them, and they knew it. But, the shorty that really stood out was the one who walked up on one of my boys and punched him in the mouth for referring to them as "high-post bitches." Yo, you had to be there to see this fly-ass sista, piped the hell out in all her bling-bling, run all up in this cat's grill like it was nothing. I was like, "Damn!" And then it hit me: she was my centerfold beauty. I looked up in the sky, saw those stars twinklin' and knew I had to have her. So, I paid my money, watched her dis cats most of the night, then waited. And the minute the D.J. slid in some slow cuts, I macked my way over to her, snatched her up on the dance floor and got my groove on. Surprisingly, her mean ass didn't black on me.

Man, listen. The minute her body touched mine, I bricked up. She felt so damn good in my arms that I didn't realize I was squeezing her almost half to death until she snapped, "Do you think you can back the fuck up off me and pull your dick from outta my leg?" Yo, she had me so damn horny I had the shakes. Word up. But, she damn sure wasn't impressed with the feel of my stiff dick like *most* chicks were. And she made that very clear when she slammed her car door in my face, then drove off, leaving me standing in the middle of an empty parking lot dumbfounded.

Yo, I had her on the brain bad but had no idea how or where I'd run into her again. I wanted to get up between those hips in the worst way. Word up. But, after that night, I didn't see any other traces of her until almost a year later—when I walked up in my spot and there she was, laughing and chilling with my roommate along with another fine-ass honey. Talk about miracles happening. The woman of my dreams was up in that piece with Brit. Now wasn't that some shit? Here I was, daydreaming about her ass, and this little nigga had already scooped her up. Yo, I ain't gonna front. I was kinda jealous. But it was all good in the hood. I pulled him to the side and asked, "Yo, B, who's that?"

"Those are my girls, Indy and Chyna."

"Hmm. So who's the chick with all the ice?"

"Oh, that's Indy. She's fly, right?"

"She aiight," I said, frontin' like a muhfucka. "How you know her?"

He looked at me, grinning. "Why, you like her?"

"Nah, nigga," I snapped. "I'm just asking."

"Yea, right," he said, smiling. "We met last summer at the Labor Day Greekfest in Virginia Beach. She just transferred to Hampton. And—"

"Oh, word?" I asked with a little more interest than I had anticipated.

"Yea. And Chyna goes to State (referring to Norfolk State), but you wouldn't know anything about that since you don't go to class." Yo, even back then B was on my case about shit. Matter of fact, he was the only cat who could get that, 'cause anyone else woulda caught a quick one to the ribs. But he was right. School was just a front. I was only there because it was a condition of my probation, and it allowed me to get my hustle on, feel me?

Anyway, like I was sayin', B was getting ready to tell me more about Chyna but I didn't care about all that. I was only interested in the shorty with the hazel eyes and the fatty banger and I wanted to know one thing. "Did you smash it?" I asked in a hushed tone, gesturing my head toward the living room. He laughed in my face.

"Boy, is that all you think about? Everyone's not a pussy hound like you." And that's all he said. Never said whether he did or didn't. And still won't. Not that it matters now. "Hey, Indy," he called out, smirking. "Come here."

She walked out—nah, fuck that! She switched out—into the hallway with a confidence I had never seen in any female. Man, listen. Her ass had a shake that would hypnotize the toughest nigga; and still does. "Yes," she, responded, looking me up and down with those sexy-ass eyes, then giving her attention to Brit. He introduced us. I nodded and winked. She twisted her face up and said, "We've already met."

"Really?" Brit asked with surprise, giving me an under-eyed stare. "Well, Tee wants to ask you something." I damn near choked when he said that, walking off with a big-ass smile on his face. She put her hand on her hip, cocking her head to one side.

"And what might that be?"

I licked my lips, walking up on her.

She rolled her eyes, flicking her hand in my face. "Boy, please..."

Aye yo, let me not beat you in the head 'bout all this. So to make a long story short, Indy gave me no work. And I got the sense the only reason she tolerated me—at first—was because of Brit. But over time, I charmed her enough to at least get some time alone with her. But she made it very clear, "Nigga, don't think you getting some pussy."

"Nah, baby," I said, smiling.

She rolled her eyes, twisting her lips up.

"Don't baby me. I'm not your baby nor do I intend on having your baby."

"I feel you," I said, lowering my voice. "My bad."

She folded her arms, cocked her head to the side and stared at me.

"Check it. All I wanna do is spend some time with you."

"Humph," she snapped. "Well...time is money, and money is time. And I don't have enough of either to be wasting. So you had betta come right."

I smiled, knowing then she was gonna give me a run for my money. Funny thing, she did then, and she still does. But it's peace. Yo, even back then she was no joke, and definitely about business. I mean she was so driven and determined. And she knew exactly what she wanted outta life. I think that's what really intensified my desires, along with the fact she wasn't givin' up the pussy. Oh, she was givin' it up. She just wasn't lettin' me hit it. So, what I'm sayin' is, I waited a long damn time to bag her ass, know what I mean?

I closed my eyes tighter. This time I saw her lying up in that hospital bed in a coma with her head bandaged and face swollen. I didn't have the strength or the desire to leave her bedside. And when her monitor went dead, it was like someone was shutting off my airway. I was losing a piece of me. I begged God. I pleaded with him to not take her from me. And I swore I'd never let her go. I went up in that hospital chapel and prayed like I had never prayed before. And I cried tears I never knew were in me. That was the first time I had ever cried over a woman. It was then I realized that I needed her love the way I needed oxygen. I needed it to survive.

Yo, fuck tryna hold out. Of all the things we've gone through, of all the beefs—the one thing I know, shit ain't right without Indy in my life. I can't eat, can't sleep and I can't get her out of my mind. Yeah, the nigga got it bad for her ass. I can't front. I'm a sucka for her little ass. But, don't get it fucked up, what she did still doesn't sit right with me, but it ain't something we can't work through. I mean if she's not ready to have kids, then I can't force it on her, right?

Bottom line: It was time to pull myself up from outta this fuckin' dark hole before I ended up being put away somewhere. But, the first thing I needed was a good workout, then a hot shower. I did about ten sets of crunches, squats and one-arm push-ups. When I finished, I did about fifty overhand, then underhand pull-ups, and two-hundred jumping jacks. By the time I knocked all that out, it had definitely made me feel better. I went into the bathroom, turned on the water, brushed my teeth and tongue, then gargled with some Listerine. When I dropped my boxers, I was greeted by the smell of over a week-old funk and sweat. *Damn, nigga. Your musty ass does stink*, my mind scolded as I picked my underwear up, tossing them in the garbage, then stepping into the shower. *This shit with Indy got my groove all fucked up.*

I grabbed Brit's eucalyptus liquid body cleanser, poured some into my washcloth and went to work. Yo, that shit is the bomb. Word up! I must have spent an hour under the water, washing and scrubbing my ass and balls squeaky clean. That's one thing I've never been down with, not hitting the shower. Hell—back in my hustling and straggling days—if I didn't do anything else, I always showered or at least washed up. I learned a long time ago, a cat had to have a clean dick, ass and balls 'cause you never knew when a chick wanted to jump down on her knees. No chick wants to suck on funky nuts unless she's a fiend. Word up. Some of them trick asses would do almost anything for a hit. I kept on scrubbing and washing until I was raw, feeling so fresh and so clean.

When I finished my shower, I shaved, then stood in front of the mirror behind the door, using some of B's mango butter to oil myself down. I stared at my shiny body, then rubbed the tattoo—*Indy's man* etched in a heart with roses entwining—over my left breast. Flashes of her lovemaking brought on a semi-hard-on. I wanted to jerk my shit off but I didn't have the energy. *Damn!* I thought, squeezing my dick. *Brit's right. It's time to take my ass home.* I wrapped my towel around me, going back into my temporary cave, walking over to the desk, then hitting the space bar on my laptop.

When the document reappeared, I scrolled through it one last time before saving it on disc. I smiled at the finished product: Two hundred and forty-five pages of my next book, *Keeper of My Heart*, completed in less than two weeks. "Indy, with all that's in me…this one's for you, girl. No matter what," I said, shutting the computer off, turning on the stereo, then lying down. An overdue sleep was beginning to take over.

I woke up to my stomach growling. *Fuck, I'm hungry as hell*, I thought as I yawned and stretched, glancing over at the clock. It was 6:30. Damn. I had slept for almost six hours. Yo, whoever was cooking, that shit smelled good as hell. Smelled almost like someone was actually in this spot hitting the pots. Hell, I almost thought so the way the aroma slid under the door and wafted around the room. My stomach growled again. I got up, opened the bedroom door and took a whiff. Aye, yo. I wasn't buggin.' Someone was up in this piece. *It must be Brit*, I thought as I went back into the room to slip on my jeans to see what had made him change his mind about bouncin' for the weekend. *He must have dropped the boys off at his mother's*, I reasoned 'cause I didn't hear them running around the house.

When I got downstairs, there was a white rug in the middle of the floor and white candles were lit everywhere. Phyllis Hyman was softly playing in the background. I tiptoed through the dining room toward the kitchen.

The dining room table was set for two. There were flowers all over the place. Orchids, roses, and some other shit I've never seen or heard of. I walked in the kitchen and almost passed out. Word is bond. I shook my head, smiling to myself. That damn Brit is always doing something.

"Yo, what you doing here?" I asked, feeling shock and surprise overwhelm me. It was Indy, standing in the middle of the kitchen, wearing an apron, cooking her ass off. Aye yo, I ain't gonna front, I was happy as hell to see her. But I wasn't gonna let her know it. There was no damn way I was giving her the satisfaction of knowing I'm strung the fuck out. Feel me? Then again, knowing B's ass, he'd already told her any damn way.

"Hi," she said, giving me a faint smile. Damn, I wanted to grab her little ass and tongue her down. But I refused to fold. "Umm...I thought you might be hungry."

I folded my arms and leaned up against the frame of the doorway, trying to keep my eyes from undressing her. I shifted them over to the pots she had on the stove. When my stomach growled louder, I pressed my arms into my ribcage to keep it from jumping out of my body. I stood there, watching her move from one end of the kitchen to the other. *What the fuck kind of getup is that?* I thought to myself, trying to figure out what the hell she had on underneath her apron. It looked like an old oversized, granny housecoat. It was long, striped and had a big collar, which she had buttoned up to her neck. I looked down at her feet. She was wearing heels. Looked like boots. *Damn, her ass is really buggin'.*

"Oh, word. That's the only reason you drove way out here?"

"And because I've missed you."

"Is that it?"

"No, that's not it, Tee," she said, rinsing, then wiping her hands. She walked over toward me, touching my face. I didn't budge. I didn't blink an eye. "I was wrong for what I did. I apologize for pulling that gun on you and for all the nasty things I said. I didn't mean any of it. But, I won't apologize for taking those pills." I raised my eyebrow but kept my mouth shut. "However, I do apologize for not discussing it with you first. I was wrong for keeping that from you. And I'm hoping you can forgive me."

"Oh, yeah," I said, sidestepping her. "Yo, you can cancel that."

"What?"

"You heard me. You think you can come up in here and hit me with a weak-ass apology and shit supposed to be peace. Shit ain't sweet. And I ain't beat. So, you gonna have to come at me a little better than what you just dished out." *Nah, hold up. I know I just told ya'll how much I missed her and how messed up I've been, but fuck that. I wasn't letting her off the hook that easy.* I took a seat at the kitchen table, folding my arms across my chest. "And what the fuck did you do with my dog?"

"He's fine," she continued in her sweet tone.

"Where is he?"

"Safe."

Safe? What the fuck does that mean? I stared at her ass. "That's fucked up what you did."

"I know," she said, pausing. "Look, Tee. You have every right to be mad at me. But, come home and be mad at me. I can't sleep. I haven't been able to think straight." *Oh, okay. Maybe she hasn't been shakin' and movin' like I thought.*

"That's too bad," I said, trying to contain my real feelings. "I've been sleeping just fine. Maybe you should go get that checked." Her eyes tightened but she gave a forced smile.

"The doctor ordered my husband home."

"Well, the last I remember, *you* told him to get the fuck outta your life."

"Well, I want him back, and I want him home."

"Oh, yeah? And what you gonna do to keep him, if he decides to come home?"

"Love him," she responded, walking back over to me. She stood between my legs, placing her hands on my shoulders. "Honor him." She leaned in, kissed me on the forehead, then attempted to kiss me on the lips. I jerked my head outta the way.

"And?" I pushed, spreading my legs wider, placing my hands on my knees. She looked good as hell standing there in her little white apron. Yea, even in that funny-ass outfit underneath. She massaged my shoulders. I felt my dick beginning to stiffen.

350

"I'm not perfect."

"I know that," I said, trying to ignore the way her hands were making me feel. I could feel my tension melting away. The smell of her perfume was making me horny. "But you've always been perfect enough for me."

She smiled. I stared at her. "So, you're gonna love me, and honor me. But are you gonna obey me?"

She stopped her magic hands in mid motion, twisting her face up. "I came here to apologize to you. Not to obey you."

"Well, then," I said, getting up, causing her to stumble backward. I brushed past her. "I guess it's a wrap. 'Cause I want a wife who's gonna love, honor *and* obey me."

"Humph," she grunted. "Then I guess it is. 'Cause I obey no man. The best I can do is love you. I can even be faithful and devoted to you. And I'm even willing to compromise. But obeying you, please. You got the wrong one."

I held back my smile. She continued.

"Look, coming here to apologize is a big thing for me."

"Well, when you love someone, nothing's too big of a deal. You do what you gotta do to make things right."

"I know that. And I do love you, Damascus Miles. And I want to make things right. That's why I'm here."

"Why are you here again?" I asked, smirking.

She sighed. "I'm here because I know I was wrong. Dead wrong. I know I really crossed the line and I apologize."

"Yeah, you *really* showed your ass."

"And I'm sorry."

"Okay, so what does being sorry mean?"

"It means I'm here to ask if you can find it in your heart to forgive me for my ill actions. It means I love you. It means I've missed you and I want you home." I had to catch myself from smiling.

"How much do you love me?"

"Enough to want to make my marriage work."

"How much did you miss me?"

"Enough to know I want to spend the rest of my life with you, but I'm—"

"But are you in 'in love' with me?"

She tilted her head from one side to the other, shifting her weight from under her feet.

"Yes," she said in a hushed tone.

"I can't hear you," I snapped, holding in my smile.

"Yes!" Okay, I was satisfied so there was no need for her to continue, feel me? I had heard what I wanted to hear. "Tee, I'm really so—"

"Aye, yo. Shut up," I said, walking over to her, then grabbing her around the waist. "You always talking out your damn neck." I was surprised when she didn't open her mouth to say something slick. "I know you're used to living by your own rules, but, we need to get something clear: there's a new player in the game and the rules have changed. Ya heard?"

She cocked her head to one side.

"I said you got that?"

"I heard you," she said, trying to press her body into me. I backed away.

"Rule number one, if there's no trust, there'll be no us. Feel me? I need to know that the woman I love is not tryna play me."

"Tee," she said in her sexy voice, "You have all of me."

"Yeah, aiight. We'll see. Rule number two, if something's on your mind you need to communicate your feelings with me. I'm not a mind reader. And I don't have a crystal ball. We need to be able to talk about anything at anytime, got that?"

"I know."

"Rule number—"

"Damn," she snapped. "How many rules are you giving me?"

"Aye, yo," I said, giving her a stern look, "as many as I want. You got a problem with that?"

Her lips curled up. "Nope."

"Yeah, that's what I thought." She glared at me. I smirked. "Yo, is there a problem?"

"No," she said, trying her best to be sweet. "Anything else."

"Yeah," I snapped. I decided to flip it up a bit and hit her with some of the shit she used to hit me with just to fuck with her. "Rule number three, you'll get no more of this good dick until you learn to behave. Until then, you're on punishment. And no dildos allowed in the house. If it's not my dick stickin' you, then you don't get stuck." She looked at me in disbelief, but said nothing. "I mean it, Indera."

"Oh, you're joking, right?"

"Nah, I'm serious as hell. If I gotta go cold turkey, you gotta tough it out too." She placed her hands on her hips. "Rule number four, if you don't lick, I don't stick. If you want this dick, you gotta lick it and lick it good." I wanted to add, "And when you suck it, you betta swallow it. I don't want you wastin' none of this sweet nut," but I figured I betta not push it. So I said, "And when I do decide to give you this loving, I expect you to let me get up in that pussy even if we're beefing. One thing has nothing to do with the other. So don't deny me what's mine. Understood?"

"Humph."

"That's not the response I'm looking for."

"I hear you," she said, staring at me like I was out of my mind. She tried to kiss me again, but I put my finger up to her lips instead.

"Unh-huh. There'll be none of that," I warned, teasing her. "I'm not giving up any more of this tongue until you start acting like a wife. We are partners, not colleagues or co-workers. I expect you to *co-operate* in this marriage. Not try to run the show all the damn time. Understood?"

"I hear you."

"Nah, that's not what I asked you. I asked you if you understood."

"I understand, Tee. Anything else?"

"Rule number five, Ease up on the power moves. You're a married woman now, and you have a husband who *wants*...Nah, fuck that—needs—to spend quality time with his wife."

"Okay, is that it?" Damn, she was really being cooperative for a change.

"Rule number six, No fuckin' guns in the house. You wanna play 'shoot 'em up, bang-bang,' then take your ass in the woods and hunt."

She cracked a smile.

"Aye, yo. I'm not playing with your little ass. No guns. Got that?"

"Yeah, I got it," she said, removing her apron and unbuttoning her dress. I tried my damnedest to act unmoved. But when she stepped out of that big frumpy dress wearing a denim, hot pant jumpsuit, zipped down to the center of her chest and rocking a pair of thigh-high boots, I almost lost it. She was lookin' too damn good. *Nah nigga. Don't play yourself.* I walked back over to the table and sat down. My dick throbbed. *Easy, dawg*, I said to myself, tightly pressing my legs shut in hopes it would ease the heat swelling in my nuts.

"Where the hell you learn to shoot like that anyway?"

"I've been going to the shooting range twice a week for the last two years." She explained that after her shooting ordeal in the salon she knew it was time to be armed and ready in case someone else wanted to try it on her time. Damn, I couldn't blame her. I know when I was out there makin' moves I had to be strapped "just in case."

"I'm licensed to kill," she continued. "And I keep my Glock cocked. So, you come at me wrong, I'm shooting first and asking questions later." The minute she said that, I thought about fine-ass Pam Grier in that movie *Sheba, Baby* when she played a gun-toting private eye.

"Oh, yea? Well, I suggest you leave that Sheba Shayne shit to the cops. Now are there any more hidden talents you've kept from me?"

"No."

I kept my eyes locked on her. "Is there anything else you've been doing that I need to know about?"

"Nope," she said, going back over to the stove. She pulled off the lids to each pot and stirred. I was getting weak from hunger. And my dick was getting hard by the minute staring at those thick hips and the way her ass cheeks peeked from under them shorts. *Damn, she done got thicker than a muhfucka*, I thought, keeping my eye on her every move. She opened the oven, parting her legs, then bending over. I licked my lips. Yeah, she knew what she was doing. She was fuckin' with me. But, it was all gravy. I kept pressin' on without jumpin' her sexy bones.

"Aye, yo. What's for dinner?"

"It's a surprise," she said, smiling. "I hope you're hungry."

"Yeah, I'm starved," I replied, realizing I hadn't eaten a decent meal in weeks. Not that I had much of an appetite. But the only thing up in B's spot is Soymilk, grain cereal, fruit, yogurt, lettuce, and jugs of water. Yo, he came back from L.A. on some real wholesome kick. A cat like me would starve to death on that shit.

I got up and went into the dining room to be fed. She served curry chicken, rice and peas, cabbage and fried plantains. And for dessert, she made peach cobbler. Yo, the girl put her thing down. After three helpings, I damn near licked my plate clean.

"Aye, yo, where in the hell you learn to cook like that?" I asked, helping her clear the table. I still couldn't get over how she threw down. Since she never cooked for me, and was so adamant about not being in the kitchen, I had resigned myself that she couldn't do anything but burn water.

"My father's wife," she said, getting lost in thought. "I used to be that bitch's cook, remember?" Yo, I had forgotten. Indy would have to cook and clean for her stepmother and would get beat if everything wasn't to her liking. Damn, if she weren't already dead, I could kill her myself for the way she mistreated her. That woman treated Indy worse than a slave. "It's the only decent thing she taught me."

"Damn well too," I added. "So, is there any chance I can get fed like this on a regular?"

"Nope."

"Well," I said, smirking. "The way to a man's heart is through his stomach. So, rule number seven, I expect you to have my meals cooked and ready to be served the minute I walk through the door."

"You know what?" she snapped. "You're really pressing your luck, Mister."

"Okay, how 'bout a home-cooked meal three times a week."

"Lick my ass, how 'bout that?"

I laughed. "Rule number eight, 'you do as you're told.'"

"Humph."

"Why'd you do it?" I asked, lying across the sofa with my arms folded behind my head, staring up at the ceiling while Indy sat on the rug in the middle of the floor. Phyllis Hyman continued to softly play in the background. "If you didn't want kids why didn't you just say it, instead of tryna be on some slick shit?" I turned my head toward her, waiting for her response.

"Tee, it's not that I don't or didn't want children. It's just that I was…I mean…I'm scared." I must have given her a confused look because she continued before I could ask why she was scared. She took a deep breath. "I'm scared of giving birth, then dying, leaving my child without a mother. I don't want my child to experience that kind of emptiness." Damn. This was about to get deep. I sat up, giving her my undivided attention.

"Baby, I know losing your mom has been hard for you, but what makes you think the same thing that happened to her will happen to you?"

She closed her eyes, covering her face. "Because her mother died when she was three years old." I gave her that look again. "I don't think I ever told you this, but all the women on my mother's side have died at early ages. And, all of their children had to grow up without them in their lives. My mother was forty when she died, my grandmother forty and both of my mother's sisters died when they were in their late thirties. With the exception of my mother, they all died from cancer.

"I've always accepted the possibility that I might die young. Which is why I do all the things I do. Before I leave this earth, I want to know I've made a difference in many lives, Tee. That's why I make the moves I do. I want to be remembered long after I'm gone. So, everything I do, I do in honor of my mother's death. But, the one thing I don't want to do is die, then have my child being raised by another woman."

Damn. I rubbed my chin.

"Damn, Indy. What makes you think I'd do something like that?" Yo, she must have forgotten all the shit I went through after my moms was killed, bouncing from one foster home to another, being beaten and abused. "Baby, we both have had terrible childhoods. Don't you know if something were to happen to you, I'd be lost? But I would never allow our child, or children, be mistreated by anyone. And I damn sure wouldn't abandon them. Believe that."

"I believe you," she said, pausing while staring at me. I kept my eyes locked on hers. She smiled. "But the thought is sometimes there. After all the shit I've been through…I don't want my child to be mistreated, abused or neglected."

"I know, baby. I know." My head was starting to hurt. I knew all too well her pain 'cause her pain and mine were one in the same. I found my mother lying in a pool of blood. Hers died in her arms. AnnaMae Miles may not have had the money or education or the kind of love Indy's had for her. But, the one thing I believe in my heart is that she loved me in her own special way. She had to. Either way, death had taken both of them away.

"My life hasn't been the same," she said, pulling her knees up to her chest, then wrapping her arms around her shins. "I have more money than I could ever spend in one lifetime because that's what my mother left me. But not one cent of it can ever bring her back. Do you know I'd give up everything just to have her here with me? A part of me died on that floor with her. And, after all these years, I still haven't been able to pick myself up from up off it. I miss her, Tee. So the thought of having children scared me. That's why I took those pills. I needed to be sure that I don't have any traces of cancer in my body or any signs of an aneurysm. And being beat in my head hasn't helped matters any. I've worried that it would cause me to have a brain tumor or something in the future."

Flashes of her lying up in the hospital with tubes coming out of her caught up with me. I pressed my temples to control my thoughts. If I could have gotten my hands on the cat who had hurt her, I'd have split his shit myself. "Indy, damn. Why didn't you share this with me? Don't you know whatever you're going through, I'm here for you? When you go through it, I go through it. Yo, we in this shit together. For life! Nothing or no one can disrupt what we have. Don't you understand that?"

She nodded.

"You shouldn't ever have to bear anything alone, baby. I got your back, girl. Always."

"I know."

Yo, my head felt like a drum being pounded on. I wanted to say more, but my words seemed to lump together in my throat. Damn. I had no idea. I swallowed hard and got down on the floor with her, reaching for her hand. She placed hers in mine.

"Do you?" I asked in almost a whisper. She nodded again, rocking back and forth. "Then promise me, from here on out, you won't keep things from me."

"I'll try."

"Come here, girl," I said, pulling her into my arms. I tightly held her, kissing her on her forehead. "You're stuck with me for life, baby. I'm not going anywhere. When you're ready, I'm ready. Got that?"

"I hear you, Tee."

"Children or not, I love the hell out of you."

"And I love you," she said, closing her eyes, then gazing back at me. "You are all the man I'll ever need, Tee. And I'm so sorry for hurting you. Can you forgive me?"

"No doubt, baby. All was forgiven the minute you walked through that door." She looked up at me with those pretty-ass eyes and I couldn't resist her any longer. I kissed her lips, slowly at first, then with more intensity, prying her mouth open with my tongue. We let 'em dart and dance to a beat of their own until neither of us could stand it anymore.

Yo, fuck the rules! Some rules are made to be broken. I was makin' love to my wife. Word up! I laid her on her back, peeled off her clothes, sucking and licking on her nipples until I reached her navel. I slowly blew in it, then stuck my tongue in. I kissed all over her body, spreading her legs wide open. Yo, that pussy was nice 'n wet. Just how I like it. I licked it. Stuck my tongue deep in it, kissing its sweetness while sticking my finger in her ass. When I could no longer take the throbbing in my balls, I pulled my finger outta her ass, sucked its essence from my finger, then took off my jeans. I pulled her legs up over her head, rubbed the length of my heavy dick over her pussy a few times, then slid myself deep inside of her, moving in and out nice 'n slow. Damn. That pussy was hot. She matched my rhythm, stroke for stroke. Gripped me. Pulled me in. Arched her back, threw her hips forward, giving up all that good pussy. My pussy.

"Damn, baby, that's right. Give me that wet pussy…Yeah, baby. Work it."

"Hmm. It's all yours, Tee. Hmm. Take your pussy, baby. Uh. Hmm. Give me that dick. Hmm. Uh. Fuck me, baby. Ooh, you make my pussy so wet."

"Yeah, baby. Hmm. Just like that."

"Uh. Uh," she moaned in between strokes. "I love you, baby."

I stuck my tongue deep in her mouth, sucking and licking her lips. "I love you too," I whispered, pumping all of my love into her.

Yo, we sweated and moaned, called out each other's name, expanding and exploring the depths of our emotions and desires for each other. Then in the middle of the sky, I met the only woman I'll ever love on the moon, spilling my seeds in her. And before I knew what had come over me, I pulled out my dick and went down on her. Damn right! Right in the middle of Brit's living room, I sucked and licked her pussy with my thick nut buried inside of her. Word up. I ate her like she was an all-night sushi bar until her creamy pussy dripped her juices along with mine. Then, shifting my body around, Indy took my dick in her mouth and sucked me until I came again, swallowing every drop. Now that's wassup.

Yo, we were wrapped up in each other's arms all sweaty and sticky, enjoying the effects of making up, feel me? Then Indy put her soft lips to my ear, whispering the sweetest words I could ever imagine. I tongued her down, then positioned myself behind her in the spoon position, lifting her right leg up while sliding my dick back in her wet hole, making love to her all over again. She moaned, clutching my dick with her pussy. Yo, it was gonna be a long night 'cause I was gonna wear that back out until the sun came up, ya heard?

2I

INDERA: *Dear Mama*

Girl, the whole time I was driving up to Brit's, I was trying to figure out what I was going to say to let Tee know how bad I felt for going off on him the way I did. And then I remembered a time when Chyna and Ryan were having marital problems and I wondered how she could stay in her marriage. She simply said to me, when I had trouble accepting her reason for holding on, "Everything is not always cut-and-dry in relationships. And until you fall in love or find someone you're capable of loving, you'll never understand." Well, I can now tell my dear friend that I *am* in love, and I understand all too well that loving someone goes way beyond feelings. It's about will: the will to love. And I will *not* let my actions destroy Tee's love for me. *I've been waiting all my life for you…I wanna be the only man you'll ever need.* "You are the only man for me," I said aloud, pressing down on the accelerator. Let me tell you, apologizing and asking for forgiveness aren't two of my most prominent characteristics. I just hoped Tee would accept it and be able to forgive me.

When I finally reached his place I gathered my bags, then headed for the door. To be honest, I was nervous. And, believe me when I tell you, there are not many things that make me nervous. But, facing Tee—the man I pledged my love to, then turned around and pulled a gun on—was one thing that had me on pins and needles.

Once I entered the house, I almost chickened out. I thought about cooking him some food, leaving him a note, then waiting for him to call me. But, when I peeked in the bedroom and saw him sleeping, I knew I had to play my position and let the chips fall where they may. I fucked it up, and I needed to clean it up. You don't know how bad I wanted to crawl up in bed with him and lie in his arms. I missed him. From his light snore to his boxers being in the middle of the floor, I missed my man. And I didn't realize how much until then. He looked so peaceful. I walked over to him with my hand on my stomach, gazing at his nude body. I smiled and quietly walked back out, shutting the door behind me. Yes, Chile. Miss Indy is strung, okay.

I went downstairs, strategically placing candles and flowers around the living room. Then I rolled open the white fur rug I had custom-ordered from Gucci. Chile, I had transformed Britton's living room into something out of *Lifestyles of the Rich and Famous*, okay.

Anyway, I was so deep in thought trying to make sure everything was perfect, the food, the atmosphere and *me*, that I didn't hear him when he walked into the kitchen. But the minute I heard his voice, the only thing I wanted to do was jump up in his arms and kiss him all over. He looked so damn sexy, standing there bare-chested.

Look. I know I can be a nasty bitch sometimes…Oh, don't give me that look, like I don't deserve or appreciate him. I love that man. I *do* appreciate him. And I'm not letting him go. Please. So one of you hungry vultures can try to get your claws in him. Ha! *Not*. So you might as well set your sights on someone else, 'cause that man is taken. And we both know he's *not* going anywhere. So, shoo!

Oh my God! Did you see how he tried to act like he wasn't happy to see me? Please! You and I both knew the real deal. The man is head over heels for me. That's one of the reasons why I took my behind up to Brit's to get him, besides the fact that I'm crazy about his ass as well. Girl, it took everything in me not to laugh when he sat on his hands just to keep them off of me. I played it cool, though, since I *was* in the doghouse for a minute, if you know what I mean. But when I stepped out of that old raggedy housecoat, I knew he wouldn't be able to hold out too much longer. He can't resist this soft ass and hot pussy. That's why I wore that sexy little number by Yves St. Laurent, okay.

See. There's nothing wrong with a little feminine allure to keep your man just where you want him—in the palm of your hand. Oh, sure it can backfire from time to time. But, when you know how to captivate and seduce your man physically *and* mentally, it always works out in your favor. Trust and believe. He'll be ready to fall at your feet in no time. Or in Tee's case, suck my hot pussy with his nut in me.

Chile, I almost lost my mind when he placed his mouth on my wet box, licking and slurping me. I knew then, it was nothing but love—oh, okay; and a little freaky-deaky—for him to take it there *and* for me to sword-swallow his dick, then gulp down his creamy cum. And can you believe, I didn't gag or spill one damn drop. I sucked and swallowed, then kissed him until we were ready to go again. Chile, last night was definitely the point of no return for us.

Anyway, I have something I want to tell you. And don't you dare say anything until I'm done. Whatever you do, don't say, "I knew it!" or I'm putting your ass outta my house. Are we straight on that? Good. Now, here goes...

As you know, I had to stop by to see my doctor before driving up to see Tee to discuss all of the lab work I had done. Let me tell you. I had every-thing from an EEG, EKG to a MRI and mammogram done on me, along with everything else in between. And I was wrecked from the time I got the call to come in until the time I left my house to get to my appointment. The minute I walked through my doctor's posh Park Avenue office, I was on the verge of falling over the edge. Thank goodness I didn't have to wait to be seen, otherwise I think I would have turned into a basket case.

"Indy," Giovanna had said, hugging me. I could smell citrus fruits clinging to her jet-black ringlets. I inhaled its fragrance. "Please come inside and have a seat." She closed the door and sat behind her huge mahogany desk. "I'm glad you were able to come so quickly."

Giovanna and I have a long history together. Besides the fact that we attended the same ritzy boarding school in Connecticut, we were friends. It was there, in the lavish confines of our school, that my friend—the youngest and only daughter of Sicilian immigrants who own and operate several Italian bakeries throughout New York—would teach me the true meaning behind money, power, and respect. Chile, I'll never forget the time our whole school was on a ski trip in Switzerland when these two snotty white girls made racist comments to the both of us. I can't recall offhand exactly what they called us; but whatever it was, it wasn't cute. And sweet-faced Giovanna showed me another side of her that sure wasn't pretty when she went into her designer bag, pulling out two pair of spiked brass knuckles.

"Here, put these on," she'd said, tossing a pair over to me, then slipping her fingers through the ring holes.

"Um, what do I do with these?" I had asked, staring at them in my hands, unfamiliar with their use. Her facial expression changed. Hardened.

"Look," she'd snapped, giving me a cold stare. "There's no time for discussion. Just slide them over your damn fingers and let's go."

"But..."

"But nothing! Those bratty bitches just disrespected us to our faces. That is not accepted or tolerated. See, where I come from, money and power go hand in hand 'cause without one, you can't have the other. But, neither money nor power guarantee respect. So you have to demand it... And respect *will* be given, be it by choice or force. 'Cause without all three, you're nothing."

"What if we get in trouble?"

She tossed her thick, curly hair to the side. "My father will take care of it." She walked off, heading toward the circle of rich girls, giggling. I ran to catch up with her. "So, are you in or out? 'Cause if not, I'll handle it myself. *No one* disrespects me and gets away with it."

"In," I said, slipping on my shiny weapon. We walked in silence, approaching them saying nothing with words and everything with fists, leaving blood everywhere. That day sealed our friendship. And it was our blood-sister pact that allowed me to be embraced—with open arms—by one of the most notorious organized crime families in the world.

I glanced around her office, admiring all of her degrees and community service awards hanging on her walls. There were pictures of her with her husband and three children, along with photos of her with some of her celebrity patients. I smiled.

"Well, when you called me, it sounded urgent." I felt my breathing quicken.

"How are you feeling today?" she asked, flipping through my chart.

"Girl, let's cut to the chase," I said, shifting in my seat, wanting to get right to the point. I crossed my legs and rubbed my cross. "Tell me. Am I dying?" Chile, the stress of wondering if I'd live to see another year has shaken my nerves over the past several months. So I had no time for local chitchat. I needed to know.

"Well," she began. "Every test we have run on you has come back normal. Indy, based on all of your results, I'd say you were a very healthy woman." She looked up at me smiling. I took a deep breath, growing impatient.

"Then what the hell is wrong with me?"

She pushed her glasses down over the bridge of her nose, looking up at me.

"You're pregnant."

"Whaaaat?!" I screamed. "Bitch, you must be crazy."

"No. *I'm* not crazy. But *you* are pregnant."

"How?" I asked, flabbergasted. Chile, my mouth hit the floor. "There must be some kind of mistake."

"No, there's no mistake."

"Ugh!"

"Sounds like this is not exactly the news you had anticipated."

"*Exactly,*" I replied, holding my face in my hands, shaking my head, then looking up at her. "There has to be some kind of mistake. I mean, a few months ago, I took an EPT to be sure because I wasn't feeling well. And it came back negative. Then I went to two other Duane Reades and bought a different brand of tests from each store and they were also negative. And, four months ago, I had you give me a test, and that, too, was negative. You need to give me another test."

"I really don't think that's necessary." I gave her one of my raised-eyebrow stares. But she dismissed it. She explained how birth control pills typically have a three to five percent failure rate. But if a woman takes her pills regularly and is not late or doesn't miss any, the pregnancy rate is only one percent.

"No," I said, quickly shaking my head. "I took my pills regularly, as pre-scribed. Every damn day, so please tell me how the hell did I get pregnant?"

"Indy," she continued, treading lightly. "When you gave me the urine sample, yes, it was negative. But your most recent blood work came back positive, showing high levels of beta HCG. There is no mistake. You are *very* pregnant."

Oh, don't ya'll give me that "I told you so" look. Unh-huh! Did some-one just say *I knew it?* Well, I tell you what. Get out. No, I'm serious. Get the fuck out! I told you to not say it, and you did. So somebody escort her ass out of here before it gets ugly up in here. That's right. Get that player-hatin'-I'll-fuck-your-man-for-pennies ho outta here. Now where was I? Oh, yea. Giovanna was explaining how the hell I got pregnant.

"And," she continued, "if you remember, we did change your prescription and lower your dosage due to the nausea and bleeding you were experi-encing. And if you were on any medications, certain prescriptions can reduce the pills' effectiveness."

"I still can't understand this. I mean. My period comes like clockwork."

"Some women continue to menstruate during pregnancy."

"Oh, no!" I snapped. "I've been taking those pills and …Oh, my God!"

"Indy," she responded, sensing my concern. She got up, walking around her desk to sit in the chair next to me. "Many women inadvertently take oral contraceptives unaware that they are already pregnant. But, there's no need to be concerned about the pills causing birth defects any more than the background rate of birth defects that normally occur…"

"But—"

"Listen. Before we start jumping to conclusions, lets schedule a Level 2 ultrasound and an amniocentesis to be sure."

All this time I thought my mood swings were due to some neurological problem as a result of my head trauma and come to find out it's because I'm pregnant, causing my hormones to be out of whack. I felt like scream-ing, *I don't believe this shit. I'm going to have a baby. I'm going to be a mother.* I wanted to faint. "What in the world am I going to do with a baby?"

"Love it," she said, smiling and patting my hand. "You have nothing to worry about."

"That's easy for you to say."

We stood up, gave each other a long hug, then I walked out of her office dazed and confused.

So there you have it. I'm as pregnant as the day is long. Oh, go 'head and say it. Yes, you told me. So what! Well, I guess that's what I get for trying to be slick, huh?

Humph. Anyway, after Tee rocked my body from head to toe, front to back, I whispered in his ear, "You're gonna be a daddy."

His face lit up. "Say word!"

"Word," I said, imitating someone tryna be down. He laughed.

"Oh, shit! Nah, hold up. When? How?" I told him all about my doctor's visit and reassured him that this wasn't one of my ploys to get back in his good graces. Chile, I think that was the happiest I've ever seen him since our wedding day. Oh my God! I'm really pregnant. I mean, I know what Giovanna said, but I still can't believe it. The reality of me becoming a mother hasn't hit me yet.

Anyway, the next morning I got up and cooked breakfast: scrambled eggs, French toast, home fries, and turkey bacon. Hmm-hmm. Oh, please. Don't think this is gonna be on some regular. I did what I had to do to get back in my man's good graces. I mean, we've peaced things up, but he's still a little wary of me, and rightfully so. So, I'll feed him and fuck him real good for a minute, then it's back to business as usual, okay. Girl, you know how we do to keep our men where we want 'em.

Anyway, after we ate, Tee and I cleaned up Brit's house, showered, then headed for home. I dropped him off where he had hidden his truck, then I told him I needed to make a few stops before I went back to Brooklyn, so he went on without me. I needed to visit the one person who loved me more than life itself: my mother. With the recent news of being pregnant, I needed to sit and feel her presence. Spend some quality time with her, know what I'm sayin'?

As I drove through Rye, nearing the entrance to the cemetery that was now her home, I began to feel overwhelmed with emotions. Usually when I come out here, I'm at ease. But, for some reason, today things were so different. It's been a little over thirty years since her death, yet it still seems like yesterday. I mean, despite what goes on in my life, there's not a day that goes by that I don't think about her. Miss her. If you only knew how much I yearn to hear her voice, to feel her touch. No matter how old I get, in my heart I will always be her little girl. Her princess.

I flipped open my visor, checked my hair for any signs of dishevelment, then freshened up my lips with a fresh coat of toasted-almond lipstick. I gave myself one last once-over before opening my door and heading toward her gravesite. When I approached the black-granite headstone, I noticed that someone had placed beautiful pink roses in the marble vase secured in front of her headstone. I kissed the top of her stone, then laid my face on it.

"Hello, Momma," I whispered, rubbing my hands along its smooth surface. The stone was cold against my skin. "I miss you so much. Why'd you have to leave me?" One by one, tears began to roll down my face. I kneeled down in front of her stone and traced the inscription: *In Loving Memory. Nandi Akusa Mahkhandi-Fleet. Beloved mother. Devoted wife. 1929-1969.*

I removed the gold locket from around my neck and kissed the front of it before opening it. I stared at the picture inside. Hot tears continued to fall, burning my eyes as they rolled down the sides of my face. "Why Momma?" Before I knew what had come over me, I was sobbing. "God, why'd you have to take my mother from me? Why?"

"Momma, my life hasn't been the same without you," I said aloud, wiping my face with the back of my hands. Although I felt emotionally drained from everything else going on in my life, I still wept years of emptiness away. I thought I was all cried out. But at that moment, I purged years of loneliness and sadness that I've kept hidden deep inside of me, twisting and tearing at my heart. I don't think anyone can truly understand the extent of my loss or feel the scars I've carried around since the death of my mother. I realize there is nothing that will bring her back. Not tears. Not self-pity. Not prayer. Not one damn thing will give me back what I lost: my mother's love.

In losing my mother, I lost me. Bit by bit. Every time I was beaten or molested or neglected, a piece of my spirit was chipped away. My mother's death was truly the beginning of my end. I know some of you look at me like I'm crazy. Well, I'm not. Trust and believe, I'm far from it. But I'll tell you who is: the bitch who beat and tortured me is crazy. The mother-fucker who crept in my bed and molested me over and over is crazy. The weak-ass nigga who drugged and raped me is crazy. And all of them were crazy to think that I'd let them get away with hurting me. You see, anyone who does anything to jeopardize the mental, physical, or emotional well-being of a child is the fucking crazy one, okay. Not me. I am living and breathing proof that a child's life is influenced by the behaviors of adults. I have every material thing imaginable and I want for nothing. But, make no mistake. I'd have given up every single dime my mother left me to have a safe, healthy childhood. Maybe I wouldn't be the way I am.

I know me better than anyone else. And I know I have baggage from my childhood. But it is shit I try very hard to keep tucked away in the far corners of my past. And what I've learned is that the locks of my pain only snap open when someone really presses my last nerve. Then I go off. I take out all of my anger and hurt on them not caring what the consequences will be. It's like once I go off, there's no stopping me. Chile, I know I have the potential to become very volatile. And I know it's not healthy. Lord knows I do.

"Indy," Brit had said a few days prior to coming out to my house. "I think you need to get your ass in counseling before you end up in jail."

"I don't need damn counseling. What I need is for people to stay the hell in their lanes and out of my way."

"Humph. If you ask me, sounds like you're in denial." There was a moment of silence before he continued, "I just finished reading this book called *Shattered Souls*. I think you should check it out…It was almost like reading our own life stories."

"Boy, please," I said, sucking my teeth, "I'm not in denial and I have no time for self-help books."

"It's not a self-help book. Well, not in the traditional sense. It's a well-written novel that I think you'd be able to relate to and appreciate. You might even enjoy it. I think it could help you. We all have issues, Indy. It's just a matter of how you deal with them. Do you let them control you, or are you in control of them?"

Like I have time to sit around reading novels, I thought dismissing his suggestion. "I don't deny having issues. But I don't need to be up in some stranger's face, spilling my heart out, either. I have you for that."

"Hmm."

"I'm fine," I continued, sighing, "as long as I'm not set off. I always warn you before I snap so you have a chance to pull over and take it down instead of catching it. But if you insist, then it's on. It's not like I look for conflicts. If anything, I try to avoid them."

"True. But the problem is, once someone sets you off, you don't go off and be done with it; you take it to the extreme."

"I do not."

"The hell if you don't," he snapped. "Let's look at everything—and I do mean *everything*—you've done to people who you feel have wronged you. Now you tell me, don't you think you could have dealt with them in a more rational manner? And don't respond without thinking through what I'm asking."

I thought about it for a minute before responding. "Nope. I learned a long time ago, you get what you give. If you bring it, I'm gonna sling it. Simple as that."

"Indy, I think we need to keep it real."

"Okay, let's," I said with a tinge of sarcasm.

"Look, I know what you've been through. And I understand your pain. But, my God, when do you think you'll let it go. I mean, you tell the girls you work with how important it is for them to not hold on to their anger and how important it is for them to learn forgiveness. Yet, you can't live by your own words. You say one thing to those girls, then in the next breath, you're ready to pick up the phone and have someone cut up, beat up or buried. When are *you* gonna let go? When will you learn to forgive? Don't you think it's time you live by example and not by fault?"

Once again, everything Brit said was true. He was hitting me left and right with so many things, I couldn't think straight. "I don't know," I said, sighing. "I just don't know."

"Well, I suggest you start with prayer. Because at this point, God is the only one who is going to be able to help you. I love you, girl. Now, I don't know what's gotten into you lately, but you've really been bugging. You blacked on Chyna in the worst way. You almost shot up your husband, and you've even been snippy with me. I don't know what's going on, but something is, and you need help to get it under control." When he finished with me, I was speechless, okay.

Anyway, I rubbed my stomach and closed my eyes, taking in everything Britton has said to me over the years, and—for the first time, in a long time—silently prayed, asking God to give me the strength, courage and wisdom to be a good mother. I asked Him to show me how to be forgiving of those who have wronged me. Oh, please. Don't ask. I don't know where that came from—considering there are a few things I still need to take care of. But it fell from my mouth nonetheless. It sure did. Chile, by the time I was finished praying, I was all broken down.

Then I felt someone's soft hand touch my face. I looked around but didn't see anyone. *"I love you, my sweet child."*

"Momma?"

"Yes, baby. I'm here."

Heavy tears fell. "Why'd you have to leave me, Momma?"

"Sweetheart, I am the soft winds that have blown around you, the sweet rain that has soothed your sorrows, the warm sun that has brightened your days. I am the shining star that has guided you through the darkest hours. I've never left you, my sweet child. I've been with you every step of the way."

"But I miss you so much." I couldn't control the weeping. Tears and snot were everywhere.

"Don't cry, baby. I am right here, and here," she said, placing her hand over my heart, then lightly kissing my forehead. *"If there's an empty space in your soul, fill it with memories of my love for you. Close your eyes and listen with your heart. You will always see and feel me."*

I sobbed uncontrollably.

"Sssh," she said in her soothing tone, cradling me in her arms. *"Don't let your spirit be burdened with sorrow. There's no need to weep. Lift up your heart. There is nothing you can do, except live a better life in memory of me. And rejoice. For I am in God's care now. I am in paradise. I am free."*

At that moment, I smiled, feeling safer than I have ever felt in my life.

Then I thanked God for the time I did have with my mother on earth. Her soothing voice, her sweet smile; the twinkle in her eyes, her gentle touch, and the feel of her loving arms around me would always be with me. If you're lucky enough to still have your mother in your life, pick up the phone and let her know how much you appreciate her, reach out and hug her; let her know how much you love her. I wiped my tears as quickly as they fell.

"I love you, Momma."

"And, from my soul to yours...I love you more." A soft wind blew, and she was gone. But this time, I was okay 'cause she would always be alive in my heart. I was finally at peace with her death. I kissed the tip of my finger, placing it on the stone, then tracing the letters over her name, smiling. I stood up to leave, startled by the voice in back of me.

"I miss her too."

I almost passed out. "What are you doing here?" I asked, turning around to face him.

"I've come here every month since her death."

"So those flowers are from you?" I inquired, pointing over at the bouquet.

He nodded. "I know how much she loved flowers." He went on to explain that since her death he has flown in to spend time with her, bringing her fresh flowers and asking for her forgiveness.

I stood there, staring into the face of a man who had eyes like mine: almond-shaped and hazel. They were bright and sparkling. It was an uncanny feeling. I've been so blinded by my anger and hatred that I never clearly saw how handsome he was. His light-brown hair was neatly cut and sprinkled with gray. And with the exception of a thin mustache and neatly trimmed goatee, his face was smooth, and clear. I looked down at his expensive loafers, then back into his eyes. "She loved you more," I said in almost a whisper, turning my head back to her grave.

"And I loved her."

"Really?" I asked disbelievingly.

"Yes," he said, softly. "And I've never stopped loving her or you."

"Bullshit," I snapped, removing strands of my hair from my face. "Love would have kept you home with your family. Not in the streets with your whores."

He stared over at my mother's headstone, reminiscing. "I came to the States when I was seventeen years old with nothing but dreams of marrying your mother and making it big. I did both, but with a price." He rubbed his chin. "The more money I made, the more involved and complicated my life became. The streets became more demanding of me. And we slowly drifted apart. She wanted me to choose between her, and the life I had become accustomed to. And I couldn't."

I felt dizzy. He was standing there, telling me how my mother's parents disowned her once she married him. A self-made-millionaire. A poor boy who had gone through life wearing hand-me-down clothes, and walking two miles to school with holes in the bottom of his shoes. He accused my mother of keeping him from me because of the life he'd refused to give up. She'd spend his money but would no longer allow him to share her bed. He blamed her for his infidelity throughout their marriage. She'd turn her back to his extramarital affairs and business dealings as long as he maintained her lifestyle, and stayed away from *me*, or she'd have all of his business transactions under federal investigation.

I stood there, eyeing him in disbelief. My mother had died, and—instead of being there for me—he'd shipped me off to a fucking boarding school. Why? Because he claims that was the arrangement between my mother, her attorneys and him. Even if that's true, why didn't he visit? And why the hell did it take him three years to show up to get me? There was no legitimate answer he could give me. So he stood there in his designer clothes and fancy jewels fast-talking me. He was really full of shit, feeding me that bull.

"I know. I— "

I put my hand up, stopping him before he could finish. "Please," I said, shaking my head. "I don't want to hear anymore." I felt the tears coming, but I kept them in check. I felt my anger swelling, pushing up against the gates of my rage.

"Indera, we need to talk."

"No," I snapped, gathering my blanket from off the ground, then walking past him. "We have nothing to talk about." He ran up behind me, grabbing my arm and swinging me around.

"You can't keep running from me."

"Why can't I?" I screeched. "You ran from me. Now get your mother-fucking hand off of me." I yanked my arm from out of his grasp. "If you *ever*," I snapped, clenching my teeth, "put your hands on me again, you'll be lying in a box next to my mother."

He snatched my arm again, this time with more force. The sparkle I had seen in his eyes only minutes before had faded. The veins in his forehead popped out. He didn't yell, but his voice was cold. "Don't *you* ever threaten me. Or it will be *you* in that box. I am still your father."

I glared at him, slapping his damn face. "Kiss my ass! Do you think I give a fuck about you *still* being my father? Being in a box next to my mother would have been a whole lot better than being abandoned by you, and abused by your fucking wife. So, fuck you!"

When he tightened his grip instead of letting go, I slapped him again. He didn't budge. He stared me down. I slapped him again, leaving my print on the side of his face. "Get your fucking hands off of me." When I raised my hand to slap him for the fourth time, he grabbed me by the wrist with his other hand, yanking my arm down.

"If slapping me makes you feel better, then fine. But we're going to talk *today*."

I stared through him. "Let. Me. Go," I demanded in a low, controlled tone. He didn't. "You really don't know who you're fucking with, do you?"

The left side of his mouth curved into an eerie smile, causing the hairs on the back of my neck to rise. "Let me explain something to you, my dear daughter. I know whom I'm dealing with. See. You are me, and I am you. We are one in the same. Both cut from the same cloth." I couldn't believe he'd stood there and allowed that to fall from his damn mouth.

Granted he's cleaned his money up, and now owns a variety of business ventures in the States and abroad. Still in all, he was a man with organized ties in Colombia; a former drug kingpin: the head of a thirty-million-dollar-a-year, narcotics-trafficking network—a crime that carries a mandatory life sentence. And to add to his resume, he's a cold-blooded killer when crossed. Huh? Oh. Don't even go there. I've *never* killed anyone, okay. I maim, *not* murder. Don't get it twisted. And as far as what happened to Grace, she was already dead. Hello.

"I'm nothing like you," I snapped, tightening my jaws.

"Take a long look in my eyes," he challenged, squeezing my arm tighter. "And tell me what *you* see." I matched his stare, holding back the burning sensation of tears. "That's right. You see yourself in me. And I've always seen me in you. That fire that burns inside of you is real. And is dangerous when toyed with." He loosened his grasp on me, lowering his voice. "So, I know very well what you're capable of. You're a Fleet."

"I hate you!"

"The blood on my hands," he spat, "is the same blood on yours. Don't ever forget that."

I almost gagged when he said that. And before I knew it, my emotions had gotten the best of me. If I had had my gun on me, I would have blown his face off, right there. "I hate you!" I screamed, slapping and punching. He stood there, taking blow for blow without flinching. I banged my fists in his chest, crying. "Fuck you!" I banged, and screamed, and slapped and punched him until I was exhausted. And then he did the unthinkable: He grabbed me in his arms and held me tight. And I fell into his embrace, sobbing.

"That's right. Let it all out."

"I hate you! I hate you! I hate you!" I screamed into his chest. He tightened his arms around me. "No, you don't. As hard as you've tried, your heart won't let you." I continued wailing. I was really out of control emotionally. "I'd give my life to take back all the hurt and pain you've endured."

"But you can't," I said, backing out of his arms. I stared him in his eyes. "You weren't there when I needed you."

"But I'm here now. If you'd just let me. All I want is a chance to make it up to you."

"You had your chance."

"It's never too late," he said, handing me his monogrammed handkerchief, "to start over."

I wiped my face, then blew my nose into the crisp, white material. I shook my head, inhaling his Dior. "I'm afraid it is, for me."

"Open up you heart and let me in. Let me love you."

"I have no space in my heart for you," I said, turning to leave him standing there.

"How can you expect to be forgiven," he snapped, "if you can't forgive? I am still your father, Indera. And whether you believe or not, I love you. And I'm not leaving. So, you don't have to open your heart to me, but at least make peace with me, and with yourself." I stopped in my tracks, turning to face him. Over his shoulder, I saw my mother, walking toward me. Her arms were extended open.

"My sweet child. It's time for you to let go of your bitterness. For every sin you've committed, through God's grace and mercy, you've been forgiven. Now it's time for you to forgive those who have trespassed against you. Though your father may not have been there when I was here on earth in the way I wanted him to be, he has come here faithfully to be with me. And I have forgiven him."

She wrapped her arms around me, wiping my tears. *"Go to him,"* she whispered, gently pushing me forward. *"Remember, I am always with you."* And then she was gone. I took a deep breath, walking closer toward the man I've hated, and loved, all in the same breath. I stared him in his eyes, then reached up and touched his face. His skin was soft. He really was a handsome man.

"I am willing to try to forgive you," I said, hugging him as tears fell from my eyes. "And I do want to be at peace. I'll call you when I'm ready to talk." I reached up, kissed him on the cheek and headed for my car, leaving him in thought and with the image of me driving off, never looking back.

22

CELESTE: *This Time I'll Be Sweeter*

As the days collided into weeks, I found myself immersed in planning and preparing for the Weaves and Wonders Grand Opening, anticipating the appearance of that one special guest—among all the other hundred or so supporters who were invited to partake in Indera's business endeavor—to waltz in with open arms. Everyone was there: media and news reporters, the elite and downtrodden, young and old. Even the mayor of Hartford graced the event with his presence to welcome Indera to the Greater Hartford area. Surprisingly, other salon owners also stopped in to wish her well and embrace her into their community.

And as the day sped by, I busied myself with making sure everything ran smooth while checking and double-checking my watch against the clock on the wall. Everything was perfect. Everyone was in place. Nothing was missing, except the moment when Britton would walk through the door. And I'd saunter up to him wearing a smile as bright as sunshine. I had rehearsed this in my mind over and over. I knew the tape. Unfortunately, I wouldn't have a chance to play it. He never showed up. And my heart crashed a thousand times.

"Celeste, is everything all right?" Indera asked, feigning concern. "You seem a bit upset."

I forced a smile. "I'm fine, Indy. Thanks. I'm just a little tired from the excitement. I guess all the last-minute running around has caught up with me."

She returned my smile, patting my arm. "Hmm. I see. Well, you go on and get yourself some rest. I can handle things from here. You did a wonderful job. I couldn't have done it without you." Her tone sounded sincere, but there was something in her eyes that told me otherwise. She handed me a folded check. "Here's the balance for your services along with a bonus to show my appreciation for all of your hard work."

I opened up the check, glancing at the amount written in the box. I almost fainted. Working for her wasn't an easy task by any means; but, I wasn't expecting what I saw: a check amount for twenty-thousand dollars. "Thank you," I said, glancing over at the door when it opened. My face must have shown my dismay when a young woman walked in.

"Celeste, are you sure everything is okay. You keep looking over at the door as if you're expecting someone." If I didn't know any better, I would have sworn her eyes were laughing at me.

I nodded my head. "Everything's fine," I said, mustering the strength to mask my disappointment. "I was expecting a good friend to stop by."

She tilted her head, lifting her brow. "Hmm. So that's why you're all laid out in this fierce little number. And here I thought you got all dressed up for me." She chuckled. I half-smiled. "Well, we still have another hour or so before we shut down. Hopefully, he'll show by then."

She startled me. "I never said it was a him," I replied, catching her smirk. "Girlfriend, you didn't have to. It's obvious."

"Indera, darling," a regal woman said, walking over to us. It was hard to tell how old she was, but she had clearly aged well. I admired her beauty and grace. She was stylishly dressed in a hunter-green Chanel dress and matching hat. She removed her designer shades. Indera smiled when she approached us. "There you are, my dear." They embraced.

"Soror, it's so good to see," Indy said, beaming. "I didn't think you would make it."

"Now you know I wouldn't have missed this for the world." She rubbed the side of Indy's face. "Your mother would be so proud of you." I turned my face, swallowing my pain. *You shameless fool, I don't know whose child you are but you surely can't belong to me. Embarrassing my good family name.*

"Oh, excuse me. Soror, this is Celeste. Celeste, this is Soror Augustina Wells." We both smiled. "Celeste is a member of the Omicron Alpha Alpha Chapter."

She smiled.

I cleared my throat. "Nice meeting you, soror," I said, extending my hand to shake hers. I quickly glanced down at the diamond and gold bracelets draped around her wrist.

"Likewise," she replied, clasping her hand over mine. Her eyes bore into mine. "My goodness. You have a remarkable resemblance to a soror I went to school with. Oh, dear. What was that child's name." She pressed the tip of her neatly manicured finger on the center of her forehead as if there were an imaginary button to push on her memory. She chuckled. "Thanks to old age, I can't seem to remember her real name right now, but we called her Avia for short." I shifted my eyes. Indera stared at me. "Where are you from, dear?"

"D.C.," I said, pausing. My heartbeat quickened. "But I live here in Hartford."

"That's where she was from," she offered, shaking her head.

"Isn't that interesting," Indera said, smiling. "Soror, do you remember her last name. Maybe Celeste has heard of her." The walls were closing in on me. Somehow I felt as if I were being boxed in. Prey being hunted.

"God rest her soul," Augustina continued. "She and her charming husband, along with their youngest child, were killed in an automobile accident some years ago." I felt the space of floor under my feet open up. I was being pulled down.

"Oh, that's terrible," Indera said, placing her hand over her chest. "Did they have any other children?"

Time stopped, along with my breathing.

"If I'm not mistaken, there's an older daughter. But last I heard, she had taken to the streets. Poor thing."

I nervously twisted the ends of my scarf.

Two other women walked over to us. Both were dressed in flowing green dresses. They greeted us and were introduced as sorors who had also pledged at Spelman around the same time Indera's mother and my mother had pledged. "Soror, what in the Heaven was Avia's last name?" Augustina asked one of the women.

"Avia? Didn't she pledge on the spring '48 line?" the woman asked, looking over at her counterpart.

"I don't think so," her counterpart offered. "Indera's mother was on that line." Sweat rolled down my back. Indera seemed amused. "Avia pledged fall '50."

"She most certainly did," Augustina declared. She snapped her fingers. "Randolph. That's it. Avia Randolph…"

"Umm. Excuse me for one moment, ladies," Indy said, gracefully leaving the group. She had a big wide "the-cat-just-ate-the-canary" grin on her face. "I need to check on something. I'll be right back." They waved her on, dragging me down memory lane. I kept my smile painted on my face as these women unknowingly pieced together my life.

"…Actually that was her married name. Her husband was a professor of philosophy at Howard." Tension was beginning to coil its way around my neck. I was slowly suffocating.

"Humph," one of the women said, shaking her head. "It was an awful tragedy the way they were killed."

"I know. It came as such a shock to us all," Augustina said, pausing.

I needed air.

"I'm sorry, sorors," I said abruptly. "But I really have to get going. It was a pleasure meeting you all." I excused myself, gathered my things and hurriedly left the building without saying good-bye.

By the time I arrived home my thoughts were so cluttered with worry that I barely had enough strength to shower. I needed to tie and knot the strings of my life before everything unraveled right before my eyes. I tossed and turned for hours before finally drifting off to sleep with streaks of lies running from my eyes.

The shrill sound of the phone shook me from a restless slumber. I rubbed my eyes, focusing on the time. It was eight in the morning. I picked up, and the minute the word "hello" fell from my mouth a strange yet familiar greeting lured me through the phone: *"You have a collect call from… Lonnie…at the District of Columbia state penitentiary. To accept this call, please do not use three-way or call-waiting features or you will be disconnected. To accept this call…"* Against my better judgment, I waited for the computerized recording to finish and pressed one. "Hello?"

"Long time, no hear, baby," a low voice said against the rattle of voices and sounds in the background. I shifted the receiver from one ear to the other as a sweaty paste coated the palms of my hands. I pressed the phone deep into my ear, straining to hear everything. Listening to nothing.

"Who is this?" I asked, twirling my worries around the phone's cord with my fingers.

"It's the past you tried to run from," he said coolly. "But I'm on your heels, baby. Remember that." I cringed, hoping my mind was playing tricks on me. Hoping that I'd wake up and realize it was a sick, twisted dream. Unfortunately, my mind wasn't deceiving me, and my eyes were as wide as the hole I was sinking in.

"How'd you get my number?" I asked in a fearful whisper.

"Oh, don't you worry your sweet little head about that. I got my eyes and ears on you, baby. And I'm gonna find you. So ready or not, here I come—"

"Don't call my house again," I snapped, interrupting him, "'cause if you do, I'll call up there and tell the authorities you're harassing and threatening me."

A wicked and cruel laugh escaped from him as I slammed down the phone, nervously pacing the floor. *He can't get to me*, I reasoned in my head. *By the time he gets out, I'll be long gone.* I racked my brain trying to figure out who might have given him my phone number. My mind went blank as an unsettling chill ran along my spine. No one knew where I was. When I left D.C., I left without saying a word to anyone. So as far as anyone from my past knew, I was long gone. I jumped when the phone rang again. This time, I let the answering machine pick up.

"Celeste, girl. It's Rochelle. Call me when you get in."

I raced over to the phone, picking up just before she hung up. "Hello."

"Hmm. I see you're screening calls today."

"Something like that," I said, blowing out my relief.

"Is everything okay?" she asked, genuinely concerned.

"I just got a disturbing phone call so I'm a little on edge. That's all."

"Anything you want to talk about?"

"No. Not really," I stated, sitting on the edge of my bed, staring at my toes. I needed a pedicure, badly. I made a mental note to make myself an appointment the minute I hung up with her. "Maybe some other time," I offered. "I'd rather forget it for now."

"Then it's forgotten. Just know I'm a phone call away." I smiled. That's one of the reasons I appreciate her friendship. No matter what, she never pushes or tries to probe into my life. She accepts what I'm willing to share with her with open arms. Not that I've told her much about my sordid past. As much as I would like to, I can't disclose to her the part of my life I'm desperately trying so hard to forget.

"Guess what we'll be wearing to the charity ball tomorrow night?" she asked, changing the subject.

"What?" I asked, happy to get my mind off the previous call.

"Full-length mink coats."

"Get out of here. You're kidding, right?"

"Absolutely not," she replied. "I just picked them up a few hours ago. And they're gorgeous. We'll be stepping up in that piece sharp."

"I can't wait," I responded gleefully. I had already purchased my dress, shoes and other accessories. The mink would set it off just right. I smiled, imagining the look on Indera's face when I walked up in her celebrity ball. She had made it a point to say my services were no longer needed when I'd asked her about coordinating the event for her. Nor would she be extending an invitation for me to attend. When I offered to buy a ticket, she declined the sale, stating it was best if I didn't show my face. I was pissed to say the least.

"And why is that?" I had asked with indignation in my tone. She shifted in her seat, crossing her legs at the ankles like the lady she was, then tilted her head as if she didn't comprehend the question. "I don't understand your abrupt attitude toward me."

She twisted her face up. "Ugh! Girlfriend, please; you being a sneaky bitch is the reason for my abruptness."

"Excuse you?"

"You heard me," she said, eyeing me. "You're a sneaky, lying bitch."

"I don't appreciate the way you're speaking to me," I said, getting up from my desk. "So perhaps you should leave." I walked over toward the door, preparing to open it. "I've done nothing but be nice to you, and all you can think to do is be nasty."

"Oh please," she snapped, ensconcing deeper in the armchair, clearly not planning to leave anytime soon. I shut the door, then walked back over to my desk, sitting on its edge. I folded my arms in front of me. "Your reason for being nice to me, as you put it, was purely motive driven. And we both know what drove you to seek me out, don't we?"

"Indy, I have no idea what you're talking about." I held in my breath, hoping she hadn't figured out my plot. Truth be told, I was quickly learning that I had underestimated her. The possibility of her finding me out hadn't been factored into the plan.

"Okay. Well, let's try this. Does the name Britton ring a bell for you?" She tilted her head, waiting for my reaction.

I breathed in the air around me, held it for several moments, then slowly released it through my nose. She knew. "How long have you known?" I asked, fidgeting with the wedding band hanging from around my neck.

"Long enough." So that would explain why he wasn't at the opening. I was sure she somehow conveniently kept him from showing up.

"Does Britton know?"

"Of course not. Why would I want to tell him about you?"

"Because he has the right to know."

"Humph. Well, as far as he's concerned, you're somewhere dead with a needle stuck in your arm." I cringed.

"Well, I'm not."

"Too bad for him," she said callously.

"So what are you going to do?" I asked, hoping she lacked the ability to influence any decisions he made regarding our future together.

"Not a damn thing," she responded, getting up from her seat. "Except to suggest you go crawl back in whatever hole you came out of."

"I love him. And I want him back."

"Britton has gone on with his life, so you should do the same."

"Britton is my life," I snapped, raising my voice. "And whether you like it or not, Indy, he is going to find out that I'm alive and well. And if I can help it, we *will* be together."

She laughed. "Bitch, you're delusional. But I'll leave you with this, stay away from him—"

"Or what?" I snapped, standing to my feet.

She smiled. "You can fill in the blanks." She walked out of my office, leaving me standing in the middle of the floor, fuming.

Rochelle's voice broke my reverie.

"…And wait until you see the dress I picked up," she continued. "It's a real showstopper. Girl, I haven't been out anywhere fancy in so long, I feel like I'm preparing for my prom."

"I know what you mean," I said, chuckling. "So tell me about these mink coats."

"Girl," she purred. "They're absolutely plush and luxurious. You'll be stepping out in a brown one and I'll be wearing black."

"Ooh, I can't wait," I said, pausing when reality slapped me in the face. Money was tight. Although, I was finally able to catch up on all my bills and even pay a few of them off, I couldn't get too happy spending. With the exception of a few dollars I had managed to save out of the money I earned from the Weaves and Wonders event, I was still living paycheck to paycheck. I could hit hard times in the blink of an eye if I wasn't careful how I spent my money.

"Girl, I can't afford a mink right now."

She laughed. "Relax. They're rented."

"Whew," I said, relaxing. "For a minute there, I thought I was going to have to dig in my savings again."

"Don't worry. Your little nest egg is safe. A friend of mine works at a furrier so I was able to get them discounted."

"That's a relief," I said, laughing. The phone line buzzed. "Hey Ro, can you hold for a minute, someone's on the other line."

"Sure."

I clicked over. "Hello." No one answered. "Hello." *Whoever it was, they must have hung up*, I reasoned, clicking back over to my conversation with Rochelle. "Okay, I'm back."

"As I was saying, my friend is renting the coats to me for almost nothing. That Indera bitch is going to be shocked when she sees us stepping up in there."

"I bet she will," I said, relishing the thought of seeing her face.

The ballroom was absolutely elegant. Large round tables were smartly dressed with crisp white linen tablecloths while tall crystal vases centered in the middle of each table were filled with a bouquet of fresh lilies. The room was quickly filling with men and women donned in formal wear. I spotted Tradawna walking toward one of the tables with a very attractive gentleman in a black tux. She was stylishly dressed in a black gown with a plunging back drape. I smiled to myself, then quickly scanned the room, hoping to catch a glimpse of Britton. The thought of finally laying eyes on him had my heart doing somersaults. I took in a deep breath of disappointment when I didn't see anyone who remotely resembled him.

"Relax, girl," Rochelle said, sensing my anxiety. "The night's still young. He'll be here."

I reluctantly smiled, glancing down at my watch. She was right. It was only a little after seven. "I know," I said, toying with the ends of my scarf. "I'll be glad when all this is finally over." I looked around the room one last time. I spotted Indera to the left of me, wearing a beautiful green, double-strapped, ankle-length gown. Her hair was pinned up with a cascade of curls around her face. The lighting from the huge chandeliers made the diamonds around her neck glow.

"Just look at her," Rochelle huffed, glaring over at her. She lowered her voice. "As much as I dislike her, I have to give it to her. The bitch is fierce." I nodded in agreement.

"That she is," I said, shifting my weight from one foot to the other. I had only had my heels on for less than an hour and my feet were already killing me. "Remind me to never buy another pair of six-inches again. By the time this night is over, I'm going to need a new set of feet."

She chuckled. "Well," she offered lightly, "if you're lucky, you'll have that fine man of yours rubbing those bad boys for you from now on."

"That *is* the plan," I replied, smiling. "And this time, I'm not letting him get away." *Lord, please don't let anything go wrong.*

"That's the spirit. Now let's go freshen up before it's time for your grand appearance."

"I'm right behind you," I said, following her to the bathroom. We both relieved ourselves, washed our hands, then stood in front of large oval mirrors neatly centered over marble basins. I pulled out my MAC lipstick, then neatly applied a fresh coat. I smacked my lips together and dabbed the corners of my mouth with a napkin.

"Girl, even down to the damn bathroom," Rochelle stated, rummaging through her beaded handbag, "this place is fabulous." She pulled out her cosmetic case, yanking out her compact and dabbing her face with pressed powder. "I can't stand this shine on my nose and forehead. I look like a damn walking light bulb."

I laughed, readjusting my scarf so that it would hang loosely around my neck. "Girl," I offered, staring over at her, "you look fine. By the way, I love your dress." She wore a burgundy form-fitting gown with a daring neckline and a thigh-high slit. Her days at Bally's had finally paid off and tonight she was forty pounds lighter, and leaving nothing to the imagination.

"Why thank you," she said, breaking into a wide smile. "When I saw it, it had my name written all over it. Take me. Take me. Take me." She broke out in laughter, pulling out the tag. "And bring me back in the morning." I smiled, nodding knowingly. First thing Monday morning Rochelle would be at Nordstrom standing in line to return her find. I don't always agree with her shopping tactics but I've been known to return a few things here and there myself, provided I don't stain it. Rochelle could care less. Ring around the collar, makeup smudges, sweat stains. It didn't matter. As long as she had the receipt, she was bringing it back.

"You're a mess," I said, swatting at her playfully, heading for the door. "Come on, let's go mingle." As I was about to reach for the handle, the door swung open, almost slamming into me. I instinctively jumped backward.

"Oh, excuse…" Her eyes locked on mine. "What in the world are you doing here?"

"Hello, Indy," I said with a slight smile. "I'm here to celebrate and support a good cause." She glanced over at Rochelle who was giving her an under-eyed glare. Indy smirked, brushing past me.

"Well, I'd advise you…" she stated, then paused, tossing her head over toward Rochelle, "and the chicken-head to leave before I have you both thrown out."

I held my breath, fully aware of what was to come. "Chicken-head? Bitch, who you calling a chicken-head?" Rochelle asked, snapping her hand on her hip and rolling her neck. "You're the damn chicken-head."

Indy turned to face her. "Excuse you."

"You heard me, bitch."

Indy smiled. I clutched my imaginary pearls. Rochelle stared her down.

"*Like I said,*" Indy repeated, returning her attention to me. "You and this chicken-head need to leave. This is a private event and neither of you were invited. So I suggest you find your way out."

"Well, for your information," Rochelle snapped. "We paid our five-hundred dollars, and we're staying. So get over yourself."

"I'm not talking to you."

"Yeah, but you were talking about me. So as far as I'm concerned you were talking to me. And I'm not the one. Understand?" Rochelle paused for effect, shifting her weight before continuing. "'Cause contrary to popular belief, if you keep talking slick, I'll beat your ass up in here, pregnant or not."

Oh Lord. Please don't let my night turn into a night of battle.

"You know what," Indy snapped. "I'm gonna let you get that for the moment, sweetie. But don't let the belly fool you. 'Cause the minute you feel froggish and try to leap, I will stomp your teeth in, trust and believe."

"Indy, there's really no need for all this hostility," I stated, catching Rochelle's eye. She smirked. "We're here to have a good time. And like I said, support a wonderful cause."

Indy turned toward the mirror, softly tugging at her curls, then twirling them back in place. Her hair was laid. She smoothed down her eyebrows with her neatly manicured fingers, then stared at me through the mirror. "Hmm. Sounds good. But I'm not buying."

"Think what you like," I said. "But the fact of the matter is we had no intentions of missing such a well-publicized event."

She laughed. "Oh, come off of it. You think you're going to use my affair to stage your little plan to get Britton back. Well, you're in for a rude awakening."

"It's not what I think," I replied, coolly. "It's what I know. And there's nothing you or anyone else can do about it. So I suggest *you* find a way to get used to it. Now if you'll excuse us, we were on way out to join the crowd."

"Umm. Celeste," she said, turning around to face me. "Before you go, do tell me. How was life behind bars?"

My mouth dropped open. "What in the world are you talking about?"

"Why, soror," she said snidely. "Don't look so surprised. I mean, I couldn't imagine spending ten years of my life in prison. But then again," she said, walking toward me. "I wasn't the one on crack."

How in the world did she find all this out? "You don't know what you're talking about."

"Oh, I don't?" she snapped. "Well then, let's try this. Celeste Munley-Randolph. The daughter of Octavia and Horace Randolph; mother of three children: a daughter you never wanted, a son you killed from your drug use, and another you tossed in a trash bin to die." She rubbed her belly. "Hmm. Maybe the next time you get pregnant—oops. I forgot. Poor thing, had to have her insides pulled out."

I felt weak at the knees. "Where did you get this information?" I asked, fighting back my tears. In one breath, layer by layer, she was peeling back my secrets and exposing me. The only way she could have found out about my hysterectomy was by having someone access my prison records. "How dare you," I quavered, "pry into my personal business."

"No," she snapped, clenching her teeth. "How dare *you* try to stunt me. You fake-ass bitch. The gall of you to think you could get to Britton through me with all of your lies. Well, guess what, dear. I made it my business to know just whom I was dealing with. Unfortunately you didn't do your own homework. 'Cause if you had, you would have known that you were treading very treacherous waters trying to grin in my face."

I literarily felt numb all over. "You shut your mouth," Rochelle snapped, coming to my defense.

Indy put the palm of her hand up at Rochelle as if to stop her. "Talk to the hand, ho. 'Cause I'm really not feeling you. But I got something for your stink ass. See. I know all about you too, Miss Quick Drawers. Ever since your husband left you, you've been fucking everything under the sun. Umm. From what I've been told, you have a case of the alphabet soup. Is that ABC or HIV?"

"You know what," Rochelle said, throwing down her clutch. "I will fuck you up." Rochelle went to lunge at her. I jumped in the middle, holding her back.

"Let it go," I snapped. "It's not worth it." Indy didn't budge.

"No. Let *her* go," she egged. Rochelle glared at her, breathing heavy.

"I'll beat your ass."

"Let it go," I repeated.

Indy's eyes bore into her. Her lips curled into a smirk. "Girlfriend, I never open my mouth to say anything unless I'm sure what I'm talking about. So, if the truth hurts, oh well. Your little threats and half-assed gestures to come at me don't move me one way or the other. So when you bring it, you better be prepared to swing it." She turned her back on us, facing the mirror again. She finished primping while keeping an eye on us.

Rochelle stared her down. I held her tighter.

Indy turned back around, facing us. She tilted her head and crossed her arms over her chest.

"Come on," I said, pulling Rochelle toward the door. "It's not worth it. Let it go."

Rochelle continued to resist but then calmed down. When her breathing slowed, I let her go but I stayed in front of her. "She really don't know who she's fucking with," she said, looking at me. "And you're right. She's not worth the trouble. But you don't have to stand here and listen to this stuck-up bitch's shit, either."

I took in a deep breath, blowing it out slowly. "I'm fine," I said, forcing a wide smile and turning my attention to Indy. "Tonight," I continued, swallowing my anguish, "I'm here to see my husband. And nothing you say or do will stop me. So you can have me thrown out if you'd like. But tonight, I will see him. Even if it means I have to sit outside and wait for him."

The door opened. "Oh, here you are," a tall slender woman, wearing a green-beaded tunic gown, said, looking at Indy. "The Master of Ceremonies is getting ready to introduce you."

"I'll be right out," Indy replied, peeling her eyes off me. "I just need to finish up in here."

"All right. I'll let him know," the young woman said, slowly backing her way out of the doorway. When the door closed, Indy continued.

"Now where were we?" she asked, looking from me to Rochelle. She glanced down at her diamond-faced timepiece. "On second thought, I'd love to hang around and chat, but I do have guests to greet." She sauntered toward the door, then stopped in her tracks, turning around. She snapped open her Louis Vuitton croissant handbag, pulling out ten one-hundred-dollar bills, then throwing them at us. "Here's your refunds. I expect both of you trifling bitches to see yourself out. But if you stay, it's at your own risk."

"Fuck you," Rochelle spat.

She laughed harshly. "I'll keep that in mind." Then with nothing else said, she clicked on her heels and walked out the door like nothing ever happened, leaving Rochelle and me baffled.

"Humph," Rochelle said, picking up the crisp bills from the floor. "That bitch is crazy."

"I think she's a little bit more than crazy," I stated, still trying to regain my composure. I walked back over to the sink, staring at myself in the mirror. I was literally shaken. I couldn't believe Indy had managed to break into my locker of lies, and plunder through my secrets. Her words plunged through me, unclogging a host of painful memories. My mother had revealed the truth, and my reflection in the mirror confirmed it. *On the outside, you're a beautifully wrapped package. But on the inside, you're nothing more than a bag of rotted trash. You disgust me.* I shook the words from my thoughts. There was no sense in allowing my mother to ruin the rest of my evening. Indera had already succeeded in dampening my mood.

"Well, she's lucky you stepped in when you did. And it's a good thing that chick walked up in here, because she was about to get cut up real good."

"Take it from me," I offered. "It wouldn't have been worth all the trouble..." I paused for a split second, feeling myself being pulled back into my cell. Not the one erected from steel and concrete, but the one created in the corners of my mind from feelings of solitude and emptiness. The one that crippled me emotionally, causing me to use drugs as my crutch through life. My self-built cell, painted with hurt and lies. Painfully coated with memories of losing my parents, my children, my husband, and most importantly—me to my addiction. I broke from its clutches, continuing with my conversation. "...Besides, I don't think it would have gotten that far. If I know nothing else about Indera Fleet, I do know she'd never allow herself to be caught on display, acting a fool. Not with all these high-rollers here." I leaned over the sink, desperately trying to glue myself back together.

"Are you all right?"

I nodded. "I'm fine," I said, hiding my face in the palm of my hands. "I just need a few minutes to pull myself together."

She walked over to me and rubbed my back. "Girl, don't let that bitch steal your joy. You've come too far to be knocked around or turned around. I say we go out there and have us a grand ole time. Here," she said, handing me five hundred dollars. "Compliments of Indy." I smiled, taking the bills and stuffing them in my purse. "Now fix your face, and let's go have us a few drinks and get you that man of yours."

My face brightened. The thought of finally seeing Britton replaced distress with a wide smile. "You're absolutely right." I placed my face inches away from the mirror, dabbing my eyes with a white handkerchief. I then reapplied a fresh coat of eyeliner and lipstick, straightened out my dress, threw my head up and sashayed out the door behind my only friend.

My eyes widened in awe as we made our way back to the ballroom. It was packed. Once again, Indera had outdone herself. She was standing at the podium, finishing up her speech. Rochelle had tracked down one of the waiters and returned with two flutes of bubbly. I graciously took a sip, letting it tickle my senses. I scanned the room as Indera's words clung in the air.

"...So tonight, as we celebrate Black History and the contributions and sacrifices of our forefathers, let us embrace and salute the leaders of today and tomorrow; our present and future; the men and women who have climbed the ladder of success, gaining recognition for their staunch belief that no matter what, you can be whatever you strive to be. You can do whatever you desire to do. These are the men and women who continued to knock on the doors of opportunities that were once closed on them.

"With determination, perseverance, and never-ending faith, we have come a mighty long way from the days of slavery, and Jim Crow laws. And despite every beating, despite every rape, despite every family torn apart, we were still able to rise. And we are still standing.

"And tonight. I, on behalf of the Nandi Educational and Research Foundation and its board of directors, proudly stand before you to present to you the 2001 Nandi Fleet Scholarship recipients for their excellence in education and community service. So without further ado, I introduce to you the young men and women who are carving their mark along the road of great achievers, and believers. The new generation of history makers."

One by one, she called the names of the eight high school seniors from the New York/New Jersey area: four males and four females, receiving full four-year scholarships to one of the historically black colleges/universities of their choice. She handed each one a mock check with their names written on them, shaking their hands. A few gave her loving hugs. The room shook with applause as bright lights from photographers' cameras caught the moment on film. Tomorrow Indera's good deed would be captured on the front page of every newspaper's "Society" section.

I grabbed my second glass of champagne, gulping down my envy. "Now that's what I call fine," Rochelle said, leaning into my ear, snapping me back to my reason for being there in the first place. She had finally returned from floating around the room.

"Who?" I asked, matching her whisper, then following her stare.

"Over there in the right corner, talking to the model-looking chick. Girl, that's the kind of man I could lick from head to toe." I slowly turned my head, looking over my shoulder. My heart stopped, then thumped with heavy beats.

"Oh my God," I said in almost a whisper. "It's Britton." He was standing with a curvaceous woman the color of honey, wearing a glove-fitted, royal-blue sequined skirt and tunic. He seemed enthralled by her conversation or perhaps her beauty. But none of that mattered. The moment I had been waiting for had finally come. Yet, as eager as I was to see the look on his face, I was scared to move. Too afraid to breathe, fearful of his reaction.

"Well?" Rochelle snapped.

I broke my gaze momentarily. "Huh? What did you say?"

"What are you waiting for? Go on over there and claim your place. 'Cause if you don't, I sure will."

"How do I look?" I asked, patting my hair, then smoothing down my dress.

"Like a woman who's about to score big," she said, grinning. I smiled.

"Wish me luck," I said, looking up at the ceiling for a sign, something that would dictate the course of my journey. There was none. But I knew I couldn't delay the inevitable. He needed to know I was alive, and eager to be a part of his life again.

"Go on," Rochelle said, pushing me in his direction. I smiled, then slowly made my way through the crowd. Courage kept my feet moving. And I held its hand tightly as I neared him. Perhaps it was my imagination. But the room seemed to have grown quiet and all eyes seemed fixated on me. I was floating.

"Would you like champagne, ma'am?" the waiter asked as I glided by. I nodded, taking my third flute, slowly rinsing down my nervousness. I kept my eyes on Britton as he smiled at something his acquaintance said. His dimples dipped in his cheeks as he flashed his perfectly straight teeth. He hadn't changed a bit. The woman he was with stopped talking when she saw me approaching them. And—as if prompted, Britton turned his head in my direction, locking his eyes on mine. I could see the shock on his face as his mouth opened. I cleared my throat, swallowing awkwardly as I stood face-to-face with the man who held the key to my heart.

23

BRITTON: *Sorry Doesn't Always Make It Right*

After all these years, I couldn't believe my eyes. The woman I walked out on sixteen years ago—after two years of marriage—because of her addiction and the things that came along with her use: the erratic mood swings, the lying, the stealing and the sexual indiscretions was standing before me. She looked nothing like the wild-haired, disheveled woman I used to chase down, trying to keep out of ramshackle crack dens or the glazed-eyed woman who would lock herself in the bathroom, run the shower, then come out looking half-crazed. The woman standing before me was stunning. I was speechless.

"Hello, Britton," she said, holding a flute of champagne.

"Ce-Celeste, I'm..." I paused, trying to swallow the ball of shock that stuck in my throat. I was beginning to find it hard to breathe.

"Surprised?" she asked, smiling. Her eyes sparkled.

"Yeah, to say the least," I managed to say without tripping over my words. I immediately returned my attention back to the lovely sista who had enthralled me with her charm, beauty, and grace. I kindly introduced her to Celeste. Of course, I omitted the fact she was my estranged wife. They both gave the other a cordial smile and hello.

"Britton," she said in a voice as sweet as pecan pie, "it was a pleasure meeting you. We'll have to continue our conversation *soon.*" She handed me a business card. "Call me."

I smiled, taking her hand in mine. "The pleasure was all mine. I'll be in touch." I kissed her hand and watched her glide away. *Damn!* I shifted my eyes back to Celeste. "What are you doing here?" I asked in a tone harsher than I expected. But I was totally taken off guard.

"You don't sound too pleased to see me," she responded with a look of disappointment. "I am. I mean…I'm just in a state of shock. It's been so long." I noticed Indy briskly walking toward us, rubbing her hand over her stomach. The look on her face spelled trouble.

"Brit, is everything all right?" she asked, glaring at Celeste.

"Indy, everything's fine," I indicated, scanning the room for Amir and Amar. "Indy, where are the boys?"

"They're sitting over there with Pedro." She gestured over to the right. "They're fine." Indy gave Celeste a half-eyed glare. Celeste pursed her lips. I felt like I had just gotten sucked into an inferno.

"Celeste, I thought I told you to leave."

"Indy," Celeste said. "It's no secret you don't like me, but let's try to be civil in front of all your guests." My mouth flew open.

"You two know each other?"

"We met a few months back," Celeste offered, never breaking her stare.

"Yeah," Indy concurred in a hushed tone. "I met this conniving bitch on my trip to Vegas."

"Now, soror, is that any way to speak in public? We *are* supposed to be about sisterhood. Now if you don't mind, my *husband* and I were in the middle of a conversation."

Soror? I couldn't believe Celeste had joined a sorority. She was always so opposed to belonging to any organization, especially a sorority. When she and I were at Howard together, she never had anything nice to say about Greek life. She saw pledging as a waste of time and energy.

"I don't need to join a sorority to feel like I have a sense of purpose," she had said to me when I asked her why she hadn't pledged. "Besides, I wouldn't be caught dead on somebody's line talking that 'Big Sister, *may I*' mess."

The next week, I went on line. Interestingly, she was surprisingly concerned for me and tried to be supportive even if she didn't understand why I—or anyone for that matter—would want to belong to any organization that belittled, berated *and*—in some instances—beat you before they embraced you as a member. "How can these people say they are about brotherhood and sisterhood, disrespecting you like that?" she once asked me in a hushed whisper, sneaking into the library to bring my line brothers and me something to eat. I decided to not respond because nothing I said would have made any sense to her; yet alone a difference.

"Don't 'soror' me, you barren bitch," Indy snarled, bringing me back to the present. "We both know the reason why you joined my sorority, so let's cut the bull. I let you and your crony off easy in the bathroom. But I see you wanna try me. Guests or no guests, I will slide your ass across this floor."

"Indy, please," I said with pleading eyes. I couldn't let my curiosity of wanting to know what she meant by that remark get the best of me. Nor could I allow my desire to know where her hostility originated. If I didn't try to calm this ticking bomb immediately, it would explode in any second. "It's okay."

"Don't worry, Britton," Indy said, turning her attention to me. "It's peace for the moment." She smiled, then returned her glare back to Celeste, clenching her teeth. "But, make no mistake. I'll be watching you. And the minute you slip, I'll be there to mop you up."

"Now, now," Celeste edged. "We wouldn't want you to go into early labor." Indy's nose flared. Her eyes blazed.

"If you know what's good for you," she snapped, "you had—"

"There you are," Tee said, walking up behind Indy, oblivious to the catfight that was about to erupt. He wrapped his arms around her waist, leaning in. "I was hoping I could get a dance with my beautiful wife." Indy broke her stare. "Brit, my man, what's the deal?" He smiled, shifting his eyes from Celeste to me, then to Indy.

"Not a thing, Tee." I glanced over at Celeste who looked like she had seen a ghost, then returned my attention to Tee. "I'm not sure if the two of you ever met. I'd like to introduce you to Celeste, my wife." His eyes popped wide open. Indy raised an eyebrow.

"Oh, damn! Umm. Nice to meet you."

"Nice meeting you, too."

"I just bet it is," Indy said, glaring.

"C'mon, baby, let's go. B, I'll catch you later." He grabbed Indy by the arm, whisking her away toward the dance floor—before Celeste or I had a chance to respond.

"What was that all about?" I asked visibly confused.

"Oh, it's nothing. She and I had a little disagreement, that's all."

"No. I'm not talking about that. I meant with Tee. I've never seen him scramble away so quickly in my life. Have the two of you met somewhere before?"

"Not at all," she quickly replied, fidgeting with the end of the green silk scarf neatly draped around her neck. "I mean, I vaguely remember seeing him on campus."

"Hmm, I see." I tried to remember if I had gotten cool with Tee before or after I left Celeste. *Damn. It was so long ago*, I thought, trying to search my memory. *Let me see.* When we transferred to Norfolk State, I didn't know Tee. As a matter of fact, we didn't meet until spring semester. Hmm. Celeste dropped out of school a few weeks before the fall semester ended. And since I didn't speak to anyone on campus about my marriage to her—more out of embarrassment than anything else—it was easier for me to keep that part of my life a secret. I made it a point to not bring any of my frat brothers around our apartment, not even Tee. So, I don't think anyone could have made the connection if they did happen to see her.

Besides, she rarely went out during the day anyway. She'd spend most of her days sleeping and her nights wandering the streets getting high. And when I finally left her, I brought no pictures along—with the exception of the one I carried in my wallet before finally tearing it up, and tossing it out. Otherwise, the only reminders of her were old memories. So he couldn't have known who she was. Not by face anyway.

"So when did you decide to join a sorority?" I asked once the chill of war blew over.

"A few years ago," she offered, taking a hard swallow of her last bit of champagne. She flagged one of the tuxedo-clad waiters, placing her empty flute on the silver tray, then taking another. "Champagne?"

"No thanks. I didn't know you drank."

"I have a two-drink max," she said, sipping her bubbly. I raised my eyebrow. The glassiness in her eyes revealed otherwise. But then again, what do I know. She stared at me as if she were a schoolgirl with a crush on her seventh-grade English teacher.

"What?" I asked, adjusting my cummerbund and loosening my bowtie. "Why are you looking at me like that?"

She smiled. "I was just thinking how handsome you are. Even with the braids, you haven't changed a bit."

"Thanks." I didn't know what else to say. I felt awkward, standing in the corner of this huge ballroom making small talk with the woman I once loved. The orchestra played "Inseparable" by Natalie Cole.

"I love this song. Will you dance with me?" She must have sensed my reluctance. "Just one dance," she added before I could respond.

"I'd rather not," I said, nervously glancing down at my watch.

A hint of disappointment flickered in her eyes. She half-smiled. "I understand." Another waiter passed by. She handed him her empty flute. Being this close to her after all this time seemed remarkably strange.

I returned the smile. "Maybe another time."

"I've missed you so much," she said, looking up at me. "You don't know how long I've waited for this." Her eyes glistened. I held her stare. I said nothing. I felt nothing. The only thing I heard were the chords of the song. *In-sep-arable, that's how we'll always be ...inseparable, just you and me."*

The awkwardness was getting the best of me. "I have to go check on my sons," I quickly replied and headed to their table.

"Do you mind if I tag along?"

"Daaaady," they squealed. Amir jumped down from his chair, raising his arms for me to pick him up. I lifted him up, planting him on my left hip. Amar was finishing up his third bowl of vanilla ice cream.

"I hope my two rug rats weren't given you too much trouble," I said to Pedro. He smiled.

"No sir. They were fun." His girlfriend agreed, excusing herself to get something to drink. "Excuse me," he said, getting up to follow behind her. Celeste was standing in back of me, slightly to the left, smiling. I introduced her to my boys.

"We already met," she offered. I gave here a puzzled look, but decided not to ask when, where or how. "They're adorable."

I smiled. "Thanks."

"Here, sweetheart," she said, taking a napkin from her handbag, then leaning over to wipe Amar's mouth. "Let me help you with that."

"You act like a mommy," Amir said, twisting at his head of curls. Something he only does when he's tired. Amar climbed down from his chair.

"That's not Mommy," Amar corrected, reaching up for me to pick him up too. I scooped him up and placed him on my other hip. He wrapped his arm around my neck.

"Noooo!" Amir whined. "I *said* she acts like a mommy." Celeste shifted her weight from one foot to the other, appearing slightly uncomfortable by their comments. She parted a nervous smile. I glanced down at my watch. It was 10:30 p.m. Way past our bedtimes.

"C'mon, boys," I interrupted before they said something else to make this more unbearable. "Let's get our coats so we can go. Celeste, I really need to get going. How long will you be in town?"

"Until tomorrow."

"Maybe we can get together to talk."

Her smile widened. "I'd like that. Here let me give you the number to where I'm staying." She pulled out a pen, then wrote her contact information on the back of her business card. "It was good seeing you," she said, attempting to kiss me on the cheek. I slipped the card inside my pocket.

"Nooo! Amar screamed, putting his hand in the way. "Don't kiss my daddy."

"Amar, stop being fresh," I scolded. "You know better than that. Look, I'll call you." Before she could say another thing, I quickly walked over toward Indy and Tee to say my good-byes. They both shot their eyes to the left of me. Indy rolled her eyes, then looked back up at me, parting a smile.

"I hope you had a wonderful time, despite the intrusion."

"Indy," I said reassuringly. "Everything was nice. You really outdid yourself." She smiled, standing up. She placed the palms of her hand on either side of her swollen belly. "Let me get these boys home before they break my arms."

"Drive safely," she said, leaning her head in to give us kisses. Tee and I gave each other a pound.

"I'll holla at you tomorrow," he added.

"Most def." When I turned around to get our things, I spotted Celeste standing over in the corner talking to a very attractive woman. She had grabbed another flute, making that her *third* drink for the night. They clicked their glasses, smiling. I headed toward the coat check, then hurriedly walked out into the cool night with the scent of her perfume lingering in my mind.

When the parking attendant brought my car around, I handed him his tip, buckled up my boys, then slid into the driver's seat, flipping on the radio to 98.7 KISS-FM. Lenny Green's *Kissing After Dark* was on. His deep voice seemed to melt the metal in my speakers 'cause the sound was about as smooth as he was. I smiled, shaking my head when I heard Natalie Cole's soulful voice singing, "I Can't Say No." I turned up the volume, then headed toward the Lincoln Tunnel for Jersey. I had decided to stay at my mother's since she and my stepfather were away. Besides, the ride to their house was closer than the ride to mine.

At the crack of dawn, I was up stirring around the house. I had tossed and turned all night, replaying the events of earlier that evening. I had so many questions that needed answering. Like why there was so much tension between Indy and Celeste, for starters. I wanted to know why Celeste decided to resurface after all these years of being hard to track down. It was like she had vanished off the face of the earth. And now, she was back. I went to the bathroom to relieve myself, then washed my hands and face. I stood in the mirror, pulling my braids back from my face. "Why now?" I asked aloud.

Before going downstairs to the kitchen, I checked in on the boys who were sound asleep. Amar was all the way at the foot of his bed with his arms hanging over. Amir had kicked off his covers. I pulled the covers back over him, then fixed Amar so he wouldn't fall out of the bed, banging his head. I gave them both kisses on their foreheads and tiptoed out their room, closing the door behind me.

By the time I made myself some French toast and turkey bacon, finished reading the *Star-Ledger* and cleaning up the kitchen, it was already eight-thirty. I was so glad Mr. Jay and my mom were away on their seven-day anniversary cruise. That gave me a chance to have the house to myself while I prepared for any other curve balls life may throw my way. Surprisingly, the boys were still sleeping. I savored the quiet time for a little while longer before I picked up the phone, dialing my sister's number.

"Hello?"

"Hello, who's this?" I asked, sitting at the kitchen table.

"Hi, Uncle Britton. It's Paris."

"Hey, Paris," I said, smiling. She sounded so much like my sister. "Is your mother up yet?"

"Yes. Hold on. I'll get her for you. Mom!" she yelled, half-covering the phone. "It's Uncle Britton." Someone picked up the other phone.

"Hi, Uncle Britton."

"Hi, Alona. Are you being a good girl?"

"Uh-huh."

"That's good."

"Uncle Britton, can I come over your house today?"

"Not today, sweetheart. Maybe next week, okay?"

"Okay," she said. "My mommy is being mean today."

"Is that so," I said, chuckling.

"Alona, hang up that phone," Amira snapped, picking up another line.

"Bye, Uncle Britton."

"Bye, baby." She hung up. "Good morning, Sunshine."

"Humph," she growled. "What's so good about it?"

"Oh, let me guess. Wil didn't give you your stickin' this morning?"

"Nope!" she bellowed. "That damn man is getting real stingy lately."

I shook my head. "Oh well. Pull your horny behind together. I need a favor from you."

"Hmm-hmm."

"Do you think you can watch the boys for me for a few hours?" The phone line buzzed. "Hold on for a minute." I clicked over. "Hello."

"Hello, Britton?"

"Who's this?" I asked.

"Lina," she said. My jaw dropped. I hadn't heard from her in months. "How are you?"

"Fine," I replied. "And you?"

"I'm doing well. I was thinking about you and the boys and was just wondering how you all were doing."

"We're doing good. The boys are getting big. Did you get the pictures I sent?"

"Yes. Thank you."

I almost had forgotten about Amira being on the other line. "Lina, I have my sister on the other line. Can I call you back?"

"Sure. Call me on my cell."

"I will." I clicked back over. "Amira?"

"Damn. I was getting ready to hang up on your ass."

"Sorry," I said, failing to share with her my reason for keeping her on hold for as long as I did, knowing she'd have nothing good to say. And I honestly didn't feel like hearing her mouth. "So, as I was asking, can you watch the boys for me?"

"Oh, I suppose so," she said. "It'll be nice to have the boys around since it's the only action I'll be getting today."

I laughed. "Amira, you crack me up. Thanks. I'll drop them off around one-ish."

"Hmm. You must have a hot date or something."

"Yeah, right. I wish."

"Well..." She snickered. "If you stopped being so picky maybe you would." I laughed but decided not to tell her about the last four dates I'd had with Myesha. Since that night I invited her over for dinner, we've been really hitting it off. Besides the fact that she's sexy and smart, she doesn't mind doing things that include my sons, and I like that. Interestingly, the boys have really taken to her. And her nephew seems to like me as well.

But it's still nothing to write home about. I mean, we're still in the "getting-to-know-you" stage so I'm not gonna jinx myself and make it out to be more than what it is. I like her. And she seems to like me. And that's what matters. We talk for hours on the phone, laughing and planning our next outings together. A few times, I ended up jerking off, listening to her voice. She didn't seem to mind. The only thing she said was, "Next time let me know, so I can join in." I laughed. But you better believe that's just what I did.

We haven't gotten intimate yet, but there's definitely a lot of sexual sparks flying between us. But we've both agreed to not rush into anything. And I'm cool with that, particularly until I can tie up all these loose ends with Lina—and now Celeste.

"Umm," I said, smiling. "I'll keep that in mind the next time the neighborhood bag lady tries to pick me up."

"Ugh! Please. I see you when you get here, boy."

"See ya!" I hung up, placing the phone back in its cradle with thoughts of my past. A swirl of fog filled my mind as I wondered what was going on with Lina for her to call me. Maybe she really did miss us. Clearly, there was no chance for reconciliation between her and me, but maybe she was ready to be a healthy part of our sons' lives. I picked up the phone and pressed speed dial.

"Hello, Lina?"

"Thanks for calling back," she said. There was a slight pause. "It's good to hear your voice."

"Likewise," I offered lightly. "How's the City of Angels treating you?"

"I've had better days," she responded solemnly. She was getting frustrated with Tinseltown's fickle ways. She still hadn't been able to land a part with any substance. "But, I'm doing what I gotta do."

"I hear you. Just try to stay focused. One day, you'll get that big break you so desperately want." I was honestly sincere in saying that. I mean if turning your back on your children for stardom is more important to you than them, then who am I to stand in your way. Do you. And I'll do me.

"I'm learning, what's meant for me will be for me. And if it's not then it's not meant to be." A part of me wanted to know if she was still lying on her back, or kneeling on her knees, for her ride to fame. But in the grand scheme of things, it really wasn't that significant to me. That was her cross to bear, not mine. She broke my train of thought. "So, the boys are doing well?"

"Yes. Big and busy," I shared lovingly. "They are really a blessing."

"And you are a blessing to them." I shifted the phone from one ear to the other, sitting down. I remained quiet. "I know you and I parted on some really negative energy. And I've been doing a lot of thinking lately. I know I can't take back some of the hurtful things I've said or done, but I want you to know I'm really sorry for hurting you. You didn't deserve that."

"I appreciate you saying that," I said, twisting the braids along the nape of my neck. I was searching for the right words. "We both said things that weren't right. I really wish things had turned out differently between us. But they didn't. And it's okay. I've let it go. You're my sons' mother, and I just want you to want to be in their life. Not because it's what I want. Not because it's what they need. But, because it's what you want, and need for you. But if you can't, then I'm okay with that as well. Because no matter what. They'll always have me. And I'm hoping that'll be enough." The phone line buzzed again. I excused myself, then clicked over. This time it was Indy.

"Hey, lady," I said. "Can I call you back? I have Lina on the phone."

"Humph," she grunted. "Well, make sure you call me back the minute you hang up. We need to talk ASAP." I could sense the urgency in her voice.

"I will."

"*Before* you see Celeste," she urged.

"As soon as I hang up," I reassured. We hung up. I clicked back over to Lina.

"Sorry about that, Lina."

"That's all right."

"Okay, so as I was saying, Amir and Amar need a mother in their life, Lina. And if that can't be you, then hopefully one day it'll be someone else."

"Britton, I really do love you," she said. I frowned. Didn't she just hear what I said? I shook my head.

"Lina, this isn't about me, or you loving me. This is about our sons."

"I know. You didn't give me a chance to finish. I think you are a wonderful man, and a terrific father. And I'm thankful our sons have you to parent them."

"Thank you," I said, allowing her to change the flow of our conversation. "Despite everything, I'm thankful to have them in my life. And for that, I thank you. I'm not going to lose hope that one day you'll want to feel what I feel."

"I do," she said. "Not a day goes by that I'm not thinking about them—or you. Missing them. And you. You walking out, taking our sons opened my eyes to that. Which is my reason for calling. I'm going to be in New York for a few weeks, and was hoping we could spend time together."

"Sure," I said, clinging on to what little optimism I had. "Give me a call when you get in town." We said a few more things before hanging up. Although I promised to give Amir and Amar big hugs from her, I wondered if I should even bother going through all of that. I wasn't sure if I was prepared to answer a thousand and one questions from them about the "when, where and how comes" of their mother's being. Not today. Not tomorrow—maybe, ever. I heard the rustling of feet across the floor upstairs. I looked up at the clock. It was quarter to eleven. I smiled, getting up to go upstairs to get my sons ready to spend the day with their favorite auntie.

By the time I got back from dropping the boys off and talking to Indy, it was four-thirty when the doorbell rang. It was Celeste. I welcomed her in, offering to take her coat, then ushering her into the living room. I pushed my conversation with Indy to the back of my mind, promising myself I wouldn't bring up anything she'd told me. I would give Celeste the opportunity to tell me herself where her journey through life had taken her over the last seventeen years.

"Make yourself comfortable," I said, gesturing for her to have a seat while I hung up her coat. "Can I get you something to drink?"

"No, thanks," she said, sitting on the sofa. "I'm fine." I went into the kitchen, returning with a glass of cranberry juice for myself. She was seated with her legs crossed, staring around the room. "This is a lovely place." I sat down in the chair across from her, fidgeting with my glass.

"Thanks," I said, finally taking a sip of my drink to swallow down my nervousness. I didn't know where this meeting was going. Although I knew the woman sitting in front of me, she was still a stranger in my eyes. So much time had lapsed between us. "You're looking good."

She smiled. "Thank you. And so are you."

I gave her a customary "thanks," then asked, "So what have you been doing with yourself?" She explained that a few months after I walked out on her she returned to D.C. and continued getting high until she had an outer body experience that forced her to stop using drugs. She claimed that after an episode of smoking crack all night, she started sweating profusely, hallucinating and her heart raced to the point where she actually thought she was going to die. She passed out and had to be hospitalized. She indicated that scared her enough to want to change her life around.

"I haven't touched drugs since," she said, shifting in her seat. "I've missed out on so much because of my use and I hurt so many people in the process. I want to make it up to those my use affected the most, especially you, Britton."

"Hmm. I see. Celeste, you don't have to make up anything to me."

"But I do, Britton. I know my use hurt you. And because of that, I lost you. There hasn't been a moment gone by that I haven't thought about you. Missed you."

I shifted my eyes from hers, putting my glass to my lips to take a controlled sip of my juice. The cold contents cooled my nerves. I returned my attention to her. "I've thought about you as well," I offered. "I often wondered if you were safe or somewhere dead. I kept you in my prayers. I'm really glad to see things have worked out for you."

"I've been fortunate." She looked at me, tilting her head. She smiled. "Please tell me why you gave up on me?"

"I didn't give up on you, Celeste. *You* gave up on you. I couldn't stand seeing what you were doing to yourself, to us. I couldn't take it anymore."

"So you left me."

"I tried to be there for you. I tried to love you through it all. But you ran to drugs for solace. You sought the streets instead of me. I was hurting too."

"You abandoned me when I needed you most."

"Unh-huh," I said, shaking my head. "You're not going to try to make me feel guilty for doing what I felt was best."

"Best for who, Britton? Surely not for me!"

"Look, if I had stayed, it would have only made things worse. I didn't like what you had become and I didn't like what it was doing to you, *or* me for that matter."

"I needed you, Britton."

"And I needed you. But you couldn't see that." She shifted her eyes from mine, staring at her hands in her lap. I welcomed the silence while I took a sip of the remainder of my drink. "I apologize if you feel as though I abandoned you," I continued, breaking her train of thought. "But the more I tried to hold on, the more I hurt. So I had to let go. I couldn't let you pull me down with you."

"Is that what you think I was doing, pulling you down?" she asked, looking over at me in disbelief.

"Yes, emotionally and mentally, everything was beginning to take its toll on me. Your use and lies were becoming dead weight in our marriage. Worrying myself sick night after night as to when you were going to walk through the door, or if I'd get a phone call saying something terrible had happened to you. It was wearing me down. And if I had stayed, I would have only been enabling you."

"I'm sorry, Britton, for putting you through that. I truly am. But I'm not the same person I was back then."

"And neither am I, Celeste." She stared at me, then parted her lips into a faint smile.

"But you do still love me." I wasn't sure if that was meant to be a question or a statement. But I answered the best I could.

"I will always care about you." I shifted my eyes from hers to the floor, then the ceiling. I spotted a water stain in the far left corner.

"So you're saying you don't love me, is that it?"

"I don't know what I feel for you—"

"Can you honestly look me in my eyes and say you're not still in love with me?"

"If I stood here and said I was still in love with you, I'd be lying. 'Cause the truth of the matter is, Celeste, I don't know. I mean we were so young back then. I don't know if I even really knew what love was or if what I thought I was feeling was actually love at all. I mean, everything between us happened so fast. I know I still have feelings for you. I'm just not sure what they stand for. You and I are practically strangers."

"But we were once lovers. We shared a child together and we are *still* married. I would say that makes us more than strangers, wouldn't you?"

"No. I'd say that makes us two people who share a past together; yet have traveled separate paths in life."

"So why didn't you divorce me if you feel there is nothing left between us?"

"Because I didn't know where you were, Celeste, that's why."

"And now?"

"And now, I think it's best we plan to move on with our lives." What I really meant to say is that I thought it was best to move forward because I had already moved on a long time ago. I had already detached myself from her, divorcing myself from her mentally and emotionally—or so I thought.

"But what if that's not what I want? What if I told you I wanted another chance?"

"Celeste," I sighed, shaking my head. "You can't just waltz back into my life after seventeen long years and think we can pick up where we left off. It just doesn't work like that."

"I never said it did. All I'm asking is that you not cancel us out without giving me a fair chance to prove to you I am a changed woman. That's all I'm asking." She reached for my hand but I pulled away as my thoughts swam in murky waters.

"Celeste, I need to know. Were you using drugs while you were pregnant?" Her eyes blinked in wide-eyed shock.

"Why would you ask me something like that?"

"Because I need to know if your use was the cause of—"

"How dare you," she screeched, cutting me off while tears swelled in her eyes. I had to will my lips still to keep from apologizing for something I needed an answer to. "Britton, do you have any idea what I have been through? The aching. The emptiness. I lost a child, Britton. Our child. And I have never been able to get past that." Teardrops clung to her lashes and slowly dropped, one by one until they rolled down her face.

"You still haven't answered the question. Did you kill our baby?" Although the thought that she might have been responsible for Joshua's death was tucked in the back of my mind—along with the rest of the clutter, I didn't mean for it to come out. Not like that. But I needed to know. Indy had planted the seed. And as hurtful and as accusatory as it may have sounded, I had the right to know. I braced myself for what was about to happen next. I felt it coming like one knows the smell of a summer rain before swollen clouds burst. She slapped me with the force of a lightning bolt striking an oak tree. My jaws tightened but I didn't blink. I stared at her as she began pacing the floor like a caged animal, chewing on her bottom lip.

"I loved my baby. I loved him, do you hear me, Britton?!" she screamed, pointing a finger at me. Her eyes were flooded with despair. She lowered her voice. "I carried him for nine months and loved him with every breath in me." Turning her back to me, she began weeping. My heart ached. "I loved him," she cried into her hands.

"I've never doubted that," I said, walking over to her, turning her around to face me. Removing her hands from her wet face, I lifted her chin up with my hand, stared into her tear-filled eyes, then kissed her gently on the forehead. I'm not sure why. She looked so helpless and I guess I felt badly for my ill thinking. She threw her arms around my neck, sobbing uncontrollably. I held her as she buried her face into my chest and cried her heart out, still not knowing if she stole my son's life away from me. Then again, I had to question her ability to be honest with me.

"Everything's going to be okay," I said, stroking her hair. "That's right, let it out."

"I'm so sorry, Britton," she said in almost a whisper, between sobs and hiccups. "I didn't...mean to...slap you. Can you ever forgive me?"

"There's nothing to forgive," I said, rubbing her back. At that moment, something within me was beginning to soften. I don't know why but it did. I think because of all her damn crying. Between you and me, I can't stand to see a woman cry. "What's done is done. I just wish things would have turned out differently." *Damn*, I thought to myself. *That seems to be the line of my life, considering I've had to use it twice today.*

She continued to cry as she pressed her body into mine, causing a wave of heat to go through me, starting from my feet, then slowly traveling through my body. She lifted her tear-streaked face from my chest and looked up at me with sadness in her eyes. Her pelvis rubbed against my rising nature. She kissed me on the cheek, then the lips. Slowly at first, then with more intensity as she used her tongue to find its way into my mouth. I felt myself weakening. I tried to resist but temptation was coiling its way to my libido. I gave in, parting my lips and letting our tongues dance and swirl. The smell of her perfume was intoxicating. My head began to spin. Then something Indy said to me replayed in my mind, causing the present to blur.

"She was sucking Tee's dick on a regular…"

"Whaat?! When?"

"When he was dancing in Connecticut. She and another trick friend of hers were doing Tee and his boy every time they came through." I shook my head at the news but wasn't the least bit surprised. Besides, what she did with her mouth and body wasn't any of my concern. Her hand slid down between my legs, jerking me back to my senses.

"No," I said, pulling away from her. "This isn't right."

"Why isn't it?" she asked, grabbing my hand, then rubbing her face into my palm. "I'm your wife."

"In name only," I softly responded, trying to collect myself. "It wouldn't be right."

She locked her eyes on mine. I held her stare as she reached for my face, stroking it with the back of her hand. "I love you so much. I've never stopped loving you, Britton."

"What do you want from me?" I asked, grabbing her hand from my face.

"I want my husband back."

I shook my head, taking in a deep breath, then slowly exhaling before I said, "How can you know that? There's been so much space and distance between us."

"I know because you are my past, present and future. Britton, you are all I've thought about. In my dreams, you are all I see. Please give us another chance. That's all I'm asking."

"I don't know," I said, sitting back down on the sofa. "There are too many unanswered questions. And I have my sons to think about—"

"We don't have to rush into anything," she said, sitting beside me. She leaned her back against me, draping my arm around her. "We can take it nice and slow if you'd like." I leaned my head back onto the back of the couch, closing my eyes as she continued to talk. "I don't want to come between you and your sons. I just want to be a part of your lives."

As sincere as she sounded, I wasn't too keen on the idea of having her or any other woman running in and out of my sons' lives; or mine for that matter. I need to focus on creating a stable home environment for my sons and raising them the best I know how without the interference or distraction of a relationship.

"I don't know what to tell you." I removed my arm from around her. "I'm happy you turned your life around. And I will always care about you. But I can't give you something that doesn't exist between us. I mean right now, trying to have a relationship with you or anyone else isn't a good idea. It would only complicate my life. I have too many other things to concentrate on."

The truth of the matter is, I'm reluctant to get involved with anyone. I don't have the strength, energy or desire to be with her or anyone else. Well, that's not completely true, thanks to Myesha. But there was no need to share that with Celeste. It was none of her business. All she needed to know was, I was not interested in her—*that* way. And as horny as I am, I know even occasional sex could potentially become problematic. So it's best I don't cross the line. Especially after knowing she was swabbing down Tee.

"The most I can offer you," I continued, "is friendship." And even that is questionable given the fact that she can't be honest. There's no way I can befriend a liar.

"Friendship?" she asked, shifting her body to face me; clearly disappointed. "So I guess that means you're still divorcing me." I studied her face before responding. I quickly flipped through my memory's scrapbook, seeing remnants of a beautiful young woman who walked with the confidence and air of someone who had the whole world in the palm of her hands. Now sitting before me was a woman who carried the crumbled pieces of her life in her hand like that of a jigsaw puzzle waiting to be put together.

Although she was still beautiful, her face wore the scars of a darker world. A world I'd never understand. Her eyes were glistening. Her lips trembled.

"It's for the best," I responded. Tears slowly fell from her eyes like a swollen river trickling through the cracks of a dam. As each tear fell, a puddle of memories seemed to whirl into a stream of uncertainty. I had to stand my ground. I wouldn't embrace her or nurse her pain—this time. I slowly began to lose myself in the cacophony of her wailing and pleas. However, no matter how many tears she shed, I'd always have doubts lurking in the back of my mind. I'd always wonder if she'd stoop low enough to entrap me, by purposely getting pregnant.

Even though she adamantly denied it, I'd always see my child's stiff body in the arms of a nurse and wonder if her reckless behaviors had something to do with his death. If only I would have insisted on having an autopsy done on him, instead of her convincing me to not let them cut his little body open. Maybe I wouldn't be standing here sweeping through this dust of doubt. I have no pictures of him. No memories of ever holding him; only flashes of his existence in my mind's eye.

"I'm sorry, Britton," she said, sobbing. "I love you. And I'm willing to fight to keep you."

"Celeste, you have to pull yourself together. You have to let go."

"No!" she screamed. I knitted my brows together. She was beginning to get on my nerves. She was either being overly dramatic, or she was really in need of an injection. In either case, she was losing her damn mind. *What in the hell is wrong with these hysterical-ass women?* "I can't. I lost the only man I have ever loved. And it's taken me years to find you. I won't let you go that easy."

"This is not a debate," I said, trying to be considerate of her emotional state. "You really have no choice. It is what it is. And that's that."

As easy as I tried to make this, it was apparent she was going to turn it into a more difficult situation. If I believed in my heart there was hope for us to pick up where we'd left off, I'd welcome the chance. But there isn't. And I would be less of a man if I led her to believe otherwise. Her sobs subsided. Tears still ran down her lovely face; yet she wiped each one away as quickly as it fell.

"Britton, for every mistake I've made, it has pained me. And I know in hurting myself I hurt you. I hope you know I'm truly sorry. Maybe saying I'm sorry isn't enough. But outside of my love for you, apologies are all I have."

"I'm not looking for apologies," I offered. "I'm looking for truths. Something I don't feel I could ever get from you." She lowered her eyes. I felt bad for her but I refuse to allow lies to be a part of my personal space. If there's no foundation to build anything of substance on, why bother trying to build anything at all. In the end, when everything comes tumbling down, you're left with ruins caused by bitterness.

"But I am being honest."

I shook my head.

"Do you ever think about our son?" she asked, looking up at me, clearly trying to take the focus off her. "Or have you erased him from your mind like you did me?"

"Celeste," I began, trying to muster the courage to be honest with her without building her hopes up. "Joshua's memory is etched in my mind." I couldn't believe she'd part her lips to ask me a question like that. I've done nothing but wonder what he'd be like, what my life would be like if he were alive. For years, I would see his innocent face in the still of the night and he'd be covered in white and I would stretch my arms out to him but he'd have these tiny wings on his shoulders that kept pulling him away from me. Every time I saw that image, I'd break down crying.

I stood at the head of that hospital bed coaching Celeste, anticipating his arrival, then witnessing his birth. Eagerly waiting to hold him in my arms. But my world was shattered when he came into this world stillborn. I never got the chance to hold him. I don't ever wish that kind of loss on anyone. It is so painful. Lord knows I would have given him my last breath to give him life.

But no matter how many nurses and doctors scurried around to work on him; no matter how much love I had for him, he was already gone and there was nothing anyone could do to change that. I've spent many years weeping. Although the tears may not have been visible, they fell nonetheless.

Lowering his small white casket into a damp dark ground was the hardest thing I've ever had to live through. That was over seventeen years ago. And I can still see it as clear as day—as if it were yesterday. I wanted nothing more than to pull open that coffin and hold my son, to feel him in my arms. But God needed him more.

Yes, I still hurt. I still wonder. But I no longer have that unexplainable knot of pain that seemed to twist at the core of my being. Learning to accept that everything in life happens for a reason is what helped me get through that maze of emptiness. And now when I see his face, I smile 'cause he's with me wherever I go. He's not only watching over me; he's the angel on my shoulder.

"So no, Celeste. I haven't erased him or you from my mind." She smiled, then hugged me tightly before walking over to the window.

"Tell me, Britton," she said with a deep sigh, pulling back the curtains, "when was the last time you went to his grave?"

At that moment I didn't know what to say. Guilt whirred its way through me. The last time I had gone to his gravesite was over four years ago. That was the only time since his funeral that I had gone. I had thought about going when I was in Maryland two years ago but decided against it. I had flowers sent instead. I couldn't go back.

After we buried him, I didn't feel it was necessary to go back. I don't feel I need to stand over his grave, praying and mourning when his image lives on in my mind. What was going to a cemetery going to do? I was already cheated out of having him in my life, for whatever reason, and I finally found peace with that. So am I wrong for feeling the way I do?

"It's been a while," I answered, twisting my braids along the back of my neck.

She turned to face me, gathering her things before asking, "Well, will you at least drive down there with me to see him?"

I nodded. "Sure," I said, walking her to the door.

She hugged me again, then spoke in almost a whisper. "Thank you."

I closed my eyes tightly, returning her embrace. "I'll call you one day next week to let you know when."

"I'll be waiting," she replied, kissing me on the cheek before heading toward her car. I closed the door behind her, locked it, then pressed my back up against it, banging the back of my head. *I'm sorry too, Celeste.* I thought to myself as I made my way upstairs to change my clothes, then head to Amira's. *'Cause come first thing tomorrow, I'll be on the phone with my attorney.*

24

CELESTE: *For All We Know*

L ike the sand that cascades down an hourglass, each grain was quickly slipping through my fingers. The hands of time were winding back, then forth, propelling me into a cloud of disappointment. Time was no longer on my side. It had been stolen from me. And as much as I hate to admit it, my life was beginning to twist and turn into a colorless pool of regrets.

Since my meeting with Britton, we've talked several times; but any time I attempt to talk about us rebuilding our marriage, he brushes me off, changing the subject or ending the call. He's even avoided going to the cemetery to visit our son's grave, saying he'll get back to me when he can. It's always one excuse after another. It's almost as if he doesn't want to go. Or maybe he's avoiding, going with me.

I closed my eyes. Allowed his voice to take me back to our last conversation over a week ago, then wiped a single tear away as it slid down my face. Nothing was going the way I had planned. "Britton," I had said, "I was wondering if we could meet for lunch today. I'm going to be in the city for a meeting and have a few hours to spare."

"Uh. I really wish I could, Celeste. But there's no way I can get to the city, then back to work in an hour. Things are too hectic here for me to take an extended lunch."

"No problem," I replied with anticipation swelling in my chest. "I'll come out there. We could grab something to eat and have an opportunity to talk."

I heard him sigh. "Today's really not a good day," he stated, deflating my bubble of hope. "I have a stack of monthly reports to do, and I'm short-staffed—"

"Okay, then," I interrupted, not willing to give him an out. "How 'bout after work? I promise I won't take up much of your time."

"After work's not good, either. I already have plans."

I picked my cuticles. "Britton, I feel like you're avoiding me."

"Celeste, I'm not avoiding you. I'm busy. And like I told you the last time we spoke, I have a lot of stuff going on in my life right now."

"Britton," I insisted, "we really need to talk."

"I agree. But not today."

I felt impatience taking over. I tapped the tip of my pencil on my desk, then stabbed its point into my calendar, leaving a lead dot of frustration. "When?"

"Celeste, I have to go. I'll call you when I have a moment to think straight."

Before I could say another word, he had hung up. No good-bye, only the click of the dial tone.

I opened my eyes, getting up to clear my head. I needed to write. Writing has always had a way of calming me. I opened my leather-bound journal and wrote:

My Dearest Britton:

Where do I begin? I know my addiction hurt you. It hurt me. It coerced me to do things I'm ashamed of. Things I am too embarrassed to share with you. I have cried a thousand and one tears. Tears that only wet the surface of my past, leaving the smears and smudges of my life as constant reminders that no matter how much I've changed, no matter what I do, there will always be something to remind me of who I had become; who I used to be, who I'll always be. An addict.

I know it was my self-indulgences and selfishness that chased you away. I lost you then. And, although I have found the physical you, it has become painfully clear that I lost the emotional you a long time ago. And that hurts. I had foolishly hoped we could begin anew. I had blindly believed that you'd be able to see beyond my past, and embrace the woman I've become. Yes, a woman with flaws; but a changed woman nonetheless.

I can't get you out of my mind. No matter how hard I've tried. No matter how many lovers have shared my bed—and, yes, there have been plenty due to my recklessness, I have loved you from the first moment I laid eyes on you. After all these years, your smile still affects me. I think back on that night at the ball when we reunited, and it warms me. My loins simmer in ecstasy and passion, wanting you to fill me with your love. Forever.

Britton, as hard as I try to shake it, I need to feel the strength of your manhood in between the soft space I have reserved especially for you. Even if forever never comes.

I closed my book, then sat in silence until sleep took over my body. When I awoke it was eleven p.m. I peeled myself out of the chair, then headed for bed with thoughts of Britton weighing down on my mind.

Since then, a part of me is beginning to wish I'd left well enough alone. I'd been better off not tracking him down, and let him be, instead of chasing rainbows. Since that phone conversation, I haven't been the same. It's like finality is closing in on me. And with that, my heart has been heavy. Truthfully, I hadn't anticipated his being so adamant about not wanting to rekindle what we had. I presumed he'd miss me as much as I missed him. And would jump at the chance to love me again. Silly me, huh?

I refused to consider the possibility that he had moved on with his life, leaving no room for me to reenter. The way he acts toward me, you would have never thought we had ever known each other or had shared a child together. He's not mean or anything, just indifferent. And that hurts, because I still love him. But I guess that's what I get for allowing my fantasies to control and consume me. Yet, for whatever reason, I held on to the notion that there was still a chance. No matter how slight. But when that menacing Indera showed up at my door a few weeks ago, I knew then I didn't have a snowball's chance in hell.

"I don't know what script you're reading, but you have the game twisted if you really think Britton is going to take you back," she had said during her unannounced and unwelcomed visit. "Especially if I have anything to do with it." I was seething. I wished I had never gone ahead with my scheme of trying to befriend her. She was truly a thorn in my side.

"Well. Maybe he would," I snapped, "if you minded your business and let him make up his own mind. He's a grown man."

"And he's *my* friend. So if you think I'm going to let the likes of you bring him down, you had better think again. I've given you every opportunity to bow out of his life gracefully; but you insist on still trying to have what you can't."

"Why can't you let him make his own decisions?"

"He already has," she said, grinning.

"Then you should have nothing to worry about."

"Oh, trust and believe. I'm not worried about a thing. Your slutty ass is no longer an issue."

I gave her a look of disbelief.

"What? Did I hit a nerve?"

"I think you're going a bit too far," I said, shifting my weight.

"Please," she snapped. "I know all about your nasty ass, okay?" She paused, cocking her head to the side and raising her eyebrow for effect. And then she hit me with the one thing I had thought was impossible. She threw in my face how I had solicited my body for drugs, and how I had slept with Tee the first time I met him, then continued performing fellatio on him every time he came to Connecticut up until the time he proposed to her.

Okay. I know, I know. I led you to believe my tryst with Tee was an isolated incident. It wasn't. Indy's right. Any time he came to the Connecticut area, I'd willingly drop to my knees and give him oral pleasures. I had hoped he wouldn't remember my face because it had been so long ago, and he had been with so many women—one, two, sometimes, three at a time. But he did. And his eyes told it. Which is why I got nervous when Britton introduced us at the ball, and he looked as if he had seen a ghost.

To this day, I don't know why I did what I did with him. I just did. Sadly, I received nothing in return. No hugs, no kisses, and no respect.

I know some of you might look at me like I'm trifling, but—like I told you when we were in Vegas, I honestly didn't know he was connected to Britton—or to her for that matter. I truly didn't. It wasn't until I saw their wedding picture in *Jet* that I made the connection. Otherwise, I would have never put myself in such a compromising situation. But what's done is done, and I can't take it back.

Please don't roll your eyes or suck your teeth at me. I know from the moment I introduced myself to you, I've been professing my undying love for Britton. And that remains true, regardless of my sexual indiscretions. All I ask is that you not judge me. I made some mistakes, and I've done some things I'm not proud of. But that doesn't negate my love for him. Although I held him in my heart, I'm still human. And I still had needs. I still desired to be held, no matter how temporary.

Yes, my addiction had stripped me of my self-worth, and rational reasoning. I told you all this already. It had stolen my senses, forcing me to prowl alleyways in search of its demon-like powers. Without it, I was powerless. With it, I felt like I could fly as high as I wanted. So I'd spend every dime I could get my hands on. And when I couldn't afford to pay for it, I'd offer my body for the next high. Yes. The truth is, I'd physically submit to my suppliers. But mentally, I'd always close my eyes and drift off to another place. A place where there were rainbows and sunshine. Sadly, every time I was done, there was nothing but darkness.

I stood in the middle of my living room, half-listening to Indy ramble on, spilling my life out of her mouth. I let my mind run to an abandoned building, searching for refuge. I tried to ignore the smell of a struck match as my mind traveled through the haze of my past. The snap, crackle of its flame melting against my demons—hissing and sizzling, caused my body to twitch. Thick smoke filled my lungs as I held it in, then slowly burned through my nose. My jaws rhythmically moved from side to side. I tried to escape the high. But the crackling got louder. The smell became stronger. The desire was more profound. Face quivering. Eyes bulging.

Sweat dripping. Sounds of flesh smacking against flesh amid swirling clouds of thick smoke cluttered my thoughts. Lusty. Sexually charged. I fell to my knees, taking in the crack-induced paranoia. A frozen smile painted by ashy lips. Moaning, groaning. Giving myself wantonly to anyone eager to release seeds of pleasure.

I shuddered. In a matter of minutes, Indy had come into my home and dragged me through a mangled past I have struggled to forget.

"And the only reason he remembered your nut-thirsty ass," she continued, snatching me from my haunted history, "is because you were the only dumb bitch sucking down his dick every time he was in town. Nasty trick."

My head ached, but I boldly pressed on. I couldn't let her sense my uneasiness. Otherwise, she'd toy with me the way a vulture does its prey before eating it alive. She was hovering over me, ready to swoop down. And I knew it. She had already smelled the opening of my fetid wounds.

"Okay. You're right. But it's not like I knew he'd end up marrying you. Nor did I know he was a friend of Britton's."

She rolled her eyes up in her head in exaggerated disgust. "I didn't tell you this for some weak-ass explanations. I wanted you to know that I know how nasty you are. I could really care less about you sucking Tee's dick. It was before my time."

"Then why are you here?" I rudely asked, placing my hand on my hip. I was getting really tired of her and this intrusion. In a matter of minutes, she had managed to jolt memories I'd kept tucked away. She had pulled the curtain up, flipped on the lights and unveiled my lies.

"To bid your pathetic, dick-sucking-for-crack-ass a farewell," she sneered, never raising her voice. "That's why I'm here, okay."

I took a deep breath, blowing out my angst. "How dare you pass judgment on me."

"No," she snapped. "How dare *you* try to play me."

"What is it that makes you so hateful?" I asked, squeezing my eyes tight. Irritated. Desperate. "Don't you have anything better to do besides sniffing your nose in other people's affairs?"

She placed her designer handbag on the coffee table, removing her full-length, then laying it across the arm of my sofa. She placed one hand on her hip. "Let me explain something to your trifling ass. I don't give a fuck about you, okay. And had you not tried to slime your way all up in my space we wouldn't be having this conversation because I wouldn't know you existed. But, since you wanted to get on some slick shit and try to get to Britton through me, you now have to deal with me, got it?"

I was really getting tired of biting my tongue with her. "You know what, bitch—," I said, fuming.

She chuckled, interrupting me. "Bitch?"

"Just what I said," I snapped, matching her glare. "You don't intimidate me."

She raised an eyebrow. "Girlfriend," she replied, placing her diamond-clad hand on her stomach. Even pregnant she was radiant. I hated her. "I'm glad I don't intimidate you. But I tell you what. Don't let the belly fool you."

"Nor do you scare me." I shifted my eyes, and my weight from one foot to the other. Although I said it, her surprisingly mild manner gave me the chills. *Must be the pregnancy*, I reasoned.

She smiled wickedly. Her hazel eyes seemed to turn black. Her voice was calm. Her posture composed. "That's refreshing to know. But understand this, the worst thing you could have done was try to scheme on my time. And now that you have, you stuck your hand in a hornet's nest. So you don't have to be scared. But you had better be prepared. Because I'm not *just* a bitch, I'm a dangerous bitch. And you fucked up when you failed to recognize, okay."

"You know what," I said, trying to mask my disquiet. But the truth is, I was becoming increasingly unnerved. Something inside of me told me this was the calm before the storm. But as far as I was concerned, there was nothing else she could say to rattle my cage. I truly believed there was *nothing* else she had on me. "Your threats mean nothing to me."

She clapped her hands together. "Bravo. How brave of you. Just know you have sealed your own fate, dear."

"I think it's best you get the hell out of my house!" I snapped, staring at her protruding belly. I walked toward the door, swinging it open.

"Before I forget you're pregnant and slap the shit out of you!" The cold night air cut into me.

Her smile widened. "You know, *soror*. I was just thinking the same thing. 'Cause I would truly hate to have to show you the other side of me." She slipped into her mink, slid her hands into her mink-trimmed leather gloves, then grabbed her purse. "Oh, and by the way, sweetie. The day you find the nerve to slap me, is the day your arms will be found shoved so far up your ass your hands will hang from you mouth. So leap if you want." I mean it, if she wasn't pregnant, I could have killed her. *Bitch*. I shook the thought of pushing her down the stairs—on her way out—out of my mind.

"It's too bad whoever shot you," I snarled, "didn't kill you."

"Well, he didn't," she grinned eerily. "But, I can't say you'll be so lucky." My eyes widened. "And what is that supposed to mean?"

"It means it's a wrap. So, if I were you, I'd get my affairs in order."

"Get. Out!" I shouted. "You don't frighten me, bitch!" She brushed by me, never blinking. Never saying another word. I slammed the door, shaking.

Interestingly, Britton and I did have several conversations since then, and he never mentioned knowing anything. I kept my fingers crossed that Indy was blowing smoke. So when he called me tonight saying he wanted to see me, I was flooded with emotions. At last, he was coming around. I hoped. It had been over a month since I'd last seen or heard from him. And during that time, I had wanted so bad to call him. I need-ed to hear his voice but I didn't want to smother him so I gave him space, sending flowers and cards instead. I was desperately searching for a way to convince him to let me back in his heart. Yet, no matter what I said or how hard I tried, he still refused to give me another chance. I was devas-tated when he called me, asking me to please stop sending him flowers. He said he wants me to be happy. Well, how can I be, if I don't have him? Didn't he understand that he has been my reason for living? I've held on to his memory as a source of strength. Hoping. Wishing. Praying for the chance to love him again. And all he can think about is ending what could be so beautiful; shattering everything I've dreamed of. How could he not know the depths of my love for him? I opened the door, smiling.

"Hello. Come in."

He half-smiled. "Thanks. Hello to you."

"Here, let me take your coat," I said, closing the door behind him. "I'm happy you called." He shoved his gloves in his pocket, then handed me his thick leather jacket. I walked over to the hall closet, putting my nose to the collar of his jacket, taking in his scent before hanging it up.

"Well, I'm glad you could see me on such short notice. This couldn't wait until tomorrow."

"Well, it must be important," I said, swallowing hard, "for you to drive all the way up here." His big, brown doe-like eyes caught mine. I held on to his gaze for as long as I could before guilt made me shift them. Caught in my own trappings. That's how I felt. "Can I get you something to drink?" I asked, preparing to get up from my seat.

"I've filed for divorce," he blurted out. His words came at me like a blow to the gut, knocking the wind out of me. I sat motionless. Although the news shouldn't have come as a surprise, I was speechless. We both sat in silence while I frantically searched for something to say, or do. I needed more time. I needed him.

"I see," I said, standing up and walking over to him.

"I feel it's for the best. I'd like to get the papers signed and back to my lawyer as soon as possible."

His lips were moving, but I heard nothing he said. The key to my heart belonged to him. It always has, always will. So if I were to lose any part of me tonight, then it needed to be right here, right now with him. "Britton, let's not talk about tomorrow," I said, grabbing his hand and looking him in his eyes. "Tonight, I want you to love me as if it were our last day on earth." I leaned in to kiss him.

"Celeste," he said, turning his face away and pulling his hand from mine. "We can't make time stand still."

"I know. But in our minds, we can."

"I don't think so. It is what it is. And for us, it's over. It has been for a very long time. I don't mean to sound harsh. But I just wish you'd accept it."

I heard what he said, but I refused to be defeated. I pressed on, unsnapping my robe. I let it fall off my shoulders and onto the floor, walking toward him in a black negligee. I stood inches from his face. "Make love to me," I said with pleading eyes.

He shook his head, looking at me with disdain. "Don't you get it? I'm not interested in you that way," he said, pulling out a folded set of papers. "Here are the divorce papers."

"What?" I asked, stunned. I was shocked by their presence, and the sting of reality. "I don't believe this...well, I'm not signing them. I won't let you throw away our chance to be happy together when you haven't even given us a fair chance."

"Celeste," he said, sounding frustrated. "Please don't make this any more difficult than it already is. I'd like to get this over with as soon as possible." He spoke with no emotion. Showed no facial expression. I couldn't believe this was the same soft-spoken man I've spent my life loving. I fought hard to keep my tears from falling.

My voice quavered. "I won't let you go," I warned, choking back my emotions.

"You have no choice," he responded, placing the destiny of our relationship on the glass table.

"So there's nothing I can say or do to change your mind?"

He shook his head. "You can't make me feel something I don't."

"But you haven't given it a try."

"Celeste," he said, pressing the tips of his fingers into either side of his temples. "I haven't tried because I don't want to. I believe people can change and I'm happy you've made changes in your life. I want nothing but the best for you. I truly do. But my priority is what's best for me. I don't mean to be hurtful. But I owe it to not only you, but to myself to be honest. And the truth is, I just don't love you the way you want me to."

His words felt like a knife being plunged in my heart. I turned my back to him, giving in to my emotions. Hot tears splashed from my eyes. I relented. "I'll sign them when we get back from visiting our son."

He sighed. "Why can't you sign them now?"

"You want your divorce, Britton? Fine. But I'm not signing anything until after we get back from our son's grave and then you can go on with your life."

He let out a sigh. "Thank you," he said softly. He walked up behind me, placing his hand on my shoulder.

I turned around to face him. Streaks of anguish painted my face.

"Just know I will love you forever." I know it sounded like a line in a movie or book, but it was the sincerest thing I could say. It was how I felt.

He sighed. "But it's time to let go."

"I won't."

"You deserve to be happy," he said, wiping my face with his fingertips. I grabbed his hand, squeezing it. I pressed the palm of his hand to my lips, kissing it, then closing my eyes, allowing myself to get lost in his scent for the second time. "I don't want to hurt you. I hope you can one day understand."

I let go of his hand, taking a deep breath.

"I need to be alone," I said, wiping the remainder of my tears away. "Please leave."

He nodded and gathered his coat, heading for the door. "We can go to the grave tomorrow morning. I'll be here around seven."

"I'll be ready," I responded flatly. All of a sudden he was anxious to go to our son's grave just so he could be rid of me. I wanted to scream. He gave me a faint smile and headed for the door. I watched him open it and gently shut it behind him, never looking back. Once again, he was walking out of my life.

I fell to the floor, sobbing. I must have cried for hours before I was finally able to pull myself together. I felt weak. Emotionally and mentally drained. Everything I had hoped for, everything I had envisioned would be flushed down the drain with the stroke of a pen. "I hate you, Indera Fleet!" I screamed. "Meddling bitch!"

I walked over to the table where the papers were neatly placed. I picked them up, trembling while reading each line. Tears began welling in my eyes again. I wiped my face with my hand as each one fell. I'm sorry but I won't let him go. I refuse to spend another moment of my life without him. I won't go on missing him. Wanting him. Needing him.

"God, please forgive me," I said, tearing up the documents and throwing the shredded paper toward the door. I walked over to my hall closet, standing up on my toes while reaching for a tin box tucked neatly in the far back of the top shelf. When I retrieved what I was looking for, I pulled it down, then opened it. Like I said, I had no intentions of hurting or living without him in my life. Not this time. I took the .45 and stuffed it in my pocketbook. *Tomorrow, I'll do it then—at our son's grave.*

Twenty-minutes later I heard a knock on the door and jumped up, tossing my pocketbook back in the closet. I ran over to open the door, hoping it was Britton coming back to take me in his arms. Or to at least say, he'd had a change of heart. But when I opened it, my heart sank even further.

I gasped, clutching my chest. "What are you doing here?" I asked, shocked and frightened.

"Hey, baby," he said, pushing his way through the door. "Is that any way to greet your man?"

"How'd you find me?" I asked, wrapping my arms around me in attempt to cover up my body.

"Let's just say a little birdie led me to you. You don't sound too happy to see me?"

"I-I—"

"Oh, let me guess. You thought I was that pretty nigga who just left outta here?"

Oh my God, I thought, trying to hide my panic. *He's been watching me. Who would know I was connected to him?* "How'd you get out of prison?" I asked, trying to keep calm, holding my face. He was supposed to still be locked up. After my arrest for possession of crack cocaine and reckless endangerment, I agreed to help the prosecutors get a conviction on Rocky for running a crack cocaine trade in Washington, D.C., along with weapons offenses, and rape and sodomy charges. In exchange, I'd only have to serve two to three years of a ten-year prison sentence. Rocky—with his prior criminal record—would serve twenty-five years with a mandatory fifteen years before parole eligibility. But he was five years short and out, free as a bird. Who in their right mind would let him back out on the streets?

"An angel with horns helped get me free on a bullshit technicality," he spat. "So I could get home to my bitch." He slapped me, causing me to fall to the floor. I knew enough to not scream. I slowly scooted away from him to avoid being kicked or stomped on. I needed to stay calm if I wanted to see tomorrow.

"That's good, baby," I coaxed, trying to keep my voice steady.

"So who's the bitch-ass nigga?"

"I don't know who you're talking about?" I scanned the room, trying to figure out an escape. I needed to figure out a way to get to my pocketbook.

"Aye. Don't play stupid with me. I saw him leave. But I know you weren't giving him my pussy." His face tightened. "Did you give that pretty nigga my pussy, bitch?"

I shook my head.

"Good. Now, get the fuck up," he snapped. "Before I kick your back in."

"Rocky, please," I said, getting up from the floor. "If you don't leave, I'll call the cops." I knew that was the wrong thing to say, but it was too late. I had spoken without thinking.

"What the fuck did you just say?" he asked, grabbing me by the arm, yanking me around. He flipped open a switchblade. "And tell 'em what? That your trick ass threw our son in a fucking garbage bin? Go 'head, call 'em." My eyes widened. "Oh, you didn't think I'd find out, did you?" He ran the cold blade alongside my neck. My life flashed before my eyes. "I'll split yo shit, bitch. Do you think I give a fuck about you calling the fuckin' Po-Po? I just did ten years, and—"

I took in a deep breath. "What do you want?" I asked with more force than I anticipated, masking my fear.

He laughed, taking his blade and in one swift motion, slicing the thin fabric of my silk teddy. "What the fuck you mean, 'what do I want'? I'm here to collect on my interest, bitch. So we can either do it the nice way or the rough way. Either way, I'm not leaving until I'm finished with you. But know this. If I gotta take it, I'm gonna kill you when I'm done." I swallowed hard, knowing he meant every word. I knew what he attempted that night at Rock Creek Park; he'd surely succeed this time. "Did you really think you could get away from me?" He twisted my arm.

I winced. "Oww. I-I didn't."

"Shut the fuck up!" he snapped, throwing me on the sofa. His eyes were as dark as midnight. "One word and you're dead. And when I'm finished with you, I'll do that pretty nigga of yours." My heart sank.

The last thing I'd ever want is for something horrible to happen to Britton as a result of my sordid past.

My gut told me he didn't know exactly how to find Britton, but if he saw him leaving, he might have gotten his license plate number and would be able to track him down. He'd kill him and his whole family if need be. I couldn't chance it. He didn't deserve that.

"Please, don't hurt him," I begged.

"Oh, don't you worry," he said, unbuckling his belt, then unzipping and letting his jeans fall to his ankles before kicking off his dirt-soiled boots. His manhood was enlarged with excitement. "The only thing I'm inter-ested in hurting right now is that pussy, bitch. And it better be tight." I swallowed hard and stifled the screaming in my head as his fists pounded against my flesh. I lay motionless as he used his blade to cut off my under-wear before probing my dry insides with his fingers. "Get that pussy wet," he barked, bringing his fist to my face, "or I'll beat your skull in."

Tears rolled out of my eyes as I took my hand and rubbed between my legs. "Please, Rocky," I whimpered. "Don't hurt me." He spit in his hand, stroking his erection before pushing my legs up over my head, then ram-ming his hand in me. I screamed as he punched his fist in and out, creat-ing a pain I never knew possible.

"That's right. Beg, bitch."

"Oh, God! Please help me," I screamed as he continued punching and beating my vagina. "Someone, please help me!"

"Shut the fuck up!" He pulled his fist out of me, hitting me in the mouth. Blood splashed from my mouth. "You thought you could take my drugs, and money and get away with it. Trick-ass bitch." He hit me again. "You led the fucking pigs to me and thought I wouldn't find out. Stupid, bitch! Don't you know I own you?" He hit me again, got up, ruffled through his duffle bag and came back with a roll of tape.

"Please, Rocky," I pleaded. "I'll give it to you any way you want. Just don't hurt me." I was fearful of what he'd do to me. I had crossed him. And I knew enough to know crossing him was like digging your own grave. I replayed the tape. I knew the lines. The consequences would be…*Please, someone help me! Please.*

"Oh, I'm gonna hurt you all right. And I don't want to hear nothing when I fuck the shit out of you," he growled, taping my mouth to keep me from calling for help. He swung my legs up over my head, then rammed himself inside my rectum. I lay still; held back the screams in my head. A fierce pain raced along my spine. He pounded and banged in and out until he released a stream of hatred inside of me, collapsing on top of me. His breathing was rapid. Sweat dripped from his body. The smell of his sex was putrid like death. I fought back the urge to vomit.

Time seemed to collide as he began punching me about the face and head. The world was spinning. I was too numb to feel. I was too deaf to hear. And the room twirled in a burst of kaleidoscopic colors when I closed my eyes, clinging to what was left of life. My life. A life rooted in bad karma. I was slipping.

In my clouded mind, I knew if I survived I'd never be the same. Mentally and emotionally, I was already dead. If only I could get my hands on some drugs. Just one hit to help me float away. Something to help me escape, run, flee. I needed to be free. *Take me.*

I must have passed out because when I opened my eyes he was hovering over me with an icy glare. My legs were spread apart and bent at the knees. I would submit willingly.

Silence stood between us until he got between my legs, forcing his hardened manhood between the folds of my abyss. I winced. His hot breath burned my skin as he panted, moving himself in and out of me. "When I'm done with you," he warned in between grunts, "you'll be no good to anyone." Slowly, he pulled out forcing my legs forward, up over my head. Then he took his knife and slashed and stabbed at my vagina, causing a piercing pain to shoot through my body.

There was no need for screaming, or pleading. As my mother had warned, "You live by the sword, you'll die by the sword." His wide hands found their way around my neck, pressing inward, shutting off my airway. But I refused to struggle. In moments, it would be over. I'd be free. *Please, God, forgive me for my sins.*

My mind rippled with thoughts of a place with soft, fluffy clouds. A place where there was no past or present. No secrets or lies. My eyes fluttered, rolled in back of my head. "I died loving you, Britton," is the only thing I remember my mind crying before being thrown into the ground. This time, there was no coffin, no hammering of nails. This time there'd be no woman trying to claw her way out. There was no use. She wouldn't be buried alive. Tears welled up in my eyes but evaporated before they could fall. Flashes of bright lights appeared and disappeared. And then… I embraced my fate.

25

BRITTON: *Life Goes On*

I'm reading a book called *A World in Transition: Finding Spiritual Security in Times of Change.* So far, it's very interesting. It talks about nurturing our souls and effecting lasting spiritual transformation for ourselves regardless of what is going on around us in the world. Basically, it's saying despite the turbulent times we may encounter in our lives, we need to learn how to nourish our mind, body and souls. And this book teaches you how to balance our spiritual bodies with our emotional, mental and physical bodies while transforming suffering into peace, joy and liberation. At this point in my life, that is exactly what I'm striving to do.

I say all that to say, with all the uncertainties in life—the one thing we can always be sure of is: Where there is life, there will always be death. Somewhere, somehow, someone is being born and put to rest. And no matter how hard we try to keep them separate, life and death are interconnected. Yet, regardless of how many times I accept this truth, nothing ever prepares me for the latter. Even when it's expected, it still has a way of creeping up on you, leaving you in a state of shock and confusion.

Long story short, I finally made it to Maryland—with Celeste—to pay my respects to my son, and to lay his mother to rest. Yes, that's right. It's been three weeks and I'm still stunned. I mean. One minute, I'm eager to divorce Celeste and the next minute, I'm thrust into the roll of widower, making burial plans for a woman who has no known family ties—other than me, a man who walked out on her and never looked back. It's crazy. I've racked my brain trying to make some sense out of her death—excuse me, her murder. Because that's what it was: a brutal, cold-blooded, sense-less killing.

No matter how hard I try to forget the day I walked in her apartment, finding her half-naked body lying on her blood-soaked sofa, the scene remains with me. I couldn't believe what I saw. I still can't.

Her glazed eyes haunt me. They were open and rolled upward, as if she painfully accepted her life's ending. Her head hung back over the sofa's armrest. Her face was beaten and bloody. The nightgown she had tried to seduce me in the night before had been sliced open, and a shiny, metal handle—an object police later identified as a knife—protruded from her pelvis where she had been stabbed numerous times before her killer buried its blade deep in her. Her vagina was…I struggled to keep the contents in my stomach from spilling out. Everything I had eaten for breakfast, stuck in my throat before gushing out all over the carpet. Her killer had cut and stabbed the essence of her womanhood.

Every gory detail is etched in my mind like the carvings of a sculpture. Permanent reminders. That for every beginning there is always an end. And sometimes the core of false hopes, half-truths and hidden secrets is the middle of one's demise. I believe this to be true for Celeste. She was a woman who lived behind many masks. Masks she used to hide her drug use, and her criminal behaviors. A sick, twisted façade of what she wanted people to see, and believe.

Indy had filled in all the missing blanks with what information she knew about Celeste. A part of me wanted to not believe what she'd said about her. Where or how Indy got these facts was irrelevant to me. Because, no matter her past, she didn't deserve to die the way she did. Tortured. No matter what she did, she was still a human being.

There had been no sign of forced entry. The homicide detectives searched the place from top to bottom, dusting for evidence. The only thing tangible found was a gun in her pocketbook, loaded with two bullets. Fingerprints and semen confirmed their beliefs that the same man whom I found lying on the floor next to her with his throat slit from ear to ear was the attacker. I shook my head. Interestingly, there were no other fingerprints in the house, except for hers and his. He killed, and got killed. Why?

Whatever the reason, two things were surely clear: There was still a murderer lurking the streets. And Celeste and her attacker had a history together. The Hartford Police identified him as Lonnie Swenton, a drug-dealing menace from Southeast Washington, D.C. who had been released from prison two days prior to Celeste's murder. The reasons for his early release were unclear and, truthfully, unimportant to me. I had already heard more than I wanted. Knew more than I needed. Indy had offered to help me box up her things in hope of linking together the rest of this mystery. But I declined.

I love Indy to death and appreciated her offer, but the idea of her helping me go through Celeste's things didn't seem right. Particularly knowing that there was bad blood between them, for whatever reasons. I didn't even feel comfortable packing up her belongings myself. But I did. And in doing so, it appeared that Celeste was either very much infatuated—or extremely obsessed—with me. She had a collage of pictures of me from the early eighties, during my days at Howard and Norfolk State. And over two-hundred-and-fifty poems and letters written in a journal addressed to me. A part of me felt as if I were invading her privacy by reading them. But I did anyway. She had poured her heart onto each page, spilling out her emotions. Declaring her adoration for me. A love she knew I could never return. Yet, she held on hoping.

I slowly flipped through her book inked with pain and passion, running my fingers across the flow of her pen pressed against each page. Absorbing her heartfelt urgency. Feeling her angst. Stealing a peek into her pleasures. Subconsciously, there was one letter and a poem that I committed to memory. Why I'm not sure. But I'll share with you.

My Darling,

I once fell, trapped in the moments of doubt. To be preyed upon by the vultures of confusion. My heart emptied its contents into a bottomless pit of a time. Nothing seemed to subside the physical pain. Nothing seemed to alleviate the emotional strain. Fear of rejection held my heart captive. So I lived my life in darkness, never seeing the happiness placed before me. I knew nothing of true love and passion. I was blinded by emptiness. Numbed by bitterness. Deafened by loneliness. But then came you. Strong. Determined. Committed.

You see, my Love. Even before I knew you existed, when you were just a figment of my imagination, you gave me a reason to live. Became my ray of hope. I needed you. Wanted you. Had to have you.

My knight in shining armor, you freed me from the shackles of despair, turned my weaknesses inside out, opened up the valves of my heart. Showed me with the touch of a hand, the brush of soft lips, the whisper of sweet words that I was worth loving. And for that, I am forever grateful for your presence in my life. For it is you that represents all that I've become, all that I will be. I will continue to miss you, my sweet Britton, until I am safely wrapped in your arms again. From now to eternity, I will always love you. I will always need you.

Your loving wife,
Celeste

Come Inside the World Within

Britton, my love,
There's a world within
Hidden with untouched treasures
Awaiting to be enjoyed
Awaiting to be explored
Come, my love, come
Come sail across its enchanted waters of love
Come stroll along its magical sands of pleasure
Come drink from its cup of endless delight
Wet
Warm
Mystical
Come, my love, come
There's a world within
Enriched with inescapable excitement
Awaiting to be shared

Come breathe its air of everlasting happiness
Come soar its skies of unforgettable memories
Come grip its horizon
Tantalizing
Mesmerizing
Hypnotizing
Come, my love, come
There's a world within
Filled with nature's most precious secrets
Awaiting to be revealed
Come ski the hills of passion
Come pick the lilies of romance
Come taste the fruit of erotic desires
Delectable
Sexual
Multiple Orgasmic
Come, my love, come
Come inside the world within

I read a few more pages, then closed my eyes, replaying memories of our past together. I couldn't recall what I had said, or done to make her feel the way she did. When I think back, our romance was rushed and rather short-lived. But who am I to question the impact someone has on another person's life. What she felt was her reality. Those were her feelings, not mine. And I guess that's all that really mattered.

When I came across her diary, I fought the urge to break into her book of secrets. I didn't need to know them. So I placed it—along with her journal, in the casket with her. Those were her thoughts, desires, dreams and fears. She could take them with her. If for nothing else, I needed to respect that part of her life.

I allowed my mind to drift along the outskirts of time, reminiscing in no particular direction. Moments with Celeste—our first kiss, the first time we made love, our wedding, the loss of our son, the loss of her spirit—

all splashed around in my head. Somehow, I floated back to her apartment, then rode the tide of scattered images: remnants of my divorce papers torn to pieces and strewn across her floor. Splattered blood. I blinked my eyes from past to present, and saw Celeste standing in front of me with outstretched hands covered by black gloves. Her face was hidden behind a veil. Her eyes were darkened by misery. She called out to me. Low. Soft. Removed her face covering, then mouthed the words *I love you* before disappearing behind a fog. The only thing left was the silhouette of a beautiful woman beat down by drugs and deception; scarred by lechery and lies. I shuddered.

Somewhere between the short, balding Reverend Miller's eulogy and Celeste's casket being slowly lowered in the ground on top of our son, I looked around and felt myself choking up. It was too much, and really sad to see that Celeste didn't have many, if any, healthy relationships. The only mourners at her gravesite were an uncle she hadn't seen in over twenty years, a husband who had walked out of her life, a few of her sorority sisters, and a woman who knew very little about who she was—her only friend, Rochelle, who sobbed uncontrollably. I wrapped my arm around her, tried to console her as best I could against the March winds. Then I closed my eyes and prayed for Celeste's soul. She had burned many bridges along her journey in life. Her dishonesty had cost her everything.

I let my mind savor thoughts about the love of my own family and friends, and realized how blessed I was. Tears began to stream down my cheeks. Not because of her death. Or the pain Rochelle felt. But because I knew God was a good God. He knew just how much Celeste could bear, and He knew life here on earth for her was dark. Whatever the plan, she had to be in a better place. Wherever that may be.

I stood there under the green canopy, zoning in and out as the reverend's wife sang "His Eye is on the Sparrow." I've always loved that song. The words touched me. Opened up the gates of my tear ducts. I pulled stems of flowers out of the six floral arrangements, then tossed them onto her casket as it descended into the earth. Then one by one, my tears fell with an exigency I didn't understand. She just had to be free.

When Mrs. Miller finished, I shook her and the Reverend's hand, hugged Celeste's uncle, though we had never met, then told Rochelle I'd keep her in my thoughts and prayers. We embraced then I headed toward my car, leaving a part of my past behind.

"How are you holding up?" Myesha asked as I climbed back into the driver's side of the car. I turned the key in the ignition and started up the engine. I turned to face her, feeling whatever sadness I had dissipate. She took my hand into hers. Squeezed it ever so gently. The concern in her eyes warmed me.

The last four months we've been dating exclusively. And it's been nothing like anything I've ever experienced or imagined. It's like she was made for me, and only me. That's crazy, right. I mean. I've only known her for a short period of time, yet it feels as if I've known her my whole life. This ordeal with Celeste has reconfirmed the saying that life is too short. Nothing is promised to us. And nothing is gained by taking life for granted. We need to live each day as if it were going to be our last. Living, loving, and forgiving. For tomorrow truly isn't promised.

"I'm blessed," I finally said, kissing her hand. Everything with her felt so right. Special. I was glad she wanted—no insisted—on riding down to Maryland with me. Every day since that awful morning, Myesha has been by my side, helping me get through this. Listening. Loving. She stared into my eyes, allowing me into her soul. I leaned in and kissed her on the mouth. Her soft lips melted away my tension. I wanted this feeling to last forever. It had to.

A part of me was beginning to feel guilty for feeling the way I did. Happy. Should I have been sad? I mean here I was just pulling out of a cemetery where the mother of my firstborn had been lowered in the ground less than ten minutes. And my heart was skipping rope instead of drowning in sorrow. My thoughts bobbed and weaved as I tried to rationalize what I was feeling. Yes, I was saddened by Celeste's death. But life for *me* wasn't sad. I had a lot to live for, a lot to be thankful for. I glanced back over at the beautiful woman sitting next to me, and smiled. I was falling.

Instead of driving back to Jersey, we agreed to stay overnight with Chyna and Ryan. I hadn't seen her since her return from Slovenia, and hadn't really had a chance to talk with her since her falling-out with Indy. I missed her. And besides, it gave her a chance to meet Myesha. Indy had already met her, and liked her. "She's the one," she had said in my ear, pulling me to the side out of earshot of Myesha. "I hope your moody behind doesn't mess it up." I laughed at her remark. But the fact of the matter is that I am moody. However, the difference with this relationship from the others is that she respects my personal space. And she doesn't come with a whole lot of baggage or drama.

Chyna and Myesha really hit it off, which was nice. They ended up spending the whole afternoon out shopping and having "girl talk" while Ryan and I kicked back and shot pool and watched the NCAA championship. You know for all the years I've know Ryan, he and I never really rapped like two men would. So I'm glad we had the opportunity to. I really admire the brotha. And one thing is definitely for sure: he loves the ground Chyna walks on. You can really see it in his eyes and hers for that matter.

"You know, Ryan," I said, "I've never told you this, but I'm glad Chyna has you in her life." He gave me a look of astonishment, clearly taken back by my comment.

He smiled, extending his hand to me. "Thank you. Coming from you, that really means a lot." I shook his hand, returning the smile.

"I know you and Chyna have had your share of ups and downs, but I'm glad to see the two of you were able to weather the storms. I really admire your commitment to your marriage."

"When you love someone," he said, looking over at me, leaning back in his seat, "you fight to stay together. And you let no one or nothing come between you, especially not pride, or guilt. I had to learn the hard way. And it almost cost me the only woman I've ever loved."

"I guess what they say about love being able to conquer all things holds true," I said, taking a sip of my cranberry juice.

He pursed his lips, rubbing his chin and nodding. "Only when you're anchored."

Damn, I thought to myself. *Now that's deep*. Silence took over for a beat. There was nothing else to say. That one word—anchored—said it all. I laid my head back, closed my eyes and imagined being anchored in love, by love.

An hour later, I was awakened by the stroke of Myesha's hand across my face. Ryan had left me on the sofa, snoring while he went upstairs to his study. "Hey sexy," she said, planting a kiss on my lips. "Miss me?"

I smiled, opening my eyes. "Immensely," I said, stretching then glancing down at my watch. It was a little after eight. She slipped a piece of Dentyne in her mouth, then leaned over and slid her cinnamon-flavored tongue in my mouth. I slowly sucked on her tongue, then kissed her with more intensity before coming up for air. "Hmm. Yeah. I definitely missed you."

She grinned, plopping down beside me. "Hungry?"

"A little," I replied, yawning. "Excuse me."

"Hey, sleepyhead," Chyna said, standing in the doorway. "We could hear you all the way outside." They both laughed.

"You even chased Ryan up outta here," Myesha added.

"Oh, you got jokes," I said, picking up a pillow and playfully clunking her over the head. "You both are real funny." I folded my arms across my chest, feigning a pout.

"Aww. My baby's feelings are hurt."

"He'll get over it," Chyna said, "when he gets a taste of the jerk chicken and rice and peas we brought back." I perked up, rubbing my stomach. Chyna and Myesha had stopped by the Negril Jamaican Eatery in Mitchellville and picked up a smorgasbord of Jamaican cuisine, including their slamming banana cake.

"Did someone say jerk chicken?"

"And chicken patties."

"Hmm," I moaned. "That's music to my ears."

"Then let's eat," Chyna said, heading back into the kitchen. "I'm going to go up and get Ryan, so ya'll go on and help yourselves."

"You don't have to tell me twice," I said, jumping up from my seat and taking Myesha by the hand, leading her toward the feast.

After dinner, Myesha helped Chyna with the dishes, then excused herself to get ready for bed. Ryan hung around for a few minutes more, then got up to turn in as well.

"Hey, Ryan," I said, getting up to shake his hand. "It was good talking with you."

"Likewise, man. If I don't see you in the morning, have a safe trip back."

"Thanks."

He kissed Chyna on the side of her head. "Good night."

"Good night," she said. "I'll be up shortly." He nodded and headed up the spiral staircase, allowing Chyna and me an opportunity to get caught up.

Chyna busied herself around the kitchen, putting away dishes and filling her teakettle with fresh water. She sat it on the stove, turning the flames up high, then sat down across from me at the breakfast nook.

"So how have things been going?" I asked, giving her a look of concern. "How's Sarina doing?"

"Some days are better than others," she said. "Sarina is stable. Which is a good thing. But I don't know how well she'll do once she's released." She indicated Sarina was admitted to an in-patient psychiatric hospital in Baltimore where she's been since they picked her up from Indy's.

"I can only imagine how hard it's been on you and Ryan."

She sighed. "If you only knew. Sometimes I don't know if I'm coming or going. But somehow we manage to get through it."

I smiled, reaching over and taking her hand. "Everything is going to be all right. It'll all work out. I've kept Sarina in my prayers."

"Thanks," she said, getting up to the whistling of the kettle. "I really appreciate that. Would you like some tea?"

I shook my head. "No. I'm fine. Thanks." She filled her teacup with water and sat back down. "So, what do the doctors say about her condition?"

"Nothing that we don't already know. Sarina's chances of living a normal life are great as long as she complies with treatment and medications. If she doesn't, she'll end up hospitalized again." She shook her head, letting out a soft sigh. I waited quietly in between her pause. "Right now, she's as compliant as they come, saying and doing all the right things. But we've been down this road before. I can only hope that this time, she really means it."

"You'll have to keep it in prayer." She nodded knowingly. "So when will she be home?"

"They expect to release her in another two weeks or so, depending on how she does on her next evaluation. But Ryan has been pushing for them to keep her longer."

"Hmm. And how do you feel about that?" I asked, watching her blow into her cup. She seemed to have gotten lost in its steam. She took three small sips and looked back up.

"I don't know, Britton. The thought of her being locked away upsets me, but if she is going to continue to refuse to stay on her medications, then continued hospitalization is for the best. There's nothing else I can do. I've done all I can. And quite frankly, I'm drained. She is finally going to have to want to help herself."

My heart went out to her. I didn't know much about the disorder. But I had read somewhere that a sixth of people with schizophrenia died by their own hands, often in response to psychotic symptoms that could be managed and well-controlled with medication. But like Sarina, so many people with the diagnosis refused to stay on their medicines long enough to live a fulfilling life. The road to recovery was a lifelong process.

"She will," I said optimistically.

"I hope so," she replied, leaning back in her chair, taking a deep breath. We allowed a comfortable silence to take over for a moment. She took two more sips of her mint tea and asked, "How's Indy doing?"

"She's doing all right," I offered, shifting in my seat. I leaned forward, placing my forearms up on the table. "I take it the two of you still aren't speaking." Of course, I already knew that to be the case, but I decided to say it anyway.

"Basically."

"Well, I'll be glad when the two of you patch things up."

"That would be nice. But I really don't know if things between us could ever be the same." I gave her an understanding look. "We have had our disagreements over the years, but never to this degree. She really said some hurtful things."

"I know," I stated. "But you know she loves you."

"And I love her. But she has to know she can't just say whatever she wants however she wants, and expect people to accept it. Sometimes she has no regard for other people's feelings." Although I had to agree with what she said, I kept my comments to myself.

"Well," I said, leaning back, "I don't know if I should tell you this or not, since the two of you aren't friends anymore…"

"I never said that," she snapped. "I'm just distancing myself from her for a while."

"…Well, so you know," I continued as if conspiring to release top-secret information, "she's pregnant."

"Whaat?!" she asked in disbelief.

"You heard me," I said, grinning.

She covered her mouth in shock. "Oh, my. That's a surprise."

"To say the least," I stated. "Girlfriend had been walking around five-and-a-half-months' pregnant, and didn't even know it."

"*Five-and-a-half months?*" she repeated.

I nodded. "She's due in like two-and-half more months."

She shook her head in disbelief. "Talk about surprises. How is she taking the news?"

"I don't think it's hit her yet. She's been in a state of shock. But Tee, on the other hand, is ecstatic."

"I can imagine," she said, getting up and walking over to the sink where she washed her cup and spoon, then dried and put them away. "Finding out you're that far along in your pregnancy sure doesn't give her or anyone time to get used to the idea."

I chuckled. "And Tee's been catching hell."

"Poor thing," she said sympathetically. "I'm sure he has. Hmm. That would explain her nasty mood swings."

"Oh, she's extra bitchy now," I said laughing. "She even snaps on me."

Her eyes widened. "Now that's serious."

I *tsked*. "Not hardly," I said. "I don't pay her behind any mind."

She smiled, shaking her head. "I can't believe she's going to be a mother."

"Well, believe it. 'Cause you're about to become an aunt. So you and Miss Indy had better work things out before this baby comes. We've gone through too much together for us *all* not to be a part of this new beginning."

I stood up and walked over to her, giving her a hug. "Our friendship can weather any storm, including Indy's mean ass. Our bond is too strong."

"You're right," she agreed. "But you don't know what it felt like to walk in and see my child tied up like a wild animal. That really hurt me." Chyna explained how Sarina's two top and bottom front teeth had been knocked loose, and she had three large lumps in her head from Indy hitting her in the head with an object. She also had a gash over her left eye, which required seven sutures.

"Chyna, I know Sarina is your daughter, but you know as well as I do that she can be violent. She attacked Indy in her own home, so she did what she needed to do to defend herself. Would you have preferred she called the police on her?"

"Sounds like you want me to choose the lesser of two evils."

"Well, tell me what would you have done? As a matter of fact, what do you think could or would have happened to her if she had gone after someone else?"

She clasped her hands behind her head, pulling stress from her neck. "She'd probably be dead," she replied, lowering her voice. She sighed. "I know you're right. Ryan has been saying the same thing to me."

"Then maybe you should take a closer look at it, and see it for what it was. It wasn't a personal attack on you or your friendship with Indy. It was about Sarina—a grown woman, regardless of her illness—who disrespected the wrong person, and got her behind whipped."

"But she—"

I cut her off before she could finish her sentence. "No, Chyna. What she did was attack a woman in her own home. A woman who just happened to be Indy. And on top of that, she's pregnant. Now what do you think would have happened if Indy had miscarried as a result of all of this?"

Her face knitted with worry. I continued before she could respond. "Don't make excuses for Sarina. That's part of her problem. You've always tried to defend her behaviors. Whether you are aware of it or not, you've done a lot of enabling where Sarina is concerned."

I had hoped I wasn't being too blunt. But it was time Chyna woke up. We all knew Sarina was disturbed, but that didn't give her the right to assault people. Whether she's in her right frame of mind or not, it doesn't make her behaviors acceptable.

"You're right," Chyna asserted. "And Lord knows I'd hate to think what the repercussions would have been if something had happened to Indy or her unborn child. The ramifications would…" She paused, shaking her head. She pressed the inside corners of her eyes with her thumb and index fingers in an attempt to hold back the tears. "…I know my daughter's condition is serious, and…But being her mother, it's hard to separate what I know in my heart to be true, and what in my head I want to believe."

I nodded, giving her a look of reassurance. "I know."

We talked a bit more about Sarina's mental state, then talked about her sons. Her face seemed to light up as she spoke. She stated Jayson was following in Ryan's footsteps, wanting to operate and manage one or two of his father's four funeral parlors. He was twenty-four, and dating a thirty-six-year-old woman who Chyna didn't approve of because of the age difference.

"But I just mind my business," she replied, raising her hands up in mock surrender. "He's a grown man who can make his own decisions."

"Responsible ones at that," I added.

She sighed. "Very. I just wish he'd find someone closer to his own age. That woman is only a few years younger than me. And I'm supposed to embrace her as a potential daughter-in-law. The thought sickens me." I shook my head, but said nothing for or against it. It shouldn't really matter as long as they were both two consenting adults of sound mind and body. As far as I was concerned, love came in all different shapes, sizes and ages. Of course, it was easy for me to say that now. But I wondered if I would have the same attitude if Amir or Amar came home with a woman almost old enough to be their mother. I erased the thought from my mind.

She continued. Ryan Jr., was bored to death—no pun intended—with the idea of being a mortician and making a living out of burying people, and wanted nothing to do with the funeral parlor business. After only being home for a year, he missed the military life and had re-enlisted in the Army to serve and protect for another four years. Chyna wasn't happy with the possibility of him being shipped overseas, but she supported him wholeheartedly.

A part of her had hoped his girlfriend of almost three years would have been able to convince him otherwise, but finding out he was about to become a father only confirmed in his mind he was doing the right thing.

"I can't believe you're going to be a grandmother," I responded, shaking my head with a wide smile on my face.

"Me either," she said, chuckling. "I just hope I don't start looking like one." I looked my friend up and down, head-to-toe. She was almost forty and didn't look a day over thirty. She was flawless. And had the grace and presence of a runway model. Her green eyes had the sparkle of precious gems. Her waist-length hair was in one big braid, and twisting around on the top of her head like a crown. She reminded me of a princess.

I smiled. "There has to be something in the water," I replied, laughing. "'Cause where I'm standing I can't even imagine it. Not in a million years."

She giggled. "Boy, you're too much. I have a lot to be thankful for. I'm blessed."

"And, as Indy would say, well kept," I added. She smiled. I could tell the way she held my gaze that she missed her sista. She leaned her back against the counter, then folded her arms across her chest. I decided to leave well enough alone. In my heart, I knew they'd work it out in the only way two sisters could. "And what's up with Mr. Morehouse?" I asked, talking about her youngest son, Kayin. "He should be graduating soon."

"In eight weeks." She smiled. "I can't believe how fast time flew. It seems like yesterday when we were helping him move into his dorm room." She shook her head admiringly. "Now he's living in his own apartment, driving his own car, and graduating from college." Her voice was colored with pride.

"Too bad he pledged the wrong fraternity," I remarked, feigning disgust.

She chuckled. "Don't hate."

"Oh, all right," I said, grinning. "I guess he's entitled to one mistake."

She returned the smile. "I'll be sure to tell him you have finally found it in your heart to forgive him."

"Now let's not go that far," I snapped, slapping my forehead teasingly. "I said I'd excuse him for his error. But his love for my niece has given him amnesty from a showdown."

She laughed. "Well, thank goodness for Noelle." Over the years, Chyna has really grown fond of my niece, and vice-versa. Like myself, Chyna knew it was only a matter of time before they would end up married. Amira would probably lose her mind, but she'd get over it. For some reason, she still struggled with the idea of Noelle getting involved with "a pretty boy."

"Ah. Young love," I said in a singsong tone.

"Hmm. Speaking of love," she responded. "Myesha is a lovely woman." I grinned. "Thanks. I take it that means you like her."

"Absolutely," she said gleefully. "I really enjoyed spending the day with her. She really seems to love you."

I gave her a look of shock when she said the "L "word. I know I was really feeling her vibe, but *love* hadn't really crossed my mind. Particularly since we'd only been dating for such a short period of time. But when it comes to one's emotions how can you measure the depths of what someone feels based on time? There was a point in my life when I thought I could. But now I have to wonder because, if I'm really honest with myself, Myesha has my nose wide open.

"You know, Chyna," I said, smiling. "I'm really big on her too. She's everything I could want in a woman."

"Oh, please," she said, playfully swatting her hand at me. "What's this 'I'm really big on her too' mess? You love her, don't you?"

I widened my smile. "I'm not sure what it is I'm feeling," I said, staring into my friend's beautiful eyes. There was a long pause before I added, "She's really special. And I know I want what we have to continue. But my track record in relationships makes me leery."

She returned the smile, wrapping her arms around me. "Follow your heart, Britton." She kissed me on the cheek. "She wants the same thing."

I grinned. "Hmm. Sounds like you know something I don't."

"Call it woman's intuition."

I laughed.

"What's so funny?" she questioned, raising her eyebrow.

"Nothing," I said, shaking my head. "That's the same thing Amira and my mother said when they met her."

"Well then, that should say it all."

"And it does," I said, beaming. I was feeling really good. All of the special women in my life had confirmed what I already knew—Myesha was the one for me. I faked a yawn, covering my mouth. "Hmm. 'Scuse me. I'm beat," I stated, raising my eyebrows up and down. "I think I better turn in."

She chuckled. "That sounds like a good idea," she replied, winking. We hugged. "Sweet dreams."

"Hmm. If I have my way, it won't be just a dream." She smiled, waving me on. I blew her a kiss, then went upstairs to snuggle up with the wonderful woman in my life.

Once we returned to New York, the rest of the week breezed by without incident. And I was glad. I was looking forward to spending the weekend with Myesha, along with her nephew and the twins. I think the boys looked forward to our family-oriented outings just as much as I did. I walked over to the window and peered out, hoping it didn't rain or wasn't going to be too cold. Because as we all know, March weather is always so unpredictable.

As I was about to step away from the window, a cherry-red Navigator pulled up in front of my door. I squinted my eyes, trying to figure out who was behind the tinted windows. The passenger-side door opened and a woman wearing a black leather skirt and black cashmere sweater stepped out. Her hair was cut in a sassy pageboy style. Damn, she was bad. "Oh, shit!" I snapped once I recognized who she was. "I don't believe this." I almost passed out. Little did I know, it wasn't going to be the weather I would need to be worried about.

I swung the door open before she could ring the bell. "Lina," I said in a tone laced with shock and annoyance. "This is a surprise."

"Hello, Britton," she said, walking in before I actually invited her in. I stepped aside. "I bet I'm the last person you expected to see." She smiled, moving in to give me a hug. I cordially accepted the embrace but quickly stepped back, staring at her.

"To say the least," I said, trying to keep my composure. But inside I was screaming, "Your inconsiderate ass was supposed to be here six weeks ago!"

"I apologize for not coming sooner, but I had three auditions."

I raised an eyebrow. "And you couldn't get to a phone?"

"I said I'm sorry," she offered in an unbothered tone. Well, she might have been unmoved, but I wanted to blow a gasket. She actually had the audacity to think it would be okay for her to pop up unannounced with an "I'm sorry" like that would be the fix-all to her damn thoughtlessness. She had no idea what I've had to go through the last few weeks. I knew I shouldn't have let her speak to the boys when she called here wanting to talk with them. But against my better judgment I did. And I paid for it. From that day forward, they both asked nonstop, "Daddy, is Mommy gonna come today."

"No. Not today," I had responded.

"When, tomorrow?"

"Hopefully next week," I replied, hoping to soothe their minds for the moment.

"Daddy, is next week gonna be a long time?" Amir asked.

I forced a smile. "I hope not, little man." He looked up at me, tilting his head as if contemplating whether or not my answer was good enough. His eyes bore into mine.

"Are we gonna get a new mommy?" I lowered my head, then knelt down in front of him. I hugged him. That was the safest thing for me to do. At that moment, I honestly didn't know what to say. What in the world do you say to a child with an inquisitive mind without saying too much?

I sighed, refocusing my attention on Lina. *Still confused. And still chasing stars*, I thought to myself. *Some things will never change.*

"Lina, not for nothing. But sorry just doesn't cut it. Every day since you spoke to Amir and Amar they have been bugging me about when you were coming to see them. And every day I have been giving them one excuse after another."

"Do you mind if I have a seat?" I shook my head. She sat down on the sofa, crossing her legs. The slit of her skirt pulled back, revealing her smooth thigh. "Britton, I didn't come all the way out here to argue with you."

I gave her a look of astonishment. "Is that what you think we're doing, arguing? I'm just expressing my concern with your insensitivity."

"Okay then," she responded, picking up the silver-framed picture of Amar and Amir, "concern taken. I'll be more mindful in the future." She studied the photo, stealing a moment of reflection. I welcomed the silence. "I can't believe how big they've gotten," she said in almost a whisper. "They're every bit of you."

I stared at her disbelievingly. She didn't get it—and never would. So what was the use of making an issue out of it? I decided to let the conversation take its course in another direction. I thought about asking her who was in the truck waiting for her, but decided against it. It really wasn't any of my concern. I took in a deep breath, attempting to check my attitude. "I know," I agreed, sitting on the arm of the sofa. "If I didn't know better, I'd think they were cloned. But they have your smile," I offered.

She shrugged slightly. "I guess. Speaking of which, where are they?"

"They're not here," I said almost ruefully. A part of me was glad they were out with Myesha. It served her right for popping up late and wrong. But she was still their mother. She had a right to see them. And that fact, as much as I would like to blot it from the truth, is what compelled me to pick up the phone to call Myesha on her cell, asking her to bring the boys home. "They should be home within the next half-hour," I said, hanging the phone up.

She smiled. "Thanks. I really appreciate it."

I nodded.

"The next time," she added lightly, "I'll make sure I call." It almost sounded thoughtful.

"That's probably a good idea," I said, walking over to sit in the chair on the other side of the room. I stretched out my legs, crossing them at the ankles. She glanced down at her watch. I studied her. On the outside, she was really a beautiful woman. Too bad she was so damn rotten to the core. "So how long are you gonna be in town?" I asked, trying to keep the conversation easy.

"Just for a few more days," she said, running her fingers through her neatly cropped hair. "I have to get back to L.A. for an audition."

"Hmm, I see." I folded my hands in my lap. "So how long have you been in town?"

She shifted in her seat. "A couple of days," she coolly responded. I raised my eyebrow. *And she's just now getting here*, I thought to myself. *She's really pathetic.* "I would have come by sooner but—"

"Lina," I stated, cutting her off before she said something to set me off, "it's really not that serious. You don't have to explain yourself to me. The fact that you were able to find time out of your busy schedule to drop by is enough." Yes, I was being sarcastic. Oh well.

She locked her eyes on me. I glanced down at my watch, wondering what was taking Myesha so long. "Britton, do you ever think about me?"

I tilted my head, looking at her like she was out of her damn mind. "For what?" I asked. I guess my tone matched my thoughts.

She shrugged her shoulders. "I don't know. I was just wondering."

I sighed. "To be very honest with you, Lina. I try very hard not to. I mean, you made your choice, and I made mine. And I'm very comfortable with it."

"I guess I can't blame you," she said. "I really wish things would have turned out differently for us."

I squinted at her. "How so?" I asked, curious to see where she was trying to go with this. She and I hadn't really had a civil conversation since I'd left California. And the few phone conversations we've had over the last several months have been strained. I'm sure part of that is due to my attitude toward her. Okay, most of it is. But truthfully, I really don't want my indifference toward her to create any further friction between us, particularly if she's trying to establish a relationship in our sons' lives.

She scooted up to the edge of her seat. "I don't know. I mean, I still think about the time we first met in the Dominican Republic, and how much fun we had. Everything seemed so perfect."

I followed behind her down memory lane, then smiled knowingly. "Yeah.

It seemed perfect at that time in our lives. And we did have some memorable moments." I became quiet, then blew the recollection of fonder times out of my mind. "But it wasn't meant to be anything more than that. In all honesty, everything between us happened too fast."

She nodded, then forced a smile. "Britton, I didn't mean to hurt you."

I bit my lip in thought. For some reason, Celeste popped in my head. This conversation was beginning to seem all too familiar to me. I had definitely been down this road once before. And once again, I was going to have to make a detour. Like in my relationship with Celeste, Lina and I had come to a fork in the road, and we both chose to take separate paths. There was nothing wrong with that. As far as I was concerned, turning back to trudge through the bickering and misunderstandings was out of the question.

"Lina, you didn't hurt me. You disappointed me. Those are two different feelings. But I don't—I mean, I can't blame you totally. I contributed to our conflicts. And I'm responsible for how I reacted in response to our disputes. We tried, and it just didn't work."

"Did we really?" she asked, gazing at me. I leaned forward in my seat, placing my elbows on my knees and clasping my hands together. I looked down at my watch. Myesha would be walking through the door at any minute with the boys. I needed to change the direction of this conversation—now.

I sighed. "I know I did. But that doesn't really matter now."

"Why doesn't it?"

"Because for one, you're in L.A., and I'm here."

"You could consider moving back."

I shook my head. "Not hardly," I responded. "I'm happy right where I am. And even if I wasn't, the West Coast is the last place I'd return to. And for two, the only thing that matters now is whether or not you are going to be a part of our sons' lives."

"I would like to."

I kept my face void of expression. "And what does that mean?"

"It means I can't make any promises."

"You mean you *don't* want to make promises you can't keep," I corrected, eyeing her through slants of disgust.

"Britton, how can I? There's a three-thousand-mile gap between us."

"Move back to New York then," I said in a tone that was more of a dare than suggestive. "If you really want to be in our sons' lives, then make a way."

She lowered her eyes, then returned her eyes to mine, matching my stare. "I can't do that. My life is in L.A."

"And mine is here with my sons. So it's obvious we have nothing else to discuss."

"It's clear you're still angry with me."

"Not angry," I retorted. "Disgusted."

"Well, for the sake of our sons, I was hoping we could at least be friends."

"Lina," I huffed, "you can't even be a mother to *our* sons. So what makes you think we can be friends? That is not possible." And I meant that. I'm agreeable to being cordial and even friendly; but friends, no way, no how. There's no way I can embrace anyone who willingly turns their back on (or abuses) their children. Children don't ask to be born. They are brought into this world by either choice or chance."

"Let's not do this, Britton. I came all the way out here to see them. So let's start there." I felt like getting up, giving her a standing ovation for her gesture, then telling her to get the hell out. But I remained seated.

"And what about tomorrow, or the next day or day after that? What then? There's something very wrong with this picture."

"Britton, what do you want me to say?"

"Do you really have to ask?" I snapped. "On second thought, don't even answer that. If you don't know by now then I guess you'll never know. It's obvious you can't give them what they need."

"Maybe I can't," she relented. "Not that I don't want to. I have dreams of something much bigger than being a mother. I know that might sound cruel. But, it's true."

I sat for what seemed like hours listening to her rationalize her neglecting her duties as a mother by saying how children weren't in the cards for her. That she knew in her heart if she put her dreams on hold, she'd be unhappy, and would end up bitter. She was a walking billboard for the word "selfish." But those were her feelings, and somehow I needed to try to accept them for what they were. I needed to let go of any hope of her being an active part of their lives. I knew this. But it still hurt. Because in the end, I'd be the one who'd have to find the right words to answer all the "whys" and "how comes."

"So you abandon our sons instead."

"I—"

"Let me explain something to you. I have always kept the door open for you to be a part of our their lives. But, it is not a revolving one. I will not let you think you can flounce in and out whenever you feel like it. You can freewheel around the world in search of fame if you so choose. But make no mistake. You will not have free reins to disrupt *my* sons' lives with your flightiness. If you can't make any long-term commitments to them, then I would rather you stay away. And let us go on with our lives. Amir and Amar are going to be loved with or without you in their lives."

She looked at me wide-eyed and confused. "Are you seeing someone?" she asked. What that had to do with what we were talking about and why that was a concern of hers was beyond me, but I answered nonetheless.

I nodded. "Yes, I am."

"Are you happy?"

"Very."

She forced a smile. "And the boys, do they like her?"

"They seem to. Why?"

"Just asking. What's her name?" she asked. The doorbell rang. I knew it wasn't Myesha because the door was unlocked, and she would have walked in

"Myesha," I shared, getting up to answer the door. It was the driver of the truck, Carmen, Lina's best friend and one of Tee's past sex kittens. She was stylishly dressed in a pair of black leather pants, a black mohair sweater, and black leather heels. And of course she was adorned in her trademark jewelry: name-plated earrings, thick gold chains and gold bangles. I smiled, inviting her in.

"Hello, Britton," she said in a voice that almost purred. "It's been a long time."

"Yes, it has," I replied. "You're looking good."

"Likewise," she offered, bouncing from one foot to the other. "Can I use your bathroom?"

"Sure," I said, pointing down the hallway. "It's the door on your left-hand side." She scurried down toward the bathroom, closing the door behind her. She let out an audible sigh as she relieved herself.

Lina and I said nothing else. My mind was made up. She had to go. If she wanted to visit with Amir and Amar, then she'd have to schedule a time that was convenient for me. And first thing Monday morning, I was going to be in touch with my attorney. I was going to take Amira's and Indy's advice, and file for child support. Not that I wanted or needed her money. But she needed to be held accountable some kind of way. Hell, when a man abandons his family, society still expects him to be financially responsible for his children. And when he doesn't, he's labeled a "dead-beat dad." Well, it's no different for a woman who turns her back on hers.

When I heard the sound of a car pulling up, I exhaled relief, and apprehension in one quick breath. Lina shifted in her seat, then stole a peek out of the window through the white sheer curtains. The expression on her face confirmed it was Myesha.

When she walked through the door with Amir and Amar in tow, I immediately jumped out of my seat to take her by the hand, and introduced her to Lina. They cordially acknowledged one another with customary smiles, and with Myesha extending her hand out to her.

"Nice to finally meet you," she said. Lina smiled, shaking her hand. "Hi, Daddy," Amir and Amar chimed in unison, dragging bags from FAO Schwarz. I smiled. Myesha had taken them into the city to shop. They walked right past Lina without recognizing who she was. For a split second, I thought I saw hurt paint the pupils of her eyes. But, of course, I was wrong.

"Hey there," I said, giving them both hugs. "You have fun?"

They both nodded their heads. "Yes. We got new toys."

My smile widened. "Wow." Lina looked from the boys to Myesha, then back over at me. Carmen walked out of the bathroom, drying her hands on a paper towel. Her eyes seemed to be locked on Myesha as if she were sizing her up. I introduced them. Myesha graciously extended her hand, giving Carmen a firm grip. She turned her attention to me.

"How's Tee doing?" she asked with a hint of seduction.

"Happily married," I replied.

She smiled. "Well, tell him I said hi."

"I'll let him know you asked about him."

She widened her smile, then looked over at Lina who informed her she'd be ready to leave in another twenty minutes or so. I raised my eyebrow. Carmen excused herself, returning to the comforts of her truck.

"Look who's here to see you," I said, trying to muster as much enthusiasm humanly possible. "It's Mommy." It almost killed me to let those words fall from my mouth. She was being given a title she hadn't earned. A privilege she had no right to.

"That's my mommy?" Amar asked unsure of what I had said. Amir hid behind me, peeking around my leg. I pulled him in front of me.

I nodded, trying to ignore the awkwardness that filled the room. "Yes, Amar. That's Mommy."

Lina got up from her seat. "Hi, sweeties," she said softly, opening up her arms. Amar took leery steps toward her before walking into her embrace. Amir backed away, reaching up for me to pick him up. He started rubbing his eyes and whining. I reluctantly pushed him forward. Felt like I was forcing him to do something we both knew wasn't deserved. But I insisted. He slowly dragged himself toward her. She wrapped her arms around him, squeezing both of them close to her, deep into her bosom. "It's so good to see you. You've gotten so big." Myesha locked her arm around my waist as a sign of support and solidarity. If I didn't know before, I knew now. She and I were one.

Lina looked up at us, then shifted her attention back to the boys, doting over them for another five minutes or so before saying, "Umm, Mya, right?"

"No. Myesha," she politely corrected.

"Oh. I'm sorry. Myesha. Pretty name."

"Thanks."

She straightened her back, rubbing Amar on his head. Amir ran back over to me, raising up on his toes and extending his arms in the air. I picked him up. He wrapped his arms around my neck. I got the message loud and clear: Don't let me go. Amar slowly made his way back over to me. He stood on my feet, raising his arms up to be picked up. I shifted Amir over on my right hip, then lifted Amar up, placing him on my left one.

"Britton tells me the two of you are dating."

Myesha gave me a quick glance before responding, "That's correct."

"Which means you spend a lot of time with my sons." Myesha gave me one of those looks that said, "I'll beat her down if she tries it."

"Lina, I think you better go," I said.

"I'm not looking to start trouble. I just want to know. As a matter of fact, I think I have a right to know."

"Oh, really?" I said.

"No. It's all right," Myesha stated calmly. "Yes, I do spend a lot of time with *your* sons. And?"

Lina smiled. Myesha planted one hand on her hip. I took a deep breath. The room seemed much smaller. Lina asked, "Britton, do you mind if Myesha and I have a few moments alone?"

"No," I snapped. "You need to go."

"Britton, it's okay," Myesha said reassuringly. "Why don't you take the boys upstairs for their nap?" I looked over at Lina, then Myesha. I didn't sense tension in the air, but it felt uncomfortable just the same. The air around me seemed to get thinner.

"It'll only be a minute," Lina indicated. I didn't budge.

"Anything you have to say, you can say it in front of me."

"I need to talk to her, from one woman to another."

"About what?" I demanded.

Myesha walked over to me, touching my arm. She repeated, "It's okay. I'd like to have a few words with her as well."

"You sure?" I asked. She nodded, nudging me toward the stairs with both boys in my arms half asleep. I glanced back at Lina, then decided to walk over to her. I whispered, "Don't start no mess, Lina."

She reached out and rubbed each boys' face with the back of her hand. She kissed the tips of her index and middle fingers, then placed them gently on their foreheads. Her eyes became misty. "I have no regrets, Britton. And I know in my heart I've done the right thing. I just hope they won't grow up hating me too much."

"It won't be my doing," I assured her.

She forced a smile. "I'd really like a moment alone with Myesha, then I'll go."

I looked over at Myesha. She nodded, allowing her smile to melt away my reluctance. I headed toward the stairs, leaving my past and present in the same room. Lord only knew what the future would look like when I returned.

Forty-eight minutes; that's how long the two of them were downstairs talking before I finally heard the door open, then close. I had come down twice to make sure the two of them were still breathing, and each time I was politely dismissed. I even found myself lingering at the top of the staircase trying to eavesdrop, but could hear nothing but an occasional chuckle or sniffle. In all honesty, the suspense of not knowing what the hell they were talking about was driving me crazy.

So the minute I heard the door open, I raced to the window and peeked out, seeing Myesha giving Lina a hug, and Lina wiping her eyes. She hopped in the truck, then rode off, staring straight ahead.

The minute Myesha walked back in, I was downstairs sitting on the sofa, waiting to be filled in. "So what was that all about?" I asked.

She plopped down beside me, lifting my arm up, then leaning in to me. My arm wrapped around her. "She wanted to know how serious our relationship was, and how I felt about you and the boys."

"For what?" I snapped.

"Because she wants them to have a mother. Something she's not able to be to them."

"Well, that's decent of her, considering she's deserted them."

She turned to face me. "In her own small way, I believe she really does love them."

I raised my eyebrow, shaking my head in disbelief. "Well, she sure as hell has a funny way of showing it."

"She has her own story to tell."

"And so does the Pope, but that doesn't make what she's doing right."

She took my hand in hers. Our fingers interlocked. "That's her cross to bear, not yours. Or ours." *Ours.* The way she said that sounded permanent. "I told her that I loved you. That I planned on growing old with you. I told her I adored your sons, and had enough room in my heart to love and nurture them as if they were my own." I couldn't believe what I was hearing. She was one remarkable woman. It was too good to be true. "I told her that I wasn't trying to take her place, but I was more than willing to be the mother she wasn't able to be."

"And what did she have to say?"

"She asked me to look after them, and you. And I promised I would."

"You sure about this?"

She nodded. "Very."

"I'm not always the easiest person to be around."

"I don't give up easy."

"But are you sure?"

She tilted her head and squinted her eyes. "I'm in this for the long haul."

I kissed her. "The road could get a little bumpy."

She kissed me back. "Then I'll buckle up, and ride it out."

"We can be a handful," I said.

"I can handle it. I welcome it with open arms."

I stood up, paced the floor, then stood in the center of the room. "You're the first woman I've been involved with since leaving L.A. And I promised myself I wouldn't have a lot of women running in and out of my sons' lives. They need stability."

She stood up, walked toward me. "I'm a stable woman. And I'm not running anywhere." Her brown eyes twinkled as she stepped into me. Her voice lowered into a seductive whisper. "I know what I want out of life. And who I want in it." As I held her gaze, my heart was beating so hard against my chest that I thought it would give out from overload. No one had ever made me feel like this.

"You are so beautiful," I whispered, so that only she could hear me. She held my eyes. I lightly brushed my lips against hers, then kissed her purposefully. I wrapped my arms around her, pulling her into me. She let her hands trace up and down the spine of my back.

I closed my eyes while my tongue lingered around in her mouth, and allowed my mind to sail back to the Dominican Republic with its sandy white beaches, and mesmerizing aqua-colored waters. Amir and Amar splashed about while Myesha stood in the middle of my paradise, wearing a flowing white linen dress. Painted toes gripping the warmth of the sand beneath her. She was with child. My child.

I smiled.

"What's so funny?" she asked.

I slowly shook my head, gazing at her with lust and anticipation. "For the first time in my life…" I paused, kissing her with more passion and intensity before breaking away. "This feels so right." The feel of her breasts against my chest ignited a fire in me. I needed, wanted, her in my life for as long as there was breath in me. "…I feel so complete with you."

"I love you, Britton."

And then, without giving it any thought, I slowly knelt on one knee, and looked up at her, taking her hand in mine. I slowly kissed and sucked on her fingers as if sucking the nectar of the world's sweetest mango. I buried my face in the center of her being, then looked up into the brightness of her smile. "Will you marry us?" I asked with loving eyes. The tears streaming down her face were the only answer I needed.

26

SARINA: *Wild Is The Wind*

Don't be fooled by what you see. I am what I am. Illogical. Accept me or not. I am what I am. Illusional. A mirage of sights and sounds held together by rippled tides of confusion. Don't be fooled by what you see. I am what I am. Erratic. Humph. That's what I thought while walking to my shrink's office for what would be the last time. Today is my celebration. My emancipation if you will.

You see. I've finally come from under the stairwell, emerging from cobwebs, and dust balls. Floating. Gliding in and out of sanity. And at last, I'm going home. That's right. I'm spreading my wings and fleeing this coop once and for all. Chicken coop, pigeon coop, dodo-bird coop. And that's exactly what this place has been. A wired cage for a bunch of scatterbrain fools, cackling and cawing.

Yes, sirreeeee buddy. I'm out. One-hundred and seventy days. That's approximately four-thousand-one-hundred-and-eighty hours of locked doors and barred windows. That's all it took. And in only a few hours, I'll be free.

Well, free in the physical sense. Mentally, I'll still be a prisoner. Shackled to a string of thoughts and sounds. You see my mind still plays tricks on me, but not as much as it used to. I think the medications, along with my desire to never set foot in this Godforsaken hellhole again, has helped emancipate me from the voices that hide in the crevices of my head. I don't think about cheeking my pills like I had in the past, either. Which is a good thing. Probably because I'm afraid of what I'll hear, or be told to do. Or maybe it's the fact that Chyna—I mean, my mother—would love nothing more than to have me put away for the rest of my life.

Oh, she says she wants me home, but I don't believe half of what comes out of her mouth. I wouldn't be in all this mess in the first place if it weren't for her, sticking her hands all up in my cookie jar, minding my damn business. "I feel it's the safest place for her…, " I overheard her saying one day on the phone. "…I'm worried about her, and just want what's best for her." *Wrong*. Worried my ass. The only thing she's ever been worried about is what the neighbors think. It's always been what was best for *her*. She's even brainwashed my father into believing an institution is the best place for me. The cotton-ball nerve of her!

If she could have her way, they'd be locking me up, and throwing away the key. Have me put away like an old, raggedy sweater. Tossed away and forgotten. Trapped in a trunk with a bunch of moths that'd slowly eat my existence away—bit by bit, until there was nothing left but strands of yarn. Yes. That's exactly what she'd try to do if it were left up to her. But, little does she know, I'm not going to give her the satisfaction. I'm going home, and this time—for good. I've had four months to rehearse my lines. And finally, it's show time.

"Hello, Sarina," Dr. Burchell says, walking into his office, holding my file in his thick hand. His long, spidery fingers catch my attention. I shift in my seat, feeling the urge to spread open my legs, stick my finger in my hot pot, then stir my juices. I haven't had sex in months. And here he comes, wearing jeans—Gap, maybe 501's—that politely hug his manliness. Hmmm. He looks…tasty. I wonder if he's a boxer or brief kinda guy. "How are you feeling today?"

I casually lick my lips. "Horny," I want to say; but I part a smile and bat my eyes instead, inviting him into my space. As crazy and cluttered as it may be, it's mine just the same. And today, I welcome the prodding of my shrink.

For a white man, he's cute. Sandy-brown hair that's curly on top and neatly cut on the sides, a neatly trimmed mustache, sideburns that curve around his jaw line, and a goatee. His nose is thicker than it should be; makes me wonder if he has a taste of Africa running through his blood. He looks to be in his early forties, late thirties. Six foot, strong arms with

big veins. His wet, full lips entice me. And, now, I feel my panties beginning to stick to the folds of my coochie. Damn him.

"I'm fine," I say coolly.

He returns my smile, sitting across from me in his plush, burgundy
leather chair. For the first time, I take in his office. Cherrywood desk,
walls adorned with certificates and degrees. Wall-to-floor bookshelf
filled with psychoanalytical mumbo-jumbo. I see he collects coffee mugs
from different states and countries. Well-traveled, I think.

The room seems to have a coziness, and life of its own; separate from
the starch-white floors and gray walls on the other side of his door. I
breathe in the air around him; let his scent linger on the tip of my nose,
then look in the center of his crotch. The way he sits is inviting. I smile
again; this time wide, showing teeth. He's amusingly unaware of my lust.

"Good," he says, his eyes lock onto mine. "Well, this is our last session
before you leave us." I stare at him, through him. Wondering if he wants
me to clap or cry. I do neither; I stare, then blink. "Since you've already
been cleared, this is more of a formality than anything else."

I blink again. "Am I cured?" I ask, knowing damn well there's no cure
for what I have. But I ask anyway. Just for the hell of it.

His forehead seems to have a shine. Almost looks as if he's glowing. For
a split second, he reminds me of a lightning bug. I stifle a snicker. "No. I
wouldn't say you're cured. But I can definitely say, your condition appears
stable."

Okay. So my *condition* seems stable. Hip, hip hooray! Now, does that
mean I'm a stable person? Or just riding the wave of sanity? I don't bother
asking him for the answer I already know. I'm stable enough to ride the
wave.

"So how do you feel about going home?" he asks, plopping my life in
the center of his lap, covering the lump of happiness between his legs. I
strain to steal another glimpse before he begins scribbling something in
my file. I envy the pen between his fingers. I want to kiss the tips of each
one. Feel them stroke the heat between my legs. I press my thighs close
together, shutting off my thoughts. I need to stay focused.

I shrug my shoulders. "What's there to feel?" I ask, regaining my composure. "It's not like I'm going to another planet, or something. Home is home."

"Ah. But is it a home you're looking forward to returning to?" Now what kind of stupid-ass question is that? I want to inquire, but I restrain myself. I accept the fact that I may be one pill away from crazy—but if you ask me, anyplace is better than this nuthouse.

"Sure I am," I finally respond, crossing, then uncrossing my legs. I start to get wet as his blue eyes wash over me. I find myself slipping into an ocean of fantasies. But then I remember where I am, and what my goal is. I shift in my seat. Seeing him in his gray polo—despite its designer emblem—reminds me of how much I hate this place. *Why'd he have to wear that color?* I ask myself. *Gray is so institutional.* "I want to get back to my life outside of these walls."

"Sarina, tell me. And what do you expect life to be like outside of here?"

I really do like him. But today he's starting to get on my damn nerves; ruffle my fucking feathers. I just want to get out of here. Doesn't he know this? I raise my brow, wondering if what he's asked is supposed to be a trick question. I close my eyes, and think on it for a moment. I roll my eyeballs around in their sockets, then bite down on my lip to keep from laughing. The idea of living without ringing phones sounding like fire alarms, or not seeing doors in a wall where no door exists fascinates me. Being able to look into someone's face while they're talking without seeing long, slimy tongues hanging from their mouths, or fearing I'd be eaten alive excites me.

Preoccupation. Obsession. Compulsion. I don't think you can begin to imagine what my life has been like, running from an overstimulated imagination. Hiding from a distorted reality. Feeling like someone else's thoughts are being inserted into your own head, stealing yours. Believing you're Satin's lovechild, the whore of Babylon. *No*, I think—remembering a Langston Hughes poem, *Life for me ain't been no crystal stair.*

"Sane," I finally say, opening my eyes. "Yeah. That's it. I expect life to be sane. I don't want to feel like I'm on the brink."

He smiles, understanding all too well what I mean. He's been there too; felt what I've felt. Bodiless. He's heard voices, making it hard to distinguish between reality and nightmares. Seen faces melt in front of him the way an ice cream cone does, leaving sticky blurs. Has chased his thoughts racing forty miles a minute. Has locked himself in his room, believing people were outside trying to get him.

Yes, my psychiatrist is also a nut. Oh, okay. Maybe "nut" is a bit extreme. He's touched. But you'd never know it. He appears to be a man who has everything under control. That's probably why I like him, along with the fact I suspect he has a fat ding-dong. HeeHeeHee.

One time, I bit it off and stuck it deep in my coochie. Other times, I've spent many nights imagining him dangling it in front of me, slapping me in the mouth with his hardness. Teasing me until I greedily swallow him down. I choke on the thought of his white gooey nut, hitting the back of my throat, while his dick hairs coil through my teeth and wrap around my tonsils. HeeHeeHee. Right now, I visualize bending over, grabbing my ankles and letting him stick it in, nice and slow. I clear my esophagus. Oh, how I want him. *Take me. I am the whore of Babylon.* HeeHeeHee.

Oh, don't get me wrong. My attraction for him runs much deeper than my hunger for him. He's the first doctor I've had who wasn't afraid to admit he was crazy. The others looked it, acted it, but denied it. And I could see right through them. Usually, I play therapist, probing his mind, trying to understand my…umm…infirmity—yeah, that's it—through his experiences. Somehow, his past accounts of believing he could fly and thinking the noises made by cars and planes were machine guns firing at him have been helpful to me. He's been sort of an inspiration for me. He doesn't let his *condition* hinder him. And he uses his experiences, the good, the bad, and the ugly to help others. I admire him for that. His honesty has touched me. Today, I stare at him, long and hard, and realize I am going to miss him.

"Have you given any thought as to what you want to do when you get out of here?" What the fuck is this, twenty questions? Geesh.

Roll a blunt and suck your dick, I think. The thoughts roll into words, then stick on the tip of my tongue. I open my mouth to speak; lucky for him, nothing comes out. I consider his question in my mind. Hmm. If the voices don't come back to steal my sanity, I'd like to finish design school, become a well-known fashion designer. Shoot. Maybe I'll just get any ole job to get out, mix and mingle. Not that I need one. After all, I have Sarina Creations to display my exclusive fashions. I marvel at the thought of all those jealous bitches drooling over my delectable haute couture creations. Hmm.

Well, I guess if I really wanted to do something daring, I could write poetry or something. Maybe become a poet laureate. Win a Nobel Peace Prize. Oh, how sweet that would be. My first poem would be titled: "Lick me, stick me." And would go something like…Ahem. Umm. Okay, here goes.

Lick me,
stick me.
Fuck me all night.
Dick me from the front,
dick me from the back
pin me down and lick me,
stick me
bang my back out all night.
I need a dick in my mouth
Need a dick in my ass
Need a dick in my coochie-oochie
So stick me, lick me,
dick me all fuckin' night.

HeeHeeHee. Oh, I know you think I'm a trip. But who cares. The fact of the matter is, I really don't know what I might do. But I can say this much, right now I just want to get out of here. Maybe drink a forty and fuck. HeeHeeHee.

Oh, I almost forgot what I was getting ready to tell you, before I broke out into my poetic flow. HeeHeeHee. Umm. Oh, yeah. I may not have many aspirations, but one thing's for sure: I want nothing to do with my father's old nasty funeral homes. The thought of formaldehyde and dead bodies makes my stomach roll into a ball. There's nothing worse than the stench of death. That's what this place reminds me of, a breeding ground for the walking dead. It's what I hate the most. So, thanks. But no thanks. I want nothing to do with the family business. But I sure will spend up the money. HeeHeeHee.

Don't I want to be able to take care of myself? Now what kind of dumb question is that? Of course I do, silly. However, the idea of becoming self-sufficient frightens me, and excites me all in one beat.

Truthfully, I've never had a job. Well, that's not completely true. I did work at Loews Movie Theater for two weeks before paranoia and delusions crept in. I was like eighteen, almost nineteen. I'd be standing behind the counter saying, "Welcome to Loews Theaters." Then one day something inside of me snapped. I started hearing screaming and becoming agitated for no apparent reason. I was having trouble following any train of thought and voices were chanting in my head, "You will die…You must die." Before I knew it, I was screaming at customers because every time someone came to my line I thought they were plotting to kill me. How could I tell anyone that I had this person inside of my head, telling me what to do, think and say?

Well, I've been told that persons with schizophrenia have deficits in social and communication skills, which oftentimes makes it difficult for them to maintain employment, or function in vocational settings. Please. That's a bunch of horse piss if you ask me. I'm very social, and very skilled at communicating how I feel. Is it my fault people misinterpret my behaviors? So what if I have a tendency to talk to myself? And—yes—I can become quite animated. Big deal. It's not like I'm always talking to someone only I can see in my mind's eye. Sometimes, I'm rehearsing—or replaying, as they say. You know, replaying a situation in my head over and over again, oftentimes speaking to myself out loud. Is it compulsion? Yep. So what.

Still, I've refused to accept that I have…umm…what they call a mental illness. No. I won't accept that. I don't want to be crazy. But I know there's something wrong with me. And I don't want to be locked away. I don't deserve to be. I just go off from time to time. I have to believe that I can control whatever is going on with me. I just have to.

They—doctors in white coats, with fancy degrees, who are crazier than me—say my denial is what has kept me from acknowledging that I am schizophrenic. And they state my refutation is out of fear. Well, who the cocka-doodle-do are *they* to label me?

"I really don't know," I say reluctantly, "what I'm going to do. Sometimes I feel like I'm going to drift the rest of my life away." I'm not sure if what I say is imagined or real. Wrapped in a cocoon are my thoughts and feelings. The surreal seems real. Fact becomes fiction, and fiction becomes reality. Yet, for some reason, I feel compelled to share with him my trepidation. But I don't. I wonder if opening up would liberate me. Today, I feel so conflicted.

"Sarina, don't lose hope," he offers almost sympathetically. "You can do, and be, anything you set your mind to. This here," he says, gesturing with his hands, "doesn't have to be your life. I'm living proof. Despite three hospitalizations, and two suicide attempts, look at me: a man who has suffered and survived. I'm a survivor. And you can be too…"

Hope. Don't lose hope. I repeat it in my head several times, trying to make the words seem real. Possible. I read something in the Bible about hope, and I frantically dig through my brain, trying to remember where, what verse. I come up blank. Oh, well.

"I'm not you," I say softly. "I won't be so lucky." I want to say more. But I don't. If I tell him I feel like I'm trapped in a closet—stuck in an invisible box, he may use it against me. I like him. Want to fuck him. But I don't trust him. He still has the power to control me, and destroy me with the stroke of a pen.

He smiles reassuringly. "It's not about luck. It's about getting honest with yourself about your illness. It's about accepting the fact that you have a brain disease that is treatable." He watches me. And I let him. I want to be his display. Give him something to really look at. I throw my head back, and allow thoughts of his tongue dragging across my body to arouse me. My nipples harden. *Hmmm. Fuck me. I'm the whore of Babylon.* I hear him talking but I can't make out the words. I concentrate on the voice. "Sarina, you understand the only way you can live a normal, healthy life is by taking your medications daily. Maybe for the rest of your life."

I nod, returning my attention to him. "I know," I relent in a seductive whisper. I agree with him because it's what I'm supposed to do; still I don't like the idea of taking them. The side effects are unbearable, and sometimes disabling; but I understand the ramifications if I stop taking them. Nevertheless, I abhor them. They make me fat, and funky, and really tired.

Prozac makes me feel lethargic. Haldol makes me catatonic. And I hate the shots of haloperidol these wacky-ass nurses inject in me every time I'm hospitalized. However, I despise the voices even more. They control me. But, right now, I need them to stay wherever they are; well hidden to ensure I get out of this place, and stay out. So, I'll take the meds—no matter what. Well, at least until I know I'm home free. Then I'll cut down on my dosage. It's not like I won't be taking them, I'll just be making an adjustment. Like taking my pills every other day. There shouldn't be any problems with that.

I can recall the number of times I stopped my medicine thinking it was poisoning me, or believing I was better. Each time, the delusions and paranoia would return. I hate being paralyzed by hallucinations. Being consumed by demons with fangs devouring me has kept me awake many nights, roaming the house looking for them. I chuckle at the thought of Chyna thinking I was up ransacking her house. Ha! If only life could have been so simple.

"Good," he says, folding my file shut. He leans in, resting his elbows on his thighs and cupping his hands under his chin. His gaze warms me. I want him to suck my panties off me. Maybe in another life, for now I keep my desires to myself. "Do you still hate your mother?" he asks. His question takes me by surprise.

Do I still hate my mother? I repeat the question in my head, wondering if what I say will be held against me. Right now, I'm not certain if I hate her or not. I used to. But today, I'm not so sure. Sometimes I blame her for my *condition*. Other times, I blame myself. I've inherited a family curse that spared my brothers but has plagued me.

From the way I look, to the way I think, and act. Growing up I always thought I was strange. You know, a little different from the kids my age. Although I managed to get A's and B's in school, I sometimes had a habit of staring straight ahead, even when someone was talking to me. (I still do.) Or I'd *know* everyone was talking about me. And I'd fight them. (I still do that too. HeeHeeHee). I'd beat the drawers right off of them without blinking an eye. Then in my senior year, I stopped going to classes. I'd be up all day and all night for two and three days, then I'd feel like I was crashing and want to sleep for days on end. And when I wasn't sleeping, I spent my time daydreaming.

So I went through life not having many friends. But I didn't care. I had Pecola, my special friend. I could see her and hear her, but no one else could. She was my secret. And I felt lucky to have someone who needed me to protect them. Sadly, she only existed in my head. Only belonged in my little world. But now she's gone. Buried deep in my psyche. And, even after knowing all of this, I still miss her.

Wanna hear something even more crazy? My own mother—with all of her education in counseling—couldn't even figure out what was going on with me. Not that I made it easy for her. HeeHeeHee. I kept my paranoia and delusions to myself. I had to. Otherwise, she would have diagnosed me a long time ago. Stamped me disturbed and put me away. No. She and my father didn't need to know what was going on with me. They'd have never understood. So, as far as they were concerned, I was being a typical rebellious teenager—and, perhaps, a bit eccentric. HeeHeeHee. I guess to some extent I was. I did what I wanted, when I wanted. The difference now is that they know there's something wrong with me. HeeHeeHee. But I still do what I damn well please.

I remember my first hospitalization; the first time I was told I was paranoid schizophrenic. I laughed hysterically, thinking the beady-eyed psychiatrist had bumped his big head. There was some kind of mistake.

Then my mother decided to share her family tree—the one with its twisted roots, and rotten fruit—with me, divulging the facts about manic-depression and schizophrenia being illnesses that have affected the women in her family. Well, why wasn't she walking around crazed? Mighty funny she wasn't hearing voices, or seeing things that didn't exist. I sat in my chair across from her and my shrink, watching their faces fade in and out. Become blotchy blurs. She was a liar. He was a quack. There was no other reasonable explanation.

Many times I've looked myself in the mirror and have seen her reflection. Her green eyes mesmerize me. Her creamy skin, and silky hair taunt me. Things I will never have. Someone I'll never be. Yet, everything I wish I was. I have so much anger toward her. An anger that seems to fester, then boil over to the point where I hurt me in order to hurt her. She's everything I'm supposed to be. Everything I'm not.

I rub the gash over my eye. Sometimes it still aches. It's a constant reminder of that heifer, Indy. That's why I beat her ass. High-priced hooch. HeeHeeHee. Yet, I'm the crazy one. Oh, I don't dwell on it. But, one day, Miss Hoity-toity will get hers. Watch and see. Wanna hear something funny? Sometimes, I imagine myself turning into a cockatrice—you know, the mythical serpent hatched from a cock's egg who has the power to kill by its glance. HeeHeeHee. Well, I'd stare that bitch down, and kill her dead.

I look up at Dr. Burchell, and shake my head. "No," I finally say, "I don't hate her." Maybe I do, but today is not the day to decide. Streaks of light sneaking through the slits of his blinds catch my attention, and I lose focus.

I envision myself in another place, in a world where voices and sights aren't a part of me. Someplace far. Where my head isn't infested with disturbing thoughts or sounds. I've always wanted to be someone special, but it's hard imagining it as a possibility when you're not playing with a full deck. And right now, no matter how many times its been shuffled, the hand life has dealt me is one jumbled mess. The light glows, then flutters in my mind. I see Dr. Burchell's lips moving, but I don't hear what he's saying until the tail end.

"…loves you?"

"Huh?" I ask, catching the inquisitive look on his face.

"I said, do you think she loves you?"

"Do I think who loves me?"

"Your mother." I keep from twisting my face. Does he really think I give a cat's ass either way? I want to tell him so, but I know better.

I stare at him blankly for a minute.

"I think she tries to."

He tilts his head, rubbing his chin. "Do you love her?"

I get up from my seat, and raise my hands up over my head, stretching and pacing the floor. His questioning is getting on my nerves. I feel like screaming on him. But I don't. I want to go home. "Sometimes," I respond in almost a whisper.

"What would you like to be different between the two of you?" His voice is low, and soothing.

"Nothing," I snap.

"Are you sure about that?"

"Of course I'm sure. What kind of question is that?" But I already know the answer he wants. He wants me to say how much I want a close mother-daughter relationship with her. He wants to hear how much I need her. Well, he can clutch pig balls with his teeth before he hears any of that. He watches me pace. He notices everything. Instinctively, I stop and return to my seat.

For a split second, I imagine having his babies. Beautiful boys, maybe even a girl, with sandy-colored hair and bright eyes. My twat twitches with anticipation. I want so bad to welcome him into my wetness. I clamp my legs shut.

"Just wondering." He pauses for a beat. "You're a very talented woman."

I force a smile, assuming he's talking about the sketches in my sketch-pad—the ones of mannequins posing, styling in my designs—since he hasn't been exposed to any other talents of mine. HeeHeeHee.

"Maybe, one day, I'll decide to do something with it," I offer.

"Well, whatever you choose to do, I hope you realize you're a very lucky woman."

I raise my brow. "Really?"

"Absolutely. You have the love and encouragement of your family. Something many people don't have."

I restrain from sucking my teeth. I have a father who treats me like a fragile piece of glass, three brothers who stay clear of me, and a mother who devotes her every waking hour trying to mind my business. Get real. I want to laugh at the absurdity.

"Well, that's just handy-dandy. But I'd rather have the love and support of a man."

He nods understandingly. "Be patient. Love will come knocking all in due time. But first, you must be willing to work on *you.*"

I tilt my head and purse my lips, seemingly annoyed. "What else do I possibly need to work on?" I ask.

"Sarina, despite your progress, you still seem resistant to the notion that you have an illness that is debilitating. Particularly, if you opt to be non-compliant with treatment and medications." *How many damn times is he going to say this to me? I already said I was going to take the goddamn, stinking pills.* I feel like rolling my eyes up in my head. But I will them still. "Sarina, I just want you to understand that living with schizophrenia is very possible, and manageable." Yeah. Yeah. Yeah. Yada. Yada. Yada.

Everything goes over my head. He pauses to take in my expression. There's none. I'm as blank as a sheet of paper. And then, he says, "You're a very beautiful woman. Don't be a victim of circumstance."

The word "beautiful" rings in my ears. He called *me* beautiful. The remark sounds so foreign to me. No man has ever said I was *beautiful.* It has to be a joke. I hold my breath and wait for the laughter to come. It doesn't. I don't know how to respond. Can't think of anything to say. I'm frozen for a moment before glancing down at his hand. I don't see a wedding band. Can't recall ever seeing one.

"Are you married?" I decide to ask.

He shakes his head. "No."

"Engaged?"

He shakes his head, again; this time smiling. "No."

"Gay?"

"No." His eyes never leave mine. He never blinks. "I'm just a man patient-ly waiting."

For some reason, I feel hopeful. I smile, savoring my fantasies. "Mind if I wait with you?"

He lets out a nervous chuckle, then glances down at his watch. I smile. A voice blares out from his intercom, disrupting the mood I've created in my mind. I want to slap it off his desk. "Dr. Burchell, your assistance is needed on West Wing."

"I'll be right there," he says, grabbing my file from his lap, then getting up to toss it on his desk. "Well, Sarina. I think it's time to get you signed out of here before…" He clears his throat, shifting his tone. "Your family should be here any minute to pick you up." *Nooooo!* I want to scream. *Not until we finish our conversation.* He walks over to me. I remain planted stubbornly in my seat, only because I'm not ready to leave him. I want to hear what he was about to say before that fucking interruption. I'm almost willing to sabotage my release; just for another session, or two.

Truthfully, he'd be my only reason for staying in this dungeon of despair. His crotch is now eye level, and I want to reach out and touch. "Sarina, you be safe," he continues, extending his hand for me to shake. I look at it, and my mouth waters. I want to lick and lap it. I shake it instead. He holds onto it longer than I think he should. But I don't mind. "Stay beautiful."

I finally get up from my seat before I do or say something I regret. "Thank you, Doc," I reply, parting a smile as bright as sunshine. For the first time, in my life I feel special; yet sad. I feel the tears fighting their way to the surface, but I hold them back. I am happy and scared. I lean in and gently kiss him on his cheek. I want more, but I don't press it.

Now I'm certain he can smell the lust on my breath. See the desire in my eyes. The way he looks at me tells me so. My panties are soaked against my flesh. I step closer. However, he pulls away before I…

"Come on, let's get you checked out."

"Can you continue being my shrink?" I ask sheepishly.

"I'll refer you to one of my colleagues," he replies casually. "My job is done." His words discourage me. I don't want another doctor. But I don't let my disappointment show. I understand there's a fine line between ethical and unethical. The envelope was already pushed to the edge. I decide to push it a little farther.

"Can I call you sometimes?"

He smiles, opening the door. I quickly walk behind him, almost stepping on the back of his heels. The unfamiliar scent of his cologne is intoxicating. He ignores me.

"Well," I say impatiently.

"I'd love to hear how your progress in treatment is going," is all he says, moving swiftly toward the nurse's station, leaving me feeling like a jilted Jezebel.

That is not what I want to hear; I half-smile while heading for the ladies room. Once inside, I remove my lust-stained panties, wipe my hairy cavern, then quickly step back into his office and place them—neatly folded with the crotch outward—on top of his desk. HeeHeeHee. *I should wipe his face with them*, I think as I walk toward the smiling nurses with the bugged eyes and big teeth. Free as a bird. Yeah, that's me.

The minute I get outside, I drop to my knees and kiss the asphalt. For some reason this hospitalization seems to have been the most difficult. My father stares at me with concern. I see it in his eyes. But he keeps his thoughts to himself. And I let him. I'm not the least bit interested in hearing anything other than why the hell my so-called mother didn't have the decency to come fetch me with him. She sends him by himself. And for some odd reason, my mood is spoiled like rotten meat.

He places my suitcase in the cargo space, then gets in his new Mercedes truck. *I hate these trucks*, I think. *They're so damn ugly.* I run my hand over the dashboard to feel its newness, then settle back in the leather seat. "Your mother," he begins as he slips behind the wheel, turning the ignition key, "had an emergency she couldn't get out of. But we're going to meet her for lunch."

"I'm not hungry," I reply dryly, staring straight ahead. I feel his eyes on me, but I don't acknowledge them. I remain focused on nothing. "I want to go home."

"Okay. Sure," he says. His tone sounds filled with what I think is disappointment. I can't be sure. And I really don't care. "It's going to be good to have you home. We've missed you, sweetheart."

I turn to face him, but say nothing. *We, who?* I want to know. He can't possibly be referring to my mother. Not the woman who was too damn busy to…Humph. And then she wonders why there's so much dissension between us. And I'm sure my brothers haven't given me a second thought since I took off for New York. None of them have come to see me—the nutty sister. I don't blame them though. I wouldn't visit me either.

I lean my head back on the headrest, closing my eyes. Thoughts of Dr. Burchell force me to snap my legs shut. Oh, how I miss him already.

My father's voice disrupts me. He's on his cell, apparently talking to my mother. "Hey," I overhear him saying, "Sarina and I are gonna head on home. She's not up to lunch right now…I know, but she should probably get some rest.…All right then, see you when you get home…Love you, too." *Humph*, I think. *The bitch didn't even ask to speak to me.*

I press my eyelids together tightly, ignoring my father's glances. I can feel his eyes on me. But I choose a nap over him. I want to go home and luckily, the ride from Baltimore to Fort Washington was uneventful. Before I realize it, we're pulling up to 1501 Ginger Crest, and I'm being shaken from my sleep.

I run my hands over my hair. It's grown in, and is a knotty mess. Oh, how I've missed my wigs. It'll be nice to have long hair cascading over my shoulders again. I haven't worn a wig in months, thanks to that stupid hospital, acting all paranoid. What the hell did they think I'd do with damn horsehair, hang myself?

I cautiously open my door, then step out of the truck while my father hurries to get my suitcase. I close the door, wondering if he'll buy me a car. *Hmm. Probably. If I behave*, I muse. A convertible Lex or Benz would be nice. The thought of driving like a bat out of hell with the top down, and my wig blowing in the wind causes the corners of my lips to curve into a slight smile.

Yes, I'll have to be good for Daddy. There was a time when I had him wrapped around my fingers. I could get anything I want. But now, thanks to my mother, I'm not so sure. But it'll be worth a try.

I pick up my pace. Feel an extra bounce in my step as I make a beeline for the stoned pathway alongside of the house. I don't want to go through the house. I want to walk around the back of the house to the comforts of my own place. I throw my father a quick wave. "Okay, Dad. I'll see you later," I say. "I'm going to lie down."

Without a second thought, he clears his throat, stealing my joy. "We've moved you back into the house," he says in a-matter-of-fact tone, heading for the front door.

I stop in my tracks unsure of what he's saying. I had to hear him wrong. "Excuse me?"

"Your mother and I closed up the carriage house," he indicates. "We've moved all of your belongings back upstairs."

I feel a tantrum brewing. I want to yell, throw rocks at him. I stare him down. One, one-thousand; two, one-thousand; three, one-thousand…I count to ten. "Why?" I calmly ask, turning around to follow him in the house. I want to argue, but I won't. Not with him.

"Your mother and I thought it was best," he responds, opening the front door. There goes that word again, *best*. Yeah, right.

I bite my lower lip. "Humph." Is the only thing I say, stomping up the double-wide staircase to my living quarters where I crumble to my neatly made, king-sized bed. I fall off to sleep, wondering what else my mother would do to agitate me.

When I finally awaken, it's already four-thirty in the afternoon. I'm starving. The house is quiet, too quiet. But I'm smart enough to know that I'm not left alone. I walk into my bathroom, shower and then find an orange one-piece body suit hidden in the back of my closet. I was pleased to see no one—meaning my mother—had gone through my things. I pull out a pair of black and orange leather pumas, slip them on, then shake out one of my colored wigs, the orange one with the black streak, and bob cut. I look into the mirror and smile. *Yes, it's good to be home*, I think, opening my door and sashaying my way down the long hallway toward the spiral stairs that lead down to the kitchen—pivoting and posing as if I'm modeling.

As soon as I get to the top of the staircase, I can hear them talking. My parents. I quietly lean my back against the wall, then slide down, squatting and listening.

"How's she been so far?" my mother asks.

"Not bad," my father replies. "She's been sleep since we got home."

"Did you check on her?"

"Of course I did. She was out like a light." *Well, you wouldn't have gotten in if you didn't remove the locks on my damn door.* Can you believe that? They actually had the nerve to take all the locks off my doors. And to top it off, they turned my phone line off. How dare they do this to me! Hold me hostage. Force me to endure this cruel punishment.

"How'd she take not moving back into the cottage?" my mother asks.

"She didn't. She stomped up the stairs, and I haven't seen her since."

"Well," my mother says, sounding as if she's moving around in the kitchen. I hear a door open, then close, most likely the pantry. "I want to give her a few days to settle in, then I'm going to schedule her for an appointment with Dr. Brock, the psychiatrist Dr. Burchell referred her to. I don't want her to be without treatment for too long."

I roll my eyes. She really makes me sick. I get up, deciding I've had enough of their conversation, then wind around and down the stairs, making my presence known. My debut.

The minute I see Chyna, I want to scream. She's cut off all of her hair. *What the hell was she thinking?* I stare at her in disbelief—certain she only did it to spite me, just another way for her to get under my daggone nerves. She's standing with a big, billboard smile on her face. And I want to scratch it off her. I force a smile instead.

"Hello," she says, walking over to hug me. My body stiffens, but I accept her arms around me. "Welcome home, sweetheart."

I'm as stiff as a board. I say nothing. Just think it. *Oh, please.*

"Hey there, baby girl," my father says, smiling. "How'd you sleep?"

"Like a moth trapped in a jar," I respond, going into the refrigerator to get something to drink. Neither one of them respond. They let the remark go over their heads. And I'm glad. Orange juice, grapefruit juice, spring water, cranberry juice. So many choices, so little time. I choose the cranberry juice, pouring it into a crystal tumbler.

"Are you hungry?" my mother asks. "I thought we could go out to eat."

I shake my head. "I don't want anything to eat. And I don't want to go out."

"Are you sure?" she probes.

I fold my arms, leaning up against the counter. Then I sip my juice and nod. "Yep."

My father glances at me, but says nothing. I can tell something's going through his mind. I can see his thoughts. He doesn't have much patience for my attitude. *I better be nice.* I gotta get out of this house, but go where? It's not like I have any friends.

"Can I use the car?" I ask, staring down at my sneaker-clad feet. I see my mother in my peripheral vision, looking over at my father.

"Where would you like to go?" my father asks, getting up from his chair. He's extremely tall, and reminds me of the Jolly Green Giant. On second thought, he looks more like a black Hulk with his big muscles.

"Out for some fresh air," I reply. He walks over to me, wrapping his huge arm around me, then pulling me into him. He plants a deep kiss on the top of my head. He doesn't immediately say "no."

"That sounds like a plan," he says, squeezing me into him. My mother looks shocked, but keeps her mouth shut. Surprisingly. I smile inside, feeling victorious.

"Thanks, Daddy," I coo. Yes! I scream inside. I'm going to get out of this rattrap. Find me a liquor store, then get my drink and fuck on. Someone was going to lick me, then stick me. HeeHeeHee.

"No problem. Let me go up and change my clothes, then we can head on out."

Whaat?! He has to be pulling my leg. Didn't he just hear me ask if *I* could use—like in drive—his car my damn self. "Umm. I was hoping to go out on my own," I indicate. "I won't be out long." I catch my mother sitting in her chair with a smug look plastered all over her face. *She thinks she's cute. Let's see how pretty she is when I scratch her face up.*

He shook his head. "I'll take you wherever you need to go." *Oh, what is this shit*, I think, *Driving Miss Daisy?*

"Forget it," I snap, breaking out of his embrace. "I'll call a cab. Can I have some money?"

He reaches in his pocket, and pulls out a wad of money. I salivate. "Here you go," he offers, peeling back his green and handing me a five-dollar bill. What the hell am I supposed to do with five damn dollars? I want to scream on him.

I raise my eyebrow, glaring down at his outstretched hand. "If that's the best you can do," I state, "then thanks, but no thanks. You can keep that chicken change," I blurt out, fuming. I stomp off up the stairs and back into my room, yelling. "I hate this goddamn house."

Early in the damn morning, there's a knock on my door. And it annoys me. I had snuggled with sweet thoughts of Dr. Burchell and had planned on playing in my coochie, sticking my hairbrush inside of me. Oh, no! Not the bristle end, silly—the handle. But the knock on my door dried up my wet dream. I let out a loud grunt of frustration. I'm as mad as a pit bull right now. I can already tell today isn't going to be a good day.

"Sarina, sweetheart," my mother says, peeking inside. "Is everything okay?" *Sarina sweetheart.* The sound of her voice makes my skin crawl. I've been home for less than six days, and she's asked me the same damn question at least sixty times. Well, maybe not sixty. But it damn sure feels like it. Something inside of me wants to let loose a string of curse words. But I don't. I'm still on my best behavior, taking my pills every other day.

I open my mouth to call her by her first name. However, something stops me. I take a deep breath, and smile as if I'm on *Candid Camera.* "Everything's just ducky," I reply. But in actuality it's not. I don't want to stay in this house with her. I want my own space, my carriage house. The one tucked away in the backyard. The place she took away from me. Moved me right out of it so she can have me up under her nose.

"Your father and I decided you should stay in the main house for a bit," she had said when I had asked her for the keys to get into *my* place.

"And how long is a *bit*?" I had asked as calm and collected as I could.

"Just for a few more days," she replies.

Well, that was five days ago, and I'm still stuck in this house with her. She ain't nothing but a low-down liar. I frown when I notice she's already walked in without being invited. I want to scream, "*Don't fucking invade my space.*" I count to ten instead, then sit up in my bed. I rub my eyes, then focus on her.

"I thought we could go shopping today," she says excitedly.

I hate to burst her bubble, but I do anyway. "I don't want to go shopping." I get out of my bed buck-naked and stretch.

"Are you sure?"

I nod, turning my back on her. I bend over, giving her a full view of my black ass. The ass I want to tell her to kiss. I look under my bed for my slippers. When I find them, I turn back around to face her, slipping them on my feet. "There's really no need for you to be so nice to me," I state, keeping my voice steady. I manage to not sound hostile. Only to the point. "You don't like me, and I don't like you. So let's cut right to the cow's ass."

She clutches her arms, seemingly appalled. She's careful to keep her eyes on mine. Heaven's forbid she steals a peek at my titties. I feel like squeezing and licking them to make her uncomfortable. But I restrain myself. "Sarina," she says calmly, "why would you say something like that?"

"Because it's the truth."

She sighs. "Well, sweetheart. I'm sorry if you feel that way. But the truth of the matter is, I love you. And I'm here for you. Hopefully, one day, you'll realize that."

I roll my eyes, plopping down on the bed. Not concerned about covering my nude body.

"All I want is for you to be well and safe. All I've ever hoped for is that you be able to live a normal life."

I suck my teeth. "Yeah, right. Then why'd you have me put away? Do you really think having me locked away, like I'm some rabid animal—for the rest of my life—is going to make me well, or keep me safe?" I contain my agitation, fully aware that, if I act out, she'd have me hauled off in an ambulance, preparing my next stint in a looney bin. The Nut Hut. *It's not what you say*, I remind myself. *It's how you say it.*

"Sarina, you weren't in your right frame of mind. Your father, and I—"

"Don't you bring my father into this," I warn, holding up the palm of my hand to stop her. "This is nothing but your doing. So you leave him out of it." She stares at me blankly for a minute, releasing a heavy frustrated sigh, before realizing the suggestion.

"You really think I want you committed, don't you?"

I return her stare, tilting my head. "Don't you?"

Her voice quavers. Tears begin to surface, but she holds them back. "Sarina, there is no need for you to be combative. This is your home. And this is where I want you. But I'm really getting tired of this tug-of-war with you. Nothing I say, or do, is ever right. I'm tired of your constant scrutiny and I'm tired of the hurtful remarks. Whether you want to accept it or not, I am your mother, the woman who carried you for nine months."

I dismiss her melodrama. "I don't want to be anywhere around you."

"I'm sorry you feel that way. But, know this: I will continue to love you no matter what."

I pucker my lips up as if I've just sucked on a lemon. Bitterness sticks under the roof of my mouth. "I want to move back into my place."

"Absolutely not," she states.

"Why?"

"Because it's for the best." There is that fucking word again. I hate it. I hate it. I hate it.

"Drop dead," I snap.

She doesn't blink. Doesn't even raise her voice. "I don't know why I continue to allow you to talk to me any kind of way. Well, as of today— it stops. If you want out of this house, fine. I will assist you with finding your own place. But you will not remain on this property or in this house with your attitude. First thing tomorrow morning you will get your wish." She walks out, leaving my door wide open.

I feel myself falling off the wave. Sliding. How dare she threaten to put me out? I have no money, and nowhere to go. I can't believe she's spoken to me like that. I storm over to the door, cursing her under my breath. But smart enough to know, she's in control of my freedom. I slam it hard, and scream at the top of my lungs.

27

CHYNA: *Change Is Gonna Come*

I'm telling you. Sarina really makes me want to pull my hair out. As you can see, she's just downright nasty toward me. And instead of dealing with her accordingly, I always end up making excuses for her. Enabling her to think she can continue disrespecting me. Not anymore. I will no longer be her personal doormat for her to walk and stomp on. The buck stops here. And *this* time I mean it.

Every time Sarina deteriorates and ends up in the hospital, Ryan becomes insistent that we consider alternatives for her. And each time, I've refused to bear in mind any placement other than home. Because home—with her family—is where I believed she should be. However, there is only so much abuse and disrespect I can take. At this point, I have reached my limit. Period.

Don't get me wrong. I am still very prayerful, and hopeful that one day Sarina will get better. But I also know when it's time to stop fooling myself. I am very clear with the reality that *nothing* will change with Sarina unless she is ready to accept that a problem does exist. I am fully aware that almost everyone with a mental illness—particularly schizophrenia—initially denies they have it. Sadly, some deny it all their lives. As I said before, I denied it existed in my family, for years. So I understand. But, I can no longer carry Sarina through this journey. It's something she has to want for herself. Until she is willing to ask for help in coping with her illness— then and only then—will she begin to recover! Yes, I am scared for my child. But I will not dwell on it. Not now, not anymore.

From the beginning, I've gone through a range of emotions, from denial to sadness. From shame and guilt to confusion and dismay. And, over the years, I have searched frantically for answers that will never be found. Well, I'm done. I'm done blaming myself. And I'm done being held hostage by the whims and antics of Sarina. My child needs help, but she doesn't think so. And that's the bottom line.

I have been more than patient with Sarina, as understanding as I can be, and extremely supportive. Yet, she continues to give me her rear end to kiss. Well, I'm through. I hope I'm not sounding too harsh. But enough is enough. I'm not turning my back on her, but I'm definitely not going to give her my back to kick in, either.

I've thought this over long and hard, and I meant what I said when I told her she was going to get her wish. She wants out of this house, then she'll get it. I don't care how much it costs or how far away it is. She is going to get all the supervision and help she needs 'cause I surely can't give it to her. So I've been diligently working on finding her a structured place to live, because this one is no longer the residence for her. It hurts, but it's the truth. And the truth I can live with; Sarina, I can't.

And the first thing I did last Tuesday when I woke up was pick up the phone and call Dr. Burchell to discuss my concerns, then I made an appointment for her with Dr. Brock. I was relieved when his secretary called back with an appointment for that same afternoon. And I was surprised when she didn't put up a fight to go. I'm certain her compliance was because Ryan was going along but it didn't matter to me. My only concern was that she got dressed and hopped in the car without saying one word—to me that is. She had a lot to say to her father, though.

"Why is that woman always messing with me?" she asked him as if I weren't sitting in the same car with them.

"Hunh?" Ryan asked, visibly confused. But I knew whom she was referring to. I sat there, face forward, playing the invisible role. "What woman are you talking about, Sarina?"

She clucked her tongue, tossing her head in my direction. "Your wife."

He looked over at me. I pursed my lips, pulling my shades down from the top of my head, and covering my eyes. "My *wife*," he snapped, "happens to be *your* mother. And I don't want to ever hear you address her like that again. Do you understand me?" He glowered at her through his rearview mirror.

"Well, excuuuuuuse the H-E-double-L out of me."

"You are really starting to try my nerves with your foolishness," he continued, bearing off I-295.

"Dang," she snapped. "I said, my bad. I just wanted to see what you were going to say. Like I thought—you'd defend her, rather than keeping her away from your only daughter." I flipped down my lighted visor, pretending to fix my hair. I watched her behind my colored lenses. *I don't know what in the world is wrong with her*, I thought to myself. *I hope she's not cheeking her meds again.*

"Sarina," Ryan continued, lowering his voice, "your mother and I want to help you. But for whatever reason, you continue to fight us every step of the way."

She leaned forward, peering over his shoulder. "Humph. You want to help, then let me be. Stop treating me like a child. I'm a grown woman."

Ryan glanced over at me. I gave him a look, but continued in my silence. "If you want to be treated like a woman, then you need to start acting like one. And part of being grown—as you say—is being responsible. Something you haven't been."

She snorted, rolling her eyes up in her head. "Well, I don't know why I have to see this stupid shrink. I'm fine. But since it was her idea, you're just willing to go along with it. Did you ever stop to think that maybe she's the one with the problem?"

He shook his head, clearly getting frustrated. "Sarina, do me a favor," he urged. "Sit back and keep quiet. I don't want to hear another negative word come from out of your mouth."

She made a mocking face behind his back, then started humming a tune, which sounded like "It's A Thin Line Between Love and Hate." *Lord, give me strength*, is the only thing I asked thoughtfully.

As hurt and upset as I have been with Indy for what she did to Sarina—

and said to me, I can truly understand why she went off. Not that I accept it. But I do understand. And believe me. If I were a different kind of woman, and parent, I'd probably want to slap her face off too. But me being who I am, and knowing what I know about my child's issues, I continue to practice undying patience. There is a light at the end of this long, dreary tunnel. I have to believe that—for my own sanity. Lord knows I do.

For some reason, Indy's voice rang in my head, her words cutting through me. *You deserve whatever you get. I hope she beats your ass. Maybe then, you'll wake the fuck up.* I had to wonder. Did I really? Was this the price I had to pay for keeping my family history a secret? My thoughts drifted back two years. There was no rhyme or reason for what Sarina tried to do to me; other than her delusions took over, coercing her to harm me. I was out in the backyard, pruning my rose garden when Sarina snuck up behind me. The minute I felt something wet hit across my back and neck area, I turned around, startled—to find Sarina standing over me, holding an opened can of lighter fluid, smirking. "It's time, devil bitch." She tossed fluid in my face—thank God, missing my eyes.

The only thing I could do was scream, and scramble away on my knees—before my daughter could toss a lit match on me. Had I not been fast enough, she would have set me on fire. I had to actually wrestle Sarina down, rolling around in my garden while she screamed obscenities, and threats to kill me. Sarina clawed at my face, and bit my arm determined to leave a trail of hatred.

I tried to restrain her, but she was too strong for me. I yelled at the top of my lungs for someone to help me. I'm not sure who called the police; if Jayson hadn't come home when he did, there's no telling what might have happened. I watched Sarina being hauled off in cuffs, with an eerie smirk on her face. The same face my grandmother had on hers the day she killed her husband. The image of my body being burned at the hands of my own daughter still frightens me. And it has opened my eyes to the sad realization that my child—when she becomes actively psychotic—would stop at nothing to injure me—or worse, kill me. *You deserve whatever you get.*

Wrong! I don't deserve to live in fear and I refuse to. As long as Sarina continues to take her illness lightly, and sabotage her treatment, she will continue to be a threat to not only her own safety—but mine as well. So, as much as it hurts me, I agree with Ryan. Sarina has to go.

The rest of ride to the doctor's Mitchellville office was disturbingly quiet. Ryan, Sarina and I rode in silence somewhere lost in our own thoughts for the most part of the twenty-minute or so trip. A few times Ryan glanced back in his rearview mirror at Sarina, then over at me. Why, I wasn't sure. But it caused me to look back over my shoulder to find her staring at me, almost as if she were trying to burn a hole through me. Instead of saying something to her, I ignored her. I was invisible.

Dr. Brock's office was located in a brick structure with huge windows, making it look like the building was made out of glass. Ryan parked, then the three of us walked through an impressive atrium toward the elevators. The minute we stepped onto the elevator, Ryan and I stepped to the back, while Sarina stood in front of us. Then she had the audacity to scratch in the crack of her behind, digging as if she had lost the rest of her good sense, and common courtesy. Scratched and dug as if Ryan and I weren't there.

"Sarina," Ryan said, clearly disgusted, "do you mind?"

She looked back at him, us. "Something's slowly crawling in the crack of my ass…" She caught the look Ryan gave her. "…Oh, my bad. I mean, booty hole."

He shook his head. I ignored her, sucking in my bottom lip remembering something Kayin had said to me during his last visit home. "Something needs to be done with her. She's too over the top." I had to agree. Most of what she does seems so unreal. Fictional, if you ask me. But it happens. Oh, I know. Unbelievable. Well, trust me. I know I'd have a hard time believing it myself if I didn't hear it, and see it firsthand.

She scratched again.

I was sure she was doing it just to get under *my* skin. It was as if she wanted me to say something to her. But I had no intentions of giving her the satisfaction. I stood behind my shades and focused on the flashing numbers for each floor. "Well, is all that digging necessary?" Ryan asked.

She smacked her lips. "Uh, yeah. If you gotta itch, you scratch. Helllo."

I glimpsed over at Ryan. The veins in the side of his neck had popped out. I grabbed his hand and squeezed it. His posture seemed to relax.

"You know what, young lady. You are really pressing your luck. So I'd suggest you chill out, right now. Do you understand?"

She sucked her teeth. "Yessssss, Daaaaady," she replied sarcastically, then stepped off the elevator when the door opened for the ninth floor.

"She's really trying my nerves," he said in a tone low enough only I heard.

"Don't let her get to you," I offered calmly. "She wants you to get all riled up."

"Well, it's working," he said flatly.

Ryan and I waited in the waiting room area while Sarina followed behind a red-haired nurse with wide hips. Sarina—not caring who was watching her—strutted, swinging her hips mockingly behind the slightly pigeon-toed woman. Ryan shook his head. I sat still, idly flipping through a *Time* magazine.

"Dr. Burchell," I said, closing the magazine, "says we should hear something from Project Hope within the next few days for a placement screening." Project Hope was a specialized day treatment program in Bowie that had opened six months ago, providing extensive services— ranging from residential housing, counseling, case management, crisis stabilization and medication monitoring—to adults with mental illness. The facility itself has three psychiatrists, three social workers, and six case managers who are responsible for ensuring live-in residents and outpatient clients receive the appropriate interventions and services. I had heard about the program during a NAMI meeting in Baltimore, and was impressed with what it had to offer. It reminded me of Green Door in Northwest D.C. And it was where Sarina needed to be.

"Are you sure you want to go through with this?" he asked, rubbing the back of my hand.

I nodded. "It's the best thing for her recovery. Sarina needs to be out on her own, away from us, even if it is only a few miles away. She needs to learn to be self-sufficient. Something she'll never learn as long as I keep rescuing her."

I really believed in my heart that Project Hope would give Sarina the encouragement she needed to live a healthy, productive life as a contributing member of society. In addition to providing Sarina with living quarters, the program would teach her money management techniques, how to live on a budget, and offer vocational training and job placement.

He smiled knowingly. "You know my sentiments on this. I'm all for it. Been for a long time. I'm glad you've finally accepted it as an option." I stared at him, nodding wearily. As torn up as I was about my decision, I knew it was the right thing for all of us. If she wasn't successful there, then there'd be no other choice but to have her committed. There was a sharp ache in the pit of my soul. The last thing I ever wanted was my daughter to be locked away indefinitely. She was twenty years old, and I was still running behind her, trying to make her want to be responsible. What would her life be like when she turned thirty—or forty? There was no way I could continue chasing her around the rest of her life. And Ryan was done, hunting her down every time she decided to take off. "Don't worry, sweetheart," he continued, "we're gonna get through this, together."

"I truly hope so," I replied, reaching for his hand, then locking my fingers through his. "I don't know what I'd do without you." He pulled my hand up to his lips, then gently kissed it.

"Likewise," he said lovingly.

I smiled, leaning my head back, closing my eyes, and waiting for Sarina to finish with Dr. Brock. Somehow, some way, change was definitely gonna come. It had to.

A whole hour and forty-five minutes had come and gone before Sarina finally came out from her appointment. She seemed calmer. But maybe it was my imagination, or my wishful thinking.

"Sarina," I heard behind her, "you forgot your pocketbook."

"Oh, heehee." Sarina giggled, turning back to get it. A tall, very attractive woman with beautiful Hershey-colored skin, and stylishly dressed, walked up to Sarina handing her her denim-and-rhinestone bag. "I knew I was missing something. Thank you."

"A bag as nice as that could easily walk off," she said, admiring Sarina's creativeness. Her bag matched her denim jumper and floppy hat perfectly. I'll admit the bag was definitely different. Actually the whole outfit was... let me see, what's the word I'm looking for? Interesting. The jumper hugged Sarina's small waist, then molded over her curvaceous hips. The back was cut out. The sleeves and legs flared open and were trimmed in rhinestones, as were the edges of her hat. That's Sarina for you.

"You didn't go in it, did you?" she asked, opening her bag, then rummaging through it to make sure everything was in it.

"Of course not," the woman said, a hint of seriousness on her face.

"I don't like anyone going through my shit...I mean, stuff."

"Sarina, believe me. I would never think to go through someone else's purse unless I didn't know who it belonged to, and needed to find out contact information."

"Humph," Sarina replied. "Isn't that special." The woman looked over at Ryan and me and smiled. She walked over to us letting Sarina's remark go over her head.

"Hello, you must be Mr. and Mrs. Littles. I'm Dr. Brock." Ryan stood up and shook her hand. I did the same.

"Nice to meet you," Ryan said. I smiled in agreement.

"I hope you didn't mind the wait. Sarina and I were getting acquainted, and before I knew it, we had gone over our time."

I shook my head. "No problem at all," I said.

"Not at all," Ryan chimed in, wrapping his arm around my waist.

"Well, I'm looking forward to working with Sarina. We drew blood work to check her levels. And discussed the possibility of trying her on another medication."

"Don't be telling them all my daggone business," Sarina snapped, slamming her right hand on her hip. "They know too much of my business as it is."

"Sarina," Dr. Brock assured, "what you and I talk about stays between us. But since your parents are handling your medical care, there are some things they should know."

Sarina rolled her eyes. "Well, keep it brief and basic."

Dr. Brock smiled. "Of course. As you wish."

"Humph. Where's the bathroom? I need to drain my sewage."

"Three doors down the hall on your right," Dr. Brock said, pointing her in the direction she needed to go. She returned her attention to Ryan and me.

"She's a very interesting young lady."

"That's putting it mildly," Ryan said.

"I'd like to see her in about two weeks."

"No problem," I said. "We'll make sure she gets here."

"Good. You can make the appointment with my secretary."

"Okay, thanks," Ryan said, removing his arm from around me. "Honey, I'll go over and make her appointment, and settle up the bill. Be right back." I nodded. She must have sensed my worries.

"Mrs. Littles," she said, lightly touching me on the arm, "she's going to be just fine. She has a lot of work to do. But she's going to get through it."

"Thank you. I really needed to hear that. She has been really trying."

"I understand, believe me. Schizophrenia can be very overwhelming for family members, let alone the patient. So imagine what she's going through."

"I do," I replied. I was sure Dr. Brock already knew my family history of mental illness so I didn't feel a need to say anything more about it. I understood all too well the effects mental illness had on everyone.

Ryan walked back over to us, placing a white appointment card in his wallet. "Okay, we're all set."

"Perfect. Umm. Just so you know," she continued, shifting from Ryan to me. "I've been in contact with Dr. Burchell regarding Sarina, and he has discussed your concerns with me. I agree placement might be for the best for now, at least until Sarina becomes more compliant." Sarina walked over to us, cutting her eyes at me. "Sarina. It was a pleasure speaking with you today. And I look forward to our next session."

"Well, I'm not."

"Why's that?" Dr. Brock asked.

"I already told you. I prefer men. I have no interest sitting up in your crusty face every week."

"I assure you it won't be too grueling."

"If you say so," Sarina huffed, glancing at her watch. "I don't like interacting with bitches—oops, heehee. I mean, women." Ryan glared at her. I acted like I didn't hear a word she'd said. Nothing that came out of her mouth surprised me anymore. Dr. Brock didn't seem a bit fazed by her comment, either.

"Well then, it should prove to be quite interesting."

"Oh, please," Sarina snapped, walking off toward the door, then opening it. I smiled. "Thank you, Doc."

"Don't thank me yet." She shook my hand, then Ryan's. "But you're very welcome, just the same. Enjoy the rest of your day."

"Umm. Can we cut the chitchat and get outta here. I'm tired."

"Sarina, see you in two weeks," Dr. Brock said, turning to go back to her office.

"Yeah, whatever," Sarina snapped. Ryan and I headed toward the door with Sarina following behind.

"Do you think I can use the phone?!" Sarina yelled into the phone. She had picked up the phone in the study. And it was her fourth time picking it up in a matter of two minutes.

"Sarina," I calmly said, "I am still on the phone. When I am done you can use it."

Bam. She slammed the phone down into the receiver.

"Britton, I'm sorry about—"

I heard the phone pick up again. "Well, how long you gonna be?"

"Sarina, will you please get off the phone. I *said* I would let you know when I'm done." *Bam.*

I let out a long, frustrated breath of air.

"Uh-oh," Britton replied, "sounds like Miss Sarina is cranked up."

"What else is new," I replied. "She's been home a little over three weeks and has been *cranked* up since day one."

"Why? You would think she'd be happy to be home."

"Yeah. You would think. But she's not." I paused, sighing. "I guess, Ryan and I haven't made matters any easier for her."

"Oh?"

"Well, we told her she couldn't move back into the carriage house, then we took her private phone line, and removed the locks from all of her doors. If she wants to make calls she has to make them from the main phone. On top of that, she has no money, and no way of getting around unless Ryan or I take her. And unfortunately, all this doesn't sit well with her, especially the idea of me chauffeuring her around."

He chuckled. "Sounds almost like still being in the hospital. But, given her track record, it's probably for her own good. At least until she proves herself."

"That's the same thing Ryan said. He's adamant about not giving in to her, *this* time. Which has always been hard for me."

"Do you think she's taking her medication?" he asked concerned.

"Well," I said, "I watch her take it, but I can't be so sure. She could be bringing them back up once I leave the room. All I know, something is going on. I can't put my finger on it. I mean she's not behaving bizarrely or anything. But she's definitely not acting right. And it goes beyond her being her typical nasty self."

"Hmm. I see. Has she had her blood levels checked yet?"

"The other day," I said, glancing up at the clock. It was already noon. *The mail should be here*, I thought walking to the door, then stepping outside to the mailbox. "The lab results should be in sometime on Thursday. As a matter of fact, she has her next appointment with Dr. Brock tomorrow. At first she hemmed and hawed about going back, but she seems to be okay with it now."

"Well, that's a start, considering she never likes any of her psychiatrists."

"You're right about that. But, I think her being a woman, and a woman of color, makes a difference."

"Hmm. Well, let's hope she can encourage, inspire, and motivate Sarina to want to get better, and stay better."

"That would be a godsend," I said, hopeful. "In the meantime, I've been working diligently with Dr. Burchell to get her into a day treatment program. She needs intensive treatment, and ongoing support. We have an assessment appointment scheduled for next week. I'm praying she's eligible." I grabbed the eight or so pieces of mail, then shuffled through each piece, walking back to the kitchen.

"I don't see why she wouldn't be. As long as she meets the criteria, there shouldn't be a problem."

"Well," I sighed, "if it is, then I'll just keep searching until I find one that will take her. The sooner the better."

"Hmm. Sounds like you have everything under control."

"Britton," I said, "I don't know about all that. It seems like Sarina is bent on making my life miserable because we've set limits on her."

"Don't worry," he offered, "a little tough love never hurt anyone. She'll survive."

"Yeah. But will I?"

"Sure you will. Just keep your head up. Everything's gonna work out."

"I truly hope you're right," I said, plopping the mail on the breakfast nook counter, then pulling out a stool and sitting down. Most of the mail was junk, but there was one piece that caught my eye. An elegant ivory-colored and gold-embossed envelope with a New York return address. I slit it open with a fingernail, pulling out a matching card. The gold letters read *Surprise Shower*. It was an invitation. I opened the flap, and read: *The friends of Indera and Damascus Miles would like to invite you to celebrate in the upcoming birth of their firstborn on Saturday, March 31st, 2001 at six thirty in the p.m.* I felt a pang in my heart. A twinge of jealousy and regret shot through me. When Britton had asked me to help with the planning, I had declined because I was angry. And I refused to swallow my pride. But in the pit of my soul, I know I should have been involved in every way, sending out her invitations and whatnot. Not someone else. But instead, she and I were at odds.

Since our blow-up, Indy had called twice, leaving a message both times. Of course, I didn't return her calls. And I suppose she got the hint because I haven't heard from her since. I need time. And right now there's too much going on with Sarina for me to deal with Indy. But, in time, I will.

"I am," he said. I didn't respond. "Hello, are you still there?"

"I'm sorry. I was reading the invitation I just got in the mail for Indy's shower."

"Oh, good. Trying to keep this shindig under wraps from her has been a task and a half. There's not much that can get past her."

I half-smiled, wondering how on earth they were going to pull this party off without her finding out and pulling the plug on their plans.

"That's for sure," I concurred. "When is she due?"

"Sometime the end of April, I think."

"Wow, that soon." Despite everything, I was truly happy for her.

"Yep. That's what happens when you wake up one morning to learn you're pregnant, then find out in the next breath that you're only four months away from giving birth."

"I guess you have a point," I agreed, trying to imagine being pregnant and not having any idea. "Well, judging by the invitation, it looks like it's going to be a lovely event."

"Yeah, it should be," he said, chortling. "It better be. Indy would have a fit if it weren't. I can see her now, throwing Swedish meatballs at us for everything not being *fierce*, as she would say." I couldn't help but chuckle myself at the thought of Indy going off. I shook my head. He continued, "I'm kind of excited about it, though. I don't think anyone has ever surprised Indy with anything. Other than the news that she was pregnant."

"I think you might be right," I said, staring at the card.

There was a slight pause.

"I am going to see you there, right?"

I massaged my left temple, then pressed the palm of my hand in the center of my forehead, fighting back an emerging headache. "I'm not sure," I said, holding the card in my hand. "I'll probably just send a gift." A part of me felt that would be the safest thing to do. I wasn't sure if I was ready to face her after all the nasty things she had said. I love Indy dearly, but... she really gets beside herself sometimes.

He sucked his teeth. "Don't you think this mess with you and Indy has gone on long enough? The two of you need to get it out in the open and clear the air so we can *all* get back to the business of being friends."

"In time," I said weakly. "But for now, I think it's best we keep our distance."

"I guess. Well, if you change your mind. I know she'd be very happy to see you. And so would I. So, hopefully, you'll find it in your heart to come."

"I'd love to see you too," I said, committing the RSVP deadline to memory. In all honesty, I really did miss Indy. She was the one person, besides Britton, with whom I shared everything. But now—with so much space between us, it seemed like that was a lifetime ago. "I have two weeks to decide. But, like I said, if I don't show up, I will send a gift or something."

"Well, the fact that you haven't said you wouldn't come is a start. So, I won't press the issue. But I will say this, then I'm done: Life is too short, Chyna, to hold on to grudges. And our friendship is much bigger than that. So, if you love Indy, or miss her, please let her know and work on forgiving her."

I took in a deep breath, then slowly exhaled. "You're right, Britton. And I know I have to eventually talk this out with her."

"Exactly," he snapped, sounding relieved. "And the sooner the better." I smiled. It was so typical of him to try to play peacemaker and mender of all things, including our friendship. That's probably why I love his spirit. "Well, my sista and dear friend, I gotta go. But please call me, if there's anything I can do."

I smiled. "Thanks. I sure will."

"And remember, tomorrow isn't promised to us. So don't let today slip away. True friendship runs deeper than shallow words and pride. I love you, girl."

"And I love you. Give those handsome boys a big hug from their Aunt Chyna."

"Sure will. Take care."

"You too." We hung up. But my thoughts of the camaraderie Indy and I shared lingered on. We had a long history together. A friendship that transcended understanding. We had truly been sisters, or so I thought. Can someone, please, tell me how someone who supposedly loves you can say such nasty, hurtful things without an ounce of remorse? How could Indy dismiss my feelings, disrespect my child to my face, then expect for me to just accept it as okay. Well, it's not. My friend of over twenty-some-odd years hurt me. Her disregard for my feelings might have been shallow; but her words cut me, deeply. And right now, I don't know if I can get past that.

I took the invitation, stuffed it back in its envelope, then stuck it in my wooden "things to do" box on the wall. I had some serious thinking to do. I wasn't sure what I intended to do; but the one thing I did know, the closeness Indy and I once shared had definitely changed.

Wednesday morning, the day of Sarina's appointment, she shocked Ryan and me when she came down the stairs for breakfast, wearing a white terry-cloth bathrobe and black heeled boots. She had face cream smeared all over her face, and had big pink rollers dangling from the ends of her shoulder-length, burgundy-colored wig. Our surprise wasn't from what she looked like, or what she was wearing; it was that she hadn't come down once for meals since being home.

"Good morning," I had said the minute her foot hit the last step to come down into the kitchen.

"Humph," she said. "I guess." I let it go. It was better than her usual—ignoring me.

"Hey, sweetheart," Ryan said, looking up from one of his favorite portions of *The Washington Post*—the obituary section. As morbid as that seems to me, he seems to enjoy keeping abreast of who's departed this world. "You're up, awful early."

She pulled out a chair, then plopped down, swiveling around. I glanced up at the clock. It was 7:15 a.m. *That's unusual*, I thought, *her appointment isn't until eleven*. Since being home, she hadn't made it a priority to get up before noon, *unless* she was forced to. I didn't say a word. Simply smiled approvingly.

"Mmm-hmm," she said, picking up a piece of turkey bacon, then smelling it before taking a small bite. She frowned up her nose, then put the remaining piece of meat inside a napkin, laying it on the table. I was relieved when she didn't put it back on the platter. Progress comes in all forms. "Yes, I am," she continued, glancing over at me. "Up and at 'em."

Ryan looked over at me, surprised and seemingly pleased. "Well, it's good to see you this morning," he said cheerfully.

"Well, today's the day I catch my worms," she replied, pouring herself some orange juice from the crystal pitcher into a coffee cup.

"Oh," Ryan asked inquisitively.

"Yep. I wanted to let both of you know that I'm old enough, and grown enough, to go to my own appointments without the two of you following behind me. So, today, I'm going to see *my* shrink, by *my* self."

I shrugged my shoulders, giving him a look. She swiveled her chair around to me, then back to Ryan. He waited for me to respond. I didn't. He cleared his throat.

"Sweetheart," he said, putting his paper down, and removing his reading glasses, "your mother and I know you're old enough to go to your own appointments. We just thought you would want some support."

"Oh my God," she snapped, "That's the biggest pot of shit...I mean, bull...I've smelled in a long time. Why don't you just tell the truth? You don't trust me. That's the real reason. Both of you think I'll run off."

Ryan looked over at me for help. But I acted as if I didn't see him. Instead, I busied myself around the kitchen, removing dishes from the dishwasher and putting them away. I knew eventually I would have to speak up, say something. But not right then.

"Listen, sweetheart—"

"I hate it when both of you call me that," she interrupted, raising her voice. "Don't call me that. It sounds so... Ugh! Just don't call me that. Ain't nothing sweet about me."

I felt a nerve pinch in my brain. "Sarina, why would you say something like that? Your father or I don't mean anything negative by calling you that. It's a term of endearment."

She glared over at me. "Well, I don't like it."

"Okay, and now we know. We won't use it again."

"I'd appreciate it," she said, looking back at her father. "Okay, so back to getting to the truth."

Ryan rubbed his chin. "Sarina, your mother and I have been worried about you. It's not that we don't want to trust you. It's that...well, you have done some things that have caused us to be a little leery."

She snorted. "So you treat me like I'm still in a nut house, by removing my locks and monitoring my calls. What kind of madness is that?"

"Sarina," I jumped in, "you want truth, then give it: Are you taking your meds?"

She sucked her teeth, glaring at me. "Yes, I'm taking my pills. Anything else." For some reason I wasn't fully convinced.

"Every day?"

Her eyes shifted. "Well, yeah. I mean...no." I raised my eyebrow. Ryan stared at her. "I mean I do take them."

I repeated the question. "Are you taking them every day, Sarina?"

"I just told you," she snapped.

"Well, I truly hope so. Like your father said, we want to be able to trust. But you'll have to earn it. We need to be able to believe that you'll do the right thing even when no one is around. That includes taking your medications." I allowed a pregnant pause to linger in the air. "That's what being a responsible adult means."

She rolled her eyes, flicking her hand in the air.

"And what's all that supposed to mean?" Ryan asked, drumming his fingers on the table.

She shrugged her shoulders, looking down at the floor.

"Your father and I have been with you every step of the way, and we want to see you become successful in life. I wish you'd stop fighting us tooth and nail."

"And I wish you'd let me out of this damn cage."

"Sarina," Ryan urged.

"No," she snapped. "I want to move back in the carriage house."

"Not until you can prove to your mother and I—"

"Prove what? That I'm not crazy anymore?"

"Sarina," I said, "that's not what your father meant."

"Who asked you," she barked, swinging around in her chair.

"Sarina, don't talk to your mother like that."

"Well, she should mind her business."

"You are my business," I retorted. "I birthed you. I nursed you. And I—"

"Deserve a damn medal," she said. "Well, lick me dry, why don't you."
I didn't blink. Didn't flinch a muscle.

"Whoa, whoa," Ryan said, holding his hands up in mock surrender,
"Sarina, now you're getting way out of hand."

"That's right, take her side."

"I'm not taking anyone's side."

"Well, it seems that way to me."

He sighed, lowering his voice. "Sarina, your mother and I just want to
make sure you get the help you need. We want you to stay well."

She burst into laughter. "You want me to stay well," she repeated, yanking her wig off her head, then slamming it on the table. "Well, how's this
for staying well: I don't need you to remind me of my craziness. I'm
reminded of it every damn morning. Every day for the rest of my life, will
be a constant reminder of what I have. So, thank you very much.

"Neither one of you have any damn idea of what I go through. Of what
my life has been like. It's been hell for me, okay. And it scares me. Maybe
I do need help. But, it's up to me to decide. Not you," she said, pointing
at her father, then me. "Or you. I have to be the one to decide. And as of
today, *I've* decided that I *don't* need either of you, tagging behind me.
Now if you don't mind, I have to get ready for my appointment."

She jumped up, snatching her wig off the table—rollers swinging every-
which-a-way, stomping up the stairs. Ryan and I were speechless.

A whole week has gone by and, believe it or not, Sarina has been civil.
Well, let me rephrase that. She's not initiating any conversations with me,

but she's definitely not creating conflict, either. So, for me, that's a blessing. And at this point, I'll take any small gesture she's willing to offer. Her appointment with Dr. Brock apparently turned out to be more productive than any of us had anticipated. And despite my curiosity, I knew better than to ask her how things went. If and whenever she wanted to share, I'd be ready to listen.

The phone broke my train of thought. I picked up on the third ring. "Hello."

"Hello, yes. May I speak to Mr. or Mrs. Littles, please?"

"This is Mrs. Littles," I responded, glancing at the caller ID. It was Project Hope. "How can I help you?"

"Hi. This is Margo Freeman from Project Hope."

"Hello, Ms. Freeman."

"I'm calling to let you know that Sarina has been approved for our residential living."

"Oh, that's great news," I said, smiling. *Yes!* I screamed inside.

"I thought you'd be pleased," she replied. "She can move in on the first of April."

"Oh my. That soon."

"Well, normally it takes several months, but we have an unexpected slot opening up."

Talk about a blessing. "Well," I replied, "this has made my day. Thank you."

"Oh, don't thank me. You can thank Dr. Burchell for his part in this. Besides the fact that he sits on our board, he highly recommended we give Sarina the spot."

"Well, I thank all of you just the same."

"And you're very welcome. Now, let's see. We'll need to have you and Sarina to come down and fill out some additional papers, then it's all set."

"You tell me when, and we're there."

"How's tomorrow at three?"

"Perfect," I replied, feeling like a ton of bricks had just been lifted off my shoulders. "See you then."

We hung up. And for the first time in months—years, I could see the light at the end of the tunnel. It was a flickering ray of hope. A well of optimism rose inside of me. My daughter was going to get the help she needed. This time, I believed in my heart, she wanted it. "Thank you, Lord!" I shouted, picking up the phone to share the news with Ryan.

28

INDERA: *Thanks For My Child*

"Come on, baby," Tee said, hurrying me along. "We're gonna be late."
I cut my eyes at him, then rolled 'em. "Don't be fuckin' rushing me!"
I snapped, trying to catch my breath. Ugh! The closer I get to my due date,
the harder it is for me to get around. And the minute I start rushing, I
start sweating. I sat on the edge of the bed, contemplating whether or
not I should just stay home. To be honest with you, I surely wasn't in the
mood to be around any of his frat brothers, or their non-descript wives.
But, because I'm *trying* to be the good wife, I'm going.

"If I wasn't so damn fat I'd be able to find something to wear."

"Baby, you look good," he said, smiling. He leaned in, plopping a kiss
on my lips. "With your fine, sexy self."

"Humph," I grunted, twisting my lips up. "Just help me put these stockings on." He knelt down in front of me, taking my foot in his hand, then
massaging it. He stuck my big toe in his mouth, then slowly licked and
sucked on it before slipping the stocking over my foot. He did the same
with the other foot. I smiled, letting a soft moan escape from me. He looked
up at me and winked, licking his lips. "Eat my pussy," I said, leaning back
on my forearms.

"There'll be none of that," he snapped, grinning. "But I'll make it up
to you after the baby comes. Believe that."

I sucked my teeth, trying to pull myself up. "You make me sick." He
reached over to help me up. "I can do it my damn self." It was difficult
but I got my big ass up without his help and waddled myself over to the

closet where I pulled out a purple Anna Sui maternity dress which looked more like a bed sheet than a damn cocktail dress. I stared at it, then threw it to the floor. "I can't believe I spent all that damn money for this damn thing." I kicked it out of the way, searching in the closet for something else to put on this fat ass of mine. Well, actually, I'm not really that big. I'm all stomach. And—keeping it real—I've only gained twenty pounds. But it's still twenty pounds too much for my liking.

Anyway, after ten minutes of cursing and snatching things off hangers, tossing them to the floor, I settled for a hunter-green Donna Karan V-neck slip dress with three-quarter-length jacket. I stood in the mirror and groaned. Chile, I looked like Miss Piggy wrapped in a silk blanket. It's like my stomach blew up overnight. I felt like smashing that damn mirror to pieces, okay. Tee must have sensed what I was thinking 'cause he spoke before I could go into another one of my tantrums.

"Baby," he offered, walking up behind me, wrapping his arms around my expanded waist. "You look beautiful." He planted warm kisses on my neck. I leaned my head back, pressing my ass into him.

"Make love to me then."

He grinned, turning me around to face him. I rubbed the lump in his pants. "You so damn nasty," he said, giving me a peck on the lips. "I promise. I'll make it up to you." I stuck my mouth out, pouting. He sucked on my lips, then slowly probed them open with his tongue. I bit him. "Oww!" he snapped, holding his bottom lip. "Why you gotta play?"

Girl, let me tell you, my pussy lips were quivering for some thrusting. Fuck going to some damn party. I wanted to get the party started with him dropping these drawers and popping these hips.

"I'm not playing," I snapped, trying to hold back tears that had already surfaced around the edges of my eyes. I don't know what the hell was the matter with me. I was on the verge of a damn breakdown or something. I wanted to be touched. *Now!*

"I want some damn dick, so since you don't want to give me none, you can take your ass to your little party without me."

His eyes widened. "Whaat?!" he snapped, sucking his teeth. "Come on, girl, stop playing. You can't have me walking up in there without you on my arm."

"I'm *not* playing," I sneered, narrowing my eyes.

"And what am I supposed to tell everyone?"

"Tell 'em your pregnant wife is sick." I paused, taking off my jacket. "Tell 'em my pussy has collapsed from dick deprivation. I don't care what you tell 'em. But I'm not going any damn where so enjoy yourself without me."

He glanced down at his watch—for the fifth damn time, shaking his head. He seemed to be panicking. *What the fuck is wrong with him*, I thought to myself. *He's not the one in a state of emergency.*

"Aiight, baby. I tell you what. Let's just go for an hour or so, then we can come on back, and I'll tighten you up just right." I gave him one of my "oh-no-the-hell-you-won't" looks, placing my hand on my round hip. And before he could open his mouth to say another thing, I flipped into bitch mode, cursing him out. And you wanna know what he did? He walked out, slamming the door behind him, leaving me standing in the middle of our bedroom wet, and agitated.

Just as I was about to take off my clothes, the phone rang. I decided to let the answering machine click on. When I heard Brit's voice I rushed over, picking up.

"Hello."

"Heeeey, Momma," he sang. "How's the mother-to-be doing?"

"Ugh! Don't ask."

"That bad, huh?"

"Worse."

He chuckled. "Still not getting any? Poor thing."

"Oh, fuck you," I groaned, smiling. That damn man knows how to brighten up my day. "Where are you?"

"Funny you should ask. I'm in the city and was hoping you and Tee could meet me. I have something I want to share with the two of you. It's rather important."

"Well, that stinking husband of mine isn't here...Wait a minute! Why are you calling here about meeting you in the city when—"

Tee burst into the bedroom, scaring me. "Are you done beefing?"

"Hold on a minute," I said into the receiver, turning my attention to Tee. "I thought you left. Wait, Brit's on the phone. Brit…Hello?" The phone was dead. "Well, he was. Something must have happened to his cell." I placed the phone back in its cradle.

"Oh word?" He shifted his eyes, glancing again at his watch. "Will you please stop tripping and let's go. I said, I'll hit you off tonight when we get back."

I tilted my head, stared at him for a few seconds, then snatched my jacket off the bed. "And you better do me right," I snapped. He smiled. "I want your tongue in my ass too."

"Aiight. You got that. Now can we go."

"I mean it. You better work me from head to toe."

"Come on," he said, patting me on my ass, then squeezing it, "the sooner we get out of here, the sooner we can get back here so I can wax that ass."

"Ooh, Daaaady!" I squealed. "That's what I'm talking 'bout."

"Surprise!" everyone yelled, as I walked through the door behind Tee. I gasped, covering my mouth. I was floored. Tee had a wide grin on his face.

"Surprise, baby," he said, leaning in to give me a kiss on the lips. I slipped my tongue in his mouth.

"Awww!" Everyone clapped. Cameras flashed. I almost gagged when I spotted Chyna standing, front and center, smiling at us. I almost didn't recognize her. Not only had she cut her butt-length hair off into an asymmetric bob, she was working the hell out of a black Versace mini dress with black knee-high boots. In all the years I've known her, I've never known her to dress so daring. It was a really good look and she wore it well. Girlfriend was *fierce!* I silently hoped my body would snap back after I had my baby.

The last thing I needed or wanted were saddlebags and a pouch. I made a mental note to hit the gym hard the minute I dropped this load. Turning into a piglet would not do, okay. Chyna was the first to walk over to hug me. Chile, you don't know how happy I was to see her.

"Okay, you two," she said, glowing. "That's what got you here in the first place." Tee and I smiled. She hugged Tee, then me. "Hey, girl. It's about time you got here. We thought we were gonna have to come to you." We embraced as if we had never missed a beat in our relationship. However, in my heart, things felt different between us. I held her tightly, keeping the container of tears sealed.

"You betta work," I snapped, backing away to get a good look at her. "I love the cut. And that dress is slammin'." I peeped Tee eyeing her on the sly. But I didn't mind 'cause girlfriend was serving us lovely with her spell-binding shape and all-eyes-on-me beauty. She could give any supermodel a damn run for their money, okay.

She smiled. "Thanks. It's the new me."

"Well, the new you is definitely working. And how's Ryan handling this new you?

"He's loving me all over again," she responded gleefully.

"I know that's right. Umm. Speaking of Ryan, where is he?"

"He couldn't get away," she said, "but he sends his wishes."

"Well, tell him I send a 'thank you.'"

She nodded, smiling. "I've missed you," she said, taking my hand and lightly squeezing it.

"I've missed you too," I said, glancing around the room at all the smiling faces. There were about sixty people in attendance. Two tables overflowed with beautifully wrapped boxes and gift bags. And you know how girlfriend likes gifts, okay. I squeezed her hand back. "It's so good to see you." She gave me a kiss.

"Of course it is," she replied jokingly. "We'll get caught up later. Right now, I'm gonna get out of the way so everyone else can greet you." Before she stepped aside, I grabbed her by the hand, then hugged her again.

"I love you," I said. "And I'm sorry for being such a bitch."

She smiled. "You can't help yourself. But we'll talk about it." She stepped in closer, placing her lips flush to my ear. "For the record, I love you too." She kissed me again on the cheek before stepping out of the way, giving the rest of the guests a chance to greet me. Tears pushed their way up to the surface, welling in my eyes. I was so overwhelmed. Next to give me a hug was Britton and the twins. Myesha was standing slightly in back of them.

"Boy, you are too much," I said, giving him a big hug and kiss. "I thought something was a little fishy when you called."

He smiled, kissing me on the cheek. "Glad you could finally make it. You always gotta be so difficult. But little did you know. We were getting ready to party without you."

"Yeah, right," I said, rolling my eyes in mock disgust. "I don't think so." I spoke to Myesha over his shoulder. "Hey, girl. It's nice seeing you again."

"Same here," she replied. "You look so pretty."

"Oh, please. I feel like Henrietta the Hippo."

"And you're probably eating like her too," Britton added, snickering.

I flicked my hand at him. "Lick my..." I caught myself just before the rest of the words fell out of my mouth.

"Hi, Auntie," the boys chimed in unison.

"Hey, babies," I said, smiling and bending over to kiss them both. Brit had 'em both rocking Sean John jumpsuits and Timbs. Amir had on a beige jumper and tan leather boots while Amar wore all brown. I smiled. "Look at ya'll. Looking all fly and whatnot." They both giggled, showing the cutest set of dimples.

"All right, let's break this up," Tee said, cutting in between the twins and Britton. "You're giving my wife too much attention."

"Don't hate," Brit said, giving Tee a fraternal handshake, then brotherly embrace.

"What's up, My," Tee said, looking over in her direction. "Good to see you."

"You too," she replied, slipping her arm in between Brit's. They really looked good together. "Thanks for inviting me."

"Come on now," he continued, glancing at Brit, then winking. "You're practically family, isn't that right, baby."

"Mmm-hmm," I agreed, smiling. More than anything, I've always wanted Britton to be happy with someone who could love him for the man he is. I'm certain Myesha is the one to do that. Of the women who've come in and out of his life, she's the only one I can honestly say I've liked. "And judging by the size of that ring, you gonna fit right in."

Britton grinned. "Sounds like ya'll tryna marry us off or something."

"Now would that be such a bad thing?" Myesha asked, feigning shock.

"Umm," he said playfully. "Let me think it over before I respond." She raised her eyebrow. Tee and I smiled. He kissed her lightly on the lips, then continued, "I think I'm going to need more time." He kissed her again, quickly slipping his tongue in her mouth, then pulling away. He smiled. "You set the date, and I'm there."

"I'm gonna hold you to that," she said, kissing him again. "Now if you'll excuse me while I go to the bathroom."

"Daddy, I have to go pee-pee," Amir said.

"You can come too," she said, smiling. Her tone was filled with love.

"I have to go pee-pee too," Amar whined.

She smiled. "Well, let me get my little men to the bathroom. Come on, boys."

"See you when you get back," Britton said, giving her a wink.

She gave me a hug, then excused herself with Amir and Amar trailing behind her. Britton's eyes danced with pride as he watched them walk off.

"You look so happy," I said, grabbing his hand.

"I am."

"And we're happy for you," Tee said, giving him a brotherly pound.

"Thanks, man. It's definitely a beautiful feeling."

"Don't I know it," Tee responded, wrapping his arm around my neck. "I couldn't imagine life any other way." He kissed me on the side of my head.

I smiled, letting go of Brit's hand. Tradawna walked up. Tee and Brit exchanged pleasantries with her, then stepped out of the way. She looked lovely in her electric-blue skirt with three-button jacket. And as usual, she served us cleavage for days. "Hey, soror," she said, giving me a hug. "You look wonderful."

"Girl, thanks," I said, grinning. "You know how I do."

"I know that's right."

"It's good to see you," I said, waving for Chyna to come over. "Thanks for coming."

"I wouldn't have missed it for the world."

I smiled as Chyna walked toward us. Four grown kids and she didn't look a day over thirty. "Tradawna, let me introduce you to my sister, and best friend. Chyna, this is Tradawna, one of our sorors."

"Hello, soror," Chyna said, extending her hand. "Nice meeting you."

"Likewise."

I noticed the line to greet me was getting longer. And as patient as everyone was, I could tell some of them were getting anxious. "Ladies, if you'll excuse me for one moment. I think I had better go greet the rest of my guests before the natives get restless. I'll be right back."

"You go 'head," they said in unison, then laughed. I smiled, leaving the two of them to get better acquainted. People grabbed and hugged me as I made my way through the crowd. It was really good to see everyone, including Giovanna and her very handsome, and very rich husband. Tee, Britton and Val had really outdone themselves with throwing me this surprise party. At first I was a little saddened when I found out Chyna wasn't a part of the planning. But I understood why. The most important thing was, she came. And had a good time. That's all that really mattered to me.

Chile. We ate, laughed, played trivia games and danced until midnight. By the time we got home, I was so damn exhausted that the only thing I wanted rubbed was my back and feet. And Tee did just that until I fell fast asleep.

Oooh! I'm miserable. I'll be so glad when I have this baby. My back hurts and this constant pressure on my bladder is the most uncomfortable feeling. You should see me racing to the bathroom 'cause I feel like I'm gonna piss all over myself, then I get there and nothing but a little drizzle comes out—or nothing at all. But let me laugh at something funny, and I'll piss all over myself. It's like I'm a walking fountain. It's disgusting.

To add to my misery, my ass has spread like the plague. It's sickening. Well, I guess sitting around eating pints of Edy's Dreamery ice cream doesn't help matters any. Chile, you have to try the Deep Dish Apple Pie, with its chunks of apples, real piecrust pieces and swirls of caramel. It's to die for. And let me tell you, right now, that's what I feel like: Death warmed over! Girl, having all this weight on my small frame is a sin. I feel like a beached whale in distress. Do you hear me? My stomach is so huge it looks like I swallowed two whole watermelons. I'm telling you, I'll be glad when I have this baby so I can get back to the gym. I'd sure like to know who in the hell said being pregnant was a wonderful feeling. Humph. I'd slap the shit out of them!

Between you and me, the closer I get to my delivery date, the more nervous I'm getting about going into the hospital. Ever since a sistafriend of mine called me, giving me the scoop about the goings-on in these hospitals I've been shook. Chile, listen. Homegirl works for the National Centers for Disease Control and Prevention and she told me that it was calculated for 2000 that ninety-thousand deaths were linked to hospital infections, the fourth leading cause of deaths in the United States behind heart disease, cancer and strokes, okay. So, you know, I am not feeling that. I'm really considering having my child at home in my own damn bed, okay.

Furthermore, girlfriend didn't stop there. She went on to disclose that since 1995, more than seventy-five percent of all hospitals have been cited for serious cleanliness and sanitation violations. "Infection rates are soaring," she stated!

In the middle of her conversation, I vaguely remembered a 1997 incident in which four babies died. A 1998 story flashed through my mind: eight children died at a Chicago pediatric medical center due to hospital-linked infections. I almost fainted. I don't know what I'd…listen. I don't even want to think about it. Giovanna wants me to stay positive. Well, that's all fine and dandy, but I need to also stay abreast of what the hell is going on in these damn hospitals, okay. I'm going to have to have my research assistants do some serious digging to see what citations, if any, have been reported on my hospital of choice. And if there are any, they'll be in for it, okay!

Oh my! Hmmm. The baby just kicked. See, look. It did it again. Ugh! That's all it does. Sometimes, I think she does all this kicking and moving around to be spiteful. Well, I'm not sure if it's a boy or girl. So, I vacillate from one to the other, depending on my mood. Right now, it's a girl. Humph. That's what I bet it is. A moody-ass girl 'cause only a girl would be doing all this hell raising inside of me—squirming and kicking the hell out of me, keeping me up all hours of the night.

And to make matters worse, I'm horny as hell! That damn husband of mine hasn't touched me in almost two months, talking about he doesn't want to hurt the baby. He pays more attention to this child inside of me than he does me. It's always the baby this, the baby that. Oh, please! I told his ass the baby wants me to have some dick. Hell, maybe a good banging would put this child to sleep at night then—*maybe*—I'll be able to get *me* a good night's rest for a damn change. But no! I have to suffer because of this baby stretching my body all out of shape and cock-blocking me. So I suggested—trying to compromise, "Just eat my pussy then."

"Nah, baby, can't do that, either."

"And why the hell not?"

"'Cause it just wouldn't be right with the baby right there," he stated, pointing under my stomach. The minute he laid his hand on my stomach, the baby kicked again. "Aye, yo. You see that? He's awake, so no lovin' for you."

"You make me sick," I whined, wrapping my arms across my chest.

"You look so cute when you pout," he said, leaning over to kiss me. I turned my head just before he hit my lips. I wanted to roll up on top of him but this damn stomach of mine was in the way. "What if you get too excited and go into labor or something?" Now, he was asking for a face slapping. He didn't get it. I *needed* excitement. I *wanted* labor. I wanted the labor of a hard dick and a strong back. I needed the excitement of a good fuck.

"Well, what difference did it make when you were eating my pussy two months ago?" I asked, snatching the covers off him.

"Two months ago," he reasoned, "You weren't due in three weeks." I rolled my eyes at him. "Come here, girl," he said, trying to kiss me again. "Let me rub your back for you."

"I don't want my damn back rubbed. I want my pussy rubbed." I took his hand and stuck it between my legs. My pussy was hot! "Well, let me hump on your hand then." I clamped my thighs shut. He yanked his hand out.

"Damn, you nasty," he said, laughing.

"This shit's not funny." I sat up, removed my nightgown, then spread open my legs. "C'mon, Tee. Let me feel your dick on my pussy. Just lay it right here," I said, pressing my two fingers between my swollen pussy lips.

"Aww, hell no! I'm not falling for that shit again." I started to laugh but I was too damn mad to. 'Cause the last time he agreed to just rub me with his dick, I had my hand on it while he rubbed it back 'n forth, over my clit and hole. Chile, I counted ten strokes, then on the eleventh stroke—just when he was about to slide his dick forward—I shoved my hips upward and locked my legs around him, causing his dick to slide right inside of me. Girl, before he could pull out, my pussy muscles had clamped around his meat. There was nothing he could do. He was trapped in my love cage.

He laughed. "I know the drill. I start rubbing my dick across that hole, then before I know it, your lips have flapped around my shit and I'm sucked inside you."

"Unh-huh. I just want to feel it. I promise."

"Nope. Not this time, baby."

I placed my left hand on my wet pussy. It was so juicy. He tried his best to ignore me. Though his mouth said "no," his dick swelled in my hand. I stroked it a few times, then took his right hand in mine, bringing it to my lips. I slowly licked and sucked his long, thick fingers. Then I attempted to place his hand back between my legs. "Play with my pussy, Tee." He still refused.

"Aye, yo. Go 'head with that." I'm telling you, I was about to blow a damn gasket. This motherfucker couldn't even rub my pussy for me. Can you believe this shit? So the fuck what if I'm pregnant! My uterus is closed up, not my damn pussy, okay. So needless to say, I cursed him out to no end and I made it very clear to him, it would be a cold day in hell before

I'd ever beg him to touch my sweetness again. And you know what he had the nerve to do? He laughed.

"Yeah right. The minute you have this little one," he said, rubbing, then kissing my stomach, "it's on and poppin'." I slapped his hand off me, got up out of bed and went into my walk-in closet, flipping open my "Indy" chest. Chile, I was like a kid in a candy store with all my hidden treats. Since he refused to give me some lovin', I'd decided I'd take matters into my own hands and handle my own damn needs. Humph.

I went downstairs to get one of the barstools in the basement, sat it in the middle of the bedroom floor, then fastened my harness over it, attaching one of my travel companions. This particular night it was going to be Kunta, my twelve-inch warrior dick, then I gave it a second thought—I didn't want to chance having my child's head banged in—and settled for Mojo, an extra-thick six-inch. It wouldn't hit the bottom of this love basket but it'd sure knock the sides around. "Yo, what the hell you doing now?" he asked, sitting up in bed.

"I'm getting ready to bust me a nut," I said, facing the mirror, preparing to mount my love tool. "So you can sit your stingy dick-havin' self right there and watch or take your ass downstairs." He didn't budge. And with that said, I pulled open my ass cheeks so he could get a back-shot view of my pussy opening up before I buried my rubber friend deep inside of me.

Chile, I closed my eyes and rode the hell out of that thing. And when I opened my eyes for one quick second to see what my captive audience was doing, that nasty fool had his dick in his hand, getting ready to beat his shit.

"Oh, no the hell you won't," I snapped, pulling up off my wet, slippery dildo. I leaned over it, then slowly licked and sucked it. "Hmm," I purred. "My pussy tastes so good. And it'll be a long damn time before you get any of it." He smiled. I rolled my eyes at him while unlatching my sex toy from its harness. I walked into the bathroom, slamming the door behind me. He thought he was gonna get his nut off at my expense. *Not!* I finished myself off, climbed into bed, then fell fast asleep, sleeping like a baby.

Humph. Well—since I'm telling you everything else—I might as well let you know how far lack of sex has taken me. I'm telling you, I'm so damn horny, all I have to do is press my fingers against my clit and I cum. *Snap!* Just like that. And I'm a wet mess. Oh, it's terrible.

Anyway, I'm a little embarrassed to tell you this. But fuck it! Last night, I was sitting up eating my third pint of Deep Dish Apple Pie when all of a sudden I got the urge to touch myself. Well, before I even realized what I was doing, I had propped two pillows up against my headboard, leaned back and opened up my legs, sticking my cold tablespoon on my pussy. Chile. Let me tell you, I almost lost my mind, it felt so damn good. You should have seen me. I'd scoop out some ice cream, eat it, then press the back of the spoon right between my pussy lips. Hmmm. Scoop. Eat. Press. Scoop. Eat. Press. Oh, I know it's terrible. But I didn't give a damn. The feeling of that cold spoon on my hot pussy was exhilarating and quite tasty—if I do say so myself. And just when I thought I was about to come, a gush of water escaped me. My water broke.

"Come on, baby. Breathe."

"Ahh!" I yelled in between contractions. Inhale. Exhale. Inhale. Exhale. The pain was excruciating. It felt like my insides were being twisted and pierced with pins. But I wanted to experience childbirth without drugs. And now I was suffering. "Ahhh! I'm gonna fuuuuck you up. Ahhh! I hate you!" With my knees bent, legs spread wide and feet dangling from stirrups, I pushed down with all that was in me. "Ahhhhhhhhh!"

"Stop pushing, Indy!" Giovanna ordered.

"Get this baby out of me!" I pleaded.

"Breathe baby," Tee said with his lips flush to my ear. "It's gonna be all right. Just remember what we learned in Lamaze."

"Fuck you!" I snapped in between contractions. "And fuck Lamaze!" I swung my arm around, hitting him in his face with my hand. "As soon as I have this baby, I'm gonna slap the shit out of you."

"Indy!" Giovanna snapped. "You have to close your mouth and concentrate."

The contractions stopped for a few seconds. "Get him and his hot-ass breath outta my damn face!" I yelled just before the next one took over. "Ahhhh!"

"I need you to listen to me. I need you to push when I say. Do you understand?"

"Yessssssss," I screamed. "This baby is killing me. It hurts." Tee grabbed my hand and lovingly stroked it. I tightened my grip around his hand. Inhale. Exhale. Inhale. Exhale. Gritting my teeth, I dug my nails deep into his flesh. "I hate you!" Tears rolled down my face as I panted. Sweat dripped. "You make me sick! Get this baby out of me!"

"You're doing fine," Giovanna assured. "You're crowning. Okay, Indy. I need you to exhale." I did. "Now push!"

I screamed and pushed. My pussy was ripping. I pushed and screamed. And in between Tee's attempts to soothe me, I saw my mother's face and heard her whisper, *"My sweet Indy, love this child as I have loved you."*

I heard my father, *"I have made mistakes but I have always loved you. Please forgive me."*

"That's it, Indy. Just like that. Here comes the head. Push, Indy."

I saw Britton, smiling at me with open arms. *"Let go of the past, Indy."*

"I can see our baby, Indy," Tee said, choking back tears. He gently wiped sweat from my face with a cool rag. "I love you, baby. That's it, Indy, breathe."

I closed my eyes tight. In my mind's eye, Chyna reached out and hugged me. *"Indy, you have so much love in you. You can do it."*

My mother lovingly rubbed my face. *"I am always with you, my sweet child."*

"Push, Indy! Push!" Giovanna ordered. Bending my head down into my chest, I grunted and pushed with a force more powerful than the winds of a tornado while she pulled my baby's head, then shoulders, then the rest of its body from my womb. I was exhausted.

"It's a girl!" Giovanna exclaimed.

"It's a girl," Tee repeated. "Indy, baby, she's beautiful!" Tee flashed a wide smile, kissing me on my sweaty forehead, placing his warm hand over mine. "I love you so much, baby."

"I know you do," I said faintly.

And with the light smack of Giovanna's hand against my child's bottom, I broke down and cried as she laid my firstborn in my arms. I was a mother.

29

DAMASCUS: *A Song For You*

On April 5, 2001, Arabia Perette Miles—came into this world, kicking and screaming at 3:20 a.m., weighing seven pounds, six ounces. Man. It was the most exhilarating experience I could have ever imagined. Right at this moment, my life has more meaning than I ever thought possible.

Witnessing the birth of my little girl was worth all the slaps and scratches I took from Indy's mean ass. Word up! She mighta fucked me up but I got a daughter in the end. So I'm happy. I peeked in Indy's room, carrying balloons and flowers to add to the other ten dozen or so flowers already sent to her by well-wishers. I quietly sat them down on the table. Her back was facing me. I thought she was crying. I softly walked over to her, almost tiptoeing, then sat on the edge of the bed. I rubbed her back. "You okay?"

"I'm fine," she replied, never turning toward me. "Just a little tired *and* sore."

I continued rubbing her back. "Thank you, baby."

"For what?"

"For being my wife, my better half; for being the mother of my child, and for completing me. I love you."

"I love you too," she said, turning her head toward me. She smiled. "My heart is yours, Tee. But I'm still gonna slap the shit out of you as soon as I regain my strength." I burst out laughing.

"Yeah, aiight. Don't you think I'm banged up enough?" I asked, showing her my bandaged hand and bruised face.

"Nope. Not until you feel all the pain I experienced in that delivery room."

"Well, can I at least get a kiss until then?"

She sucked her teeth. "I guess so. 'Cause you ain't getting any pussy."

"Yeah, aiight," I said, smiling and walking over to the other side of her bed. "The minute you get home, I'ma knock the dust off that ass."

She snickered. "Whatever."

Her left breast was out. She had just finished nursing our baby. I helped her raise the bed into sitting position, then leaned over and planted my mouth on her sweet lips. I sucked on them, sliding my tongue in her mouth. I ain't gonna front. My dick got hard, seeing her full breast exposed. She was too damn sexy. "Damn, I can't wait to get me some of that."

"Wrong answer," she said, covering her self up. "The only one sucking on these big-ass nipples is this little one here. Isn't that right, precious? Oh Tee. She's so precious. Look at her tiny fingers." I smiled. Indy was beaming. She had a really different look about her. I can't explain it. She was radiant. Her eyes were filled with love. Arabia started fussing and squirming. "Shhhhh. What's the matter with Mommy's baby? You want your daddy?" She continued squirming and fussing. I went into the bathroom to wash my hands, then came back to hold my daughter. Indy handed her to me. I took her in my arms, pulling back her pink-and-white blanket. She was so little, so delicate. A warm feeling overcame me. And just like that, she quieted. Yo, she's definitely gonna be a daddy's girl.

"Hi, baby," I said, kissing her on her smooth forehead. "Daddy loves you more than you'll ever know." I smiled at her little fingers, then slipped my pinkie in her delicate hand. She squeezed. And then without warning, I erupted into a ball of emotion. A river of tears flowed. They were sweet tears of joy. Tears of all-I-ever-hoped-life-would-be clung to the sides of my face, then dripped onto my shirt, one by one.

With Arabia nestled in the crook of my arm, I pulled her in close to my chest, over my heart so she could feel the beat of my love for her. I used my free hand to wipe my face with the sleeve of my shirt. When I turned to face Indy, she was smiling.

"What?"

"Oh nothing," she said. "You just look so happy."

"Baby, I'm happier than you'll ever know." I walked over, leaning in to plant another kiss on her soft lips. She slipped her tongue in my mouth, reaching over to feel the length of my dick. It was brick. "Damn, girl. See what you do to me?"

She squeezed. "Hmm. Just how I like it. Always ready."

I smiled. "She's asleep," I whispered, walking over to lay her in the bassinet. I pulled the pink-and-white blanket over her little body and walked back over to the bed, sitting on the edge. "Now where were we?" I asked, pressing my lips against hers. "I can't wait to get you home, girl."

She grinned, licking her lips. "How 'bout you close the door and pull those curtains shut."

I chuckled. "Oh, word." I jumped up, shutting the door, then yanking the curtains closed. I walked over to her, then stood with my legs spread apart and hands on my hips. "What you got in mind?"

"Hmm. Let's see how many licks it takes to get to the sticky stuff." I smiled as she summoned me closer with her come-hither look. She unzipped my pants, then stuck her hand inside, pulling out my snake. "Your dick is hot, baby," she whispered, slowly licking the underside of my dick. She had me so heated I was leaking precum. She licked it, then swirled her tongue around the head. I let out a deep moan as her tongue worked its magic on my wand. Word up. My left knee shook as she licked and slurped my dick down while squeezing my nut sac.

"Damn, baby. You can suck some dick."

"Whose dick is this?" she asked in between licks.

"Yours, baby," I whispered, dipping at the knees and pumping my hips. "You got me strung, girl."

"Give me that nut then." No sooner than she said that, she pulled up off my dick, then used her soft hands to jerk me off while she sucked my balls. She had me weak at the knees. And before I knew it, I bust three hot ones in her hand.

The sound of someone clearing his or her throat from behind the curtain startled us. "Ahem."

"Yo, who's that?" I asked, tryna wipe myself off. Indy wiped her hands and lips in her towel, then reached over to grab a wipe off the nightstand. I stuffed my dick back in my pants.

"I hope I'm not interrupting anything." Indy and I looked at each other as if we had been caught with our hands in the cookie jar. I pulled the curtains back. It was Britton standing there with a big-ass grin on his face, and a bouquet of balloons, a card and flowers.

"Aww. For me?" Indy said, smiling.

"No," he replied, walking over toward the bed, leaning in to give her a kiss and a hug, "they're for the baby." I reached out to give him a pound. He stared at my hands, squinted his eyes at Indy, then looked back at me. "I think you better go wash your hands first."

I bust out laughing. Indy giggled. He sniffed the air. "I know you fiends aren't in here trying to do or *just* finished doing what I think."

"Go 'head with that," I said, tryna hide my still-hard dick. Indy smiled.

"Boy, what in the world you sneaking up in here for anyway?"

"I knocked. It's not my fault you fools can't hear." He chuckled and gave Indy a serious look, frowning his face up. "What in the world are your lips doing greasy? Uh, on second thought. Don't even ask. Ya'll so daggone nasty."

Indy and I laughed. "Don't be hatin'. My baby knows how to love me right. Ain't that right, baby," I said, giving her a long passionate kiss.

She licked her lips. "You know mother has to keep her man happy. I got to get it, where I can fit it."

Brit rolled his eyes. "Ugh! Where's the baby?"

"She's over there sleeping," Indy said, pressing the remote to adjust her bed. He walked over to the other side of the room, staring into the bassinet. I went to the bathroom to take a leak. When I returned, Brit had Arabia in his arms.

"Tee, my brotha," he said, looking up at me. "She's beautiful." She squirmed when he kissed her on her forehead.

I smiled. "Thanks, man."

He placed her back down in her bed where she settled comfortably, then walked over to give me some love. We embraced for a long moment. "I'm so happy for you."

Indy was sitting up in bed, grinning. "Hey, what about me?" she asked, feigning a pout. "I'm the one who did all the damn work."

"Girl, you know I'm happy for you too," he said, walking back over to give her another hug, kissing her on the cheek. "I never thought I'd live to see this day: two of my closest friends truly happy."

"Aww!" Indy said.

"Listen," he continued, "I know visiting hours are almost over so I'm going to get going. I just want you both to know how much I appreciate you in my life. And how much Amir, Amar and I love you both for always having our backs." Indy had tears in her eyes.

"I love you, too, Britton," she said, wiping her eyes. "I owe you so much, boy."

"Please. You owe me nothing. If anyone owes anyone anything it's me."

"Boy, please."

"No, I'm serious—"

"Nah, baby boy," I said, cutting in. "Like Indy said. We owe you. You've always kept it real with us. And it's because of you that we are where we are today. Yo, you my dawg for life. You've always loved us unconditionally. You've always been there to lift us up emotionally, and you damn sure kept us in check. I got nothing but major love for you."

"And you know I'll cut a bitch over you," Indy offered. We burst into laughter.

"Don't I know it," he said, glancing down at his watch. "Look, let me get out of here. I still have to go back over to Jersey to get the boys from Mom's."

"Aiight, yo," I said, giving him a pound. "I'll holla at you. Give your mom a hug for me."

"Most definitely."

"Thanks for coming to see me," Indy said. When he hugged her again, she softly said, "I don't know what I'd do without you." She kissed his cheek.

"Nor I without you," he replied warmly, then snapped, "Now go brush your tongue, and pick those hairs from your teeth."

"Oh, boy. Kiss my ass," she snapped playfully.

"Aye, yo," I said, laughing. "That's fucked up."

He shook his head in mock disgust. "Just nasty. That's what you is. Just plain 'ole nasty heathens."

We laughed.

"Okay, I'm out."

Indy smiled. "Give those fine boys a hug and kiss for me."

"I sure will," he said as he headed for the door. "We'll come by the house one day next week."

Indy nodded.

"One," I said, placing my fist over my heart. Indy blew him a kiss. He smiled and closed the door behind him. Arabia let out a light sound, then began to stir in her bed. She started to cry. I walked over, picking her up.

"Sssh," I said, rocking her in my arms. "It's all right. Daddy's here." She began fidgeting. Her face turned beet-red as she hollered at the top of her little lungs.

"I think she's hungry," Indy said, opening up her nightgown. I handed Arabia to her. The minute Indy settled her in the crook of her arm she turned her little head toward Indy's breast and—without prompting—opened up her mouth to suckle. Yo, between you and me, I was beginning to feel a little jealous as she sucked on Indy's swollen nipple, but then found myself getting aroused. I think I was buggin' or something. But, word is bond, watching Indy—with love in her eyes—breastfeed our daughter was such a fuckin' turn-on. She was so damn sexy.

Flashes of the first time I laid eyes on her, images of our first kiss, moments of sleepless nights of passionate lovemaking, and even our first fight, shot across my mind. And I couldn't help but smile. There's no other woman I could ever imagine spending my life with. She's my everything. And together, we are two souls, united as one; two hearts beating as one: living, breathing and loving…today, tomorrow, for always. Till death do us part. Feel me?

Yo, all my life, I've wanted nothing more than a family—my own family whom I could love and be loved by. I never fully understood the depths of what that would mean. That is until this very moment. Standing here with the woman I adore—and sharing in the joy of having the most precious gift two people can bring in to this world: a child. My child. I have a new purpose in my life. It's to unconditionally love and protect the two most beautiful women in my world. For my love, and all that is within me, belongs to them—the keepers of my heart. Word up!

I leaned over, planted a kiss on the top of my daughter's head, then kissed my beautiful wife. "I love you, baby."

She smiled. "And from my soul to yours...I love you more."

Yeah, that's what I'm talking about. I smiled. My heart was truly full. And nothing else really mattered. Believe that.

30

INDERA: *Getting Late*

Baby, let me tell you. The past four months being home have been so fulfilling I don't think things can get any better than this. I have a beautiful daughter who fills my heart with so much love, a husband who loves me in every way imaginable, a wonderful set of friends, a booming career, and a gorgeous new home. I really have to agree with Tee, I couldn't imagine life any other way. I am just so thankful.

"Arabia. Araaaabia. Hey pretty girl." Oh, excuse me. She is just so precious. I couldn't resist. Chile, I never knew being a mother and wife could be so rewarding. I'm loving every minute. I sure do. I sit on my throne all day and just give orders, okay. I have a nanny who helps out with Arabia. A cook who keeps a hot meal ready for Tee, and a housekeeper who keeps this place spotless. I don't lift a finger to do shit. The Queen has arrived, okay!

And I'm spreading my divine presence everywhere I go. I guess you've heard about my newest endeavor? Well, if you haven't, you will now. Girlfriend, Miss Indy has now entered the world of cosmetics, okay. That's right. Simply Indy—a line of skincare products—will be selling alongside Patti LaBelle, Iman, Interface, and Flori Roberts. And my fragrance, Arabia, will hit Bloomingdales, Saks, Nordstroms and other fine department stores the end of this month. When I said, I was going to become a household name, that's what I meant. From hair, face and body, I'm gonna be all over you.

And as far as my other business ventures, I'm going to fall back a bit, and enjoy my life as a mother and wife—for a hot minute, that is. 'Cause you know as well as I do, there's no way I can sit still. Girlfriend has to have her hands in the middle of something. But for now, I'm completely content—*and* satisfied—with making moves from home. With Britton as the program director of Nandi's, and Coffee as the director of operations for all three Weaves and Wonders, I have nothing to worry about. Chile, I don't know what I'd do without them.

Speaking of Britton, with the expansion of the shelter to provide services to adolescent males as well, the board of directors and I have decided to offer him the position of executive director. Hell, it's the least I could do. He's the first program director I've had who has been able to manage my girls with a fair, firm, consistent hand, which is what they need. Boyfriend took my vision and ran with it. He's constantly looking for ways to reach out to parents and their children who are in crisis. And to top it off, they all love him to death. Now that's what I'm talking about.

Chile, you should see him stepping up in that piece all suited-up, dressed for success, looking like he's fresh off the cover of *GQ*. Turning heads— I might add. And now that he's cut off all those braids, and has waved it up, he's just extra F-I-N-E. All I can say is, damn. Damn. Damn. Make a bitch wanna speak in tongues. Need I say more?

Moving on. I have good news. Well—maybe not for you, but definitely for me—Britton and his lovely fiancée have moved into my brownstone and are planning to buy it—for a steal of course. Which is definitely a relief because the thought of selling it to some stranger was tearing me up. Oh, I had it on the market for a hot minute. But once I heard what a few of the prospective buyers wanted to do with it, I pulled the sign up, and took it off the market, okay. There's no way I wanted my mother's home chopped up into apartments. Not! If I'm not mistaken, my brownstone is probably one of very few in Brooklyn that is still in its original form. And that's just how I want to keep it. I don't care if it *was* going to sell for five-hundred and fifty-thousand dollars. I know it's in good hands. And at least I know Britton is close by.

Chile. For a minute I was getting worried when he started that I-want-to-go-back-to-Sousa mess. There was no way I wanted him bouncing back to the Dominican Republic. I know he's a grown man who'll do what he wants, but I would have still done whatever I could to convince him to stay. So you know I was relieved and extremely happy when he got involved with Myesha. And when he announced his engagement, I knew it was a sealed deal. Homeboy wasn't going anywhere but down the altar.

Anyway, girlfriend is the first woman that he's been involved with whom I actually like. Excuse me? I know I already said that. *And?* Humph. Well, I'm telling you again. Sooo, like I said, I really like the child. Not that it really matters 'cause Britton's known to see who he wants regardless of what I say or think.

However, it's nice to finally be able to embrace the woman in his life without reservations. Because, honey chile, let me tell you. He's had his share of some stuck-up—and crazy—bitches, okay. Oh, they're usually very pretty. But that's about it. No wonder he takes two and three years in between relationships. He needs that much time to recuperate from all of their drama.

Now I do have to admit I was a little surprised when he initially told Tee and I about his relationship, particularly his engagement, after all his mess with that trifling...I mean Lina. However, he kindly broke it down to me, nice and sweet, that is. "Indy, I love her. She's the first woman who stirs my soul. When I look into her eyes, I see my other half, the better half of me. She completes my existence. And I want to spend my entire life basking in the love we share for each other."

Hmm. How poetic. I smiled. What else could I do? My dear brother was in love, and I wasn't going to disrupt that. Besides, I already knew she was the one. Still in all, I did pull her to the side, and had one of my friendly heart-to-hearts with her. You know. Just in case she started slipping, okay. Humph. Think I didn't. "Girlfriend," I had said, "Britton is my heart. He's a good man. And I expect you to treat him right. 'Cause, baaaby, if you don't, I'm going to have to go into my trick bag on you."

She smiled. "Indy. No need for all of that. I have no intentions of doing anything but loving Britton. So, you have nothing to worry about. His heart, body and soul—*and* sons—are safe with me." Hmm. She included my godsons. Now, you know I was happy to hear that. That was a bonus.

I returned the smile, gently patting her hand. "Thank goodness. 'Cause it would hurt me to my heart, if I had to get ugly on you." She chuckled. I didn't. I pressed on. "I'm sitting here smiling with you, and having this chat because I like you, but please know I'd turn on you quicker than a rattlesnake if you ever tried to get doggish."

"I appreciate the forewarning. But it's not necessary. Like I said, you have nothing to worry about. I respect the level of loyalty and protectiveness the two of you have for each other. And I truly admire the bond the two of you share. I hope in time we can become just as close."

"Well," I responded, "just don't try to get brand-new. As long as you remain the way you are, anything's possible. In my heart, I believe you're right for Britton. And I want to trust you'll always be true to him. But, I wouldn't have rested unless I put the cards down on the table. So, if I've offended you, I apologize. I just don't want there to be any room for confusion."

"I understand," she said. "There is no confusion. And no offense taken."

I smiled, getting up. "Good. Now let's hit Fifth Avenue. My treat."

"Well all right," she replied, jumping to her feet. "I'll drive. And pay for lunch."

"Sounds like a plan." And off we went. Chile, we shopped until we dropped at every fine boutique Fifth Avenue had to offer, then ate a lovely lunch at Mr. Chows. And do you know, she never peeped a word of our conversation. 'Cause had she, I know Britton like I know the back of my hand; he'd been on the phone tryna check me. But because she kept our little chat between us, I give her mad props, okay. Miss Myesha is definitely the one for my Britton.

So, like I said. It's so good to see him with someone who truly keeps a smile on his face. And as you know, it's a far cry from that damn Lina, who I hate to keep bringing up. But I'm telling you. Every time I think about her turning her back on my beautiful godsons—and you know how I am about children—I want to slide her ass. That bitch makes me sick to my stomach, okay. However, lucky for her, I'm a changed woman. Now, don't give me that "yeah right" look. I am. Otherwise, I'd make sure she got just what she deserved. But like Britton told me a while back, "Indy, for once. Do me a favor, and mind your business. Let me deal with her."

"Well," I replied, sucking in the air around me. "I don't like how she just dismisses her children."

"Indy, in the grand scheme of things, how is that any of your concern?"

"Well—"

"Well nothing," he interrupted. "Stay out of it."

I pursed my lips, clutched my pearls and gave him a look, but I kept my mouth shut, okay. Boyfriend got real feisty. So, now I don't say anything about it. Truthfully, he was right; it's not any of my business what she does. If girlfriend wants to be on her knees sucking and fucking everything in sight instead of being a mother, then so be it. At least she had the decency to agree to let Myesha adopt Amir and Amar once she and Britton are married. So, I suppose I shouldn't be too hard on her trick ass, huh?

Yes, girlfriend is a bona-fide trickster. An X-rated flick ho. And quiet as it's kept, from what I hear from my L.A. "connects," she's the freak of the week on the set. Girlfriend can suck down two dicks without batting an eye. And has a pussy as wide as the Holland Tunnel. Ugh! Well, like I've always said, if you gotta be a ho, then be a paid one. So, I guess, in the "grand scheme of things," she's doing her and that's all that really matters. So moving along.

Hmm. Let me see. What else. Oh, yeah. Chile. Miss Sarina is finally home acting like she has some damn sense for a change. Well, she's in an independent living program from what I hear. Of course, I get the watered-down version from Britton. But, if you ask me…never mind, I'm going to keep my negative comments to myself. I'm really trying to change, okay.

Anyway, I guess being locked down for almost four months, and being drugged up like a zombie has had its benefits. I just hope for her sake she stays on her meds. Chyna and I don't talk much about Sarina since our little altercation. As a matter of fact, I don't even ask about the child. And it's probably for the best 'cause Lord knows I'd have no problem going upside her head again if I had to. And I think—if there *were* a next time—I'd have to take her down, and keep her down, if you know what I mean.

In all honesty, the only thing I regret about that whole ordeal is the strain it has put on my relationship with Chyna. She and I have always been like sisters; but there has definitely been a shift in our friendship. I think since my shower, and birth of the baby, she and I have probably spoken eight, maybe nine, times.

Sometimes, I want to pick up the phone and chat away about something exciting the baby's done, but I don't. I let her be. And that hurts. But being the diva I am, I quickly get over it. However, that's not to say I don't miss the times when we spoke almost every day, about anything and everything. Still in all, I've accepted the fact that things oftentimes change. I mean. The love between us will always be there, but there is definitely something remarkably different between us. And I'm okay with that. I've apologized, and that's really all I can do. The forgiving part is up to her.

"Indy," she had said when we finally had a chance to talk about our dispute, "I do accept your apology. But I can't accept you telling me I should have been happy I wasn't making funeral arrangements. That hurt me. To think you'd really go to that extreme bothers me."

"Well," I said, looking her in her eyes. "I didn't mean to hurt you. I was just being honest."

"I know, Indy. And that's what frightens me."

I shrugged my shoulders. "It is what it is. I don't know what else to tell you. It doesn't matter to me now, and it didn't then, that Sarina is your daughter. The fact is she came at me."

"And I feel terrible about that, especially knowing you were pregnant."

"Well, fortunately for her, nothing tragic happened."

She took in a deep breath, then slowly blew it out. "Thank goodness."

"Yeah, basically. But no matter how you look at it, Sarina had that ass-whipping coming. And hurtful or not, she'd have been in a body bag if it weren't for the fact that I love you like a sister."

She forced a painful smile. "I guess I should be thankful."

"No. Just informed. She's your child and, as her mother, I'd expect you to stand by her. That is your right. So, you stand by her. And you go through whatever it is you need to go through with her. When it's all said and done, I'll be here waiting for my friend with open arms."

She wiped tears from her eyes. "I just need some time."

I smiled, giving her a hug. "Take all the time you need." And from the bottom of my heart, I truly meant that.

Speaking of forgiveness. I've swallowed my pride, tossed out my anger, and finally forgiven my father—with the help of…umm. Oh, hold on. The phone's ringing.

"Hello."

"Hey, baby."

"Hey to you. Where are you?"

"Still in Atlanta."

"Hmm. What time is your flight?"

"Five o'clock."

"Are you coming straight home?"

"No doubt. Why?"

"'Cause I want some damn dick," I snapped.

"And I wanna give it all to you," he said, laughing. "Word up."

"Well," I giggled, "be ready to get the dust sucked off it."

He laughed. "Yeah, aiiight. You always talkin' slick."

"And I can back it up."

"We'll see. Yo, I gotta go. Give my girl a kiss for me."

"And what about me?"

"I got all the kisses you need, baby. See you tonight."

"Love you."

He blew a kiss into the phone. "Love you too."

Hmmmph. Chile. I love that man. Who would have guessed Miss Indy would ever be head over heels for a man. Girrrrl, five years ago, I would have slapped you silly if you'd even suggested it. Love is such a strange phenomenon. It really can take you out of character, having you doing some real crazy shit. I can definitely attest to that. 'Cause Lord knows I've done my share. But, I won't ever tolerate a man who beats or a man who cheats. Period. Lucky for me, I don't have either. So—using Brit's words, *again*—in the grand scheme of things I'm truly fortunate.

Oh, Lord. I'm bouncing all over the place. What was I saying before Tee called? Hmm. Oh, yeah, I was telling you how I've forgiven my father. Yep. I made a conscious decision to let go of my bitterness toward him. And in all honesty, I feel so much better. I'm really at peace, if you know what I mean.

I really believe having my daughter along with that damn book *Shattered Souls* played a big part in my willingness to let go. Yeah, I broke down and read it. Britton kept raving about it so much that it piqued my curiosity. Besides, he had bought me a hardcover copy personally autographed to me. So, it was sort of hard not to pick it up when it's right in your face, calling your name.

Anyway, let me tell you. I'm really glad I read it. Chile. I laughed, cried and screamed all in one sitting. It was one well-written piece of fiction, a definite page-turner. But, as entertaining and enlightening as it was, I was forced to do some serious soul searching. And, sadly, the one thing I realized: Britton, Tee, Chyna and myself were all—in one shape, form or fashion—a shattered soul. No matter how much money we acquired—no matter how successful we were—the memories of being abused, neglected and/or abandoned would always be with us. However, whether we allow our past to control us, or be *in* control of it, is what determines a victim from a survivor. And girlfriend, I am proud to say, I am a survivor, okay.

Through it all—chest out, head held high, I refused to let my circumstances hinder me. I've never made excuses for my actions, not that some of the things I've done in my lifetime were always right. No, I'm not admitting to any wrongdoings. I'm only saying I haven't always done right, okay.

Anyway, the reality is, I'm responsible for my life, and how I live it. Not my father. Not my dead stepmother. Not the man who sodomized me as a child. Not the men who ran a train on me. Not anyone, but me. I am who I am today because of my experiences, good and bad. And girlfriend, I love me, despite it all.

So there was no need to continue blaming him for things that happened to me in the past. He can't change any of it, even if he wanted to. Nor can I. The only thing I was able to change, wholeheartedly, was my relationship with him. Too much time has been lost between us. And I didn't want to waste another minute, holding on to regrets, okay.

Chile. I'm telling you. Having a child is the best thing that could have ever happened to me. Because seeing Tee holding Arabia in his arms, and the love in his eyes for her, made me realize how much I really missed my own father. And how much I still needed him in my life, no matter what. There was no sense of denying it any longer.

I want my children to know who their grandfather is. They'll never know their grandmother—God rest her soul—but they'll know her spirit, which lives through me. And I will do whatever I can to ensure they...yes, I said children.

Well, all right. I might as well tell you, since I've pretty much told you every-damn-thing else. I'm two months pregnant. Hmm-Hmm. I sure am. Anyway...as I was saying, I am going to make sure Arabia, and the child that grows inside of me, are always surrounded by unconditional love, okay.

Unh-huh. Don't even say it! I know what I said. But things happen, okay. I know you didn't expect me to wait six weeks before I climbed up on Tee and slid down on his juicy dick. Please. There was no way I could avoid all that meat. He was constantly brushing it up against me, pressing it into me, teasing me, taunting me with it. I couldn't take it any longer. I mean we tried to hold off; but after the seventh day, it was on and poppin' between the sheets. And the shit was good as hell, okay. Whew! Somebody hand me an ice cube to cool down. Just thinking about it gets me heated.

So yes, I'm pregnant. And Tee is ecstatic. He wants a son. And for his sake I hope this one is a boy. Because, if it isn't, he'll be out of luck 'cause sistagirl is getting her tubes tied and fried the minute I have this baby. There will *not* be another baby popping out of this sweet pussy, okay. I have things to do besides carting a whole bunch of babies. So, two will do just fine. And I'm happy about it, okay. So moving on.

"Araaaabia, hey, baby...What's Mommy's pretty girl doing?" Oh, look at her; she's the cutest thing.

Oh, shoot. Let me see, what else has been going on since we've last seen each other. Hmm. Well, Tee's second book dropped, and has been selling like crazy. Both of his books are on the *Essence* best-sellers list. And his third book, *Keeper of My Heart*, which he's dedicated to me, will be out in the spring of 2002. I'm so proud of him. His publisher has offered him another three-book deal, but he's not sure if he wants it. He says he wants to go to law school. Hell, I say, go to law school and write the books too. But whatever he decides, is all right with me. I'm gonna have his back no matter what.

And I'm pleased to announce we haven't had a fight in months. Oh, don't get it twisted. He still tries to get on my last damn nerve, sometimes. But I don't let it get to me the way I used to. Well, at least I try not. I'm really learning how to pick and choose my battles, and I suspect he's doing the same. 'Cause I know I can sure work the hell out of his nerves too, know what I'm sayin'?

Now when I start my shit, he just looks at me and sucks his teeth, then walks off. When he comes back, he hits me with, "Aiight, you done buggin' yet?" And believe it or not, I don't say another word, even when I'm *not* done. And I'm really trying not to withhold sex when he pisses me off. Although, every now and then, I have to go on strike just to keep him on his toes, if you know what I mean.

Well, between you and me. Sometimes, I purposefully do something to agitate him just so he can take his frustrations out on me sexually. Hmm. Girl, talk 'bout a good fuck-me-sweaty-until-you-collapse moment. He tries to tear this back out, okay. But little does he know, that that's how I wanted it. Oh, it's just another one of my tricks. But it works. 'Cause the minute he pops that thick love cream, he melts right in the palm of my hand, and it's love in paradise all over again. Like I told you before, brains, beauty and good pussy go a long way, okay.

But, I'll say this: Being married may require a lot of damn work, okay. However, it's sure worth it's weight in gold. Just when I think I'm ready to lose it on him, he does something that melts my heart. Like sending me this beautiful floral arrangement with a lovely card attached. Here look: *Baby, no matter the distance between us, you are always with me. I love you with all that is in me. In mind, body and soul. Flesh to flesh, soul to soul. We are one! See you when I get home, your man for life.* See what I mean. He knows just what to say to get my juices flowing. Hmm. I sure can't wait for him to get home so I can get me a taste of that nut.

"Araaaaabia, hey, baby."

Oh, shit. Look at the time! It's already three o'clock. Time sure does fly when you're having fun, doesn't it? Well, honey chile, all good things must come to an end. And this party boat has now docked. Girlfriend, I know. Just when things were starting to get good, it's time to say good-bye. Umm. I hate to see you leave too.

Now hold up, you ain't got to go home, but you damn sure got to get up outta here. I have a thousand and one things to do before Tee walks through this door. I need to hit the gym, get a facial, get my pedicure and manicure, and soak this pussy. I done already told ya'll I want my back dug out, okay? So chop, chop.

Ugh! Look at this. I'm getting all teary-eyed. I don't believe this shit. I am really gonna miss you. Well, *most* of you that is. 'Cause we all know there's always a phony bunch of bitches in the crowd, hating. Humph. Need I say more?

Now, to the rest of you, big hugs to you. We've really gotten to know each other. We've laughed, cried, and cut up something fierce. But, I've told you all you need to know. We've sat around long enough. You've eaten and drunk up everything in sight...Umm. Excuse you. What in the world are you still sitting here for? Didn't you hear what I just said? I *said* it's time to go. Get up, get those shoes on, and let's get hopping.

Excuse me? What about Celeste? Oh, I get it. Your nosey behinds wanna know if I had something to do with that child's death. Oh. My. Goodness. You stink bottoms actually suspect I did her in. Chile, please. I plead the fifth, okay. Mother ain't no fool. So, think what you want. Like I said before. I maim, *not* murder, okay.

Now, on that note *Ciao*. Excuse me, what did you say? Is this the end? Hmm. Maybe—maybe not, who knows. But if it is, I know I've made a lasting impression, and will be forever in your minds. So thanks for stopping by, and giving me your undivided attention. It's been real. *Mwah!*

ABOUT THE AUTHOR

Dywane D. Birch, a graduate of Norfolk State University and Hunter College, is the author of *Shattered Souls*, *From My Soul to Yours*, *When Loving You is Wrong*, *and Beneath the Bruises*. He is also a contributing author to the compelling compilation, *Breaking The Cycle* (2005), edited by Zane—a collection of short stories on domestic violence, which won the 2006 NAACP Image Award for outstanding literary fiction; and a contributing author to the anthology *Fantasy* (2007), a collection of erotic short stories. He has a master's degree in psychology, and is a clinically certified forensic counselor. A former director of an adolescent crisis shelter, he continues to work with adolescents and adult offenders. He currently speaks at local colleges on the issue of domestic violence while working on his fifth novel and a collection of poetry. He divides his free time between New Jersey and Maryland. You may email the author at bshatteredsouls@cs.com or visit www.myspace.com/dywaneb

SHATTERED SOULS

BY DYWANE D. BIRCH

AVAILABLE FROM STREBOR BOOKS

BRITTON: LIFE

D AMN, LIFE IS GOOD. Here I am sitting out on my terrace in the nude, listening to a Tracy Chapman CD, drinking lemonade, and taking in the most mesmerizing view of sparkling turquoise water. Right at this moment, I feel blessed and I'm thankful. I give thanks for my life—I am debt-free, stress-free, and carefree. No one believed me when I said I was packing my bags and leaving the States. But I knew, from the first time I set foot on this island four years ago, that this would become my home. Was it a difficult choice to make? No doubt. But it was something I needed to do for me. See, I am a firm believer that no one else can live your life for you. And your life shouldn't be consumed with trying to satisfy everyone else all the time. There comes a time when you have to make choices for yourself and live accordingly. And now that I've had time to reflect and to become more in tune with what my needs are, I have finally come to realize that there is a big difference between making a living and having a life. I got tired of just going through the motions. I got tired of living among the walking dead. And I was damn sure tired of putting other people's needs before my own. I knew that if I didn't make changes in my life, I would have fallen into a deep pit of depression. And I was afraid of being haunted by the "would've-could've-should've" syndrome. So, for once, I threw caution to the winds and said, "Fuck what others think or feel." I worked three jobs to save enough money to live here comfortably. I paid off all my bills, sold my town house and car, rented out my condo, and placed all my valuables in storage. Then I made sure I had access to enough emergency cash just in case things got crazy, cut up all my credit cards except for my platinum American Express, and bought a first-class ticket to the Dominican Republic. So here I am, living on one of the most beautiful tropical islands in the world, with peace of mind.

Now, don't get me wrong. I'm not saying life has always been kind to me, because it hasn't. And it damn sure isn't perfect. Trust me, I have survived my share of personal storms. Some with more wind and rain than others. But I've weathered them. From light drizzle to hurricanes, I've endured the beatings of cold droplets and heavy gales. I am convinced it was a higher power that gave me the mental and physical strength to pick myself up, brush myself off, and press on. Although the skies have cleared for now, I know lightning and thunder can still strike at any time. That's why I try my best to take nothing for granted. At this point in my life, I am better prepared, with experience and well-taught lessons, to pay closer attention to life's storm warnings. Basically, I've made a conscious choice to keep dead weight and negativity out of my life. For good!

I think the hardest part of packing up and moving was knowing I wouldn't be able to spend much time with my friends and family. When I told my mother I was moving, I thought she'd flip, but she didn't. She hugged me and said, "Good. Just make sure you have enough room for me because I'm going to need a place to stay when I come down for vacation." Then she smiled and said, "I love you very much and I just want you to be happy, so if this move makes you happy then I'm happy. You deserve it." My eyes were heavy, but I didn't let any tears surface as we embraced. I knew then I'd miss her more than I'd thought. It seems like mothers always know the right things to say at the right time.

Now, my sister, on the other hand, felt it was her duty to let me know exactly what she felt about it: "The Dominican Republic? Isn't that one of the poorest countries? Why in the world would you move there? Boy, every time I turn around, you're running off somewhere. I don't know why you gotta keep moving around. Don't you know you can't run away all your life? And what do you plan on doing down there?" My sister is four years older than me and can be overbearing and too opinionated. So, of course, when I told her I planned on doing *nothing*, I thought she was going to blow a gasket. "You mean to tell me, as hard as it is to find a good job, you are giving up a good-paying job to lay around on some beach?! Sometimes I just don't understand you. You're not going to be able to live off your savings forever." I love this girl dearly, but I wish she'd try harder to just be my big sister instead of my mother.

Yes, I gave up my full-time job as a school psychologist, a job that I'd had to struggle to keep because of all the political crap that goes on within school districts. They had a problem with me not conforming to their rules and with being too vocal. I guess I was a bit too rebellious for them. Well, I had a bigger problem with them. Anytime I had a fifteen- or sixteen-year-old in front of me who read and wrote on a third- or fourth-grade level, I wanted to know what the hell was going on. How in the hell do you just pass a child from grade to grade without ensuring that kid has mastered every task on or above grade level? Each time I had a fifteen-year-old still in the eighth grade, I wanted to know what alternative support was being offered. And what would really set me off was the school's audacity in allowing students to graduate without being properly armed educationally to survive in this world. Come on now, if children can't read or write, then that means they can't fill out an application. So how do you expect them to become self-sufficient? As far as I was concerned, someone in the school system failed those children and I wanted schools to be held accountable. I really couldn't get with the concept of just throwing students out of school or classifying them "emotionally disturbed" just because they were disruptive. Yes, there are some youth who really do have significant emotional problems, but many disruptive behaviors in the classroom are due to teachers failing to properly educate and prepare our youth for the next grade level. It just seemed like no one was *really* interested in trying to understand that maybe some kids disrupt the class because it is the only way they know how to avoid being embarrassed by the limitations we have imposed on them.

So, when we fail our youth, what do we do? We expel them. Bottom line, it just seems much easier to throw these children out of school or classify them as requiring special education than to deal with the real cause of the problems. And because many parents don't know that legally, most schools can't just drop students from their rolls—they can't suspend or expel them without providing an alternative learning environment—I would inform parents of this and challenge teachers and school officials on it, and remind them of their responsibility to properly educate our youth. So, in a nutshell, my presence in the school system wasn't welcomed with open arms. But, hey, I never cared about being liked as long as I was respected. And respect is what I got, regardless.

I also gave up my cushy part-time job as an adjunct professor teaching psychology. But that still doesn't explain why my sister should concern herself with my job security. After all, I do have marketable skills, and I'm confident that I'll have no problem getting a job when I decide to move back.

Anyway, a part of me knew what she was *really* getting at. She thinks I moved because I was running away from commitment or another failed relationship. I'll admit that when I was younger, I did use moving from place to place as an avoidance mechanism. It was my way of trying to control my feelings and ensuring I didn't get hurt. But this was different. I moved as a means of letting go. True, I pulled out of a relationship. But I didn't run off or move on because of it. I moved because I needed to be alone. I needed a sabbatical year, or two, to collect my thoughts without interruptions. I needed space to sort through my own emotional baggage, far away from family and friends. Okay, so maybe moving here was going to the extreme but sometimes I am an extremist. I'm either hot or cold. In or out. Sometimes downright impulsive. There is just no in-between with me.

To be honest with you, I could sing the blues all day and all night about some of my impulsive behaviors and failed relationships. But why bother? It's not like I can change what's already happened. As far as I'm concerned, the past is a chapter in my life I don't wish to revisit. I am living for this second. Hoping to live for another minute. Another hour. Another day.

Nothing in life is guaranteed, so I am living for the moment. I'm just hopeful that I will continue to awake to another day, and I'm thankful when I do.

Whenever I call home to get the 411 on what's happening in the States, I get hit with the 911. Someone has either been robbed, killed, raped, beaten, or all of the above. It's really a damn shame. The U.S. is *supposed* to be one of the most advanced technological forces to be reckoned with, and it can't even properly protect its citizens. Makes you wonder what the country's priorities really are. Hell, that's probably one of the reasons I never felt connected there. Never pledged allegiance to the flag. For what? I've always questioned the U.S.'s allegiance to its people's struggles. I'm not necessarily referring to the individual struggles of being African American. Although that *is* a key issue. I'm talking about the struggles within our families. Within our communities. Within each race. Well, one thing's for sure: As long as there is no justice, there will never be peace.

I will say this: Living here has definitely given me a whole new attitude about life and the things we take for granted. Like family and *true* friends. I think sometimes we get so caught up in the hustle and bustle of just trying to survive that we tend not to tell the ones who mean the most to us how important they really are to us. I know in the past I was guilty of that, on more than one occasion. Family for me consists of my mother, my sister, and my nieces. My extended family? *Puhleeeeze.* Let's just say I don't play 'em too close. I know I can't control who I'm related to, but I can sure control how I relate to them. As far as friends go, and I mean *real* friends, I have only three—Damascus, Indy, and Chyna. That's my clique for life.

Damascus, who goes by the name Tee, is the first and only male I can honestly say I've embraced as a soul brother. Even though we've had our disagreements and a couple of fistfights, we've still been able to keep it real with each other. I've admired his strength in being able to come out on top despite having no one positive in his life to guide him. On the surface, he comes across like a self-absorbed ruffian from the 'hood who's only concerned with his own self-indulgences, but I know better. Hell, we were roommates for three years, and one thing's for sure: You never really get to know a person until you live with him. So all that slick shit he talks…let's just say I know what's underneath the steel armor. Still, he is probably one of the most conceited and sex-crazed brothas I know. I've always believed his mother meant to name him Narcissus. I swear, he is stuck in that stage of development in which his body is the object of his own erotic interest. I've always teased him about falling in love with himself the first time he saw his reflection in the mirror. But I'll give him his props; he is a smooth-looking brotha, and a lot of females are big on him. I've just always had a problem with the way he measures manhood.

Indy gets the award for having the most attitude and I love it. I like the fact that she calls it like she sees it, and she's not afraid of challenges or taking risks. She doesn't care what comes out of her mouth; if she feels it, she says it. She tells you from the gate what her expectations are, and if you can't flow with it, then she just moves on without blinking an eye. I tell her that that's not always a healthy way of handling things, but she says, "Boyfriend, please. It's my way or the highway. Besides, how you gonna give me advice you don't live by?" Anyway, aside from being angry with almost every man in the world, she is a very successful businesswoman who will not settle for anything less than the finer things in life. In layman's terms, she's materialistic as hell. But then again, people say that about me.

There's a rawness about her that is exciting and provocative and men *love* it. There's also this kinkiness about her that seems to drive men crazy, figuratively and literally. I've warned her to be careful because that could be dangerous. She has this remarkable way with words that just cracks me up. You have to hear some of the things that come out of her mouth to understand what I mean. Nevertheless, despite her sometimes sharp tongue, she is a very sweet person as long as you don't cross her. If you take her kindness for a weakness or try to play her, *watch out!* And when she says she's gonna do something, that's what she means. Trust me, she's a woman of her word.

Out of everyone, Indy is my road dog. Back in the eighties when we were away at college we used to travel back and forth, by car or plane, between Virginia and New York just to get our weekend workout in at The Paradise Garage, Nells, The Tunnel, you name it. Oh, and I can't forget about Club

Zanzibar out in Jersey. We used to tear those spots up. We'd carry our back-packs filled with bottled water, baby powder to make the floor slippery, and a facecloth and towel to wash and dry off the sweat. We'd change into our dancing gear, move toward whoever was generating the most energy, then find a nice corner to spin until daybreak. We took road trips to the Aggie-Fest in North Cacky-Lackey, the Freak-Nic in Atlanta, and the Greek Picnic in Philly (then on to the Belmar Beach in Jersey the next day). And no summer would be complete without the annual Labor Day weekend in Virginia Beach. That's where we first met and clicked. The summer of 1983.

Now, Chyna is what many brothas would refer to as a "dime-piece." She's gorgeous. She's flawless. She's just one classy, sophisticated woman who car-ries herself like a lady at all times. I don't think I can ever recall her cursing or saying anything negative about anyone. Imagine a young Lena Horne with green eyes and long, sandy brown hair that flows past her butt. She's the only one of the three of us who's married and she has four children—one daughter and three sons. Her husband, whom none of us can stand, is a successful businessman who has given her every material thing imaginable; yet there's always been something missing. We—no, let me speak for myself—*I* don't like him because I've always felt like he treats Chyna as if she were his trophy. If you met him you'd understand what I'm saying. Granted, he has a great physique, but that face…Aaaagh. Let's just say he has the body of Hercules and the face of Magilla Gorilla. Outside of that, I just don't feel he appreciates her the way she should be appreciated, nor has he encouraged her to do anything other than be dependent on him. So I consider her knocked up and locked up by a man who likes being in full control of her. But I do give her a lot of credit, and I'm proud of her. Even though she was a young teenage mother and wife, she still didn't let that hinder her from completing her undergraduate studies and then going on to grad school to obtain two master's degrees. It's too bad she's done nothing with them. She chose to be a full-time mother and wife instead, for which I commend her. Having a home filled with love is something she's always wanted. Well, she has a gorgeous home in pristine suburbia; I just wonder how much love her husband has been able to fill it with.

The four of us are different yet so much alike. We come from different backgrounds, but our struggles…let's just say we've been able to look to one another for support, encouragement, and understanding. That's probably why our friendship has survived for fifteen years. Now, I'll be the first to admit, Indy's mouth has sometimes created tension among us, probably because she says what she feels. But she says what needs to be said out of concern— nothing more, nothing less. In any event, there's mutual respect among us, and nothing any one of us says to the other would or could put a wedge between us. Hell, our friendship has been sealed with tears, laughter, and *unconditional* love. Besides, I know all their secrets.

I'm sure one of the reasons I love being in the Dominican Republic is because there is a sense of family and community. The community *is* your family. An outsider who has gained their *confianza* will be embraced as family. Believe me, it's not something easily gained. Personally, I like the fact that trust is highly valued here. It's too bad it's not the same way back home. Maybe the world would be a better place to live if it was. There just seems to be a lot of phoniness at home. I have never been able to get with the superficial people and smiling faces who'll stab you in the back with the same hand they extend to you. There's always some type of hidden agenda. That's cool, but I'm not the one. And I'm definitely not with all the negative energy they generate. I only wish we could embrace one another for who we are instead of for what we have. Perhaps a pot of peace and happiness would be found on the other side of that rainbow of madness we slide across.

Here, life is sweet and simple. There's not that sense of urgency that you experience back home. Everyone is so laid-back and friendly. I have to admit, I've had to make some adjustments in my attitude and get used to not having many of the expensive luxuries I thought I could never live without like my 325i convertible, the fifty-two-inch-screen TV I hardly turned on, and the convenience of buses and subways. It really took me a while to get used to riding a moped to and fro. I haven't got up the nerve to upgrade to a motor-cycle yet. But I'd rather do that than ride in a passenger van that carries people and animals together. I tried that once and threw up from the thick July heat, the smell of sweaty bodies, and the odor of funky farm animals.

I also had to get used to the fact that here, friends and relationships are more important than work or being on time for appointments. Sometimes I laugh trying to imagine waltzing or whistling into work forty minutes late because I was talking to a friend. Ha. Not in Jersey. Friendships and family are definitely not priorities there. The one thing I still struggle with is the fact that privacy is unimportant here more so in the rural areas. Now, I don't mind company from time to time, but this popping in and out is not my cup of tea. Here, doors are kept open and it is considered strange to close them and not accept visitors anytime, day or night. Whether invited or not, guests will be offered something to drink and asked to stay if mealtime is near. Hell, back home, if you came to my spot unannounced, I wouldn't let you in. And if you continued banging on my door or ringing my doorbell, I might just throw a mixture of bleach and shit down on you. But I'm changing. Slowly.

Well, I don't know about you, but I'm gonna finish listening to my Tracy Chapman CD, finish reading this book by Ernest Gaines, *A Lesson Before Dying*, then pack my luggage. In two days, I'm off on a seven-day Carnival cruise. Yes, this is truly the life. And I have to agree with Tracy Chapman: "Heaven's here on earth."

At 5:00 a.m. I was up pacing the oak wood floor in my bedroom. I couldn't sleep. My mind raced with thoughts of the character in that book I read last night. The book was deep. I really hate it when a book can stir up feelings in me. I felt angry, sad, and happy all in one reading. I think what touched me the most was his diary to the teacher. I honestly had tears in my eyes and for a minute, I almost allowed them to flow. Almost. But I opted to run. I ran two miles in the sand along the water's edge. The wet sand felt good under my feet, and when the cool water pulled back into the ocean, I could feel myself being gently pulled in too. I ran fast and hard against the ocean's soft morning breeze. I needed to outrun my thoughts before they caught up with me before the tears I felt for the character in that book overwhelmed me. So I ran and ran and ran until it hurt. Until I could think of nothing else except getting home and back to bed.

Before I even got through the door, the phone rang, and I knew it could be only one of five people calling. But I guessed it was my sister because she's the only one who calls me all hours of the day and night. She seems to think that because I don't have to get up to go to work every morning there are no time restrictions on when she should call.

"Good morning, snookems," I said while glancing over at the round wood clock hanging over the door. Six-thirty a.m. This better be good.

"Hey, Brit," she said in a sullen tone. "You're up awful early. What are you doing?"

"I was just sitting here waiting for you to call," I said sarcastically. "What's wrong?"

"It's Daddy. And before you go off, just listen to me, okay?"

I asked her to hold on, lit two sandalwood incense sticks, pulled off my wet clothes, sat on a wooden barstool, then took two deep breaths and picked up the phone. "I'm listening."

"Daddy's real sick and he really wants to see you. He knows you won't call him or accept any calls from him, but he wants to talk to you."

"About what? I have nothing to talk about and I'm not interested in seeing him."

"My God, Brit," she said with annoyance. "Can't you just let go of whatever it is that's been eating away at you? Our father is dying, and the least you can do is give him a chance. I don't know what you think he's done to you or hasn't done for you, but he's tried to be there for you. You've always pushed him away."

"Look, we've gone over this a thousand times already. I don't have any ill feelings toward him. I just have no use for him. I let go a long time ago. Now, I'm sorry to hear about his health but I can't feel something I—"

"No one is asking you to *feel* anything," she snapped. "All I'm asking is that you, for once, stop being so damn selfish. Just go see him or at least call him. Please. He's our father and he needs you. You owe him a chance."